THE ESSENTIAL PROSE OF JOHN MILTON

The Essential Prose of John Milton

Edited by William Kerrigan,
John Rumrich,
and Stephen M. Fallon

MODERN LIBRARY
NEW YORK

2013 Modern Library Paperback Edition

Published in the United States by Modern Library,
an imprint of The Random House Publishing Group,
a division of Random House, Inc., New York.

MODERN LIBRARY and the TORCHBEARER Design are registered
trademarks of Random House, Inc.

Originally published as part of *The Complete Poetry and Essential Prose of John Milton* in hardcover in the United States by Modern Library,
an imprint of The Random House Publishing Group,
a division of Random House, Inc., in 2007.

Grateful acknowledgment is made to Yale University Press
for permission to reprint material from three volumes from
The Complete Prose Works of John Milton, edited by Maurice Kelley
and John Carey: vol. 1 (copyright © 1953 by Yale University), vol. 4
(copyright © 1966 by Yale University), and vol. 6 (copyright © 1973
by Yale University). Reprinted by permission.

ISBN 978-0-8129-8372-2
eBook ISBN 978-0-679-64559-7

www.modernlibrary.com

147492925

Contents

List of Illustrations

Both illustrations are used with permission.

Introduction

John Milton wrote most of the poetry for which he is celebrated when he was either in his twenties or in his fifties and sixties. During his thirties and forties—at the time of life when Shakespeare wrote most of his plays (and all of his mature ones)—Milton composed relatively little verse: 16 sonnets, 17 psalm translations, and occasional poems amounting to 107 lines in Latin and 4 in Greek. Instead of more poetry he wrote enough prose to fill nearly seven of the eight hefty volumes that make up the Yale edition of his *Complete Prose Works.* Early in this period, in a passage from *The Reason of Church Government* (1642), at once self-deprecating and self-promoting, he expressed his frustration that the political and social turmoil of the time seemed to require controversial prose and left little leisure for poetry: "I should not choose this manner of writing, wherein knowing myself inferior to myself, led by the genial power of nature to another task, I have the use, as I may account it, but of my left hand" (p. 87). Yet his contemporaries knew him better for this not-so-genial prose than for the poetry he believed himself born to write.

Modern readers may find this historical fact difficult to digest because his prose writings are not so immediately pertinent now as they were in their original historical circumstances. Had Milton never written a line of verse, an academic audience might still have found its way to several of the prose works, most likely including *Of Education, The Doctrine and Discipline of Divorce, and The Tenure of Kings and Magistrates. Areopagitica* would perhaps have reached a wider audience, both for its rhetorical brilliance and its landmark contribution to the developing case for freedom of expression. But without the poetry to spark our interest, few today would read much of the prose. And that would have been our loss, as the vigorous, combative, and often luminous prose gathered in this volume suggests. Milton championed causes that provoked and sometimes outraged his first readers and remain controversially relevant today inasmuch as they address the definition of marriage, the desirability of religious toleration, the separation of church and state, and the duty of the individual when confronted with tyranny.

This edition includes the complete texts of several of Milton's most salient prose works along with extensive selections from others. We have modernized spelling and punctuation in the interest of readability. Perusing the texts in their original spelling and punctuation would more literally approximate the experience of a seventeenth-century audience. In a more substantial way it would diverge from that experience. The frequent capitalizations, variations in spelling, and long and serpentine sentences characteristic of prose printed during the early modern period would be as strange and off-putting to today's readers as they were familiar and unremarkable to our seventeenth-century predecessors. The editor who would modernize Milton's prose nevertheless confronts an intractable dilemma. His language can lack the coherence and more definite structure found in most modern sentences, which are rendered more readily intelligible by logically ordered rather than rhetorical punctuation and relatively frequent end-stops. The second sentence of *Of Reformation,* for example, runs to 375 words. Modernizing, we break this unit up into three sentences of 191, 88, and 96 words. Of course any editorial choice is a compromise, and we are painfully aware that the gain in readability comes at the cost of damping the forward thrust of Milton's prose as well as its intellectual flex and amplitude. Versions of these texts with original spelling and punctuation are available online and in university libraries, and we hope that readers drawn to a particular passage or work will consult them.

The prose selections in this volume largely correspond, though with significant additions, to the selections in our *Complete Poetry and Essential Prose of John Milton.* We have gathered and selected prose works first of all for their intrinsic excellence. Few would question the merit of Milton's abiding classics *Areopagitica,* the first book devoted to freedom of the press, and *Of Education,* his remarkable outline for the reform of contemporary pedagogy. There is also a great deal of fascinating self-reflection throughout his polemical tracts, scattered like the dismembered body of an autobiography. We have reprinted such excerpts from *The Reason of Church Government, An Apology for Smectymnuus,* and the *Second Defense of the English People,* as well as a group of his familiar letters and two of his early "prolusions," or academic exercises. Our selections from the polemical *Of Reformation* and *Eikonoklastes* display the fervor of Milton's religious and political commitments. In a significant addition to the works represented in our earlier volume, this updated edition includes a sampling of *Milton's Commonplace Book,* which opens a window on decades of Milton's reading and on his remarkably engaged and critical reliance on others' arguments as he goes about constructing his own.

Early on, though confident in his powers as a poet, Milton seems somewhat uneasy in the medium of prose. The result in his early polemics directed at the bishops (here, *Of Reformation, The Reason of Church Government,* and *An Apology for Smectymnuus*) is a vivid, image-laden style that at times becomes undisciplined. A quieter, more assured style marks the two divorce tracts, *The Doctrine and Discipline of Divorce* and *Tetrachordon.* We reprint substantial portions of these books. Increasingly viewed as pivotal in Milton's career, they reflect the chastening experience of his initially unhappy first marriage as he faces the challenge of interpreting Scripture against the grain of its apparent sense. In two other works, *The Tenure of Kings and Magistrates* (which in this edition, with the inclusion of Milton's citations of Reformed authorities, is complete) and *The Ready and Easy Way*, the reader will be able to follow the full development of arguments that establish Milton as a major political thinker and simultaneously show him reacting in personal ways to the pressure of great events, as one king is beheaded and another, his son, is crowned eleven years later. The final set of selections, from Milton's theological treatise *Christian Doctrine*, though reduced from the selections in our *Complete Poetry and Essential Prose*, remains extensive. After two decades of unpersuasive challenges, the question of Milton's authorship of this unorthodox treatise has been firmly settled in the affirmative. We are convinced of its signal importance for understanding the beliefs embedded in his major poems.

The fortunes of Milton's prose have varied with time. The prose works have been more intensely read (or at least cited) over the last forty years than they were during Milton's lifetime. Even the undeniably great *Areopagitica* made no great splash when first published. The 1644 edition was the only edition until 1697, nearly a quarter century after Milton's death. The *Eikonoklastes* fared somewhat better, with the first edition of 1649 followed by a second in 1650, but the brevity of the interval presumably owes more to the interests and sponsorship of the ruling Council of State than it does to public demand for the book. In stark contrast, the book's target, Charles I's *Eikon Basilike*, was wildly popular, going through thirty-five editions in the first year in London alone, not counting those printed elsewhere.

Many of Milton's prose works are radically polemical, so much so that Restoration readers, whether out of prudence or conviction, generally chose either to ignore the prose or to condemn it as a blot on the poet's reputation. The attack on episcopacy infuriated supporters of the Church of England; the defense of divorce for incompatibility put him at odds with the literal sense of the Gospels; the advocacy of bringing to justice a king turned tyrant made him anathema among triumphant and often vindictive royalists. John Egerton, the Earl of Bridgewater, who played the role of the Elder Brother in Milton's *Masque Presented at Ludlow Castle*, inscribed his copy of Milton's *Defense of the English People*, now in the Huntington Library, "*Liber igni, Author furcâ, dignissimi*/the book is most deserving of burning, the author of the gallows." Egerton's harsh judgment epitomizes a general hostility toward Milton during the Restoration, when Cavalier writers entertained their readers by imagining his humiliation and execution or by deriding his blindness and otherwise denigrating him and his work. In the early 1660s, before the appearance of his late, major poems could begin to blunt the edge of notoriety he had earned as a prose controversialist, Milton vividly paints the situation in which he found himself, "fall'n on evil days,/... and evil tongues;/In darkness, and with dangers compassed round,/And solitude" (*Paradise Lost* 7.25–28). The official cultural attitude during the Restoration seems to have been that Milton's vicious attacks on Charles had consigned him and all his works to oblivion, as the Royalist poet and biographer William Winstanley insisted in his *Lives of the Most Famous English Poets*: "his fame is gone out like a candle in a snuff, and his memory will always stink, which might have ever lived in honorable repute had not he been a notorious traitor and most impiously and villainously belied that blessed martyr, King Charles the First" (195).

In subsequent decades, as admiration for Milton's late masterpieces nonetheless became increasingly widespread, critics and editors sought to insulate the author's poetry from the contaminating touch of his still intensely divisive prose, a diffuse cultural project that partly accounts for the preoccupation of early eighteenth-century critics with the sublime as an aesthetic category permitting appreciation of the awe-inspiring emotional power of great art even when it concerned or evoked politically terrifying subjects or events. Aubrey's impatience to see Milton's long-suppressed sonnets in praise of Cromwell and Fairfax anticipates such aesthetic theory: "Were they made in commendation of the devil, 'twere all one to me; 'tis the ὕψος [sublime] that I look after" (p. xxvii). The aversion to Milton's prose persists to some extent today, as the recent, failed effort to separate the poet from his theological treatise suggests. Ironically, the wishful denial of the treatise's rightful attribution faintly echoes the official if covert Restoration effort to suppress Milton's still unpublished writings after his death, along with any criminal opinions they might contain. That policy put Milton's theological manuscript in the closet for a century and a half and left readers free to construe his epic as a bulwark of the Christian tradition. One fortunate outcome of the recent efforts to deny the Miltonic provenance of what he described as "his dearest and best possession," however, has been renewed attention to the complicated pertinence of Milton's heretical theology to his poetry and vice versa.

That which made Milton notorious among royalists and Tories made him a hero for republicans and Whigs, though a generation passed before the rehabilitation of Milton's prose could even begin. The first edition of Milton's collected prose, compiled by John Toland, an Irish Whig philosopher and freethinker, was not printed until 1697. Thomas Birch produced the eighteenth century's only edition of Milton's prose in 1738. Six versions of the collected or selected prose appeared in the nineteenth century (edited by Charles Symmons, 1806; George Burnett, 1809; Robert Fletcher, 1833; Rufus Griswold, 1845; John Mitford, 1851; J. A. St. John, 1853). Griswold's was the first American edition, but the American Founders, and particularly Jefferson, acquired earlier editions from overseas and were influenced by them (see 269–70). The two major editions of Milton's collected prose in the twentieth century were both American, the Columbia *Works of John Milton,* including the poetry (1931–38) and the magisterial, scholarly Yale *Complete Prose Works of John Milton* (1953–82).

The notable increase in the interest in Milton beginning in the last decades of the twentieth century can be traced to two factors: the professionalization and rapid expansion of Milton studies, for which the prose works represented a relatively untilled field, and the resonance between the temper of the times and Milton's oppositional attitude toward authority. The radical Milton appealed to academics in the 1960s through the '80s and beyond, if less so to undergraduates after the '70s. In this century, Milton's theological commitments have attracted more critical scrutiny than ever, particularly for their impact on his late poetry and indeed on critical evaluation of that poetry.

Why read Milton's prose now? We read Milton's prose because of his poetry, of course, but also for the perspective afforded by the prose on crucial events in English history and Milton's experience of them. The prose works gathered in this volume are invaluable contexts for Milton's poems. The attacks on bishops in the anti-prelatical tracts and on tyrants (and Charles I) in his political tracts tell us something about Milton's attitude toward religious and civil authority and by extension help us to understand the seductive power of Satan in *Paradise Lost* and *Paradise Regained.* A careful reading of Milton's discussion of free will and virtue in *Areopagitica* will illuminate his dramas of choice, from the *Masque* through his epics and on to *Samson Agonistes.* To wrestle with Milton's arguments on marriage, divorce, and the relation of man and woman in the divorce tracts is to be armed against simplistic understandings of gender in Milton, whether one is tempted to call him a misogynist or a feminist. While one must be careful to avoid reducing poetry to dogma, surveying the independent and often heretical tenets elaborated in the *Christian Doctrine* brings into focus the idiosyncratic fertility of Milton's retelling of the Genesis story in epic form.

Reading the prose provides another perspective on Milton the man and writer. Coleridge said that "it is a sense of [his] intense egotism that gives me the greatest pleasure in reading Milton's works. The egotism of such a man is a revelation of spirit."[1] The selections in this volume include most of the passages of dispersed autobiography and self-representation in Milton's prose. We learn something of who Milton was, who he thought he was, and who he wanted readers to think he was. Separating these senses is itself part of the challenge and pleasure of reading Milton. Milton carefully crafted his image, which he then deployed to purchase authority for his prose and his verse.

And, finally, we read the prose because it is often a poet's prose, with brilliantly rendered figures and complex expressive structures that show us the form and pressure of the events and ideas Milton experienced, celebrated, confronted, mourned, and suffered. In the prose as in the poetry (if not as continuously), Milton writes in a style that "by certain vital signs it had, was likely to live" (p. 88). We can witness the development of Milton's style over the years and his deftness in fitting form to rhetorical purpose (Corns 1982). Readers of Milton's prose have their favorite passages. Most would include *Areopagitica*'s celebrated description of the life of books,

1. *From Specimens of the Table Talk of the Late Samuel Taylor Coleridge,* ed. Henry Nelson Coleridge, 2 vols. (London, 1835), 2:241.

> For books are not absolutely dead things, but do contain a potency of life in them to be as active as that soul was whose progeny they are; nay, they do preserve as in a vial the purest efficacy and extraction of that living intellect that bred them. I know they are as lively and as vigorously productive as those fabulous dragon's teeth, and, being sown up and down, may chance to spring up armed men. And yet, on the other hand, unless wariness be used, as good almost kill a man as kill a good book. Who kills a man kills a reasonable creature, God's image, but he who destroys a good book kills reason itself, kills the image of God, as it were, in the eye. Many a man lives a burden to the earth, but a good book is the precious lifeblood of a master spirit, embalmed and treasured up on purpose to a life beyond life. (p. 178)

Libraries extract sentences from this passage to carve over their doors, and with good reason. Milton intends his account of a good book more seriously than most today would credit. By "precious lifeblood" he means active intellectual potency. Be forewarned that he lies in wait to shape and to sway his readers.

We have edited the English prose works from the early editions indicated in the headnotes. The translations from Milton's non-English prose (here, the *Commonplace Book, Prolusions, Familiar Letters,* the *Second Defense of the English People,* and *Christian Doctrine*) are taken with permission from the Yale University Press edition of the *Complete Prose Works.* Deviations from these translations are detailed in our notes to the texts. For their help and advice in compiling the present volume the editors wish to thank Christopher Chapman, Rebecca Flores, David Harper, Dustin Stewart, and Maryam Zomorodian.

References and Abbreviations

Most of the many editions, books, and articles cited in the notes and headnotes can be found, alphabetized by author, in Works Cited at the end of this volume. Where an author's surname is given without a date, it means that only one of this author's works has been cited in the edition. Where a name is coupled with a date, it means that at least two works by this author have been cited. Multiple entries in Works Cited are arranged chronologically. Books that Milton refers to in passing in his prose works receive a full citation in our notes and do not reappear in Works Cited.

We use these abbreviations for works by John Milton:

1637	*A Masque Presented at Ludlow Castle* (1637).
1645	*Poems of Mr. John Milton* (1645).
1667	*Paradise Lost. A Poem Written in Ten Books* (1667).
1671	*Paradise Regained. A Poem in IV Books. To which is added Samson Agonistes* (1671).
1674	*Paradise Lost. A Poem in Twelve Books. The Second Edition . . .* (1674).
BMS	Bridgewater manuscript of *Masque.*
CMS	Manuscript of poems by Milton at Trinity College, Cambridge.
Yale	*Complete Prose Works of John Milton,* ed. Don M. Wolfe et al. (8 vols., Yale Univ. Press, 1953–80).
Animad	*Animadversions on the Remonstrant's Defense*
Apology	*An Apology for Smectymnuus*
Areop	*Areopagitica*
CD	*Christian Doctrine*
Damon	*Epitaph for Damon*
DDD	*The Doctrine and Discipline of Divorce*
Eikon	*Eikonoklastes*
Il Pens	*Il Penseroso*
L'All	*L'Allegro*
Lyc	*Lycidas*
Masque	*A Masque Presented at Ludlow Castle*
Nat Ode	*On the Morning of Christ's Nativity*

Of Ed	*Of Education*
Of Ref	*Of Reformation*
PL	*Paradise Lost*
PR	*Paradise Regained*
RCG	*The Reason of Church Government Urged Against Prelaty*
REW	*The Ready and Easy Way to Establish a Free Commonwealth*
SA	*Samson Agonistes*
TKM	*The Tenure of Kings and Magistrates*
1Def	*Pro Populo Anglicano Defensio* (*A Defense of the English People*)
2Def	*Defensio Secunda* (*Second Defense of the English People*)

We use the following abbreviations for works by Shakespeare:

ADO	*Much Ado About Nothing*
ANT	*Antony and Cleopatra*
AWW	*All's Well That Ends Well*
AYL	*As You Like It*
COR	*Coriolanus*
HAM	*Hamlet*
1H4	*The First Part of King Henry the Fourth*
2H4	*The Second Part of King Henry the Fourth*
H5	*King Henry the Fifth*
JC	*Julius Caesar*
LLL	*Love's Labor's Lost*
LR	*King Lear*
MAC	*Macbeth*
MM	*Measure for Measure*
MND	*A Midsummer Night's Dream*
MV	*The Merchant of Venice*
OTH	*Othello*
ROM	*Romeo and Juliet*
R2	*King Richard the Second*
R3	*King Richard the Third*
TMP	*The Tempest*
TN	*Twelfth Night*
TRO	*Troilus and Cressida*
VEN	*Venus and Adonis*
WIV	*The Merry Wives of Windsor*
WT	*The Winter's Tale*

Unless otherwise indicated, we quote the Bible from the *AV* (King James Version), and use standard abbreviations when referring to its books; we sometimes cite *Geneva* (*The Geneva Bible*, 1588). Poetry in English, except where otherwise indicated, we cite from the Oxford authors series. Classical works are cited from the Loeb Classical Library unless otherwise noted, with standard abbreviations, such as, prominently, *Il.* and *Od.* for Homer's *Iliad* and *Odyssey*, *Ec.* and *Aen.* for Vergil's *Eclogues* and *Aeneid*, and *Her.* and *Met.* for Ovid's *Heroides* and *Metamorphoses.*

We also use these abbreviations:

Edmund Spenser, *SC*, *FQ* *The Shepheardes Calender*, *The Faerie Queene*

A Chronology of Milton's Life

1608 (December 9) John Milton born on Bread Street in London.

1615 (November 24?) Brother Christopher born.

1620 (?) Enters St. Paul's School under the headmastership of Alexander Gill, Sr. Begins his friendship with Charles Diodati. Thomas Young tutors Milton at home.

1625 (February 12) Admitted to Christ's College, Cambridge.

1629 (March 26) Receives his B.A. degree. In December writes *On the Morning of Christ's Nativity.*

1632 (July 3) Receives his M.A. degree. Retires to his father's country house at Hammersmith for continued study.

1634 (September 29) *A Masque* performed at Ludlow Castle in Wales.

1635 or 36 Moves with his parents to Horton.

1637 *A Masque* published (dated 1637 but possibly published in 1638). Mother, Sara, dies in Horton on April 3. *Lycidas* written in November and published the next year.

1638–9 Milton tours the Continent from April or May 1638 to July or August 1639. Charles Diodati dies in August 1638.

1639 Settles in London, where he makes his living as a tutor.

1641 Earliest antiprelatical tracts—*Of Reformation* (May), *Of Prelatical Episcopacy* (June or July), *Animadversions on the Remonstrant's Defense* (July)—published.

1642 Publishes *The Reason of Church Government* (January or February) and *An Apology for Smectymnuus* (April). Marries Mary Powell in June or July. In August she leaves him and the Civil War begins.

1643 *The Doctrine and Discipline of Divorce* published in August.

1644 The second edition of *The Doctrine and Discipline of Divorce* published in February; *Of Education* in June; *The Judgment of Martin Bucer* in August; *Areopagitica* in November.

1645 Two more divorce pamphlets, *Tetrachordon* and *Colasterion,* published in March. Reconciles with Mary in July or August and moves to a larger house in Barbican in September.

1646 *Poems of Mr. John Milton* published in January, dated 1645. Daughter Anne born July 29.

1647 (March 13) On or about this date his father dies, leaving Milton the Bread Street house and a moderate estate. (September–October) Moves to a smaller house in High Holborn.

1648 (October 25) Daughter Mary born.

1649 (January 30) Charles I executed. *Eikon Basilike* published a week later. (February 13) *The Tenure of Kings and Magistrates* published, with a second edition in September. (March 15) Appointed Secretary for Foreign Tongues and ordered to answer *Eikon Basilike.* (May 11) Salmasius's *Defensio Regia* arrives in England. (October 6) *Eikonoklastes* published, answering *Eikon Basilike.*

1651 (February 24) The *Pro Populo Anglicano Defensio* (*A Defense of the English People*) published, answering Salmasius. (March 16) Son John born.

1652 (February or March) Total blindness descends. Daughter Deborah born May 2. Wife Mary dies on May 5. Son John dies in June.

1653 Duties as Secretary for Foreign Tongues are reduced by the addition of an assistant. Cromwell installed as Protector in December.

1654 *Defensio Secunda* (*Second Defense of the English People*) published in May.

1655 Milton is pensioned in April and though he continues to work for the Protectorate, devotes more time to private studies. *Pro Se Defensio* (*Defense of Himself*) published in August.

1656 (November 12) Marries Katharine Woodcock.

1657 (October 19) Daughter Katharine born.

1658 Probably begins work on *Paradise Lost.* Wife Katharine dies on February 3. Daughter Katharine dies on March 17. Cromwell dies in September, succeeded by his son Richard.

1659 *A Treatise of Civil Power* published in February. Richard Cromwell resigns in May. *Considerations Touching the Likeliest Means to Remove Hirelings out of the Church* published in August.

1660 *The Ready and Easy Way to Establish a Free Commonwealth* published in February, with a second edition in April. Charles II proclaimed king in May. Milton arrested and imprisoned between September and November and released in December.

1663 (February 24) Marries Elizabeth Minshull. Moves to a house in Artillery Walk, near Bunhill Fields.

1665 Around June, moves to Chalfont St. Giles to avoid the London plague.

1667 (October or November) *Paradise Lost* published as a poem in ten books.

1670 (around November 1) *History of Britain* published.

1670 *Paradise Regained* and *Samson Agonistes* published.

1672 *Artis Logicae* (*The Art of Logic*) published.

1673 *Of True Religion* published. An enlarged edition of *Poems* published, also including *Of Education.*

1674 *Epistolae Familiarum* (*Familiar Letters*) published, including his *Prolusions. Paradise Lost. A Poem in Twelve Books* published around July 1. Milton dies November 9 or 10 and is buried in St. Giles, Cripplegate.

Minutes of the Life of Mr. John Milton

John Aubrey

There are several seventeenth-century Milton biographers, including the anonymous biographer (most likely Milton's friend Cyriack Skinner), the Oxford historian Anthony à Wood, Milton's nephew and former student Edward Phillips, and the deist John Toland. One can find their works in Helen Darbishire's *The Early Lives of Milton* (1932), which attributes the anonymous biography to Edward Phillips's brother, John. We choose to print the biographical notes gathered by the antiquarian John Aubrey, which are notable for their author's extraordinary attention to personal details and efforts to verify his information by consulting those who knew Milton well, including the poet's widow, his brother, and some of his friends.

Aubrey's manuscript notes are loosely organized, partly chronologically and partly by the person interviewed. Our text follows the chronologically arranged version established by Andrew Clark (2:62–72). Those wanting to identify the sources of individual comments may consult Clark's edition or Darbishire's. We have reproduced Clark's interpolated headings, but we have in some places made different choices in our inclusions and exclusions. We have also modernized the text, changing punctuation and spelling. Aubrey's notes are peppered with ellipses, where he leaves blanks to be filled in should further information appear. Bracketed ellipses in our text indicate places where we omit material found in Clark's edition; otherwise the ellipses are Aubrey's.

[His parentage]

His mother was a Bradshaw.

Mr. John Milton was of an Oxfordshire family.

His grandfather, . . . , (a Roman Catholic), of Holton, in Oxfordshire, near Shotover.

His father was brought up in the University of Oxon, at Christ Church, and his grandfather disinherited him because he kept not to the Catholic religion (he found a Bible in English in his chamber). So thereupon he came to London, and became a scrivener (brought up by a friend of his; was not an apprentice) and got a plentiful estate by it, and left it off many years before he died. He was an ingenious man; delighted in music; composed many songs now in print, especially that of *Oriana*.[1]

I have been told that the father composed a song of fourscore parts for the Landgrave of Hesse, for which [his] highness sent a medal of gold, or a noble present. He died about 1647; buried in Cripplegate church, from his house in the Barbican.

[His birth]

His son John was born in Bread Street, in London, at the Spread Eagle, which was his house (he had also in that street another house, the Rose, and other houses in other places).

He was born Anno Domini . . . the . . . day of . . . , about . . . o'clock in the . . .

(John Milton was born the 9th of December, 1608, *die Veneris*,[2] half an hour after 6 in the morning.)

[His precocity]

Anno Domini 1619, he was ten years old, as by his picture; and was then a poet.

[School, college, and travel]

His schoolmaster then was a Puritan, in Essex, who cut his hair short.

He went to school to old Mr. Gill, at Paul's School. Went at his own charge only to Christ's College in Cambridge at fifteen, where he stayed eight years at least. Then he traveled into France and Italy (had Sir H. Wotton's commendatory letters). At Geneva he contracted a great friendship with the learned Dr. Diodati of Geneva (*vide* his poems). He was acquainted with Sir Henry Wotton, ambassador at Venice, who delighted in his company. He was several years <*Quaere*, how many? *Resp.*, two years> beyond sea, and returned to England just upon the breaking out of the civil wars.

From his brother, Christopher Milton: When he went to school, when he was very young, he studied very hard and sat up very late, commonly till twelve or

1. ***Oriana:*** Milton's father contributed a song, "Fair Orian," to *The Triumphs of Oriana* (1601), a volume of songs dedicated to Queen Elizabeth I.
2. ***die Veneris:*** Venus's Day, i.e., Friday.

one o'clock at night, and his father ordered the maid to sit up for him; and in those years (10) composed many copies of verses which might well become a riper age. And was a very hard student in the university, and performed all his exercises there with very good applause. His first tutor there was Mr. Chapell; from whom receiving some unkindness <whipped him>; he was afterwards (though it seemed contrary to the rules of the college) transferred to the tuition of one Mr. Tovell,[3] who died parson of Lutterworth.

He went to travel about the year 1638 and was abroad about a year's space, chiefly in Italy.

[Return to England]

Immediately after his return he took a lodging at Mr. Russell's, a tailor, in St. Bride's churchyard, and took into his tuition his [Milton's] sister's two sons, Edward and John Phillips, the first 10, the other 9 years of age; and in a year's time made them capable of interpreting a Latin author at sight, etc., and within three years they went through the best of Latin and Greek poets: Lucretius and Manilius <and with him the use of the globes and some rudiments of arithmetic and geometry> of the Latins; Hesiod, Aratus, Dionysius Afer, Oppian, Apollonii *Argonautica,* and Quintus Calaber. Cato, Varro, and Columella *De re rustica* were the very first authors they learned. As he was severe on the one hand, so he was most familiar and free in his conversation to those to whom most sour in his way of education. N.B. he made his nephews songsters, and sing, from the time they were with him.

[First wife and children]

He married his first wife, Mary Powell of Fosthill,[4] at Shotover, in Oxonshire, Anno Domini . . . ; by whom he had four children. [He] hath two daughters living: Deborah was his amanuensis (he taught her Latin, and to read Greeke to him when he had lost his eyesight, which was anno Domini . . .).

[Separation from his first wife]

She went from him to her mother's at . . . in the king's quarters, near Oxford, anno Domini . . . ; and wrote the *Triplechord* about divorce.[5]

Two opinions do not well on the same bolster. She was a . . . Royalist, and went to her mother to the King's quarters, near Oxford. I have perhaps so much charity to her that she might not wrong his bed: but what man, especially con-

3. I.e., Nathaniel Tovey.
4. I.e., Forest Hill.
5. **Triplechord** ***about divorce:*** most likely *Tetrachordon* (four strings).

templative, would like to have a young wife environed and stormed by the sons of Mars, and those of the enemy party?

His first wife (Mrs. Powell, a Royalist) was brought up and lived where there was a great deal of company and merriment <dancing, etc.>. And when she came to live with her husband, at Mr. Russell's in St. Bride's churchyard, she found it very solitary; no company came to her; oftentimes heard his nephews beaten and cry. This life was irksome to her, and so she went to her parents at Fosthill. He sent for her, after some time; and I think his servant was evilly entreated: but as for manner of wronging his bed, I never heard the least suspicions; nor had he, of that, any jealousy.

[Second wife]

He had a middle wife, whose name was Katharine Woodcock. No child living by her.

[Third wife]

He married his second [sic] wife, Elizabeth Minshull, anno . . . (the year before the sickness): a gentle person, a peaceful and agreeable humor.

[His public employment]

He was Latin secretary to the Parliament.

[His blindness]

His sight began to fail him at first upon his writing against Salmasius, and before 'twas full completed one eye absolutely failed. Upon the writing of other books after that, his other eye decayed.

His eyesight was decaying about 20 years before his death. His father read without spectacles at 84. His mother had very weak eyes, and used spectacles presently after she was thirty years old.

[Writings after his blindness]

After he was blind he wrote these following books, viz.: *Paradise Lost, Paradise Regained, Grammar, Dictionary* (imperfect).

I heard that after he was blind that he was writing a Latin dictionary (in the hands of Moses Pitt). *Vidua affirmat*[6] she gave all his papers (among which this

6. **Vidua affirmat:** His widow maintains.

dictionary, imperfect) to his nephew, a sister's son, that he brought up . . . Phillips, who lives near the Maypole in the Strand. She has a great many letters by her from learned men, his acquaintance, both of England and beyond the sea.

[His later residences]

He lived in several places, e.g., Holborn near Kingsgate. He died in Bunhill, opposite the Artillery-garden wall.

[His death and burial]

He died of the gout, struck in the 9th or 10th of November, 1674, as appears by his apothecary's book.

He lies buried in St. Giles Cripplegate, upper end of the chancel at the right hand, *vide* his gravestone. Memorandum: his stone is now removed, for about two years since (now 1681) the two steps to the communion table were raised. I guess John Speed[7] and he lie together.

[Personal characteristics]

His harmonical and ingenious soul did lodge in a beautiful and well-proportioned body—*"In toto nusquam corpore menda fuit,"* Ovid.[8]

He was a spare man. He was scarce so tall as I am, [. . .] of middle stature.

He had auburn hair. His complexion exceeding fair—he was so fair that they called him *the Lady of Christ's College.* Oval face. His eye a dark gray.

He had a delicate tuneable voice, and had good skill. His father instructed him. He had an organ in his house; he played on that most.

Of a very cheerful humor. He would be cheerful even in his gout-fits, and sing.

He was very healthy and free from all diseases: seldom took any physic (only sometimes he took manna):[9] only towards his latter end he was visited with the gout, spring and fall.

He had a very good memory; but I believe that his excellent method of thinking and disposing did much to help his memory.

7. ***John Speed:*** author of *The History of Great Britain,* he is buried in St. Giles, as is John Foxe, author of *The Book of Martyrs* and *Acts and Monuments.*

8. 1 *Amores* 5.18: "There was not a blemish on her body."

9. ***manna:*** a mild laxative.

He pronounced the letter R <*littera canina*[10]> very hard (a certain sign of a satirical wit—from John Dryden.).

[Portraits of him]

Write his name in red letters on his pictures, with his widow, to preserve.[11]

His widow has his picture, drawn very well and like, when a Cambridge-scholar, which ought to be engraven; for the pictures before his books are not *at all* like him.

[His habits]

His exercise was chiefly walking.

He was an early riser <*scil.* at 4 a clock *manè*[12]>; yea, after he lost his sight. He had a man read to him. The first thing he read was the Hebrew bible, and that was at 4 h. *manè*, 1/2 h. plus. Then he contemplated.

At 7 his man came to him again, and then read to him again and wrote till dinner; the writing was as much as the reading. His (2nd) daughter, Deborah, could read to him in Latin, Italian and French, and Greek. [She] married in Dublin to one Mr. Clarke <sells silk, etc.>; very like her father. The other sister is Mary, more like her mother.

After dinner he used to walk 3 or 4 hours at a time (he always had a garden where he lived); went to bed about 9.

Temperate man, rarely drank between meals.

Extreme pleasant in his conversation and at dinner, supper, etc; but satirical.

[Notes about some of his works]

From Mr. E. Phillips:—All the time of writing his *Paradise Lost*, his vein began at the autumnal equinoctial, and ceased at the vernal or thereabouts (I believe about May); and this was 4 or 5 years of his doing it. He began about 2 years before the king came in, and finished about three years after the king's restoration.[13]

In the 4th book of *Paradise Lost* there are about six verses of Satan's exclamation to the sun, which Mr. E. Phillips remembers about 15 or 16 years before ever

10. **littera canina:** dog letter, so called because making a continuous *r* sound resembles a dog's growl when threatening attack.

11. A note to himself.

12. **Scil. . . . manè:** It is well known (*scilicet*) . . . in the morning.

13. I.e., Milton composed his epic between 1658 and 1663.

his poem was thought of, which verses were intended for the beginning of a tragedy which he had designed, but was diverted from it by other business.

Whatever he wrote against monarchy was out of no animosity to the king's person, or out of any faction or interest, but out of a pure zeal to the liberty of mankind, which he thought would be greater under a free state than under a monarchial government. His being so conversant in Livy and the Roman authors, and the greatness he saw done by the Roman commonwealth, and the virtue of their great commanders induced him to.

From Mr. Abraham Hill:—Memorandum: his sharp writing against Alexander More, of Holland, upon a mistake, notwithstanding he had given him by the ambassador all satisfaction to the contrary: viz. that the book called *Clamor* was writ by Peter du Moulin. Well, that was all one; he having writ it,[14] it should go into the world; one of them was as bad as the other.

Memorandum:—Mr. Theodore Haak. Regiae Societatis Socius, hath translated half his *Paradise Lost* into High Dutch in such blank verse, which is very well liked of by Germanus Fabricius, Professor at Heidelberg, who sent to Mr. Haak a letter upon this translation: *"incredibile est quantum nos omnes affecerit gravitas styli, et copia lectissimorum verborum,"*[15] etc.—*vide* the letter.

Mr. John Milton made two admirable panegyrics, as to sublimity of wit, one on Oliver Cromwell, and the other on Thomas, Lord Fairfax, both which his nephew Mr. Phillips hath. But he hath hung back these two years, as to imparting copies to me for the collection of mine [. . .]. Were they made in commendation of the devil, 'twere all one to me: 'tis the ὕψος[16] that I look after. I have been told that 'tis beyond Waller's or anything in that kind.[17] [. . .]

[His acquaintance]

He was visited much by learned [men]; more than he did desire.

He was mightily importuned to go into France and Italy. Foreigners came much to see him, and much admired him, and offered to him great preferments to come over to them; and the only inducement of several foreigners that came over into England was chiefly to see Oliver Protector and Mr. John Milton; and would see the house and chamber where he was born. He was much more admired abroad than at home.

14. Milton published his *Second Defense of the English People* (1654), with its attack on More as the author of the *Cry of the King's Blood* (*Regii Sanguinis Clamor*), even after learning that another had written the book.
15. "It is incredible how much the dignity of his style and his most excellent diction have affected all of us."
16. ὕψος: loftiness, altitude.
17. We omit here a catalog of Milton's works.

His familiar learned acquaintance were Mr. Andrew Marvell, Mr. Skinner, Dr. Pagett, M.D.

Mr. . . . [Cyriack] Skinner, who was his disciple.

John Dryden, Esq., Poet Laureate, who very much admires him, and went to him to have leave to put his *Paradise Lost* into a drama in rhyme. Mr. Milton received him civilly, and told him *he would give him leave to tag his verses.*[18]

His widow assures me that Mr. T. Hobbes was not one of his acquaintance, that her husband did not like him at all, but he would acknowledge him to be a man of great parts, and a learned man. Their interests and tenets did run counter to each other, *vide* Mr. Hobbes' *Behemoth.*

18. John Dryden's *The State of Innocence, and Fall of Man: An Opera Written in Heroique Verse,* based on *Paradise Lost,* was published in 1677. A *tag* was an ornamental, metal-tipped lace or string that dangled from a garment.

THE ESSENTIAL PROSE OF JOHN MILTON

Familiar Letters

This section contains ten letters. With the exception of the so-called "Letter to a Friend," which was composed in English and for which there is a separate headnote, the letters by Milton are in Latin and cannot be regarded as mere mail, documents that have somehow survived from a private correspondence. "You ask what I am thinking of?" Milton writes to Diodati. "So help me God, an immortality of fame." However personal the thought may have been, it belongs as well to the genre in which Milton is writing. For the Latin familiar letter fused private and public, friendship and literary ambition. In Milton's day, such letters were written with an eye toward publication. As authors did the usual business of letter writing (thanking, requesting, praising, criticizing, excusing, seducing, opining, joking), they simultaneously demonstrated their mastery of Latin style, imitating the precedents of Cicero, Ovid, and Seneca. Milton published his *Epistolae Familiarum* in 1674, the last year of his life (see introduction to *Prolusions*). This book has been translated and annotated by Phyllis B. and E. M. W. Tillyard (1932).

The earliest of these ten pieces, probably, are the undated Greek letters sent to Milton by Charles Diodati, the great friend of his childhood. Together with the two Latin letters dated in September 1637 from Milton to Diodati, they convey the jocular yet somewhat tense idealism of this friendship. Diodati, who eventually studied medicine, chides Milton for his rigorous and possibly debilitating programs of self-study. Milton, for his part, readily confesses that his temperament "allows no delay, no rest, no anxiety . . . about scarcely anything to distract me, until I attain my object and complete some great period, as it were, of my studies." He pursues the idea of the beautiful as diligently as Ceres "sought her daughter Prosperina." The analogy is itself a pursuit of the beautiful.

In the 1628 letter to Alexander Gill, one of his teachers at St. Paul's grammar school, and son of its headmaster, Milton speaks diffidently of verses that he has sent, "light-minded nonsense" composed for a commencement ceremony at his college. Yet he is clearly eager for his former teacher, himself a poet, to evaluate them and to respond by sending verses of his own for Milton to read. Evidently, the scholasticism of Cambridge and the lack of preparation of his fellow students, clergy in training for the most part, had aroused Milton's skepticism and a corresponding nostalgia for the humanist training he received at St. Paul's.

The poet and statesman Sir Henry Wotton writes in 1638 to thank Milton for his gift of the anonymous 1638 edition of *A Masque.* After complimenting the work ("I must plainly confess to have seen yet nothing parallel in our language"), he proceeds to offer aid and advice with regard to the young poet's forthcoming trip to the Continent. Perhaps at the urging of the publisher, this letter was printed before *A Masque* in the 1645 *Poems.* It was omitted in the second edition of 1673.

Milton's letter to the Vatican librarian, Lukas Holste, was written during his second stay in Florence. Having just returned from Rome, Milton thanks Holste for his courtesies, praises his patron, Cardinal Barberini, and in his eager approval of Holste's various scholarly projects savors the humanist ideal of a republic of learning unspoiled by religious and political differences.

The Athens-born Leonard Philaras was a scholar, diplomat, and champion of Greek liberty. Visting London in 1654, he asked the blind Milton to supply him with an account of his symptoms in the hope that a French physician, François Thévenin, might be able to treat him. Milton's reply is our main authority for any attempt to diagnose his condition. Though he hopes for the best, Milton is clearly resigned to his blindness, and the letter closes with evocations of *Sonnet 22.*

This representative selection of Milton's private correspondence concludes with one of his two 1657 letters to Henry De Brass, a young man who wrote to ask Milton, then nearing fifty and totally blind, for his evaluation of Latin historians. Students who read Milton's *History of Britain* will find that he attempts to achieve the same brevity of style for which he praises Sallust. Milton no doubt felt that his experience as Latin Secretary for the Commonwealth had also made him equal to the task of "writing worthily of worthy deeds." The self-consciousness and worry that seem to break through his youthful letters have faded, and Milton's benign attitude toward his correspondent calls to mind the generosity the young Milton was shown by Sir Henry Wotton nearly twenty years before.

Our texts of the Greek and Latin letters follow the translations in the Yale edition of Milton's prose. We print the text of *Letter to a Friend* from a facsimile of the *CMS* (Wright 1972, 6–7).

Diodati Greets Milton Cheerfully[1]

The present state of the weather seems to be quite jealous of the arrangements we made when lately we parted, for it has been stormy and unsettled for two whole days now. But nevertheless, so much do I desire your company that in my longing I dream of and all but prophesy fair weather and calm, and everything golden for tomorrow, so that we may enjoy our fill of philosophical and learned conversation. Therefore I wished to write you to invite and encourage you, in fear lest you turn your mind to other plans, despairing of sunshine and enjoyment, for the time at least. But be of good cheer, my friend, and stand by the plans we made together, and adopt a festive spirit, gayer than that of today. For tomorrow all will be fair; the air and the sun and the river, and trees and little birds and earth and men will laugh and dance with us as we make holiday—but let this be said with humility. Only do you be ready to set out when called, or even uncalled, to come to me, who long to see you. "For Menelaus, good at the war-cry, came to him unbidden."[2] Farewell.

1. Two undated letters to Milton by his boyhood friend Charles Diodati (d. 1638) survive. Both are in Greek. On their friendship and correspondence, see Parker (1968, 1:59–61), Kerrigan (1983, 48–50), and Rumrich (1999). In this volume, see *Elegies 1* and *6, Damon,* and *Sonnet 4.* His name does not appear in Milton's English verse or in his prose.
2. Homer, *Il.* 2.408. Other Greek heroes must be called to Agamemnon's tent for a midnight council, but *Menelaus,* because of his heartfelt sympathy with his brother, comes without being bidden.

Diodati Greets Milton

I have no complaint with my present way of life with this one exception, that I lack some noble soul skilled in conversation. Such a person I do miss; but there is abundance, of everything else here in the country. For what is lacking when the days are long, the countryside most lovely with flowers, and waving and teeming with leaves, on every branch a nightingale or goldfinch, or some other little bird singing and warbling in rivalry? Where are walks of utmost variety, a table neither scant nor overburdened, and quiet sleep. Could I but add to these a good companion, learned and initiate, I would be happier than the King of Persia. Still there is always something lacking in human affairs, wherefore one must be moderate. But you, extraordinary man, why do you despise the gifts of nature? Why such inexcusable perseverance, bending over books and studies day and night? Live, laugh, enjoy your youth and the hours, and stop reading the serious, the light, and the indolent works of ancient wise men, wearing yourself out the while. I, who in all other things am your inferior, in this one thing, in knowing the proper limit of labor, both seem to myself, and am, your better. Farewell, and be merry, but not in the manner of Sardanapalus in Soli.[3]

3. **Sardanapalus:** Greek name of a seventh-century Assyrian king, probably an amalgamation of several Assyrian kings. Classical authors present him as a sybaritic transvestite. *Soli* was a town in Cyprus under Assyrian control. Parker confuses it with a coastal town in Asia Minor by the same name (1968, 1:60).

To Alexander Gill[1]

In my former letter I did not so much answer you, as avoid the duty of answering;[2] and so I silently promised that another letter would soon follow, in which I should reply at somewhat greater length to your most friendly challenge. But even if I had not promised, it must be confessed that this letter is your most rightful due; for I think that each one of your letters cannot be repaid except by two of mine, or if it be reckoned more accurately, not even by a hundred of mine. Included with this letter, behold that project about which I wrote you somewhat more obscurely, a problem on which, when your letter reached me, I was laboring with great effort, harried by the shortness of time. For by chance a certain Fellow of our House,[3] who was going to act as respondent in the philosophical disputation at this academic assembly, entrusted to my puerility the verses which annual custom requires to be written on the questions, he himself being long past light-minded nonsense of that kind and more intent on serious things.[4] It is these, printed, that I have sent you, since I knew you to be the keenest judge of poetry in general and the most honest judge of mine. Now if you will deign to send me yours in turn, there will certainly be no one who will enjoy them more, though there will be, I confess, one who will better appraise their merit. Indeed whenever I remember your almost constant conversations with me (which even in Athens itself, nay in the very Academy, I long for and

1. Alexander Gill the younger (c. 1597–1644) was the son of the headmaster of St. Paul's school and taught there. He was already a published poet and, shortly after Milton wrote this letter, found himself in prison for unguarded expression of his political opinions (Parker 1968, 1:50–51).
2. Although two other letters to Gill survive, neither appears to be the letter to which Milton here refers.
3. **Fellow of our House:** that is, a graduate of Milton's college now in its employ.
4. Various short works have been proposed as candidates for the verses entrusted to Milton, among them *That Nature Does Not Suffer from Old Age* and *Of the Platonic Idea as Understood by Aristotle*. Both were composed around this time. The annual assembly to which Milton refers was Commencement, held on July 1, 1628, the day before the date of this letter.

need), I think immediately, not without sorrow, of how much benefit my absence has cheated me—me who never left you without a visible increase and growth of knowledge, quite as if I had been to some market of learning. There is really hardly anyone among us, as far as I know, who, almost completely unskilled and unlearned in philology and philosophy alike, does not flutter off to theology unfledged, quite content to touch that also most lightly, learning barely enough for sticking together a short harangue by any method whatever and patching it with worn-out pieces from various sources—a practice carried far enough to make one fear that the priestly ignorance of a former age may gradually attack our clergy.[5] And so, finding almost no intellectual companions here, I should longingly look straight to London, did I not consider retiring into a deeply literary leisure during this summer vacation and hiding as it were in the cloisters of the Muses. But since you already do so every day, I think it almost a crime to interrupt you longer with my noise at present. Farewell.

Cambridge, July 2, 1628.

5. See *Of Education* for a more developed version of Milton's critique of the universities' scholastic curriculum.

Letter to a Friend

The so-called "Letter to a Friend" survives in two drafts in the Trinity College manuscript (*CMS*) of Milton's minor poems, which also contains seven pages of notes for projected tragedies. Like those notes and the manuscript poems, which show evidence of considerable revision, the "Letter" opens a window on the mind of the young Milton. The intended recipient (we have no evidence that the letter was ever sent) is not specified. An emerging consensus pointed to Thomas Young, Presbyterian minister and Milton's tutor from 1618 to 1620 (from Milton's tenth through twelfth years), but recently Barbara Lewalski (2000) has taken the letter's composition in English as evidence that the recipient was neither a minister nor a university acquaintance. In any event, we know from the drafts themselves that the "friend" had questioned why Milton had not yet entered the ministry. William Riley Parker's persuasive dating of the letter in 1633 relies on this fact, as Milton would have become eligible for the ministry on his twenty-fourth birthday, in December 1632.

While we print what in the manuscript appears to be the final state of the draft letter, to look at the two drafts with their forests of strikeouts and interlinear and marginal additions is to see Milton in the process of composing himself (Fallon 2007). Although the tone is defensive in places, the revision process tends toward the effacement or qualification of hints of possible blameworthiness. The letter contains in small compass several themes that will become familiar in Milton's later writing: a concern with belatedness, a sense of special vocation, and an insistence on personal rectitude. One can also witness here one of Milton's favorite strategies, turning defense against criticism into assertion of unusual virtue and propriety. Note, for example, how he uses the parable of the laborers in the vineyard, in which those workers who come late receive the same reward as those who have worked all day. This apparent injustice calls for parabolic interpretation, the burden of which seems to be a rebuke to the self-righteous, who think they deserve more from God than others, and a demonstration of the mercy of God, who saves even those who come late. Milton reads the parable in a strained and self-referential manner, however, implying that the workers hired in the eleventh hour are less the objects of divine indulgence than they are particularly meritorious for having spent the earlier hours diligently preparing to serve well.

Sir,

Besides that in sundry other respects I must acknowledge me to profit by you whenever we meet, you are often to me, and were yesterday especially, as a good watchman to admonish that the hours of the night pass on (for so I call my life, as yet obscure and unserviceable to mankind) and that the day with me is at hand wherein Christ commands all to labor while there is light.[1] Which because I am persuaded you do to no other purpose than out of a true desire that God should be honored in everyone, I therefore think myself bound, though unasked, to give you account, as oft as occasion is, of this my tardy moving, according to the precept of my conscience, which I firmly trust is not without God. Yet now I will not strain for any set apology, but only refer myself to what my mind shall have at any time to declare herself at her best ease.

But if you think, as you said, that too much love of learning is in fault, and that I have given up myself to dream away my years in the arms of studious retirement like Endymion with the moon,[2] as the tale of Latmos goes,[3] yet consider that if it were no more but the mere love of learning, whether it proceed from a principle bad, good, or natural, it could not have held out thus long against so strong opposition on the other side of every kind. For if it be bad,[4]

1. Milton alludes to several biblical passages simultaneously here. The imperative to work while it is light is taken from John 9.3–4 and 12.35–36, but the watchman comes from Isa. 21.11–12, a passage often applied to ministers, as Lewalski notes (2000), and also from Matth. 24.42–44 and 25.13–14, passages that bracket the parable of the wise and foolish virgins and precede the parable of the talents, to which Milton alludes later.
2. **moon:** The moon goddess Selene, enchanted by the sight of the shepherd *Endymion* sleeping on Mount *Latmos,* visited him nightly and bore him fifty daughters. Various traditions explain Endymion's sleep: according to one, Selene placed him in an unbroken sleep so that she could enjoy him undisturbed; in another, particularly suited to this context, Endymion, offered anything he might desire by Zeus, chose eternal sleep with eternal youth.
3. **goes:** The manuscript reads, in error, "of goes."
4. **bad:** Here *bad* replaces the scratched-out "evil in me," one example among many in which Milton, as he revises, softens or excises suggestions of his own deficiency or delinquency.

why should not all the fond hopes that forward youth and vanity are fledge with, together with gain, pride, and ambition, call me forward more powerfully than a poor, regardless, and unprofitable sin of curiosity should be able to withhold me, whereby a man cuts himself off from all action, and becomes the most helpless, pusillanimous, and unweaponed creature in the world,[5] the most unfit and unable to do that which all mortals most aspire to, either to defend and be useful to his friends or to offend his enemies? Or if it be to be thought an natural proneness, there is against it a much more potent inclination inbred which about this time of a man's life solicits most, the desire of house and family of his own, to which nothing is esteemed more helpful than the early entering into credible employment, and nothing more hindering than this affected solitariness. And though this were enough, yet there is to this another act, if not of pure yet of refined nature, no less available to dissuade prolonged obscurity, a desire of honor and repute and immortal fame[6] seated in the breast of every true scholar, which all make haste to by the readiest ways of publishing and divulging conceived merits, as well those that shall as those that never shall obtain it. Nature therefore would presently work the more prevalent way if there were nothing but the inferior bent of herself to restrain her.

Lastly, this love of learning, as it is the pursuit of something good, it would sooner follow the more excellent and supreme good known and presented, and so be quickly diverted from the empty and fantastic chase of shadows and notions to the solid good flowing from due and timely obedience to that command in the gospel set out by the terrible seizing of him that hid the talent.[7] It is more probable therefore that not the endless delight of speculation but this very consideration of that great commandment does not press forward as soon as may be to undergo, but keeps off with a sacred reverence and religious advisement how best to undergo, not taking thought of being late so it give advantage to be more fit; for those that were latest lost nothing when the master of the vineyard came to give each one his hire.[8] And here I am come to a stream-head copious enough to disburden itself like Nilus at seven mouths into an ocean, but then I should also run into a reciprocal contradiction of ebbing and flowing at once, and do that which I excuse myself for not doing, preach and not preach. Yet that you may see that I am something suspicious of myself, and do take notice of a certain belatedness in me, I am the bolder to send you some of my nightward thoughts some while since (because they come in not altogether unfitly) made up in a Petrarchan stanza, which I told you of.[9]

5. **world:** The ms. reads "word," not "world." While we adopt the standard reading here, to be *unweaponed . . . in the word* is an explicable meaning in the context of a defense of delaying entry into the clergy.

6. **fame:** The description of the desire for fame as an *act, if not of pure yet of refined nature* foreshadows the description of fame in *Lyc* 71, as "that last infirmity of noble mind."

7. Matt. 25.14–30.

8. Matt. 20.1–16.

9. *Sonnet 7.* Milton copies the sonnet into the first draft of the letter; the second draft contains not the sonnet itself but a placeholder ("after the stanza").

How soon hath Time the subtle thief of youth
Stol'n on his wing my three and twentieth year!
My hasting days fly on with full career,
But my late spring no bud or blossom shew'th.
Perhaps my semblance might deceive the truth,
That I to manhood am arrived so near,
And inward ripeness doth much less appear,
That some more timely-happy spirits endu'th.
Yet be it less or more, or soon or slow,
It shall be still in strictest measure even
To that same lot, however mean or high,
Toward which Time leads me, and the will of Heav'n;
All is, if I have grace to use it so,
As ever in my great Taskmaster's eye.

after the stanza [*Sonnet 7*]

By this I believe you may well repent of having made mention at all of this matter, for if I have not all this while won you to this, I have certainly wearied you to it. This therefore alone may be a sufficient reason for me to keep me as I am, lest having thus tired you singly, I should deal worse with a whole congregation, and spoil all the patience of a parish. For I myself do not only see my own tediousness, but now grow offended with it that has hindered me thus long from coming to the last and best period of my letter, and that which must now chiefly work my pardon, that I am

Your true and unfeigned friend.

To Charles Diodati

Now at last I plainly see that you are trying to outdo me once in obstinate silence. If so, congratulations; have your little glory; see, I write first. Yet certainly, if ever we should debate the reasons why neither has written to the other for so long, do not doubt that I shall be much more excused than you. Obviously so, since I am naturally slow and lazy to write, as you well know; whereas you on the other hand, whether by nature or by habit, can usually be drawn into this sort of correspondence with ease. At the same time it is in my favor that your habit of studying permits you to pause frequently, visit friends, write much, and sometimes make a journey. But my temperament allows no delay, no rest, no anxiety—or at least thought—about scarcely anything to distract me, until I attain my object and complete some great period, as it were, of my studies. And wholly for this reason, not another please, has it happened that I undertake even courtesies more tardily than you. In returning them, however, my Diodati, I am not such a laggard; for I have never committed the crime of letting any letter of yours go unanswered by another of mine. How is it that you, as I hear, have written letters to the bookseller, even oftener to your brother, either of whom could conveniently enough, because of nearness, have been responsible for passing letters on to me—had there been any? But what I really complain of is that you, although you promised that you would visit us whenever you left the city, did not keep your promises. If you had once actually thought of these neglected promises, you would not have lacked immediate reason for writing. And so I had all these things to declaim against you, with reason I think; you will see to the answers yourself. But meanwhile, pray, how is everything? Are you quite well? Are there in those parts any fairly learned people with whom you can associate pleasantly and with whom you can talk, as we have been used to talking? When do you return? How long do you plan to linger among those Hyperboreans?[1] I should like you to answer these questions one by one. But you must not suppose that it is only now that I have your affairs at heart; for know that at the beginning of autumn I turned aside from a journey to see your brother, with the intention of finding out what you were doing. Again recently, when the news had been brought to me accidentally at London (by I know not whom) that you were in the city, immediately and as if by storm I hurried to your lodging, but " 'twas the vision of a shadow,"[2] for nowhere would you appear. Wherefore, if you conveniently can, fly hither with all speed and settle in some place which may offer brighter hope that somehow we may visit each other at least sometimes. Would that you could be as much my rustic neighbor as you are my urban one, but this as it pleases God. I wish I could say more, both about myself and about my studies, but I should prefer to do it in person. Furthermore, tomorrow we return to that country place of ours, and the journey presses so close that I have scarcely been able to throw these words hastily on paper. Farewell.

London, Septemb. [November?] 2. 1637.

1. **Hyperboreans:** those who dwell in the far north, literally "above the north wind." Diodati's actual whereabouts at the time are unknown.
2. Pindar, *Pyth.* 8.95. "In Milton's copy of Pindar at Harvard, the passage containing these words . . . is underlined" (Yale 1:324n4). In context it is an observation on the transience of human life.

To the Same

I see now why you wish me so many healths, when my other friends in their letters usually manage to wish me only one: you evidently want me to know that to those mere wishes which were all that you yourself could formerly and others can still offer, there are just now added to your art as well, and the whole mass as it were of medical power. For you bid me be well six hundred times, as well as I wish to be, and so on. Certainly you must have recently been made Health's very steward, you so squander the whole store of salubrity; or rather

Health herself must doubtless now be your parasite,[1] you so act the king and order her to obey. And so I congratulate you and must thank you on two scores, both for your friendship and for your excellent skill. Indeed, since we had agreed upon it, I long expected letters from you; but though I had not yet received any, I did not, believe me, allow my old affection towards you to cool because of such a trifle. On the contrary, I had already suspected that you would use that very same excuse for tardiness which you have used at the beginning of your letter, and rightly so, considering the intimacy of our friendship. For I do not wish true friendship to be weighed by letters and salutations, which may all be false, but on either hand to rest and sustain itself upon the deep roots of the soul, and, begun with sincere and blameless motives, even though mutual courtesies cease, to be free for life from suspicion and blame. For fostering such a friendship there is need not so much for writing as for a living remembrance of virtues on both sides. Even if you had not written, that obligation would not necessarily remain unfulfilled. Your worth writes to me instead and inscribes real letters on my inmost consciousness; your candor of character writes, and your love of right; your genius writes too (by no means an ordinary one) and further recommends you to me. Therefore do not try to terrorize me, now that you hold that tyrannical citadel of medicine, as if you would take back your six hundred healths, withdrawing them little by little, to the last one, should I by chance desert friendship, which God forbid. And so remove that terrible battery which you seem to have trained on me, forbidding me to be sick without your permission. For lest you threaten too much, know that I cannot help loving people like you. For though I do not know what else God may have decreed for me, this certainly is true: he has instilled into me, if into anyone, a vehement love[2] of the beautiful. Not so diligently is Ceres, according to the Fables, said to have sought her daughter Proserpina, as I seek for this idea of the beautiful, as if for some glorious image, throughout all the shapes and forms of things ("for many are the shapes of things divine"); day and night I search and follow its lead eagerly as if by certain clear traces.[3] Whence it happens that if I find anywhere one who, despising the warped judgment of the public, dares to feel and speak and be that which the greatest wisdom throughout all ages has taught to be best, I shall cling to him immediately from a kind of necessity. But if I, whether by nature or by my fate, am so equipped that I can by no effort and labor of mine rise to such glory and height of fame, still, I think that neither men nor Gods forbid me to reverence and honor those who have attained that glory or who are successfully aspiring to it. But now I know you wish your curiosity satisfied. You make many anxious inquiries, even about what I am thinking. Listen, Diodati, but in secret, lest I blush;

1. **parasite:** one who obtains the hospitality or patronage of the powerful by being obsequious.
2. **vehement love:** Milton breaks from Latin to put this phrase in Greek. Cp. Adam's "vehemence of love" in the Argument to *PL* 9.
3. Milton refers to the search of Ceres for Proserpina after she had been taken to the underworld by Hades. The quoted passage is in Greek and appears in several of Euripides' tragedies, e.g., the concluding chorus of *Bacchae*.

and let me talk to you grandiloquently for a while. You ask what I am thinking of? So help me God, an immortality of fame.[4] What am I doing? Growing my wings and practicing flight.[5] But my Pegasus still raises himself on very tender wings. Let me be wise on my humble level. I shall now tell you seriously what I am planning: to move into some one of the Inns of Court,[6] wherever there is a pleasant and shady walk; for that dwelling will be more satisfactory, both for companionship, if I wish to remain at home, and as a more suitable headquarters, if I choose to venture forth. Where I am now, as you know, I live in obscurity and cramped quarters. You shall also hear about my studies. By continued reading I have brought the affairs of the Greeks to the time when they ceased to be Greeks. I have been occupied for a long time by the obscure history of the Italians under the Longobards, Franks, and Germans, to the time when liberty was granted them by Rudolph, King of Germany. From there it will be better to read separately about what each state did by its own effort.[7] But what about you? How long will you act the son of the family and devote yourself to domestic matters, forgetting urban companionships? For unless this step-motherly warfare be more hazardous than either the Dacian or Sarmatian, you must certainly hurry, and at least make your winter quarters with us.[8] Meanwhile, if you conveniently can, please send me Giustiniani, Historian of the Veneti.[9] On my word I shall see either that he is well cared for until your arrival, or, if you prefer, that he is returned to you shortly. Farewell.

London, Septemb. [November?] 23. 1637.

4. **immortality of fame:** Milton's Latin text simply reads "immortality" [*immortalitatem*], without mention of fame.
5. **Growing my wings:** Milton interjects the Greek verb for sprouting wings (πτεροφυῶ), which in this context suggests the winged soul's quest for immortality in Plato's *Phaedrus* (246e–252c). The Latin verb translated as "practicing" (*meditor*) is better rendered as "contemplating."
6. **Inns of Court:** public houses in the legal district of London.
7. At the time he wrote this letter, Milton's course of private study (1632–38) was drawing to an end. For what he read when, see Hanford 1921.
8. ***Dacian, Sarmatian:*** references to intermittent, fierce second-century conflicts between Rome and tribal forces in central Europe. The reference to *winter quarters* (Lat. *hiberna*) continues the allusion to Roman military history.
9. Milton refers either to Justianus Bernardus, *De Origine Urbis Venetiarum Rebusque ab Ipsa Gestis Historia* (Venice, 1492) or to later translations into Italian.

Sir Henry Wotton to Milton[1]

From the College, this 13. of April, 1638.

SIR,

It was a special favor, when you lately bestowed upon me here, the first taste of your acquaintance, though no longer then to make me know that I wanted

1. By the time he befriended Milton, Wotton (1568–1639) was nearing the end of a remarkable life, during which he was the admired friend of John Donne, George Herbert, and Izaak Walton among others. After his employment by the Earl of Essex in gathering foreign intelligence, he spent long periods abroad as King James's ambassador. He returned to England in 1624 and was made Provost of Eton.

more time to value it, and to enjoy it rightly; and in truth, if I could then have imagined your farther stay in these parts, which I understood afterwards by Mr. *H.*,[2] I would have been bold in our vulgar phrase to mend my draft (for you left me with an extreme thirst) and to have begged your conversation again, jointly with your said learned Friend, at a poor meal or two, that we might have banded together[3] some good Authors of the ancient time: among which, I observed you to have been familiar.

Since your going, you have charged me with new obligations, both for a very kind letter from you dated the sixth of this month, and for a dainty piece of entertainment which came therewith. Wherein I should much commend the tragical part, if the lyrical did not ravish me with a certain Doric delicacy in your songs and odes, whereunto I must plainly confess to have seen yet nothing parallel in our language: *Ipsa mollities.*[4] But I must not omit to tell you, that I now only owe you thanks for intimating unto me (how modestly so ever) the true artificer. For the work itself, I had viewed some good while before, with singular delight, having received it from our common friend Mr. *R.* in the very close of the late *R*'s Poems, printed at *Oxford,* whereunto it was added (as I now suppose) that the accessory might help out the principal, according to the art of stationers, and to leave the reader *con la bocca dolce.*[5]

Now sir, concerning your travels, wherein I may challenge a little more privilege of discourse with you; I suppose you will not blanch[6] Paris in your way; therefore I have been bold to trouble you with a few lines to Mr. M.B., whom you shall easily find attending the young Lord S. as his governor, and you may surely receive from him good directions for the shaping of your farther journey into Italy, where he did reside by my choice some time for the King, after mine own recess from Venice.[7]

I should think that your best line will be through the whole length of France to Marseilles, and thence by Sea to Genoa, whence the passage into Tuscany is as diurnal as a Gravesend barge:[8] I hasten as you do to Florence, or Siena, the rather to tell you a short story from the interest you have given me in your safety.

2. **Mr. *H.*:** "Probably John Hales, former fellow of Merton and now retired to a private fellowship at Eton" (Yale 1:340).
3. **banded together:** discussed in a group, bandied about.
4. **tragical:** dramatic, that part which imitates an action; **lyrical:** musically expressive; ***Doric:*** simple, rustic; ***Ipsa mollities:*** softness itself.
5. **Mr. *R.*:** Perhaps John Rouse, Oxford librarian (see Milton's ode addressed to him) or Humphrey Robinson, a major London book trader. No volume of poetry published at Oxford about the time of this letter is known to have been bound with Milton's *Masque,* though Thomas Randolph's *Poems* (Oxford, 1638) has been proposed (Yale 1:341). Wotton suggests that the stationer's art of putting a profitable book together is like that of planning a successful meal, which ought to end *con la bocca dolce* (with a sweet taste).
6. **blanch:** omit, fail to see.
7. Michael Branthwaite, who had assisted Wotton in Venice, was serving as tutor to James Scudamore, son of the English ambassador in Paris, John Scudamore. In *2Def,* Milton says the elder Scudamore introduced him to Hugo Grotius and otherwise helped him on his way (see p. 343).
8. **Diurnal . . . barge:** regularly recurring each day, like the *Gravesend barge* (a ferry).

At Siena I was tabled in the House of one Alberto Scipioni an old Roman Courtier in dangerous times, having been steward to the Duca di Pagliano, who with all his family were strangled, save this only man that escaped by foresight of the tempest. With him I had often much chat of those affairs; into which he took pleasure to look back from his native harbor; and at my departure toward Rome (which had been the center of his experience) I had won confidence enough to beg his advice, how I might carry myself securely there, without offense of others, or of mine own conscience. *Signor Arrigo mio* (says he) *I pensieri stretti, & il viso sciolto* will go safely over the whole world: Of which *Delphian* Oracle (for so I have found it) your judgment doth need no commentary;[9] and therefore (sir) I will commit you with it to the best of all securities, God's dear love, remaining

Your friend as much at command
as any of longer date
Henry Wootton.

Postscript.

SIR, I have expressly sent this my foot-boy to prevent[10] *your departure without some acknowledgement from me of the receipt of your obliging letter, having myself through some business, I know not how, neglected the ordinary conveyance. In any part where I shall understand you fixed, I shall be glad, and diligent to entertain you with home-novelties;*[11] *even for some fomentation*[12] *of our friendship, too soon interrupted in the cradle.*

9. Wotton took the passage in Italian to mean: "My Signor Harry, your thoughts close, and your countenance loose"; he had given the same advice to others (Yale 1:342). The entire paragraph suggests that Wotton wanted to impress upon Milton the need of a Protestant for discretion while traveling in Roman Catholic countries, especially Italy.
10. **prevent:** arrive before.
11. **home-novelties:** news of home.
12. **fomentation:** stimulation.

To Lukas Holste in the Vatican at Rome[1]

Although I can remember (and often do) many courteous and cordial favors which I have received in my hasty journey through Italy, still, I do not know whether I can rightly say that I have had greater tokens of kindness from anyone on such short acquaintance than from you. For when I went up to the Vatican to meet you, you received me with greatest kindness, though I was utterly unknown to you, unless perhaps I had been previously mentioned by Alessandro Cherubini.[2] At once courteously admitted to the Library, I was permitted to browse through the invaluable collection of books, and also the numerous

1. Born in Germany, *Lukas Holste* (Lat. Holstenius, 1596–1661) became a protégé of Cardinal Francesco Barberini, converted to Roman Catholicism, and by the time of Milton's visit worked in the Vatican Library. It was there in 1952 that the original manuscript of this letter was discovered.
2. Milton made his acquaintance in Rome. He died at twenty-eight, and little is known of him.

Greek authors in manuscript annotated by your nightly toil. Some of these, as yet unseen by our generation, seemed as if in readiness for action, like Vergil's

> —souls shut deep within a green valley, and about to cross the threshold of the upper world;

they seemed to demand only the ready hands of the printer and a delivery into the world.[3] Some, already edited by your labor, are being eagerly received everywhere by the learned; and I am sent forth enriched by your gift of two copies of one of these. Next, I could not help believing it the result of your mentioning me to Cardinal Francesco Barberini, that when, a few days later, he gave that public musical entertainment with truly Roman magnificence, he himself, waiting at the door, singled me out in so great a throng and, almost seizing me by the hand, welcomed me in an exceedingly honorable manner. When on this account I paid my respects to him the following day, it was again you yourself who gained both access for me and an opportunity to converse—an opportunity which, considering how important the man (though certainly no one of highest rank could be more kindly nor more courteous) and considering the time and place, was really rather ample than scant.[4] I am sure I do not know, most learned Holstenius, whether I alone have found you such a friend and host, or whether, remembering that you gave three years' work to scholarship at Oxford, you want to honor all Englishmen with attentions of that sort.[5] If the latter, you are indeed handsomely paying our—nay partly even your—England for what you learned there; and you deserve equal thanks in the name of each of us privately and of the country publicly. But if the former, if you have distinguished me from the rest and esteemed me enough to want my friendship, I both congratulate myself on your opinion and at the same time consider it due more to your generosity than to my merit. That commission which I understood you to have given me concerning the inspection of a Medicean codex,[6] I have faithfully referred to my friends, who, however, display scant hope of accomplishing the matter at present. In that library nothing can be copied except by previous permission, nor may one even bring a pen to the tables. They say, however, that Giovanni Battista Doni[7] is at Rome; he is expected daily, having

3. Milton quotes the *Aeneid* (6.679–80). His writings often represent books as bearing the lively potency of their authors; see Milton's poem *On Shakespeare* and *Areop* (p. 178).
4. Although in his writings Milton repeatedly registers a characteristically Puritan disdain for Roman Catholic presumption of religious and political authority, he was capable of maintaining amicable and dutiful relations with individual members of that church, including, as this letter indicates, one so powerful as Cardinal Barberini. While in Rome, he ate dinner with other Englishmen at the English Jesuit College and, at the cardinal's musical evening, may have heard Leonora Baroni sing. Her singing inspired three poems (*Ad Leonoram Romae Canentam* and two additional poems *Ad Eandem* ["to the same"]).
5. Beginning in 1622, Holste performed research in Oxford and London.
6. **codex:** an unbound manuscript of some ancient classic. Since Milton sends the letter from Florence, home of the Medicis, he evidently refers to a manuscript in a library there. No more specific identification has been made of the library or manuscript in question.
7. **Doni:** another favorite of the Barberinis, admired for his learning in the arts and sciences both. He was a native of Florence but frequently stayed in Rome.

been called to Florence to give the public lectureship in Greek literature; and they say that through him you can easily obtain what you wish. Yet it would have given me very great pleasure if so eminently desirable a project could have been at least slightly furthered by my poor efforts, for it is a shame that in so worthy and splendid an undertaking you should not have the help of all men everywhere and their learning and fortunes. Finally, you will have bound me by a new obligation if you extend my most respectful greetings to his Eminence the Cardinal, whose great virtues and zeal for what is right, so ready to further all the liberal arts, are always before my eyes—also that gentle and, may I say, humble loftiness of spirit, which alone has taught him to distinguish himself by effacing himself, and about which it can be truly said, as of Ceres in Callimachus, though in a different sense: "Feet to the earth still cling, while the head is touching Olympus."[8] Such humility can prove to most other princes how alien to and how far different from true magnanimity are their surly arrogance and courtly haughtiness. Nor do I think that while he lives anyone will any longer miss the Estensi, Farnesi, or Medici, formerly the patrons of learned men. Farewell, most learned Holstenius, and if there is anyone who highly appreciates yourself and your works, please count me another of his kind, if you think it worthwhile, in whatever part of the world I may be.

Florence, March 30. 1639.

8. Callimachus, *Hymn 6, To Demeter,* 58.

To Leonard Philaras[1]

To Leonard Philaras, Athenian,

Since I have been from boyhood a worshipper of all things Greek and of your Athens first and foremost, I have always been most firmly convinced that this city would someday nobly recompense my goodwill towards her. Nor has the ancient spirit of your noble country belied my prophecy, but has given me you, both an Attic brother and a very loving one: it was you who addressed me most kindly by letter, though far distant and knowing me only by my writings;[2] and afterwards, arriving unexpectedly in London, you continued that kindness by going to see one who could not see, even in that misfortune which has made me more respectable to none, more despicable perhaps to many. And so, since you tell me that I should not give up all hope of regaining my sight, that you have a friend and intimate in the Paris physician Thévenot[3] (especially outstanding as an occulist), whom you will consult about my eyes if only I send you the means by which he can diagnose the causes and symptoms of the disease, I

1. For the circumstances that occasioned this letter, see the introduction.
2. He wrote to congratulate Milton on his *Defense of the English People.*
3. **Thévenot:** François Thévenin (Lat: *Tevenotus*). He died in 1656.

shall do what you urge, that I may not seem to refuse aid whencesoever offered, perhaps divinely.

It is ten years, I think, more or less, since I noticed my sight becoming weak and growing dim, and at the same time my spleen and all my viscera burdened and shaken with flatulence. And even in the morning, if I began as usual to read, I noticed that my eyes felt immediate pain deep within and turned from reading, though later refreshed after moderate bodily exercise; as often as I looked at a lamp, a sort of rainbow seemed to obscure it. Soon a mist appearing in the left part of the left eye (for that eye became clouded some years before the other) removed from my sight everything on that side. Objects further forward too seemed smaller, if I chanced to close my right eye. The other eye also failing slowly and gradually over a period of almost three years, some months before my sight was completely destroyed, everything which I distinguished when I myself was still seemed to swim, now to the right, now to the left. Certain permanent vapors seem to have settled upon my entire forehead and temples, which press and oppress my eyes with a sort of sleepy heaviness, especially from mealtime to evening, so that I often think of the Salmydessian seer Phineus in the *Argonauts,*

> All round him then there grew
> A purple thickness; and he thought the earth
> Whirling beneath his feet, and so he sank,
> Speechless at length, into a feeble sleep.[4]

But I must not omit that, while considerable sight still remained, when I would first go to bed and lie on one side or the other, abundant light would dart from my closed eyes; then, as sight daily diminished, colors proportionately darker would burst forth with violence and a sort of crash from within; but now, pure black, marked as if with extinguished or ashy light, and as if interwoven with it, pours forth. Yet the mist which always hovers before my eyes both night and day seems always to be approaching white rather than black; and upon the eyes turning, it admits a minute quantity of light as if through a crack.

Although some glimmer of hope too may radiate from that physician, I prepare and resign myself as if the case were quite incurable; and I often reflect that since many days of darkness are destined to everyone, as the wise man warns, mine thus far, by the signal kindness of Providence, between leisure and study, and the voices and visits of friends, are much more mild than those lethal ones.[5] But if, as it is written, man shall not live by bread alone, but by every word that proceedeth out of the mouth of God,[6] why should one not likewise find comfort in believing that he cannot see by the eyes alone, but by the guid-

4. Apollonius of Rhodes, *Argonautica* 2.205–8.

5. Milton alludes to Eccles. 11.8: "But if a man live many years, and rejoice in them all; yet let him remember the days of darkness; for they shall be many. All that cometh is vanity."

6. Deut. 8.3, quoted by Jesus to Satan, Matt. 4.4.

ance and wisdom of God. Indeed while he himself looks out for me and provides for me, which he does, and takes me as if by the hand and leads me throughout life, surely, since it has pleased him, I shall be pleased to grant my eyes a holiday. And you, my Philaras, whatever happens, I bid you farewell with a spirit no less stout and bold than if I were Lynceus.[7]

Westminster, September 28, 1654.

7. **Lynceus:** one of the Argonauts. His eyes were so sharp that he could see even through the earth.

To the Most Distinguished Mr. Henry de Brass[1]

I see, sir, that you, like very few of today's youth who wander through foreign lands, travel rightly and wisely, not for childish aims, but in the manner of ancient philosophers, to gather richer learning from every source. Yet whenever I regard what you write, you seem to have come abroad not so much to acquire foreign knowledge as to impart knowledge to others, to barter good merchandise rather than to buy it. And I wish that it were as easy for me to assist and promote those admirable studies of yours in every way as it is truly agreeable and pleasant that one of your distinguished talents should ask it of me. Yet as to your writing that you have decided to write to me and ask me to resolve those problems about which for many ages historians seem to have been in the dark, I have certainly never assumed nor would I dare assume anything of the sort. Concerning what you write of Sallust, I will say frankly, since you wish me to say freely what I think, that I prefer Sallust to any other Latin historian whatever, which was also the nearly unanimous opinion of the ancients. Your Tacitus has his merits, but certainly the greatest of these in my judgment is that he imitated Sallust with all his might. As far as I can tell from what you write, my discussing these matters personally with you seems to have made you feel almost the same way yourself about that most sagacious writer; and you even ask me, since he said at the beginning of the *Bellum Catilinae* that history is extremely difficult to write "because the style must be equal to the deeds," just how I think a historian could acquire such a style.[2] I think thus: he who would write worthily of worthy deeds ought to write with no less largeness of spirit and experience of the world than he who did them, so that he can comprehend and judge as an equal even the greatest, and, having comprehended, can narrate

1. As he grew older and achieved public prominence, Milton's private letters become more assured and, when he addresses younger men, particularly former pupils, magnanimous and avuncular. Although little is known about Henry De Brass beyond what Milton's letters to him tell us, Milton's tone toward him is characteristic of this period, and what he says provides valuable insight into his opinions on writing history.
2. "Milton does not use quotation marks, but his '*quod facta dictis exaequanda sunt*' are the exact words of Sallust, *Bellum Catilinae,* 3.2" (Yale 7:501).

them gravely and clearly in plain and temperate language.[3] For I do not insist on ornate language; I ask for a historian, not an orator. Nor would I favor injecting frequent maxims or judgments on historical exploits, lest by breaking the chain of events, the historian invade the province of the political writer; if, in explaining plans and narrating deeds, he follows to the best of his ability not his own invention or conjecture but the truth, he truly fulfills his function. I would also add of Sallust, what he himself praised most highly in Cato, that he can accomplish much in few words, which I believe no one can do without sharp judgment and a certain restraint. There are many in whose writing you will miss neither grace of style nor abundance of fact, but in my opinion the chief among the Latins who can join brevity with abundance, that is, who can say much in few words, is Sallust. I think these should be the excellences of the historian who expects to do justice to great deeds in words. But why should I say all this to you, who, with your ability, could reach these conclusions yourself, and who have entered a course on which if you proceed you will soon be able to consult no one more learned than yourself? And though you need no one's urging, still, lest I seem wholly unresponsive to your great need for my authority, I strongly urge and advise you to persevere. Farewell, and congratulations on your own excellence and on your zeal for gaining wisdom.

From Westminster, July 15, 1657.

3. Cp. *Apology*, p. 98.

Introduction to Prolusions

Toward the end of Milton's life, the bookseller Brabazon Aylmer planned a volume of his correspondence. Originally it was to have contained a group of familiar letters written over the years to various correspondents and a larger batch of letters of state composed by Milton during his tenure as Latin Secretary for the Cromwell government. But Aylmer was denied permission to reprint the state papers, and through an intermediary sought a replacement from the author. So it was that seven orations or "prolusions" composed during Milton's years at Cambridge University came to be published with his familiar letters in a 1674 volume entitled *Epistolarum Familiarum Liber Unus: Quibus Accesserunt, Ejusdem, jam olim in Collegio Adolescentis, Prolusiones Quaedam Oratoriae.* "I had no hesitation in publishing them," Aylmer said in his preface, "youthful work though they are, in the hope that I should find them as saleable (which is my chief personal concern) as those who originally heard them delivered found them enjoyable."

The prolusions show the young Milton already adept in the techniques of rhetoric and disputation later to be displayed in such argumentative masterpieces as *Paradise Lost, Paradise Regained,* and *Samson Agonistes.* For a modern student, they also offer a small window onto a lost tradition of pedagogy. The positions to be defended (that day is superior to night, that knowledge makes men happier than ignorance) were assigned. The student was expected to produce an oration defending the position in well-turned Latin, with appropriate allusions to classical literature and mythology, then to deliver the oration in persuasive fashion, and afterward, perhaps, to defend its position against objections from the audience. Such exercises were intended to produce men who, rarely at a loss for words, relished debate and associated winning an argument with superior learning. Milton, whether as poet or as prose controversialist, clearly drew much of his power from the seedbed of this training. The two prolusions we have chosen for this edition (1 and 7) anticipate memorable moments in a variety of his later works, including *Lycidas, Of Education, Areopagitica, Paradise Lost,* and *Paradise Regained.*

Our texts follow the translations in volume one of the Yale edition of Milton's prose works.

PROLUSION 1

DELIVERED IN COLLEGE

WHETHER DAY OR NIGHT IS THE MORE EXCELLENT

It is a frequent maxim of the most eminent masters of rhetoric, as you know well, Members of the University, that in every style of oration, whether demonstrative, deliberative, or judicial,[1] the speaker must begin by winning the good will of his audience; without it he cannot make any impression upon them, nor succeed as he would wish in his cause. If this be so (and, to tell the truth, I know that the learned are all agreed in regarding it as an established axiom), how unfortunate I am and to what a pass am I brought this day! At the very outset of my oration I fear I shall have to say something contrary to all the rules of oratory and be forced to depart from the first and chief duty of an orator. For how can I hope for your good-will, when in all this great assembly I encounter none but hostile glances, so that my task seems to be to placate the implacable? So provocative of animosity, even in the home of learning, is the rivalry of those who pursue different studies or whose opinions differ concerning studies they pursue in common. However, I care not if "Polydamas and the women of Troy prefer Labeo to me;—a trifle this."[2]

Yet to prevent complete despair, I see here and there, if I do not mistake, some who without a word show clearly by their looks how well they wish me. The approval of these, few though they be, is more precious to me than that of the countless hosts of the ignorant, who lack all intelligence, reasoning power, and sound judgment, and who pride themselves on the ridiculous effervescing froth of their verbiage. Stripped of their covering of patches borrowed from newfangled authors, they will prove to have no more in them than a serpent's slough, and once they have come to the end of their stock of phrases and platitudes you will find them unable to utter so much as a syllable, as dumb as the

1. **demonstrative:** describing in a laudatory or disparaging manner, such as panegyric or invective; **deliberative:** characterized by careful consideration in order to arrive at a decision; **judicial:** appropriate for legal controversy, critical or judicious.

2. Attius Labeo, author of a Latin translation of the *Iliad,* symbolized for Persius (34–62 C.E.) the Hellenization of Roman culture (*Satires* I.4, 50). Polydamas and the Trojan ladies represent an unworthy audience.

frogs of Seriphus.[3] How difficult even Heraclitus would find it, were he still alive, to keep a straight face at the sight of these speechifiers (if I may call them so without offence), first grandly spouting their lines in the tragic part of Euripides' Orestes, or as the mad Hercules in his dying agony, and then, their slender stock of phrases exhausted and their glory all gone, drawing in their horns and crawling off like snails.[4]

But to return to the point, from which I have wandered a little. If there is anyone who has refused peace on any terms and declared war *à mort*[5] against me, I will for once stoop to beg and entreat him to lay aside his animosity for a moment and show himself an unbiased judge in this debate, and not to allow the speaker's fault (if such there be) to prejudice the best and most deserving of causes. If you consider that I have spoken with too much sharpness and bitterness, I confess, that I have done so intentionally, for I wish the beginning of my speech to resemble the first gleam of dawn, which presages the fairest day when overcast.

The question whether Day or Night is preferable is no common theme of discussion, and it is now my duty, the task meted out to me this morning, to probe the subject thoroughly and radically,[6] though it might seem better suited to a poetical exercise than to a contest of rhetoric.

Did I say that Night had declared war on Day? What should this portend? What means this daring enterprise? Are the Titans waging anew their ancient war, and renewing the battle of Phlegra's plain?[7] Has Earth brought forth new offspring of portentous stature to flout the gods of heaven? Or has Typhoeus forced his way from beneath the bulk of Etna piled upon him? Or last, has Briareus eluded Cerberus and escaped from his fetters of adamant?[8] What can it possibly be that has now thrice roused the hopes of the gods of hell to rule the empire of the heavens? Does Night so scorn the thunderbolt of Jove? Cares she nothing for the matchless might of Pallas,[9] which wrought such havoc in days of old among the Earth-born brothers? Has she forgotten Bacchus's[10] triumph over the shattered band of Giants, renowned through all the space of heaven?

3. **Seriphus:** an Aegean island turned to stone by Perseus; proverbially even its frogs were dumb as rocks.
4. **Heraclitus:** (c. 500 B.C.E.) Greek philosopher noted for his mournful attitude; **Orestes:** matricidal hero of Greek myth, driven insane by avenging furies; **Hercules:** An unbearably painful poison caused his madness and death.
5. **à mort:** to the death (French).
6. **radically:** to the root.
7. **Phlegra's plain:** In Greek myth, the Olympian gods defeated the giants on the ground out of which their mother (Earth) delivered them, Phlegra, the westernmost prong of the Chalcidicean peninsula in the Aegean. See *PL* 1.198–99n and 577n.
8. **Typhoeus:** Earth-born monster buried beneath Mount *Etna* by Zeus and deemed responsible for its volcanic unrest; **Briareus:** hundred-armed giant imprisoned in Tartarus, classical hell guarded by *Cerberus,* the three-headed dog.
9. **Pallas:** title of Athena, Greek goddess of wisdom.
10. **Bacchus:** aided Zeus in defending Olympus from the Giants' assault.

No, none of these. Full well she remembers, to her grief, how of those brothers most were slain by Jove, and the survivors driven in headlong flight even to the furthest corners of the underworld. Not for war, but for something far other, does she now anxiously prepare. Her thoughts now turn to complaints and accusations, and, womanlike, after a brave fight with tooth and nail, she proceeds to argument or rather abuse, to try, I suppose, whether her hands or her tongue are the better weapon. But I will soon show how unadvised, how arrogant, and how ill-founded is her claim to supremacy, compared with Day's. And indeed I see Day herself, awakened by the crowing of the cock, hastening hither more swiftly than is her wont, to hear her own praise.

Now since it is generally agreed that to be of noble lineage and to trace one's descent back to kings or gods of old is an essential qualification for honors and dignity, it behooves us to inquire, first, which of the two is of nobler birth, secondly, which can trace back her descent the furthest, and thirdly, which is of the greater service to mankind?

I find it stated by the most ancient authorities on mythology that Demogorgon,[11] the ancestor of all the gods (whom I suppose to be identical with the Chaos of the ancients), was the father of Earth, among his many children. Night was the child of Earth, by an unknown father (though Hesiod gives a slightly different pedigree and calls Night the child of Chaos, in the line "From Chaos sprang Erebus and black Night").[12] Whatever her parentage, when she had reached marriageable age, the shepherd Phanes asked her to wife. Her mother consented, but she herself opposed the match, refusing to contract an alliance with a man she did not know and had never seen, and one moreover whose style of life was so different from her own. Annoyed at the rebuff, and with his love turned to hatred, Phanes in his indignation pursued this dusky daughter of Earth through all the length and breadth of the world to slay her. She now feared his enmity as much as she had previously scorned his love. Therefore she did not feel secure enough even among the most distant peoples or in the most remote places, nor even in the very bosom of her mother, but fled for refuge, secretly and by stealth, to the incestuous embrace of her brother Erebus. Thus she found at once a release from her pressing fears and a husband who was certainly very like herself. From this pretty pair Aether and Day are said to have sprung, according to Hesiod, whom I have already quoted:

> From Night again sprang Ether and the Day
> Whom she conceived and bore by Erebus' embrace.[13]

11. **Demogorgon:** In *PL,* Milton does not make him identical to Chaos but does place him in his court; see 2.965 and note.
12. Milton is quoting Hesiod (*Theog.* 123).
13. In Hesiod, both *Night* and *Erebus* are accounted primeval offspring of Chaos; their union produces *Ether* (upper air or sky) and *Day.* Milton here quotes *Theog.* 124–25.

But the more cultured Muses and Philosophy herself, the neighbor of the gods, forbid us to place entire confidence in the poets who have given the gods their forms, especially the Greek poets; and no one should regard it as a reproach to them that in a question of such importance they hardly seem sufficiently reliable authorities. For if any of them has departed from the truth to some slight extent, the blame should not be laid upon their genius, which is most divine, but upon the perverse and blind ignorance of the age, which at that time was all-pervading. They have attained an ample meed of honor and of glory by gathering together in one place and forming into organized communities men who previously roamed like beasts at random through the forests and mountains, and by being the first to teach, by their divine inspiration, all the sciences which are known today, arraying them in the charming cloak of fable; and their best title to everlasting fame (and that no mean one) is that they have left to their successors the full development of that knowledge of the arts which they so happily began.

Do not then, whoever you are, hastily accuse me of arrogance, in shattering or altering the statements of all the ancient poets, without any authority to support me. For I am not taking upon myself to do that, but am only attempting to bring them to the test of reason, and thereby to examine whether they can bear the scrutiny of strict truth.

First, then, the story that makes Night the child of Earth is a learned and elegant allegory of antiquity; for what is it that makes night envelop the world but the dense and solid earth, coming between the sun's light and our horizon?

Then, as to the statements of the mythologists, calling Night sometimes fatherless, sometimes motherless, these too are pleasing fictions, if we understand them to signify that she was a bastard or a changeling, or else that her parents refused for very shame to acknowledge so infamous and ignoble a child. But why they should believe that Phanes, endowed as he was with a wondrous and superhuman beauty, was so much in love with Night, a mere mulatto or silhouette, as even to wish to marry her, seems a problem hopelessly difficult to solve, unless the phenomenal scarcity of females at that time left him no choice.

But now let us come to close quarters with our subject. The ancients interpret Phanes as the sun or the day, and in relating that he at first sought Night in marriage and then pursued her to avenge his rejection, they mean only to signify the alternation of day and night. But why should they have thought it necessary, in order to show this, to represent Phanes as a suitor for the hand of Night, when their perpetual alternation and mutual repulsion, as it were, could be indicated far better by the figure of an innate and unremitting hatred? For it is well known that light and darkness have been divided from one another by an implacable hatred from the very beginning of time. It is in fact my opinion that Night got her Greek name of *euphrone*[14] for the very reason that she showed

14. **euphrone:** the kindly time, euphemism for *night.* The related Greek adjective, *euphroneon,* means "with kind or prudent mind."

caution and good sense in refusing to bind herself in wedlock to Phanes; for if she had once submitted to his embrace she would doubtless have been destroyed by his beams and by his unendurable radiance, and either annihilated altogether or utterly consumed by fire; like Semele, who, legend says, perished by fire, against the will of her lover Jove. For this reason, with a proper regard for her security, she preferred Erebus to Phanes. With reference to this, Martial aptly and wittily says, "Worst of husbands, worst of wives, I wonder not that you agree so well."[15]

It is, I think, proper to mention with what a handsome family, how like their mother, she presented her husband—namely Misery, Envy, Fear, Deceit, Fraud, Obstinacy, Poverty, Want, Hunger, Fretfulness, Sickness, Old Age, Pallor, Darkness, Sleep, Death and Charon,[16] her last child; so that the proverb *from a bad crow a bad egg* is exactly applicable to this case.

There are, however, some who maintain that Night also bore Aether and Day to her husband Erebus. But who in his senses would not howl down and turn out the advocate of such a theory, as he would anyone who seriously propounded Democritus' notions or the fairytales of childhood?[17] Is it indeed probable on the face of it that black and gloomy Night should be the mother of a child so comely, so sweet, so universally beloved and desired? Such a child; as soon as conceived, would have caused her mother's death by her birth before due time, would have driven her father Erebus into headlong flight, and forced old Charon to hide his dazzled eyes beneath the waters of the Styx and flee to seek what refuge he might in the realms below, as fast as his oars and sails could carry him. No, so far from being born in Hades, Day has never even shown her face there, nor can she find entrance even through a chink or cranny, except in defiance of Fate's decree. Nay, I dare rather declare that Day is older than Night, and that when the world had but newly emerged from Chaos, Day shed her wide-spreading rays over it, before ever the turn of Night had come—unless indeed we are so perverse as to call by the name of Night that foul and murky darkness, or regard it as identical with Demogorgon.[18]

Therefore I hold that Day is the eldest daughter of Heaven,[19] or rather of his son, begotten by him, it is said, to be the comfort of the race of men and the terror of the infernal gods, for fear lest Night should rule unopposed, lest Ghosts and Furies and all that loathsome brood of monsters, unchecked by any barrier between Earth and Hades, should leave the pit of Hell and make their way even

15. Milton refers to one of Martial's *Epigrams* (8.35), which actually concludes to opposite effect: "I wonder you don't agree" [*Mirror non bene convenire vobis*].

16. **Charon:** In Greek myth, the ferryman Charon conveys the dead across the river Styx.

17. The reference is to the Greek atomic theory of matter, founded by *Democritus* (c. 460–357 B.C.E.), and its ethical and religious ramifications.

18. In Book 2 of *PL*, Milton presents Night in just this way, describing her as "eldest" (894) and identifying Chaos as her realm (133).

19. In Greek myth *Heaven* (Gk. *Ouranos*) and Earth (*Gaia*) produce numerous children, among them Hyperion, the original sun god and presumably the *son* of Heaven to whom Milton refers.

to the upper world, and lest wretched Man, enveloped and surrounded by murky darkness, should suffer even in this life the tortures of the damned.

So far, Members of the University, I have endeavored to drag from their deep and dark hiding-places the obscure children of Night; you will immediately perceive how worthy they are of their parentage—especially if I should first devote the best of my small powers to the praise of Day, though Day herself must far transcend the eloquence of all who sing her praise.

In the first place, there is assuredly no need to describe to you how welcome and how desirable Day is to every living thing. Even the birds cannot hide their delight, but leave their nests at peep of dawn and noise it abroad from the treetops in sweetest song, or darting upwards as near as they may to the sun, take their flight to welcome the returning day. First of all these the wakeful cock acclaims the sun's coming, and like a herald bids mankind shake off the bonds of sleep, and rise and run with joy to greet the new-born day. The kids skip in the meadows, and beasts of every kind leap and gambol in delight. The sad heliotrope, who all night long has gazed toward the east, awaiting her beloved Sun, now smiles and beams at her lover's approach. The marigold too and rose, to add their share to the joy of all, open their petals and shed abroad their perfume, which they have kept for the Sun alone, and would not give to Night, shutting themselves up within their little leaves at fall of evening. And all the other flowers raise their heads, drooping and weighed down with dew, and offer themselves to the Sun, mutely begging him to kiss away the tear-drops which his absence brought. The Earth too decks herself in lovelier robes to honor the Sun's coming, and the clouds, arrayed in garb of every hue, attend the rising god in festive train and long procession. And last, that nothing may be lacking to proclaim his praise, the Persians and the Libyans give him divine honors; the Rhodians too have dedicated to his glory that far-famed Colossus of astounding size, created by the miraculous art of Chares of Lindus;[20] to the Sun too, we are told, the American Indians even to this day make sacrifice with incense and with every kind of ritual. You yourselves, Members of the University, must bear witness how delightful, how welcome, how long-awaited is the light of morning, since it recalls you to the cultured Muses from whom cruel Night parted you still unsatisfied and athirst. Saturn, hurled down to Hades from highest heaven, bears witness how gladly he would return to the light of day from that dread gloom, would Jove but grant the boon. Lastly, it is manifest that Pluto himself far preferred light to his own kingdom of darkness, since he so often strove to gain the realm of heaven. Thus Orpheus says with truth and with poetic skill in his hymn to Dawn—"Then of a truth do mortal men rejoice, nor is there one who flees thy face which shines above, when thou dost shake sweet sleep from their eyes. Every man is glad, and every creeping thing, all the tribes of beast and bird, and all the many creatures of the deep."[21]

20. **Chares:** Greek sculptor from *Lindus* (Rhodes). The Colossus of Rhodes, completed in 280 B.C.E., was a gigantic bronze statue of the sun god, deemed one of the seven wonders of the ancient world.

21. The Orphic *Hymn to Dawn* (28.7–11).

Nor is this to be wondered at, when we reflect that Day serves for use as well as pleasure, and is alone fitted to further the business of life; for who would have the hardihood to sail the wide and boundless seas, without a hope that Day would dawn? He would cross the ocean even as the ghosts cross Lethe and Acheron,[22] beset on every hand by fearsome darkness. Every man would then pass his life in his own mean hovel, hardly daring even to creep outside, so that the dissolution of human society must needs follow. To no purpose would Apelles have pictured Venus rising from the waves, in vain would Zeuxis have painted Helen, if dark, dense night hid from our eyes these wondrous sights.[23] In vain too would the earth bring forth in abundance vines twining in many a winding trail, in vain nobly towering trees; in vain would she deck herself anew with buds and blossoms, as with stars, striving to imitate the heaven above. Then indeed that noblest of the senses, sight, would lose its use to every creature; yes, and the light of the world's eye being quenched, all things would fade and perish utterly; nor would the men who dwelt upon the darkened earth long survive this tragedy, since nothing would be left to support their life, nor any means of staying the lapse of all things into the primeval Chaos.[24]

One might continue on this strain with unabating flow, but Day herself in modesty would not permit the full recital, but would hasten her downward course toward the sunset to check her advocate's extravagances. My day is now indeed already drawing to its close, and will soon give place to night, to prevent your saying in jest that this is the longest day though the season is midwinter. This alone I ask, that by your leave I may add a few words which I cannot well omit.

With good reason, then, have the poets declared that Night springs from Hell, since by no means whatever could so many grievous ills descend upon mankind from any other quarter. For when night falls all things grow foul and vile, no difference can then be seen between a Helen and a Canidia,[25] a precious jewel and a common stone (but that some gems have power to outshine the darkness). Then too the loveliest spots strike horror to the heart, a horror gathering force from a silence deep and sad. All creatures lingering in the fields, be they man or beast, hasten to house or lair for refuge; then, hiding their heads beneath their coverings, they shut their eyes against the dread aspect of Night. None may be seen abroad save thieves and rogues who fear the light, who, breathing murder and rapine, lie in wait to rob honest folk of their goods and

22. **Lethe and Acheron:** Rivers of hell. Cp. *PL* 2.575–86.

23. **Apelles:** Court painter in Macedon, fourth century B.C.E., he was considered the greatest of Greek painters. Though none of his paintings survived, description of his work did and inspired Renaissance painters, Botticelli among them. **Zeuxis:** famous Greek painter of the fifth century B.C.E. His celebrated painting of *Helen* (of Troy) was for the temple of Hera at Croton.

24. Cp. *PL* 4.664–66: "Minist'ring light prepared, they set and rise; / Lest total darkness should by night regain / Her old possession, and extinguish life."

25. **Helen:** the most beautiful woman; **Canidia:** a frightful witch (Horace, *Satires* 1.8.23–50).

wander forth by night alone, lest day betray them. For Day lays bare all crimes, nor ever suffers wrongdoing to pollute her light. None will you meet save ghosts and specters, and fearsome goblins who follow in Night's train from the realms below; it is their boast that all night long they rule the earth and share it with mankind. To this end, I think, night sharpens our hearing, that our ears may catch the sooner and our hearts perceive with greater dread the groans of specters, the screeching of owls and nightbirds, and the roaring of lions that prowl in search of prey. Hence clearly is revealed that man's deceit who says that night brings respite from their fears to men and lulls every care to rest. How false and vain is this opinion they know well from their own bitter experience who have ever felt the pangs of guilty consciences; they are beset by Sphinxes and Harpies, Gorgons and Chimaeras,[26] who hunt their victims down with flaming torches in their hands; those poor wretches too know it full well who have no friend to help or succor them, none to assuage their grief with words of comfort, but must pour out their useless plaints to senseless stones, longing and praying for the dawn of day. For this reason did that choicest poet Ovid rightly call Night the mighty foster-mother of cares.[27]

Some indeed say that it is above all by night that our bodies, broken and worn out by the labors of the day, are revived and restored. But this is the merciful ordinance of God, for which we owe no gratitude to Night. But even were it so, sleep is not a thing so precious that Night deserves honor for the bestowal of it. For when we betake ourselves to sleep, we do in truth but confess ourselves poor and feeble creatures, whose puny frames cannot endure even a little while without repose. And, to be sure, what is sleep but the image and semblance of death? Hence in Homer Sleep and Death are twins, conceived together and born at a single birth.[28]

Lastly, it is thanks to the sun that the moon, and the other stars display their fires by night, for they have no light to radiate but such as they borrow from the sun.

Who then but a son of darkness, a robber, a gamester, or one whose wont it is to spend his nights in the company of harlots and snore away his days—who, I ask, but such a fellow would have undertaken to defend a cause so odious and discreditable? I wonder that he dare so much as look upon this sun, or share with other men, without a qualm, that light which he is slandering so ungratefully. He deserves to share the fate of Python,[29] slain by the stroke of the sun's hostile rays. He deserves to pass a long and loathsome life imprisoned in Cimmerian darkness.[30] He deserves, above all, to see sleep overcoming his hearers even as he speaks, so that his best eloquence affects them no more than an idle

26. **Sphinxes and Harpies, Gorgons and Chimaeras:** a gallery of fearsome classical monsters; *PL* 2.628.
27. *Letters from the Black Sea* 1.2.41–42.
28. *Il.* 14.230. See also 11.280, where death is described as "the sleep of bronze."
29. **Python:** monstrous serpent slain by Apollo.
30. In Homer, the Cimmerians dwell on the far shore of the western ocean, where the sun doesn't shine (*Od.* 11.13-22). Cp. *L'All* 10.

dream, till, drowsy himself, he is cheated into taking his hearers' nods and snores for nods of approval and murmurs of praise as he ends his speech.

But I see the black brows of Night, and note the advance of darkness; I must withdraw, lest Night overtake me unawares.

I beg you then, my hearers, since Night is but the passing and the death of Day, not to give death the preference over life, but graciously to honor my cause with your votes; so may the Muses prosper your studies, and Dawn, the friend of the Muses, hear your prayers; and may the Sun, who sees and hears all things, hearken to all in this assembly who honor and support his cause. I have done.

PROLUSION 7

DELIVERED IN THE COLLEGE CHAPEL IN DEFENSE OF LEARNING AN ORATION

LEARNING BRINGS MORE BLESSINGS TO MEN THAN IGNORANCE

Although, gentlemen, nothing could give me greater pleasure and satisfaction than your presence here, than this eager crowd in cap and gown, or than the honorable office of speaker, which I have already once or twice discharged before you gladly enough, I must, to be candid, confess that I scarcely ever undertake these speeches of my own free will; even though my own disposition and the trend of my studies make no impediment. In fact, if the choice had been offered me, I could well have dispensed with this evening's task. For I have learnt from the writings and sayings of wise men that nothing common or mediocre can be tolerated in an orator any more than in a poet, and that he who would be an orator in reality as well as by repute must first acquire a thorough knowledge of all the arts and sciences to form a complete background to his own calling. Since however this is impossible at my age, I would rather endeavor truly to deserve that reputation by long and concentrated study and by the preliminary acquisition of that background, than snatch at a false repute by a premature and hastily acquired eloquence.[1]

Afire and aglow with these plans and notions, I found that there was no more serious hindrance or obstacle than the loss of time caused by these constant interruptions, while nothing better promoted the development and well-being of the mind, contrary to what is the case with the body, than a cultured and liberal leisure. This I believe to be the meaning of Hesiod's holy sleep and Endymion's

1. Cp. Milton's sense of his own belatedness in *Sonnet 7* and *Letter to a Friend.*

nightly meetings with the moon;[2] this was the significance of Prometheus' withdrawal, under the guidance of Mercury, to the lofty solitude of the Caucasus, where at last he became the wisest of gods and men, so that his advice was sought by Jupiter himself concerning the marriage of Thetis.[3] I can myself call to witness the woods and rivers and the beloved village elms, under whose shade I enjoyed in the summer just passed (if I may tell the secrets of goddesses) such sweet intercourse with the Muses, as I still remember with delight. There I too, amid rural scenes and woodland solitudes, felt that I had enjoyed a season of growth in a life of seclusion.

I might indeed have hoped to find here also the same opportunity for retirement, had not the distressing task of speaking been unseasonably imposed upon me. This so cruelly deprived me of my holy slumbers, so tormented my mind, intent upon other things, and so hindered and hampered me in the hard and arduous pursuit of learning, that I gave up all hope of finding any peace and began sadly to think how far removed I was from that tranquility which learning had at first promised me, how hard my life was like to be amid this turmoil and agitation, and that all attempts to pursue learning had best be abandoned. And so, almost beside myself, I rashly determined on singing the praise of ignorance, since that was not subject to these disturbances, and I proposed as the theme of dispute the question whether art or ignorance bestowed greater blessings on its devotees. I know not how it is, but somehow either my destiny or my disposition forbade me to give up my old devotion to the Muses; indeed, blind chance itself seemed of a sudden to be endowed with prudence and foresight and to join in the prohibition. Sooner than I could have expected, Ignorance had found her champion, and the defense of learning devolved on me. I am delighted thus to have been played with, and am not ashamed to confess that I owe the restoration of my sight to Fortune, who is herself blind. For this she deserves my gratitude. Now I may at any rate be permitted to sing the praises of learning, from whose embrace I have been torn, and as it were assuage my longing for the absent beloved by speaking of her. This can now hardly be called an interruption, for who would regard it as an interruption when he is called upon to praise or defend the object of his affection, his admiration, and his deepest desire?

But, gentlemen, it is my opinion that the power of eloquence is most manifest when it deals with subjects which rouse no particular enthusiasm. Those which most stir our admiration can hardly be compassed within the bounds of

2. **Hesiod's holy sleep:** presumably refers to the contemplative pastoral life in which the Muses called to Hesiod as he pastured his sheep under Mount Helicon. **Endymion:** The goddess of the moon came down to him as he was sleeping in a cave in Latmos. Cp. *Letter to a Friend* (p. 8).

3. The more usual version of the story is that Jupiter sent Mercury to bind *Prometheus* to Mount Caucasus as punishment for bringing fire to humanity. Jupiter's need to learn the bridal secret of the nymph *Thetis* (that her son would be greater than his father) brings him to request the guidance of Prometheus.

a speech: the very abundance of material is a drawback, and the multiplicity of subjects narrows and confines the swelling stream of eloquence. I am now suffering from this excess of material: that which should be my strength makes me weak, and that which should be my defense makes me defenseless. So I must make my choice, or at least mention only in passing rather than discuss at length the numerous arguments on whose powerful support our cause relies for its defense and security. On this occasion it seems to me that my efforts must be directed entirely to showing how and to what extent learning and ignorance respectively promote that happiness which is the aim of every one of us. With this question I shall easily deal in my speech, nor need I be over-anxious about what objections Folly may bring against knowledge, or ignorance against learning. Yet the very ability of ignorance to raise any objection, to make a speech, or even to open her lips in this great and learned assembly, she has received as a favor, or rather an alms, from learning.

It is, I think, a belief familiar and generally accepted that the great Creator of the world, while constituting all else fleeting and perishable, infused into man, besides what was mortal, a certain divine spirit, a part of himself, as it were, which is immortal, imperishable, and exempt from death and extinction. After wandering about upon the Earth for some time, like some heavenly visitant, in holiness and righteousness, this spirit was to take its flight upward to the heaven whence it had come and to return once more to the abode and home which was its birthright. It follows that nothing can be reckoned as a cause of our happiness which does not somehow take into account both that everlasting life and our ordinary life here on Earth. This eternal life, as almost everyone admits, is to be found in contemplation alone, by which the mind is uplifted, without the aid of the body, and gathered within itself so that it attains, to its inexpressible joy, a life akin to that of the immortal gods. But without art the mind is fruitless, joyless, and altogether null and void. For who can worthily gaze upon and contemplate the ideas of things human or divine, unless he possesses a mind trained and ennobled by learning and study, without which he can know practically nothing of them: for indeed every approach to the happy life seems barred to the man who has no part in learning. God would indeed seem to have endowed us to no purpose, or even to our distress, with this soul which is capable and indeed insatiably desirous of the highest wisdom, if he had not intended us to strive with all our might toward the lofty understanding of those things, for which he had at our creation instilled so great a longing into the human mind. Survey from every angle the entire aspect of these things and you will perceive that the great Artificer of this mighty fabric established it for His own glory. The more deeply we delve into the wondrous wisdom, the marvelous skill, and the astounding variety of its creation (which we cannot do without the aid of learning), the greater grows the wonder and awe we feel for its Creator and the louder the praises we offer Him, which we believe and are fully persuaded that He delights to accept. Can we indeed believe, my hearers, that the vast spaces of boundless air are illuminated and adorned with everlasting lights, that these are endowed with such rapidity of motion and pass through such intricate revolutions, merely to serve as a lantern for base and slothful men, and to light the path of the idle and the sluggard here below? Do we perceive no purpose in the luxuriance of fruit and herb beyond the short-lived beauty of verdure? Of a truth, if we are so little able to appraise their value that we make no effort to go beyond the crass perceptions of the senses, we shall show ourselves not merely servile and abject, but ungracious and wicked before the goodness of God; for by our unresponsiveness and grudging spirit He is deprived of much of the glory which is His due, and of the reverence which His mighty power exacts.[4] If then Learning is our guide and leader in the search after happiness, if it is ordained and approved by almighty God, and most conformable to His glory, surely it cannot but bring the greatest blessings upon those who follow after it.

I am well aware, gentlemen, that this contemplation, by which we strive to reach the highest goal, cannot partake of true happiness unless it is conjoined with integrity of life and uprightness of character. I know, too, that many men eminent for learning have been of bad character, and slaves to anger, hatred, and evil passions, while on the other hand many utterly ignorant men have shown themselves righteous and just. What of it? Does it follow that ignorance is more blessed? By no means. For the truth is, gentlemen, that though the corrupt morals of their country and the evil communications of the illiterate have in some instances lured into wicked courses a few men distinguished for their learning, yet the influence of a single wise and prudent man has often kept loyal to their duty a large number of men who lacked the advantages of Learning. And indeed a single household, even a single individual, endowed with the gifts of Art and Wisdom, may often prove to be a great gift of God, and sufficient to lead a whole state to righteousness. But where no Arts flourish, where all scholarship is banished, there you will find no single trace of a good man, but savagery and barbarity stalk abroad. As instances of this I adduce no one country, province, or race alone, but Europe itself, forming as it does one fourth of the entire globe. Throughout this continent a few hundred years ago all the noble arts had perished and the Muses had deserted all the universities of the day, over which they had long presided; blind illiteracy had penetrated and entrenched itself everywhere, nothing was heard in the schools but the absurd doctrines of driveling monks, and that profane and hideous monster, Ignorance, assumed the gown and lorded it on our empty platforms and pulpits and in our deserted professorial chairs. Then Piety went in mourning, and Religion sickened and flagged, so that only after prolonged suffering, and hardly even to this very day, has she recovered from her grievous wound.

But, gentlemen, it is, I believe, an established maxim of philosophy that the

4. In *PL*, the themes sounded in the paragraph recur in various forms; cp. 3.694–704, 4.657–76, 8.10–38.

cognizance of every art and science appertains to the intellect only and that the home and sanctuary of virtue and uprightness is the will. But all agree that while the human intellect shines forth as the lord and governor of all the other faculties, it guides and illuminates with its radiance the will also, which would else be blind, and the will shines with a borrowed light, even as the moon does. So, even though we grant and willingly concede that virtue without learning is more conducive to happiness than learning without virtue, yet when these two are once wedded in happy union as they surely ought to be, and often are, then indeed Knowledge raises her head aloft and shows herself far superior, and shining forth takes her seat on high beside the king and governor, Intellect, and gazes upon the doings of the Will below as upon some object lying far beneath her feet; and thereafter for evermore she claims as her right all excellence and splendor and a majesty next to that of God himself.[5]

Let us now leave these heights to consider our ordinary life, and see what advantages learning and ignorance respectively can offer in private and in public life. I will say nothing of the argument that learning is the fairest ornament of youth, the strong defense of manhood, and the glory and solace of age. Nor will I mention that many men highly honored in their day, and even some of the greatest men of ancient Rome, after performing many noble deeds and winning great glory by their exploits, turned from the strife and turmoil of ambition to the study of literature as into a port and welcome refuge. Clearly these honored sages realized that the best part of the life which yet remained to them must be spent to the best advantage. They were first among men; they wished by virtue of these arts to be not the last among the gods. They had once striven for glory, and now strove for immortality. Their warfare against the foes of their country had been far other, but now that they were facing death, the greatest enemy of mankind, these were the weapons they took up, these the legions they enrolled, and these the resources from which they derived their strength.

But the chief part of human happiness is derived from the society of one's fellows and the formation of friendships, and it is often asserted that the learned are as a rule hard to please, lacking in courtesy, odd in manner, and seldom gifted with the gracious address that wins men's hearts. I admit that a man who is almost entirely absorbed and immersed in study finds it much easier to converse with gods than with men, either because he habitually associates with the gods but is unaccustomed to human affairs and a stranger among them, or because the mind, expanding through constant meditation on things divine and therefore feeling cramped within the narrow limits of the body, is less expert in the nicer formalities of social life. But if such a man once forms a worthy and congenial friendship, there is none who cultivates it more assiduously. For what can we imagine more delightful and happy than those conversations of learned

5. The relation between will and intellect that Milton here expresses hierarchically becomes an equation in later works: "reason is but choosing" (*Areop*, p. 192); "reason also is choice" (*PL* 3.108).

and wise men, such as those which the divine Plato is said often to have held in the shade of that famous plane-tree, conversations which all mankind might well have flocked to hear in spell-bound silence?[6] But gross talk and mutual incitement to indulge in luxury and lust is the friendship of ignorance, or rather the ignorance of friendship.

Moreover if this human happiness consists in the honorable and liberal joys of the mind, such a pleasure is to be found in study and learning as far surpasses every other. What a thing it is to grasp the nature of the whole firmament and of its stars, all the movements and changes of the atmosphere, whether it strikes terror into ignorant minds by the majestic roll of thunder or by fiery comets, or whether it freezes into snow or hail, or whether again it falls softly and gently in showers of dew; then perfectly to understand the shifting winds and all the exhalations and vapors which earth and sea give forth; next to know the hidden virtues of plants and metals and understand the nature and the feelings, if that may be, of every living creature; next the delicate structure of the human body and the art of keeping it in health; and, to crown all, the divine might and power of the soul, and any knowledge we may have gained concerning those beings which we call spirits and genii and daemons.[7] There is an infinite number of subjects besides these, a great part of which might be learnt in less time than it would take to enumerate them all. So at length, my hearers, when universal learning has once completed its cycle, the spirit of man, no longer confined within this dark prison-house, will reach out far and wide, till it fills the whole world and the space far beyond with the expansion of its divine greatness. Then at last most of the chances and changes of the world will be so quickly perceived that to him who holds this stronghold of wisdom hardly anything can happen in his life which is unforeseen or fortuitous. He will indeed seem to be one whose rule and dominion the stars obey, to whose command earth and sea hearken, and whom winds and tempests serve; to whom, lastly, Mother Nature herself has surrendered, as if indeed some god had abdicated the throne of the world and entrusted its rights, laws, and administration to him as governor.

Besides this, what delight it affords to the mind to take its flight through the history and geography of every nation and to observe the changes in the conditions of kingdoms, races, cities, and peoples, to the increase of wisdom and righteousness. This, my hearers, is to live in every period of the world's history, and to be as it were coeval with time itself. And indeed, while we look to the future for the glory of our name, this will be to extend and stretch our lives backward before our birth, and to wrest from grudging Fate a kind of retrospective immortality. I pass over a pleasure with which none can compare—to be the

6. In the *Phaedrus*, Socrates converses with his friend under the shade of a plane tree. For friendship and learning in the Platonic tradition, cp. the letters between Milton and Diodati.

7. The word translated as *spirits* is *lares*, Latin for guardian deities of households; *genii* perform a similar function for individuals. Although *daemons* are in one sense the Greek equivalents of *genii*, Milton uses the term to indicate a broader category of supernatural being, intermediate between gods and men as occasion demands, such as the Attendant Spirit in *A Mask*.

oracle of many nations, to find one's home regarded as a kind of temple, to be a man whom kings and states invite to come to them, whom men from near and far flock to visit, while to others it is a matter for pride if they have but set eyes on him once. These are the rewards of study, these are the prizes which learning can and often does bestow upon her votaries in private life.

What, then, of public life? It is true that few have been raised to the height of majesty through a reputation for learning, and not many more through a reputation for uprightness. Such men certainly enjoy a kingdom in themselves far more glorious than any earthly dominion; and who can lay claim to a twofold sovereignty without incurring the charge of ambition? I will, however, add this one thing more: that there have hitherto been but two men who have ruled the whole world, as by divine right, and shared an empire over all kings and princes equal to that of the gods themselves; namely Alexander the Great and Augustus, both of whom were students of philosophy.[8] It is as though Providence had specially singled them out as examples to humanity, to show to what sort of man the helm or reins of government should be entrusted.

But, it may be objected, many nations have won fame by their deeds or their wealth, without owing anything to learning. We know of but few Spartans, for example, who took any interest in liberal education, and the Romans only admitted philosophy within the walls of their city after a long time. But the Spartans found a lawgiver in Lycurgus, who was both a philosopher and so ardent a student of poetry that he was the first to gather together with extreme care the writings of Homer, which were scattered throughout Ionia.[9] The Romans, hardly able to support themselves after the various risings and disturbances which had taken place in the city, sent ambassadors to beg for the Decemviral Laws, also called the Twelve Tables, from Athens, which was at that time foremost in the study of the liberal Arts.[10]

How are we to answer the objection that the Turks of today have acquired an extensive dominion over the wealthy kingdoms of Asia in spite of being entirely devoid of culture? For my part, I have certainly never heard of anything in that state which deserves to be regarded as an example to us—if indeed one should dignify with the name of "state" the power which a horde of utter barbarians united by complicity in crime has seized by violence and murder. The provision of the necessaries of life, and their maintenance when acquired, we owe not to art but to nature; greedy attacks on the property of others, mutual assistance for purposes of plunder, and criminal conspiracy are the outcome of

8. Aristotle instructed *Alexander the Great* (356–23 B.C.E.); *Augustus* (63 B.C.E.–14 C.E.), the first Roman emperor, was interested in philosophy and literature as a means of encouraging social morality.

9. **Lycurgus:** legendary lawgiver of seventh-century B.C.E. (?) Sparta who, according to Plutarch (*Lives* 1.215), was introduced to Homer's works while in *Ionia* and made them widely known. *Ionia* is a storied region on the west coast of Asia Minor (Turkey).

10. **Decemviral:** refers to the ten men appointed in 451 B.C.E. to compile the laws brought back from Athens. They inscribed them on *twelve tables.* This paragraph rehearses examples that Milton later uses in his survey of the history of learning in *Areop.*

the perversion of nature. Some kind of justice indeed is exercised in such states, as might be expected; for while the other virtues are easily put to flight, Justice from her throne compels homage, for without her even the most unjust states would soon fall into decay. I must not, however, omit to mention that the Saracens,[11] to whom the Turks are indebted almost for their existence, enlarged their empire as much by the study of liberal culture as by force of arms.

If we go back to antiquity, we shall find that some states owed not merely their laws but their very foundation to culture. The oldest progenitors of every race are said to have wandered through the woods and mountains, seeking their livelihood after the fashion of wild beasts, with head erect but stooping posture. One might well think that they shared everything with the animals, except the dignity of their form; the same caves, the same dens, afforded them shelter from rain and frost. There were then no cities, no marble palaces, no shining altars or temples of the gods; they had no religion to guide them, no laws or law-courts, no bridal torches, no festal dance, no song at the joyful board, no funeral rites, no mourning, hardly even a grave paid honor to the dead. There were no feasts, no games; no sound of music was ever heard: all these refinements were then lacking which idleness now misuses to foster luxury. Then of a sudden the Arts and Sciences breathed their divine breath into the savage breasts of men, and instilling into them the knowledge of themselves, gently drew them to dwell together within the walls of cities. Therefore of a surety cities may well expect to have a long and happy history under the direction of those guides by whom they were first of all founded, then firmly based on laws, and finally fortified by wise counsels.

What now of ignorance? I perceive, gentlemen, that Ignorance is struck blind and senseless, skulks at a distance, casts about for a way of escape, and complains that life is short and art long. But if we do but remove two great obstacles to our studies, namely first our bad methods of teaching the arts, and secondly our lack of enthusiasm, we shall find that, with all deference to Galen or whoever may have been the author of the saying, quite the contrary is the truth, and that life is long and art short.[12] There is nothing so excellent and at the same time so exacting as art, nothing more sluggish and languid than ourselves. We allow ourselves to be outdone by laborers and husbandmen in working after dark and before dawn; they show greater energy in a mean occupation, to gain a miserable livelihood, than we do in the noblest of occupations, to win a life of true happiness. Though we aspire to the highest and best of human conditions we can endure neither hard work nor yet the reproach of idleness; in fact we are ashamed of owning the very character which we hate not to have imputed to us.

But, we object, our health forbids late hours and hard study. It is a shameful

11. **Saracens:** Used broadly, as here, it means Arabs in general.

12. The saying actually originates with the Greek physician Hippocrates (c. 460–c. 370 B.C.E.). Milton may be drawing on Seneca, who attributes the saying to "the greatest of healers" (*On the Brevity of Life* 1).

admission that we neglect to cultivate our minds out of consideration for our bodies, whose health all should be ready to impair if thereby their minds might gain the more. Yet those who make this excuse are certainly for the most part worthless fellows; for though they disregard every consideration of their time, their talents, and their health, and give themselves up to gluttony, to drinking like whales, and to spending their nights in gaming and debauchery, they never complain that they are any the worse for it. Since, then, it is their constant habit and practice to show eagerness and energy in the pursuit of vice, but listlessness and lethargy where any activity of virtue or intelligence is concerned, they cannot lay the blame on nature or the shortness of life with any show of truth or justice. But if we were to set ourselves to live modestly and temperately, and to tame the first impulses of headstrong youth by reason and steady devotion to study, keeping the divine vigor of our minds unstained and uncontaminated by any impurity or pollution, we should be astonished to find, gentlemen, looking back over a period of years, how great a distance we had covered and across how wide a sea of learning we had sailed, without a check on our voyage.

This voyage, too, will be much shortened if we know how to select branches of learning that are useful, and what is useful within them. In the first place, how many despicable quibbles there are in grammar and rhetoric! One may hear the teachers of them talking sometimes like savages and sometimes like babies. What about logic? That is indeed the queen of the Arts, if taught as it should be, but unfortunately how much foolishness there is in reason! Its teachers are not like men at all, but like finches which live on thorns and thistles. "O iron stomachs of the harvesters!"[13] What am I to say of that branch of learning which the Peripatetics call metaphysics?[14] It is not, as the authority of great men would have me believe, an exceedingly rich art; it is, I say, not an art at all, but a sinister rock, a Lernian bog[15] of fallacies, devised to cause shipwreck and pestilence. These are the wounds, to which I have already referred, which the ignorance of gownsmen inflicts; and this monkish disease has already infected natural philosophy to a considerable extent; the mathematicians too are afflicted with a longing for the petty triumph of demonstrative rhetoric. If we disregard and curtail all these subjects, which can be of no use to us, as we should, we shall be surprised to find how many whole years we shall save. Jurisprudence in particular suffers much from our confused methods of teaching, and from what is even worse, a jargon which one might well take for some Red Indian dialect,[16] or even no human speech at all. Often, when I have heard our lawyers shouting at each other in this lingo, it has occurred to me to wonder whether men who had neither a human tongue nor human speech could have any human feelings either. I do indeed fear that sacred justice will pay no atten-

13. Horace, *Epodes* 3.4: "O dura Messorum ilia!" *Stomachs* is a euphemism for bowels.
14. **Peripatetics:** philosophers in the Aristotelian tradition, such as the scholastics.
15. **Lernian bog:** noisome marshes of Lerna, near Argos, where Hercules confronted the Hydra.
16. **Red Indian dialect:** The Latin text reads *Americanus,* "American."

tion to us and that she will never understand our complaints and wrongs, as she cannot speak our language.

Therefore, gentlemen, if from our childhood onward we never allow a day to pass by without its lesson and diligent study, if we are wise enough to rule out of every art what is irrelevant, superfluous, or unprofitable, we shall assuredly, before we have attained the age of Alexander the Great, have made ourselves masters of something greater and more glorious than that world of his. And so far from complaining of the shortness of life and the slowness of Art, I think we shall be more likely to weep and wail, as Alexander did, because there are no more worlds for us to conquer.[17]

Ignorance is breathing her last, and you are now watching her final efforts and her dying struggle. She declares that glory is mankind's most powerful incentive, and that whereas a long succession and course of years has bestowed glory on the illustrious men of old, we live under the shadow of the world's old age and decrepitude, and of the impending dissolution of all things, so that even if we leave behind us anything deserving of everlasting fame, the scope of our glory is narrowed, since there will be few succeeding generations to remember us. It is therefore to no purpose that we produce so many books and noble monuments of learning, seeing that the approaching conflagration of the world will destroy them all.[18] I do not deny that this may indeed be so; but yet to have no thought of glory when we do well is above all glory. The ancients could indeed derive no satisfaction from the empty praise of men, seeing that no joy or knowledge of it could reach them when they were dead and gone. But we may hope for an eternal life, which will never allow the memory of the good deeds we performed on earth to perish; in which, if we have done well here, we shall ourselves be present to hear our praise; and in which, according to a wise philosophy held by many, those who have lived temperately and devoted all their time to noble arts, and have thus been of service to mankind, will be rewarded by the bestowal of a wisdom matchless and supreme over all others.[19]

Let the idle now cease to upbraid us with the uncertainties and perplexities of learning, which are indeed the fault not so much of learning as of the frailty of man. It is this consideration, gentlemen, which disproves or mitigates or compensates for Socrates' famous ignorance and the Skeptics' timid suspension of judgment.[20]

And finally, we may well ask, what is the happiness which Ignorance

17. *Of Education* develops some of the pedagogical reforms suggested in these paragraphs, with a particular eye toward efficient use of students' time.

18. The idea that time had almost run its course and the world had long been in decline was prevalent in the Renaissance. The *conflagration* to which Milton refers is apocalyptic.

19. Cp. *Lyc* 70–84.

20. *Socrates* was celebrated by the Oracle at Delphi as the wisest man alive because, he explained, he recognized his own ignorance (Plato, *Apology* 21a–b). The *Skeptics* of classical Greece argued that there were no adequate grounds for certainty as to the truth of any proposition. Hence they suspended judgment.

promises? To enjoy what one possesses, to have no enemies, to be beyond the reach of all care and trouble, to pass one's life in peace and quiet so far as may be—this is but the life of a beast, or of some bird which builds its little nest in the farthest depths of the forest as near to the sky as it can, in security, rears its offspring, flits about in search of sustenance without fear of the fowler, and pours forth its sweet melodies at dawn and dusk. Why should one ask for that divine activity of the mind in addition? Well, if such is the argument, we will offer Ignorance Circe's cup, and bid her throw off her human shape, walk no longer erect, and betake her to the beasts.[21] To the beasts, did I say? They will surely refuse to receive so infamous a guest, at any rate if they are either endowed with some kind of inferior reasoning power, as many maintain, or guided by some powerful instinct, enabling them to practice the arts, or something resembling the arts, among themselves. For Plutarch tells us that in the pursuit of game, dogs show some knowledge of dialectic, and if they chance to come to cross-roads, they obviously make use of a disjunctive syllogism. Aristotle points out that the nightingale in some sort instructs her offspring in the principles of music. Almost every animal is its own physician, and many of them have given valuable lessons in medicine to man; the Egyptian ibis teaches us the value of purgatives, the hippopotamus that of blood-letting. Who can maintain that creatures which so often give us warning of coming wind, rain, floods, or fair weather, know nothing of astronomy? What prudent and strict ethics are shown by those geese which check their dangerous loquacity by holding pebbles in their beaks as they fly over Mount Taurus! Our domestic economy owes much to the ants, our commonwealth to the bees, while military science admits its indebtedness to the cranes for the practice of posting sentinels and for the triangular formation in battle.[22] The beasts are too wise to admit Ignorance to their fellowship and society; they will force her to a lower station. What then? To stocks and stones? Why even trees, bushes, and whole woods once tore up their roots and hurried to hear the skilful strains of Orpheus. Often, too, they were endowed with mysterious powers and uttered divine oracles, as for instance did the oaks of Dodona. Rocks, too, show a certain aptitude for learning in that they reply to the sacred words of poets; will not these also reject Ignorance? Therefore, driven lower than any kind of beast, lower than stocks and stones, lower than any natural species, will Ignorance be permitted to find repose in the famous "non-existent" of the Epicureans?[23] No,

21. In Homer, the enchantress Circe uses her charmed cup and wand to transform Odysseus's men into swine (*Od.* 10.230–50).

22. In his *Apology for Raymond Sebond* (2.12), Montaigne had argued similarly but at greater length that beasts "reason not contemptibly" (*PL* 8.374) and included many of the same examples as Milton, including the syllogizing dog (known as "Chrysippus's dog"), a classical commonplace of considerable vogue in seventeenth-century philosophy.

23. A fundamental premise of Epicurean philosophy, one that contradicts the Christian doctrine of creation *ex nihilo,* is that nothing can come into being from that which is nonexistent. In his *Christian Doctrine,* the heretical Milton sides with the Epicureans on this point (1.7).

not even there; for Ignorance must be something yet worse, yet more vile, yet more wretched, in a word the very depth of degradation.

I come now to you, my clever hearers, for even without any words of mine I see in you not so much arguments on my side as darts which I shall hurl at Ignorance till she is slain. I have sounded the attack, do you rush into battle; put this enemy to flight, drive her from your porticos and walks. If you allow her to exist, you yourselves will be that which you know to be the most wretched thing in the world. This cause is the personal concern of you all. So, if I have perchance spoken at much greater length than is customary in this place, not forgetting that this was demanded by the importance of the subject, you will, I hope, pardon me, my judges, since it is one more proof of the interest I feel in you, of my zeal on your behalf, and of the nights of toil and wakefulness I consented to endure for your sakes. I have done.

Introduction to Milton's *Commonplace Book*

John Milton's *Commonplace Book* was not discovered until 1874, lying unsuspected among the manuscripts of Sir Fredrick Graham in Netherby Hall, Cumberland. It evidently came into the library of the Graham family as a bribe offered by Daniel Skinner, the feckless amanuensis who served Milton in his final years. After Milton died, Skinner had possession of several of his unpublished manuscripts, including that of the *Commonplace Book.* Seeking a post in Paris, he seems to have made a present of it to Richard Graham, Viscount Preston (1645–95), who eventually brought it home with him to the northern border of England (Kelley, 1949). Like *Christian Doctrine,* another manuscript in Skinner's possession that did not come to light until the nineteenth century, the *Commonplace Book* offers a most revealing if long shuttered window on Milton's intellectual breadth and process. It provides critical context for understanding works Milton wrote for a public audience and does so from a broader, secular perspective than that afforded by the narrower ambit of a systematic theological treatise.

A commonplace book was a particular kind of reading notebook in widespread use among the educated and consequential in early modern Europe. Readers compiled quotations in them, often indexed (as were Milton's) under headings or "places" that the reader deemed current or apt. Under such organizational headings the reader would copy out memorably expressed points of wisdom as well as telling examples and observations that might jog the mind into detailed recollection or supply ammunition for attacking or advancing an argument (as Milton's often did). A conscientiously kept commonplace book becomes in effect the trail left by a wayfaring mind, in some instances over decades of reading. The trail left by Milton's reading stretches from the 1630s into the last decade of his life and includes excerpts from about ninety authors writing in Greek, Latin, Italian, French, and English. Most of the entries date from the 1630s and 1640s, when Milton was most active as a scholar and polemicist, and are remarkable for their intellectual engagement and scholarly precision. Milton's citations were exact enough to permit James Holly Hanford to reconstruct Milton's intellectual itinerary in "The Chronology of Milton's Private Studies" (1921), a fundamental contribution to Milton studies that has been usefully supplemented in the works of subsequent scholars (Mohl 1969, Poole

2009, Fulton 2010). The small sample we have included here reflects a persistent concern with how a Christian committed to purity should participate in a morally ambiguous world.

Our text is taken with permission from volume one of the Yale edition of the *Complete Prose.* Deletions of entries within headings are indicated by ellipses in brackets. We have in most cases silently deleted Milton's abbreviated notations of sources within entries and supplied the full citations in our annotations and list of works cited. Our text sometimes deviates from the translations in the Yale edition, and where the change is substantial, we have noted our rationale. For advice concerning certain translations, we are grateful to William Poole, whose new edition of the complete *Commonplace Book* is forthcoming in volume 9 of the Clarendon Milton.

MILTON'S *COMMONPLACE BOOK*

Ethical Index

Moral Evil

In moral evil much good can be mixed and that with remarkable cunning. "No one combines poison with gall, and with hellebore, but with savory sauces and delicacies. . . . So the devil steeps whatever deadly dish he prepares in God's dearest benefits" &c.[1]

Why does God permit evil? So that reason may stand firm with virtue. For the good is made known, is made clear, and is exercised by evil. As Lactantius says . . . , that reason and intelligence may have the opportunity to exercise themselves by choosing the things that are good, by fleeing from the things that are evil.[2]

Of the Good Man

[. . . .]

A good man by some reckoning seems to surpass even the angels, to the extent that, enclosed in a weak and earthly body and always struggling with his passions, he nevertheless aspires to lead a life like that of the inhabitants of heaven.[3]

[. . . .]

1. Tertullian (p. 102). Except for minor omissions, Milton's Latin quotation, drawn from *De Spectaculis* (*Of Public Shows*), is exact. Advocating abstinence, Tertullian (c. 160–c. 225) urges his Christian audience to forsake the pagan entertainments of ancient Rome.
2. Milton paraphrases Lactantius (pp. 376–78). We render "*ut ratio virtuti constare possit*" as "so that reason may stand firm with virtue" instead of following the Yale translation ("so that the account can stand correct with goodness"). The Latin "*constare*" articulates Milton's fundamental conviction that reason and will are functionally inseparable, or as Milton's God puts it: "reason also is choice" (*PL* 3.108). Milton's citations of Lactantius commonly refer to his best-known work, *Divinarum Institutionum Libri VII* (*The Divine Institutes in Seven Books*), which presented Christianity in a manner meant to confront and persuade philosophically minded pagans. Though posthumously condemned as a heretic, Lactantius (c. 250–c. 325) was beloved of Renaissance authors for his eloquent Latin style.
3. John Chrysostom (c. 347–407) was Archbishop of Constantinople and the best known of Greek early church fathers (pp. 16–17). Milton cites a point made near the end of Chrysostom's Twelfth Homily, in *Sixty-Seven Homilies on the Book of Genesis* (pp. 16–17).

Of Lust

Pederasty or sodomy. "What can be sacred to those who would debase the age that is weak and in need of protection, so that it is destroyed and defiled through their own lust?"[4]

[. . .]

Of Poetry

[. . . .]

Basil tells us that poetry was taught by God to kindle in the minds of men a zeal for virtue. "For when the Holy Spirit saw that mankind could be led with difficulty to virtue and that we are neglectful of upright living because of our proneness to pleasure, what did it do? It mixed with the doctrines the delight of melody so that we might unconsciously receive the benefit of the discourse through the charm and smoothness of the sounds."[5]

[. . . .]

Of Reproof

Luther refrained neither from harshness nor from jests that were now and then even a little shameful.[6]

Economic Index

Adultery

The Protestants, those of Orleans, when that city was in their possession, used to punish adultery by death: a practice which the courtiers resented so violently that they vowed they would be, on account of it, always estranged from the Protestants.[7]

Divorce

The reason why it ought to be permitted is that, as physicians and almost all others acknowledge, [copulation] without love is cold, unpleasant, unfruitful,

4. Milton's quotation of Lactantius' Latin is nearly exact (p. 511). See note 2 above. The Yale translation renders the Greek nouns ("*paiderastia*" "*arrhenokoitia*") in Milton's caption as "lust for boys or men." We have substituted more literal translations.
5. Milton's summary sentence was originally written in Latin; the quotation of Basil's *Homilies on the Psalms* in Greek (p. 126). An influential theologian in the Nicene era church, Basil (c. 330–79) became a Bishop notable for charitable work in Cappadocia—in modern-day Turkey.
6. John Sleidan (1506–56) in his *Commentaries* (p. 261) describes a harshly derisive vernacular polemic written by Luther against the Pope. Milton evidently approved.
7. The French historian Jacques Auguste de Thou (Thuanus) (1553–1617), a pious Catholic nonetheless committed to religious toleration, relates the narrative on which Milton bases this summation (2:241). Concerning capital punishment for adultery, Milton, in *Colasterion*, the last of his divorce tracts, contends that scripture "appoints many things, and yet leaves the circumstance to man's discretion" (Yale 2:730).

noxious, bestial, abominable. Therefore it is intolerable that either one, or at least the innocent one, should be bound unwillingly by so monstrous a fetter.[8]

Political Index

The State

[....]

The form of state to be fitted to the people's disposition: some live best under monarchy; others otherwise. So that the conversions of commonwealths happen not always through ambition or malice. As among the Romans who after their infancy were ripe for a more free government than monarchy, being in a manner all fit to be Kings. Afterward grown unruly, and impotent with overmuch prosperity were either for their profit, or their punishment fit to be curbed with a lordly and dreadful monarchy; which was the error of the noble Brutus and Cassius, who felt themselves of spirit to free an nation but considered not that the nation was not fit to be free, whilst forgetting their old justice and fortitude which was made to rule, they became slaves to their own ambition and luxury.[9]

"Separation between religion and the state cannot be."[10]

Hospital, the very wise chancellor of France, was of the opposite opinion. "Many," he says, "can be citizens who are by no means Christians, and he who is far from the bosom of the Church does not cease to be a loyal citizen, and we can live peacefully with those who do not reverence the same religious rites as we do."[11]

A commonwealth is preferable to a monarchy: "because more excellent men come from a commonwealth than from a kingdom; because in the former virtue is honored most of the time and is not feared as in the kingdom," &c.[12]

Love of Country

This virtue should be sought by philosophers cautiously. For a blind and carnal love of country should not carry us off to plundering and bloodshed and hatred of neighboring countries, so that we may enrich our country in power, wealth, or glory; for so did the pagans act. It behooves Christians, however, to cultivate

8. The description of copulation without love closely follows the description of Johann Benedict Sinibaldus, a leading seventeenth-century Roman physician (15). The final sentence is Milton's observation (Cp. *DDD*, 126–27, 151].

9. This entry, written in English, reads like the quick outline of steps in an argument. Milton does not indicate a source, perhaps because he was drawing on the familiar work of Sir Thomas Smith (1513–77). See *The Commonwealth of England*, especially chapters 4–5 of Book 1.

10. This assertion is taken from the preface to Camden's *Annales*.

11. Milton again quotes Thuanus, 2:71.

12. The quotation from *The Art of War* by Machiavelli (1469–1527) is in Italian, p. 63.

peace among themselves and not seek the property of others. For this reason Lactantius attacks philosophy.[13]

[. . . .]

King

Sigonius writes that Diocletian was the first of the Romans to permit himself to be worshipped; whereas before him all the Roman emperors had been satisfied with the consular salute. This assertion others make about Constantine.[14]

What the early Christians decided about this, Justin Martyr, writing to the Emperor Antoninus Pius, makes clear in his belief, founded upon the teaching of Christ, that we should give to Caesar the things which are Caesar's and to God the things which are God's; "therefore," he says, "we worship God alone, and in other matters we gladly serve you," in which he plainly assigns "worship" to God alone, and "willing service" to kings.[15]

[. . . .]

Whether monarchy be a power absolute. Sir Tho. Smith answereth that neither it nor any other kind of commonwealth is pure an[d] absolute in his kind, no more than elements are pure in nature, or the complexions and temperatures in a body, but mixed with other, "for that nature . . . will not suffer it." [. . .] And in the 9th c[hapter] that the act of a k[ing] "neither approved by the people, nor established by act of parliament" is "taken for nothing either to bind the k[ing], his successors, or his subjects."[16]

[. . . .]

Definition of Sir Tho. Smith is "A K[ing] who is by succession or election commeth with good will of the people to his government, and doth administer the com[mon]wealth by the laws of the same and by equity, and doth seek the profit of the people as his own." And on the contrary, "he that comes by force, breaks laws at his pleasure, makes other without consent of the people, and regardeth not the wealth of the commons, but the advancement of himself, his faction, and his kindred" he defines for a tyrant.[17]

[. . . .]

13. Lactantius, Book 6, chapter 6. See note 2 above.
14. in *De Occidentali Imperio,* Italian historian Carolus Sigonius (Carlo Sigonio) (c. 1524–84) relates the history of the Western Roman Empire from the time of Diocletian (245–313) to its fall. Diocletian persecuted Christians and renewed former Roman religious practices in an effort to invigorate the empire. Milton's reference is to Book 1, p. 20.
15. Milton quotes from Justin Martyr's *Second Defense of Christians to Antoninus Pius,* p. 64.
16. Milton summarizes the single paragraph of Smith's chapter 6, entitled "That Commonwealths or Governments are not most commonly simple, but mixed" (p. 5). He then quotes from chapter 9, "Of the Name of the King, and the Administration of England" (p. 9).
17. Smith, p. 6.

Of Religion. To What Extent it Concerns the State

[...]

That the confounding of ecclesiastical and political government (when, that is to say, the magistrate acts as minister of the Church and the minister of the Church acts as magistrate) is equally destructive to both religion and the State, Dante, the Tuscan poet, shows:[18]

> Rome, that made the good world, used to have
> Two suns, which made clear to see
> The one way and the other: that of God and that of the world.
> The one has extinguished the other; and the sword
> Is joined with the crozier; and the one and the other
> Must perforce go ill together:
> Because, being joined, the one does not fear the other.

And a little further on.

> Say henceforth that the Church of Rome,
> By confounding in herself two powers,
> Falls into the mire, and fouls herself and her burden.

The opinions of men concerning religion should be free in a republic, or under good princes. While Machiavelli praises such princes, he says, among other good things, that under them you will see golden times, "where each man can hold and defend the opinion that he wishes."[19] See the Theological Index, Of Not Forcing Religion.

Various Forms of Government

Republican form. Machiavelli much prefers a republican form to monarchy, citing reasons by no means stupid throughout the 58th chapter of Book 1 of his *Discorsi* and in Book 3, chapter 34, where he argues that a republic makes fewer mistakes than a prince does in choosing its magistrates or councilors.[20]

To return to the very source of government, either by enacting good laws or by reducing magistrates to the ranks of ordinary citizens or by restoring the control of things to the decision of the people, is often beneficial. See

18. We substitute "confounding" for Yale's "combining" to render Milton's "*confusionem*" (from "*confusio,*" literally "to fuse together."). Milton quotes Dante exactly from canto 16 of *Purgatorio,* in Bernardino Daniello of Lucca's edition of the *Divine Comedy,* p. 349.
19. Milton quotes Machiavelli's *Discorsi,* p. 27. The subsequent reference to "the Theological Index" has been taken as an indication that Milton had a separate document in which he collected citations that would appear in *Christian Doctrine.*
20. See Machiavelli, p. 282, for the claim that the people choose magistrates more wisely than a prince does.

Machiavelli *Discorsi*: Book 3, chapter 1, where he says that this is very healthful for a republic just as it is for a mixed government &c.[21]

James Kennedy, Archbishop of St Andrews, censured and rejected government by women in a long speech.[22]

Public Shows

Tertullian, in the book which he wrote on public shows, condemns their use and closes them to Christians. And indeed not merely with arguments (which tear to pieces only the pagan games) does he show that he ought to fetter with scruples of conscience the mind of the careful and wise Christian so that he would not venture to see any dramatic poem composed by a poet by no means unskilled. Nevertheless he does that best in the epilogue of his book as, for instance, with concise and powerful style he stirs up the mind of the Christian to better plays, that is, divine and heavenly plays, which, in great number and of great value, the Christian can anticipate the coming of Christ and the Last Judgment.[23] Cyprian, or someone else rolled the same stone in a book composed on the same theme.[24] And Lactantius with arguments by no means stronger considers the whole dramatic art in moral error.[25] Not even once does he seem to have reflected that, although the little corruptions in the theater deservedly should be removed, it is by no means necessary for that reason that all practice of the dramatic arts should be completely done away with; on the contrary it would rather be absurd beyond measure. For what in all philosophy is more important or more sacred or more exalted than a tragedy rightly produced; what more useful for seeing at a single view the events and changes of human life? The same writer likewise in the following chapter seems to wish that the whole art of music might be carried from our midst.[26]

Of Military Discipline

[....]

If a magistrate shall order the leader of an army into an attack or battle with certain danger for all, it seems to be a part of the commander's duty to state his own opinion. If however a magistrate unversed in war shall still obstinately pursue the matter, it is not honorable for a commander to destroy his own army on account of the inexperience and stubbornness of one man or even of a whole

21. Machiavelli, p. 203.
22. The quotation of James Kennedy appears in Buchanan, p. 131.
23. Tertullian, pp. 102–103. See note 1, above.
24. Cp. Cyprian, p. 3.
25. Milton again refers to Lactantius' *Divine Institutes*. The title of Book 6, chapter 20, is "Of the Senses and Their Pleasures Both in Beast and Man and of the Pleasures of the Eyes and of Public Shows." See especially p. 503.
26. The title of Book 6, chapter 21, of Lactantius' *Divine Institutes* is "Of the Pleasures of the Ears, and of Sacred Literature" (pp. 507–509).

people. See the case of Malatesta, who refused to comply with the ruinous advice of the Florentine dictator.[27]

[. . . .]

Of Sedition

[. . . .]

Against all sedition Luther writes most venerably and prudently, both to the people and to the magistrate, saying that together they should do away with the causes of sedition: the people by waiting patiently and by settling the matter quietly through highly esteemed arbiters; the magistrate by at least leaving off cruelly oppressing, robbing, and ruining the people.

The Emperor loads with many charges the leaders of the Protestants, when they defend themselves; charges, namely, of rebellion, contempt of magistrate, &c., as happens today.[28]

The rebellion of a people has often been the means of their regaining their freedom, and therefore they should not be blamed, because very often they act from just causes and complaints. Witness Machiavelli: "I say that those who condemn the riots between the nobles and the common people thereby, in my estimation, blame those things that were the principal means of keeping Rome free."[29] For good laws were derived from those disturbances, &c.

Tyrant

Whether it is permissible to withdraw one's allegiance from a tyrant. Rinaldo, Count of Caserta, when Manfred, King of Naples, had committed adultery with the wife of the Count, sent to Rome to the Pope and to King Charles of Anjou, who were there together, a friend of his to determine before the College "whether it was permissible for a vassal in such a case to be resentful toward his king and to withdraw allegiance from him; what was decided by both knights and scholars was that as the vassal is bound to sacrifice his life and blood for his king, so likewise the good king is bound to maintain loyalty to his vassal, and that since the king had injured him in such a heinous wrong, it was permissible for the vassal to withdraw his allegiance, because in such a case the king loses the title of king and acquires the name of tyrant."[30]

27. Milton cites Jovius (Paolo Giovio), 2:170ff, who portrays Malatesta Baglioni (1491–1531) as a prudent hero. Modern authorities describe his actions as traitorous. We use "magistrate unversed in war" to translate "*sin magistratus be expers*" rather than adhere to Yale's "magistrate having no part in war."

28. Milton cites Sleidan's *Commentaries* (see note 6) on Luther, sedition, and the Emperor, pp. 71–72, 292–93. We use "most venerably and prudently to translate Milton's "*sanctissime et prudentissime*" rather than follow Yale's "most justly and most wisely."

29. Milton quotes from Book 1, chapter 4, of the *Discorsi,* p. 12. The last sentence summarizes Machiavelli's rationale for approving such riots.

30. Milton draws on the history of Angelo di Costanzo, which he quotes exactly (p. 16).

people. See the case of Manlius, who refused to comply with the [illegible] vice of the [illegible] dictators.

Sedition

[illegible] other [illegible] when [illegible] are [illegible] and [illegible] both in the [illegible] magistrate saying [illegible] should [illegible] the [illegible] the people [illegible] and [illegible] a higher [illegible] the magistrate by [illegible] oppressing, robbing, and [illegible] the people.

[illegible] the [illegible] charges [illegible] rebellion [illegible]

[illegible] a people has often [illegible] the means of their regaining their freedom, [illegible] they should not be blamed [illegible] Machiavelli [illegible] the common people [illegible] the principal means of keeping Rome [illegible] those [illegible]

Tyrant

[illegible] it is permissible [illegible] Count of Caserta, [illegible] King of Naples, [illegible] the Pope and [illegible] King [illegible] whether [illegible] vassal [illegible] England [illegible] the name of tyrant.

Controversial Prose

Introduction to Selections from *Of Reformation*

In May 1641 appeared the first prose work that Milton wrote for publication, *Of Reformation, Touching Church-Discipline in England and the Causes that hitherto have hindered it. Two Books, Written to a Friend.* Over the next eleven months, there followed four additional antiprelatical tracts, or works attacking the legitimacy of episcopacy. By his own account in the 1654 *Second Defense,* Milton entered the lists late: "As Parliament acted with vigor, the haughtiness of the bishops began to deflate. As soon as freedom of speech . . . became possible, all mouths were opened against them. . . . I decided . . . to devote to this conflict all my talents and all my active powers" (see pp. 345–46). In the 1630s, well before freedom of speech was possible, others—notably William Prynne, Henry Burton, and John Bastwick—had opened their mouths against bishops and been punished with imprisonment, branding, and the loss of their ears. The bishops were in retreat by the time Milton published *Of Reformation*: the House of Commons had charged Archbishop Laud with high treason, imprisoned him in the Tower, and pressed for exclusion of the bishops from the House of Lords. The increasingly powerful "Root and Branch" faction in Parliament, headed by Sir Henry Vane and Oliver Cromwell, sought not only to strip the bishops of secular power but also to remove them from the church altogether. Nearly twenty years later, it would require real physical courage for Milton to publish his antimonarchic prose works on the eve of a nearly universally popular Restoration, but with his antiprelatical tracts he could expect to meet an approving audience. He nevertheless published the work anonymously.

Milton had been trained to compose arguments in Latin (see the *Prolusions*), and *Of Reformation* betrays his lack of experience with vernacular prose. Long, convoluted, and sometimes broken sentences make this the most difficult of Milton's prose works to read in unmodernized form (even here, with sentences repunctuated and often divided, some difficulty remains). Don M. Wolfe has compared the tract's prose with "a hard pine log full of knots and unexpected twirls, rarely straight and smooth and easy to follow" (Yale 1:108). *Of Reformation* continues to be read, despite its difficult prose, for the brilliance of its imagery.

Milton would claim months later that, in the medium of prose, he had the use only of his "left hand" (*RCG,* p. 87), but the poet's right hand is manifest in *Of Reformation.* He unleashes a torrent of graphic images suggesting the bestial nature of the bishops and the disease and deformity they have inflicted upon a once pure church. Typical is his charge that under episcopal government "the obscene and surfeited priest scruples not to paw and mammock the sacramental bread as familiarly as his tavern biscuit" (p. 60). In the most famous set piece in the work, Milton compares episcopacy to a head-size "wen" growing from the neck of the body commonwealth, "a swollen tumor," "a bottle of vicious and hardened excrements," "a heap of hard and loathsome uncleanness, [which is] to the head a foul disfigurement and burden" (p. 70).

The vivid and often grotesque imagery overlays and sometimes overwhelms the structure of the tract's argument. Milton outlines the corruption of the church; laments that reformation, while beginning in England under Wycliffe, has stalled because of popish bishops; and traces the thwarting of reformation to three groups: "antiquitarians," as Milton calls them, "libertines," and "politicians." The bulk of Book 1 is occupied with an attack on antiquitarians, or those who defend episcopacy by way of the church fathers; here Milton contends that early bishops lived modestly and were elected by their flocks, that the texts of the fathers are at times contradictory and at times corrupt, and that the fathers themselves pointed to Scripture as the only authority. At the end of Book 1, Milton quickly dispatches the libertines, who fear that change in church government will restrain their licentiousness. In Book 2, Milton argues, against the politicians, that bishops undermine rather than support kings.

Milton would prove to be a quick study, and later works show a marked improvement in argumentation and readability as the author adjusts to what he calls "the cool element of prose" (see p. 87). Thomas N. Corns (1982) has demonstrated that, already by the mid-1640s, Milton moved toward a more functional, readable style, more sparing of imagery and neologisms.

The text of our selection is based on the copy of the first edition in the British Library's Thomason Collection.

Selections from

OF REFORMATION TOUCHING CHURCH-DISCIPLINE IN ENGLAND, AND THE CAUSES THAT HITHERTO HAVE HINDERED IT. TWO BOOKS, WRITTEN TO A FRIEND. 1641.

Sir,

Amidst those deep and retired thoughts which, with every man Christianly instructed, ought to be most frequent of God and of his miraculous ways and works amongst men, and of our religion and worship to be performed to him; after the story of our Savior Christ, suffering to the lowest bent of weakness in the flesh and presently triumphing to the highest pitch of glory in the spirit, which drew up his body also, till we in both be united to him in the revelation of his kingdom; I do not know of anything more worthy to take up the whole passion of pity on the one side and joy on the other, than to consider first the foul and sudden corruption, and then after many a tedious age the long-deferred, but much more wonderful and happy reformation of the church in these latter days. Sad it is to think how that doctrine of the gospel, planted by teachers divinely inspired and by them winnowed and sifted from the chaff of over-dated ceremonies, and refined to such a spiritual height and temper of purity and knowledge of the creator, that the body, with all the circumstances of time and place, were purified by the affections of the regenerate soul and nothing left impure, but sin; faith needing not the weak and fallible office of the senses, to be either the ushers or interpreters of heavenly mysteries, save where our Lord himself in his sacraments ordained; that such a doctrine should, through the grossness and blindness of her professors and the fraud of deceivable traditions, drag so downwards as to backslide one way into the Jewish beggary of old cast rudiments and stumble forward another way into the new-vomited paganism of sensual idolatry:[1] attributing purity or impurity to

1. The perspective of this complex temporal figure is primitive (and by extension reformed) Christianity; Milton castigates the Anglican Church for ***backsliding*** to a liturgy as highly articulated as the Jewish ceremonial law abrogated by Christ and for ***stumbling forward*** to the idolatrous ***paganism*** of the Roman Catholic Church, to which the Anglican Church, after the Reformation, has returned like a dog to its vomit (Prov. 26.11, 2 Pet. 2.22).

things indifferent, that they might bring the inward acts of the spirit to the outward and customary eye-service of the body, as if they could make God earthly and fleshly because they could not make themselves heavenly and spiritual.

They began to draw down all the divine intercourse betwixt God and the soul, yea, the very shape of God himself, into an exterior and bodily form; urgently pretending a necessity and obligement of joining the body in a formal reverence and worship circumscribed, they hallowed it, they fumed it, they sprinkled it, they bedecked it, not in robes of pure innocency, but of pure linen with other deformed and fantastic dresses in palls and miters, gold and gewgaws fetched from Aaron's old wardrobe, or the flamin's vestry.[2] Then was the priest set to con his motions and his postures, his liturgies and his lurries,[3] till the soul by this means of over-bodying herself, given up justly to fleshly delights, bated her wing apace downward; and finding the ease she had from her visible and sensuous colleague, the body, in performance of religious duties, her pinions now broken and flagging, shifted off from herself the labor of high soaring anymore, forgot her heavenly flight, and left the dull and droiling carcass to plod on in the old road and drudging trade of outward conformity.

And here, out of question from her perverse conceiting of God and holy things, she had fallen to believe no God at all, had not custom and the worm of conscience nipped her incredulity. Hence to all the duties of evangelical grace, instead of the adoptive and cheerful boldness which our new alliance with God requires, came servile and thrall-like fear; for in very deed, the superstitious man by his good will is an atheist, but being scared from thence by the pangs and gripes of a boiling conscience, all in a pudder[4] shuffles up to himself such a God and such a worship as is most agreeable to remedy his fear, which fear of his, as also is his hope, fixed only upon the flesh, renders likewise the whole faculty of his apprehension, carnal. And all the inward acts of worship, issuing from the native strength of soul, run out lavishly to the upper skin and there harden into a crust of formality. Hence men came to scan the scriptures by the letter, and in the covenant of our redemption magnified the external signs more than the quickening power of the spirit; and yet looking on them through their own guiltiness with a servile fear (and finding as little comfort, or rather terror from them again), they knew not how to hide their slavish approach to God's behests, by them not understood nor worthily received, but by cloaking their servile crouching to all religious presentments, sometimes lawful, sometimes

2. **palls, miters:** ecclesiastical vestments used by both the Roman and English churches; **Aaron's old wardrobe:** a reference to elaborate Jewish ritual clothing (Exod. 28), the *flamin's vestry* to the robes of ancient Roman priests.

3. **con his motions:** learn how to position and move his body during the liturgy; **lurries:** memorized or set lessons. Milton ridicules the prescribed and formulaic nature of Anglican (and Roman Catholic) liturgy.

4. **in a pudder:** in a tizzy.

idolatrous, under the name of humility, and terming the piebald frippery and ostentation of ceremonies, decency.[5]

Then was baptism changed into a kind of exorcism, and water sanctified by Christ's institute thought little enough to wash off the original spot without the scratch or cross impression of a priest's forefinger. And that feast of free grace[6] and adoption to which Christ invited his disciples to sit as brethren and coheirs of the happy covenant which at that table was to be sealed to them, even that feast of love and heavenly-admitted fellowship, the seal of filial grace, became the subject of horror and glouting[7] adoration, pageanted about like a dreadful idol, which sometimes deceives well-meaning men and beguiles them of their reward by their voluntary humility, which, indeed, is fleshly pride, preferring a foolish sacrifice and the rudiments of the world (as Saint Paul to Colossians [2.8] explaineth) before a savory obedience to Christ's example. Such was Peter's unseasonable humility, as then his knowledge was small, when Christ came to wash his feet; who, at an impertinent time, would needs strain courtesy with his master, and falling troublesomely upon the lowly, all-wise, and unexaminable intention of Christ in what he went with resolution to do, so provoked by his interruption the meek Lord, that he threatened to exclude him from his heavenly portion unless he could be content to be less arrogant and stiff-necked in his humility.[8]

But to dwell no longer in characterizing the depravities of the church and how they sprung and how they took increase, when I recall to mind at last, after so many dark ages wherein the huge overshadowing train of error had almost swept all the stars out of the firmament[9] of the church, how the bright and blissful reformation (by divine power) struck through the black and settled night of ignorance and antichristian tyranny, methinks a sovereign and reviving joy must needs rush into the bosom of him that reads or hears, and the sweet odor of the returning gospel imbathe his soul with the fragrancy of heaven. Then was the sacred Bible sought out of the dusty corners where profane falsehood and neglect had thrown it; the schools opened; divine and human learning raked out of the embers of forgotten tongues, the princes and cities trooping apace to the new erected banner of salvation; the martyrs, with the unresistible might of weakness, shaking the powers of darkness and scorning the fiery rage of the old red dragon.

The pleasing pursuit of these thoughts hath ofttimes led me into a serious question and debatement with myself, how it should come to pass that England (having had this grace and honor from God to be the first that should set up a

5. **decency:** a shorthand term for the uniform liturgy promoted by Laud, who decried the lack "of uniform and decent order in too many Churches" (*A Relation of the Conference* [1639], 3).

6. **feast of free grace:** i.e., the Lord's Supper.

7. **glouting:** looking sullen, frowning.

8. See John 13.5–11.

9. See Rev. 12.4. Throughout the tract, as here and at the end of the paragraph, Milton draws on the imagery of the apocalyptic final book of the Bible.

standard for the recovery of lost truth and blow the first evangelic trumpet to the nations, holding up, as from a hill,[10] the new lamp of saving light to all Christendom) should now be last and most unsettled in the enjoyment of that peace whereof she taught the way to others. Although indeed our Wycliffe's preaching,[11] at which all the succeeding reformers more effectually lighted their tapers, was to his countrymen but a short blaze soon damped and stifled by the pope and prelates for six or seven kings' reigns, yet methinks the precedency which God gave this island, to be the first restorer of buried truth, should have been followed with more happy success and sooner attained perfection in which as yet we are amongst the last. For, albeit in purity of doctrine we agree with our brethren, yet in discipline, which is the execution and applying of doctrine home, and laying the salve to the very orifice of the wound, yea, tenting[12] and searching to the core, without which pulpit preaching is but shooting at rovers,[13] in this we are no better than a schism from all the reformation and a sore scandal to them. For while we hold ordination to belong only to bishops, as our prelates do, we must of necessity hold also their ministers to be no ministers, and shortly after their church to be no church. Not to speak of those senseless ceremonies which we only retain as a dangerous earnest of sliding back to Rome, and serving merely either as a mist to cover nakedness where true grace is extinguished or as an interlude to set out the pomp of prelatism. Certainly it would be worth the while, therefore, and the pains, to inquire more particularly, what and how many the chief causes have been that have still hindered our uniform consent to the rest of the churches abroad, at this time especially when the kingdom is in a good propensity thereto, and all men in prayers, in hopes, or in disputes, either for or against it.

Yet will I not insist on that which may seem to be the cause on God's part (as his judgment on our sins, the trial of his own, the unmasking of hypocrites), nor shall I stay to speak of the continual eagerness and extreme diligence of the pope and papists to stop the furtherance of reformation, which know they have no hold or hope of England their lost darling, longer than the government of bishops bolsters them out; and therefore plot all they can to uphold them, as may be seen by the book of Santa Clara,[14] the popish priest in defense of bishops, which came out piping hot much about the time that one of our own prelates, out of an ominous fear, had writ on the same argument, as if they had joined their forces like good confederates to support one falling Babel.

10. See Matt. 5.14.

11. **Wycliffe:** John Wycliffe, well over a century before Martin Luther, articulated several central Reformation tenets, including the right of each believer to interpret Scripture and opposition to transubstantiation and papal infallibility. In 1380 he published the first English Bible. English Protestants pointed proudly to Wycliffe as the first reformer; Milton laments the irony that Wycliffe's nation is now less reformed than its continental neighbors.

12. **tenting:** probing a wound.

13. **shooting at rovers:** long-distance archery, in which arrows rarely hit the target.

14. **Santa Clara:** Franciscus a Sancta Clara, a Franciscan priest, was born Christopher Davenport; he converted to Catholicism in 1617. Milton refers to his *Apologia Episcoporum seu Sacri Magistatus* (1640).

But I shall chiefly endeavor to declare those causes that hinder the forwarding of true discipline which are among ourselves. . . .

[*The omitted section offers a survey of missed opportunities for full reformation in England in the sixteenth century; Milton insists that the martyrdom of Cranmer, Latimer, and Ridley does not prove the lawfulness of prelacy, even as the martyrdom of various Christian heretics does not prove the truth of their doctrines.*]

And here withal I invoke the immortal deity, revealer and judge of secrets, that wherever I have in this book plainly and roundly (though worthily and truly) laid open the faults and blemishes of fathers,[15] martyrs, or Christian emperors, or have otherwise inveighed against error and superstition with vehement expressions, I have done it neither out of malice, nor list to speak evil, nor any vainglory, but of mere necessity to vindicate the spotless truth from an ignominious bondage, whose native worth is now become of such a low esteem that she is like to find small credit with us for what she can say, unless she can bring a ticket from Cranmer, Latimer, and Ridley,[16] or prove herself a retainer to Constantine[17] and wear his badge. More tolerable it were for the church of God that all these names were utterly abolished, like the brazen serpent,[18] than that men's fond opinion should thus idolize them, and the heavenly truth be thus captivated.

Now to proceed, whatsoever the bishops were, it seems they themselves were unsatisfied in matters of religion, as they then stood, by that commission granted to eight bishops, eight other divines, eight civilians, eight common lawyers, to frame ecclesiastical constitutions;[19] which no wonder if it came to nothing, for (as Hayward[20] relates) both their professions and their ends were different. Lastly, we all know by examples that exact reformation is not perfected at the first push, and those unwieldy times of Edward VI may hold some plea by this excuse: Now let any reasonable man judge whether that king's reign be a fit time from whence to pattern out the constitution of a church discipline, much less that it should yield occasion from whence to foster and establish the continuance of imperfection with the commendatory subscriptions of confessors and martyrs, to entitle and engage a glorious name to a gross corruption. It was not episcopacy that wrought in them the heavenly fortitude of martyrdom,

15. **fathers:** church fathers.
16. **Cranmer, Latimer, and Ridley:** Thomas Cranmer, Hugh Latimer, and Nicholas Ridley were Anglican bishops executed by the Catholic Queen Mary in 1555 and 1556; they are celebrated as martyrs of the Reformation in John Foxe's influential *Acts and Monuments* (1563). Milton is markedly idiosyncratic in taking a critical view of the three in this work. On Milton's assumption of the prophetic role of *freeing truth from an ignominious bondage,* see Kerrigan 1974, Suh.
17. **retainer to Constantine:** i.e., a Roman Catholic.
18. See Num. 21.9.
19. Cranmer proposed unsuccessfully a thirty-two-member commission to reform canon law in 1544.
20. **Hayward:** John Hayward, author of *The Life and Reign of King Edward the Sixth* (1630).

as little is it that martyrdom can make good episcopacy. But it was episcopacy that led the good and holy men, through the temptation of the enemy and the snare of this present world, to many blameworthy and opprobrious actions. And it is still episcopacy that before all our eyes worsens and slugs the most learned and seeming religious of our ministers, who no sooner advanced to it but, like a seething pot set to cool, sensibly exhale and reek out the greatest part of that zeal, and those gifts which were formerly in them, settling in a skinny congealment of ease and sloth at the top. And if they keep their learning by some potent sway of nature, 'tis a rare chance, but their devotion most commonly comes to that queasy temper of lukewarmness that gives a vomit to God[21] himself....

[*Milton concludes his survey of missed opportunities in the previous century. He answers those who point to the great antiquity of Christian bishops first by arguing that early Christian bishops, unlike their modern successors, were elected by their flocks.*]

Thus then[22] did the spirit of unity and meekness inspire and animate every joint and sinew of the mystical body, but now the gravest and worthiest minister, a true bishop of his fold, shall be reviled and ruffled by an insulting and only canon-wise prelate, as if he were some slight, paltry companion. And the people of God, redeemed and washed with Christ's blood and dignified with so many glorious titles of saints and sons in the gospel, are now no better reputed than impure ethnics and lay dogs; stones and pillars and crucifixes have now the honor and the alms due to Christ's living members. The table of communion, now become a table of separation,[23] stands like an exalted platform upon the brow of the quire, fortified with bulwark and barricado to keep off the profane touch of the laics, whilst the obscene and surfeited priest scruples not to paw and mammock[24] the sacramental bread as familiarly as his tavern biscuit. And thus the people, vilified and rejected by them, give over the earnest study of virtue and godliness as a thing of greater purity than they need, and the search of divine knowledge as a mystery too high for their capacities and only for churchmen to meddle with, which is that the prelates desire—that when they have brought us back to popish blindness we might commit to their dispose the whole managing of our salvation, for they think it was never fair world with them since that time. But he that will mold a modern bishop into a primitive must yield him to be elected by the popular voice, undiocesed, unrevenued, unlorded, and leave him nothing but brotherly equality, matchless temperance, frequent fasting, incessant prayer, and preaching, continual watchings and

21. See Rev. 3.16.
22. **then:** in the early church, when bishops relied on the consent of their flocks.
23. Milton, like other Puritans, objected to Laud's returning the communion table to the old position of the altar, against the chancel wall at the east end of the church, most distant from the congregation.
24. **mammock:** to tear into shreds.

labors in his ministry, which what a rich booty it would be, what a plump endowment to the many-benefice-gaping mouth of a prelate, what a relish it would give to his canary-sucking and swan-eating palate, let old Bishop Mountain[25] judge for me.

How little therefore those ancient times make for modern bishops hath been plainly discoursed. But let them make for them as much as they will, yet why we ought not stand to their arbitrament shall now appear by a threefold corruption which will be found upon them. 1. The best times were spreadingly infected. 2. The best men of those times foully tainted. 3. The best writings of those men dangerously adulterated. These positions are to be made good out of those times witnessing of themselves.

[*In a lengthy section omitted here, Milton argues that corruption already touched the early church, that the writings of the church fathers have not always been reliably transmitted, and that the fathers themselves pointed to Scripture rather than to their own writings as authoritative.*]

But not to be endless in quotations, it may chance to be objected that there be many opinions in the fathers which have no ground in scripture. So much the less, may I say, should we follow them, for their own words shall condemn them and acquit us that lean not on them; otherwise these their words shall acquit them and condemn us. But it will be replied, the scriptures are difficult to be understood and therefore require the explanation of the fathers. 'Tis true there be some books, and especially some places in those books, that remain clouded; yet ever that which is most necessary to be known is most easy, and that which is most difficult so far expounds itself ever as to tell us how little it imports our saving knowledge. Hence, to infer a general obscurity over all the text is a mere suggestion of the devil to dissuade men from reading it, and casts an aspersion of dishonor both upon the mercy, truth, and wisdom of God. We count it no gentleness or fair dealing in a man of power amongst us to require strict and punctual obedience, and yet give out all his commands ambiguous and obscure; we should think he had a plot upon us; certainly such commands were no commands but snares.

The very essence of truth is plainness and brightness; the darkness and crookedness is our own. The wisdom of God created understanding fit and proportionable to truth, the object and end of it, as the eye to the thing visible. If our understanding have a film of ignorance over it or be blear with gazing on other false glisterings, what is that to truth? If we will but purge with sovereign eyesalve that intellectual ray which God hath planted in us, then we would believe the scriptures protesting their own plainness and perspicuity, calling to them to be instructed not only the wise and learned, but the simple, the poor,

25. **Bishop Mountain:** George Montaigne (1569–1628) rose from modest beginnings to become Archbishop of York.

the babes, foretelling an extraordinary effusion of God's spirit upon every age and sex, attributing to all men—and requiring from them—the ability of searching, trying, examining all things, and by the spirit discerning that which is good. And as the scriptures themselves pronounce their own plainness, so do the Fathers testify of them. . . .

[*Milton contrasts the clarity of Scripture with the "knotty Africanisms, the pampered metaphors, the intricate and involved sentences of the fathers."*]

I trust they for whom God hath reserved the honor of reforming this church will easily perceive their adversaries' drift in thus calling for antiquity. They fear the plain field of the scriptures; the chase is too hot; they seek the dark, the bushy, the tangled forest; they would imbosk.[26] They feel themselves struck in the transparent streams of divine truth; they would plunge and tumble and think to lie hid in the foul weeds and muddy waters, where no plummet can reach the bottom. But let them beat themselves like whales, and spend their oil till they be dredged ashore, though wherefore should the ministers give them so much line for shifts and delays? Wherefore should they not urge only the gospel, and hold it ever in their faces like a mirror of diamond, till it dazzle and pierce their misty eyeballs, maintaining it the honor of its absolute sufficiency and supremacy inviolable? For if the scripture be for reformation, and antiquity to boot, 'tis but an advantage to the dozen, 'tis no winning cast. And though antiquity be against it, while the scriptures be for it, the cause is as good as ought to be wished, antiquity itself sitting judge.

But to draw to an end: the second sort[27] of those that may be justly numbered among the hinderers of reformation are libertines. These suggest that the discipline sought would be intolerable: for one bishop now in a diocese we should then have a pope in every parish.[28] It will not be requisite to answer these men, but only to discover them; for reason they have none, but lust and licentiousness, and therefore answer can have none. It is not any discipline that they could live under, it is the corruption and remissness of discipline that they seek. Episcopacy duly executed, yea the Turkish and Jewish rigor against whoring and drinking, the dear and tender discipline of a father, the sociable and loving reproof of a brother, the bosom admonition of a friend is a presbytery and a consistory to them. 'Tis only the merry friar in Chaucer can disple[29] them.

26. **imbosk:** conceal themselves.

27. **second sort:** The three sorts are the "antiquitarians," whose arguments Milton has addressed in the body of the first book, the "libertines," whom he dispatches in a single paragraph here, and the "politicians," whom he answers in the second book.

28. A common charge against Presbyterian church government.

29. **disple:** to subject to religious discipline or penance.

Full sweetly heard he confession,
And pleasant was his absolution,
He was an easy man to give penance.[30]

And so I leave them, and refer the political discourse of episcopacy to a second book.

The Second Book

Sir,

It is a work good and prudent to be able to guide one man, of larger extended virtue to order well one house; but to govern a nation piously and justly, which only is to say happily, is for a spirit of the greatest size and divinest metal. And certainly of no less a mind, nor of less excellence in another way, were they who by writing laid the solid and true foundations of this science, which being of greatest importance to the life of man, yet there is no art that hath been more cankered in her principles, more soiled and slubbered with aphorisming pedantry than the art of policy, and that most, where a man would think should least be, in Christian commonwealths. They teach not that to govern well is to train up a nation in true wisdom and virtue and that which springs from thence, magnanimity (take heed of that), and that which is our beginning, regeneration, and happiest end, likeness to God, which in one word we call godliness; and that this is the true flourishing of a land, other things follow as the shadow does the substance. To teach thus were mere pulpitry to them. This is the masterpiece of a modern politician, how to qualify and mold the sufferance and subjection of the people to the length of that foot that is to tread on their necks, how rapine may serve itself with the fair and honorable pretences of public good, how the puny law may be brought under the wardship and control of lust and will. In which attempt, if they fall short, then must a superficial color of reputation by all means direct or indirect be gotten to wash over the unsightly bruise of honor.

To make men governable in this manner, their precepts mainly tend to break a national spirit and courage by countenancing open riot, luxury, and ignorance, till having thus disfigured and made men beneath men, as Juno in the fable of Io,[31] they deliver up the poor transformed heifer of the commonwealth to be stung and vexed with the breeze[32] and goad of oppression under the cus-

30. *Canterbury Tales,* "General Prologue," 221–23.
31. Zeus changed *Io* into a cow to protect her from the jealousy of Hera, who first set hundred-eyed *Argus* to watch Io and then sent a gadfly to drive Io through the world (Apollodorus, *Library* 2.1.3).
32. **breeze:** stinging insect, gadfly.

tody of some Argus with a hundred eyes of jealousy. To be plainer, sir, how to solder, how to stop a leak, how to keep up the floating carcass of a crazy and diseased monarchy or state betwixt wind and water, swimming still upon her own dead lees, that now is the deep design of a politician.

Alas, sir! a commonwealth ought to be but as one huge Christian personage, one mighty growth and stature of an honest man, as big and compact in virtue as in body. For look what the grounds and causes are of single happiness to one man, the same ye shall find them to a whole state, as Aristotle, both in his *Ethics* and *Politics*, from the principles of reason lays down.[33] By consequence, therefore, that which is good and agreeable to monarchy will appear soonest to be so by being good and agreeable to the true welfare of every Christian, and that which can be justly proved hurtful and offensive to every true Christian will be evinced to be alike hurtful to monarchy; for God forbid that we should separate and distinguish the end and good of a monarch from the end and good of the monarchy, or of that from Christianity.

How then this third and last sort that hinder reformation[34] will justify that it stands not with reason of state, I much muse. For certain I am, the Bible is shut against them, as certain that neither Plato nor Aristotle is for their turns.[35] What they can bring us now from the schools of Loyola with his Jesuits or their Malvezzi that can cut Tacitus into slivers and steaks,[36] we shall presently hear. They allege, 1. that the church government must be conformable to the civil polity; next, that no form of church government is agreeable to monarchy but that of bishops. Must church government that is appointed in the Gospel, and has chief respect to the soul, be conformable and pliant to civil, that is arbitrary, and chiefly conversant about the visible and external part of man? This is the very maxim that molded the calves of Bethel and of Dan; this was the quintessence of Jeroboam's policy:[37] he made religion conform to his politic interests, and this was the sin that watched over the Israelites till their final captivity. If this state principle come from the prelates, as they affect to be counted statists, let them look back to Eleutherius,[38] bishop of Rome, and see what he thought of the policy of England. Being required by Lucius, the first Christian king of this island, to give his counsel for the founding of religious laws, little thought he of this sage caution, but bids him betake himself to the Old and New Testa-

33. See Aristotle, *Nichomachean Ethics* 1.9 (1099b30) and *Politics* 7.2 (1324a5).

34. Politicians; see note 27.

35. I.e., neither the Bible, Plato, nor Aristotle endorses what Milton calls in the first paragraph of this book the "masterpiece of a modern politician."

36. St. Ignatius of *Loyola* (1491–1556) founded the *Jesuits;* Virgilio *Malvezzi* (1595–1654) is the author of *Discourses upon Cornelius Tacitus,* an English translation of which appeared in 1642.

37. See 1 Kings 12.26-33. Because Rehoboam held Jerusalem with the Temple, his rival *Jeroboam* set up golden calves in *Bethel* and *Dan,* places he controlled, in order to shore up his authority with religious observance and sentiment.

38. According to tradition, *Lucius,* King of the Britons in the second century, sent to Rome to request from *Eleutherius* that he be made a Christian. See Bede's *Church History* 1.4 and Geoffrey of Monmouth's *History of Britain* 4.19.

ment and receive direction from them how to administer both church and commonwealth; that he was God's vicar and, therefore, to rule by God's laws; that the edicts of Caesar we may at all times disallow, but the statutes of God for no reason we may reject.

Now, certain if church-government be taught in the gospel, as the bishops dare not deny, we may well conclude of what late standing this position is, newly calculated for the altitude of bishop elevation and lettuce for their lips. But by what example can they show that the form of church discipline must be minted and modeled out to secular pretences? The ancient republic of the Jews is evident to have run through all the changes of civil estate, if we survey the story from the giving of the law to the Herods, yet did one manner of priestly government serve without inconvenience to all these temporal mutations: it served the mild aristocracy of elective dukes and heads of tribes joined with them, the dictatorship of the judges, the easy or hard-handed monarchies, the domestic or foreign tyrannies, lastly the Roman senate from without, the Jewish senate at home with the Galilean Tetrarch (yet the Levites had some right to deal in civil affairs).[39] But seeing the evangelical precept forbids churchmen to intermeddle with worldly employments,[40] what interweavings or interworkings can knit the minister and the magistrate in their several functions to the regard of any precise correspondency?

Seeing that the churchman's office is only to teach men the Christian faith, to exhort all, to encourage the good, to admonish the bad (privately, the less offender, publicly, the scandalous and stubborn), to censure and separate from the communion of Christ's flock the contagious and incorrigible, to receive with joy and fatherly compassion the penitent, all this must be done, and more than this is beyond any church authority. What is all this either here or there to the temporal regiment of weal public, whether it be popular, princely, or monarchical? Where doth it entrench upon the temporal governor, where does it come in his walk? Where does it make inroad upon his jurisdiction? Indeed if the minister's part be rightly discharged, it renders him the people more conscionable, quiet, and easy to be governed, if otherwise his life and doctrine will declare him. If, therefore, the constitution of the church be already set down by divine prescript, as all sides confess, then can she not be a handmaid to wait on civil commodities and respects; and if the nature and limits of church discipline be such as are either helpful to all political estates indifferently, or have no particular relation to any, then is there no necessity, nor indeed possibility, of linking the one with the other in special conformation.

Now for their second conclusion, "That no form of church government is agreeable to monarchy, but that of bishops,"[41] although it fall to pieces of itself

39. See 2 Chron. 19.8–11.

40. See Matt. 20.25–26.

41. James I in 1603 stated this principle both prophetically and pithily: "No bishop, no king" (see Yale 1:15–16).

by that which hath been said: yet to give them play front and rear, it shall be my task to prove that episcopacy, with that authority which it challenges in England, is not only not agreeable, but tending to the destruction of monarchy. While the primitive pastors of the church of God labored faithfully in their ministry, tending only their sheep, and not seeking but avoiding all worldly matters as clogs[42] (and indeed derogations and debasements to their high calling), little needed the princes and potentates of the earth, which way so ever the gospel was spread, to study ways how to make a coherence between the church's polity and theirs. Therefore, when Pilate heard once our Savior Christ professing that "his kingdom was not of this world" [John 18.36], he thought the man could not stand much in Caesar's light, nor much endamage the Roman empire: for if the life of Christ be hid to this world, much more is his scepter unoperative but in spiritual things.

And thus lived, for two or three ages, the successors of the apostles. But when through Constantine's lavish superstition they forsook their first love and set themselves up two gods instead, Mammon and their belly,[43] then taking advantage of the spiritual power which they had on men's consciences, they began to cast a longing eye to get the body also and bodily things into their command; upon which their carnal desires, the spirit daily quenching and dying in them, they knew no way to keep themselves up from falling to nothing, but by bolstering and supporting their inward rottenness by a carnal and outward strength. For a while they rather privily sought opportunity than hastily disclosed their project, but when Constantine was dead, and three or four emperors more, their drift became notorious and offensive to the whole world. For while Theodosius the younger reigned, thus writes Socrates the historian in his 7th book, 11th chapter: "Now began an ill name to stick upon the bishops of Rome and Alexandria, who beyond their priestly bounds now long ago had stepped into principality."[44] And this was scarce eighty years since their raising from the meanest worldly condition. Of courtesy now let any man tell me, if they draw to themselves a temporal strength and power out of Caesar's dominion, is not Caesar's empire thereby diminished? But this was a stolen bit, hitherto he was but a caterpillar secretly gnawing at monarchy, the next time you shall see him a wolf, a lion, lifting his paw against his raiser, as Petrarch expressed it, and finally an open enemy and subverter of the Greek empire. Philippicus and Leo,[45] with diverse other emperors after them, not without the advice of their patriarchs and at length of a whole eastern council of three hundred thirty-eight bishops, threw the images out of the churches as being decreed idolatrous. Upon

42. **clogs:** originally denoted wooden blocks tied to legs in order to impede motion.

43. See Matt. 6.24: "Ye cannot serve God and mammon."

44. **Socrates:** Scholasticus lived in the fifth century. Milton translates from his *Church History* 8.11.

45. *Philippicus*, Emperor of Constantinople (711–713), abolished the canons of the Sixth Council of Constantinople, which had called for images of Christ as a human being; his successor *Leo* III, who reigned from 717 to 741, issued a series of edicts against image worship in the 720s.

this goodly occasion the bishop of Rome[46] not only seizes the city and all the territory about into his own hands, and makes himself lord thereof, which till then was governed by a Greek magistrate, but absolves all Italy of their tribute and obedience due to the emperor, because he obeyed God's commandment in abolishing idolatry.

Mark, sir, here how the pope came by St. Peter's patrimony, as he feigns it; not the donation of Constantine, but idolatry and rebellion got it him. Ye need but read Sigonius,[47] one of his own sect, to know the story at large. And now to shroud himself against a storm from the Greek continent and provide a champion to bear him out in these practices, he takes upon him by papal sentence to unthrone Chilpericus, the rightful King of France, and gives the kingdom to Pepin for no other cause but that he seemed to him the more active man.[48] If he were a friend herein to monarchy I know not, but to the monarch I need not ask what he was.

Having thus made Pepin his fast friend, he calls him into Italy against Aistulphus the Lombard, that warred upon him for his late usurpation of Rome as belonging to Ravenna, which he had newly won.[49] Pepin, not unobedient to the pope's call, passing into Italy, frees him out of danger and wins for him the whole exarchate[50] of Ravenna, which, though it had been almost immediately before the hereditary possession of that monarchy which was his chief patron and benefactor, yet he takes and keeps it to himself as lawful prize and given to Saint Peter. What a dangerous fallacy is this, when a spiritual man may snatch to himself any temporal dignity or dominion, under pretence of receiving it for the church's use? Thus he claims Naples, Sicily, England, and what not? To be short, under show of his zeal against the errors of the Greek church, he never ceased baiting and goring the successors of his best lord Constantine, what by his barking curses and excommunications, what by his hindering the western princes from aiding them against the Saracens and Turks, unless when they humored him. So that it may be truly affirmed, he was the subversion and fall of that monarchy which was the hoisting of him. This, besides Petrarch whom I have cited, our Chaucer also hath observed,[51] and gives from hence a caution to England to beware of her bishops in time, for that their ends and aims are no more friendly to monarchy than the pope's.

46. **bishop of Rome:** Pope Gregory III.

47. **Sigonius:** Carlo Sigonius (1523–1584), a historian, was the author of *De Regno Italiae,* the *sect* is Roman Catholicism.

48. Pope Zacharias, Gregory III's successor, took the crown of France from Chilperic and bestowed it on Pepin in 751. Milton notes this case and that of Leo in the preceding paragraph in his *Commonplace Book* (Yale 1:444).

49. Milton continues here to follow Sigonius.

50. **exarchate:** the territory of an exarch, or governor of an outlying province under the Byzantine emperors.

51. *The Plowman's Tale,* from which Milton quotes in the next paragraph, does not appear to have been written by Chaucer. Nevertheless, sixteenth-century editors accepted it as Chaucer's, as did Spenser and Milton.

Thus he brings in the Plowman speaking, 2nd Part, stanza 28.

> The Emperor yafe the pope sometime
> So high lordship him about
> That at last the silly kime,[52]
> The proud pope put him out;
> So of this realm is no doubt,
> But lords beware and them defend,
> For now these folks be wonders stout,
> The king and lords now this amend.

And in the next stanza, which begins the third part of the tale, he argues that they ought not to be lords.

> Moses Law forbode it tho
> That priests should no Lordship welde[53]
> Christ's gospel biddeth also,
> That they should not lordships held
> Ne Christ's apostles were never so bold
> No such Lordships to hem embrace
> But smeren[54] her Sheep, and keep her Fold.

And so forward. Whether the bishops of England have deserved thus to be feared by men so wise as our Chaucer is esteemed, and how agreeable to our monarchy and monarchs their demeanor has been, he that is but meanly read in our chronicles needs not be instructed. Have they not been as the Canaanites and Philistims[55] to this kingdom? What treasons, what revolts to the pope, what rebellions, and those the basest and most pretenseless, have they not been chief in? What could monarchy think when Becket durst challenge the custody of Rochester Castle and the Tower of London, as appertaining to his signory (to omit his other insolencies and affronts to regal majesty, till the lashes inflicted on the anointed body of the king washed off the holy unction with his blood drawn by the polluted hands of bishops, abbots, and monks)?[56]

What good upholders of royalty were the bishops when, by their rebellious opposition against King John, Normandy was lost, he himself deposed, and this kingdom made over to the pope?[57] When the Bishop of Winchester durst tell

52. **kime:** simpleton, fool.
53. **welde:** wield.
54. **smeren:** smear, to rub (sheep) with a mixture to keep wet out of the fleece and prevent disease or vermin.
55. **Philistims:** Philistines.
56. In this account of Thomas à Becket, Archbishop of Canterbury, Milton follows Raphael Holinshed's *Chronicles of England, Scotland and Ireland* (1587), 3.70, and John Speed's *History of Great Britain* (1627), p. 467.
57. In this paragraph, Milton continues to follow Speed and Holinshed (see Yale 1.581).

the nobles, the pillars of the realm, that there were no peers in England, as in France, but that the king might do what he pleased, what could tyranny say more? It would be petty now if I should insist upon the rendering up of Tournay by Wolsey's treason,[58] the excommunications, cursings, and interdicts upon the whole land. For haply I shall be cut off short by a reply, that these were the faults of the men and their popish errors, not of episcopacy, that hath now renounced the pope and is a Protestant. Yes, sure, as wise and famous men have suspected and feared the Protestant episcopacy in England, as those that have feared the papal.

You know, sir, what was the judgment of Padre Paolo,[59] the great Venetian antagonist of the pope, for it is extant in the hands of many men, whereby he declares his fear that when the hierarchy of England shall light into the hands of busy and audacious men, or shall meet with Princes tractable to the prelacy, then much mischief is like to ensue. And can it be nearer hand,[60] than when bishops shall openly affirm that "no bishop, no king"?[61] A trim paradox, and that ye may know where they have been a begging for it, I will fetch you the twin brother to it out of the Jesuit's cell; they, feeling the axe of God's reformation hewing at the old and hollow trunk of papacy and finding the Spaniard their surest friend and safest refuge, to sooth him up in his dream of a fifth monarchy, and withal to uphold the decrepit papalty, have invented this super-politic aphorism, as one terms it, "one pope and one king."[62]

Surely there is not any prince in Christendom who, hearing this rare sophistry, can choose but smile, and if we be not blind at home, we may as well perceive that this worthy motto, "no bishop, no king," is of the same batch and infanted out of the same fears, a mere ague-cake[63] coagulated of a certain fever they have, presaging their time to be but short. And now, like those that are sinking, they catch round at that which is likeliest to hold them up, and would persuade regal power that if they dive he must after. But what greater debasement can there be to royal dignity, whose towering and steadfast heighth rests upon the unmovable foundations of justice and heroic virtue, than to chain it in a dependence of subsisting (or ruining) to the painted battlements and gaudy rottenness of prelatry, which want but one puff of the king's to blow them down like a pasteboard house built of court-cards.[64] Sir, the little ado which methinks

58. Cardinal Thomas *Wolsey*, Archbishop of York, was the power behind Henry VIII's throne from 1515 until shortly before his death in disgrace in 1530.

59. **Padre Paolo:** Paolo Sarpi (1552–1623), author of a history of the Counter-Reformation Council of Trent, was a religious reformer. His opposition to the papacy arises in part from tension between his native Venice and Rome.

60. **nearer hand:** i.e., nearer at hand.

61. See note 41.

62. Milton may have in mind the Dominican Tommaso Campanella's *De Monarchia Hispanica* (1640); *the Spaniard* is the King of Spain.

63. **ague-cake:** a fever-induced enlargement of the liver or spleen.

64. **court-cards:** face cards in a deck of playing cards.

I find in untacking these pleasant sophisms, puts me into the mood to tell you a tale ere I proceed further; and Menenius Agrippa[65] to speed us.

A Tale

Upon a time the body summoned all the members to meet in the guild for the common good (as Aesop's chronicles aver many stranger accidents). The head by right takes the first seat, and next to it a huge and monstrous wen, little less than the head itself, growing to it by a narrower excrescency. The members amazed began to ask one another what he was that took place next their chief. None could resolve. Whereat the wen, though unwieldy, with much ado gets up and bespeaks the assembly to this purpose: that as in place he was second to the head, so by due of merit; that he was to it an ornament and strength, and of special near relation; and that if the head should fail, none were fitter than himself to step into his place; therefore he thought it for the honor of the body that such dignities and rich endowments should be decreed him, as did adorn and set out the noblest members. To this was answered, that it should be consulted. Then was a wise and learned philosopher sent for, that knew all the charters, laws, and tenures of the body. On him it is imposed by all, as chief committee,[66] to examine and discuss the claim and petition of right put in by the wen; who soon perceiving the matter and wondering at the boldness of such a swollen tumor, "wilt thou," quoth he "that art but a bottle of vicious and hardened excrements, contend with the lawful and freeborn members, whose certain number is set by ancient and unrepealable statute? Head thou art none, though thou receive this huge substance from it. What office bearest thou? What good canst thou show by thee done to the commonweal? The wen, not easily dashed, replies that his office was his glory, for so oft as the soul would retire out of the head from over the steaming vapors of the lower parts to divine contemplation, with him she found the purest and quietest retreat, as being most remote from soil and disturbance. "Lourdan,"[67] quoth the philosopher, "thy folly is as great as thy filth. Know that all the faculties of the soul are confined of old to their several vessels and ventricles, from which they cannot part without dissolution of the whole body, and that thou containest no good thing in thee, but a heap of hard and loathsome uncleanness, and art to the head a foul disfigurement and burden; when I have cut thee off and opened thee, as by the help of these implements I will do, all men shall see."

But to return whence was digressed, seeing that the throne of a king, as the

65. In the next paragraph, Milton adapts a story from Livy's *Roman History* 2.32. In Livy, *Menenius Agrippa* pacifies an army protesting the actions of the consuls with an allegory of the debilitating effect of the revolt of the body's members against the belly, which seems to take but not to give. Milton's version is more graphic, and the emphasis changes; now a truly useless part attempts to aggrandize itself; thus Milton expresses what he sees as the grasping emptiness of episcopacy. Shakespeare dramatizes the episode of Menenius Agrippa in the first scene of *Coriolanus*.

66. **committee:** a person to whom some task or trust is committed.

67. **Lourdan:** sluggard, loafer.

wise King Solomon often remembers us,[68] is established in justice, which is the universal justice that Aristotle so much praises,[69] containing in it all other virtues, it may assure us that the fall of prelacy, whose actions are so far distant from justice, cannot shake the least fringe that borders the royal canopy, but that their standing doth continually oppose and lay battery to regal safety, shall by that which follows easily appear. Amongst many secondary and accessory causes that support monarchy, these are not of least reckoning, though common to all other states: the love of the subjects, the multitude and valor of the people, and store of treasure. In all these things hath the kingdom been of late sore weakened, and chiefly by the prelates. First, let any man consider, that if any prince shall suffer under him a commission of authority to be exercised till all the land groan and cry out as against a whip of scorpions, whether this be not likely to lessen and keel[70] the affections of the subject? Next, what numbers of faithful and freeborn Englishmen and good Christians have been constrained to forsake their dearest home, their friends, and kindred, whom nothing but the wide ocean and the savage deserts of America could hide and shelter from the fury of the bishops?

O sir, if we could but see the shape of our dear mother England, as poets are wont to give a personal form to what they please, how would she appear, think ye, but in a mourning weed[71] with ashes upon her head and tears abundantly flowing from her eyes, to behold so many of her children exposed at once and thrust from things of dearest necessity, because their conscience could not assent to things which the bishops thought indifferent? What more binding than conscience? What more free than indifferency? Cruel then must that indifferency needs be that shall violate the strict necessity of the conscience, merciless and inhumane that free choice and liberty that shall break asunder the bonds of religion. Let the astrologer be dismayed at the portentous blaze of comets, and impressions in the air, as foretelling troubles and changes to states; I shall believe there cannot be a more ill-boding sign to a nation (God turn the omen from us) than when the inhabitants, to avoid insufferable grievances at home, are enforced by heaps to forsake their native country.

Now whereas the only remedy and amends against the depopulation and thinness of a land within is the borrowed strength of firm alliance from without, these priestly policies of theirs, having thus exhausted our domestic forces, have gone the way also to leave us as naked of our firmest and faithfulest neighbors abroad, by disparaging and alienating from us all Protestant princes and commonwealths, who are not ignorant that our prelates, and as many as they can infect, account them no better than a sort of sacrilegious and puritanical rebels, preferring the Spaniard, our deadly enemy, before them, and set all orthodox writers at naught in comparison of the Jesuits, who are indeed the only corrupters of youth and good learning; and I have heard many wise and learned

68. Prov. 16.12.
69. Aristotle, *Nichomachean Ethics* 5.1 (1130a10).
70. **keel:** make less eager or ardent.
71. **weed:** garment.

men in Italy say as much. It cannot be that the strongest knot of confederacy should not daily slacken when religion, which is the chief engagement of our league, shall be turned to their reproach. Hence it is that the prosperous and prudent states of the United Provinces (whom we ought to love, if not for themselves yet for our own good work in them, they having been in a manner planted and erected by us, and having been since to us the faithful watchmen and discoverers of many a popish and Austrian complotted treason,[72] and with us the partners of many a bloody and victorious battle),[73] whom the similitude of manners and language, the commodity of traffic, which founded the old Burgundian league betwixt us,[74] but chiefly religion should bind to us immortally, even such friends as these, out of some principles instilled into us by the prelates, have been often dismissed with distasteful answers and sometimes unfriendly actions. Nor is it to be considered to the breach of confederate nations whose mutual interest is of such high consequence, though their merchants bicker in the East Indies;[75] neither is it safe or wary, or indeed Christianly, that the French king, of a different faith, should afford our nearest allies as good protection as we.[76] Sir, I persuade myself, if our zeal to true religion and the brotherly usage of our truest friends were as notorious to the world as our prelatical schism and captivity to rochet[77] apothegms, we had ere this seen our old conquerors and afterward liege-men, the Normans, together with the Britains, our proper colony, and all the Gascoins that are the rightful dowry of our ancient kings,[78] come with cap and knee, desiring the shadow of the English scepter to defend them from the hot persecutions and taxes of the French. But when they come hither and see a tympany[79] of Spaniolized bishops swaggering in the foretop of the state and meddling to turn and dandle the royal ball with unskillful and pedantic palms, no marvel though they think it as unsafe to commit religion and liberty to their arbitrating as to a synagogue of Jesuits.

But what do I stand reckoning upon advantages and gains lost by the misrule and turbulency of the prelates? What do I pick up so thriftily their scatterings and diminishings of the meaner subject, whilst they by their seditious practices have endangered to lose the king one third of his main stock? What have they

72. Early in Elizabeth's reign, there were several plots to depose her and restore Catholic worship. One plot involved marrying the Catholic Duke of Norfolk, who had Spanish ties, to the Catholic Mary, Queen of Scots; another would have had Mary marry Don John of Austria.

73. English soldiers had fought against Spain as allies of the Dutch in the late sixteenth and early seventeenth centuries.

74. The *Burgundian league* of 1339 called for the settling of Flemish weavers in England, a leading wool producer; Milton apparently follows Speed's *History*.

75. Dutch and English traders competed forcefully for dominance in Asia, leading to intermittent armed conflict.

76. While the Catholic Louis XIII of France supported the Protestant Dutch against Catholic Spain, Charles I temporized and at times wished to ally himself with Spain.

77. **rochet:** a linen garment worn by bishops.

78. Milton laments England's relinquishing, owing to military defeats, its claims to French provinces.

79. **tympany:** a swelling, in this case, of pride and arrogance; the bishops are *Spaniolized* because won over to the cause of Catholic Spain.

not done to banish him from his own native country? But to speak of this as it ought would ask a volume by itself.

Thus as they have unpeopled the kingdom by expulsion of so many thousands, as they have endeavored to lay the skirts of it bare by disheartening and dishonoring our loyalest confederates abroad, so have they hamstrung the valor of the subject by seeking to effeminate us all at home. Well knows every wise nation that their liberty consists in manly and honest labors, in sobriety and rigorous honor to the marriage bed, which in both sexes should be bred up from chaste hopes to loyal enjoyments; and when the people slacken and fall to looseness and riot, then do they as much as if they had laid down their necks for some wily tyrant to get up and ride. Thus learnt Cyrus to tame the Lydians,[80] whom by arms he could not, whilst they kept themselves from luxury; with one easy proclamation to set up stews,[81] dancing, feasting, and dicing, he made them soon his slaves. I know not what drift the prelates had, whose brokers they were to prepare and supple us either for a foreign invasion or domestic oppression. But this I am sure, they took the ready way to despoil us both of manhood and grace at once, and that in the shamefullest and ungodliest manner upon that day which God's law and even our own reason hath consecrated, that we might have one day at least of seven set apart wherein to examine and increase our knowledge of God, to meditate and commune of our faith, our hope, our eternal city in heaven, and to quicken, withal, the study and exercise of charity. At such a time that men should be plucked from their soberest and saddest thoughts, and by the bishops, the pretended fathers of the church, instigated by public edict, and with earnest endeavor pushed forward to gaming, jigging, wassailing, and mixed dancing is a horror to think.[82] Thus did the reprobate hireling priest Balaam seek to subdue the Israelites to Moab, if not by force then by this devilish policy, to draw them from the sanctuary of God to the luxurious and ribald feasts of Baal-peor.[83] Thus have they trespassed not only against the monarchy of England, but of heaven also, as others, I doubt not, can prosecute against them.

I proceed within my own bounds to show you next what good agents they are about the revenues and riches of the kingdom, which declares of what moment they are to monarchy, or what avail. Two leeches they have that still suck and suck the kingdom: their ceremonies and their courts. If any man will contend that ceremonies be lawful under the gospel, he may be answered otherwhere. This doubtless that they ought to be many and overcostly, no true Protestant will affirm. Now I appeal to all wise men, what an excessive waste of treasury hath been within these few years in this land, not in the expedient but

80. *Cyrus* was taught to subdue the *Lydians* by encouraging them to wear luxurious clothing and to pursue music and dance (see Herodotus, *Histories* 1.155).

81. **stews:** brothels.

82. Like other Puritans, Milton decried Charles's 1633 *Book of Sports,* which encouraged the activities listed here; see Marcus 1986.

83. See Num. 22.5–41; 24; 25.1–3.

in the idolatrous erection of temples beautified exquisitely to outvie the papists, the costly and dear-bought scandals and snares of images, pictures, rich copes,[84] gorgeous altar-cloths. And by the courses they took and the opinions they held, it was not likely any stay would be, or any end of their madness, where a pious pretext is so ready at hand to cover their insatiate desires. What can we suppose this will come to? What other materials than these have built up the spiritual Babel to the height of her abominations? Believe it, sir, right truly it may be said, that Antichrist is Mammon's son. The sour leaven[85] of human traditions mixed in one putrefied mass with the poisonous dregs of hypocrisy in the hearts of prelates, that lie basking in the sunny warmth of wealth and promotion, is the serpent's egg that will hatch an Antichrist wheresoever and engender the same monster as big or little as the lump is which breeds him. If the splendor of gold and silver begin to lord it once again in the church of England, we shall see Antichrist[86] shortly wallow here, though his chief kennel be at Rome. If they had one thought upon God's glory and the advancement of Christian faith, they would be a means that with these expenses, thus profusely thrown away in trash, rather churches and schools might be built where they cry out for want and more added where too few are; a moderate maintenance distributed to every painful[87] minister that now scarce sustains his family with bread, while the prelates revel like Belshazzar with their full carouses in goblets and vessels of gold snatched from God's temple.[88] Which (I hope) the worthy men of our land will consider.

Now then for their courts. What a mass of money is drawn from the veins into the ulcers of the kingdom this way, their extortions, their open corruptions, the multitude of hungry and ravenous harpies that swarm about their offices declare sufficiently. And what though all this go not oversea? 'Twere better it did: better a penurious kingdom, than where excessive wealth flows into the graceless and injurious hands of common sponges to the impoverishing of good and loyal men, and that by such execrable, such irreligious courses.

If the sacred and dreadful works of holy discipline, censure, penance, excommunication, and absolution (where no profane thing ought to have access, nothing to be assistant but sage and Christianly admonition, brotherly love, flaming charity, and zeal; and then according to the effects, paternal sorrow, or paternal joy, mild severity melting compassion), if such divine ministries as these, wherein the angel of the church represents the person of Christ Jesus, must lie prostitute to sordid fees and not pass to and fro between our Savior

84. **copes:** ceremonial capes worn by priests.

85. Matt. 16.6.

86. **Antichrist:** i.e., the pope.

87. **painful:** painstaking, diligent.

88. Dan. 5.1–30. Belshazzar's revelry with the temple goblets prompted the miraculous writing, interpreted by Daniel, convicting the king of pride and blasphemy and predicting his downfall (he was slain that night). Milton, assuming Daniel's role, warns the bishops of their imminent fall.

(that of free grace redeemed us) and the submissive penitent, without the truckage[89] of perishing coin and the butcherly execution of tormentors, rooks, and rakeshames[90] sold to lucre, then have the Babylonish merchants of souls just excuse. Hitherto, sir, you have heard how the prelates have weakened and withdrawn the external accomplishments of kingly prosperity—the love of the people, their multitude, their valor, their wealth—mining and sapping the outworks and redoubts of monarchy, now hear how they strike at the very heart and vitals.

We know that monarchy is made up of two parts, the liberty of the subject and the supremacy of the king. I begin at the root. See what gentle and benign fathers they have been to our liberty. Their trade being, by the same alchemy that the pope uses to extract heaps of gold and silver out of the drossy bullion of the people's sins, and justly fearing that the quick-sighted Protestant's eye cleared in great part from the mist of superstition may at one time or other look with a good judgment into these their deceitful pedlaries,[91] to gain as many associates of guiltiness as they can, and to infect the temporal magistrate with the like lawless though not sacrilegious extortion, see a while what they do: they engage themselves to preach and persuade an assertion for truth the most false, and to this monarchy the most pernicious and destructive that could be chosen. What more baneful to monarchy than a popular commotion, for the dissolution of monarchy slides aptest into democraty;[92] and what stirs the Englishmen, as our wisest writers have observed, sooner to rebellion than violent and heavy hands upon their goods and purses? Yet these devout prelates, spite of our great charter and the souls of our progenitors that wrested their liberties out of the Norman grip with their dearest blood and highest prowess, for these many years have not ceased in their pulpits wrenching and spraining the text, to set at naught and trample under foot all the most sacred and lifeblood laws, statutes, and acts of Parliament that are the holy covenant of union and marriage between the king and his realm, by proscribing and confiscating from us all the right we have to our own bodies, goods, and liberties. What is this, but to blow a trumpet and proclaim a fire-cross[93] to a hereditary and perpetual civil war? Thus much against the subject's liberty hath been assaulted by them. . . .

[*In an omitted section, Milton offers examples of bishops and the pope challenging the secular authority of kings and emperors, praises God for frustrating the designs of prelates, and exhorts the English and Scottish to remain united in their pursuit of pure worship and civil justice.*]

89. **truckage:** barter.
90. **rakeshames:** ill-behaved, dissolute persons.
91. **pedlaries:** the base practices of a pedlar.
92. **democraty:** democracy.
93. **fire-cross:** a signal used in the Scottish Highlands to summon men to gather at the sudden outbreak of war.

Sir, you have now at length this question for the time, and as my memory would best serve me in such a copious and vast theme, fully handled, and you yourself may judge whether prelacy be the only church government agreeable to monarchy. Seeing, therefore, the perilous and confused estate into which we are fallen, and that,[94] to the certain knowledge of all men, through the irreligious pride and hateful tyranny of prelates (as the innumerable and grievous complaints of every shire cry out), if we will now resolve to settle affairs either according to pure religion or sound policy, we must first of all begin roundly to cashier and cut away from the public body the noisome and diseased tumor of prelacy and come from schism to unity with our neighbor reformed sister churches, which with the blessing of peace and pure doctrine have now long time flourished and, doubtless with all hearty joy and gratulation, will meet[95] and welcome our Christian union with them, as they have been all this while grieved at our strangeness and little better than separation from them. And for the discipline propounded,[96] seeing that it hath been inevitably proved that the natural and fundamental causes of political happiness in all governments are the same and that this church discipline is taught in the word of God, and, as we see, agrees according to wish with all such states as have received it, we may infallibly assure ourselves that it will as well agree with monarchy, though all the tribe of aphorismers and politicasters would persuade us there be secret and mysterious reasons against it. For upon the settling hereof mark what nourishing and cordial restorements to the state will follow: the ministers of the gospel attending only to the work of salvation, everyone within his limited charge; besides the diffusive blessing of God upon all our actions, the king shall sit without an old disturber,[97] a daily encroacher and intruder; shall rid his kingdom of a strong sequestered and collateral power; a confronting miter, whose potent wealth and wakeful ambition he had just cause to hold in jealousy: not to repeat the other present evils which only their removal will remove. And because things simply pure are inconsistent in the mass of nature, nor are the elements or humors in man's body exactly homogeneal, and hence the best founded commonwealths and least barbarous have aimed at a certain mixture and temperament, partaking the several virtues of each other state, that each part drawing to itself may keep up a steady and even uprightness in common.

There is no civil government that hath been known, no not the Spartan, not

94. **that:** i.e., the falling into the *perilous and confused state* just mentioned.

95. The spine of this complicated clause is as follows: *sister churches, which . . . have . . . flourished and . . . will meet.*

96. **the discipline propounded:** Presbyterian church government. By the mid-1640s, moved in part by the violent reaction of former Presbyterian allies to his argument for divorce, Milton would repudiate Presbyterianism and advocate Independency, or the self-governance of individual congregations; see his poem on the subject, *On the New Forcers of Conscience,* which ends "New *Presbyter* is but old *Priest* writ large."

97. **old disturber:** episcopacy in general, and perhaps Archbishop William Laud in particular.

the Roman, though both for this respect so much praised by the wise Polybius,[98] more divinely and harmoniously tuned, more equally balanced as it were by the hand and scale of justice, than is the commonwealth of England: where, under a free and untutored monarch, the noblest, worthiest, and most prudent men, with full approbation and suffrage of the people, have in their power the supreme and final determination of highest affairs. Now if conformity of church discipline to the civil be so desired, there can be nothing more parallel, more uniform, than when under the sovereign prince, Christ's vicegerent, using the scepter of David, according to God's law, the godliest, the wisest, and learnedest ministers in their several charges have the instructing and disciplining of God's people, by whose full and free election they are consecrated to that holy and equal aristocracy. And why should not the piety and conscience of Englishmen as members of the church be trusted in the election of pastors to functions that nothing concern a monarch, as well as their worldly wisdoms are privileged as members of the state in suffraging their knights and burgesses to matters that concern him nearly? And if in weighing these several offices, their difference in time and quality be cast in, I know they will not turn the beam of equal judgment the moiety of a scruple. . . .

[*In a brief omitted section, Milton, while elaborating on the parallels between the English secular government and Presbyterian church government, insists that ministers should not share in the elaborate honors and large stipends given to legislators and judges.*]

Here I might have ended, but that some objections, which I have heard commonly flying about, press me to the endeavor of an answer. We must not run, they say, into sudden extremes. This is a fallacious rule unless understood only of the actions of virtue about things indifferent, for if it be found that those two extremes be vice and virtue, falsehood and truth, the greater extremity of virtue and superlative truth we run into, the more virtuous and the more wise we become; and he that, flying from degenerate and traditional corruption, fears to shoot himself too far into the meeting embraces of a divinely-warranted reformation, had better not have run at all. And for the suddenness, it cannot be feared. Who should oppose it? The papists? They dare not. The Protestants otherwise affected? They were mad. There is nothing will be removed but what to them is professedly indifferent. The long affection which the people have born to it, what for itself, what for the odiousness of prelates, is evident. From the first year of Queen Elizabeth, it hath still been more and more propounded, desired, and beseeched, yea sometimes favorably forwarded by the Parliaments themselves. Yet if it were sudden and swift, provided still it be from worse to better, certainly we ought to hie us from evil like

98. See Polybius, *Histories* 6.48 and 6.12.

a torrent, and rid ourselves of corrupt discipline as we would shake fire out of our bosoms.

Speedy and vehement were the reformations of all the good kings of Judah,[99] though the people had been nuzzled in idolatry never so long before. They feared not the bugbear of danger, nor the lion in the way that the sluggish and timorous politician thinks he sees. No more did our brethren of the reformed churches abroad; they ventured (God being their guide) out of rigid popery into that which we in mockery call precise Puritanism, and yet we see no inconvenience befell them.

Let us not dally with God when he offers us a full blessing, to take as much of it as we think will serve our ends and turn him back the rest upon his hands, lest in his anger he snatch all from us again. Next, they allege the antiquity of episcopacy through all ages. What it was in the apostles' time, that questionless it must be still, and therein I trust the ministers will be able to satisfy the parliament. But if episcopacy be taken for prelacy,[100] all the ages they can deduce it through will make it no more venerable than papacy.

Most certain it is (as all our stories bear witness) that ever since their coming to the see[101] of Canterbury for near twelve hundred years, to speak of them in general, they have been in England to our souls a sad and doleful succession of illiterate and blind guides; to our purses and goods a wasteful band of robbers, a perpetual havoc and rapine; to our state a continual hydra of mischief and molestation, the forge of discord and rebellion. This is the trophy of their antiquity and boasted succession through so many ages. And for those prelate-martyrs[102] they glory of, they are to be judged what they were by the gospel and not the gospel to be tried by them. . . .

[*In a substantial omitted section, Milton answers a series of objections against Presbyterian church government: if episcopacy is woven into the common law, it can be woven out; not only is government by assembly true to the practice of the early church but it does not carry with it the danger of the meddling in politics by lordly and overweening bishops; on the continent, churches governed by assemblies do not intrude in secular affairs as bishops had done before the Reformation.*]

But let us not for fear of a scarecrow, or else through hatred to be reformed, stand hankering and politizing, when God with spread hands testifies to us and points us out the way to our peace.

Let us not be so overcredulous, unless God hath blinded us, as to trust our dear souls into the hands of men that beg so devoutly for the pride and gluttony

99. **good kings of Judah:** Asa (1 Kings 15.9–15), Hezekiah (2 Kings 18.4), and Josiah (2 Kings 23.1–25) have been proposed as instances.

100. Milton here distinguishes between episcopacy and prelacy; the bishops of the early church, according to Milton, did not claim lordship over their flocks.

101. **see:** diocese.

102. **prelate-martyrs:** a reference to Cranmer, Latimer, and Ridley (see note 16).

of their own backs and bellies, that sue and solicit so eagerly, not for the saving of souls, the consideration of which can have here no place at all, but for their bishoprics, deaneries, prebends, and chanonies.[103] How can these men not be corrupt, whose very cause is the bribe of their own pleading, whose mouths cannot open without the strong breath and loud stench of avarice, simony,[104] and sacrilege, embezzling the treasury of the church on painted and gilded walls of temples wherein God hath testified to have no delight, warming their palace kitchens, and from thence their unctuous and epicurean paunches, with the alms of the blind, the lame, the impotent, the aged, the orphan, the widow? For with these the treasury of Christ ought to be, here must be his jewels bestowed, his rich cabinet must be emptied here, as the constant martyr Saint Lawrence taught the Roman praetor.[105]

Sir, would you know what the remonstrance of these men[106] would have, what their petition[107] implies? They entreat us that we would not be weary of those insupportable grievances that our shoulders have hitherto cracked under. They beseech us that we would think 'em fit to be our justices of peace, our lords, our highest officers of state, though they come furnished with no more experience than they learnt between the cook and the manciple,[108] or more profoundly at the college audit, or the regent house, or (to come to their deepest insight) at their patron's table. They would request us to endure still the rustling of their silken cassocks, and that we would burst our midriffs rather than laugh to see them under sail in all their lawn and sarsenet,[109] their shrouds and tackle,[110] with geometrical rhomboids[111] upon their heads. They would bear us in hand that we must of duty still appear before them once a year in Jerusalem[112] like good circumcised males and females to be taxed by the poll,[113] to be sconsed our head money, our tuppences in their chaunlerly[114] shop-book of Easter. They pray us that it would please us to let them still hale us and worry us with their bandogs[115] and pursuivants;[116] and that it would please the

103. **chanonies:** canonries; a *canonry* is the benefice of a canon, a priest attached to a cathedral.

104. **simony:** the exchanging of rites and blessings for money.

105. Demanded under torture to hand over the riches of the church, St. Lawrence collected the poor and brought them to his persecutor. See Augustine, *Sermon* 302.9.

106. **these men:** the bishops.

107. **their petition:** A dismissive reference to *The Humble Petition of the University of Oxford, in Behalf of Episcopacy and Cathedrals,* published a month before *Of Reformation.*

108. **manciple:** a purchasing agent for a monastery.

109. **lawn:** fine linen, used in bishops' wide sleeves; **sarsenet:** a very fine and soft silk.

110. **shrouds and tackle:** parts of a ship's rigging; *shrouds* are ropes deployed in pairs to help brace the masthead; the ropes and pulleys with which the sails are deployed are the *tackle.* Milton often compares Satan to a sailing ship in *PL* (2.636–43, 4.159–65, 9.513–15).

111. **geometrical rhomboids:** miters.

112. It was the duty of Jewish men to appear once a year at the Temple in Jerusalem.

113. In Milton's time, a *tuppence* was required at Easter as a *poll* tax from parishioners old enough to take communion.

114. **chaunlerly:** relating to a chandler, or petty shopkeeper.

115. **bandogs:** mastiffs or bloodhounds.

116. **pursuivants:** warrant officers.

Parliament that they may yet have the whipping, fleecing, and flaying of us in their diabolical courts,[117] to tear the flesh from our bones, and into our wide wounds, instead of balm, to power in the oil of tartar, vitriol, and mercury. Surely a right reasonable innocent and soft-hearted petition! O the relenting bowels of the fathers! Can this be granted them unless God have smitten us with frenzy from above and with a dazzling giddiness at noonday?

Should not those men[118] rather be heard that come to plead against their own preferments, their worldly advantages, their own abundance; for honor and obedience to God's word, the conversion of souls, the Christian peace of the land, and union of the reformed catholic church,[119] the unappropriating and unmonopolizing the rewards of learning and industry from the greasy clutch of ignorance and high feeding? We have tried already, and miserably felt, what ambition, worldly glory, and immoderate wealth can do: what the boisterous and contradictional hand of a temporal, earthly, and corporeal spirituality can avail to the edifying of Christ's holy church. Were it such a desperate hazard to put to the venture the universal votes of Christ's congregation, the fellowly and friendly yoke of a teaching and laborious ministry, the pastor-like and apostolic imitation of meek and unlordly discipline, the gentle and benevolent mediocrity of church-maintenance,[120] without the ignoble hucksterage of piddling tithes?[121] Were it such an incurable mischief to make a little trial what all this would do to the flourishing and growing up of Christ's mystical body? As rather to use every poor shift and, if that serve not, to threaten uproar and combustion and shake the brand of civil discord?[122]

O sir, I do now feel myself enwrapped on the sudden into those mazes and labyrinths of dreadful and hideous thoughts, that which way to get out or which way to end I know not, unless I turn mine eyes and with your help lift up my hands to that eternal and propitious throne, where nothing is readier than grace and refuge to the distresses of mortal suppliants. And it were a shame to leave these serious thoughts less piously than the heathen were wont to conclude their graver discourses.

Thou therefore that sits in light and glory unapproachable, parent of angels and men! next thee I implore omnipotent king, redeemer of that lost remnant whose nature thou didst assume, ineffable and everlasting love! and thou the third subsistence of divine infinitude, illumining Spirit, the joy and solace of created things! One tri-personal godhead![123] look upon this thy poor and almost

117. **diabolical courts:** The bishops were particularly hated for their ecclesiastical courts.

118. **those men:** i.e., moderate Puritans.

119. **reformed catholic church:** the universal Protestant church, not the Roman Catholic Church.

120. **mediocrity of church-maintenance:** supporting ministers sufficiently but not luxuriously.

121. Milton's unwavering position that ministers should be supported by voluntary offerings rather than enforced tithes is the central subject of his 1659 work *Considerations Touching the Likeliest Means to Remove Hirelings out of the Church.*

122. Milton refers to the first and second Bishops' Wars of 1639 and 1640.

123. Milton would later reject Trinitarian beliefs, as is evident in *CD* 1.5 and in *Paradise Lost,* where, e.g., the Son lacks the Father's omnipresence (7.584–92).

spent and expiring church, leave her not thus a prey to these importunate wolves that wait and think long till they devour thy tender flock, these wild boars that have broke into thy vineyard, and left the print of their polluting hoofs on the souls of thy servants. O let them not bring about their damned designs, that stand now at the entrance of the bottomless pit, expecting the watchword to open and let out those dreadful locusts and scorpions to re-involve us in that pitchy cloud of infernal darkness, where we shall never more see the sun of thy truth again, never hope for the cheerful dawn, never more hear the bird of morning sing. Be moved with pity at the afflicted state of this our shaken monarchy, that now lies laboring under her throes and struggling against the grudges of more dreaded calamities.

O thou that, after the impetuous rage of five bloody inundations[124] and the succeeding sword of intestine war, soaking the land in her own gore, didst pity the sad and ceaseless revolution of our swift and thick-coming sorrows when we were quite breathless, of thy free grace didst motion peace and terms of covenant with us, and having first well-nigh freed us from antichristian thraldom, didst build up this Britannic empire to a glorious and enviable height with all her daughter islands about her, stay us in this felicity, let not the obstinacy of our half-obedience and will-worship bring forth that viper of sedition that for these fourscore years hath been breeding to eat through the entrails of our peace, but let her cast her abortive spawn without the danger of this travailing and throbbing kingdom. That we may still remember in our solemn thanksgivings, how for us the northern ocean even to the frozen Thule[125] was scattered with the proud shipwrecks of the Spanish armado, and the very maw of hell ransacked and made to give up her concealed destruction ere she could vent it in that horrible and damned blast.[126]

O how much more glorious will those former deliverances appear, when we shall know them not only to have saved us from the greatest miseries past but to have reserved us for greatest happiness to come. Hitherto thou has but freed us, and that not fully, from the unjust and tyrannous claim of thy foes; now unite us entirely and appropriate us to thyself, tie us everlastingly in willing homage to the prerogative of thy eternal throne.

And now we know, oh thou our most certain hope and defense, that thine enemies have been consulting all the sorceries of the great whore,[127] and have

124. **five bloody inundations:** most likely the five invasions of England by Romans, Picts and Scots, Anglo-Saxons, Danes, and Normans, described by Milton in his *History of Britain.*

125. **Thule:** Early geographers assigned this name to a land north of Britain, supposed to be the world's most northerly region. Milton gives dramatic emphasis to the 1588 English victory over the Spanish Armada.

126. A reference to the discovery of the Gunpowder Plot of 1605, which Milton celebrated in several juvenile poems (see the three poems titled "In proditionem bombaricam" and especially the mini-epic *On the Fifth of November*).

127. **great whore:** the Roman Catholic Church, associated by Protestants generally and Puritans in particular with the Whore of Babylon of Rev. 17.1.

joined their plots with that sad intelligencing tyrant[128] that mischiefs the world with his mines of Ophir, and lies thirsting to revenge his naval ruins that have larded our seas. But let them all take counsel together, and let it come to naught; let them decree, and do thou cancel it; let them gather themselves, and be scattered; let them embattle themselves, and be broken; let them embattle and be broken; for thou art with us.

Then, amidst the hymns and hallelujahs of saints, some one may perhaps be heard offering at high strains in new and lofty measures to sing and celebrate thy divine mercies and marvelous judgments in this land throughout all ages; whereby this great and warlike nation instructed and inured to the fervent and continual practice of truth and righteousness, and casting far from her the rags of her old vices, may press on hard to that high and happy emulation to be found the soberest, wisest, and most Christian people at that day when thou, the eternal and shortly expected king, shalt open the clouds to judge the several kingdoms of the world and, distributing national honors and rewards to religious and just commonwealths, shall put an end to all earthly tyrannies, proclaiming thy universal and mild monarchy through heaven and earth.[129] Where they undoubtedly that by their labors, counsels, and prayers have been earnest for the common good of religion and their country shall receive, above the inferior orders of the blessed, the regal addition of principalities, legions, and thrones into their glorious titles,[130] and in supereminence of beatific vision progressing the dateless and irrevoluble circle of eternity shall clasp inseparable hands with joy and bliss in overmeasure forever.

But they contrary that by the impairing and diminution of true faith, the distresses and servitude of their country, aspire to high dignity, rule, and promotion here, after a shameful end in this life (which God grant them) shall be thrown down eternally into the darkest and deepest gulf of hell, where, under the despiteful control, the trample and spurn of all the other damned that in the anguish of their torture shall have no other ease than to exercise a raving and bestial tyranny over them as their slaves and negroes, they shall remain in that plight forever, the basest, the lowermost, the most dejected, most underfoot, and downtrodden vassals of perdition.

The End

128. **sad intelligencing tyrant:** i.e., the Roman Catholic throne of Spain, which employed the gold of South America (described here with the biblical term *mines of Ophir* [1 Kings 10.11]) to further its goal of extirpating Protestantism.

129. A reference to the Second Coming of Christ (Matt. 24.29–25.46).

130. I.e., the heroes of reformation will join the angels in Heaven; *principalities* and *thrones* are two of the nine orders of angels (like other Protestants, Milton sometimes used the order names employed in the Roman Church without committing himself to the hierarchical arrangement of the orders).

A Selection from

THE REASON OF CHURCH GOVERNMENT URGED AGAINST PRELATY, THE SECOND BOOK

The Reason of Church Government Urged against Prelaty is the fourth of five works, published in the span of a year, attacking the episcopal hierarchy of the Church of England. Published in January or February 1642, *The Reason of Church Government* is the longest of these so-called antiprelatical tracts, and the first to which Milton affixed his name. The immediate occasion was the appearance in 1641 of *Certain Briefe Treatises, Written by Diverse Learned Men, Concerning the Ancient and Moderne Government of the Church,* which contained arguments in favor of episcopacy by Anglican champions such as Archbishop James Ussher, Lancelot Andrewes, and Richard Hooker. *The Reason of Church Government* is more moderate in its rhetoric than some of Milton's other tracts, notably the *Animadversions* and *An Apology for Smectymnuus,* which engage in harsh personal attacks.

While Milton's arguments against episcopacy hold interest for specialists, the tract is most often read for the remarkable autobiographical passage that takes up most of the Preface to Book 2. A relative unknown taking on illustrious elders, Milton probably believed it necessary to authorize his arguments by presenting himself as learned and virtuous, a rhetorical tactic known as the "ethical proof." But he goes well beyond the conventions of ethical proof. With characteristic egotism, Milton numbers himself among God's "selected heralds" and compares himself with the prophet Isaiah (Kerrigan 1974). He acknowledges an unbounded poetic ambition, promising to do for England what Homer did for Greece and Vergil for Rome, and, as a Christian, to trump them by writing a true epic to challenge their fictitious ones.

The text of our selection is based on the copy of the first edition in the British Library's Thomason Collection.

The Second Book

How happy were it for this frail and, as it may be truly called, mortal life of man, since all earthly things which have the name of good and convenient in our daily use are withal[1] so cumbersome and full of trouble, if knowledge yet which is the best and lightsomest possession of the mind were, as the common saying is, no burden, and that what it wanted of being a load to any part of the body, it did not with a heavy advantage overlay upon the spirit. For not to speak of that knowledge that rests in the contemplation of natural causes and dimensions,[2] which must needs be a lower wisdom as the object is low, certain it is that he who hath obtained in more than the scantest measure to know anything distinctly of God and of his true worship, and what is infallibly good and happy in the state of man's life, what in itself evil and miserable, though vulgarly not so esteemed, he that hath obtained to know this, the only high valuable wisdom indeed, remembering also that God even to a strictness requires the improvement of these his entrusted gifts,[3] cannot but sustain a sorer burden of mind (and more pressing, than any supportable toil or weight which the body can labor under), how and in what manner he shall dispose and employ those sums of knowledge and illumination which God hath sent him into this world to trade with.

And that which aggravates the burden more is that, having received amongst his allotted parcels certain precious truths of such an orient luster as no diamond can equal, which nevertheless he has in charge to put off[4] at any cheap rate, yea for nothing to them that will, the great merchants[5] of this world, fearing that this course would soon discover and disgrace the false glitter of their deceitful wares wherewith they abuse the people, like poor Indians with beads and glasses, practice by all means how they may suppress the venting of such rarities and such a cheapness as would undo them and turn their trash upon their hands. Therefore by gratifying the corrupt desires of men in fleshly doctrines, they stir them up to persecute with hatred and contempt all those that seek to bear themselves uprightly in this their spiritual factory:[6] which they foreseeing, though they cannot but testify of truth and the excellence of that heavenly traffic which they bring against what opposition or danger soever, yet needs must it sit heavily upon their spirits, that being, in God's prime intention and their own, selected heralds of peace and dispensers of treasure inestimable without price to them that have no pence, they find in the discharge of their commission that they are made the greatest variance and offense, a very sword

1. **withal:** at the same time.
2. Milton follows the tradition dividing knowledge available through the "contemplation of created things" (*PL* 5.511) from the higher knowledge available through revelation and right reason. Compare Bacon's *Advancement of Learning* 1.1.3.
3. Milton alludes to the parable of the talents (Matt. 25.14–31), as he does in *Sonnet 7* and *19*. For the importance of this parable in Milton, see Haskin 29–53.
4. **put off:** sell.
5. **great merchants:** Milton refers figuratively to the bishops.
6. **factory:** trading post. Milton distinguishes between upright traders in God's Word and the bishops who cheat the English as merchant traders cheated Native Americans or East Indians with cheap baubles.

and fire both in house and city over the whole earth.[7] This is that which the sad prophet Jeremiah laments, "Woe is me my mother, that thou hast born me a man of strife and contention" [Jer. 15:10].

And although divine inspiration must certainly have been sweet to those ancient prophets, yet the irksomeness of that truth which they brought was so unpleasant to them, that everywhere they call it a burden. Yea that mysterious book of Revelation which the great evangelist was bid to eat, as it had been some eye-brightening electuary[8] of knowledge and foresight, though it were sweet in his mouth and in the learning, it was bitter in his belly, bitter in the denouncing.[9] Nor was this hid from the wise poet Sophocles, who in that place of his tragedy where Tiresias is called to resolve King Oedipus in a matter which he knew would be grievous, brings him in bemoaning his lot, that he knew more than other men.[10] For surely to every good and peaceable man it must in nature needs be a hateful thing to be the displeaser and molester[11] of thousands; much better would it like him doubtless to be the messenger of gladness and contentment, which is his chief intended business to all mankind, but that they resist and oppose their own true happiness.

But when God commands to take the trumpet and blow a dolorous or a jarring blast, it lies not in man's will what he shall say or what he shall conceal. If he shall think to be silent, as Jeremiah did because of the reproach and derision he met with daily, and "all his familiar friends watched for his halting," to be revenged on him for speaking the truth, he would be forced to confess as he confessed, "his word was in my heart as a burning fire shut up in my bones; I was weary with forbearing, and could not stay" [Jer. 20:8-10]. Which might teach these times not suddenly to condemn all things that are sharply spoken or vehemently written as proceeding out of stomach,[12] virulence, and ill nature, but to consider rather that if the prelates have leave to say the worst that can be said and do the worst that can be done, while they strive to keep to themselves to their great pleasure and commodity those things which they ought to render up, no man can be justly offended with him that shall endeavor to impart and bestow, without any gain to himself, those sharp but saving words which would be a terror and a torment in him to keep back. For me, I have determined to lay up as the best treasure and solace of a good old age, if God vouchsafe it me, the honest liberty of free speech from my youth, where I shall think it available in so dear a concernment as the church's good. For if I be either by disposition, or what other cause too inquisitive or suspicious of myself and mine own doings, who can help it?

7. Matt. 10.34: "I come not to send peace, but a sword."
8. **electuary:** medicine mixed with syrup or honey.
9. **denouncing:** proclaiming; in Rev. 10.9, John is told by an angel to eat a scroll that "shall make thy belly bitter, but it shall be in thy mouth sweet as honey."
10. In *Oedipus the King, Tiresias* must tell *Oedipus* that he has killed his father and married his mother.
11. **molester:** disturber.
12. **stomach:** angry pride.

But this I foresee, that should the church be brought under heavy oppression, and God have given me ability the while to reason against that man that should be the author of so foul a deed, or should she by blessing from above on the industry and courage of faithful men change this her distracted estate into better days without the least furtherance or contribution of those few talents[13] which God at that present had lent me, I foresee what stories I should hear within myself, all my life after, of discourage and reproach: "Timorous and ingrateful, the church of God is now again at the foot of her insulting enemies, and thou bewailest; what matters it for thee or thy bewailing? When time was, thou couldst not find a syllable of all that thou hadst read or studied, to utter in her behalf. Yet ease and leisure was given thee for thy retired thoughts out of the sweat of other men. Thou hadst the diligence, the parts, the language of a man if a vain subject were to be adorned or beautified, but when the cause of God and his church was to be pleaded, for which purpose that tongue was given thee which thou hast, God listened if he could hear thy voice among his zealous servants, but thou wert dumb as a beast; from henceforward be that which thine own brutish silence hath made thee." Or else I should have heard on the other ear: "Slothful, and ever to be set light by, the church hath now overcome her late distresses after the unwearied labors of many her true servants that stood up in her defense; thou also wouldst take upon thee to share amongst them of their joy. But wherefore thou? Where canst thou show any word or deed of thine which might have hastened her peace? Whatever thou dost now talk, or write, or look is the alms of other men's active prudence and zeal. Dare not now to say or do anything better than thy former sloth and infancy,[14] or if thou darest, thou dost impudently to make a thrifty purchase of boldness to thyself out of the painful merits of other men. What before was thy sin, is now thy duty, to be abject and worthless." These, and such like lessons as these, I know would have been my matins duly and my evensong. But now by this little diligence, mark what a privilege I have gained with good men and saints, to claim my right of lamenting the tribulations of the church, if she should suffer, when others that have ventured nothing for her sake have not the honor to be admitted mourners. But if she lift up her drooping head and prosper, among those that have something more than wished her welfare I have my charter and freehold[15] of rejoicing to me and my heirs.

Concerning therefore this wayward[16] subject against prelaty, the touching whereof is so distasteful and disquietous to a number of men, as by what hath been said I may deserve of charitable readers to be credited that neither envy nor gall hath entered me upon this controversy, but the enforcement of conscience only and a preventive fear lest the omitting of this duty should be

13. See note 3.
14. **infancy:** speechlessness.
15. **charter and freehold:** i.e., unchallengeable right.
16. **wayward:** troublesome, likely to be offensive.

against me when I would store up to myself the good provision of peaceful hours; so lest it should be still imputed to me, as I have found it hath been, that some self-pleasing humor of vainglory hath incited me to contest with men of high estimation, now while green years are upon my head, from this needless surmisal I shall hope to dissuade the intelligent and equal[17] auditor, if I can but say successfully that which in this exigent[18] behooves me, although I would be heard only, if it might be, by the elegant and learned reader, to whom principally for a while I shall beg leave I may address myself. To him it will be no new thing though I tell him that if I hunted after praise by the ostentation of wit and learning, I should not write thus out of mine own season, when I have neither yet completed to my mind the full circle of my private studies, although I complain not of any insufficiency to the matter in hand; or were I ready to my wishes, it were a folly to commit anything elaborately composed to the careless and interrupted listening of these tumultuous times. Next, if I were wise only to mine own ends, I would certainly take such a subject as of itself might catch applause, whereas this hath all the disadvantages on the contrary, and such a subject as the publishing whereof might be delayed at pleasure, and time enough to pencil it over with all the curious[19] touches of art, even to the perfection of a faultless picture, whenas in this argument the not deferring is of great moment to the good speeding, that if solidity have leisure to do her office, art cannot have much. Lastly, I should not choose this manner of writing, wherein knowing myself inferior to myself, led by the genial power of nature to another task, I have the use, as I may account it, but of my left hand. And though I shall be foolish in saying more to this purpose, yet since it will be such a folly as wisest men going about to commit have only confessed and so committed, I may trust with more reason, because with more folly, to have courteous pardon. For although a poet soaring in the high region of his fancies[20] with his garland and singing robes about him might without apology speak more of himself than I mean to do, yet for me sitting here below in the cool element of prose, a mortal thing among many readers of no empyreal conceit,[21] to venture and divulge unusual things of myself, I shall petition to the gentler sort it may not be envy to me.

I must say, therefore, that after I had from my first years by the ceaseless diligence and care of my father, whom God recompense, been exercised to the tongues and some sciences[22] as my age would suffer,[23] by sundry masters and teachers both at home and at the schools, it was found that whether aught was

17. **equal:** impartial.
18. **exigent:** pressing circumstance.
19. **curious:** elegant.
20. **fancies:** imagination.
21. **of no empyreal conceit:** lacking sublime ideas; see *PL* 7.14.
22. **some sciences:** As a child Milton learned Latin, Greek, French, Italian, and Hebrew (see *To His Father* 79–85); by *sciences,* he means useful bodies of knowledge other than languages.
23. **suffer:** allow.

imposed me by them that had the overlooking, or betaken to of mine own choice in English or other tongue, prosing or versing, but chiefly this latter, the style, by certain vital signs it had, was likely to live. But much latelier in the private academies of Italy, whither I was favored to resort, perceiving that some trifles which I had in memory, composed at under twenty or thereabout (for the manner is that everyone must give some proof of his wit and reading there), met with acceptance above what was looked for, and other things, which I had shifted in scarcity of books and conveniences to patch up amongst them, were received with written encomiums, which the Italian is not forward to bestow on men of this side the Alps; I began thus far to assent both to them and divers of my friends here at home, and not less to an inward prompting which now grew daily upon me, that by labor and intent study (which I take to be my portion in this life) joined with the strong propensity of nature, I might perhaps leave something so written to aftertimes, as they should not willingly let it die. These thoughts at once possessed me and these other: that if I were certain to write as men buy leases, for three lives and downward,[24] there ought no regard be sooner had than to God's glory, by the honor and instruction of my country.

For which cause, and not only for that I knew it would be hard to arrive at the second rank among the Latins, I applied myself to that resolution which Ariosto followed against the persuasions of Bembo,[25] to fix all the industry and art I could unite to the adorning of my native tongue; not to make verbal curiosities the end, that were a toilsome vanity, but to be an interpreter and relater of the best and sagest things among mine own citizens throughout this island in the mother dialect. That what the greatest and choicest wits of Athens, Rome, or modern Italy, and those Hebrews of old did for their country, I, in my proportion, with this over and above of being a Christian, might do for mine: not caring to be once named abroad, though perhaps I could attain to that, but content with these British islands as my world, whose fortune hath hitherto been, that if the Athenians, as some say, made their small deeds great and renowned by their eloquent writers, England hath had her noble achievements made small by the unskillful handling of monks and mechanics.[26]

Time serves not now,[27] and perhaps I might seem too profuse to give any certain account of what the mind at home in the spacious circuits of her musing hath liberty to propose to herself, though of highest hope and hardest attempting, whether that epic form whereof the two poems of Homer and those other two of Virgil and Tasso are a diffuse, and the book of Job a brief model;[28] or whether the rules of Aristotle herein are strictly to be kept, or nature to be

24. **as men buy leases, for three lives and downward:** Leases that are in effect until the last of three specified individuals dies.

25. Ludovico *Ariosto,* sixteenth-century author of the *Orlando Furioso,* resisted the classicist Pietro *Bembo*'s urging that he write in Latin rather than Italian.

26. **mechanics:** illiterate laborers, used figuratively for the medieval monks who chronicled British history.

27. **Time serves not now:** "There is not time now," or "Now is not the time."

28. Torquato Tasso's sixteenth-century *Geruselemme Liberata* echoed Vergil's and Homer's epics in form, and in devotion to a single action. The Book of Job was read in Milton's time as a brief epic.

followed, which in them that know art and use judgment is no transgression, but an enriching of art.[29] And lastly what king or knight before the conquest might be chosen in whom to lay the pattern of a Christian hero.[30] And as Tasso gave to a prince of Italy[31] his choice whether he would command him to write of Godfrey's expedition against the infidels, or Belisarius against the Goths, or Charlemagne against the Lombards, if to the instinct of nature and the emboldening of art aught may be trusted, and that there be nothing adverse in our climate[32] or the fate of this age, it haply would be no rashness from an equal diligence and inclination to present the like offer in our own ancient stories. Or whether those dramatic constitutions, wherein Sophocles and Euripides reign, shall be found more doctrinal and exemplary to a nation, the scripture also affords us a divine pastoral drama in the Song of Solomon consisting of two persons and a double chorus, as Origen rightly judges.[33] And the apocalypse of Saint John is the majestic image of a high and stately tragedy, shutting up and intermingling her solemn scenes and acts with a sevenfold chorus of hallelujahs and harping symphonies: and this my opinion the grave authority of Pareus commenting that book is sufficient to confirm. Or if occasion shall lead to imitate those magnificent odes and hymns wherein Pindarus and Callimachus[34] are in most things worthy, some others in their frame judicious, in their matter most an end[35] faulty. But those frequent songs throughout the law and prophets beyond all these, not in their divine argument alone, but in the very critical art of composition, may be easily made appear over all the kinds of lyric poesy to be incomparable.

These abilities, wheresoever they be found, are the inspired gift of God rarely bestowed, but yet to some (though most abuse) in every nation; and are of power beside the office of a pulpit to inbreed and cherish in a great people the seeds of virtue and public civility, to allay the perturbations of the mind and set the affections in right tune, to celebrate in glorious and lofty hymns the throne and equipage of God's almightiness and what he works and what he suffers to be wrought with high providence in his church, to sing the victorious agonies of martyrs and saints, the deeds and triumphs of just and pious nations doing valiantly through faith against the enemies of Christ, to deplore the general relapses of kingdoms and states from justice and God's true worship. Lastly, whatsoever in religion is holy and sublime, in virtue amiable or grave, whatsoever hath passion or admiration in all the changes of that which is called

29. Milton alludes to a vigorous Italian critical debate concerning the rule of epic form, with some favoring Tasso's Vergilian epic following Aristotle's rules (*Poetics* 26) and others defending the multiple plot and interlaced form favored by Ariosto, a model to which Spenser's *Faerie Queene* is indebted.
30. Milton years earlier had anticipated writing an epic of King Arthur (See *Manso* 80–84).
31. **prince of Italy:** Alfonso II, Duke of Ferrara.
32. Milton wonders in *PL* 9.44–46 if an epic can be written in England's damp, cold climate.
33. In his *Prologue to the Song of Songs,* cited by David Paraeus.
34. **Pindarus and Callimachus:** Pindar is famous for his odes, and Callimachus for his hymns.
35. **an end:** in the end.

fortune from without, or the wily subtleties and refluxes of man's thoughts from within, all these things with a solid and treatable smoothness to paint out and describe. Teaching over the whole book of sanctity and virtue through all the instances of example with such delight, to those especially of soft and delicious[36] temper, who will not so much as look upon Truth herself unless they see her elegantly dressed, that whereas the paths of honesty and good life appear now rugged and difficult, though they be indeed easy and pleasant, they would then appear to all men both easy and pleasant though they were rugged and difficult indeed.[37] And what a benefit this would be to our youth and gentry may be soon guessed by what we know of the corruption and bane which they suck in daily from the writings and interludes of libidinous and ignorant poetasters, who having scarce ever heard of that which is the main consistence of a true poem, the choice of such persons as they ought to introduce, and what is moral and decent to each one, do for the most part lap up vicious principles in sweet pills to be swallowed down, and make the taste of virtuous documents harsh and sour.

But because the spirit of man cannot demean itself lively in this body without some recreating intermission of labor and serious things, it were happy for the commonwealth if our magistrates, as in those famous governments of old, would take into their care, not only the deciding of our contentious law cases and brawls, but the managing of our public sports and festival pastimes, that they might be, not such as were authorized a while since, the provocations of drunkenness and lust,[38] but such as may inure and harden our bodies by martial exercises to all warlike skill and performance, and may civilize, adorn, and make discreet our minds by the learned and affable meeting of frequent academies, and the procurement of wise and artful recitations sweetened with eloquent and graceful enticements to the love and practice of justice, temperance, and fortitude, instructing and bettering the nation at all opportunities, that the call of wisdom and virtue may be heard everywhere, as Solomon saith, "she crieth without, she uttereth her voice in the streets, in the top of high places, in the chief concourse, and in the openings of the gates" [Prov. 1:20-21, 8:2-3]. Whether this may not be not only in pulpits but after another persuasive method, at set and solemn panegyries,[39] in theaters, porches,[40] or what other place or way may win most upon the people to receive at once both recreation and instruction, let them in authority consult.

36. **delicious:** sensuous.
37. Following Sidney's *Defense of Poetry* and his Italian predecessors, Milton voices a Renaissance critical commonplace, that poets can teach virtue by means of attractive examples.
38. Milton glances disapprovingly at the 1633 *Book of Sports,* by which Charles I promoted games, sports, and dancing on Sundays. As in *Of Education,* he proposes instead martial exercises and attendance at the kinds of literary and scientific academies he visited in Italy.
39. **panegyries:** religious festivals.
40. **porches:** church entranceways; medieval English drama originated in liturgical plays on church porches.

The thing which I had to say, and those intentions which have lived within me ever since I could conceive myself anything worth to my country, I return to crave excuse that urgent reason hath plucked from me by an abortive and foredated discovery.[41] And the accomplishment of them lies not but in a power above man's to promise; but that none hath by more studious ways endeavored, and with more unwearied spirit that none shall, that I dare almost aver of myself as far as life and free leisure will extend; and that the land had once enfranchised herself from this impertinent yoke of prelaty, under whose inquisitorious and tyrannical duncery no free and splendid wit can flourish. Neither do I think it shame to covenant with any knowing reader, that for some few years yet I may go on trust with him toward the payment of what I am now indebted, as being a work not to be raised from the heat of youth or the vapors of wine, like that which flows at waste from the pen[42] of some vulgar amorist or the trencher fury of a rhyming parasite, nor to be obtained by the invocation of Dame Memory and her siren daughters, but by devout prayer to that eternal Spirit who can enrich with all utterance and knowledge, and sends out his seraphim with the hallowed fire of his altar to touch and purify the lips of whom he pleases.[43] To this must be added industrious and select reading, steady observation, insight into all seemly and generous arts and affairs, till which in some measure be compassed, at mine own peril and cost I refuse not to sustain this expectation from as many as are not loath to hazard so much credulity upon the best pledges that I can give them.

Although it nothing content me to have disclosed thus much beforehand, but that I trust hereby to make it manifest with what small willingness I endure to interrupt the pursuit of no less hopes than these, and leave a calm and pleasing solitariness fed with cheerful and confident thoughts, to embark in a troubled sea of noises and hoarse disputes, put from beholding the bright countenance of truth in the quiet and still air of delightful studies to come into the dim reflection of hollow antiquities sold by the seeming bulk, and there be fain to club[44] quotations with men whose learning and belief lies in marginal stuffings, who when they have like good sumpters[45] laid ye down their horseload of citations and fathers at your door, with a rhapsody of who and who were bishops here or there, ye may take off their packsaddles, their day's work is done, and episcopacy, as they think, stoutly vindicated. Let any gentle apprehension that can distinguish learned pains from unlearned drudgery imagine what pleasure or profoundness can be in this, or what honor to deal against such adversaries. But were it the meanest under-service, if God by his secretary con-

41. **abortive and foredated discovery:** premature disclosure; Milton indicated earlier that he did not intend to discuss himself (see note 26).

42. For this double entendre Milton may be indebted to Shakespeare's *Sonnet 129* ("The expense of spirit in a waste of shame").

43. Isa. 6.6–7.

44. **club:** collect and trade.

45. **sumpters:** packhorse drivers.

science enjoin it, it were sad for me if I should draw back, for me especially, now when all men offer their aid to help ease and lighten the difficult labors of the church, to whose service by the intentions of my parents and friends I was destined of a child, and in mine own resolutions; till coming to some maturity of years and perceiving what tyranny had invaded the church, that he who would take orders must subscribe slave, and take an oath withal, which unless he took with a conscience that would retch, he must either straight perjure or split his faith, I thought it better to prefer a blameless silence before the sacred office of speaking bought and begun with servitude and forswearing. Howsoever, thus church-outed by the prelates,[46] hence may appear the right I have to meddle in these matters, as before the necessity and constraint appeared.

46. Because of his opposition to Archbishop William Laud and to the institution of episcopacy, Milton found himself unable in conscience to become a minister of the Church of England, the expected end of his Cambridge education.

A Selection from

AN APOLOGY FOR SMECTYMNUUS

The full title of Milton's final antiprelatical pamphlet, *An Apology against a Pamphlet Called A Modest Confutation of the Animadversions upon the Remonstrant against Smectymnuus,* tells us something about how the pamphlet wars unfolded, in a tangled skein of argument, reply, and ad hominem attack. The odd name "Smectymnuus" is composed of the initials of five Puritans—Stephen Marshall, Edmund Calamy, Thomas Young (Milton's childhood tutor), Matthew Newcomen, and William Spurstow—who a year earlier (March 1641) had attacked Bishop Joseph Hall's *Humble Remonstrance,* a moderate defense of episcopacy. Hall replied with *A Defence of the Humble Remonstrance, against . . . Smectymnuus* (April 1641), a work that Milton savaged in his anonymous *Animadversions* (July 1641). Late that year or early in the next appeared an anonymous reply, *A Modest Confutation of a Slanderous and Scurrilous Libell, Entituled, Animadversions,* which returned Milton's personal attacks, though with considerably less savagery. Milton, stung nevertheless, responded in *An Apology for Smectymnuus* (April 1642) with a bitter attack on Hall and his son Robert, whom he assumed, perhaps correctly, to be the authors of the *Confutation.* Like *The Reason of Church Government, An Apology* is now read most often for Milton's autobiographical portrait. Its greater emphasis on his ethical development and the virtuous tenor of his daily life derives from a perceived need to counter the confuter's personal attack. Milton emphasizes the chastity that he regarded as an essential and enabling virtue of the true Christian poet and asserts memorably that one wishing, like himself, to be a great poet "ought himself to be a true poem" (p. 98).

Our selection is based on the copy of the first edition in the Huntington Library (105678).

Thus having spent his first onset not in confuting but in a reasonless defaming of the book, the method of his malice hurries him[1] to attempt the like against the author;[2] not by proofs and testimonies, but "having no certain notice of me," as he professes, "further than what he gathers from the *Animadversions,*" blunders

1. **him:** the author of *A Modest Confutation,* whom Milton assumed to be Bishop Joseph Hall or his son; there may be an echo of Polonius on the "method" in Hamlet's "madness" (*Hamlet* 2.2).

2. **the author:** Milton.

at me for the rest and flings out stray crimes at a venture, which he could never, though he be a serpent, suck from anything that I have written, but from his own stuffed magazine[3] and hoard of slanderous inventions, over and above that which he converted to venom in the drawing. To me, readers, it happens as a singular contentment, and let it be to good men no slight satisfaction, that the slanderer here confesses he has "no further notice of me than his own conjecture." Although it had been honest to have inquired before he uttered such infamous words, and I am credibly informed he did inquire, but finding small comfort from the intelligence which he received, whereon to ground the falsities which he had provided, thought it is his likeliest course under a pretended ignorance to let drive at random, lest he should lose his odd ends which from some penurious Book of Characters[4] he had been culling out and would fain apply. Not caring to burden me with those vices whereof, among whom my conversation hath been, I have been ever least suspected; perhaps not without some subtlety to cast me into envy by bringing on me a necessity to enter into mine own praises. In which argument I know every wise man is more unwillingly drawn to speak than the most repining ear can be averse to hear.

Nevertheless, since I dare not wish to pass this life unpersecuted of slanderous tongues, for God hath told us that to be generally praised is woeful,[5] I shall rely on his promise to free the innocent from causeless aspersions.[6] Whereof nothing sooner can assure me than if I shall feel him now assisting me in the just vindication of myself, which yet I could defer, it being more meet that to those other matters of public debatement in this book I should give attendance first, but that I fear it would but harm the truth for me to reason in her behalf, so long as I should suffer my honest estimation to lie unpurged from these insolent suspicions. And if I shall be large or unwonted in justifying myself to those who know me not, for else it would be needless, let them consider that a short slander will ofttimes reach farther than a long apology; and that he who will do justly to all men, must begin from knowing how, if it so happen, to be not unjust to himself.

I must be thought, if this libeler (for now he shows himself to be so) can find belief, after an inordinate and riotous youth spent at the university, to have been at length "vomited out thence."[7] For which commodious lie, that he may be encouraged in the trade another time, I thank him; for it hath given me an apt occasion to acknowledge publicly with all grateful mind that more than ordinary favor and respect which I found above any of my equals[8] at the hands of those courteous and learned men, the fellows of that college wherein I spent

3. **magazine:** storehouse.
4. **Book of Characters:** Joseph Hall's 1608 *Characters of Virtues and Vices,* an example of the popular genre of witty character sketches, established his literary reputation.
5. Luke 6.26.
6. Matt. 5.11–12.
7. The confuter apparently refers to Milton's rustication (or suspension) from Cambridge in 1626. See *Elegy 1* for Milton's contemporary version of the episode.
8. **equals:** fellow students.

some years: who at my parting, after I had taken two degrees, as the manner is, signified many ways how much better it would content them that I would stay; as by many letters full of kindness and loving respect, both before that time and long after, I was assured of their singular good affection towards me. Which being likewise propense[9] to all such as were for their studious and civil life worthy of esteem, I could not wrong their judgments and upright intentions so much as to think I had that regard from them for other cause than that I might be still encouraged to proceed in the honest and laudable courses of which they apprehended I had given good proof. And to those ingenuous and friendly men who were ever the countenancers of virtuous and hopeful wits, I wish the best and happiest things that friends in absence wish one to another. As for the common approbation or dislike of that place as now it is, that I should esteem or disesteem myself or any other the more for that, too simple and too credulous is the confuter, if he think to obtain with me or any right discerner. Of small practice were that physician who could not judge by what both she or her sister[10] hath of long time vomited, that the worser stuff she strongly keeps in her stomach, but the better she is ever kecking[11] at, and is queasy. She vomits now out of sickness, but ere it be well with her, she must vomit by strong physic.

In the meanwhile that "suburb sink,"[12] as this rude scavenger calls it (and more than scurrilously taunts it with the "plague," having a worse plague in his middle entrail), that suburb wherein I dwell shall be in my account a more honorable place than his university; which, as in the time of her better health and mine own younger judgment, I never greatly admired, so now much less. But he follows me to the city, still usurping[13] and forging beyond his book notice, which only he affirms to have had, "and where my morning haunts are he wisses[14] not." 'Tis wonder that, being so rare an alchemist of slander, he could not extract that as well as the university vomit and the suburb sink which his art could distill so cunningly, but because his limbec[15] fails him, to give him and envy the more vexation, I'll tell him. Those morning haunts are where they should be, at home, not sleeping or concocting[16] the surfeits of an irregular feast, but up and stirring—in winter often ere the sound of any bell awake men to labor or to devotion, in summer as oft with the bird that first rouses or not too much tardier—to read good authors, or cause them to be read, till the attention be weary or memory have his full fraught: then, with useful and generous labors preserving the body's health and hardiness, to render lightsome, clear, and not lumpish obedience to the mind, to the cause of religion, and our country's liberty, when it shall

9. **propense:** inclined.
10. **her sister:** Oxford.
11. **kecking:** retching.
12. **sink:** cesspool; the confuter accused Milton of visiting brothels in London suburbs.
13. **usurping:** going beyond his evidence.
14. **wisses:** knows.
15. **limbec:** an alembic, an alchemist's distilling device.
16. **concocting:** digesting.

require firm hearts in sound bodies to stand and cover their stations, rather than to see the ruin of our protestation[17] and the enforcement of a slavish life.

These are the morning practices. Proceed now to the afternoon: "in playhouses," he says, "and the bordellos." Your intelligence, unfaithful spy of Canaan?[18] He gives in his evidence, that "there he hath traced me." Take him at his word, readers, but let him bring good sureties ere ye dismiss him, that while he pretended to dog others, he did not turn in for his own pleasure. For so much in effect he concludes against himself, not contented to be caught in every other gin,[19] but he must be such a novice as to be still hampered in his own hemp. In the *Animadversions*,[20] saith he, I find the mention of old cloaks, false beards, nightwalkers, and salt lotion,[21] therefore, the animadverter haunts playhouses and bordellos, for if he did not, how could he speak of such gear? Now that he may know what it is to be a child, and yet to meddle with edged tools, I turn his antistrophon[22] upon his own head; the confuter knows that these things are the furniture of playhouses and bordellos, therefore by the same reason the *confuter himself hath been traced in those places.* Was it such a dissolute speech, telling of some politicians who were wont to eavesdrop in disguises, to say they were often liable to a night-walking cudgeller, or the emptying of a urinal? What if I had writ as your friend the author of the aforesaid mime, *Mundus alter et idem*,[23] to have been ravished like some young Cephalus or Hylas by a troop of camping housewives in Viraginea, and that he was there forced to swear himself an uxorious varlet, then after a long servitude to have come into Aphrodisia, that pleasant country that gave such a sweet smell to his nostrils among the shameless courtesans of Desvergonia?[24] Surely he would have then concluded me as constant at the bordello as the galley-slave at his oar.

But since there is such necessity to the hearsay of a tire,[25] a periwig, or a vizard,[26] that plays must have been seen, what difficulty was there in that, when in the colleges so many of the young divines, and those in next aptitude to divinity, have been seen so oft upon the stage writhing and unboning their clergy limbs to all the antic and dishonest gestures of Trinculos,[27] buffoons, and bawds, prostituting the shame of that ministry which either they had, or were nigh

17. **protestation:** In the Protestation of May 3, 1641, the House of Commons affirmed English opposition to Roman Catholicism and reasserted English rights and liberties.

18. Returning from *Canaan,* Moses' spies "made all the congregation to murmur against him, by bringing up a slander upon the land" (Num. 14.36).

19. **gin:** trap.

20. ***Animadversions:*** Milton's earlier antiprelatical tract, attacked in *A Modest Confutation.*

21. **salt lotion:** perhaps a euphemism for semen.

22. **antistrophon:** a rhetorical figure turning an opponent's argument against him.

23. Earlier in *An Apology,* Milton ridiculed Joseph Hall's *Mundus alter et idem* as inept and frivolous.

24. *Cephalus* was taken from his wife by Aurora (Ovid, *Met.* 7.700–713); *Hylas* was seized by Hercules (Theocritus, *Idyll 13*). *Viraginea, Aphrodisia,* and *Desvergonia* are countries in Hall's imagined world, the homes respectively of viragos, erotic love, and licentiousness.

25. **tire:** costume.

26. **vizard:** mask.

27. **Trinculos:** either the character from *The Tempest* or a clown in *Albumazar,* a 1615 Cambridge University play by Thomas Tomkys.

having, to the eyes of courtiers and court ladies with their grooms and mademoiselles? There, while they acted and overacted, among other young scholars I was a spectator. They thought themselves gallant men, and I thought them fools; they made sport, and I laughed; they mispronounced, and I misliked; and, to make up the *atticism*,[28] they were out, and I hissed. Judge now whether so many good textmen were not sufficient to instruct me of false beards and vizards without more expositors. And how can this confuter take the face to object to me the seeing of that which his reverent prelates allow, and incite their young disciples to act? For if it be unlawful[29] to sit and behold a mercenary comedian personating that which is least unseemly for a hireling to do, how much more blameful is it to endure the sight of as vile things acted by persons either entered, or presently to enter into the ministry, and how much more foul and ignominious for them to be the actors?

But because, as well by this upbraiding to me the bordellos as by other suspicious glancings in his book, he would seem privily to point me out to his readers as one whose custom of life were not honest but licentious, I shall entreat to be borne with though I digress, and in a way not often trod acquaint ye with the sum of my thoughts in this matter through the course of my years and studies, although I am not ignorant how hazardous it will be to do this under the nose of the envious, as it were in skirmish to change the compact order and instead of outward actions to bring inmost thoughts into front. And I must tell ye, readers, that by this sort of men I have been already bitten at. Yet shall they not for me know how slightly they are esteemed, unless they have so much learning as to read what in Greek Απειροκαλία[30] is, which, together with envy, is the common disease of those who censure books that are not for their reading. With me it fares now as with him whose outward garment hath been injured and ill bedighted; for having no other shift, what help but to turn the inside outwards, especially if the lining be of the same or, as it is sometimes, much better? So if my name and outward demeanor be not evident enough to defend me, I must make trial if the discovery of my inmost thoughts can. Wherein of two purposes both honest and both sincere, the one perhaps I shall not miss; although I fail to gain belief with others of being such as my perpetual thoughts shall here disclose me, I may yet not fail of success in persuading some to be such really themselves, as they cannot believe me to be more than what I fain.

I had my time, readers, as other have who have good learning bestowed upon them, to be sent to those places where, the opinion was, it might be soonest attained: and as the manner is, was not unstudied in those authors which are most commended. Whereof some were grave orators and historians, whose matter methought I loved indeed, but as my age then was, so I understood them;

28. ***atticism:*** a well-turned phrase.

29. Several months later, in September 1642, Parliament closed the theaters.

30. Απειροκαλία: bad taste that leads to immoral conduct (the term is used in Plato's ***Republic*** 403c and 405b).

others were the smooth elegiac poets, whereof the schools are not scarce, whom both for the pleasing sound of their numerous[31] writing, which in imitation I found most easy and most agreeable to nature's part in me, and for their matter, which what it is there be few who know not, I was so allured to read that no recreation came to me better welcome. For that it was then those years with me which are excused though they be least severe, I may be saved the labor to remember ye. Whence having observed them to account it the chief glory of their wit, in that they were ablest to judge, to praise, and by that could esteem themselves worthiest to love those high perfections which under one or other name they took to celebrate, I thought with myself by every instinct and presage of nature, which is not wont to be false, that what emboldened them to this task might with such diligence as they used embolden me, and that what judgment, wit, or elegance was my share, would herein best appear, and best value itself, by how much more wisely and with more love of virtue I should choose (let rude ears be absent) the object of not unlike praises. For albeit these thoughts to some will seem virtuous and commendable, to others only pardonable, to a third sort perhaps idle, yet the mentioning of them now will end in serious.[32]

Nor blame it, readers, in those years to propose to themselves such a reward as the noblest dispositions above other things in this life have sometimes preferred—whereof not to be sensible when good and fair in one person meet, argues both a gross and shallow judgment, and withal[33] an ungentle and swainish[34] breast. For by the firm settling of these persuasions I became, to my best memory, so much a proficient that, if I found those authors anywhere speaking unworthy things of themselves or unchaste of those names which before they had extolled, this effect it wrought with me, from that time forward their art I still applauded, but the men I deplored; and above them all preferred the two famous renowners of Beatrice and Laura,[35] who never write but honor of them to whom they devote their verse, displaying sublime and pure thoughts without transgression. And long it was not after when I was confirmed in this opinion, that he who would not be frustrate of his hope to write well hereafter in laudable things ought himself to be a true poem, that is, a composition and pattern of the best and honorablest things—not presuming to sing high praises of heroic men or famous cities, unless he have in himself the experience and the practice of all that which is praiseworthy. These reasonings, together with a certain niceness of nature, an honest haughtiness, and self-esteem either of what I was or what I might be (which let envy call pride), and lastly that modesty whereof, though not in the title page, yet here I may be excused to make some beseeming profession, all these uniting the supply of their natural aid together,

31. **numerous:** metrical.
32. **will end in serious:** The meaning is unclear; the text may be corrupt.
33. **withal:** in addition.
34. **swainish:** low-bred.
35. Dante and Petrarch.

kept me still above those low descents of mind beneath which he must deject and plunge himself that can agree to saleable and unlawful prostitutions.

Next (for hear me out now readers), that I may tell ye whither[36] my younger feet wandered, I betook me among those lofty fables and romances, which recount in solemn cantos the deeds of knighthood founded by our victorious kings, and from hence had in renown over all Christendom.[37] There I read it in the oath of every knight that he should defend to the expense of his best blood, or of his life if it so befell him, the honor and chastity of virgin or matron. From whence even then I learnt what a noble virtue chastity sure must be, to the defense of which so many worthies by such a dear[38] adventure of themselves had sworn. And if I found in the story afterward any of them by word or deed breaking that oath, I judged it the same fault of the poet as that which is attributed to Homer, to have written indecent things of the gods.[39] Only this my mind gave me, that every free and gentle spirit, without that oath, ought to be born a knight, nor needed to expect the gilt spur or the laying of a sword upon his shoulder to stir him up both by his counsel and his arm to secure and protect the weakness of any attempted chastity. So that even those books which to many others have been the fuel of wantonness and loose living (I cannot think how, unless by divine indulgence) proved to me so many incitements, as you have heard, to the love and steadfast observation of that virtue which abhors the society of bordellos.

Thus, from the laureate fraternity of poets, riper years and the ceaseless round of study and reading led me to the shady spaces of philosophy, but chiefly to the divine volumes of Plato and his equal Xenophon.[40] Where, if I should tell ye what I learnt of chastity and love (I mean that which is truly so, whose charming cup is only virtue which she bears in her hand to those who are worthy—the rest are cheated with a thick intoxicating potion which a certain sorceress,[41] the abuser of love's name, carries about) and how the first and chiefest office of love begins and ends in the soul, producing those happy twins of her divine generation, knowledge and virtue, with such abstracted sublimities as these, it might be worth your listening, readers, as I may one day hope to have ye in a still time, when there shall be no chiding; not in these noises, the adversary, as ye know, barking at the door or searching for me at the bordellos, where it may be he has lost himself, and raps up without pity the sage and rheumatic old prelatess with all her young Corinthian laity,[42] to inquire for such a one.

36. **whither:** the text reads "whether," which, aside from its usual meaning, was a variant spelling of "whither"; either meaning fits, but "whither" seems to be the primary sense.

37. Milton may refer to medieval romances such as Malory's *Morte d'Arthur* or to Spenser's *Faerie Queene.*

38. **dear:** costly, arduous.

39. The criticism is Plato's (*Rep.* 377e).

40. **equal:** contemporary; *Xenophon's Memorabilia* records Socrates' moral teachings.

41. **sorceress:** Circe, the mother of Milton's Comus, who also tempts with a *charming cup* (*Masque* 51, 525, 811–13).

42. **Corinthian laity:** prostitutes; the association of Corinth and prostitution is ancient.

Last of all, not in time, but as perfection is last, that care was ever had of me, with my earliest capacity, not to be negligently trained in the precepts of Christian religion. This that I have hitherto related hath been to show that though Christianity had been but slightly taught me, yet a certain reservedness of natural disposition and moral discipline learnt out of the noblest philosophy, was enough to keep me in disdain of far less incontinences than this of the bordello. But having had the doctrine of holy Scripture unfolding those chaste and high mysteries with timeliest care infused, that "the body is for the Lord and the Lord for the body" [1 Cor. 6.13], thus also I argued to myself: that if unchastity in a woman, whom Saint Paul terms the glory of man, be such a scandal and dishonor, then certainly in a man, who is both the image and glory of God, it must, though commonly not so thought, be much more deflowering and dishonorable—in that he sins both against his own body, which is the perfecter sex, and his own glory, which is in the woman, and that which is worst, against the image and glory of God, which is in himself.[43] Nor did I slumber over that place expressing such high rewards of ever accompanying the Lamb, with those celestial songs to others inapprehensible, but not to those who were not defiled with women,[44] which doubtless means fornication: for marriage must not be called a defilement.

Thus large I have purposely been, that if I have been justly taxed with this crime, it may come upon me after all this my confession with a tenfold shame.

43. "Man . . . is the image and glory of God: but the woman is the glory of the man" (1 Cor. 11.7); cp. *PL* 4.299 ("He for God only, she for God in him").
44. Rev. 14.1–5; cp. the end of *Epitaph for Damon.*

Introduction to Selections from *The Doctrine and Discipline of Divorce*

In August 1643, Milton published anonymously *The Doctrine and Discipline of Divorce: Restored to the Good of Both Sexes, from the bondage of Canon Law and other mistakes, to Christian freedom, guided by the Rule of Charity. Wherein also many places of Scripture have recovered their long-lost meaning. Seasonable to be now thought on in the Reformation intended.* Early in 1644, a greatly expanded second edition appeared with a new subtitle: *Restored to the good of both Sexes, From the bondage of Canon Law and other mistakes, to the true meaning of Scripture in the Law and Gospel compared. Wherein also are set down the bad consequences of abolishing or condemning of Sin, that which the Law of God allows, and Christ abolished not. Now the second time revised and much augmented. In Two Books: To the Parliament of* England *with the Assembly.* The second edition, from which our selections are taken, includes Milton's initials on the title page and his full name affixed to a new prefatory letter to Parliament and the Westminster Assembly.

The topic was timely for both political and personal reasons. Parliament, in its efforts to settle the English church after the toppling of episcopacy and its system of canon law, had requested advice from the overwhelmingly Presbyterian Westminster Assembly. Among the topics addressed by the Assembly were marriage and divorce. Milton at this time found himself unhappily married (or deserted rather). He had met and married Mary Powell, a woman half his age, in June or July 1642. After two mutually disappointing months, she had returned to her family in Oxfordshire, and Milton was not to see her again until 1645. While it is true, as his *Commonplace Book* reveals, that Milton had been revolving ideas about marriage and divorce before he married Mary, the shock and unhappiness of his marriage is palpable in the pages of the *Doctrine and Discipline* (see Turner 188–229; Patterson 1990; and Fallon 2000). Milton himself observes in the prefatory letter that, when approaching questions like marriage and divorce, "it is incredible how cold, how dull, and far from all fellow feeling we are, without the spur of self-concernment" (p. 108).

As in his antiprelatical tracts, Milton faults the English for lagging in reformation, in this case by retaining the restrictive canon law teaching according to which divorce was allowable only for adultery and nonconsummation. He argues for divorce on wider grounds of incompatibility, mental as well as corporeal, citing Deuteronomy 24.1–2, where Moses says a man may divorce a woman when "she find[s] no favor in his eyes, because he hath found some uncleanness in her," and Genesis 2.18, where God announces that "it is not good that man should be alone; I will make him an help meet for him."

Milton insists that he is not talking about divorce for trivial causes. As true marriage is an endlessly unfolding spiritual exchange, a bonding of souls and bodies, so divorce is permitted to set free individuals who cannot achieve this union. Some couples, because of the "faultless proprieties of nature" (p. 115) resulting from the Fall, cannot love, and therefore cannot remedy each other's loneliness. Indeed, intercourse with an unloved spouse intensifies rather than remedies that loneliness. Fornication, or Moses' "uncleanness," moreover, means for Milton not only or even especially sexual sin but "continual headstrong behavior as tends to plain contempt of the husband" (p. 157).

Milton reinterprets Christ's apparently clear prohibition of divorce except for adultery in Matthew 19:3–9 as a coded teaching aimed at hard-hearted and hypocritical Pharisees. Because the Mosaic authorization of divorce is not merely positive judicial law but part of the moral law, Christ could not have prohibited divorce without involving God in the contradiction of allowing and even encouraging the Jews to sin. The emphasis on the continuing relevance of the Mosaic moral law and its value as a guide to reading the Gospel marks a departure from the antiprelatical tracts, in which Milton bridled at his opponents' efforts to invoke Jewish ritual law as precedent and justification for episcopacy.

Milton naïvely anticipated that his argument would be welcomed by his audience, and that he would "be reckoned among the public benefactors of civil and human life; above the inventors of wine and oil" (p. 116). Instead, he found himself, as he added in the second edition, subject to "evil report" as "the sole advocate of a discountenanced truth" (p. 106). Herbert Palmer, who chaired the Assembly's committee on marriage and divorce, vilified the *Doctrine and Discipline* in an August 13, 1644, sermon to Parliament as "a wicked book . . . deserving to be burnt, whose author hath been so impudent as to set his name to it and dedicate it to yourselves." A new epigraph in the second edition bears witness to the storm of criticism that greeted Milton's defense: "He that answereth a matter before he heareth it, it is folly and shame unto him" (Prov. 18.13).

The *Doctrine and Discipline,* like his other major divorce tract, *Tetrachordon,* is a divided work (Fallon 2007). Milton on the one hand mounts an argument for divorce for mutually blameless incompatibility; on the other hand he lashes out at women for disappointing the spiritual hopes of men. He articulates an ideal of nearly egalitarian, companionate marriage, and at the same time he insists, following 1 Corinthians 11.3, that man is "the head of the other sex which was made for him." He holds out a vision of chaste, redeemed sexuality, and he describes copulation in the most degrading terms ("instead of being one flesh, they will be rather two carcasses chained unnaturally together or . . . a living soul bound to a dead corpse" [p. 151]). This last division, however, is only apparent, for it is precisely Milton's idealism about the marriage bond and married sexuality that makes the loveless copulation of an unfit couple so abhorrent.

The divisions in the tract, both real and apparent, arise from and illustrate the "spur of self-concernment." The *Doctrine and Discipline* is punctuated by third-person descriptions of the virtuous young man who, like Milton, has delayed sexual gratification only to be mistaken in his choice of a mate and robbed of divinely sanctioned corporeal and spiritual intimacy. In the antiprelatical tracts and in his early poems, Milton had constructed a self-image in which prophetic gifts and prospective literary greatness are tied to his unspotted virtue and specifically his chastity. Now he contemplates the possibility of alienation from God under the weight of an unhappy marriage, and in the nation's response to his arguments on divorce finds himself vilified as a libertine. Hoping for a helpmeet and an idealized marriage as offered by God in Genesis 2.18, Milton finds himself trapped in wedlock with a woman whom apparently he does not love and with whom as a result copulation is a grinding slavery rather than a "fountain" of "the pure influence of peace and love" arising from "the soul's lawful contentment" (p. 121). The *Doctrine and Discipline* embodies both an idealized hope and the bitterness of failed expectations.

One can read the traces of the *Doctrine and Discipline*'s wrestling with gender relations through *Paradise Lost* and beyond LaBreche. The assertion of male superiority found in the epic and the first divorce tract, however, is the common coin of Milton's time (and of the Bible). Milton's signature contribution, a vision of marriage built around the spiritual conversation between man and woman, informs his portrayal of Adam and Eve at its deepest levels. The vision is lyrically expressed, significantly by Eve, in one of the loveliest speeches in the poem ("With thee conversing I forget all time" [4.639–56]).

Ultimately, Milton's hope that he would be counted, by virtue of his argument on divorce, among "public benefactors of civil and human life" was not entirely misplaced. His conception of marriage as a union of "fit conversing soul[s]" (p. 123) and (in his best and happiest moments) as a yoking of equals or near equals was ahead of its time (Halkett 1970). If we think that unhappily married couples should be able to divorce without demonstrating adultery or their inability to consummate marriage, then we have followed Milton where virtually none of his contemporaries was willing to go. As a theorist of marriage and divorce, Milton has drawn the sustained and admiring attention of one of America's leading contemporary philosophers, Stanley Cavell, who with the poet as his powerful if improbable guide traces through Hollywood comedies the linked fates of marriage and freedom.

Our text is based on the copy of the second edition in the British Library's Thomason Collection (E.31[5]), supplemented by the identification in the Yale Prose edition of several press corrections not in our copy text.

Selections from

THE DOCTRINE AND DISCIPLINE OF DIVORCE

Matt. 13.52. Every scribe instructed to the kingdom of heaven is like the master of a house which bringeth out of his treasury things new and old.

Prov. 18.13. He that answereth a matter before he heareth it, it is folly and shame unto him.

TO THE PARLIAMENT OF ENGLAND, WITH THE ASSEMBLY.

If it were seriously asked (and it would be no untimely question, renowned Parliament, select Assembly) who of all teachers and masters that have ever taught hath drawn the most disciples after him, both in religion and in manners, it might be not untruly answered, custom.[1] Though virtue be commended for the most persuasive in her theory, and conscience in the plain demonstration of the spirit finds most evincing,[2] yet whether it be the secret of divine will or the original blindness[3] we are born in, so it happens for the most part that custom still is silently received for the best instructor. Except it be because her method is so glib and easy, in some manner like to that vision of Ezekiel,[4] rolling up her sudden book of implicit knowledge for him that will to take and swallow down at pleasure, which proving but of bad nourishment in the concoction,[5] as it was heedless in the devouring, puffs up unhealthily a certain big face of pretended learning mistaken among credulous men for the wholesome habit of soundness and good constitution, but is indeed no other than that sworn visage of counterfeit knowledge and literature, which not only in private mars our education, but

1. As in the *Tenure of Kings and Magistrates,* five years later, Milton begins with an attack on custom.
2. **evincing:** convincing.
3. **original blindness:** spiritual blindness resulting from Original Sin.
4. In Ezek. 3.1–3, the prophet consumes God's words in the form of a scroll; Milton, oddly, compares Ezekiel's roll to the false teaching of Custom. In *The Reason of Church Government,* Milton compares himself with St. John, who alludes to Ezekiel when describing in Revelation his own consumption of God's word in the form of a scroll: "though it were sweet in his mouth and in the learning, it was bitter in his belly, bitter in the denouncing" (p. 85).
5. **concoction:** digestion.

also in public is the common climber into every chair where either religion is preached or law reported; filling each estate of life and profession with abject and servile principles, depressing the high and heaven-born spirit of man far beneath the condition wherein either God created him or sin hath sunk him.[6]

To pursue the allegory, custom being but a mere face, as echo is a mere voice, rests not in her unaccomplishment until by secret inclination she accorporate[7] herself with error, who being a blind and serpentine body[8] without a head willingly accepts what he wants and supplies what her incompleteness went seeking. Hence it is that error supports custom, custom countenances error. And these two between them would persecute and chase away all truth and solid wisdom out of humane life, were it not that God, rather than man, once in many ages calls together the prudent and religious counsels of men deputed to repress the encroachments and to work off the inveterate blots and obscurities wrought upon our minds by the subtle insinuating of error and custom: who, with the numerous and vulgar train of their followers, make it their chief design to envy and cry down the industry of free reasoning under the terms of humor[9] and innovation,[10] as if the womb of teeming truth were to be closed up if she presume to bring forth aught that sorts not with their unchewed notions and suppositions. Against which notorious injury and abuse of man's free soul to testify and oppose the utmost that study and true labor can attain, heretofore the incitement of men reputed grave hath led me among others. And now the duty and the right of an instructed Christian calls me through the chance of good or evil report, to be the sole advocate of a discountenanced truth:[11] a high enterprise, Lords and Commons, a high enterprise and a hard, and such as every seventh son of a seventh son[12] does not venture on.

Nor have I amidst the clamor of so much envy and impertinence whither to appeal, but to the concourse of so much piety and wisdom here assembled. Bringing in my hands an ancient and most necessary, most charitable, and yet most injured statute of Moses[13]: not repealed ever by him who only had the authority,[14] but thrown aside with much inconsiderate neglect under the rubbish of canonical ignorance, as once the whole law was by some such like con-

6. Milton suggests that, by blindly following custom, we bring ourselves lower than we have been brought by Original Sin, thus implying, as he argues in *Christian Doctrine* (1.7), that the human race is not wholly depraved after the Fall.

7. **accorporate:** incorporate.

8. **serpentine body:** Milton borrows from Spenser's allegorical embodiment of Error (*FQ* 1.1.13-24).

9. **humor:** fancy (literally, an idea resulting not from reason but from the predominance of one of the four bodily humors or fluids—blood, phlegm, black bile, and yellow bile).

10. **innovation:** Milton is anxious to deflect the charge that his argument is unprecedented (thus the title, *Doctrine and Discipline of Divorce: Restored* . . .).

11. While Milton was relatively late in his attack on episcopacy, he was far ahead of his time in his argument for divorce on the grounds of mutual incompatibility.

12. **seventh son of a seventh son:** one marked out for greatness.

13. **statute of Moses:** The Mosaic Law allowing divorce in Deut. 24.1–2.

14. I.e., Jesus.

veyance[15] in Josiah's time.[16] And he who shall endeavor the amendment of any old neglected grievance in church or state, or in the daily course of life, if he be gifted with abilities of mind that may raise him to so high an undertaking, I grant he hath already much whereof not to repent him. Yet let me aread[17] him, not to be the foreman of any misjudged opinion, unless his resolutions be firmly seated in a square and constant mind, not conscious to itself of any deserved blame, and regardless of ungrounded suspicions. For this let him be sure, he shall be boarded[18] presently by the ruder sort, but not by discreet and well-nurtured men, with a thousand idle descants[19] and surmises. Who when they cannot confute the least joint or sinew of any passage in the book, yet God forbid that truth should be truth, because they have a boisterous conceit of some pretences in the writer. But were they not more busy and inquisitive than the apostle[20] commends, they would hear him at least, "rejoicing, so the truth be preached, whether of envy or other pretence whatsoever." For truth is as impossible to be soiled by any outward touch as the sunbeam. Though this ill hap wait on her nativity, that she never comes into the world but like a bastard to the ignominy of him that brought her forth: till time, the midwife rather than the mother of truth, have washed and salted the infant, declared her legitimate, and churched the father of his young Minerva, from the needless causes of his purgation.[21] Yourselves can best witness this, worthy patriots, and better will, no doubt, hereafter. For who among ye of the foremost that have travailed in her behalf to the good of church or state, hath not been often traduced to be the agent of his own by-ends, under pretext of reformation. So much the more I shall not be unjust to hope that however infamy or envy may work in other men to do her fretful will against this discourse, yet that the experience of your own uprightness misinterpreted will put ye in mind to give it free audience and generous construction.

What though the brood of Belial,[22] the draff of men, to whom no liberty is pleasing, but unbridled and vagabond lust without pale or partition, will laugh broad perhaps to see so great a strength of scripture mustering up in favor, as they suppose, of their debaucheries? They will know better when they shall hence learn that honest liberty is the greatest foe to dishonest license. And what

15. **conveyance:** underhanded dealing.
16. See 2 Kings 22 and 23.
17. **aread:** advise, counsel.
18. **boarded:** attacked.
19. **descants:** remarks or criticisms.
20. **apostle:** Paul (Milton paraphrases Phil. 1.18).
21. Having given birth to his controversial argument as Jupiter gave birth to Minerva (or Wisdom), Milton expects to be misjudged as unclean, like the Hebrew and Anglican women subject to purification (Anglican "churching") after childbirth.
22. **brood of Belial:** The "children of Belial" is a label for enemies of God in Deut. 13.13 and Judg. 19.22. Milton, who would come to associate the term with the dissoluteness of the Cavaliers, condemns "the sons/Of Belial, flown with insolence and wine" (*PL* 1.501–2).

though others out of a waterish and queasy conscience, because ever crazy and never yet sound, will rail and fancy to themselves that injury and license is the best of this book? Did not the distemper of their own stomachs affect them with a dizzy megrim,[23] they would soon tie up their tongues, and discern themselves like that Assyrian blasphemer,[24] all this while reproaching not man but the Almighty, "the holy one of Israel," whom they do not deny to have belawgiven[25] his own sacred people with this very allowance which they now call injury and license and dare cry shame on, and will do yet a while, till they get a little cordial sobriety to settle their qualming zeal.

But this question concerns not us perhaps. Indeed man's disposition though prone to search after vain curiosities, yet when points of difficulty are to be discussed, appertaining to the removal of unreasonable wrong and burden from the perplexed life of our brother, it is incredible how cold, how dull, and far from all fellow feeling we are, without the spur of self-concernment. Yet if the wisdom, the justice, the purity of God be to be cleared from foulest imputations which are not yet avoided, if charity be not to be degraded and trodden down under a civil ordinance, if matrimony be not to be advanced like that exalted perdition, written of to the Thessalonians, "above all that is called God,"[26] or goodness, nay, against them both, then I dare affirm there will be found in the contents of this book that which may concern us all. You it concerns chiefly, worthies in Parliament, on whom, as on our deliverers, all our grievances and cares by the merit of your eminence and fortitude are devolved. Me it concerns next, having with much labor and faithful diligence first found out, or at least with a fearless and communicative candor first published to the manifest good of Christendom, that which, calling to witness every thing mortal and immortal, I believe unfeignedly to be true. Let not other men think their conscience bound to search continually after truth, to pray for enlightening from above to publish what they think they have so obtained, and debar me from conceiving myself tied by the same duties.

Ye have now, doubtless by the favor and appointment of God, ye have now in your hands a great and populous nation to reform; from what corruption, what blindness in religion, ye know well; in what a degenerate and fallen spirit from the apprehension of native liberty and true manliness, I'm sure ye find: with what unbounded license rushing to whoredoms and adulteries, needs not long enquiry: insomuch that the fears which men have of too strict a discipline perhaps exceed the hopes that can be in others of ever introducing it with any great success. What if I should tell ye now of dispensations and indulgences,[27]

23. **megrim:** headache, migraine.
24. **Assyrian blasphemer:** Milton paraphrases and quotes Isaiah's rebuke of Sennacherib, king of Assyria (2 Kings 19.22).
25. **belawgiven:** provided with a system of laws (Milton's coinage, not to our knowledge taken up by others).
26. To set (mistaken) marriage law above Christian charity is to repeat the error of "the son of *perdition*" who "*exalteth* himself above all that is called God" (2 Thess. 2.3–4).
27. **indulgences:** Milton suggests that if divorce is sinful, the Mosaic Law allowing it resembles the corrupt Roman Catholic doctrine of indulgences, which allowed the wealthy to buy their way out of sins.

to give a little the reins, to let them play and nibble with the bait a while; a people as hard of heart as that Egyptian colony[28] that went to Canaan. This is the common doctrine that adulterous and injurious divorces were not connived only, but with eye open allowed of old for hardness of heart. But that opinion, I trust, by then this following argument hath been well read, will be left for one of the mysteries of an indulgent antichrist to farm out incest by and those his other tributary pollutions. What middle way can be taken then, may some interrupt, if we must neither turn to the right nor to the left,[29] and that the people hate to be reformed? Mark then, judges and lawgivers, and ye whose office is to be our teachers, for I will utter now a doctrine, if ever any other, though neglected or not understood, yet of great and powerful importance to the governing of mankind. He who wisely would restrain the reasonable soul of man within due bounds, must first himself know perfectly how far the territory and dominion extends of just and honest liberty. As little must he offer to bind that which God hath loosened, as to loosen that which he hath bound. The ignorance and mistake of this high point hath heaped up one huge half of all the misery that hath been since Adam. In the Gospel we shall read a supercilious crew of masters, whose holiness, or rather whose evil eye, grieving that God should be so facile to man, was to set straiter limits to obedience than God had set, to enslave the dignity of man, to put a garrison upon his neck of empty and over-dignified precepts. And we shall read our Savior never more grieved and troubled than to meet with such a peevish madness among men against their own freedom.[30] How can we expect him to be less offended with us, when much of the same folly shall be found yet remaining where it least ought, to the perishing of thousands.

The greatest burden in the world is superstition, not only of ceremonies in the church but of imaginary and scarecrow sins at home. What greater weakening, what more subtle stratagem against our Christian warfare,[31] when, besides the gross body of real transgressions to encounter, we shall be terrified by a vain and shadowy menacing of faults that are not? When things indifferent[32] shall be set to overfront us under the banners of sin, what wonder if we be routed, and by this art of our adversary fall into the subjection of worst and deadliest offences. The superstition of the papist is, "touch not, taste not" [Col. 2.21],[33] when God bids both, and ours is, "part not, separate not," when God and charity both permits and commands. "Let all your things be done with charity," saith St. Paul

28. **Egyptian colony:** the Israelites, whose "hardness of heart," according to Jesus in Matt. 19.8 and Mark 10.5, was the reason Mosaic Law allowed divorce; Milton will reinterpret these passages.

29. See 2 Chron. 34.2.

30. Christ (Matt. 23) reprimanded the Pharisees for enforcing religious laws stricter than those in the Bible.

31. For *Christian warfare*, see 2 Cor. 10.4 and 1 Tim. 1.18; see also *Areop* (p. 187).

32. **things indifferent:** actions neither commanded nor forbidden in Scripture.

33. Milton quotes Paul's rebuke to those who, despite living in Christ, still consider themselves "subject to ordinances."

[1 Cor. 16.14], and his master saith, "She is the fulfilling of the Law" [Rom. 13.10].[34] Yet now a civil, an indifferent, a sometime dissuaded law of marriage, must be forced upon us to fulfill, not only without charity but against her. No place in heaven or earth, except hell, where charity may not enter: yet marriage, the ordinance of our solace and contentment, the remedy of our loneliness, will not admit now either of charity or mercy to come in and mediate or pacify the fierceness of this gentle ordinance, the unremedied loneliness of this remedy.

Advise ye well, supreme senate, if charity be thus excluded and expulsed, how ye will defend the untainted honor of your own actions and proceedings. He who marries, intends as little to conspire his own ruin, as he that swears allegiance: and as a whole people is in proportion to an ill government, so is one man to an ill marriage.[35] If they, against any authority, covenant, or statute, may by the sovereign edict of charity save not only their lives but honest liberties from unworthy bondage, as well may he against any private covenant, which he never entered to his mischief, redeem himself from unsupportable disturbances to honest peace and just contentment. And much the rather, for that to resist the highest magistrate though tyrannizing God never gave us express allowance, only he gave us reason, charity, nature, and good example to bear us out; but in this economical[36] misfortune thus to demean ourselves, besides the warrant of those four great directors,[37] which doth as justly belong hither, we have an express law of God, and such a law as whereof our Savior with a solemn threat forbid the abrogating.[38] For no effect of tyranny can sit more heavy on the commonwealth than this household unhappiness on the family. And farewell all hope of true reformation in the state, while such an evil as this lies undiscerned or unregarded in the house: on the redress whereof depends not only the spiritful and orderly life of our grown men, but the willing and careful education of our children.

Let this, therefore, be new examined: this tenure and freehold of mankind, this native and domestic charter given us by a greater Lord than that Saxon king the Confessor.[39] Let the statutes of God be turned over, be scanned anew, and considered, not altogether by the narrow intellectuals of quotationists and commonplacers, but (as was the ancient right of councils)[40] by men of what liberal profession soever, of eminent spirit and breeding joined with a diffuse and various knowledge of divine and human things; able to balance and define good

34. Milton in fact quotes Paul, not *his master,* Jesus, but Paul echoes here Jesus' teaching in Matt. 22.37–40. For the conception of Christian liberty, centrally important to Milton, see Barker (1942) and Bennett.

35. Ingeniously, Milton relates the spouse asserting a right to freedom from a bad marriage to his audience in Parliament, who had asserted their right to freedom from the misgovernment of Charles I and his advisers. On seventeenth-century authors' application of family analogies and metaphors in political contexts, see Ng.

36. **economical:** household, domestic (the Greek root *oikos* means "household").

37. **four great directors:** i.e., the gifts enumerated earlier in the sentence.

38. Christ insists that "one jot or one tittle shall in no wise pass from the law" (Matt. 5.18).

39. Edward the Confessor (d. 1066), last of the Saxon kings, was widely and deeply revered.

40. Milton consistently championed the role of laypersons in theological and ecclesiastical deliberation.

and evil, right and wrong, throughout every state of life; able to show us the ways of the Lord, straight and faithful as they are, not full of cranks and contradictions and pit-falling dispenses, but with divine insight and benignity measured out to the proportion of each mind and spirit, each temper and disposition, created so different each from other, and yet by the skill of wise conducting all to become uniform in virtue.

To expedite these knots were worthy a learned and memorable Synod; while our enemies expect to see the expectation of the church tired out with dependencies and independencies[41] how they will compound, and in what calends.[42] Doubt not, worthy senators, to vindicate the sacred honor and judgment of Moses, your predecessor, from the shallow commenting of scholastics and canonists. Doubt not after him to reach out your steady hands to the misinformed and wearied life of man, to restore this his lost heritage into the household state. Wherewith be sure that peace and love, the best subsistence of a Christian family, will return home from whence they are now banished; places of prostitution will be less haunted, the neighbor's bed less attempted, the yoke of prudent and manly discipline will be generally submitted to; sober and well ordered living will soon spring up in the commonwealth.

Ye have an author great beyond exception, Moses; and one yet greater, he who hedged in from abolishing every smallest jot and tittle[43] of precious equity contained in that Law, with a more accurate and lasting Masoreth[44] than either the synagogue of Ezra,[45] or the Galilean school at Tiberias[46] hath left us. Whatever else ye can enact, will scarce concern a third part of the British name, but the benefit and good of this your magnanimous example will easily spread far beyond the banks of Tweed and the Norman isles.[47] It would not be the first or second time since our ancient druids (by whom this island was the cathedral of philosophy to France) left off their pagan rites, that England hath had this honor vouchsafed from heaven, to give out reformation to the world. Who was it but our English Constantine[48] that baptized the Roman Empire? Who but the Northumbrian Willibrode and Winifride of Devon[49] with their followers were the first apostles of Germany? Who but Alcuin[50] and Wyckliffe[51] our country-

41. **dependencies and independencies:** Presbyterians and Independents.
42. **calends:** date.
43. See note 37.
44. **Masoreth:** rabbinical scholars' textual commentary on the Hebrew Scriptures in the form of marginal notes.
45. **synagogue of Ezra:** established in the time of Ezra (fifth century B.C.E.), the "Great Synagogue" assumed the responsibility of maintaining the text of the Torah.
46. **Tiberias:** famous center of rabbinical scholarship on the Sea of Galilee.
47. **Norman isles:** the Channel Islands.
48. Milton shared the erroneous belief that the Emperor Constantine, who Christianized the Roman Empire, was English by birth.
49. *Willibrode* and *Winifride*, also known as St. Boniface, evangelized parts of Germany. They were successively bishops of Utrecht in the eighth century.
50. **Alcuin:** Alcuin, one of the leading intellectual figures of his age, was instrumental in the revival of learning at the court of Charlemagne in the eighth century.
51. **Wycliffe:** John Wycliffe was a fourteenth-century harbinger of the Reformation.

men opened the eyes of Europe, the one in arts, the other in religion. Let not England forget her precedence of teaching nations how to live.

Know, worthies, know and exercise the privilege of your honored country. A greater title I here bring ye than is either in the power or in the policy of Rome to give her monarchs. This glorious act will style ye the defenders of charity.[52] Nor is this yet the highest inscription that will adorn so religious and so holy a defense as this. Behold here the pure and sacred law of God and his yet purer and more sacred name, offering themselves to you first, of all Christian reformers, to be acquitted from the long suffered ungodly attribute of patronizing adultery. Defer not to wipe off instantly these imputative blurs and stains cast by rude fancies upon the throne and beauty itself of inviolable holiness, lest some other people more devout and wise than we bereave us this offered immortal glory, our wonted prerogative, of being the first asserters in every great vindication.

For me, as far as my part leads me, I have already my greatest gain, assurance and inward satisfaction to have done in this nothing unworthy of an honest life and studies well employed. With what event among the wise and right understanding handful of men I am secure. But how among the drove of custom and prejudice this will be relished by such whose capacity, since their youth run ahead into the easy creek of a system or a medulla,[53] sails there at will under the blown physiognomy of their unlabored rudiments; for them what their taste will be, I have also surety sufficient, from the entire league that hath been ever between formal ignorance and grave obstinacy. Yet, when I remember the little that our savior could prevail about this doctrine of charity against the crabbed textuists of his time, I make no wonder, but rest confident that who so prefers either matrimony or other ordinance before the good of man and the plain exigence of charity, let him profess papist, or Protestant, or what he will, he is no better than a pharisee and understands not the Gospel: whom as a misinterpreter of Christ I openly protest against, and provoke him to the trial of this truth before all the world. And let him bethink him withal how he will solder up the shifting flaws of his ungirt permissions, his venial and unvenial dispenses,[54] wherewith the law of God pardoning and unpardoning hath been shamefully branded for want of heed in glossing, to have eluded and baffled out all faith and chastity from the marriage bed of that holy seed with politic and judicial adulteries.

I seek not to seduce the simple and illiterate. My errand is to find out the choicest and the learnedest, who have this high gift of wisdom to answer solidly or to be convinced. I crave it from the piety, the learning, and the prudence which is housed in this place. It might perhaps more fitly have been written in

52. Milton echoes the title held by British monarchs since 1521, "Defender of the Faith."

53. **medulla:** marrow; used in titles of various digests of knowledge, notably William Ames's 1623 *Medulla Theologica,* which influenced Milton's *Christian Doctrine.*

54. **venial and unvenial dispenses:** dispensations for minor and mortal sins.

another tongue, and I had done so, but that the esteem I have of my country's judgment and the love I bear to my native language to serve it first with what I endeavor, made me speak it thus, ere I assay the verdict of outlandish readers.[55] And perhaps also here I might have ended nameless, but that the address of these lines chiefly to the Parliament of England might have seemed ungrateful not to acknowledge by whose religious care, unwearied watchfulness, courageous and heroic resolutions, I enjoy the peace and studious leisure to remain,

The honorer and attendant of their noble worth and virtues,

John Milton

THE DOCTRINE AND DISCIPLINE OF DIVORCE;

Restored to the good of both sexes

BOOK I

THE PREFACE.

That man is the occasion of his own miseries in most of those evils which he imputes to God's inflicting. The absurdity of our canonists in their decrees about divorce. The Christian imperial laws framed with more equity. The opinion of Hugo Grotius, *and* Paulus Fagius: *And the purpose, in general, of this discourse.*

Many men, whether it be their fate or fond[56] opinion, easily persuade themselves, if God would but be pleased a while to withdraw his just punishments from us and to restrain what power either the devil or any earthly enemy hath to work us woe, that then man's nature would find immediate rest and releasement from all evils. But verily they who think so, if they be such as have a mind large enough to take into their thoughts a general survey of human things, would soon prove themselves in that opinion far deceived. For though it were granted us by divine indulgence to be exempt from all that can be harmful to us from without, yet the perverseness of our folly is so bent that we should never lin[57] hammering out of our own hearts, as it were out of a flint, the seeds and sparkles of new misery to ourselves, till all were in a blaze again. And no marvel if out of our own hearts, for they are evil; but even out of those things which God meant us either for a principal good or a pure contentment, we are still hatching and contriving upon ourselves matter of continual sorrow and perplexity. What greater good to man than that revealed rule whereby God vouch-

55. Stung by the outcry against his writings on divorce, Milton would come to regret having published them in English. See *2Def.* "One thing only could I wish, that I had not written it in the vernacular, for then I would not have met with vernacular readers, who are usually ignorant of their own good, and laugh at the misfortunes of others" (p. 341).

56. **fond:** foolish.

57. **lin:** cease.

safes to show us how he would be worshipped? And yet that not rightly understood became the cause that once a famous man in Israel could not but oblige his conscience to be the sacrificer, or, if not, the jailor of his innocent and only daughter;[58] and was the cause ofttimes that armies of valiant men have given up their throats to a heathenish enemy on the Sabbath day, fondly thinking their defensive resistance to be as then a work unlawful.[59]

What thing more instituted to the solace and delight of man than marriage? And yet the misinterpreting of some scripture directed mainly against the abusers of the law for divorce given by Moses[60] hath changed the blessing of matrimony not seldom into a familiar and coinhabiting mischief, at least into a drooping and disconsolate household captivity without refuge or redemption. So ungoverned and so wild a race doth superstition run us from one extreme of abused liberty into the other of unmerciful restraint. For although God in the first ordaining of marriage taught us to what end he did it, in words expressly implying the apt and cheerful conversation[61] of man with woman, to comfort and refresh him against the evil of solitary life, not mentioning the purpose of generation till afterwards, as being but a secondary end in dignity, though not in necessity; yet now, if any two be but once handed in the church and have tasted in any sort the nuptial bed, let them find themselves never so mistaken in their dispositions through any error, concealment, or misadventure, that through their different tempers, thoughts, and constitutions, they can neither be to one another a remedy against loneliness, nor live in any union or contentment all their days, yet they shall, so they be but found suitably weaponed to the least possibility of sensual enjoyment, be made, spite of antipathy,[62] to fadge together and combine as they may to their unspeakable wearisomeness and despair of all sociable delight in the ordinance which God established to that very end.

What a calamity is this, and as the wise man, if he were alive, would sigh out in his own phrase, what a "sore evil is this under the sun!"[63] All which we can refer justly to no other author than the canon law[64] and her adherents, not consulting with charity, the interpreter and guide of our faith, but resting in the mere element of the text; doubtless by the policy of the devil to make that gracious ordinance become unsupportable, that what with men not daring to venture upon wedlock, and what with men wearied out of it, all inordinate license might abound.

58. For the story of Jephthah, which recalls the story of Agamemnon and Iphigenia, see Judg. 11.29–40.

59. Mattathias's followers, for example, attacked by Antiochus on the Sabbath, allowed themselves to be massacred (1 Macc. 2.31–38).

60. See the discussion of Matt. 5.31–32 in 2.8.

61. **conversation:** companionship, intimacy.

62. **antipathy:** an incompatibility grounded in nature and therefore involuntary; this conception will play a major role in Milton's argument for divorce. See, e.g., his reference two paragraphs hence to the "faultless proprieties of nature" and the "secret power of nature's impression." On the implications of Milton's argument for the question of freedom and necessity, see Nichols.

63. Eccles. 5.13; the *wise man* is Solomon.

64. **canon law:** ecclesiastical or church law.

It was for many ages that marriage lay in disgrace with most of the ancient doctors as a work of the flesh, almost a defilement, wholly denied to priests and the second time dissuaded to all, as he that reads Tertullian or Jerome[65] may see at large. Afterwards it was thought so sacramental that no adultery or desertion could dissolve it, and this is the sense of our canon courts in England to this day, but in no other reformed church else.[66] Yet there remains in them also a burden on it as heavy as the other two were disgraceful or superstitious, and of as much iniquity, crossing a law not only written by Moses, but charactered in us by nature, of more antiquity and deeper ground than marriage itself; which law is to force nothing against the faultless proprieties of nature. Yet that this may be colorably done, our Savior's words touching divorce are as it were congealed into a stony rigor, inconsistent both with his doctrine and his office, and that which he preached only to the conscience is by canonical tyranny snatched into the compulsive censure of a judicial court, where laws are imposed even against the venerable and secret power of nature's impression, to love whatever cause be found to loathe—which is a heinous barbarism both against the honor of marriage, the dignity of man and his soul, the goodness of Christianity, and all the humane respects of civility. Notwithstanding that some the wisest and gravest among the Christian Emperors who had about them to consult with, those of the Fathers then living, who for their learning and holiness of life are still with us in great renown, have made their statutes and edicts concerning this debate far more easy and relenting in many necessary cases, wherein the canon is inflexible. And Hugo Grotius,[67] a man of these times, one of the best learned, seems not obscurely to adhere in his persuasion to the equity of those imperial decrees in his notes upon the Evangelists, much allaying the outward roughness of the text, which hath for the most part been too immoderately expounded, and excites the diligence of others to enquire further into this question, as containing many points that have not yet been explained. Which ever likely to remain intricate and hopeless upon the suppositions commonly stuck to, the authority of Paulus Fagius,[68] one so learned and so eminent in England once, if it might persuade, would straight acquaint us with a solution of these differences, no less prudent than compendious. He, in his comment on the Pentateuch, doubted not to maintain that divorces might be as lawfully permitted by the magistrate to Christians as they were to the Jews.

65. *Tertullian* (c. 160–c. 230) and *St. Jerome* (c. 340–420) emphasized the superiority of the celibate life to the married life. Chaucer's Wife of Bath in her Prologue (674–76) also yokes the two church fathers in her criticism of the church's hostility to sexuality.

66. The Anglican Church, to Milton's dismay, is aligned with the Roman Catholic Church against the continental Protestant churches in its assertion of the sacramental nature and indissolubility of marriage.

67. **Hugo Grotius:** In arguing for divorce, Milton was influenced by the *Annotationes in Libros Evangeliorum* (1641) of the eminent Dutch scholar Hugo Grotius (1583–1645) who like Milton treated the fall of man in verse, in his 1601 *Adamus Exul.* Milton met Grotius in Paris in 1638.

68. **Paulus Fagius:** The eminent German reformer Paulus Fagius (1504–49) spent the last months of his life in England as Cambridge's Professor of Hebrew. He became a hero of the Protestant cause after his body was disinterred and desecrated during Mary's reign.

But because he is but brief, and these things of great consequence not to be kept obscure, I shall conceive it nothing above my duty, either for the difficulty or the censure that may pass thereon, to communicate such thoughts as I also have had, and do offer them now in this general labor of reformation to the candid view both of church and magistrate; especially because I see it the hope of good men, that those irregular and unspiritual courts have spun their utmost date in this land; and some better course must now be constituted.[69] This, therefore, shall be the task and period[70] of this discourse to prove, first, that other reasons of divorce besides adultery were by the Law of Moses, and are yet to be allowed by the Christian magistrate as a piece of justice, and that the words of Christ are not hereby contraried. Next, that to prohibit absolutely any divorce whatsoever, except those which Moses excepted, is against the reason of law, as in due place I shall show out of Fagius, with many additions. He, therefore, who by adventuring shall be so happy as with success to light the way of such an expedient liberty and truth as this, shall restore the much wronged and over-sorrowed state of matrimony, not only to those merciful and life-giving remedies of Moses, but, as much as may be, to that serene and blissful condition it was in at the beginning;[71] and shall deserve of all apprehensive men (considering the troubles and distempers which for want of this insight have been so oft in kingdoms, in states and families) shall deserve to be reckoned among the public benefactors of civil and human life; above the inventors of wine and oil. For this is a far dearer, far nobler, and more desirable cherishing to man's life, unworthily exposed to sadness and mistake, which he shall vindicate.

Not that license and levity and unconsented breach of faith should herein be countenanced, but that some conscionable and tender pity might be had of those who have unwarily, in a thing they never practiced before, made themselves the bondmen of a luckless and helpless matrimony. In which argument, he whose courage can serve him to give the first onset, must look for two several oppositions: the one from those who having sworn themselves to long custom and the letter of the text, will not out of the road; the other from those whose gross and vulgar apprehensions conceit but low of matrimonial purposes, and in the work of male and female think they have all. Nevertheless, it shall be here sought by due ways to be made appear that those words of God in the institution, promising a meet help against loneliness,[72] and those words of Christ, "That his yoke is easy, and his burden light" [Matt. 11.30], were not spoken in vain; for if the knot of marriage may in no case be dissolved but for adultery, all the burdens and services of the Law are not so intolerable.

69. Milton sees Parliament's recent abolition of ecclesiastical courts as an opportunity to reform marriage and divorce law in England.

70. **period:** aim.

71. I.e., in Eden before the Fall.

72. "And God said, It is not good that man should be alone" (Gen. 2.18).

This only is desired of them who are minded to judge hardly of thus maintaining, that they would be still and hear all out, nor think it equal to answer deliberate reason with sudden heat and noise; remembering this, that many truths now of reverend esteem and credit had their birth and beginning once from singular and private thoughts, while the most of men were otherwise possessed, and had the fate at first to be generally exploded and exclaimed on by many violent opposers. Yet I may err perhaps in soothing myself that this present truth revived will deserve on all hands to be not sinisterly received,[73] in that it undertakes the cure of an inveterate disease crept into the best part of human society; and to do this with no smarting corrosive, but with a smooth and pleasing lesson, which received hath the virtue to soften and dispel rooted and knotty sorrows; and, without enchantment (if that be feared) or spell used, hath regard at once both to serious pity and upright honesty that tends to the redeeming and restoring of none but such as are the object of compassion, having in an ill hour hampered themselves to the utter dispatch of all their most beloved comforts and repose for this life's term.

But if we shall obstinately dislike this new overture of unexpected ease and recovery, what remains but to deplore the frowardness of our hopeless condition, which neither can endure the estate we are in, nor admit of remedy either sharp or sweet. Sharp we ourselves distaste, and sweet, under whose hands we are, is scrupled and suspected as too luscious. In such a posture Christ found the Jews, who were neither won with the austerity of John the Baptist, and thought it too much license to follow freely the charming pipe of him who sounded and proclaimed liberty and relief to all distresses. Yet truth, in some age or other, will find her witness and shall be justified at last by her own children.[74]

CHAP. I

The position, proved by the Law of Moses. That Law expounded and asserted to a moral and charitable use, first by Paulus Fagius, *next with other additions.*

To remove, therefore, if it be possible, this great and sad oppression which through the strictness of a literal interpreting hath invaded and disturbed the dearest and most peaceable estate of household society, to the over-burdening if not the over-whelming of many Christians better worth than to be so deserted of the church's considerate care, this position shall be laid down, first proving, then answering what may be objected either from scripture or light of reason:

73. As is often the case, Milton's syntax becomes knotted when he writes about how his motives and actions will be judged.

74. See Luke 7.31–35 and Matt. 11.16–19 for Jesus' comment on those who found John the Baptist's model too severe and his own too permissive. The passage in Luke ends, "Wisdom is justified of all her children."

That indisposition, unfitness, or contrariety of mind, arising from a cause in nature unchangeable, hindering and ever likely to hinder the main benefits of conjugal society, which are solace and peace, is a greater reason of divorce than natural frigidity, especially if there be no children, and that there be mutual consent.

This I gather from the Law in Deut. 24.1: "When a man hath taken a wife and married her, and it come to pass that she find no favor in his eyes, because he hath found some uncleanness in her, let him write her a bill of divorcement, and give it in her hand, and send her out of his house," etc. This law, if the words of Christ may be admitted into our belief, shall never, while the world stands, for him be abrogated. First, therefore, I here set down what learned Fagius hath observed on this law: "the law of God," saith he, "permitted divorce for the help of human weakness. For every one that of necessity separates, cannot live single. That Christ denied divorce to his own hinders not, for what is that to the unregenerate, who hath not attained such perfection? Let not the remedy be despised which was given to weakness. And when Christ saith, who marries the divorced commits adultery, it is to be understood if he had any plot in the divorce." The rest I reserve until it be disputed how the magistrate is to do herein. From hence we may plainly discern a twofold consideration in this law: first, the end of the lawgiver and the proper act of the law, to command or to allow something just and honest or indifferent; secondly, his sufferance from some accidental result of evil by this allowance, which the law cannot remedy. For if this law have no other end or act but only the allowance of a sin, though never to so good intention, that law is no law but sin muffled in the robe of law, or law disguised in the loose garment of sin. Both which are too foul hypotheses to save the phenomenon of our Savior's answer to the Pharisees about this matter.[75] And I trust anon by the help of an infallible guide to perfect such Prutenic tables[76] as shall mend the astronomy of our wide expositors.

The cause of divorce mentioned in the law is translated "some uncleanness," but in the Hebrew it sounds "nakedness of aught, or any real nakedness," which by all the learned interpreters is referred to the mind as well as to the body. And what greater nakedness or unfitness of mind than that which hinders ever the solace and peaceful society of the married couple, and what hinders that more than the unfitness and defectiveness of an unconjugal mind? The cause, therefore, of divorce expressed in the position cannot but agree with that described in the best and equalest sense of Moses' Law. Which, being a matter of pure charity, is plainly moral, and more now in force than ever, therefore surely lawful. For if under the Law such was God's gracious indulgence as not to suffer the ordinance of his goodness and favor through any error to be seared and

75. See Matt. 19.3–9; see 2.1.

76. **Prutenic tables:** Copernicus's planetary tables, published under a title honoring the Duke of Prussia in 1551; they were superseded by Kepler's Rudolphine tables in 1627. Milton's appropriate reference to outmoded tables demonstrates scientific knowledge and rhetorical adroitness.

stigmatized upon his servants to their misery and thraldom, much less will he suffer it now under the covenant of grace, by abrogating his former grant of remedy and relief. But the first institution will be objected to have ordained marriage inseparable. To that a little patience until this first part have amply discoursed the grave and pious reasons of this divorcive law, and then I doubt not but with one gentle stroking to wipe away ten thousand tears out of the life of man. Yet thus much I shall now insist on, that whatever the institution were, it could not be so enormous,[77] nor so rebellious against both nature and reason, as to exalt itself above the end and person for whom it was instituted.

CHAP. 2

The first reason of this law grounded on the prime reason of matrimony. That no covenant whatsoever obliges against the main end both of itself and of the parties covenanting.

For all sense and equity reclaims[78] that any law or covenant, how solemn or strait soever, either between God and man, or man and man, though of God's joining, should bind against a prime and principal scope of its own institution, and of both or either party covenanting: neither can it be of force to engage a blameless creature to his own perpetual sorrow, mistaken for his expected solace, without suffering charity to step in and do a confessed good work of parting those whom nothing holds together but this of God's joining, falsely supposed against the express end of his own ordinance. And what his chief end was of creating woman to be joined with man, his own instituting words declare, and are infallible to inform us what is marriage and what is no marriage, unless we can think them set there to no purpose: "It is not good," saith he, "that man should be alone; I will make him a helpmeet for him" [Gen. 2.18]. From which words so plain, less cannot be concluded, nor is by any learned interpreter, than that in God's intention a meet and happy conversation is the chiefest and the noblest end of marriage, for we find here no expression so necessarily implying carnal knowledge as this prevention of loneliness to the mind and spirit of man. To this, Fagius, Calvin, Paræus, Rivetus,[79] as willingly and largely assent as can be wished.

And indeed it is a greater blessing from God, more worthy so excellent a creature as man is, and a higher end to honor and sanctify the league of marriage, whenas the solace and satisfaction of the mind is regarded and provided for before the sensitive pleasing of the body. And with all generous persons married thus it is that where the mind and person pleases aptly, there some unaccomplishment of the body's delight may be better born with than when the

77. **enormous:** outside the rule (or "norm").
78. **reclaims:** vigorously denies.
79. David *Paræus* (1548–1622) and André *Rivet* (1572–1651) were prominent Calvinist theologians.

mind hangs off in an unclosing disproportion, though the body be as it ought; for there all corporal delight will soon become unsavory and contemptible. And the solitariness of man, which God had namely and principally ordered to prevent by marriage, hath no remedy, but lies under a worse condition than the loneliest single life. For in single life the absence and remoteness of a helper might inure him to expect his own comforts out of himself, or to seek with hope, but here the continual sight of his deluded thoughts, without cure, must needs be to him, if especially his complexion[80] incline him to melancholy, a daily trouble and pain of loss in some degree like that which reprobates feel.

Lest therefore so noble a creature as man should be shut up incurably under a worse evil by an easy mistake in that ordinance which God gave him to remedy a less evil, reaping to himself sorrow while he went to rid away solitariness, it cannot avoid to be concluded that if the woman be naturally so of disposition[81] as will not help to remove but help to increase that same God-forbidden loneliness (which will in time draw on with it a general discomfort and dejection of mind not beseeming either Christian profession or moral conversation, unprofitable and dangerous to the commonwealth, when the household estate, out of which must flourish forth the vigor and spirit of all public enterprises, is so ill-contented and procured at home and cannot be supported), such a marriage can be no marriage, whereto the most honest end is wanting. And the aggrieved person shall do more manly, to be extraordinary and singular in claiming the due right whereof he is frustrated, than to piece up his lost contentment by visiting the stews, or stepping to his neighbor's bed, which is the common shift in this misfortune, or else by suffering his useful life to waste away and be lost under a secret affliction of an unconscionable size to human strength. Against all which evils, the mercy of this Mosaic Law was graciously exhibited.

CHAP. 3

The ignorance and iniquity of canon law providing for the right of the body in marriage, but nothing for the wrongs and grievances of the mind. An objection, that the mind should be better looked to before contract, answered.

How vain therefore is it, and how preposterous in the canon law, to have made such careful provision against the impediment of carnal performance, and to have had no care about the unconversing inability of mind, so defective to the purest and most sacred end of matrimony; and that the vessel of voluptuous enjoyment must be made good to him that has taken it upon trust without any

80. **complexion:** the proportions of one's four bodily humors.
81. Milton once again ascribes marital failure to a kind of bodily determinism, related to *complexion* (see note 61).

caution, whenas the mind, from whence must flow the acts of peace and love (a far more precious mixture than the quintessence of an excrement), though it be found never so deficient and unable to perform the best duty of marriage in a cheerful and agreeable conversation, shall be thought good enough, how ever flat and melancholious it be, and must serve, though to the eternal disturbance and languishing of him that complains him. Yet wisdom and charity, weighing God's own institution, would think that the pining of a sad spirit wedded to loneliness should deserve to be freed, as well as the impatience of a sensual desire so providently relieved. 'Tis read to us in the liturgy that "we must not marry to satisfy the fleshly appetite, like brute beasts that have no understanding";[82] but the canon so runs as if it dreamt of no other matter than such an appetite to be satisfied; for if it happen that nature hath stopped or extinguished the veins of sensuality, that marriage is annulled. But though all the faculties of the understanding and conversing part after trial appear to be so ill and so aversely met through nature's unalterable working[83] as that neither peace nor any sociable contentment can follow, 'tis as nothing—the contract shall stand as firm as ever, betide what will. What is this but secretly to instruct us that however many grave reasons are pretended to the married life, yet that nothing indeed is thought worth regard therein, but the prescribed satisfaction of an irrational heat? Which cannot be but ignominious to the state of marriage, dishonorable to the undervalued soul of man and even to Christian doctrine itself; while it seems more moved at the disappointing of an impetuous nerve than at the ingenuous grievance of a mind unreasonably yoked, and to place more of marriage in the channel of concupiscence,[84] than in the pure influence of peace and love, whereof the soul's lawful contentment is the only fountain.

But some are ready to object that the disposition ought seriously to be considered before. But let them know again that for all the wariness can be used, it may yet befall a discreet man to be mistaken in his choice, and we have plenty of examples.[85] The soberest and best governed men are least practiced in these affairs; and who knows not that the bashful muteness of a virgin may oft-times hide all the unliveliness and natural sloth which is really unfit for conversation. Nor is there that freedom of access granted or presumed as may suffice to a perfect discerning till too late; and where any indisposition is suspected, what more usual than the persuasion of friends, that acquaintance, as it increases, will amend all. And lastly, it is not strange though many who have spent their youth chastely are in some things not so quick-sighted, while they haste too ea-

82. Milton closely paraphrases from the marriage service in the Anglican Book of Common Prayer.

83. For *nature's unalterable working*, see note 61.

84. *Impetuous nerve* and *channel of concupiscence* are graphic anatomical images, balanced against the indefinite but erotically charged image that follows of a *fountain* pouring forth *peace and love.*

85. Milton adds the last clause to the second edition; it may mark his attempt to deflect attention from himself in this otherwise patently self-regarding paragraph.

gerly to light the nuptial torch.[86] Nor is it, therefore, that for a modest error a man should forfeit so great a happiness and no charitable means to release him, since they who have lived most loosely by reason of their bold accustoming prove most successful in their matches, because their wild affections, unsettling at will, have been as so many divorces to teach them experience. Whenas the sober man honoring the appearance of modesty, and hoping well of every social virtue under that veil, may easily chance to meet, if not with a body impenetrable, yet often with a mind to all other due conversation inaccessible, and to all the more estimable and superior purposes of matrimony useless and almost lifeless. And what a solace, what a fit help such a consort would be through the whole life of a man, is less pain to conjecture than to have experience.

CHAP. 4

The second reason of this law, because without it, marriage, as it happens oft, is not a remedy of that which it promises, as any rational creature would expect. That marriage, if we pattern from the beginning as our Savior bids, was not properly the remedy of lust, but the fulfilling of conjugal love and helpfulness.

And that we may further see what a violent and cruel thing it is to force the continuing of those together whom God and nature in the gentlest end of marriage never joined, diverse evils and extremities that follow upon such a compulsion shall here be set in view. Of evils, the first and greatest is that hereby a most absurd and rash imputation is fixed upon God and his holy laws, of conniving and dispensing with open and common adultery among his chosen people, a thing which the rankest politician would think it shame and disworship that his laws should countenance. How and in what manner this comes to pass I shall reserve till the course of method brings on the unfolding of many scriptures. Next, the Law and Gospel are hereby made liable to more than one contradiction, which I refer also thither. Lastly, the supreme dictate of charity is hereby many ways neglected and violated, which I shall forthwith address to prove. First, we know Saint Paul saith, "It is better to marry than to burn" [1 Cor. 7.9]. Marriage, therefore, was given as a remedy of that trouble—but what might this burning mean? Certainly not the mere motion of carnal lust, not the mere goad of a sensitive desire; God does not principally take care for such cattle.[87] What is it then but that desire which God put into Adam in paradise before he knew the sin of incontinence—that desire which God saw it was not good that man should be left alone to burn in—the desire and longing to put off an unkindly solitariness by uniting another body, but not without a fit soul, to his in the cheerful society of wedlock. Which if it were so needful before the fall, when man was much more perfect in himself, how much more is it needful

86. See *PL* 11.589–90: "Then all in heat / They light the nuptial torch."
87. See *PL* 8.579–94.

now against all the sorrows and casualties of this life to have an intimate and speaking help, a ready and reviving associate in marriage? Whereof who misses by chancing on a mute and spiritless mate, remains more alone than before, and in a burning less to be contained than that which is fleshly, and more to be considered, as being more deeply rooted even in the faultless innocence of nature.

As for that other burning, which is but as it were the venom of a lusty and over-abounding concoction, strict life and labor with the abatement of a full diet may keep that low and obedient enough: but this pure and more inbred desire of joining to itself in conjugal fellowship a fit conversing soul (which desire is properly called love) "is stronger than death," as the spouse of Christ thought, "many waters cannot quench it, neither can the floods drown it" [Song of Solomon 8.6–7].[88] This is that rational burning that marriage is to remedy, not to be allayed with fasting, nor with any penance to be subdued, which how can he assuage who by mishap hath met the unmeetest and most unsuitable[89] mind? Who hath the power to struggle with an intelligible flame, not in paradise to be resisted, become now more ardent by being failed of what in reason it looked for, and even then most unquenched when the importunity of a provender[90] burning is well enough appeased and yet the soul hath obtained nothing of what it justly desires? Certainly, such a one forbidden to divorce is in effect forbidden to marry, and compelled to greater difficulties than in a single life. For if there be not a more human burning which marriage must satisfy, or else may be dissolved, than that of copulation, marriage cannot be honorable for the mere[91] reducing and terminating of lust between two; seeing many beasts in voluntary and chosen couples live together as unadulterously and are as truly married in that respect.

But all ingenuous men will see that the dignity and blessing of marriage is placed rather in the mutual enjoyment of that which the wanting soul needfully seeks than of that which the plenteous body would jollily give away. Hence it is that Plato in his festival discourse brings in Socrates relating what he feigned to have learnt from the prophetess Diotima, how Love was the son of Penury, begot of Plenty in the garden of Jupiter.[92] Which divinely sorts with that which in effect Moses tells us, that love was the son of loneliness, begot in paradise by that sociable and helpful aptitude which God implanted between man and woman toward each other. The same also is that burning mentioned by Saint Paul, whereof marriage ought to be the remedy; the flesh hath other natural and easy curbs which are in the power of any temperate man. When, therefore, this original and sinless penury or loneliness of the soul cannot lay itself down by

88. Milton follows a typical reading of the Song of Solomon, according to which the lover is Christ and the woman is the church.

89. The original reading—*most unmeetest and unsuitable*—was corrected in some but not all copies of the second edition.

90. **provender:** livestock feed. By this term, here used as an adjective, Milton suggests that sexual appetite is lower than the appetite for rational companionship.

91. We choose the reading of 1643, "meer," over the second editon's "meet."

92. In Plato's *Symposium* 203, Diotima relates an allegory of the birth of Eros (or Love) from the union of Poverty and Plenty. Milton goes on to compare this allegory to Gen. 2.18.

the side of such a meet and acceptable union as God ordained in marriage, at least in some proportion, it cannot conceive and bring forth love, but remains utterly unmarried under a formal wedlock and still burns in the proper meaning of Saint Paul. Then enters hate, not that hate that sins, but that which only is natural dissatisfaction and the turning aside from a mistaken object; if that mistake have done injury, it fails not to dismiss with recompense, for to retain still, and not be able to love, is to heap up more injury. Thence this wise and pious law of dismission now defended took beginning.

He therefore who, lacking of his due in the most native and human end of marriage, thinks it better to part than to live sadly and injuriously to that cheerful covenant (for not to be beloved and yet retained, is the greatest injury to a gentle spirit) he, I say, who[93] therefore seeks to part, is one who highly honors the married life and would not stain it, and the reasons which now move him to divorce are equal to the best of those that could first warrant him to marry. For, as was plainly shown, both the hate which now diverts him and the loneliness which leads him still powerfully to seek a fit help, hath not the least grain of a sin in it, if he be worthy to understand himself.

CHAP. 5

The third reason of this law, because without it, he who hath happened where he finds nothing but remediless offences and discontents, is in more and greater temptations than ever before.

Thirdly, yet it is next to be feared, if he must be still bound without reason by a deaf rigor, that when he perceives the just expectance of his mind defeated, he will begin even against law to cast about where he may find his satisfaction more complete, unless he be a thing heroically virtuous,[94] and that are not the common lump of men for whom chiefly the laws ought to be made—though not to their sins, yet to their unsinning weaknesses, it being above their strength to endure the lonely estate, which while they shunned they are fallen into. And yet there follows upon this a worse temptation. For if he be such as hath spent his youth unblamably and laid up his chiefest earthly comforts in the enjoyment of a contented marriage, nor did neglect that furtherance which was to be obtained therein by constant prayers, when he shall find himself bound fast to an uncomplying discord of nature—or, as it oft happens, to an image of earth and phlegm[95]—with whom he looked to be the copartner of a sweet and glad-

93. For the oscillation between the third person and the occulted first person in the locution *he, I say, who* and in the tract more generally, see Patterson 1990.

94. Contrast the heroic virtue Milton ascribes to himself in the *Apology* and *The Reason of Church Government.* Here Milton, who may need a divorce, indirectly associates himself with the *common lump of men.*

95. An excess of *phlegm,* one of the four bodily humors, was thought to cause apathy and sluggishness.

some society, and sees withal that his bondage is now inevitable, though he be almost the strongest Christian, he will be ready to despair in virtue and mutine[96] against divine providence. And this doubtless is the reason of those lapses and that melancholy despair which we see in many wedded persons, though they understand it not, or pretend other causes because they know no remedy, and is of extreme danger. Therefore when human frailty surcharged is at such a loss, charity ought to venture much and use bold physic, lest an over-tossed faith endanger to shipwreck.

CHAP. 6

The fourth reason of this law, that God regards love and peace in the family more than a compulsive performance of marriage, which is more broke by a grievous continuance than by a needful divorce.

Fourthly, marriage is a covenant the very being whereof consists not in a forced cohabitation and counterfeit performance of duties, but in unfeigned love and peace. And of matrimonial love, no doubt but that was chiefly meant, which by the ancient sages was thus parabled: that Love, if he be not twin-born, yet hath a brother wondrous like him, called Anteros,[97] whom while he seeks all about, his chance is to meet with many false and feigning desires that wander singly up and down in his likeness. By them in their borrowed garb, Love, though not wholly blind, as poets wrong him,[98] yet having but one eye, as being born an archer aiming, and that eye not the quickest in this dark region here below, which is not Love's proper sphere, partly out of the simplicity and credulity which is native to him, often deceived, embraces and consorts him with these obvious and suborned striplings, as if they were his mother's own sons, for so he thinks them, while they subtly keep themselves most on his blind side. But after a while, as his manner is, when soaring up into the high tower of his apogæum,[99] above the shadow of the earth, he darts out the direct rays of his then most piercing eyesight upon the impostures and trim disguises that were used with him, and discerns that this is not his genuine brother, as he imagined, he has no longer the power to hold fellowship with such a personated mate. For straight his arrows lose their golden heads and shed their purple feathers, his silken

96. **mutine:** mutiny.

97. *Anteros* appears in Plato's *Phaedrus* (255d); later mythographers filled in the story of Aphrodite's giving birth to this younger brother of Eros after she had been told that Eros would waste away unless he could see his likeness in another. For the tradition, see R. V. Merrill, "Eros and Anteros," *Speculum* 19 (1944): 265–84.

98. Spenser has E.K. in *SC* comment on the familiar (but, in Milton's eyes, erroneous because postclassical) image of Eros or Cupid as blind: "he is described of the poets to be . . . blindfolded because he maketh no difference of personages" (gloss to "March," l. 81).

99. **apogæum:** point in a celestial body's orbit most distant from the earth.

braids[100] untwine and slip their knots, and that original and fiery virtue given him by fate all on a sudden goes out and leaves him undeified and despoiled of all his force: till finding Anteros at last, he kindles and repairs the almost faded ammunition of his deity by the reflection of a coequal and homogeneal fire.

Thus mine author[101] sung it to me, and by the leave of those who would be counted the only grave ones, this is no mere amatorious novel (though to be wise and skilful in these matters, men heretofore of greatest name in virtue have esteemed it one of the highest arcs that human contemplation circling upward can make from the glassy sea[102] whereon she stands), but this is a deep and serious verity, showing us that love in marriage cannot live nor subsist unless it be mutual; and where love cannot be, there can be left of wedlock nothing but the empty husk of an outside matrimony as undelightful and unpleasing to God as any other kind of hypocrisy. So far is his command from tying men to the observance of duties which there is no help for, but they must be dissembled. If Solomon's advice be not overfrolic, "Live joyfully," saith he, "with the wife whom thou lovest, all thy days, for that is thy portion" [Eccles. 9.9]. How then, where we find it impossible to rejoice or to love, can we obey this precept? How miserably do we defraud ourselves of that comfortable portion which God gives us, by striving vainly to glue an error together which God and nature will not join, adding but more vexation and violence to that blissful society by our importunate superstition that will not hearken to Saint Paul, I Cor. 7[.15], who, speaking of marriage and divorce, determines plain enough in general that God therein "hath called us to peace" and not "to bondage." Yea, God himself commands in his Law more than once, and by his prophet Malachi, as Calvin and the best translations read, that "he who hates let him divorce";[103] that is, he who cannot love. Hence is it that the rabbins, and Maimonides (famous among the rest) in a book of his set forth by Buxtorfius, tells us that "divorce was permitted by Moses to preserve peace in marriage and quiet in the family."[104] Surely the Jews had their saving peace about them as well as we, yet care was taken that this wholesome provision for household peace should also be allowed them; and must this be denied to Christians? O perverseness! That the Law should be made more provident of peacemaking than the Gospel! That the Gospel should be put to beg a most necessary help of mercy from the Law, but must not have it. And that to grind in the mill of an undelighted and servile

100. The *braids* of Eros's bowstrings unravel.

101. No source has been found; *mine author* may well be Milton's invention, like Socrates' Diotima in the dialogue in which Anteros is found (see note 97).

102. **glassy sea:** Cp. the "sea of glass" in Rev. 4.6.

103. The translation of Mal. 2.16 was hotly contested. Milton's here differs from the *AV:* "For the Lord . . . saith that he hateth putting away [i.e., divorcing]."

104. Milton cites *The Guide for the Perplexed* of Moses *Maimonides* (1135–1204), the great synthesizer of rabbinic Judaism and Aristotelianism; Johann *Buxtorf* (1599–1664) translated the *Guide* into Latin in 1629.

copulation,[105] must be the only forced work of a Christian marriage, ofttimes with such a yoke-fellow, from whom both love and peace, both nature and religion, mourns to be separated.

I cannot therefore be so diffident, as not securely to conclude that he who can receive nothing of the most important helps in marriage, being thereby disenabled to return that duty which is his with a clear and hearty countenance, and thus continues to grieve whom he would not, and is no less grieved, that man ought even for love's sake and peace to move divorce upon good and liberal conditions to the divorced. And it is a less breach of wedlock to part with wise and quiet consent betimes, than still to soil and profane that mystery of joy and union[106] with a polluting sadness and perpetual distemper. For it is not the outward continuing of marriage that keeps whole that covenant, but whosoever does most according to peace and love, whether in marriage or in divorce, he it is that breaks marriage least; it being so often written that "Love only is the fulfilling of every Commandment" [Rom. 13.10].

CHAP. 7

The fifth reason, that nothing more hinders and disturbs the whole life of a Christian than a matrimony found to be incurably unfit, and doth the same in effect that an Idolatrous match.

Fifthly, as those priests of old were not to be long in sorrow, or if they were, they could not rightly execute their function,[107] so every true Christian in a higher order of priesthood[108] is a person dedicate to joy and peace, offering himself a lively sacrifice of praise and thanksgiving. And there is no Christian duty that is not to be seasoned and set off with cheerfulness, which in a thousand outward and intermitting crosses may yet be done well, as in this vale of tears; but in such a bosom affliction as this, crushing the very foundation of his inmost nature, when he shall be forced to love against a possibility and to use dissimulation against his soul in the perpetual and ceaseless duties of a husband, doubtless his whole duty of serving God must needs be blurred and tainted with a sad unpreparedness and dejection of spirit, wherein God has no delight. Who sees not, therefore, how much more Christianly[109] it would be to break by divorce that which is more broken by undue and forcible keeping, rather than "to cover the Altar of the Lord with continual tears, so that he regardeth not the offering any more" [Mal. 2.13]; rather than that the whole worship of a Christ-

105. Foreshadowing *Samson Agonistes,* in which Samson grinds in a mill (35–41) and recoils from the touch of Dalila (951–54).

106. See Eph. 5.31–32.

107. For Jewish law's restriction on the mourning of priests, see Lev. 21.1–6 and Ezek. 44.25–27.

108. Milton endorses the Reformation principle of the priesthood of all believers.

109. The original reading—*Christianity*—was corrected in some but not all copies of the second edition.

ian man's life should languish and fade away beneath the weight of an immeasurable grief and discouragement? And because some think the children of a second matrimony succeeding a divorce would not be a holy seed, it hindered not the Jews from being so. And why should we not think them more holy than the offspring of a former, ill-twisted wedlock, begotten only out of a bestial necessity, without any true love or contentment or joy to their parents, so that in some sense we may call them the "children of wrath" [Eph. 2.3] and anguish, which will as little conduce to their sanctifying, as if they had been bastards? For nothing more than disturbance of mind suspends us from approaching to God. Such a disturbance especially as both assaults our faith and trust in God's providence, and ends, if there be not a miracle of virtue on either side,[110] not only in bitterness and wrath, the canker of devotion, but in a desperate and vicious carelessness, when he sees himself (without fault of his) trained by a deceitful bait into a snare of misery, betrayed by an alluring ordinance and then made the thrall of heaviness and discomfort by an undivorcing law of God (as he erroneously thinks, but of man's iniquity, as the truth is). For that God prefers the free and cheerful worship of a Christian before the grievous and exacted observance of an unhappy marriage, besides that the general maxims of religion assure us, will be more manifest by drawing a parallel argument from the ground of divorcing an idolatress, which was lest he should alienate his heart from the true worship of God. And what difference is there whether she pervert him to superstition by her enticing sorcery or disenable him in the whole service of God through the disturbance of her unhelpful and unfit society, and so drive him at last through murmuring[111] and despair to thoughts of atheism? Neither doth it lessen the cause of separating in that the one willingly allures him from the faith, the other perhaps unwillingly drives him, for in the account of God it comes all to one that the wife loses him a servant; and therefore by all the united force of the decalogue she ought to be disbanded, unless we must set marriage above God and charity, which is the doctrine of devils, no less than forbidding to marry.[112]

CHAP. 8

That an idolatrous heretic ought to be divorced after a convenient space given to hope of conversion. That place of Corinth. 7 restored from a twofold erroneous exposition; and that the common expositors flatly contradict the moral law. . . .

110. Although the unhappily married Milton argues that we need divorce in part because we are not *miracles of virtue,* he had consistently described himself as extraordinarily virtuous (see note 94).

111. **murmuring:** complaint (the term is used often in the Bible for complaining of or resistance to God; see, e.g., Psalm 106:25 and Phil 2:14–16).

112. Milton condemns the prohibition of divorce by associating it with the Roman Catholic prescription of priestly celibacy.

CHAP. 9

That adultery is not the greatest breach of matrimony, that there may be other violations as great.

Now whether idolatry or adultery be the greatest violation of marriage if any demand, let him thus consider that among Christian writers touching matrimony there be three chief ends thereof agreed on: Godly society, next civil, and thirdly, that of the marriage-bed.[113] Of these, the first in name to be the highest and most excellent, no baptized man can deny; nor that idolatry smites directly against this prime end, nor that such as the violated end is, such is the violation: but he who affirms adultery to be the highest breach, affirms the bed to be the highest of marriage, which is in truth a gross and boorish opinion, how common soever; as far from the countenance of scripture, as from the light of all clean philosophy or civil nature. And out of question the cheerful help that may be in marriage toward sanctity of life is the purest and so the noblest end of that contract. But if the particular of each person be considered, then of those three ends which God appointed, that to him is greatest which is most necessary; and marriage is then most broken to him when he utterly wants the fruition of that which he most sought therein, whether it were religious, civil, or corporal society. Of which wants to do him right by divorce only for the last and meanest is a perverse injury, and the pretended reason of it as frigid as frigidity itself, which the Code[114] and canon are only sensible of.

Thus much of this controversy. I now return to the former argument.[115] And having shown that disproportion, contrariety, or numbness of mind may justly be divorced, by proving already that the prohibition thereof opposes the express end of God's institution, suffers not marriage to satisfy that intellectual and innocent desire (which God himself kindled in man to be the bond of wedlock) but only to remedy a sublunary and bestial burning, which frugal diet without marriage would easily chasten. Next, that it drives many to transgress the conjugal bed, while the soul wanders after that satisfaction which it had hope to find at home, but hath missed. Or else it sits repining even to atheism, finding itself hardly dealt with, but misdeeming the cause to be in God's Law, which is in man's unrighteous ignorance. I have shown also how it unties the inward knot of marriage, which is peace and love (if that can be untied which was never knit), while it aims to keep fast the outward formality; how it lets perish the Christian man to compel impossibly the married man.

113. Milton leaves out a principal end mentioned by most Christian writers, the procreation of children.
114. **Code:** an apparent reference to the Justinian Code, standing in here for all civil law.
115. **former argument:** the argument of the eighth chapter.

CHAP. 10

The sixth reason of this law, that to prohibit divorce sought for natural causes is against nature.

The sixth place declares this prohibition to be as respectless of human nature as it is of religion, and therefore is not of God. He teaches that an unlawful marriage may be lawfully divorced, and that those who having thoroughly discerned each other's disposition, which ofttimes cannot be till after matrimony, shall then find a powerful reluctance and recoil of nature on either side blasting all the content of their mutual society, that such persons are not lawfully married; to use the apostle's words, "say I these things as a man, or saith not the Law also the same? For it is written" [1 Cor. 9.8-9]; Deut. 22[.9-10], "Thou shalt not sow thy vineyard with divers seeds, lest thou defile both. Thou shalt not plow with an ox and an ass together," and the like. I follow the pattern of Saint Paul's reasoning: "Doth God care for asses and oxen," how ill they yoke together, "or is it not said altogether for our sakes? For our sakes no doubt this is written" [1 Cor. 9.9-10].[116] Yea, the apostle himself in the fore-cited 2 *Cor.* 6.14. alludes from that place of Deut. to forbid misyoking marriage, as by the Greek word is evident, though he instance but in one example of mismatching with an infidel. Yet next to that what can be a fouler incongruity, a greater violence to the reverend secret of nature, than to force a mixture of minds that cannot unite, and to sow the furrow of man's nativity[117] with seed of two incoherent and uncombining dispositions? Which act being kindly and voluntary, as it ought, the Apostle in the language he wrote called *eunoia,* and the Latin "benevolence,"[118] intimating the original thereof to be in the understanding and the will. If not, surely there is nothing which might more properly be called a malevolence rather, and is the most injurious and unnatural tribute that can be extorted from a person endowed with reason, to be made pay out the best substance of his body, and of his soul too, as some think,[119] when either for just and powerful causes he cannot like or from unequal causes finds not recompense. And that there is a hidden efficacy of love and hatred in man as well as in other kinds, not moral but natural, which though not always in the choice, yet in the success of marriage will ever be most predominant, besides daily experience, the author of Ecclesiasticus,

116. The passage from 1 Corinthians interprets Deut. 25.4; Milton claims to interpret in Pauline fashion the passage from Deut. 22.9–10.

117. **furrow of man's nativity:** vagina; Milton's descriptions of sexuality in the tract are graphic (see note 83) even when metaphorical.

118. See 1 Cor. 7.3.

119. As Milton himself argues in *CD* 1.7, where he refers to "Aristotle's argument, which I think a very strong one indeed, that if the soul is wholly contained in all the body and wholly in any given part of that body, how can the human seed, that intimate and most noble part of the body, be imagined destitute and devoid of the soul of the parents, or at least of the father, when communicated to the son in the act of generation?" Milton's divorce tracts contain foreshadowings of his mature materialist monism.

whose wisdom hath set him next the Bible, acknowledges, 13.16: "A man," saith he, "will cleave to his like." But what might be the cause, whether each one's allotted genius or proper star, or whether the supernal influence of schemes and angular aspects or this elemental crasis[120] here below, whether all these jointly or singly meeting friendly, or unfriendly in either party, I dare not, with the men I am likest to clash, appear so much a philosopher as to conjecture. The ancient proverb in Homer less abstruse entitles[121] this work of leading each like person to his like peculiarly to God himself,[122] which is plain enough also by his naming of a meet or like help in the first espousal instituted. And that every woman is meet for every man, none so absurd as to affirm. Seeing then there is indeed a twofold seminary or stock in nature, from whence are derived the issues of love and hatred distinctly flowing through the whole mass of created things, and that God's doing ever is to bring the due likenesses and harmonies of his works together, except when out of two contraries met to their own destruction he molds a third existence, and that it is error or some evil angel which either blindly or maliciously hath drawn together in two persons ill embarked in wedlock the sleeping discords and enmities of nature lulled on purpose with some false bait, that they may wake to agony and strife later than prevention could have wished; if from the bent of just and honest intentions beginning what was begun and so continuing, all that is equal, all that is fair and possible hath been tried and no accommodation likely to succeed, what folly is it still to stand combating and battering against invincible causes and effects, with evil upon evil, till either the best of our days be lingered out, or ended with some speeding sorrow? The wise Ecclesiasticus advises rather, 37.27, "My son, prove thy soul in thy life, see what is evil for it, and give not that unto it." Reason he had to say so; for if the noisomeness or disfigurement of body can soon destroy the sympathy of mind to wedlock duties, much more will the annoyance and trouble of mind infuse itself into all the faculties and acts of the body, to render them invalid, unkindly, and even unholy against the fundamental law book of nature, which Moses never thwarts, but reverences. Therefore he commands us to force nothing against sympathy[123] or natural order, no not upon the most abject creatures, to show that such an indignity cannot be offered to man without an impious crime. And certainly those divine meditating words, of finding out a meet and like help to man, have in them a consideration of more than the indefinite likeness of womanhood, nor are they to be made waste paper on for the dullness of Canon divinity, no nor those other allegoric precepts of beneficence fetched out of the closet of nature to teach us goodness and compassion in not compelling together unmatchable societies (or if they meet through mischance, by all consequence to disjoin them), as God and

120. **crasis:** combining of elements.

121. **entitles:** assigns.

122. Milton paraphrases *Od.* 17.218.

123. See note 62.

nature signifies and lectures to us not only by those recited decrees, but even by the first and last of all his visible works, when by his divorcing command[124] the world first rose out of chaos, nor can be renewed again out of confusion but by the separating of unmeet consorts.

CHAP. 11

The seventh reason, that sometimes continuance in marriage may be evidently the shortening or endangering of life to either party, both law and divinity concluding that life is to be preferred before marriage, the intended solace of life. . . .

CHAP. 12

The eighth reason, it is probable, or rather certain, that every one who happens to marry hath not the calling, and therefore upon unfitness found and considered force ought not to be used. . . .

CHAP. 13

The ninth reason, because marriage is not a mere carnal coition but a human society; where that cannot reasonably be had, there can be no true matrimony. Marriage compared with all other covenants and vows warrantably broken for the good of man. Marriage, the papist's sacrament, and unfit marriage, the Protestant's idol.

Ninthly, I suppose it will be allowed us that marriage is a human society, and that all human society must proceed from the mind rather than the body, else it would be but a kind of animal or beastish meeting. If the mind, therefore, cannot have that due company by marriage that it may reasonably and humanly desire, that marriage can be no human society, but a certain formality or gilding over of little better than a brutish congress, and so in very wisdom and pureness to be dissolved.

But marriage is more than human, "the covenant of God" (Prov. 2. 17), therefore man cannot dissolve it. I answer, if it be more than human so much the more it argues the chief society thereof to be in the soul rather than in the body, and the greatest breach thereof to be unfitness of mind rather than defect of body; for the body can have least affinity in a covenant more than human, so that the reason of dissolving holds good the rather. Again I answer, that the Sabbath is a higher institution, a command of the first table,[125] for the breach whereof God hath far more and oftener testified his anger than for divorces, which from Moses to Malachi he never took displeasure at, nor then neither if

124. Gen. 1.4: "And God divided the light from the darkness."

125. I.e., among the first three of the Ten Commandments, those prescribing man's duty directly to God (Deut. 5.6–21).

we mark the text,[126] and yet as oft as the good of man is concerned, he not only permits but commands to break the Sabbath. What covenant more contracted with God and less in man's power than the vow which hath once past his lips? Yet if it be found rash, if offensive, if unfruitful either to God's glory or the good of man, our doctrine forces not error and unwillingness irksomely to keep it, but counsels wisdom and better thoughts boldly to break it. Therefore to enjoin the indissoluble keeping of a marriage found unfit against the good of man both soul and body, as hath been evidenced, is to make an idol of marriage, to advance it above the worship of God and the good of man, to make it a transcendent command, above both the second and first table, which is a most prodigious doctrine.

Next, whereas they cite out of the Proverbs that it is "the covenant of God," and therefore more than human, that consequence is manifestly false; for so the covenant which Zedechiah made with the infidel king of Babel, is called the Covenant of God" (Ezek. 17.19), which would be strange to hear counted more than a human covenant. So every covenant between man and man bound by oath may be called the covenant of God, because God therein is attested. So of marriage he is the author and the witness yet hence will not follow any divine astriction more than what is subordinate to the glory of God and the main good of either party. For as the glory of God and their esteemed fitness one for the other was the motive which led them both at first to think without other revelation that God had joined them together, so when it shall be found by their apparent unfitness that their continuing to be man and wife is against the glory of God and their mutual happiness, it may assure them that God never joined them; who hath revealed his gracious will not to set the ordinance above the man for whom it was ordained, not to canonize marriage either as a tyranness or a goddess over the enfranchised life and soul of man. For wherein can God delight, wherein be worshipped, wherein be glorified by the forcible continuing of an improper and ill-yoking couple? He that loved not to see the disparity of several cattle at the plow[127] cannot be pleased with vast unmeetness in marriage. Where can be the peace and love which must invite God to such a house? May it not be feared that the not divorcing of such a helpless disagreement will be the divorcing of God finally from such a place?

But it is a trial of our patience, they say. I grant it, but which of Job's afflictions were sent him with that law that he might not use means to remove any of them if he could? And what if it subvert our patience and our faith too? Who shall answer for the perishing of all those souls perishing by stubborn expositions of particular and inferior precepts against the general and supreme rule of charity? They dare not affirm that marriage is either a sacrament or a mystery,[128] though all those sacred things give place to man, and yet they invest it

126. See the discussion of Mal. 2.16 in Chapter 6.

127. Deut. 22.10; see note 116.

128. Milton brands his opponents by association with Roman Catholics, who, unlike Protestants, view marriage as a sacrament.

with such an awful sanctity, and give such adamantine chains to bind with, as if it were to be worshipped like some Indian deity, when it can confer no blessing upon us but works more and more to our misery. To such teachers the saying of Saint Peter at the council of Jerusalem will do well to be applied, "Why tempt ye God to put a yoke upon the necks" of Christian men, which neither the Jews, God's ancient people, "nor we are able to bear" [Acts 15.10], and nothing but unwary expounding hath brought upon us.

CHAP. 14

Considerations concerning Familism, Antinomianism, and why it may be thought that such opinions may proceed from the undue restraint of some just liberty, than which no greater cause to contemn discipline.

To these considerations this also may be added as no improbable conjecture: seeing that sort of men who follow Anabaptism, Familism, Antinomianism,[129] and other fanatic dreams (if we understand them not amiss)[130] be such most commonly as are by nature addicted to religion, of life also not debauched, and that their opinions having full swing do end in satisfaction of the flesh, it may come[131] with reason into the thoughts of a wise man, whether all this proceed not partly, if not chiefly, from the restraint of some lawful liberty, which ought to be given men and is denied them—as by physic we learn in menstruous bodies, where nature's current hath been stopped, that the suffocation and upward forcing of some lower part affects the head and inward sense with dotage and idle fancies. And, on the other hand, whether the rest of vulgar men not so religiously professing do not give themselves much the more to whoredom and adulteries, loving the corrupt and venial discipline of clergy courts, but hating to hear of perfect reformation; whenas they foresee that then fornication shall be austerely censured, adultery punished, and marriage the appointed refuge of nature, though it hap to be never so incongruous and displeasing, must yet of force be worn out, when it can be to no other purpose but of strife and hatred, a thing odious to God.[132] This may be worth the study of skillful men in theology and the reason of things; and lastly to examine whether some undue and ill-grounded strictness upon the blameless nature of man be not the cause, in

129. *Anabaptism,* named for its condemnation of infant baptism, originated in Germany in the early sixteenth century. The Family of Love was founded by Hendrik Niclaes in Friesland in 1540. *Antinomianism* is a generic term for the doctrine, held by the Familists, Ranters, and other radical sectarians, that Christians are freed from the moral law.

130. This parenthesis, a significant qualification of the criticism of sectarians, is new to the second edition; this may suggest that the experience of writing, and being criticized for, his argument for divorce contributed to Milton's move toward the radical sectarians.

131. Second edition reads "it may be come." Either the compositor erred or Milton meant "perhaps it is with reason concluded that..."

132. It is very difficult to construe this sentence, which may be corrupt.

those places where already reformation is, that the discipline of the church, so often and so unavoidably broken, is brought into contempt and derision. And if it be thus, let those who are still bent to hold this obstinate literality, so prepare themselves as to share in the account for all these transgressions, when it shall be demanded at the last day by one who will scan and sift things with more than a literal wisdom of equity. For if these reasons be duly pondered and that the Gospel is more jealous of laying on excessive burdens than ever the Law was, lest the soul of a Christian, which is inestimable, should be over-tempted and cast away, considering also that many properties of nature, which the power of regeneration itself never alters, may cause dislike of conversing even between the most sanctified, which continually grating in harsh tune together may breed some jar and discord, and that end in rancor and strife, a thing so opposite both to marriage and to Christianity, it would perhaps be less scandal to divorce a natural disparity than to link violently together an unchristian dissention, committing two ensnared souls inevitably to kindle one another, not with the fire of love, but with a hatred inconcilable, who, were they dissevered, would be straight friends in any other relation. But if an alphabetical servility[133] must be still urged, it may so fall out that the true church may unwittingly use as much cruelty in forbidding to divorce, as the church of antichrist doth willfully in forbidding to marry.

THE SECOND BOOK

CHAP. I

The ordinance of Sabbath and marriage compared. Hyperbole no infrequent figure in the Gospel. Excess cured by contrary excess. Christ neither did nor could abrogate the law of divorce, but only reprove the abuse thereof.

Hitherto the position undertaken hath been declared and proved by a law of God, that law proved to be moral and unabolishable for many reasons equal, honest, charitable, just, annexed thereto. It follows now that those places of scripture which have a seeming to revoke the prudence of Moses, or rather that merciful decree of God, be forthwith explained and reconciled. For what are all these reasonings worth, will some reply, whenas the words of Christ are plainly against all divorce, "except in case of fornication" [Matt. 5.32]? To whom he whose mind were to answer no more but this, "except also in case of charity," might safely appeal to the more plain words of Christ in defense of so excepting. "Thou shalt do no manner of work" saith the commandment of the Sabbath [Exod. 20.10]. Yes, saith Christ, works of charity.[134] And shall we be more severe

133. **alphabetical servility:** obedience to the letter (as opposed to the spirit) of the law.
134. See Luke 13.10–17, 14.1–6.

in paraphrasing the considerate and tender Gospel than he was in expounding the rigid and peremptory law? What was ever in all appearance less made for man, and more for God alone, than the Sabbath? Yet when the good of man comes into the scales, we hear that voice of infinite goodness and benignity that "Sabbath was made for man, not man for Sabbath" [Mark 2.27]. What thing ever was more made for man alone and less for God than marriage? And shall we load it with a cruel and senseless bondage utterly against both the good of man and the glory of God? Let who so will now listen. I want neither pall nor miter, I stay neither for ordination nor induction, but in the firm faith of a knowing Christian, which is the best and truest endowment of the keys,[135] I pronounce, the man who shall bind so cruelly a good and gracious ordinance of God hath not in that the spirit of Christ. Yet that every text of scripture seeming opposite may be attended with a due exposition, this other part ensues and makes account to find no slender arguments for this assertion out of those very scriptures which are commonly urged against it.

First therefore let us remember, as a thing not to be denied, that all places of scripture wherein just reason of doubt arises from the letter are to be expounded by considering upon what occasion everything is set down, and by comparing other texts. The occasion which induced our Savior to speak of divorce was either to convince the extravagance of the Pharisees in that point, or to give a sharp and vehement answer to a tempting question.[136] And in such cases that we are not to repose all upon the literal terms of so many words, many instances will teach us: wherein we may plainly discover how Christ meant not to be taken word for word, but like a wise physician, administering one excess against another to reduce us to a perfect mean. Where the Pharisees were strict, there Christ seems remiss; where they were too remiss, he saw it needful to seem most severe. In one place he censures an unchaste look to be adultery already committed, another time he passes over actual adultery with less reproof than for an unchaste look, not so heavily condemning secret weakness as open malice.[137] So here he may be justly thought to have given this rigid sentence against divorce not to cut off all remedy from a good man who finds himself consuming away in a disconsolate and unenjoyed matrimony, but to lay a bridle upon the bold abuses of those overweening rabbis; which he could not more effectually do than by a countersway of restraint curbing their wild exorbitance almost into the other extreme, as when we bow things the contrary way to make them come to their natural straightness. And that this was the only intention of Christ is most evident if we attend but to his own words and protestation made in the same sermon, not many verses before he treats of divorcing,

135. Cp. Milton's claim in *CD* 1.29 that the "keys of the kingdom of heaven are not entrusted to [Peter] alone" but "with everyone else who professes the same faith."

136. See Matt. 19.3–9.

137. See Matt. 5.28, "Whosoever looketh on a woman to lust after her hath committed adultery with her already in his heart," and John 8.11, where Christ tells the woman taken in adultery, "Neither do I condemn thee; go, and sin no more."

that he came not to abrogate from the Law "one jot or tittle" [Matt. 5.18] and denounces against them that shall so teach.

But Saint Luke, the verse immediately before-going that of divorce, inserts the same caveat,[138] as if the latter could not be understood without the former; and as a witness to produce against this our willful mistake of abrogating, which must needs confirm us that whatever else in the political law of more special relation to the Jews might cease to us, yet that of those precepts concerning divorce, not one of them was repealed by the doctrine of Christ, unless we have vowed not to believe his own cautious and immediate profession. For if these our Savior's words inveigh against all divorce and condemn it as adultery, except it be for adultery, and be not rather understood against the abuse of those divorces permitted in the Law, then is that law of Moses, Deut. 24.1. not only repealed and wholly annulled against the promise of Christ and his known profession not to meddle in matters judicial, but, that which is more strange, the very substance and purpose of that law is contradicted and convinced both of injustice and impurity, as having authorized and maintained legal adultery by statute. Moses also cannot scape to be guilty of unequal and unwise decrees, punishing one act of secret adultery by death and permitting a whole life of open adultery by law. And albeit lawyers write that some political edicts, though not approved, are yet allowed to the scum of the people and the necessity of the times, these excuses have but a weak pulse. For first, we read not that the scoundrel people, but the choicest, the wisest, the holiest of that nation have frequently used these laws, or such as these, in the best and holiest times. Secondly, be it yielded that in matters not very bad or impure, a human lawgiver may slacken something of that which is exactly good, to the disposition of the people and the times, but if the perfect, the pure, the righteous Law of God (for so are all his statutes and his judgments) be found to have allowed smoothly, without any certain reprehension, that which Christ afterward declares to be adultery, how can we free this Law from the horrible indictment of being both impure, unjust, and fallacious?

CHAP. 2

How divorce was permitted for hardness of heart, cannot be understood by the common exposition. That the Law cannot permit, much less enact, a permission of sin.

Neither will it serve to say this was permitted for the hardness of their hearts, in that sense as it is usually explained,[139] for the Law were then but a corrupt

138. Luke 16.17–18: "And it is easier for heaven and earth to pass, than one tittle of the law to fall. Whosoever putteth away his wife and marrieth another, committeth adultery."

139. The Yale editor cites the arguments of Paræus (see note 78) and the prominent English Calvinist William Perkins that Mosaic Law allowed divorce, despite its sinfulness, to prevent greater sin.

and erroneous schoolmaster,[140] teaching us to dash against a vital maxim of religion by doing foul evil in hope of some uncertain good.

This only text not to be matched again throughout the whole scripture, whereby God in his perfect Law should seem to have granted to the hard hearts of his holy people under his own hand a civil immunity and free charter to live and die in a long successive adultery under a covenant of works, till the Messiah, and then that indulgent permission to be strictly denied by a covenant of grace; besides the incoherence of such a doctrine, cannot, must not be thus interpreted, to the raising of a paradox never known till then, only hanging by the twined thread of one doubtful scripture, against so many other rules and leading principles of religion, of justice, and purity of life. For what could be granted more either to the fear or to the lust of any tyrant, or politician,[141] than this authority of Moses thus expounded, which opens him a way at will to dam up justice, and not only to admit of any Romish or Austrian[142] dispenses, but to enact a statute of that which he dares not seem to approve, even to legitimate vice, to make sin itself, the ever alien and vassal sin, a free citizen of the commonwealth, pretending only these or these plausible reasons. And well he might, all the while that Moses shall be alleged to have done as much without showing any reason at all. Yet this could not enter into the heart of David, Psal. 94.20, how any such authority as endeavors "to fashion wickedness by a law" should derive itself from God. And Isaiah lays "woe upon them that decree unrighteous decrees," 10.1. Now which of these two is the better lawgiver, and which deserves most a woe, he that gives out an edict singly unjust, or he that confirms to generations a fixed and unmolested impunity of that which is not only held to be unjust but also unclean, and both in a high degree, not only, as they themselves affirm, an injurious expulsion of one wife, but also an unclean freedom by more than a patent to wed another adulterously? How can we therefore with safety thus dangerously confine the free simplicity of our Savior's meaning to that which merely amounts from so many letters, whenas it can consist neither with his former and cautionary words, nor with other more pure and holy principles, nor finally with the scope of charity, commanding by his express commission in a higher strain. But all rather of necessity must be understood as only against the abuse of that wise and ingenuous liberty which Moses gave, and to terrify a roving conscience from sinning under that pretext.

140. Paul compares the law to a schoolmaster in Gal. 3.24.

141. **politician:** This word is usually derogatory in Milton.

142. For the Protestant Milton, Rome is the seat of hostile foreign intrigue, and in his *Commonplace Book* (Yale 1:503) he records from Camden's *Annales* John of Austria's plot to invade England and depose Elizabeth.

CHAP. 3

That to allow sin by law is against the nature of law, the end of the lawgiver, and the good of the people. Impossible therefore in the Law of God. That it makes God the author of sin, more than anything objected by the Jesuits or Arminians against predestination.

[*In an omitted section of several pages, Milton maintains by argument and authority that God could not have allowed sin (divorce) by law. "Sin," he writes, "can have no tenure by law at all, but is rather an eternal outlaw, and in hostility with law past all atonement: both diagonal contraries, as much allowing one another, as day and night together in one hemisphere."*]

If it be affirmed that God as being Lord may do what he will, yet we must know that God hath not two wills, but one will, much less two contrary.[143] If he once willed adultery should be sinful and to be punished by death, all his omnipotence will not allow him to will the allowance that his holiest people might, as it were by his own antinomy or counter-statute, live unreproved in the same fact, as he himself esteemed it according to our common explainers. The hidden ways of his providence we adore and search not, but the Law is his revealed will, his complete, his evident, and certain will. Herein he appears to us as it were in human shape, enters into covenant with us, swears to keep it, binds himself like a just lawgiver to his own prescriptions, gives himself to be understood by men, judges and is judged, measures and is commensurate to right reason; cannot require less of us in one cantle[144] of his Law than in another, his legal justice cannot be so fickle and so variable, sometimes like a devouring fire[145] and by and by connivent[146] in the embers, or, if I may so say, oscitant[147] and supine. The vigor of his law could no more remit than the hallowed fire on his altar could be let go out.[148] The lamps that burnt before him might need snuffing, but the light of his law never. Of this also more beneath, in discussing a solution of Rivetus.[149]

The Jesuits and that sect among us which is named of Arminius[150] are wont

143. Cp. *CD* 1.4, p. 414, where Milton denies the Calvinist assertion of God's twofold will: the revealed will by which he calls all to believe and the secret will by which he withholds from some the grace necessary for belief.

144. **cantle:** nook or section.

145. Exod. 24.17.

146. **connivent:** dozing.

147. **oscitant:** drowsy.

148. Lev. 6.13.

149. In the next chapter, here omitted.

150. **Arminius:** Jacob Arminius (1560–1609), a theologian of the Reformed Church of the Netherlands, having been assigned to refute attacks on Calvinist predestination, became convinced by those attacks. His defense of universal, sufficient, and resistible grace against the Calvinist tenets of particular and irresistible grace, which for Arminius amounted to making God the author of sin, was condemned at the Synod of Dort. Milton's later understanding of grace and salvation, both in *CD* 1.3–4 and in *Paradise Lost,* is firmly Arminian. See Danielson and S. Fallon (1999).

to charge us of making God the author of sin in two degrees especially, not to speak of his permissions. 1. Because we hold that he hath decreed some to damnation and consequently to sin, say they. Next, because those means which are of saving knowledge to others, he makes to them an occasion of greater sin. Yet considering the perfection wherein man was created and might have stood, no decree necessitating his free will, but subsequent though not in time yet in order to causes which were in his own power, they might methinks be persuaded to absolve both God and us.[151] When as the doctrine of Plato and Chrysippus[152] with their followers the Academics and the Stoics, who knew not what a consummate and most adorned Pandora was bestowed upon Adam to be the nurse and guide of his arbitrary[153] happiness and perseverance, I mean his native innocence and perfection, which might have kept him from being our true Epimetheus,[154] and though they taught of virtue and vice to be both the gift of divine destiny, they could yet find reasons not invalid, to justify the counsels of God and fate from the insulsity[155] of mortal tongues: that man's own free will self-corrupted is the adequate and sufficient cause of his disobedience besides fate, as Homer also wanted not to express both in his *Iliad* and *Odyssey*.[156] And Manilius, the poet, although in his fourth book he tells of some "created both to sin and punishment," yet without murmuring and with an industrious cheerfulness he acquits the deity.[157] They were not ignorant in their heathen lore that it is most God-like to punish those who of his creatures became his enemies with the greatest punishment; and they could attain also to think that the greatest, when God himself throws a man furthest from him, which then they held he did, when he blinded, hardened, and stirred up his offenders to finish and pile up their disparate work since they had undertaken it. To banish forever into a local hell, whether in the air or in the center, or in that uttermost and bottomless gulf of chaos, deeper from holy bliss than the world's diameter multiplied, they thought not a punishing so proper and proportionate for God to inflict as to punish sin with sin. Thus were the common sort of Gentiles wont to think, without any wry thoughts cast upon divine governance. And therefore Cicero, not in his Tusculan or Campanian retirements among the learned wits of that age but even in the senate to a mixed auditory (though he were sparing otherwise to broach his philosophy among statists and lawyers) yet as to this point,

151. I.e., the bondage to sin, having resulted from Adam and Eve's sin, is the responsibility of the human race and not of God.

152. *Plato's Laws* contains the argument that evil derives from the wills of individuals (10.904); *Chrysippus* (280–7 B.C.E.) was reported to have taught that human beings, because their wills are free, are responsible for the outcomes of their choices.

153. **arbitrary:** up to one's choice.

154. *Epimetheus,* by opening *Pandora*'s box, released the evils that have since plagued human beings; cp. *PL* 4.714–19.

155. **insulsity:** stupidity, senselessness.

156. Milton seems to refer to the opening lines of the *Iliad,* concerning Achilles' wrath; for the *Odyssey,* see the passages (1.7 and 1.32ff) quoted at the end of *CD* 1.4.

157. See Marcus Manilius's *Astronomicon* (4.108–18).

both in his *Oration against Piso* and in that which is about the answers of the soothsayers against Clodius, he declares it publicly as no paradox to common ears that God cannot punish man more, nor make him more miserable, than still by making him more sinful.[158] Thus we see how in this controversy the justice of God stood upright even among heathen disputers. But if anyone be truly and not pretendedly zealous for God's honor, here I call him forth before men and angels, to use his best and most advised skill lest God more unavoidably than ever yet, and in the guiltiest manner, be made the author of sin—if he shall not only deliver over and incite his enemies by rebukes to sin as a punishment, but shall by patent under his own broad seal allow his friends whom he would sanctify and save, whom he would unite to himself and not disjoin, whom he would correct by wholesome chastening and not punish as he doth the damned by lewd sinning, if he shall allow these in his Law (the perfect rule of his own purest will and our most edified conscience) the perpetrating of an odious and manifold sin without the lest contesting. 'Tis wondered how there can be in God a secret and a revealed will; and yet what wonder if there be in man two answerable causes. But here there must be two revealed wills grappling in a fraternal war with one another without any reasonable cause apprehended. This cannot be less than to engraft sin into the substance of the Law, which Law is to provoke sin by crossing and forbidding, not by complying with it. Nay this is, which I tremble in uttering, to incarnate sin into the unpunishing and well-pleased will of God. To avoid these dreadful consequences that tread upon the heels of those allowances to sin will be a task of far more difficulty than to appease those minds which perhaps out of a vigilant and wary conscience except against predestination. Thus finally we may conclude, that a law wholly giving license cannot upon any good consideration be given to a holy people, for hardness of heart in the vulgar sense.

CHAP. 4

That if divorce be no command, no more is marriage. That divorce could be no dispensation if it were sinful. The Solution of Rivetus, *that God dispensed by some unknown way, ought not to satisfy a Christian mind. . . .*

CHAP. 5

What a dispensation is. . . .

158. Hughes notes that "in the oration to the Senate *On Behalf of Milo* (86) *Cicero* dramatically described the Latian gods as having been outraged by Clodius, and as having inspired him and his gang with the madness that drove them to their deaths in their lawless attack on Milo. . . . In the oration *Against Piso* (20) Cicero asserted that the extreme crimes of the wicked are 'the most inevitable of the penalties ordained for them by the immortal gods.' "

CHAP. 6

That the Jew had no more right to this supposed dispense than the Christian hath and rather not so much. . . .

CHAP. 7

That the Gospel is apter to dispense than the Law. Paræus *answered. . . .*

CHAP. 8

The true sense how Moses suffered divorce for hardness of heart.

What may we do then to salve this seeming inconsistence?[159] I must not dissemble that I am confident that it can be done no other way than this.

Moses (Deut. 24.1) established a grave and prudent law, full of moral equity, full of due consideration towards nature, that cannot be resisted, a law consenting with the laws of wisest men and civilest nations: that "when a man hath married a wife, if it come to pass he cannot love her by reason of some displeasing natural quality or unfitness in her, let him write her a bill of divorce."[160] The intent of which law undoubtedly was this, that if any good and peaceable man should discover some helpless disagreement or dislike either of mind or body, whereby he could not cheerfully perform the duty of a husband without the perpetual dissembling of offense and disturbance to his spirit, rather than to live uncomfortably and unhappily both to himself and to his wife, rather than to continue undertaking a duty which he could not possibly discharge, he might dismiss her whom he could not tolerably and so not conscionably retain. And this law the spirit of God by the mouth of Solomon (Prov. 30.21,23) testifies to be a good and a necessary law, by granting it that "a hated woman" (for so the Hebrew word signifies, rather than odious, though it come all to one), "that a hated woman when she is married is a thing that the earth cannot bear." What follows then but that the charitable law must remedy what nature cannot undergo.

Now that many licentious and hardhearted men took hold of this law to cloak their bad purposes is nothing strange to believe. And these were they, not for whom Moses made the law, God forbid, but whose hardness of heart taking ill advantage by this law he held it better to suffer as by accident, where it could not be detected, rather than good men should lose their just and lawful privilege of remedy. Christ therefore having to answer these tempting Pharisees, ac-

159. I.e., between Moses' permitting and the Gospel's apparent prohibiting of divorce.

160. Milton here quotes Deut. 24.1, though his "by reason of some displeasing natural quality or unfitness in her" replaces the *AV*'s "because he hath found some uncleanness in her."

cording as his custom was, not meaning to inform their proud ignorance what Moses did in the true intent of the law, which they had ill cited, suppressing the true cause for which Moses gave it and extending it to every slight matter, tells them their own, what Moses was forced to suffer by their abuse of his law; which is yet more plain if we mark that our Savior in the fifth of Matth[ew] cites not the Law of Moses but the Pharisaical tradition falsely grounded upon that Law.[161] And in those other places, chap. 19 and Mark 10, the Pharisees cite the law but conceal the wise and human reason there expressed, which our Savior corrects not in them whose pride deserved not his instruction, only returns them what is proper to them: "Moses for the hardness of your heart suffered you," that is, such as you, "to put away your wives" [Matt. 19.8]; and "to you he wrote this precept" [Mark 10.5] for that cause, which "to you" must be read with an impression[162] and understood limitedly of such as covered ill purposes under that law. For it was seasonable that they should hear their own unbounded license rebuked, but not seasonable for them to hear a good man's requisite liberty explained.

But us he hath taught better, if we have ears to hear. He himself acknowledged it to be a law (Mark 10), and being a law of God it must have an undoubted "end of charity, which may be used with a pure heart, a good conscience, and faith unfeigned" [1 Tim. 1.5], as was heard. It cannot allow sin, but is purposely to resist sin, as by the same chapter to Timothy appears. There we learn also "that the Law is good, if a man use it lawfully" [1 Tim. 1.8]. Out of doubt then there must be a certain good in this Law which Moses willingly allowed. And there might be an unlawful use made thereof by hypocrites, and that was it which Moses unwillingly suffered, foreseeing it in general but not able to discern it in particulars. Christ therefore mentions not here what Moses and the Law intended; for good men might know that by many other rules, and the scornful Pharisees were not fit to be told until they could employ that knowledge they had less abusively. Only he acquaints them with what Moses by them was put to suffer.

CHAP. 9

The words of the institution how to be understood, and of our Savior's answer to his disciples.

And to entertain a little their overweening arrogance as best befitted, and to amaze them yet further, because they thought it no hard matter to fulfill the Law, he draws them up to that unseparable institution which God ordained in

161. Matt. 5.31: "It hath been said, Whosoever shall put away his wife, let him give her a writing of divorcement."

162. **impression:** emphasis.

the beginning before the fall, when man and woman were both perfect and could have no cause to separate; just as in the same chapter he stands not to contend with the arrogant young man who boasted his observance of the whole Law, whether he had indeed kept it or not, but screws him up higher to a task of that perfection which no man is bound to imitate.[163] And in like manner that pattern of the first institution he set before the opinionative Pharisees to dazzle them and not to bind us. For this is a solid rule, that every command given with a reason binds our obedience no otherwise than that reason holds. Of this sort was that command in Eden: "therefore shall a man cleave to his wife and they shall be one flesh" [Gen. 2.24], which we see is no absolute command, but with an inference: "therefore." The reason then must be first considered, that[164] our obedience be not mis-obedience. The first is, for it is not single, because the wife is to the husband "flesh of his flesh," as in the verse going before. But this reason cannot be sufficient of itself; for why then should he for his wife leave his father and mother, with whom he is far more "flesh of flesh and bone of bone," as being made of their substance? And, besides, it can be but a sorry and ignoble society of life whose inseparable injunction depends merely upon flesh and bones.[165] Therefore we must look higher, since Christ himself recalls us to the beginning, and we shall find that the primitive reason of never divorcing was that sacred and not vain promise of God to remedy man's loneliness by "making him a meet help for him" [Gen 2.18], though not now in perfection as at first, yet still in proportion as things now are.[166] And this is repeated (verse 20) when all other creatures were fitly associated and brought to Adam, as if the divine power had been in some care and deep thought because "there was not yet found a help meet for man." And can we so slightly depress the all-wise purpose of a deliberating God, as if his consultation had produced no other good for man but to join him with an accidental companion of propagation, which his sudden word had already made for every beast? Nay, a far less good to man it will be found, if she must at all adventures be fastened upon him individually.[167] And therefore even plain sense and equity and, which is above them both, the all-interpreting voice of charity herself cries loud that this primitive reason, this consulted promise of God "to make a meet help," is the only cause that gives authority to this command of not divorcing, to be a command. And it might be further added that if the true definition of a wife were asked in good earnest, this clause of being "a meet help" would show itself so necessary and so essential in that demonstrative argument, that it might be logically concluded, therefore, she who naturally and perpetually is no meet help, can be no wife, which clearly takes away the difficulty of dismissing of such a one.

163. Matt. 19.16–22.
164. **that:** so that.
165. Cp. *PL* 8.499: "And they shall be one flesh, one heart, one soul."
166. Milton's argument for divorce will depend in part on the possibility of incompatibility that results from the Fall.
167. **individually:** indivisibly, inseparably.

If this be not thought enough, I answer yet further, that marriage, unless it mean a fit and tolerable marriage, is not inseparable neither by nature nor institution. Not by nature, for then those Mosaic divorces had been against nature, if separable and inseparable be contraries, as who doubts they be? And what is against nature is against law, if soundest philosophy abuse us not.[168] By this reckoning Moses should be most un-Mosaic, that is, most illegal, not to say most unnatural. Nor is it inseparable by the first institution: for then no second institution in the same law for so many causes could dissolve it; it being most unworthy a human (as Plato's judgment is in the fourth book of his *Laws*)[169] much more a divine lawgiver to write two several decrees upon the same thing. But what would Plato have deemed if the one of these were good, the other evil to be done? Lastly, suppose it be inseparable by institution, yet in competition with higher things, as religion and charity in mainest matters, and when the chief end is frustrate for which it was ordained (as hath been shown), if still it must remain inseparable, it holds a strange and lawless propriety from all other works of God under heaven.

From these many considerations we may safely gather that so much of the first institution as our Savior mentions, for he mentions not all, was but to quell and put to nonplus the tempting Pharisees and to lay open their ignorance and shallow understanding of the scriptures. For, saith he, "have ye not read that he which made them at the beginning, made them male and female, and said, 'for this cause shall a man cleave to his wife'?" [Matt. 19.4-5]; which these blind usurpers of Moses' chair could not gainsay: as if this single respect of male and female were sufficient against a thousand inconveniences and mischiefs to clog a rational creature to his endless sorrow unrelinquishably, under the guileful superscription of his intended solace and comfort. What if they had thus answered, master, if thou mean to make wedlock as inseparable as it was from the beginning, let it be made also a fit society as God meant it, which we shall soon understand it ought to be if thou recite the whole reason of the law? Doubtless our Savior had applauded their just answer. For then they had expounded this command of paradise, even as Moses himself expounds it by his laws of divorce, that is, with due and wise regard had to the premises and reasons of the first command, according to which, without unclean and temporizing permissions, he instructs us in this imperfect state what we may lawfully do about divorce.

But if it be thought that the disciples, offended at the rigor of Christ's answer, could yet obtain no mitigation of the former sentence pronounced to the Pharisees, it may be fully answered that our Savior continues the same reply to his disciples, as men leavened with the same customary license which the Pharisees maintained and displeased at the removing of a traditional abuse whereto they had so long not unwillingly been used. It was no time then to contend with

168. Cp. Aquinas, *Summa Theologica* 1–2. Q 95. art 2: "A human law has so much the nature of law, as it is consistent with the law of nature."

169. In *Laws* 4 (719d), Plato argues that the lawgiver must make only one law about the same thing.

their slow and prejudicial belief, in a thing wherein an ordinary measure of light in scripture (with some attention) might afterwards inform them well enough. And yet ere Christ had finished this argument, they might have picked out of his own concluding words an answer more to their minds, and in effect the same with that which hath been all this while entreating audience. "All men," said he, "cannot receive this saying, save they to whom it is given; he that is able to receive it let him receive it" [Matt. 19.11–12]. What saying is this which is left to a man's choice to receive or not receive? What but the married life? Was our Savior then so mild and favorable to the weakness of a single man, and is he turned on the sudden so rigorous and inexorable to the distresses and extremities of an ill-wedded man? Did he so graciously give leave to change the better single life for the worse married life? Did he open so to us this hazardous and accidental door of marriage to shut upon us like the gate of death without retracting or returning, without permitting to change the worst, most insupportable, most unchristian mischance of marriage for all the mischiefs and sorrows that can ensue, being an ordinance which was especially given as a cordial and exhilarating cup of solace the better to bear our other crosses and afflictions? Questionless, this were a hardheartedness of undivorcing worse than that in the Jews which they say extorted the allowance from Moses, and is utterly dissonant from all the doctrine of our Savior.

After these considerations, therefore, to take a law out of paradise given in time of original perfection, and to take it barely without those just and equal inferences and reasons which mainly establish it (nor so much as admitting those needful and safe allowances wherewith Moses himself interprets it to the fallen condition of man), argues nothing in us but rashness and contempt of those means that God left us in his pure and chaste law, without which it will not be possible for us to perform the strict imposition of this command; or, if we strive beyond our strength, we shall strive to obey it otherwise than God commands it. And lamented experience daily teaches the bitter and vain fruits of this our presumption, forcing men in a thing wherein we are not able to judge either of their strength or of their sufferance. Whom neither one vice nor other by natural addiction, but only marriage ruins; which doubtless is not the fault of that ordinance, for God gave it as a blessing, nor always of man's mis-choosing, it being an error above wisdom to prevent, as examples of wisest men so mistaken manifest. It is the fault therefore of a perverse opinion that will have it continued in despite of nature and reason, when indeed it was never truly joined. All those expositors upon the fifth of Matthew confess the Law of Moses to be the Law of the Lord wherein no addition or diminution hath place; yet coming to the point of divorce, as if they feared not to be called least in the kingdom of heaven,[170] any slight evasion will content them to reconcile those contradictions which they make between Christ and Moses, between Christ and Christ.[171]

170. Matt. 5.19.

171. Milton might be said here to displace the charges of evasion and contradiction that might be brought against his own reading of Matt. 19.

CHAP. 10

The vain shift of those who make the law of divorce to be only the premises of a succeeding law. . . .

CHAP. 11

The other shift of saying divorce was permitted by law, but not approved. More of the institution. . . .

CHAP. 12

The third shift of them who esteem it a mere judicial law. Proved again to be a law of moral equity. . . .

CHAP. 13

The ridiculous opinion, that divorce was permitted from the custom in Egypt. That Moses gave not this law unwillingly. Perkins *confesses this law was not abrogated. . . .*

CHAP. 14

That Beza's *opinion of regulating sin by a politic law cannot be sound.*

Yet Beza's opinion is that a politic law (but what politic law I know not, unless one of Machiavel's) may regulate sin,[172] may bear indeed, I grant, with imperfection for a time, as those canons of the Apostles did in ceremonial things. But as for sin, the essence of it cannot consist with rule, and if the Law fall to regulate sin, and not to take it utterly away, it necessarily confirms and establishes sin. To make a regularity of sin by law, either the Law must straighten sin into no sin, or sin must crook the Law into no law. The judicial law can serve to no other end than to be the protector and champion of religion and honest civility, as is set down plainly (Rom. 13),[173] and is but the arm of moral law, which can no more be separate from justice than justice from virtue. Their office also in a different manner steers the same course: the one teaches what is good by precept, the other unteaches what is bad by punishment. But if we give way to politic dispensations of lewd uncleanness, the first good consequence of such a relax will be

172. Milton has in mind the *Annotationes Majores in Novum Testamentum* (1594) of Calvin's successor in Geneva, Theodore *Beza* (1519–1605); commenting on Matt. 19.8, Beza distinguishes between moral law, which always commands the good and prohibits evil, and civil law, which must at times regulate sins that it cannot abolish.

173. Rom. 13.1: "For there is no power but of God: the powers that be are ordained of God."

the justifying of papal stews,[174] joined with a toleration of epidemic whoredom. Justice must revolt from the end of her authority, and become the patron of that whereof she was created the punisher. The example of usury, which is commonly alleged, makes against the allegation which it brings, as I touched before. Besides that usury, so much as is permitted by the magistrate and demanded with common equity, is neither against the word of God nor the rule of charity, as hath been often discussed by men of eminent learning and judgment.[175] There must be therefore some other example found out to show us wherein civil policy may with warrant from God settle wickedness by law, and make that lawful which is lawless. Although I doubt not but, upon deeper consideration, that which is true in physic will be found as true in policy, that as of bad pulses those that beat most in order are much worse than those that keep the most inordinate circuit, so of popular vices those that may be committed legally will be more pernicious than those that are left to their own course at peril, not under a stinted privilege to sin orderly and regularly, which is an implicit contradiction, but under due and fearless execution of punishment.

The political law, since it cannot regulate vice, is to restrain it, by using all means to root it out. But if it suffer the weed to grow up to any pleasurable or contented height upon what pretext soever, it fastens the root, it prunes and dresses vice, as if it were a good plant. Let no man doubt therefore to affirm that it is not so hurtful or dishonorable to a commonwealth, nor so much to the hardening of hearts, when those worse faults pretended to be feared, are committed by who so dares under strict and executed penalty, as when those less faults, tolerated for fear of greater, harden their faces, not their hearts only, under the protection of public authority. For what less indignity were this, than as if Justice herself, the queen of virtues, descending from her sceptered royalty, instead of conquering should compound and treat with sin, her eternal adversary and rebel, upon ignoble terms? Or as if the judicial law were like that untrusty steward in the Gospel, and, instead of calling in the debts of his moral master, should give out subtle and sly acquittances to keep himself from begging?[176] Or let us person him like some wretched itinerary judge, who, to gratify his delinquents before him, would let them basely break his head, lest they should pull him from the bench and throw him over the bar. Unless we had rather think both moral and judicial full of malice and deadly purpose conspired to let the debtor Israelite, the seed of Abraham, run on upon a bankrout[177] score, flattered with insufficient and ensnaring discharges, that so he might be haled to a more cruel forfeit for all the indulgent arrears which

174. Protestant polemicists often charged that the papacy allowed and, by taxation, profited from Roman brothels.

175. Milton's father was a usurer; Milton met and married Mary Powell while visiting her family to collect on a loan from his father to hers.

176. See Luke 16.1–8.

177. **bankrout:** bankrupt.

those judicial acquitments had engaged him in. No, no, this cannot be, that the Law whose integrity and faithfulness is next to God, should be either the shameless broker of our impurities or the intended instrument of our destruction. The method of holy correction, such as became the commonwealth of Israel, is not to bribe sin with sin, to capitulate and hire out one crime with another; but, with more noble and graceful severity than Popilius the Roman legate used with Antiochus,[178] to limit and level out the direct way from vice to virtue, with straightest and exactest lines on either side, not winding or indenting so much as to the right hand of fair pretences. Violence indeed and insurrection may force the law to suffer what it cannot mend, but to write a decree in allowance of sin, as soon can the hand of Justice rot off. Let this be ever concluded as a truth that will outlive the faith of those that seek to bear it down.

CHAP. 15

That divorce was not given for wives only, as Beza *and* Paræus *write. More of the institution.*

Lastly, if divorce were granted, as Beza and others say,[179] not for men but to release afflicted wives, certainly it is not only a dispensation, but a most merciful law; and why it should not yet be in force, being wholly as needful, I know not what can be in cause but senseless cruelty. But yet to say divorce was granted for relief of wives, rather than of husbands is but weakly conjectured, and is manifest the extreme shift of a huddled exposition. Whenas it could not be found how hardness of heart should be lessened by liberty of divorce, a fancy was devised to hide the flaw by commenting that divorce was permitted only for the help of wives. Palpably uxorious! Who can be ignorant that woman was created for man and not man for woman, and that a husband may be injured as insufferably in marriage as a wife. What an injury is it after wedlock not to be beloved, what to be slighted, what to be contended with in point of house-rule who shall be the head, not for any parity of wisdom (for that were something reasonable) but out of a female pride? "I suffer not," saith St. Paul, "the woman to usurp authority over the man."[180] If the apostle could not suffer it, into what mould is he mortified that can? Solomon saith, "that a bad wife is to her husband as rottenness to his bones, a continual dropping: better dwell in a corner of the housetop, or in the wilderness" than with such a one.[181] "Who so hideth her hideth the wind, and one of the four mischiefs that the earth cannot bear."[182] If the spirit of

178. Gaius *Popilius* stopped *Antiochus* IV's invasion of Egypt by commanding him not to step outside a circle drawn about him until he agreed to the terms of the Roman Senate (Polybius, *Histories* 29.27).

179. Milton refers to Beza's *Annotationes Majores in Novum Testamentum* (see note 165) and David Paræus's *Operum Theologicorum* (1605), 1.784.

180. 1 Tim. 2.12.

181. Milton stitches together Prov. 12.4, 19.13, 21.9, 21.19.

182. Milton quotes Prov. 27.16 and digests Prov. 30.21–23.

God wrote such aggravations as these and, as may be guessed by these similitudes, counsels the man rather to divorce than to live with such a colleague, and yet on the other side expresses nothing of the wife's suffering with a bad husband, is it not most likely that God in his Law had more pity towards man thus wedlocked than towards the woman that was created for another? The same spirit relates to us the course which the Medes and Persians took by occasion of Vashti, whose mere denial to come at her husband's sending lost her the being queen any longer and set up a wholesome law, "that every man should bear rule in his own house" [Esth. 1.22]. And the divine relater shows us not the least sign of disliking what was done. How should he, if Moses long before was nothing less mindful of the honor and preeminence due to man? So that to say divorce was granted for woman rather than man was but fondly invented.

Esteeming therefore to have asserted thus an injured law of Moses from the unwarranted and guilty name of a dispensation, to be again a most equal and requisite law, we have the word of Christ himself, that he came not to alter the least tittle of it, and signifies no small displeasure against him that shall teach to do so. On which relying, I shall not much waver to affirm that those words which are made to intimate as if they forbade all divorce but for adultery (though Moses have constituted otherwise), those words taken circumscriptly,[183] without regard to any precedent law of Moses or attestation of Christ himself or without care to preserve those his fundamental and superior laws of nature and charity to which all other ordinances give up their seals, are as much against plain equity and the mercy of religion, as those words of "take, eat, this is my body" [Matt. 26.26; Mark 14.22], elementally understood,[184] are against nature and sense.

And surely the restoring of this degraded law hath well recompensed the diligence was used, by enlightening us further to find out wherefore Christ took off the Pharisees from alleging the law and referred them to the first institution, not condemning, altering, or abolishing this precept of divorce, which is plainly moral, for that were against his truth, his promise, and his prophetic office. But knowing how fallaciously they had cited and concealed the particular and natural reason of the law, that they might justify any froward reason of their own, he lets go that sophistry unconvinced, for that had been to teach them else, which his purpose was not. And since they had taken a liberty which the law gave not, he amuses[185] and repels their tempting pride with a perfection of paradise, which the law required not. Not thereby to oblige our performance to that whereto the law never enjoined the fallen estate of man; for if the first in-

183. **circumscriptly:** out of context.

184. **elementally understood:** i.e., understood as referring literally to the transformation of *elements* (bread and wine to body and blood); Milton brands the common teaching on divorce by association with Roman Catholic notions of the Eucharist.

185. **amuses:** baffles, perplexes.

stitution must make wedlock, whatever happen, inseparable to us, it must make it also as perfect, as meetly helpful, and as comfortable, as God promised it should be, at least in some degree. Otherwise it is not equal or proportionable to the strength of man that he should be reduced into such indissoluble bonds to his assured misery, if all the other conditions of that covenant be manifestly altered.

CHAP. 16

How to be understood that they must be one flesh. And how that those whom God hath joined man should not sunder.

Next he saith, "they must be one flesh" [Gen. 2.24], which, when all conjecturing is done, will be found to import no more but to make legitimate and good the carnal act, which else might seem to have something of pollution in it. And infers thus much over, that the fit union of their souls be such as may even incorporate them to love and amity, but that can never be where no correspondence is of the mind. Nay, instead of being one flesh, they will be rather two carcasses chained unnaturally together or, as it may happen, a living soul bound to a dead corpse, a punishment too like that inflicted by the tyrant Mezentius,[186] so little worthy to be received as that remedy of loneliness which God meant us. Since we know it is not the joining of another body will remove loneliness but the uniting of another compliable mind, and that it is no blessing but a torment, nay a base and brutish condition, to be one flesh, unless where nature can in some measure fix a unity of disposition.

The meaning, therefore, of these words, "For this cause shall a man leave his father and his mother, and shall cleave to his wife" [Matt. 19.5], was first to show us the dear affection which naturally grows in every not unnatural marriage, even to the leaving of parents or other familiarity whatsoever. Next, it justifies a man in so doing, that nothing is done undutifully to father or mother. But that he should be[187] here sternly commanded to cleave to his error, a disposition which to his he finds will never cement, a quotidian of sorrow and discontent in his house, let us be excused to pause a little and bethink us every way round ere we lay such a flat solecism upon the gracious and certainly not inexorable, not ruthless and flinty ordinance of marriage. For if the meaning of these words must be thus blocked up within their own letters from all equity and fair deduction, they will serve then well indeed their turn who affirm divorce to have been granted only for wives—whenas we see no word of this text binds women, but men only, what it binds. No marvel then if Salomith, sister to Herod, sent a writ

186. Vergil describes the grisly torture enacted by the cruel Etruscan king *Mezentius* (*Aen.* 8.485–88).

187. The second edition here reads, apparently erroneously, "But he that should be. . . ." We substitute the first edition's wording.

of ease to Costobarus her husband, which as Josephus there attests was lawful only to men.[188] No marvel though Placidia, the sister of Honorius, threatened the like to Earl Constantius for a trivial cause, as Photius relates from Olympiodorus.[189] No marvel any thing if letters must be turned into palisadoes[190] to stake out all requisite sense from entering to their due enlargement.

Lastly, Christ himself tells who should not be put asunder, namely those whom God hath joined. A plain solution of this great controversy, if men would but use their eyes—for when is it that God may be said to join? When the parties and their friends consent? No, surely, for that may concur to lewdest ends. Or is it when church rites are finished? Neither, for the efficacy of those depends upon the presupposed fitness of either party. Perhaps, after carnal knowledge? Least of all, for that may join persons whom neither law nor nature dares join. 'Tis left, that only then, when the minds are fitly disposed and enabled to maintain a cheerful conversation to the solace and love of each other, according as God intended and promised in the very first foundation of matrimony, "I will make him a help meet for him" [Gen. 2.18]. For surely what God intended and promised, that only can be thought to be his joining and not the contrary. So, likewise, the apostle witnesseth (1 Cor. 7.15) that in marriage "God hath called us to peace." And doubtless in what respect he hath called us to marriage, in that also he hath joined us.

The rest whom either disproportion or deadness of spirit, or something distasteful and averse in the immutable bent of nature renders unconjugal, error may have joined, but God never joined against the meaning of his own ordinance. And if he joined them not, then is there no power above their own consent to hinder them from unjoining when they cannot reap the soberest ends of being together in any tolerable sort. Neither can it be said properly that such twain were ever divorced, but only parted from each other, as two persons unconjunctive and unmarriable together. But if, whom God hath made a fit help, frowardness or private injuries hath made unfit, that being the secret of marriage God can better judge than man, neither is man indeed fit or able to decide this matter. However it be, undoubtedly a peaceful divorce is a less evil and less in scandal than a hateful, hardhearted, and destructive continuance of marriage, in the judgment of Moses and of Christ; that justifies him in choosing the less evil, which if it were an honest and civil prudence in the law, what is there in the Gospel forbidding such a kind of legal wisdom, though we should admit the common expositors?[191]

188. Josephus renders this judgment on Salome's divorce of her husband in *Antiq.* 15.7.

189. Photius relates from Olympiodorus's *Histories* the story of Photia's threatening divorce to her husband unless he removed a visiting magician (*Bibliotheca* 80).

190. **palisadoes:** a fence made of stakes.

191. **common expositors:** For this term, see Williams 1948; Milton most likely has in mind the standard Calvinist authorities previously cited.

CHAP. 17

The sentence of Christ concerning divorce how to be expounded. What Grotius *hath observed. Other additions.*

Having thus unfolded those ambiguous reasons wherewith Christ, as his wont was, gave to the Pharisees that came to sound him such an answer as they deserved, it will not be uneasy[192] to explain the sentence itself that now follows: "Whosoever shall put away his wife, except it be for fornication, and shall marry another, committeth adultery" [Matt. 19.9]. First, therefore, I will set down what is observed by Grotius upon this point, a man of general learning.[193] Next I produce what mine own thoughts gave me, before I had seen his annotations. Origen,[194] saith he, notes that Christ named adultery rather as one example of other like cases, than as one only exception. And that is frequent, not only in human but in divine laws, to express one kind of fact, whereby other causes of like nature may have the like plea: as Exod. 21.18,19,20,26, Deut. 19.5. And from the maxims of civil law he shows that even in sharpest penal laws, the same reason hath the same right: and in gentler laws that from like causes to like the law interprets rightly. But it may be objected, saith he, that nothing destroys the end of wedlock so much as adultery. To which he answers, that marriage was not ordained only for copulation, but for mutual help and comfort of life, and if we mark diligently the nature of our Savior's commands, we shall find that both their beginning and their end consists in charity, whose will is that we should so be good to others, as that we be not cruel to ourselves. And hence it appears why Mark, and Luke, and St. Paul to the Cor[inthians], mentioning this precept of Christ, add no exception, because exceptions that arise from natural equity are included silently under general terms. It would be considered, therefore, whether the same equity may not have place in other cases less frequent.

Thus far he.[195] From hence is what I add. First, that this saying of Christ, as it is usually expounded, can be no law at all, that a man for no cause should separate but for adultery, except it be a supernatural law, not binding us as we now are.[196] Had it been the law of nature, either the Jews or some other wise and civil nation would have pressed it. Or let it be so, yet that law (Deut. 24.1) whereby a man hath leave to part, whenas for just and natural cause discovered he cannot love, is a law ancienter and deeper engraven in blameless nature than the other. Therefore the inspired lawgiver, Moses, took care that this should be specified and allowed; the other he let vanish in silence, not once repeated in

192. **uneasy:** hard.
193. Milton is referring to Grotius's *Annotationes* (see note 67).
194. **Origen:** (c. 185–c. 254), a leading church father.
195. **he:** i.e., Grotius, whose argument Milton has been paraphrasing.
196. **as we now are:** i.e., after the Fall.

the volume of his law, even as the reason of it vanished with paradise. Secondly, this can be no new command, for the Gospel enjoins no new morality, save only the infinite enlargement of charity, which in this respect is called the "new commandment" by St. John, as being the accomplishment of every command.[197] Thirdly, it is no command of perfection further than it partakes of charity, which is "the bond of perfection" [Col. 3.14]. Those commands therefore which compel us to self-cruelty, above our strength, so hardly will help forward to perfection, that they hinder and set backward in all the common rudiments of Christianity, as was proved.

It being thus clear that the words of Christ can be no kind of command, as they are vulgarly taken, we shall now see in what sense they may be a command, and that an excellent one, the same with that of Moses and no other. Moses had granted that only for a natural annoyance, defect, or dislike, whether in body or mind (for so the Hebrew words plainly note),[198] which a man could not force himself to live with, he might give a bill of divorce, thereby forbidding any other cause wherein amendment or reconciliation might have place. This law, the Pharisees depraving,[199] extended to any slight contentious cause whatsoever. Christ therefore, seeing where they halted,[200] urges the negative part of that law, which is necessarily understood (for the determinate permission of Moses binds them from further license), and checking their supercilious drift, declares that no accidental, temporary, or reconcilable offence, except fornication, can justify a divorce. He touches not here those natural and perpetual hindrances of society, whether in body or mind, which are not to be removed, for such, as they are aptest to cause an unchangeable offence, so are they not capable of reconcilement because not of amendment. They do not break, indeed, but they annihilate the bands of marriage more than adultery. For that fault committed argues not always a hatred either natural or incidental against whom it is committed; neither does it infer a disability of all future helpfulness, or loyalty, or loving agreement, being once past and pardoned where it can be pardoned. But that which naturally distastes, and "finds no favor in the eyes" of matrimony, can never be concealed, never appeased, never intermitted, but proves a perpetual nullity of love and contentment, a solitude, and dead vacation[201] of all acceptable conversing. Moses therefore permits divorce, but in cases only that have no hands to join and more need separating than adultery. Christ forbids it, but in matters only that may accord,[202] and those less than fornication. Thus is Moses' law here plainly confirmed, and those causes which he permitted not a jot gainsaid.

And that this is the true meaning of this place, I prove also by no less an

197. John 13.34.
198. See 1.1.
199. I.e., this law, having been depraved by the Pharisees.
200. **halted:** fell short.
201. **vacation:** cessation.
202. **accord:** be brought into concord.

author than St. Paul himself, 1 Cor. 7.10, 11, upon which text interpreters agree that the apostle only repeats the precept of Christ; where while he speaks of "the wife's reconcilement to her husband," he puts it out of controversy that our Savior meant chiefly matters of strife and reconcilement, of which sort he would not that any difference should be the occasion of divorce, except fornication. And that we may learn better how to value a grave and prudent law of Moses, and how unadvisedly we smatter with our lips when we talk of Christ's abolishing any judicial law of his great Father (except in some circumstances which are judaical[203] rather than judicial, and need no abolishing but cease of themselves), I say again, that this recited law of Moses contains a cause of divorce greater beyond compare than that for adultery; and whoso cannot so conceive it, errs and wrongs exceedingly a law of deep wisdom for want of well fathoming. For let him mark, no man urges the just divorcing of adultery as it is a sin but as it is an injury to marriage, and though it be but once committed and that without malice, whether through importunity or opportunity, the Gospel does not therefore dissuade him who would therefore divorce; but that natural hatred whenever it arises is a greater evil in marriage than the accident of adultery, a greater defrauding, a greater injustice, and yet not blamable, he who understands not after all this representing, I doubt his will like a hard spleen draws faster than his understanding can well sanguify.[204] Nor did that man ever know or feel what it is to love truly, nor ever yet comprehend in his thoughts what the true intent of marriage is.[205] And this also will be somewhat above his reach, but yet no less a truth for lack of his perspective, that as no man apprehends what vice is so well as he who is truly virtuous; no man knows hell like him who converses most in heaven, so there is none that can estimate the evil and the affliction of a natural hatred in matrimony, unless he have a soul gentle enough and spacious enough to contemplate what is true love.

And the reason why men so disesteem this wise judging law of God and count hate or "the not finding of favor," as it is there termed, a humorous,[206] a dishonest, and slight cause of divorce, is because themselves apprehend so little of what true concord is. For if they did, they would be juster in their balancing between natural hatred and casual adultery; this being but a transient injury, and soon amended, I mean as to the party against whom the trespass is, but that other being an unspeakable and unremitting sorrow and offense, whereof no amends can be made, no cure, no ceasing but by divorce, which like a divine touch in one moment heals all, and like the word of a God, in one in-

203. **judaical:** i.e., involving only the Jewish ceremonial law as opposed to moral law.

204. **sanguify:** generate blood. Milton's figure is based on a physiological model under which the liver generates blood, which in turn is purified by the spleen—in the absence of the product of the understanding, the will labors in vain, like the spleen in the absence of blood.

205. Here and in the next sentence, Milton links his innovative teaching on divorce to an all too rare understanding of marriage. His is the *soul gentle enough and spacious enough* to understand what love is.

206. **humorous:** slight and capricious.

stant hushes outrageous tempests into a sudden stillness and peaceful calm.[207] Yet all this so great a good of God's own enlarging to us is by the hard reins of them that sit us wholly diverted and embezzled from us. Maligners of mankind! But who hath taught you to mangle thus and make more gashes in the miseries of a blameless creature with the leaden daggers of your literal decrees, to whose ease you cannot add the tithe of one small atom but by letting alone your unhelpful surgery? As for such as think wandering concupiscence to be here newly and more precisely forbidden than it was before, if the apostle can convince them, we know that we are to "know lust by the law" [Rom 7.7] and not by any new discovery of the gospel. The law of Moses knew what it permitted and the Gospel knew what it forbid. He that under a peevish conceit of debarring concupiscence shall go about to make a novice of Moses (not to say a worse thing for reverence sake) and such a one of God himself, as is a horror to think, to bind our Savior in the default of a downright promise breaking, and to bind the disunions of complaining nature in chains together and curb them with a canon bit,[208] 'tis he that commits all the whoredom and adultery which himself adjudges, besides the former guilt so manifold that lies upon him. And if none of these considerations with all their weight and gravity can avail to the dispossessing him of his precious literalism, let some one or other entreat him but to read on in the same 19 of Matth[ew], till he come to that place that says, "Some make themselves eunuchs for the kingdom of heaven's sake" [Matt. 19.12]. And if then he please to make use of Origen's knife, he may do well to be his own carver.[209]

CHAP. 18

Whether the words of our Savior be rightly expounded only of actual fornication to be the cause of divorce. The opinion of Grotius *with other reasons.*

But because we know that Christ never gave a judicial law and that the word fornication is variously significant in scripture, it will be much right done to our Savior's words to consider diligently whether it be meant here that nothing but actual fornication, proved by witness, can warrant a divorce, for so our canon law judges. Nevertheless, as I find that Grotius on this place hath observed, the Christian emperors, Theodosius the Second and Justinian, men of high wisdom and reputed piety, decreed it to be a divorsive fornication if the wife attempted either against the knowledge or obstinately against the will of her husband, such things as gave open suspicion of adulterizing: as the willful haunting of feasts and invitations with men not of her near kindred, the lying forth of her house without probable cause, the frequenting of theaters against her husband's

207. See Matt. 8.26, Mark 4.39.
208. A play on words, drawing together the *canon bit,* a kind of riding bit, with the Canon Law.
209. Origen is said to have castrated himself after reading the verse from Matthew just quoted.

mind, her endeavor to prevent or destroy conception.[210] Hence that of Jerome, "Where fornication is suspected, the wife may lawfully be divorced." Not that every motion of a jealous mind should be regarded, but that it should not be exacted to prove all things by the visibility of law witnessing, or else to hoodwink the mind: for the law is not able to judge of these things but by the rule of equity and by permitting a wise man to walk the middle way of prudent circumspection, neither wretchedly jealous nor stupidly and tamely patient: to this purpose hath Grotius in his notes. He shows also that fornication is taken in scripture for such a continual headstrong behavior as tends to plain contempt of the husband, and proves it out of Judges 19.2, where the Levite's wife is said to have played the whore against him, which Josephus and the Septuagin[211] with the Chaldaean interpret only of stubbornness and rebellion against her husband.[212] And to this I add that Kimchi[213] and the two other Rabbis who gloss the text, are in the same opinion. Ben Gersom reasons that had it been whoredom, a Jew and a Levite would have disdained to fetch her again. And this I shall contribute, that had it been whoredom, she would have chosen any other place to run to than to her father's house, it being so infamous for an Hebrew woman to play the harlot and so opprobrious to the parents. Fornication, then, in this place of the Judges is understood for stubborn disobedience against the husband, and not for adultery. . . .

CHAP. 19

Christ's manner of teaching. St. Paul *adds to this matter of divorce without command, to show the matter to be of equity, not of rigor. That the bondage of a Christian may be as much, and his peace as little in some other marriages besides idolatrous. If those arguments, therefore, be good in that one case, why not in those other? Therefore the apostle himself adds* ἐν τοῖς τοιούτοις.[214]

Thus at length we see, both by this[215] and by other places, that there is scarce any one saying in the Gospel but must be read with limitations and distinctions to be rightly understood; for Christ gives no full comments or continued discourses, but, as Demetrius the rhetorician phrases it,[216] speaks oft in monosyllables, like a master scattering the heavenly grain of his doctrine like pearl here and there, which requires a skillful and laborious gatherer who must compare the words he finds with other precepts, with the end of every ordinance, and

210. This sentence and the next two translate and paraphrase a passage from Grotius' *Annotationes.*

211. **Septuagint:** third-century Greek version of the Hebrew Scriptures.

212. Once again Milton paraphrases Grotius; as the Yale editor notes, Milton fails to mention that Grotius relates this argument without endorsing it.

213. David *Kimchi*, like Levi *ben Gersom* in the next sentence, were learned rabbis of the Middle Ages.

214. "In such cases" (1 Cor. 7.15).

215. Matt. 5.32, which Milton has been addressing in the second book.

216. In *On Style* (fourth century B.C.E.).

with the general analogy of evangelic doctrine. Otherwise many particular sayings would be but strange repugnant riddles, and the church would offend in granting divorce for frigidity, which is not here excepted with adultery but by them added. And this was it undoubtedly which gave reason to St. Paul of his own authority, as he professes, and without command from the Lord, to enlarge the seeming construction of those places in the Gospel, by adding a case wherein a person deserted, which is something less than divorced, may lawfully marry again. And having declared his opinion in one case, he leaves a further liberty for Christian prudence to determine in cases of like importance, using words so plain as are not to be shifted off, "that a brother or a sister is not under bondage in such cases," adding also that "God hath called us to peace" in marriage [1 Cor. 7.15].

Now if it be plain that a Christian may be brought into unworthy bondage, and his religious peace not only interrupted now and then but perpetually and finally hindered in wedlock by mis-yoking with a diversity of nature as well as of religion, the reasons of St. Paul cannot be made special to that one case of infidelity, but are of equal moment to a divorce wherever Christian liberty and peace are without fault equally obstructed; that the ordinance which God gave to our comfort may not be pinned upon us to our undeserved thraldom, to be cooped up, as it were, in mockery of wedlock, to a perpetual betrothed loneliness and discontent, if nothing worse ensue. There being naught else of marriage left between such but a displeasing and forced remedy against the sting of a brute desire, which fleshly accustoming[217] without the soul's union and commixture of intellectual delight, as it is rather a soiling than a fulfilling of marriage rites, so is it enough to imbase the mettle of a generous spirit, and sinks him to a low and vulgar pitch of endeavor in all his actions, or, which is worse, leaves him in a despairing plight of abject and hardened thoughts. Which condition rather than a good man should fall into, a man useful in the service of God and mankind, Christ himself hath taught us to dispense with the most sacred ordinances of his worship, even for a bodily healing to dispense with that holy and speculative rest of Sabbath,[218] much more than with the erroneous observance of an ill-knotted marriage, for the sustaining of an overcharged faith and perseverance.

CHAP. 20

The meaning of St. Paul, *that* charity believeth all things. *What is to be said to the license which is vainly feared will grow hereby. What to those who never have done prescribing patience in this case. The papist most severe against divorce, yet most easy to all license.*

217. **accustoming:** sexual intimacy.
218. See 2.1.

Of all the miseries in marriage God is to be cleared and the fault to be laid on man's unjust laws.

And though bad causes would take license by this pretext, if that cannot be remedied, upon their conscience be it who shall so do. This was that hardness of heart and abuse of a good law which Moses was content to suffer rather than good men should not have it at all to use needfully. And he who to run after one lost sheep left ninety-nine of his own flock at random in the wilderness[219] would little perplex his thought for the obduring[220] of nine-hundred and ninety such as will daily take worse liberties, whether they have permission or not. To conclude, as without charity God hath given no commandment to men, so without it neither can men rightly believe any commandment given. For every act of true faith, as well that whereby we believe the law as that whereby we endeavor[221] the law, is wrought in us by charity, according to that in the divine hymn of St. Paul, 1 Cor. 13[.7], "charity believeth all things." Not as if she were so credulous, which is the exposition hitherto current, for that were a trivial praise, but to teach us that charity is the high governess of our belief, and that we cannot safely assent to any precept written in the Bible but as charity commends it to us. Which agrees with that of the same apostle to the Ephes[ians] (4.14–15), where he tells us that the way to get a sure undoubted knowledge of things is to hold that for truth which accords most with charity. Whose unerring guidance and conduct having followed as a lodestar with all diligence and fidelity in this question, I trust, through the help of that illuminating spirit which hath favored me, to have done no everyday's work in asserting,[222] after many ages, the words of Christ with other scriptures of great concernment from burdensome and remorseless obscurity, tangled with manifold repugnances to their native luster and consent between each other; hereby also dissolving tedious and Gordian[223] difficulties which have hitherto molested the church of God and are now decided, not with the sword of Alexander but with the immaculate hands of charity to the unspeakable good of Christendom.

And let the extreme literalist sit down now and revolve whether this in all necessity be not the due result of our Savior's words. Or if he persist to be otherwise opinioned, let him well advise lest, thinking to grip fast the Gospel, he be found instead with the canon law in his fist, whose boisterous edicts tyrannizing the blessed ordinance of marriage into the quality of a most unnatural and unchristianly yoke have given the flesh this advantage to hate it and turn aside, ofttimes unwillingly, to all dissolute uncleanness, even till punishment it-

219. See Matt. 18.12–13 and Luke 15.4–6.
220. **obduring:** the act of becoming or being obdurate, or hardened.
221. **endeavor:** attempt to fulfill.
222. **asserting:** here carries the meaning of "rescuing."
223. **Gordian:** an allusion to the Gordian knot, which could not be untied.

self is weary and overcome by the incredible frequency of trading lust and uncontrolled adulteries.

Yet men whose creed is custom I doubt not but will be still endeavoring to hide the sloth of their own timorous capacities with this pretext, that for all this 'tis better to endure with patience and silence this affliction which God hath sent. And I agree 'tis true, if this be exhorted and not enjoined; but withal it will be wisely done to be as sure as may be that what man's iniquity hath laid on be not imputed to God's sending, lest under the color of an affected patience we detain ourselves at the gulf's mouth of many hideous temptations, not to be withstood without proper gifts, which, as Perkins well notes, God gives not ordinarily, no not to most earnest prayers.[224]—Therefore we pray, "Lead us not into temptation," a vain prayer, if, having led ourselves thither, we love to stay in that perilous condition. God sends remedies as well as evils, under which he who lies and groans, that may lawfully acquit himself, is accessory to his own ruin. Nor will it excuse him, though he suffer through a sluggish fearfulness to search thoroughly what is lawful, for fear of disquieting the secure falsity of an old opinion.

Who doubts not but that it may be piously said to him who would dismiss frigidity, "bear your trial, take it as if God would have you live this life of continence"? If he exhort this, I hear him as an angel, though he speak without warrant, but if he would compel me, I know him for Satan. To him who divorces an adulteress, piety might say, "pardon her, you may show much mercy, you may win a soul"; yet the law both of God and man leaves it freely to him, for God loves not to plow out the heart of our endeavors with over-hard and sad tasks. God delights not to make a drudge of virtue, whose actions must be all elective and uncônstrained. Forced virtue is as a bolt overshot[225]—it goes neither forward nor backward and does no good as it stands.

Seeing therefore that neither scripture nor reason hath laid this unjust austerity upon divorce, we may resolve that nothing else hath wrought it but that letter-bound servility of the canon doctors, supposing marriage to be a sacrament, and out of the art they have to lay unnecessary burdens upon all men, to make a fair show in the fleshly observance of matrimony, though peace and love with all other conjugal respects fare never so ill. And indeed the papists, who are the strictest forbidders of divorce, are the easiest libertines to admit of grossest uncleanness, as if they had a design by making wedlock a supportless[226] yoke, to violate it most under color of preserving it most inviolable; and withal delighting, as their mystery[227] is, to make men the day-laborers of their own af-

224. Milton paraphrases from the *Christian Oeconomie* (1609) of the leading Calvinist theologian of Elizabethan England, William Perkins (1558–1602).

225. The comparison is to a jammed lock.

226. **supportless:** unbearable, insupportable.

227. **mystery:** hidden design.

flictions, as if there were such a scarcity of miseries from abroad that we should be made to melt our choicest home blessings and coin them into crosses, for want whereby to hold commerce with patience.

If any, therefore, who shall hap to read this discourse, hath been through misadventure ill engaged in this contracted evil here complained of and finds the fits and workings of a high impatience frequently upon him, of all those wild words which men in misery think to ease themselves by uttering, let him not open his lips against the providence of heaven or tax the ways of God and his divine truth—for they are equal, easy, and not burdensome. Nor do they ever cross the just and reasonable desires of men, nor involve this our portion of mortal life into a necessity of sadness and malcontent by laws commanding over the unreducible antipathies of nature sooner or later found, but allow us to remedy and shake off those evils into which human error hath led us through the midst of our best intentions and to support our incident extremities by that authentic precept of sovereign charity, whose grand commission is to do and to dispose over all the ordinances of God to man, that love and truth may advance each other to everlasting. While we, literally superstitious through customary faintness of heart, not venturing to pierce with our free thoughts into the full latitude of nature and religion, abandon ourselves to serve under the tyranny of usurped opinions, suffering those ordinances which were allotted to our solace and reviving to trample over us and hale us into a multitude of sorrows which God never meant us. And where he set us in a fair allowance of way, with honest liberty and prudence to our guard, we never leave subtilizing and casuisting[228] till we have straitened and pared that liberal path into a razor's edge to walk on between a precipice of unnecessary mischief on either side. And starting at every false alarm, we do not know which way to set a foot forward with manly confidence and Christian resolution through the confused ringing in our ears of panic scruples and amazements.

CHAP. 21

That the matter of divorce is not to be tried by law, but by conscience, as many other sins are. The magistrate can only see that the condition of divorce be just and equal. The opinion of Fagius *and the reasons of this assertion.*

Another act of papal encroachment it was to pluck the power and arbitrament of divorce from the master of family, into whose hands God and the law of all nations had put it and Christ so left it, preaching only to the conscience and not authorizing a judicial court to toss about and divulge the unaccountable and secret reasons of disaffection between man and wife, as a thing most improperly

228. **casuisting:** practicing casuistry, a sophisticated and, in Milton's view, sophistical Roman Catholic art of moral reasoning.

answerable to any such kind of trial. But the popes of Rome, perceiving the great revenue and high authority it would give them even over princes to have the judging and deciding of such a main consequence in the life of man as was divorce, wrought so upon the superstition of those ages as to divest them of that right which God from the beginning had entrusted to the husband. By which means they subjected that ancient and naturally domestic prerogative to an external and unbefitting judicature. For although differences in divorce about dowries, jointures, and the like, besides the punishing of adultery, ought not to pass without referring, if need be, to the magistrate, yet that the absolute and final hindering of divorce cannot belong to any civil or earthly power against the will and consent of both parties, or of the husband alone, some reasons will be here urged. . . . [*In an omitted passage, Milton cites the authority of Grotius and Fagius.*]

If there remain a furlong yet to end the question, these following reasons may serve to gain it with any apprehension not too unlearned or too wayward. First, because ofttimes the causes of seeking divorce reside so deeply in the radical and innocent affections of nature as is not within the diocese of law to tamper with. Other relations may aptly enough be held together by a civil and virtuous love, but the duties of man and wife are such as are chiefly conversant in that love which is most ancient and merely[229] natural, whose two prime statutes are to join itself to that which is good and acceptable and friendly and to turn aside and depart from what is disagreeable, displeasing and unlike. Of the two this latter is the strongest and most equal to be regarded, for although a man may often be unjust in seeking that which he loves, yet he can never be unjust or blamable in retiring from his endless trouble and distaste, whenas his tarrying can redound to no true content on either side. Hate is of all things the mightiest divider, nay, is division itself. To couple hatred therefore, though wedlock try all her golden links and borrow to her aid all the iron manacles and fetters of law, it does but seek to twist a rope of sand,[230] which was a task, they say, that posed the devil. And that sluggish fiend in hell, Ocnus, whom the poems tell of, brought his idle cordage to as good effect, which never served to bind with but to feed the ass that stood at his elbow.[231] And that the restrictive law against divorce attains as little to bind anything truly in a disjointed marriage or to keep it bound, but serves only to feed the ignorance and definitive impertinence of a doltish canon, were no absurd allusion.

To hinder therefore those deep and serious regresses of nature in a reasonable soul parting from that mistaken help which he justly seeks in a person created for him, recollecting[232] himself from an unmeet help which was never

229. **merely:** entirely.

230. A proverbial expression for an impossible feat and for a fetter that does not bind; cp. George Herbert, "The Collar."

231. *Ocnus* was condemned in hell to make from straw a rope, which his ass immediately ate (Pausanias, *Description of Greece* 10.29.1–2).

232. **recollecting:** withdrawing.

meant, and to detain him by compulsion in such an unpredestined misery as this, is in diameter against[233] both nature and institution; but to interpose a jurisdictive power upon the inward and irremediable disposition of man, to command love and sympathy, to forbid dislike against the guiltless instinct of nature, is not within the province of any law to reach, and were indeed an incommodious rudeness, not a just power. For that law may bandy with nature and traverse her sage motions was an error in Callicles, the rhetorician, whom Socrates from high principles confutes in Plato's *Gorgias*.[234] If therefore divorce may be so natural and that law and nature are not to go contrary, then to forbid divorce compulsively is not only against nature, but against law.

Next, it must be remembered that all law is for some good that may be frequently attained without the admixture of a worse inconvenience, and therefore many gross faults (as ingratitude and the like, which are too far within the soul to be cured by constraint of law) are left only to be wrought on by conscience and persuasion; which made Aristotle, in the 10th of his *Ethics* to Nicomachus, aim at a kind of division of law into private or persuasive and public or compulsive.[235] Hence it is that the law forbidding divorce never attains to any good end of such prohibition, but rather multiplies evil. For if nature's resistless sway in love or hate be once compelled, it grows careless of itself, vicious, useless to friend, unserviceable and spiritless to the commonwealth, which Moses rightly foresaw, and all wise lawgivers that ever knew man, what kind of creature he was. The Parliament also and clergy of England were not ignorant of this when they consented that Harry the Eighth might put away his queen Anne of Cleve, whom he could not like after he had been wedded half a year,[236] unless it were that contrary to the proverb, they made a necessity of that which might have been a virtue in them to do. For even the freedom and eminence of man's creation gives him to be a law in this matter to himself, being the head of the other sex which was made for him,[237] whom therefore, though he ought not to injure, yet neither should he be forced to retain in society to his own overthrow, nor to hear any judge therein above himself. It being also an unseemly affront to the sequestered and veiled modesty of that sex to have her unpleasingness and other concealments bandied up and down, and aggravated in open court by those hired masters of tongue-fence.[238] . . . [*In several omitted sentences, Milton offers an example from the divorce proceedings of Henry VIII and Catherine of Aragon.*] That woman whose honor is not appeached[239] is less injured by a silent dismission, being otherwise not illiberally dealt with, than to

233. **in diameter against:** diametrically opposed to.

234. Socrates argues against Callicles that justice is inherent in things and not merely a matter of convention (*Gorgias* 482–510).

235. *Nichomachean Ethics* 10.9.

236. Henry VIII was divorced from Anne of Cleves in 1540, after six months of marriage.

237. Cp. 1 Cor. 11.3: "The head of the woman is the man."

238. **hired masters of tongue-fence:** i.e., lawyers.

239. **appeached:** impeached.

endure a clamoring debate of utterless things in a business of that civil secrecy and difficult discerning, as not to be overmuch questioned by nearest friends. Which drew that answer from the greatest and worthiest Roman of his time, Paulus Emilius, being demanded why he would put away his wife for no visible reason: "This shoe," saith he, and held it out on his foot, "is a neat shoe, a new shoe, and yet none of you know where it wrings me."[240] Much less by the unfamiliar cognizance of a feed gamester can such a private difference be examined, neither ought it.

Again, if law aim at the firm establishment and preservation of matrimonial faith, we know that cannot thrive under violent means, but is the more violated. It is not when two unfortunately met are by the canon forced to draw in that yoke an unmerciful day's work of sorrow till death unharnesse 'em, that then the law keeps marriage most unviolated and unbroken; but when the law takes order that marriage be accountant and responsible to perform that society, whether it be religious, civil, or corporal, which may be conscionably required and claimed therein, or else to be dissolved if it cannot be undergone. This is to make marriage most indissoluble, by making it a just and equal dealer, a performer of those due helps which instituted the covenant, being otherwise a most unjust contract and no more to be maintained under tuition[241] of law than the vilest fraud, or cheat, or theft that may be committed. But because this is such a secret kind of fraud or theft, as cannot be discerned by law but only by the plaintiff himself, therefore to divorce was never counted a political or civil offense neither to Jew nor Gentile, nor any judicial intendment of Christ further than could be discerned to transgress the allowance of Moses, which was of necessity so large that it doth all one as if it sent back the matter undeterminable at law and intractable by rough dealing, to have instructions and admonitions bestowed about it by them whose spiritual office is to adjure and to denounce, and so left to the conscience.

The law can only appoint the just and equal conditions of divorce, and is to look how it is an injury to the divorced. Which in truth it can be none as a mere separation: for if she consent, wherein has the law to right her? Or consent not, then is it either just and so deserved, or if unjust, such in all likelihood was the divorcer, and to part from an unjust man is a happiness and no injury to be lamented. But suppose it be an injury, the law is not able to amend it, unless she think it other than a miserable redress to return back from whence she was expelled, or but entreated to be gone, or else to live apart still married without marriage, a married widow. Last, if it be to chasten the divorcer, what law punishes a deed which is not moral but natural, a deed which cannot certainly be found to be an injury? Or how can it be punished by prohibiting the divorce, but that the innocent must equally partake both in the shame and in the smart? So

240. Milton draws the story from Plutarch, *Aemilius Paulus* 5.1–2.
241. **tuition:** protection.

that which way soever we look the law can to no rational purpose forbid divorce, it can only take care that the conditions of divorce be not injurious. Thus then we see the trial of law how impertinent it is to this question of divorce, how helpless next, and then how hurtful.

CHAP. 22

The last reason why divorce is not to be restrained by law, it being against the law of nature and of nations. The larger proof whereof referred to Mr. Selden's *Book* De jure naturali & gentium. *An objection of* Paræus *answered. How it ought to be ordered by the church. That this will not breed any worse inconvenience nor so bad as is now suffered.*

Therefore the last reason why it should not be, is the example we have not only from the noblest and wisest commonwealths, guided by the clearest light of human knowledge, but also from the divine testimonies of God himself, lawgiving in person to a sanctified people. That all this is true, whoso desires to know at large with least pains and expects not here overlong rehearsals of that which is by others already so judiciously gathered, let him hasten to be acquainted with that noble volume written by our learned Selden, *Of the Law of Nature and of Nations*,[242] a work more useful and more worthy to be perused, whosoever studies to be a great man in wisdom, equity, and justice, than all those decretals, and sumless sums,[243] which the pontifical clerks have doted on ever since that unfortunate mother famously[244] sinned thrice[245] and died impenitent of her bringing into the world those two misbegotten infants, and forever infants, Lombard & Gratian, him the compiler of canon iniquity, t'other the Tubalcain[246] of scholastic sophistry, whose overspreading barbarism hath not only infused their own bastardy upon the fruitfullest part of human learning, not only dissipated and dejected the clear light of nature in us and of nations, but hath tainted also the fountains of divine doctrine and rendered the pure and solid law of God unbeneficial to us by their calumnious dunceries.

Yet this law, which their unskilfulness hath made liable to all ignominy, the purity and wisdom of this law shall be the buckler of our dispute. Liberty of divorce we claim not, we think not, but from this law; the dignity, the faith, the authority thereof is now grown among Christians, O astonishment! A labor of

242. John Selden (1584–1654), a leading scholar and Parliamentarian, published his *De Jure Naturali et Gentium* in 1640; he is thought to have influenced Milton's thinking on divorce and other matters. See *CD* 1.10, n. 28.

243. **sumless sums:** Milton plays on the title *summa*, used for compendia or digests (e.g., Aquinas's *Summa Theologica*).

244. **famously:** notoriously.

245. According to legend, the twelfth-century writers Peter *Lombard*, Johannes *Gratian*, and Peter Comestor, reputed to be the founders of Canon Law, theology, and biblical scholarship, were brothers.

246. See Gen. 4.22, where *Tubalcain* is "an instructor of every artificer in brass and iron."

no mean difficulty and envy[247] to defend. That it should not be counted a faltering dispense, a flattering permission of sin, the bill of adultery, a snare, is the expense of all this apology. And all that we solicit is that it may be suffered to stand in the place where God set it amidst the firmament of his holy laws, to shine, as it was wont, upon the weaknesses and errors of men perishing else in the sincerity of their honest purposes. For certain there is no memory of whoredoms and adulteries left among us now, when this warranted freedom of God's own giving is made dangerous and discarded for a scroll of license. It must be your suffrages and votes, O Englishmen, that this exploded decree of God and Moses may scape and come off fair without the censure of a shameful abrogating, which, if yonder sun[248] ride sure and mean not to break word with us tomorrow, was never yet abrogated by our Savior. Give sentence, if you please, that the frivolous canon may reverse the infallible judgment of Moses and his great director.

Or if it be the reformed writers whose doctrine persuades this rather, their reasons I dare affirm are all silenced, unless it be only this: Paræus, on the Corinthians, would prove that hardness of heart in divorce is no more now to be permitted, but to be amerced with fine and imprisonment.[249] I am not willing to discover the forgettings of reverend men, yet here I must. What article or clause of the whole new covenant can Paræus bring to exasperate the judicial law upon any infirmity under the Gospel? (I say infirmity, for if it were the high hand of sin, the law as little would have endured it as the Gospel.) It would not stretch to the dividing of an inheritance;[250] it refused to condemn adultery,[251] not that these things should not be done at law, but to show that the Gospel hath not the least influence upon judicial courts, much less to make them sharper and more heavy—least of all to arraign before a temporal judge that which the Law without summons acquitted. But, saith he, the Law was the time of youth under violent affections, the Gospel in us is mature age and ought to subdue affections.[252] True, and so ought the Law too, if they be found inordinate and not merely natural and blameless.

Next, I distinguish that the time of the Law is compared to youth and pupilage in respect of the ceremonial part, which led the Jews as children through corporal and garish rudiments, until the fullness of time should reveal to them the higher lessons of faith and redemption. This is not meant of the moral part; therein it soberly concerned them not to be babies, but to be men in good earnest. The sad and awful majesty of that Law was not to be jested with. To bring a bearded nonage with lascivious dispensations before that throne had been a lewd affront, as it is now a gross mistake. But what discipline is this

247. **envy:** unpopularity.
248. A pun on *Son.*
249. Milton summarizes Paraeus's comment on 1 Cor. 7.10–11.
250. See Luke 12.13–14.
251. See John 8.3–11.
252. This sentence translates and paraphrases Paraeus's commentary on 1 Corinthians.

Paræus to nourish violent affections in youth by cockering[253] and wanton indulgences, and to chastise them in mature age with a boyish rod of correction? How much more coherent is it to Scripture that the Law as a strict schoolmaster should have punished every trespass without indulgence so baneful to youth, and that the Gospel should now correct that by admonition and reproof only, in free and mature age, which was punished with stripes in the childhood and bondage of the Law.[254] What therefore it allowed then so fairly, much less is to be whipped now, especially in penal courts, and if it ought now to trouble the conscience, why did that angry accuser and condemner law reprieve it?

So then, neither from Moses nor from Christ hath the magistrate any authority to proceed against it. But what? Shall then the disposal of that power return again to the master of family? Wherefore not? Since God there put it and the presumptuous canon thence bereft it. This only must be provided, that the ancient manner be observed in the presence of the minister and other grave selected elders, who after they shall have admonished and pressed upon him the words of our Savior, and he shall have protested in the faith of the eternal Gospel and the hope he has of happy resurrection, that otherwise than thus he cannot do, and thinks himself and this his case not contained in that prohibition of divorce which Christ pronounced, the matter not being of malice, but of nature, and so not capable of reconciling. To constrain him further were to unchristen him, to unman him, to throw the mountain of Sinai upon him, with the weight of the whole Law to boot, flat against the liberty and essence of the Gospel, and yet nothing available either to the sanctity of marriage, the good of husband, wife, or children, nothing profitable either to church or commonwealth, but hurtful and pernicious to all these respects. But this will bring in confusion.[255]

Yet these cautious mistrusters might consider that what they thus object lights not upon this book but upon that which I engage against them, the book of God and of Moses,[256] with all the wisdom and providence which had forecast the worst of confusion that could succeed, and yet thought fit of such a permission. But let them be of good cheer, it wrought so little disorder among the Jews, that from Moses till after the captivity not one of the prophets thought it worth rebuking; for that of Malachi, well looked into, will appear to be not against divorcing, but rather against keeping strange concubines to the vexation of their Hebrew wives.[257] If therefore we Christians may be thought as good and tractable as the Jews were, and certainly the prohibiters of divorce presume us to be better, then less confusion is to be feared for this among us than was among them. If we be worse or but as bad, which lamentable examples confirm

253. **cockering:** indulgent, coddling.

254. See Gal. 3.24–25.

255. Milton characterizes his opponents' position.

256. Milton suggests that attacks on his position amount to attacks on the Bible.

257. See Mal. 2.16; see 1.6, and n. 103.

we are, then have we more—or at least as much—need of this permitted law as they to whom God therefore gave it (as they say) under a harsher covenant.

Let not therefore the frailty of man go on thus inventing needless troubles to itself, to groan under the false imagination of a strictness never imposed from above, enjoining that for duty which is an impossible and vain supererogating. "Be not righteous overmuch," is the counsel of Ecclesiastes, "why shouldst thou destroy thyself?" [Eccles. 7.16]. Let us not be thus over-curious to strain at atoms,[258] and yet to stop every vent and cranny of permissive liberty, lest nature, wanting those needful pores and breathing places which God hath not debarred our weakness, either suddenly break out into some wide rupture of open vice and frantic heresy or else inwardly fester with repining and blasphemous thoughts under an unreasonable and fruitless rigor of unwarranted law. Against which evils nothing can more beseem the religion of the church or the wisdom of the state than to consider timely and provide. And in so doing, let them not doubt but they shall vindicate the misreputed honor of God and his great lawgiver, by suffering him to give his own laws according to the condition of man's nature best known to him, without the insufferable imputation of dispensing legally with many ages of ratified adultery. They shall recover the misattended words of Christ to the sincerity of their true sense from manifold contradictions and shall open them with the key of charity. Many helpless Christians they shall raise from the depth of sadness and distress, utterly unfitted as they are to serve God or man. Many they shall reclaim from obscure and giddy sects, many regain from dissolute and brutish license, many from desperate hardness, if ever that were justly pleaded. They shall set free many daughters of Israel, not wanting much of her sad plight "whom Satan had bound eighteen years" [Luke 13.16]. Man they shall restore to his just dignity and prerogative in nature, preferring the soul's free peace before the promiscuous draining of a carnal rage. Marriage, from a perilous hazard and snare, they shall reduce to be a more certain haven and retirement of happy society, when they shall judge according to God and Moses (and how not then according to Christ?), when they shall judge it more wisdom and goodness to break that covenant seemingly and keep it really, than by compulsion of law to keep it seemingly, and by compulsion of blameless nature to break it really, at least if it were ever truly joined. The vigor of discipline they may then turn with better success upon the prostitute looseness of the times, when men, finding in themselves the infirmities of former ages, shall not be constrained above the gift of God in them to unprofitable and impossible observances never required from the civilest, the wisest, the holiest nations, whose other excellencies in moral virtue they never yet could equal. Last of all, to those whose mind still is to maintain textual restrictions whereof the bare sound cannot consist sometimes with humanity, much less with charity, I would ever answer by putting them in remembrance of a command above all commands, which they seem to have forgot, and who spake it, in comparison

258. **atoms:** particles of dust; cp. Matt. 23.24: "Ye blind guides, which strain at a gnat."

whereof this, which they so exalt, is but a petty and subordinate precept): "Let them go therefore" (with whom I am loathe to couple them, yet they will needs run into the same blindness with the Pharisees),[259] "let them go therefore" and consider well what this lesson means, "I will have mercy and not sacrifice" [Matt. 9.13]; for on that "saying all the law and prophets depend" [Matt. 22.40], much more the Gospel whose end and excellence is mercy and peace. Or if they cannot learn that, how will they hear this (which yet I shall not doubt to leave with them as a conclusion)? that God the son hath put all other things under his own feet, but his commandments he hath left all under the feet of charity.

The end.

259. Milton compares his opponents to the Pharisees rebuked by Christ in Matt. 9.

AREOPAGITICA;

A

SPEECH

OF

Mr. *JOHN MILTON*

For the Liberty of UNLICENC'D PRINTING,

To the PARLAMENT of *ENGLAND*.

Τοὐλεύθερον δ' ἐκεῖνο, εἴ τις θέλει πόλει
Χρηστόν τι βούλευμ' εἰς μέσον φέρειν, ἔχων.
Καὶ ταῦθ' ὁ χρῄζων, λαμπρὸς ἔσθ', ὁ μὴ θέλων,
Σιγᾷ, τί τούτων ἐστὶν ἰσαίτερον πόλει;

Euripid. Hicetid.

This is true Liberty when free born men
Having to advise the public may speak free,
Which he who can, and will, deserv's high praise,
Who neither can nor will, may hold his peace;
What can be juster in a State then this?

Euripid. Hicetid.

LONDON,
Printed in the Yeare, 1644.

Title page to *Areopagitica* (1644).

INTRODUCTION TO *AREOPAGITICA*

Despite a Parliamentary order of June 1643 prohibiting unlicensed publications, *Areopagitica* was in November 1644 printed without license. Milton composed it as if he were speaking before Parliament, observing that its members had restored the most perverse and repressive system of censorship ever devised, one first inflicted on the English by the feared and loathed Court of the Star Chamber. King Charles and Archbishop Laud had harnessed that court's wide-ranging powers to enforce "thorough" conformity. Yet two years after abolishing the Star Chamber, Parliament reimposed its system of censorship, forbidding publication of any book "unless the same be first approved and licensed by such . . . as shall be thereto appointed." The main difference under the new regime was that the licensers were Parliament's presbyters instead of Archbishop Laud's priests—a change that Milton later observed did not extend beyond the two syllables difference in their titles (*On the New Forcers of Conscience* 20).

The expanded liberty of expression enjoyed upon the demise of the Star Chamber in 1641 did not last long, but if statistics are any guide, it was energetically exploited. Excluding serials, 867 items were published in 1640, the last full year of Stuart censorship. During 1642, the one full year in which Parliament allowed the book trade to go unregulated, that total jumped to 2,968 items. The numbers bear out Milton's stirring account of embattled Londoners "disputing, reasoning, reading, inventing, discoursing, even to a rarity and admiration, things not before discoursed or written of." Milton himself in 1641–42 produced five tracts, all of them supporting the Presbyterian assault on episcopacy. His next barrage of pamphlets, however, published in 1643–44, scandalized his former allies by advocating a scriptural right of divorce. The uproar came to a head in the second half of 1644, when the dogged divorcer was denounced in broadsides and reprobated from pulpits. In a baleful sermon preached before Parliament in August of that year, Herbert Palmer declared Milton's most current divorce tract intolerable, "deserving to be burnt" (an evaluation of Milton's controversial writings regularly repeated and sometimes acted upon in years to come). That same August, the Stationers' Company, which controlled the

London book trade, delivered a petition to the House of Commons that evidently complained of the failure of Milton and others to submit to the licensing order. On Milton's part, the defiance was real and persistent. The first edition of the *Doctrine and Discipline of Divorce* was published a month after the Licensing Order of 1643, and the second edition more than six months after. Neither was registered with the Stationers' Company—as *Areopagitica* and subsequent works were not. Although it is not clear what the perceived risk was in 1643–44 for those who chose to publish unlicensed books, we do know that the still anonymous printer of *Areopagitica* took pains to use only nondescript materials in producing the pamphlet—one that bears John Milton's name on its title page.

Milton's address to Parliament, like other of his works advocating or defending political and religious liberties, takes the form of a classical oration. Its title and the topic of censorship recall Isocrates' seventh oration, the so-called *Areopagitic Discourse* (c. 355 B.C.E.), recommending moral reform to the Athenian Council of the Areopagus (Mars hill). Several centuries later, the apostle Paul would stand on that same hill, as Milton's audience well knew, quoting Greek poetry to evangelize the Athenians (Acts 17.22–34). St. Paul hoped to persuade them that his God was the unknown deity whom their cult acknowledged and poets intimated. It was their recognition that religious truth might lie beyond their ken that allowed the Athenians to learn of a faith that seemed strange, even foolish, but one that Milton's audience, sixteen centuries later, accepted as absolutely true and the sole means of salvation.

The first part of Milton's aptly titled oration is historical and traces the invention of licensing to the Roman Catholic Inquisition. The second affirms temperance as the sole means of fostering individual virtue: temperance understood not as unreasoning habit but as a rationally informed discipline fortified in the process of confronting, identifying, and rejecting the deceptive evils of the world. "Promiscuous" reading is well suited to this virtuous exercise, or so Milton insists in a passage that remains strikingly pertinent: "They are not skilful considerers of human things who imagine to remove sin by removing the matter of sin." Even if humanity did possess innate virtue to protect from exposure to corruption, mere regulation of printing, as the third part of the argument wittily elaborates, would not suffice: "Who shall silence all the airs and madrigals that whisper softness in chambers?" The fourth part develops the claim that licensing will fail to achieve the end it seeks and instead perversely undermine the virtue of English souls. Even if a belief to which one obediently but mindlessly conformed were true, one would be no more than a "heretic in the truth." Faith not rationally tried by the believer does not in Milton's view qualify as authentic.

As social policy, Milton's advocacy of limited freedom of the press and toleration of Protestant sects, though courageous enough in its historical moment, was hardly inspiring to future generations. His representation of truth as being, in this world, partial, fragmentary, and multiple, however, continues to encourage a commitment to pluralism and tolerance as conducive rather than corrosive to human virtue. Milton claims that truth once was readily accessible, indeed wholly present in the world, but, after the era of Christ and his apostles, "straight arose a wicked race of deceivers," who "took the virgin Truth, hewed her lovely form into a thousand pieces and scattered them to the four winds." The rest of history affords "the sad friends of truth" the opportunity to recover the pieces, just as in myth Isis recovered the mangled body of her beloved Osiris. This pious effort, Milton insists, will not be complete until Christ's Second Coming, and Parliament should not in the meantime obstruct "them that continue seeking."

Readers of *Areopagitica* have long found that such moments of myth and poetic symbol possess a sudden and unqualified force missing from the oration's discursive argument. Ernst Sirluck explained this inconsistency by identifying Parliamentary factions that any proposal would need to negotiate rhetorically if it were to succeed (Yale 2:169–78). More recently, Christopher Kendrick elaborated on Sirluck's thesis to argue that the discursive argument's recurring imagery of trade and commerce signals Milton's unconscious allegiance to the emergent bourgeoisie, in whose interest freedom of expression would still be regulated. For Stanley Fish, however, Milton quite consciously recognized freedom of speech as being always conditional, a privilege extended by those in power to those of like mind (1994).

We can of course never know precisely what rhetorical strategy Milton in 1644 thought he was pursuing or what political interest he may have served, consciously or unconsciously, by his appeal to Parliament. We do know that in its own time *Areopagitica* had little or no impact. Parliament actually stepped up its efforts to suppress heretical opinion. Only a half century later, Walter Blount would publish a condensed version of Milton's oration as if it were his own composition, under the title "A Just Vindication of Learning and the Liberty of the Press." Yet the book in which Milton's oration was printed did survive, and, according to its own definition of a "good book," Milton survived with it. The material process by which "the precious life-blood of a master spirit" is "embalmed and treasured up on purpose to a life beyond life" haunts the oration's imagery and diction (Dobranski). Evidently, the vitalist materialism central to Milton's epic poetry and heretical theology is the imaginative and doctrinal culmination of a persistent tendency in his thought. His definition of a good book is famously engraved over the doorway of the main reading room of the New York Public Library. But in Milton's view, his posthumous existence, like Shakespeare's, persists not in piled stones, however inscribed, but in the minds of his readers. By the eighteenth century, especially in revolutionary America and France, Milton's oration at last found an audience in whom his version of truth might live. Since then, *Areopagitica* has in the West been widely considered the most complete and inspirational argument for freedom of the press ever composed, "the foundational essay of the free speech tradition" (Blasi).

Our text is based on the copy of the first edition in the British Library's Thomason Collection, checked against the copy held in the Carl H. Pforzheimer Library in the Harry Ransom Humanities Research Center, Austin, Texas.

AREOPAGITICA:
A SPEECH OF MR. JOHN MILTON FOR THE LIBERTY OF UNLICENSED PRINTING TO THE PARLIAMENT OF ENGLAND.

Τοὐλεύθερον δ' ἐκεῖνο, εἴ τις θέλει πόλει
Χρηστόν τι βούλευμ' εἰς μέσον φέρειν ἔχων;
Καὶ ταῦθ' ὁ χρῄζων, λαμπρὸς ἔσθ', ὁ μὴ θέλων,
Σιγᾷ. τί τούτων ἔστιν ἰσαίτερον πόλει;
Euripid. Hicetid.

This is true liberty when freeborn men
Having to advise the public may speak free,
Which he who can, and will, deserves high praise,
Who neither can nor will, may hold his peace;
What can be juster in a state than this?
[Euripid. Hicetid.[1]]

For the Liberty of Unlicensed Printing:

They who to states and governors of the commonwealth direct their speech, high court of Parliament, or wanting such access in a private condition, write that which they foresee may advance the public good, I suppose them as at the beginning of no mean endeavor, not a little altered and moved inwardly in their minds: some with doubt of what will be the success, others with fear of what will be the censure; some with hope, others with confidence of what they have to speak. And me, perhaps, each of these dispositions, as the subject was whereon I entered, may have at other times variously affected; and likely might in these foremost expressions now also disclose which of them swayed most, but that the very attempt of this address thus made, and the thought of whom it hath recourse to, hath got the power within me to a passion far more welcome than incidental to a preface.

Which though I stay not to confess ere any ask, I shall be blameless, if it be no

1. Euripides, *The Suppliants* 438.41. The passage in Greek appears with Milton's translation on the title page of the first edition. Euripides is quoting the words with which the assembly at Athens opened.

other than the joy and gratulation which it brings to all who wish and promote their country's liberty, whereof this whole discourse proposed will be a certain testimony, if not a trophy. For this is not the liberty which we can hope, that no grievance ever should arise in the commonwealth—that let no man in this world expect. But when complaints are freely heard, deeply considered, and speedily reformed, then is the utmost bound of civil liberty attained that wise men look for. To which if I now manifest by the very sound of this which I shall utter, that we are already in good part arrived, and yet from such a steep disadvantage of tyranny and superstition grounded into our principles as was beyond the manhood of a Roman recovery,[2] it will be attributed first, as is most due, to the strong assistance of God our deliverer, next to your faithful guidance and undaunted wisdom, Lords and Commons of England. Neither is it in God's esteem the diminution of his glory when honorable things are spoken of good men and worthy magistrates; which if I now first should begin to do, after so fair a progress of your laudable deeds and such a long obligement[3] upon the whole realm to your indefatigable virtues, I might be justly reckoned among the tardiest, and the unwillingest of them that praise ye.

Nevertheless, there being three principal things without which all praising is but courtship and flattery. First, when that only is praised which is solidly worth praise; next, when greatest likelihoods are brought that such things are truly and really in those persons to whom they are ascribed; the other, when he who praises, by showing that such his actual persuasion is of whom he writes, can demonstrate that he flatters not. The former two of these I have heretofore endeavored, rescuing the employment from him who went about to impair your merits with a trivial and malignant encomium;[4] the latter as belonging chiefly to mine own acquittal, that whom I so extolled I did not flatter, hath been reserved opportunely to this occasion. For he who freely magnifies what hath been nobly done, and fears not to declare as freely what might be done better, gives ye the best covenant of his fidelity and that his loyalest affection and his hope waits on your proceedings. His highest praising is not flattery, and his plainest advice is a kind of praising. For though I should affirm and hold by argument that it would fare better with truth, with learning, and the commonwealth, if one of your published orders which I should name were called in, yet at the same time it could not but much redound to the luster of your mild and equal government whenas private persons are hereby animated to think ye better pleased with public advice than other statists have been delighted heretofore with public flattery. And men will then see what difference there is

2. **Roman recovery:** The English, having cast off the yoke of King Charles and the bishops, achieved what the Romans, subject to emperors and then popes, could not.

3. **obligement:** indebtedness for benefits received. The Long Parliament first convened in November 1640, four years before the publication of *Areopagitica*.

4. In *An Apology for Smectymnuus*, Milton objects to the covert Royalism of Bishop Hall's praise of Parliament and counters it with what he deems more fitting praise (Yale 1:919–20).

between the magnanimity of a triennial parliament[5] and that jealous haughtiness of prelates and cabin counselors that usurped of late, whenas they shall observe ye in the midst of your victories and successes[6] more gently brooking written exceptions against a voted order than other courts, which had produced nothing worth memory but the weak ostentation of wealth, would have endured the least signified dislike at any sudden proclamation.

If I should thus far presume upon the meek demeanor of your civil and gentle greatness, Lords and Commons, as what your published order hath directly said, that to gainsay, I might defend myself with ease, if any should accuse me of being new or insolent, did they but know how much better I find ye esteem it to imitate the old and elegant humanity of Greece than the barbaric pride of a Hunnish and Norwegian stateliness. And out of those ages, to whose polite wisdom and letters we owe that we are not yet Goths and Jutlanders, I could name him who from his private house wrote that discourse to the Parliament of Athens[7] that persuades them to change the form of democracy which was then established. Such honor was done in those days to men who professed the study of wisdom and eloquence, not only in their own country but in other lands, that cities and seignories heard them gladly and with great respect if they had aught in public to admonish the state. Thus did Dion Prusæus, a stranger and a private orator, counsel the Rhodians against a former edict,[8] and I abound with other like examples which to set here would be superfluous. But if from the industry of a life wholly dedicated to studious labors and those natural endowments haply not the worst for two and fifty degrees of northern latitude[9] so much must be derogated as to count me not equal to any of those who had this privilege, I would obtain to be thought not so inferior as yourselves are superior to the most of them who received their counsel. And how far you excel them, be assured, Lords and Commons, there can no greater testimony appear, than when your prudent spirit acknowledges and obeys the voice of reason from what quarter soever it be heard speaking, and renders ye as willing to repeal any act of your own setting forth as any set forth by your predecessors.[10]

If ye be thus resolved, as it were injury to think ye were not, I know not what should withhold me from presenting ye with a fit instance wherein to show both that love of truth which ye eminently profess, and that uprightness of your

5. According to the Triennial Parliaments Act (February 1641), a new parliament would automatically be summoned three years after the last was dismissed.

6. Parliamentary forces had won a string of victories in the spring and summer of 1644, culminating in the battle of Marston Moor (July 2), which gave Parliament control of the north.

7. A private citizen, Isocrates addressed his *Areopagitic Discourse* (c. 355 B.C.E.) to the popular assembly of Athens.

8. The *Rhodian Discourse* of Dion Prusaeus (d. 117 C.E.) urges repeal of a law permitting replacement of the original names on public monuments.

9. Milton often blames the cold and damp northern climate for English dullness (e.g., *PL* 9.44–45).

10. This sentence ends the introduction, or *exordium;* what follows is the statement of the case, or *narratio.*

judgment which is not wont to be partial to yourselves, by judging over again that order which ye have ordained "to regulate printing, that no book, pamphlet, or paper shall be henceforth printed, unless the same be first approved and licensed by such,"[11] or at least one of such as shall be thereto appointed. For that part which preserves justly every man's copy[12] to himself or provides for the poor I touch not, only wish they be not made pretenses to abuse and persecute honest and painful[13] men who offend not in either of these particulars. But that other clause of licensing books, which we thought had died with his brother quadragesimal and matrimonial[14] when the prelates expired, I shall now attend with such a homily as shall lay before ye: first, the inventors of it to be those whom ye will be loath to own; next, what is to be thought in general of reading, whatever sort the books be; and, that this order avails nothing to the suppressing of scandalous, seditious, and libelous books, which were mainly intended to be suppressed. Last, that it will be primely to the discouragement of all learning and the stop of truth, not only by disexercising[15] and blunting our abilities in what we know already, but by hindering and cropping the discovery that might be yet further made both in religious and civil wisdom.

I deny not but that it is of greatest concernment in the church and commonwealth to have a vigilant eye how books demean themselves as well as men, and thereafter to confine, imprison, and do sharpest justice on them as malefactors. For books are not absolutely dead things, but do contain a potency of life in them to be as active as that soul was whose progeny they are; nay, they do preserve as in a vial the purest efficacy and extraction of that living intellect that bred them. I know they are as lively and as vigorously productive as those fabulous dragon's teeth, and, being sown up and down, may chance to spring up armed men.[16] And yet, on the other hand, unless wariness be used, as good almost kill a man as kill a good book. Who kills a man kills a reasonable creature, God's image, but he who destroys a good book kills reason itself, kills the image of God, as it were, in the eye. Many a man lives a burden to the earth, but a good book is the precious lifeblood of a master spirit, embalmed and treasured up on purpose to a life beyond life. 'Tis true, no age can restore a life, whereof perhaps there is no great loss, and revolutions of ages do not oft recover the loss of a rejected truth, for the want of which whole nations fare the worse. We should be wary therefore what persecution we raise against the living labors of public men, how we spill[17] that seasoned life of man preserved and stored up in books, since we see a kind of homicide may be thus committed, sometimes a martyr-

11. Milton recites (though he does not quote exactly) the text of the order.
12. **copy:** copyright.
13. **painful:** painstaking, diligent.
14. Milton refers to ecclesiastical licenses to dispense with Lenten dietary rules (*quadragesimal*) and rules requiring publication of marriage banns (*matrimonial*).
15. **disexercising:** depriving of exercise.
16. Mythical dragon's teeth were sown by both Cadmus and Jason and quickly grew into armed warriors (Ovid, *Met.* 3.101–30, 7.121–42).
17. **spill:** destroy.

dom, and if it extend to the whole impression, a kind of massacre, whereof the execution ends not in the slaying of an elemental life, but strikes at that ethereal and fifth essence,[18] the breath of reason itself, slays an immortality rather than a life. But lest I should be condemned of introducing license while I oppose licensing, I refuse not the pains to be so much historical as will serve to show what hath been done by ancient and famous commonwealths against this disorder, till the very time that this project of licensing crept out of the Inquisition,[19] was catched up by our prelates, and hath caught some of our presbyters.

In Athens, where books and wits were ever busier than in any other part of Greece, I find but only two sorts of writings which the magistrate cared to take notice of: those either blasphemous and atheistical, or libelous. Thus the books of Protagoras were by the judges of Areopagus commanded to be burnt and himself banished the territory for a discourse begun with his confessing not to know "whether there were gods or whether not." And against defaming, it was decreed that none should be traduced by name, as was the manner of *Vetus Comœdia,*[20] whereby we may guess how they censured libeling. And this course was quick enough, as Cicero writes, to quell both the desperate wits of other atheists and the open way of defaming as the event showed. Of other sects and opinions, though tending to voluptuousness and the denying of divine providence, they took no heed. Therefore we do not read that either Epicurus, or that libertine school of Cyrene, or what the Cynic impudence uttered, was ever questioned by the laws.[21] Neither is it recorded that the writings of those old comedians were suppressed, though the acting of them were forbid; and that Plato commended the reading of Aristophanes, the loosest of them all, to his royal scholar Dionysius, is commonly known, and may be excused, if holy Chrysostom, as is reported, nightly studied so much the same author and had the art to cleanse a scurrilous vehemence into the style of a rousing sermon.

That other leading city of Greece, Lacedæmon, considering that Lycurgus their lawgiver was so addicted to elegant learning as to have been the first that brought out of Ionia the scattered works of Homer, and sent the poet Thales from Crete to prepare and mollify the Spartan surliness with his smooth songs and odes, the better to plant among them law and civility, it is to be wondered how museless and unbookish they were, minding naught but the feats of war. There needed no licensing of books among them, for they disliked all but their

18. The *fifth essence,* or quintessence, is not *elemental,* like earth, air, fire, and water, but *ethereal.* From it derives Heaven and the pure intellectual substance of angels (cp. *PL* 3.714–18).

19. **Inquisition:** tribunal of the Roman Catholic Church (1232–1820) created to discover and suppress heresy.

20. **Vetus Comœdia:** The old comedy of Greece regularly attacked public figures by name; Aristophanes is the best known of the old comedians.

21. Followers of *Epicurus* (c. 341–270 B.C.E.) were associated with devotion to pleasure. *Cyrene* was the home of Hedonism, a philosophy linked to sensual self-indulgence. *Cynics* were noted for insolence to authority.

own laconic apothegms[22] and took a slight occasion to chase Archilochus out of their city, perhaps for composing in a higher strain than their own soldierly ballads and roundels could reach to; or if it were for his broad verses, they were not therein so cautious, but they were as dissolute in their promiscuous conversing,[23] whence Euripides affirms in *Andromache* that their women were all unchaste. Thus much may give us light after what sort books were prohibited among the Greeks.

The Romans also, for many ages trained up only to a military roughness, resembling most the Lacedæmonian guise, knew of learning little but what their twelve tables and the Pontific College with their augurs and flamens[24] taught them in religion and law, so unacquainted with other learning that when Carneades and Critolaus, with the Stoic Diogenes coming ambassadors to Rome, took thereby occasion to give the city a taste of their philosophy, they were suspected for seducers by no less a man than Cato the Censor, who moved it in the Senate to dismiss them speedily, and to banish all such Attic babblers out of Italy.[25] But Scipio and others of the noblest senators withstood him and his old Sabine austerity, honored and admired the men, and the Censor himself at last in his old age fell to the study of that whereof before he was so scrupulous. And yet at the same time, Nævius and Plautus, the first Latin comedians, had filled the city with all the borrowed scenes of Menander and Philemon.[26]

Then began to be considered there also what was to be done to libelous books and authors; for Nævius was quickly cast into prison for his unbridled pen and released by the tribunes upon his recantation. We read also that libels were burnt and the makers punished by Augustus. The like severity no doubt was used if aught were impiously written against their esteemed gods. Except in these two points, how the world went in books, the magistrate kept no reckoning. And therefore Lucretius without impeachment versifies his Epicurism to Memmius, and had the honor to be set forth the second time by Cicero, so great a father of the commonwealth, although himself disputes against that opinion in his own writings.[27] Nor was the satirical sharpness or naked plainness of Lucilius, or Catullus, or Flaccus, by any order prohibited. And for mat-

22. **apothegms:** pithy sayings.
23. Spartan men and women exercised naked together, a practice presumed to spur sexual license
24. **twelve tables:** earliest Roman law code. **Pontific College:** Rome's supreme religious authority. **augurs and flamens:** priests who consulted natural omens to guide public policy and priests devoted to the service of a particular deity, respectively.
25. This anecdote from the second century B.C.E. indicates the Roman republic's initial distrust of Greek intellectuals, especially as rhetorical performers (*Attic babblers*). The skeptic *Carneades* (213?–129 B.C.E.), the Aristotelian *Critolaus* (fl. second century B.C.E.), and the Stoic *Diogenes* (fl. second century B.C.E.) were opposed by the notoriously rigorous and conservative *Cato* (234–149 B.C.E.). *Scipio* the Younger (185–29 B.C.E.) was, by contrast, a leading Roman patron of Greek culture. *Censors* were elected public officials who took the census and supervised Rome's public works, finance, and morality.
26. *Menander* and *Philemon* were major authors of Athenian New Comedy; *Nævius* and *Plautus* were Roman playwrights deeply influenced by them. Though Rome came to embrace Greek learning, libel was still suppressed, as Nævius discovered when he was imprisoned for satirizing Scipio.
27. In *De Rerum Natura, Lucretius* gave epic expression to Epicurean materialism. *Memmius,* to whom the work was dedicated, was praetor in 58 B.C.E. *Cicero* was its putative editor.

ters of state, the story of Titus Livius, though it extolled that part which Pompey held, was not therefore suppressed by Octavius Cæsar of the other faction.[28] But that Naso was by him banished in his old age for the wanton poems of his youth was but a mere covert of state over some secret cause, and besides, the books were neither banished nor called in.[29] From hence we shall meet with little else but tyranny in the Roman Empire, that we may not marvel, if not so often bad as good books were silenced. I shall therefore deem to have been large enough in producing what among the ancients was punishable to write, save only which all other arguments were free to treat on.

By this time the emperors were become Christians, whose discipline in this point I do not find to have been more severe than what was formerly in practice. The books of those whom they took to be grand heretics were examined, refuted, and condemned in the general councils and not till then were prohibited or burnt by authority of the emperor. As for the writings of heathen authors, unless they were plain invectives against Christianity, as those of Porphyrius and Proclus,[30] they met with no interdict that can be cited, till about the year 400 in a Carthaginian council, wherein bishops themselves were forbid to read the books of gentiles, but heresies they might read; while others long before them, on the contrary, scrupled more the books of heretics than of gentiles. And that the primitive councils and bishops were wont only to declare what books were not commendable, passing no further, but leaving it to each one's conscience to read or to lay by, till after the year 800, is observed already by Padre Paolo, the great unmasker of the Trentine Council.[31]

After which time the popes of Rome, engrossing what they pleased of political rule into their own hands, extended their dominion over men's eyes as they had before over their judgments, burning and prohibiting to be read what they fancied not—yet sparing in their censures, and the books not many which they so dealt with; till Martin the Fifth by his bull not only prohibited, but was the first that excommunicated the reading of heretical books,[32] for about that time Wycliffe and Huss,[33] growing terrible, were they who first drove the papal court to a stricter policy of prohibiting. Which course Leo the Tenth and his successors followed, until the Council of Trent and the Spanish Inquisition, engendering together, brought forth or perfected those catalogues and expurging indexes[34]

28. The historian *Titus Livius* (Livy) praised *Pompey* highly and was alleged to have had the approval of *Octavius Cæsar* (Augustus), Pompey's victorious opponent, for doing so.

29. The licentious verse of Ovid (Publius Ovidius *Naso*) was the alleged reason for his exile by Augustus. Although Ovid was banished, his books were not.

30. Late classical Neoplatonic scholars, *Porphyrius* (or Porphyry, 233–304) and *Proclus* (or Proculus, 410–485) opposed Christianity and defended paganism.

31. *Padre Paolo* is the religious name of Pietro Sarpi (1552–1623), a leader of the Venetian opposition to the papacy's secular authority, which was affirmed by the Council of Trent (1545–63). Milton's account of censorship and church councils since 400 follows Sarpi's *History of the Council of Trent.*

32. Pope Martin the Fifth (1368–1431) in 1418 issued a bull condemning the reading of heretical works.

33. The English reformer John *Wycliffe* (c. 1329–84), and his follower, John *Huss* of Bohemia (1369–1415).

34. *Leo the Tenth* was pope from 1513 to 1521. The Church created the *index* of prohibited books in 1559.

that rake through the entrails of many an old good author with a violation worse than any could be offered to his tomb. Nor did they stay in matters heretical, but any subject that was not to their palate they either condemned in a prohibition or had it straight into the new purgatory of an index.

To fill up the measure of encroachment, their last invention was to ordain that no book, pamphlet, or paper should be printed (as if St. Peter had bequeathed them the keys of the press also out of paradise) unless it were approved and licensed under the hands of two or three glutton friars. For example:

> "Let the Chancellor Cini be pleased to see if in this present work be contained aught that may withstand the printing."
>
> Vincent Rabbatta, Vicar of Florence.

> "I have seen this present work, and find nothing athwart the Catholic faith and good manners: in witness whereof I have given, etc."
>
> Nicolò Cini, Chancellor of Florence.

> "Attending the precedent relation, it is allowed that this present work of Davanzati may be printed."
>
> Vincent Rabbatta, etc.

> "It may be printed, July 15."
>
> Friar Simon Mompei d'Amelia,
> Chancellor of the holy office in Florence.

Sure they have a conceit, if he of the bottomless pit had not long since broke prison, that this quadruple exorcism would bar him down. I fear their next design will be to get into their custody the licensing of that which they say Claudius intended, but went not through with.[35] Vouchsafe to see another of their forms the Roman stamp:

> "*Imprimatur,* If it seem good to the reverend Master of the holy Palace."
>
> Belcastro, Vicegerent.

> "Imprimatur"
>
> Friar Nicolò Rodolphi,
> Master of the holy Palace.

Sometimes five *imprimaturs* are seen together dialogue-wise in the piazza of one title page, complimenting and ducking each to other with their shaven rever-

35. The margin of the first edition quotes Suetonius's *Lives of the Caesars* (5.32) regarding the legislative officiousness of Claudius: *"Quo veniam daret statum crepitumque ventris in convivio emittendi. Sueton. in Claudio"* [He is even said to have thought of an edict allowing the privilege of breaking wind quietly or noisily at table].

ences,[36] whether the author, who stands by in perplexity at the foot of his epistle, shall to the press or to the sponge. These are the pretty responsories, these are the dear antiphonies,[37] that so bewitched of late our prelates and their chaplains with the goodly echo they made and besotted us to the gay imitation of a lordly *imprimatur,* one from Lambeth house, another from the west end of Paul's,[38] so apishly romanizing that the word of command still was set down in Latin, as if the learned grammatical pen that wrote it would cast no ink without Latin, or perhaps, as they thought, because no vulgar tongue was worthy to express the pure conceit of an *imprimatur,* but rather, as I hope, for that our English, the language of men ever famous and foremost in the achievements of liberty, will not easily find servile letters enow to spell such a dictatory presumption [in] English.[39]

And thus ye have the inventors and the original of book-licensing ripped up and drawn as lineally as any pedigree. We have it not, that can be heard of, from any ancient state, or polity, or church, nor by any statute left us by our ancestors elder or later, nor from the modern custom of any reformed city, or church abroad, but from the most antichristian council and the most tyrannous inquisition that ever inquired.

Till then books were ever as freely admitted into the world as any other birth; the issue of the brain was no more stifled than the issue of the womb; no envious Juno sat cross-legged over the nativity of any man's intellectual offspring;[40] but if it proved a monster, who denies but that it was justly burnt or sunk into the sea? But that a book, in worse condition than a peccant soul, should be to stand before a jury ere it be born to the world, and undergo yet in darkness the judgment of Rhadamanth and his colleagues ere it can pass the ferry backward into light,[41] was never heard before, till that mysterious iniquity, provoked and troubled at the first entrance of reformation, sought out new limbos and new hells wherein they might include our books also within the number of their damned.[42] And this was the rare morsel so officiously snatched up and so ill-favoredly imitated by our inquisiturient bishops and the attendant minorites, their chaplains.[43] That ye like not now these most certain authors of this licensing order, and that all sinister intention was far distant from your

36. A reference to clerics' shorn crowns (tonsures).

37. *Responsories* and *antiphonies* are verses and replies, spoken or sung by a priest and congregation.

38. *Lambeth house* is a residence of the Archbishop of Canterbury; the Bishop of London used to reside near St. *Paul's* Cathedral.

39. **enow:** the archaic plural of *enough.* The 1644 edition omits "in" before "English."

40. Juno instructed the goddess of childbirth to block the birth of Hercules by sitting cross-legged while his mother labored.

41. In classical literature, Rhadamanth, his brother Minos, and Aeacus judged the dead. Milton pictures them judging instead the unborn before they can be ferried backward across the Styx to the realm of the living.

42. *Mysterious iniquity* refers to the Church of Rome, incited by the Protestant Reformation to damn books to freshly invented infernal realms (*new limbos and new hells*).

43. Milton coins *inquisiturient* in scorn of clergy eager to play inquisitor. By referring to English chaplains as *attendant minorites,* he links them with Franciscan friars (Friars Minor).

thoughts when ye were importuned the passing it, all men who know the integrity of your actions and how ye honor truth will clear ye readily.

But some will say, what though the inventors were bad, the thing for all that may be good. It may be so; yet if that thing be no such deep invention, but obvious, and easy for any man to light on, and yet best and wisest commonwealths through all ages and occasions have forborne to use it, and falsest seducers and oppressors of men were the first who took it up, and to no other purpose but to obstruct and hinder the first approach of reformation, I am of those who believe it will be a harder alchemy than Lullius ever knew to sublimate any good use out of such an invention.[44] Yet this only is what I request to gain from this reason, that it may be held a dangerous and suspicious fruit, as certainly it deserves, for the tree that bore it, until I can dissect one by one the properties it has. But I have first to finish, as was propounded, what is to be thought in general of reading books, whatever sort they be, and whether be more the benefit or the harm that thence proceeds?

Not to insist upon the examples of Moses, Daniel, and Paul, who were skillful in all the learning of the Egyptians, Chaldeans, and Greeks, which could not probably be without reading their books of all sorts; in Paul especially, who thought it no defilement to insert into holy scripture the sentences of three Greek poets, and one of them a tragedian.[45] The question was notwithstanding sometimes controverted among the primitive doctors, but with great odds on that side which affirmed it both lawful and profitable, as was then evidently perceived, when Julian the Apostate and subtlest enemy to our faith made a decree forbidding Christians the study of heathen learning; for, said he, they wound us with our own weapons, and with our own arts and sciences they overcome us.[46] And indeed, the Christians were put so to their shifts by this crafty means, and so much in danger to decline into all ignorance, that the two Apollinarii were fain, as a man may say, to coin all the seven liberal sciences out of the Bible, reducing it into diverse forms of orations, poems, dialogues, even to the calculating of a new Christian grammar. But, sayeth the historian Socrates, the providence of God provided better than the industry of Apollinarius and his son, by taking away that illiterate law with the life of him who devised it.[47]

So great an injury they then held it to be deprived of Hellenic learning, and thought it a persecution more undermining and secretly decaying the church than the open cruelty of Decius or Diocletian.[48] And perhaps it was the same

44. **Lullius:** Raymond Lully (c. 1234–1315), renowned alchemist. *Sublimation* is the alchemical process by which base substances are refined and exalted.

45. For Moses' learning, see Acts 7.22; for Daniel's, Dan. 1.17; for Paul's, Acts 22.3. Paul quotes Greek poets at Acts 17.28, Titus 1.12, and 1 Cor. 15.33. The *tragedian* is Euripides.

46. Flavius Claudius Julianus (332–63) became Roman Emperor in 361. His policy in religion was to promote Rome's old religion and discourage Christianity.

47. In his *Ecclesiastical History,* the Greek historian Socrates Scholasticus (380–450) relates the story of the two Apollinarii and Julian's early death.

48. The Roman Emperor *Decius* (d. 251) in 249 initiated the first imperial persecution of Christians. *Diocletian,* emperor from 284 to 305, ordered the last.

politic drift that the devil whipped St. Jerome in a lenten dream for reading Cicero, or else it was a phantasm bred by the fever which had then seized him.[49] For had an angel been his discipliner, unless it were for dwelling too much upon Ciceronianisms, and had chastised the reading not the vanity, it had been plainly partial: first to correct him for grave Cicero, and not for scurril Plautus, whom he confesses to have been reading not long before; next to correct him only, and let so many more ancient fathers wax old in those pleasant and florid studies without the lash of such a tutoring apparition, insomuch that Basil teaches how some good use may be made of *Margites*, a sportful poem, not now extant, writ by Homer; and why not then of *Morgante*, an Italian romance much to the same purpose?[50]

But if it be agreed we shall be tried by visions, there is a vision recorded by Eusebius far ancienter than this tale of Jerome to the nun Eustochium, and besides, has nothing of a fever in it.[51] Dionysius Alexandrinus was, about the year 240, a person of great name in the church for piety and learning, who had wont to avail himself much against heretics by being conversant in their books; until a certain presbyter laid it scrupulously to his conscience, how he durst venture himself among those defiling volumes. The worthy man, loath to give offense, fell into a new debate with himself what was to be thought, when suddenly a vision sent from God (it is his own epistle that so avers it) confirmed him in these words: "Read any books whatever come to thy hands, for thou art sufficient both to judge aright and to examine each matter." To this revelation he assented the sooner, as he confesses, because it was answerable to that of the apostle to the Thessalonians: "Prove all things, hold fast that which is good." And he might have added another remarkable saying of the same author: "To the pure, all things are pure"; not only meats and drinks, but all kind of knowledge whether of good or evil; the knowledge cannot defile, nor consequently the books, if the will and conscience be not defiled.[52]

For books are as meats and viands are: some of good, some of evil substance, and yet God in that unapocryphal vision said without exception, "Rise Peter, kill and eat," leaving the choice to each man's discretion.[53] Wholesome meats to a vitiated stomach differ little or nothing from unwholesome, and best books to a naughty mind are not unappliable to occasions of evil. Bad meats will scarce breed good nourishment in the healthiest concoction, but herein the difference

49. In an epistle (18) identified by Milton in the next paragraph, St. Jerome (c. 342–420) relates a dream in which an angel whips him for excessive devotion to Cicero.

50. *Basil* the Great (330–379) became Bishop of Caesarea in 370. He advised reading pagan literature from a Christian perspective. *Margites* and *Il Morgante Maggiore* (by Luigi Pulci, 1431–87) are mock heroic works.

51. *Eusebius* (264–340) was the Bishop of Caesarea and the Church's first historian. In his *Ecclesiastical History* (7.7), he tells of a letter in which *Dionysius*, Bishop of Alexandria (247–65), justifies having read heretical works by claiming that a vision commanded him to read whatever came into his hands. Milton substitutes *a certain presbyter* for the scrupulous priests of the original account.

52. The apostle Paul in 1 Thess. 5.21 and Titus 1.15.

53. Acts 10.13.

is of bad books, that they to a discreet and judicious reader serve in many respects to discover, to confute, to forewarn, and to illustrate. Whereof what better witness can ye expect I should produce than one of your own now sitting in Parliament, the chief of learned men reputed in this land, Mr. Selden, whose volume of natural and national laws proves, not only by great authorities brought together, but by exquisite reasons and theorems almost mathematically demonstrative, that all opinions, yea errors, known, read, and collated, are of main service and assistance toward the speedy attainment of what is truest.[54] I conceive, therefore, that when God did enlarge the universal diet of man's body, saving ever the rules of temperance, he then also, as before, left arbitrary the dieting and repasting of our minds, as wherein every mature man might have to exercise his own leading capacity.

How great a virtue is temperance, how much of moment through the whole life of man![55] Yet God commits the managing so great a trust, without particular law or prescription, wholly to the demeanor of every grown man. And therefore when he himself tabled the Jews from heaven, that omer which was every man's daily portion of manna is computed to have been more than might have well sufficed the heartiest feeder thrice as many meals.[56] For those actions which enter into a man, rather than issue out of him and therefore defile not,[57] God uses not to captivate under a perpetual childhood of prescription but trusts him with the gift of reason to be his own chooser. There were but little work left for preaching, if law and compulsion should grow so fast upon those things which heretofore were governed only by exhortation. Solomon informs us that much reading is a weariness to the flesh,[58] but neither he, nor other inspired author tells us that such or such reading is unlawful; yet certainly had God thought good to limit us herein, it had been much more expedient to have told us what was unlawful than what was wearisome. As for the burning of those Ephesian books by St. Paul's converts, 'tis replied the books were magic—the Syriac so renders them.[59] It was a private act, a voluntary act, and leaves us to a voluntary imitation: the men in remorse burnt those books which were their own; the magistrate by this example is not appointed; these men practiced the books; another might perhaps have read them in some sort usefully.

Good and evil we know in the field of this world grow up together almost inseparably; and the knowledge of good is so involved and interwoven with the knowledge of evil, and in so many cunning resemblances hardly to be discerned, that those confused seeds which were imposed on Psyche as an inces-

54. John *Selden* (1584–1654) served in Parliament and was one of England's most distinguished scholars, especially of legal history. He begins *De Jure Naturali et Gentium juxta Disciplinam Ebraeorum* (1640) with the claim that truth is best served when dissent is published.

55. On knowledge, nourishment, and temperance, cp. *PL* 7.126–30.

56. See Exod. 16.

57. One of Jesus' sayings (Mark 7.15).

58. Eccles. 12.12.

59. See Acts 19.19.

sant labor to cull out and sort asunder, were not more intermixed.[60] It was from out the rind of one apple tasted that the knowledge of good and evil as two twins cleaving together leapt forth into the world. And perhaps this is that doom which Adam fell into of knowing good and evil, that is to say, of knowing good by evil.

As therefore the state of man now is, what wisdom can there be to choose, what continence to forbear without the knowledge of evil? He that can apprehend and consider vice with all her baits and seeming pleasures, and yet abstain, and yet distinguish, and yet prefer that which is truly better, he is the true warfaring[61] Christian. I cannot praise a fugitive and cloistered virtue, unexercised and unbreathed, that never sallies out and sees her adversary, but slinks out of the race where that immortal garland is to be run for, not without dust and heat. Assuredly we bring not innocence into the world, we bring impurity much rather: that which purifies us is trial, and trial is by what is contrary. That virtue therefore which is but a youngling in the contemplation of evil and knows not the utmost that vice promises to her followers, and rejects it, is but a blank virtue, not a pure; her whiteness is but an excremental[62] whiteness; which was the reason why our sage and serious poet, Spenser, whom I dare be known to think a better teacher than Scotus or Aquinas,[63] describing true temperance under the person of Guyon, brings him in with his palmer through the cave of Mammon and the bower of earthly bliss that he might see and know and yet abstain.[64] Since therefore the knowledge and survey of vice is in this world so necessary to the constituting of human virtue, and the scanning of error to the confirmation of truth, how can we more safely and with less danger scout into the regions of sin and falsity than by reading all manner of tractates and hearing all manner of reason? And this is the benefit which may be had of books promiscuously read.

But of the harm that may result hence, three kinds are usually reckoned. First is feared the infection that may spread. But then all human learning and controversy in religious points must remove out of the world, yea the Bible itself; for that ofttimes relates blasphemy not nicely, it describes the carnal sense of wicked men not unelegantly, it brings in holiest men passionately murmuring against providence through all the arguments of Epicurus.[65] In other great disputes it answers dubiously and darkly to the common reader; and ask a Talmudist what ails the modesty of his marginal Keri, that Moses and all the

60. Apuleius tells of Psyche and the heap of mixed seeds (*Golden Ass* 4–6).

61. Cp. Eph. 6.11. The first edition has "wayfaring," but in all known presentation copies *y* is crossed out and *r* substituted. The change is thus probably authorial.

62. **excremental:** external, superficial.

63. John Duns *Scotus* (1265–1308) and St. Thomas *Aquinas* (c. 1225–74) were scholastic philosophers much studied in the universities.

64. Milton's account of Spenser is significantly erroneous. The palmer, representing reason, does not accompany Guyon, the Knight of Temperance, into Mammon's cave.

65. That is, the skepticism of holy men as recorded in Scripture sometimes corresponds to arguments of Epicurus (see, e.g., Eccles. 8.15). **nicely:** delicately.

Prophets cannot persuade him to pronounce the textual Chetiv.[66] For these causes we all know the Bible itself put by the papist into the first rank of prohibited books. The ancientest fathers must be next removed, as Clement of Alexandria, and that Eusebian book of evangelic preparation, transmitting our ears through a hoard of heathenish obscenities to receive the gospel.[67] Who finds not that Irenæus, Epiphanius, Jerome, and others discover more heresies than they well confute, and that oft for heresy which is the truer opinion?[68]

Nor boots it to say for these and all the heathen writers of greatest infection, if it must be thought so, with whom is bound up the life of human learning, that they writ in an unknown tongue, so long as we are sure those languages are known as well to the worst of men, who are both most able and most diligent to instill the poison they suck, first into the courts of princes, acquainting them with the choicest delights and criticisms of sin. As perhaps did that Petronius whom Nero called his arbiter, the master of his revels, and that notorious ribald of Arezzo, dreaded and yet dear to the Italian courtiers.[69] I name not him for posterity's sake, whom Harry the Eighth named in merriment his vicar of hell.[70] By which compendious way all the contagion that foreign books can infuse will find a passage to the people far easier and shorter than an Indian voyage, though it could be sailed either by the north of Cataio[71] eastward or of Canada westward, while our Spanish licensing gags the English press never so severely.

But on the other side that infection which is from books of controversy in religion is more doubtful and dangerous to the learned than to the ignorant; and yet those books must be permitted untouched by the licenser. It will be hard to instance where any ignorant man hath been ever seduced by papistical book in English, unless it were commended and expounded to him by some of that clergy; and indeed all such tractates whether false or true are, as the prophecy of Isaiah was to the eunuch, not to be "understood without a guide."[72] But of our priests and doctors how many have been corrupted by studying the comments of Jesuits and Sorbonists,[73] and how fast they could transfuse that corruption into the people, our experience is both late and sad. It is not forgot,

66. When reading Hebrew Scripture aloud, the Talmudic scholar (or *Talmudist*) substitutes a gloss in the margin (*Keri*) for an actual written text (*Chetiv*) deemed inappropriate or erroneous.

67. *Clement of Alexandria* (c. 150–c. 215) was among the first Christian theologians to incorporate Greek philosophy in his writings. Eusebius in *Preparatio Evangelica* argues that the Greek tradition is inferior to the Hebrew and, like Clement, details pagan indecencies.

68. *Irenæus* (c. 130–200), *Epiphanius* (c. 315–403), and *Jerome* (c. 342–420) wrote against various heresies, which consequently became more widely known.

69. *Petronius* Arbiter (d. 66), author of *Satyricon*, is usually identified with a like-named hedonist who reportedly guided Nero in his choice of pleasures (Tacitus 16.18). Born in Arezzo, Pietro Aretino (1492–1556) was a satirist whose lewd satirical wit was so feared that potential targets paid protection money to stay on his good side.

70. Sir Francis Bryan (d. 1550), called Henry's *vicar of hell*, was notorious for his loose ways.

71. **Cataio:** Cathay, or China.

72. See Acts 8.27-39.

73. The Sorbonne in Paris was a primary institution of Roman Catholic learning.

since the acute and distinct Arminius was perverted merely by the perusing of a nameless discourse written at Delft, which at first he took in hand to confute.[74]

Seeing therefore that those books, and those in great abundance which are likeliest to taint both life and doctrine, cannot be suppressed without the fall of learning and of all ability in disputation; and that these books of either sort are most and soonest catching to the learned, from whom to the common people whatever is heretical or dissolute may quickly be conveyed; and that evil manners are as perfectly learned without books a thousand other ways which cannot be stopped; and evil doctrine not with books can propagate except a teacher guide, which he might also do without writing, and so beyond prohibiting, I am not able to unfold, how this cautelous[75] enterprise of licensing can be exempted from the number of vain and impossible attempts. And he who were pleasantly disposed could not well avoid to liken it to the exploit of that gallant man who thought to pound up the crows by shutting his park gate.

Besides another inconvenience, if learned men be the first receivers out of books and dispreaders both of vice and error, how shall the licensers themselves be confided in, unless we can confer upon them, or they assume to themselves above all others in the land, the grace of infallibility and uncorruptedness? And, again, if it be true that a wise man like a good refiner can gather gold out of the drossiest volume, and that a fool will be a fool with the best book, yea or without book, there is no reason that we should deprive a wise man of any advantage to his wisdom, while we seek to restrain from a fool that which being restrained will be no hindrance to his folly. For if there should be so much exactness always used to keep that from him which is unfit for his reading, we should in the judgment of Aristotle not only, but of Solomon and of our Savior,[76] not vouchsafe him good precepts, and by consequence not willingly admit him to good books, as being certain that a wise man will make better use of an idle pamphlet than a fool will do of sacred scripture.

'Tis next alleged we must not expose ourselves to temptations without necessity, and, next to that, not employ our time in vain things. To both these objections one answer will serve out of the grounds already laid, that to all men such books are not temptations, nor vanities, but useful drugs and materials wherewith to temper and compose effective and strong medicines which man's life cannot want.[77] The rest, as children and childish men who have not the art to qualify and prepare these working minerals, well may be exhorted to forbear, but hindered forcibly they cannot be by all the licensing that sainted inquisition

74. Jacobus *Arminius* (1560–1609) was a Dutch Calvinist whose opposition to strict predestination led to an alternative system of salvation that came to be known as Arminianism. His dissent reportedly began in an attempt to rebut criticisms of orthodox Calvinism by ministers from Delft. Milton says that Arminius was *perverted,* but *Areopagitica* is implicitly Arminian, and Milton's mature theology explicitly so (cp. *CD* 1.4).

75. **cautelous:** cautious; deceitful.

76. Aristotle, *Nicomachean Ethics* 1.3 (1095a); Prov. 23.9 (for Solomon); Matt. 7.6 (Jesus).

77. I.e., which man's life requires.

could ever yet contrive. Which is what I promised to deliver next—that this order of licensing conduces nothing to the end for which it was framed—and hath almost prevented[78] me by being clear already while thus much hath been explaining. See the ingenuity[79] of Truth, who, when she gets a free and willing hand, opens herself faster than the pace of method and discourse can overtake her.

It was the task which I began with, to show that no nation or well instituted state, if they valued books at all, did ever use this way of licensing. And it might be answered that this is a piece of prudence lately discovered. To which I return, that as it was a thing slight and obvious to think on, so if it had been difficult to find out, there wanted not among them long since who suggested such a course, which they, not following, leave us a pattern of their judgment, that it was not the not knowing but the not approving which was the cause of their not using it.

Plato, a man of high authority indeed, but least of all for his commonwealth, in the book of his *Laws,* which no city ever yet received, fed his fancy with making many edicts to his airy burgomasters, which they who otherwise admire him wish had been rather buried and excused in the genial cups of an academic night-sitting.[80] By which laws he seems to tolerate no kind of learning but by unalterable decree, consisting most of practical traditions, to the attainment whereof a library of smaller bulk than his own dialogues would be abundant. And there also enacts that no poet should so much as read to any private man what he had written until the judges and law-keepers had seen it and allowed it. But that Plato meant this law peculiarly to that commonwealth which he had imagined and to no other is evident. Why was he not else a lawgiver to himself, but a transgressor, and to be expelled by his own magistrates, both for the wanton epigrams and dialogues which he made, and his perpetual reading of Sophron Mimus and Aristophanes, books of grossest infamy, and also for commending the latter of them, though he were the malicious libeler of his chief friends, to be read by the tyrant Dionysius, who had little need of such trash to spend his time on?[81] But that he knew this licensing of poems had reference and dependence to many other provisos there set down in his fancied republic which in this world could have no place. And so neither he himself nor any magistrate or city ever imitated that course, which taken apart from those other collateral injunctions must needs be vain and fruitless.

For if they fell upon one kind of strictness, unless their care were equal to

78. **prevented:** come before (its allotted place in the oration).

79. **ingenuity:** ingenuousness, candor.

80. Plato wrote both the ***Republic,*** on the principles of an ideal society, and the ***Laws,*** on the legal code for a deserted city soon to be reestablished.

81. Plato's ***Symposium*** and ***Phaedrus*** feature drinking, loose talk, and homoeroticism. Plato admired ***Sophron Mimus*** (fifth century B.C.E.), who gave literary form to the often ribald dramatic sketches known as mime (not pantomime). Although Aristophanes mocked Socrates and friends in ***Clouds,*** Plato reportedly recommended his works to Dionysius the First of Syracuse (430–367 B.C.E.).

regulate all other things of like aptness to corrupt the mind, that single endeavor they knew would be but a fond labor, to shut and fortify one gate against corruption and be necessitated to leave others round about wide open. If we think to regulate printing, thereby to rectify manners, we must regulate all recreations and pastimes, all that is delightful to man. No music must be heard, no song be set or sung, but what is grave and Doric.[82] There must be licensing dancers, that no gesture, motion, or deportment be taught our youth but what by their allowance shall be thought honest, for such Plato was provided of. It will ask more than the work of twenty licensers to examine all the lutes, the violins, and the guitars in every house; they must not be suffered to prattle as they do, but must be licensed what they may say. And who shall silence all the airs and madrigals that whisper softness in chambers? The windows also and the balconies must be thought on—there are shrewd books with dangerous frontispieces set to sale—who shall prohibit them, shall twenty licensers? The villages also must have their visitors to inquire what lectures the bagpipe and the rebeck reads even to the balladry and the gamut of every municipal fiddler, for these are the countryman's Arcadias and his Montemayors.[83]

Next, what more national corruption for which England hears ill abroad than household gluttony; who shall be the rectors of our daily rioting? And what shall be done to inhibit the multitudes that frequent those houses where drunkenness is sold and harbored? Our garments also should be referred to the licensing of some more sober workmasters to see them cut into a less wanton garb. Who shall regulate all the mixed conversation of our youth, male and female together, as is the fashion of this country? Who shall still appoint what shall be discoursed, what presumed, and no further? Lastly, who shall forbid and separate all idle resort, all evil company? These things will be and must be; but how they shall be least hurtful, how least enticing, herein consists the grave and governing wisdom of a state.

To sequester out of the world into Atlantic and Utopian[84] polities which never can be drawn into use will not mend our condition, but to ordain wisely as in this world of evil, in the midst whereof God hath placed us unavoidably. Nor is it Plato's licensing of books will do this, which necessarily pulls along with it so many other kinds of licensing as will make us all both ridiculous and weary, and yet frustrate, but those unwritten or at least unconstraining laws of virtuous education, religious and civil nurture, which Plato there men-

82. Plato preferred Dorian music because it inspires, in Aristotle's words, "a moderate and settled temper" (*Rep.* 3.398–99; *Pol.* 8.5). Cp. *PL* 1.550.

83. *Visitors* is a euphemism for censors, here depicted as absurdly concerned with the regulation of ballads. A *rebeck* is a two- or three-stringed fiddle (cp. *L'All.* 94). Romantic or sentimental country music is in Milton's view the illiterate counterpart of literary romances, such as Sidney's *Arcadia* or *Montemayor's Diana Enamorada,* deemed morally corrosive by Puritans.

84. *Sequester* is used intransitively to mean "withdraw." Plato describes the primeval excellence of the island of Atlantis in *Critias* and *Timaeus.* Thomas More tells of an ideal island society in *Utopia* (1516), as does Francis Bacon in *New Atlantis* (1627). Milton's point is that none of these places actually exist.

tions,[85] as the bonds and ligaments of the commonwealth, the pillars and the sustainers of every written statute. These they be which will bear chief sway in such matters as these, when all licensing will be easily eluded. Impunity and remissness for certain are the bane of a commonwealth, but here the great art lies to discern in what the law is to bid restraint and punishment, and in what things persuasion only is to work. If every action which is good or evil in man at ripe years were to be under pittance, and prescription, and compulsion, what were virtue but a name, what praise could be then due to well-doing, what gramercy[86] to be sober, just, or continent?

Many there be that complain of divine providence for suffering Adam to transgress. Foolish tongues! When God gave him reason, he gave him freedom to choose, for reason is but choosing; he had been else a mere artificial Adam, such an Adam as he is in the motions.[87] We ourselves esteem not of that obedience, or love, or gift, which is of force. God therefore left him free, set before him a provoking object, ever almost in his eyes; herein consisted his merit, herein the right of his reward, the praise of his abstinence. Wherefore did he create passions within us, pleasures round about us, but that these rightly tempered are the very ingredients of virtue? They are not skillful considerers of human things who imagine to remove sin by removing the matter of sin. For, besides that it is a huge heap increasing under the very act of diminishing, though some part of it may for a time be withdrawn from some persons, it cannot from all, in such a universal thing as books are; and when this is done, yet the sin remains entire. Though ye take from a covetous man all his treasure, he has yet one jewel left—ye cannot bereave him of his covetousness. Banish all objects of lust, shut up all youth into the severest discipline that can be exercised in any hermitage, ye cannot make them chaste that came not thither so: such great care and wisdom is required to the right managing of this point.

Suppose we could expel sin by this means; look how much we thus expel of sin, so much we expel of virtue. For the matter of them both is the same; remove that, and ye remove them both alike. This justifies the high providence of God, who though he command us temperance, justice, continence, yet pours out before us even to a profuseness all desirable things and gives us minds that can wander beyond all limit and satiety. Why should we then affect a rigor contrary to the manner of God and of nature, by abridging or scanting those means which books freely permitted are, both to the trial of virtue and the exercise of truth? It would be better done to learn that the law must needs be frivolous which goes to restrain things uncertainly and yet equally working to good and to evil. And were I the chooser, a dram of well-doing should be preferred before many times as much the forcible hindrance of evil-doing. For God sure es-

85. Plato, *Laws* 1 (643–45), a passage that may have suggested the ensuing puppetry metaphor.
86. **gramercy:** occasion for thanks.
87. For the identification of reason and choice, cp. *PL* 3.95–128. **motions:** puppet shows.

teems the growth and completing of one virtuous person more than the restraint of ten vicious.

And albeit whatever thing we hear or see, sitting, walking, traveling, or conversing may be fitly called our book, and is of the same effect that writings are, yet grant the thing to be prohibited were only books, it appears that this order hitherto is far insufficient to the end which it intends. Do we not see—not once or oftener, but weekly—that continued court-libel against the Parliament and City printed, as the wet sheets can witness, and dispersed among us, for all that licensing can do?[88] Yet this is the prime service a man would think wherein this order should give proof of itself. If it were executed, you'll say. But certain, if execution be remiss or blindfold now, and in this particular, what will it be hereafter and in other books? If then the order shall not be vain and frustrate, behold a new labor, Lords and Commons, ye must repeal and proscribe all scandalous and unlicensed books already printed and divulged—after ye have drawn them up into a list, that all may know which are condemned and which not—and ordain that no foreign books be delivered out of custody till they have been read over. This office will require the whole time of not a few overseers, and those no vulgar men. There be also books which are partly useful and excellent, partly culpable and pernicious; this work will ask as many more officials to make expurgations and expunctions, that the commonwealth of learning be not damnified.[89] In fine, when the multitude of books increase upon their hands, ye must be fain to catalogue all those printers who are found frequently offending and forbid the importation of their whole suspected typography. In a word, that this your order may be exact and not deficient, ye must reform it perfectly according to the model of Trent and Seville,[90] which I know ye abhor to do.

Yet though ye should condescend to this, which God forbid, the order still would be but fruitless and defective to that end whereto ye meant it. If to prevent sects and schisms, who is so unread or so uncatechized in story that hath not heard of many sects refusing books as a hindrance and preserving their doctrine unmixed for many ages only by unwritten traditions? The Christian faith, for that was once a schism, is not unknown to have spread all over Asia ere any gospel or epistle was seen in writing. If the amendment of manners be aimed at, look into Italy and Spain, whether those places be one scruple the better, the honester, the wiser, the chaster, since all the inquisitional rigor that hath been executed upon books.

Another reason, whereby to make it plain that this order will miss the end it seeks, consider by the quality which ought to be in every licenser. It cannot be denied but that he who is made judge to sit upon the birth or death of books

88. Milton refers to the weekly Royalist newspaper, *Mercurius Aulicus*, published from 1642 to 1645.

89. **damnified:** injured or impaired.

90. Milton has already identified the Council of *Trent* (1545–63) as the historical origin of prepublication licensing. The Spanish Inquisition, instituted in 1481, had its seat in *Seville.*

whether they may be wafted into this world or not, had need to be a man above the common measure, both studious, learned, and judicious. There may be else no mean mistakes in the censure of what is passable or not, which is also no mean injury. If he be of such worth as behooves him, there cannot be a more tedious and unpleasing journey-work,[91] a greater loss of time levied upon his head, than to be made the perpetual reader of unchosen books and pamphlets, ofttimes huge volumes. There is no book that is acceptable unless at certain seasons; but to be enjoined the reading of that at all times, and in a hand scarce legible, whereof three pages would not down[92] at any time in the fairest print, is an imposition which I cannot believe how he that values time and his own studies, or is but of a sensible nostril, should be able to endure. In this one thing I crave leave of the present licensers to be pardoned for so thinking; who doubtless took this office up, looking on it through their obedience to the Parliament, whose command perhaps made all things seem easy and unlaborious to them; but that this short trial hath wearied them out already, their own expressions and excuses to them who make so many journeys to solicit their license are testimony enough. Seeing therefore those who now possess the employment by all evident signs wish themselves well rid of it, and that no man of worth, none that is not a plain unthrift of his own hours, is ever likely to succeed them, except he mean to put himself to the salary of a press corrector,[93] we may easily foresee what kind of licensers we are to expect hereafter, either ignorant, imperious, and remiss, or basely pecuniary. This is what I had to show wherein this order cannot conduce to that end whereof it bears the intention.

I lastly proceed, from the no good it can do, to the manifest hurt it causes in being first the greatest discouragement and affront that can be offered to learning and to learned men.

It was the complaint and lamentation of prelates, upon every least breath of a motion to remove pluralities[94] and distribute more equally church revenues, that then all learning would be forever dashed and discouraged. But as for that opinion, I never found cause to think that the tenth part of learning stood or fell with the clergy, nor could I ever but hold it for a sordid and unworthy speech of any churchman who had a competency left him.[95] If therefore ye be loath to dishearten utterly and discontent, not the mercenary crew of false pretenders to learning, but the free and ingenuous sort of such as evidently were born to study and love learning for itself, not for lucre or any other end but the service of God and of truth, and perhaps that lasting fame and perpetuity of praise which God and good men have consented shall be the reward of those whose published labors advance the good of mankind, then know, that so far to distrust

91. **journey-work:** day labor.
92. **down:** i.e., go down (like food or drink, as *be . . . of a sensible nostril* suggests).
93. **press corrector:** proofreader.
94. **pluralities:** the possession by clergymen of more than one benefice or living.
95. **tenth part of learning:** The phrasing suggests the system of tithing for support of the church. **competency:** income sufficient to meet living expenses.

the judgment and the honesty of one who hath but a common repute in learning, and never yet offended, as not to count him fit to print his mind without a tutor and examiner, lest he should drop a schism or something of corruption, is the greatest displeasure and indignity to a free and knowing spirit that can be put upon him.

What advantage is it to be a man over it is to be a boy at school, if we have only scaped the ferula to come under the fescue[96] of an *imprimatur;* if serious and elaborate writings, as if they were no more than the theme of a grammar lad under his pedagogue, must not be uttered without the cursory eyes of a temporizing and extemporizing licenser? He who is not trusted with his own actions, his drift not being known to be evil, and standing to the hazard of law and penalty, has no great argument to think himself reputed, in the commonwealth wherein he was born, for other than a fool or a foreigner. When a man writes to the world, he summons up all his reason and deliberation to assist him; he searches, meditates, is industrious, and likely consults and confers with his judicious friends; after all which done he takes himself to be informed in what he writes, as well as any that writ before him. If in this the most consummate act of his fidelity and ripeness, no years, no industry, no former proof of his abilities can bring him to that state of maturity, as not to be still mistrusted and suspected, unless he carry all his considerate diligence, all his midnight watchings, and expense of Palladian[97] oil, to the hasty view of an unleisured licenser, perhaps much his younger, perhaps far his inferior in judgment, perhaps one who never knew the labor of book-writing, and if he be not repulsed or slighted, must appear in print like a puny[98] with his guardian and his censor's hand on the back of his title to be his bail and surety that he is no idiot or seducer; it cannot be but a dishonor and derogation to the author, to the book, to the privilege and dignity of learning.

And what if the author shall be one so copious of fancy as to have many things well worth the adding come into his mind after licensing, while the book is yet under the press, which not seldom happens to the best and diligentest writers, and that perhaps a dozen times in one book. The printer dares not go beyond his licensed copy. So often then must the author trudge to his leave-giver, that those his new insertions may be viewed, and many a jaunt will be made, ere that licenser, for it must be the same man, can either be found, or found at leisure. Meanwhile, either the press must stand still, which is no small damage, or the author lose his accuratest thoughts and send the book forth worse than he had made it, which to a diligent writer is the greatest melancholy and vexation that can befall. And how can a man teach with authority, which is the life of teaching, how can he be a doctor in his book as he ought to be (or else had better be silent), whenas all he teaches, all he delivers, is but under the

96. **ferula:** teacher's rod; **fescue:** teacher's pointer.

97. **Palladian:** pertaining to Pallas Athena, Greek goddess of wisdom.

98. **puny:** minor, youth; someone young in learning (from French *puis-né:* later-born).

tuition, under the correction of his patriarchal licenser to blot or alter what precisely accords not with the hidebound humor which he calls his judgment?[99] When every acute reader upon the first sight of a pedantic license will be ready with these like words to ding the book a quoit's distance[100] from him: "I hate a pupil teacher; I endure not an instructor that comes to me under the wardship of an overseeing fist. I know nothing of the licenser, but that I have his own hand here for his arrogance. Who shall warrant me his judgment?"

"The state, sir," replies the stationer,[101] but has a quick return: "the state shall be my governors, but not my critics; they may be mistaken in the choice of a licenser, as easily as this licenser may be mistaken in an author; this is some common stuff"; and he might add from Sir Francis Bacon, that "such authorized books are but the language of the times."[102] For though a licenser should happen to be judicious more than ordinary, which will be a great jeopardy of the next succession, yet his very office and his commission enjoins him to let pass nothing but what is vulgarly received already.

Nay, which is more lamentable, if the work of any deceased author, though never so famous in his lifetime and even to this day, come to their hands for license to be printed or reprinted; if there be found in his book one sentence of a venturous edge, uttered in the height of zeal, and who knows whether it might not be the dictate of a divine spirit, yet not suiting with every low decrepit humor of their own, though it were Knox himself, the reformer of a kingdom that spake it, they will not pardon him their dash. The sense of that great man shall to all posterity be lost for the fearfulness or the presumptuous rashness of a perfunctory licenser. And to what an author this violence hath been lately done, and in what book of greatest consequence to be faithfully published, I could now instance, but shall forbear till a more convenient season.[103]

Yet if these things be not resented seriously and timely by them who have the remedy in their power, but that such iron molds[104] as these shall have authority to gnaw out the choicest periods of exquisitest books and to commit such a treacherous fraud against the orphan remainders of worthiest men after death, the more sorrow will belong to that hapless race of men whose misfortune it is to have understanding. Henceforth let no man care to learn or care to be more than worldly wise, for certainly in higher matters to be ignorant and

99. At his trial in March 1644, Archbishop Laud was charged with bargaining to restore England to the Catholic Church so that he might become Patriarch of Great Britain. The allusion is reinforced, according to Sirluck (*Yale* 2.533), by Milton's assertion that licensers did not just *blot* but altered what authors wrote, an offense with which Laud was also charged.

100. **ding:** throw violently. **quoit:** a ring-shaped piece of iron, the classical discus.

101. **stationer:** bookseller or publisher.

102. The quotation is rough but substantially accurate. See *A Wise and Moderate Discourse Concerning Church-Affaires,* 11 (1641), composed by Bacon in 1589 as *An Advertisement touching the Controversies of the Church of England.*

103. Works usually cited as examples include John Knox's *History of the Reformation* (1644) and Edward Coke's *Institutes of Laws of England* (1641). Both suffered cuts before publication.

104. **iron molds:** stains caused by rusty iron or ink, here used figuratively of the licensers' efforts.

slothful, to be a common, steadfast dunce, will be the only pleasant life, and only in request.

And as it is a particular disesteem of every knowing person alive, and most injurious to the written labors and monuments of the dead, so to me it seems an undervaluing and vilifying of the whole nation. I cannot set so light by all the invention, the art, the wit, the grave and solid judgment which is in England, as that it can be comprehended in any twenty capacities how good soever, much less that it should not pass except their superintendence be over it, except it be sifted and strained with their strainers, that it should be uncurrent without their manual stamp. Truth and understanding are not such wares as to be monopolized[105] and traded in by tickets and statutes and standards. We must not think to make a staple commodity of all the knowledge in the land, to mark and license it like our broadcloth and our woolpacks. What is it but a servitude like that imposed by the Philistines not to be allowed the sharpening of our own axes and coulters, but we must repair from all quarters to twenty licensing forges.[106] Had any one written and divulged erroneous things and scandalous to honest life, misusing and forfeiting the esteem had of his reason among men, if after conviction this only censure were adjudged him, that he should never henceforth write but what were first examined by an appointed officer, whose hand should be annexed to pass his credit for him that now he might be safely read, it could not be apprehended less than a disgraceful punishment. Whence to include the whole nation and those that never yet thus offended under such a diffident and suspectful prohibition may plainly be understood what a disparagement it is. So much the more whenas debtors and delinquents may walk abroad without a keeper,[107] but unoffensive books must not stir forth without a visible jailer in their title.

Nor is it to the common people less than a reproach. For if we be so jealous over them as that we dare not trust them with an English pamphlet, what do we but censure them for a giddy, vicious, and ungrounded people, in such a sick and weak estate of faith and discretion as to be able to take nothing down but through the pipe[108] of a licenser? That this is care or love of them we cannot pretend, whenas in those popish places where the laity are most hated and despised, the same strictness is used over them. Wisdom we cannot call it, because it stops but one breach of license, nor that neither whenas those corruptions which it seeks to prevent break in faster at other doors, which cannot be shut.

105. Commercial monopolies, on which Charles I had increasingly depended during the 1630s, caused great outrage and constituted a prominent Parliamentary grievance.

106. The Philistines did not permit the subject Israelites to have forges. To sharpen tools, they had to go to the Philistines (1 Sam. 13.19–21).

107. In Milton's era (and long after) debtors could be jailed, though in certain exempt districts they were able to walk without fear of apprehension. Parliament in 1643 ruled that those who had aided the king were *delinquents,* expropriated their property, and left them liable to imprisonment. By 1644, this action had been much mitigated, and relatively easy settlement was made available (Sirluck, Yale 2:536).

108. **pipe:** tube for giving medicine.

And in conclusion, it reflects to the disrepute of our ministers also, of whose labors we should hope better, and of the proficiency which their flock reaps by them, than that after all this light of the gospel which is and is to be, and all this continual preaching, they should be still frequented with such an unprincipled, unedified, and laic rabble, as that the whiff of every new pamphlet should stagger them out of their catechism and Christian walking.[109] This may have much reason to discourage the ministers, when such a low conceit is had of all their exhortations and the benefiting of their hearers, as that they are not thought fit to be turned loose to three sheets of paper without a licenser, that all the sermons, all the lectures preached, printed, vented in such numbers and such volumes as have now well nigh made all other books unsaleable, should not be armor enough against one single enchiridion, without the castle of St. Angelo of an *imprimatur*.[110]

And lest some should persuade ye, Lords and Commons, that these arguments of learned men's discouragement at this your order are mere flourishes and not real, I could recount what I have seen and heard in other countries where this kind of inquisition tyrannizes: when I have sat among their learned men, for that honor I had, and been counted happy to be born in such a place of philosophic freedom as they supposed England was, while themselves did nothing but bemoan the servile condition into which learning amongst them was brought; that this was it which had damped the glory of Italian wits; that nothing had been there written now these many years but flattery and fustian. There it was that I found and visited the famous Galileo grown old, a prisoner to the Inquisition, for thinking in astronomy otherwise than the Franciscan and Dominican licensers thought.[111] And though I knew that England then was groaning loudest under the prelatical yoke, nevertheless I took it as a pledge of future happiness that other nations were so persuaded of her liberty.

Yet was it beyond my hope that those worthies were then breathing in her air who should be her leaders to such a deliverance as shall never be forgotten by any revolution of time that this world hath to finish. When that was once begun, it was as little in my fear that what words of complaint I heard among learned men of other parts uttered against the Inquisition, the same I should hear by as learned men at home uttered in time of Parliament against an order of licensing. And that so generally, that when I had disclosed myself a companion of their discontent, I might say, if without envy, that he whom an honest quæstorship had endeared to the Sicilians was not more by them importuned against Verres,[112]

109. Christians are exhorted to walk wisely at Eph. 5.15–16 and Col. 4.5.

110. **conceit:** concept, imagination; **enchiridion:** handbook (with a pun on the Greek for "dagger"); **castle of St. Angelo:** papal prison in Rome.

111. Galileo (1564–1642) published *Dialogue on the Two Chief Systems,* which undermined church teaching on the stationary centrality of the earth, in 1632. He was made to recant and spent the rest of his life under house arrest. Milton claims to have met him in Tuscany in 1638.

112. In 75 B.C.E., Cicero served as *quaestor* (financial officer) for Sicily. Afterward, *Verres* became governor (73–71), and the Sicilians asked Cicero to prosecute him for corruption, which he did with brilliant success.

than the favorable opinion which I had among many who honor ye, and are known and respected by ye, loaded me with entreaties and persuasions that I would not despair to lay together that which just reason should bring into my mind toward the removal of an undeserved thraldom upon learning. That this is not therefore the disburdening of a particular fancy, but the common grievance of all those who had prepared their minds and studies above the vulgar pitch to advance truth in others, and from others to entertain it, thus much may satisfy.

And in their name I shall for neither friend nor foe conceal what the general murmur is: that if it come to inquisitioning again, and licensing, and that we are so timorous of ourselves and so suspicious of all men as to fear each book and the shaking of every leaf before we know what the contents are; if some who but of late were little better than silenced from preaching shall come now to silence us from reading except what they please, it cannot be guessed what is intended by some but a second tyranny over learning, and will soon put it out of controversy that bishops and presbyters are the same to us both name and thing.[113] That those evils of prelaty, which before from five or six and twenty sees[114] were distributively charged upon the whole people, will now light wholly upon learning is not obscure to us, whenas now the pastor of a small unlearned parish on the sudden shall be exalted archbishop over a large diocese of books and yet not remove but keep his other cure too, a mystical pluralist.[115] He who but of late cried down the sole ordination of every novice bachelor of art and denied sole jurisdiction over the simplest parishioner, shall now at home in his private chair assume both these over worthiest and excellentest books and ablest authors that write them.[116] This is not—ye covenants and protestations[117] that we have made!—this is not to put down prelaty; this is but to chop an episcopacy;[118] this is but to translate the palace metropolitan[119] from one kind of dominion into another; this is but an old canonical sleight of commuting our penance.

To startle thus betimes at a mere unlicensed pamphlet will after a while be afraid of every conventicle, and a while after will make a conventicle of every Christian meeting.[120] But I am certain that a state governed by the rules of jus-

113. In supporting Presbyterian opposition to episcopal hierarchy, Milton had argued that *bishop* and *presbyter* were in Scripture synonymous terms for "priest" (Yale 1:650). He suggests that presbyters now risk becoming the same as bishops in more than name. Cp. *On the New Forcers of Conscience.*

114. **sees:** seats of episcopal power.

115. **mystical pluralist:** By overseeing "a large diocese of books," while simultaneously remaining in his local parish, the pastor mysteriously manages to occupy two places at once.

116. Presbyterians had disputed the sole right of bishops to ordain new ministers and exercise spiritual authority, yet they now assume similar rights over authors and books.

117. **covenants and protestations:** Milton invokes various resolutions in Scotland and England from 1638 to 1643 that spelled out Presbyterian opposition to episcopal discipline and upheld the rights and liberties of the people.

118. **chop an episcopacy:** exchange one church hierarchy for another.

119. **palace metropolitan:** residence of the presiding bishop. The Archbishop of Canterbury resided in Lambeth Palace.

120. **To startle:** to take fright (corresponds with [*to*] *be afraid of*); **conventicle:** a meeting of religious nonconformists, held secretly to avoid persecution.

tice and fortitude, or a church built and founded upon the rock of faith and true knowledge, cannot be so pusillanimous. While things are yet not constituted in religion,[121] that freedom of writing should be restrained by a discipline imitated from the prelates, and learnt by them from the Inquisition to shut us up all again into the breast of a licenser, must needs give cause of doubt and discouragement to all learned and religious men. Who cannot but discern the fineness[122] of this politic drift and who are the contrivers, that while bishops were to be baited down, then all presses might be open; it was the people's birthright and privilege in time of Parliament; it was the breaking forth of light.

But now, the bishops abrogated and voided out of the church, as if our Reformation sought no more but to make room for others into their seats under another name, the episcopal arts begin to bud again, the cruse[123] of truth must run no more oil, liberty of printing must be enthralled again under a prelatical commission of twenty, the privilege of the people nullified, and, which is worse, the freedom of learning must groan again, and to her old fetters—all this the Parliament yet sitting. Although their own late arguments and defenses against the prelates might remember them that this obstructing violence meets for the most part with an event utterly opposite to the end which it drives at: instead of suppressing sects and schisms, it raises them and invests them with a reputation. "The punishing of wits enhances their authority," sayeth the Viscount St. Albans,[124] "and a forbidden writing is thought to be a certain spark of truth that flies up in the faces of them who seek to tread it out." This order, therefore, may prove a nursing mother to sects, but I shall easily show how it will be a stepdame to Truth, and first by disenabling us to the maintenance of what is known already.

Well knows he who uses to consider, that our faith and knowledge thrives by exercise as well as our limbs and complexion.[125] Truth is compared in scripture to a streaming fountain; if her waters flow not in a perpetual progression they sicken into a muddy pool of conformity and tradition. A man may be a heretic in the truth; and if he believe things only because his pastor says so or the Assembly[126] so determines, without knowing other reason, though his belief be true, yet the very truth he holds becomes his heresy. There is not any burden that some would gladlier post off to another than the charge and care of their religion. There be (who knows not that there be?) of Protestants and professors who live and die in as arrant an implicit faith as any lay papist of Loretto.[127] A

121. The episcopacy had been uprooted, and a new church discipline had not yet been settled.

122. **fineness:** cunning, subtle strategy (finesse).

123. In 1 Kings 17.12–16, a widow's small jar (*cruse*) of oil never fails, as Elijah promised.

124. Sir Francis Bacon, whose *Wise and Moderate Discourse Concerning Church-Affaires* is again quoted, from the same page as previously. See note 102.

125. **uses:** is accustomed to; **complexion:** bodily constitution; natural disposition.

126. The Westminster Assembly of divines was convened to advise Parliament on church affairs.

127. The *those* preceding *who* in this sentence is understood. **professors:** Puritans who publicly declare their faith; **implicit:** blindly trusting; **Loretto:** Italian shrine to which it was believed angels had transported Mary and Jesus' house from Nazareth.

wealthy man, addicted to his pleasure and to his profits, finds religion to be a traffic so entangled and of so many piddling accounts that of all mysteries[128] he cannot skill to keep a stock going upon that trade. What should he do? Fain he would have the name to be religious; fain he would bear up with his neighbors in that. What does he, therefore, but resolves to give over toiling and to find himself out some factor to whose care and credit he may commit the whole managing of his religious affairs; some divine of note and estimation that must be. To him he adheres, resigns the whole warehouse of his religion with all the locks and keys into his custody; and indeed makes the very person of that man his religion; esteems his associating with him a sufficient evidence and commendatory of his own piety. So that a man may say his religion is now no more within himself, but is become a dividual movable,[129] and goes and comes near him according as that good man frequents the house. He entertains him, gives him gifts, feasts him, lodges him; his religion comes home at night, prays, is liberally supped, and sumptuously laid to sleep, rises, is saluted, and after the malmsey or some well spiced brewage, and better breakfasted than he whose morning appetite would have gladly fed on green figs between Bethany and Jerusalem,[130] his religion walks abroad at eight and leaves his kind entertainer in the shop trading all day without his religion.

Another sort there be who, when they hear that all things shall be ordered, all things regulated and settled, nothing written but what passes through the customhouse of certain publicans that have the tunnaging and the poundaging of all freespoken truth,[131] will straight give themselves up into your hands, make 'em and cut 'em out what religion ye please. There be delights, there be recreations and jolly pastimes that will fetch the day about from sun to sun, and rock the tedious year as in a delightful dream. What need they torture their heads with that which others have taken so strictly and so unalterably into their own purveying? These are the fruits which a dull ease and cessation of our knowledge will bring forth among the people. How goodly, and how to be wished, were such an obedient unanimity as this; what a fine conformity would it starch us all into? Doubtless a staunch and solid piece of framework as any January could freeze together.

Nor much better will be the consequence even among the clergy themselves. It is no new thing never heard of before, for a parochial minister, who has his reward and is at his Hercules' pillars[132] in a warm benefice, to be easily in-

128. **mysteries:** professions, occupations, trades.

129. **dividual movable:** separable piece of property or commodity.

130. Hungry, Jesus sought figs to eat on the way from Bethany to Jerusalem (Matt. 11.12–14).

131. **publicans:** tax collectors; **tunnaging and poundaging:** excise taxes on wine (by the tun) and other commodities. Sirluck complains that the modernization of "tunnage to tonnage . . . betrays a misconception." But "*tonnage* is the more usual form," according to the *OED* (1.1), and has been since the fifteenth century.

132. **Hercules' pillars:** rocks on either side of the Strait of Gibraltar, anciently thought to mark the western limit of the world and to have been established by Hercules.

clinable, if he have nothing else that may rouse up his studies, to finish his circuit in an English concordance and a topic folio,[133] the gatherings and savings of a sober graduateship, a harmony and a catena,[134] treading the constant round of certain common doctrinal heads, attended with their uses, motives, marks, and means; out of which, as out of an alphabet or sol-fa, by forming and transforming, joining and disjoining variously, a little bookcraft, and two hours' meditation, might furnish him unspeakably to the performance of more than a weekly charge of sermoning—not to reckon up the infinite helps of interlinearies, breviaries, synopses, and other loitering gear.

But as for the multitude of sermons ready printed and piled up on every text that is not difficult, our London trading St. Thomas in his vestry and add to boot St. Martin and St. Hugh have not within their hallowed limits more vendible ware of all sorts ready made: so that penury he never need fear of pulpit provision, having where so plenteously to refresh his magazine.[135] But if his rear and flanks be not impaled,[136] if his back door be not secured by the rigid licenser, but that a bold book may now and then issue forth and give the assault to some of his old collections in their trenches, it will concern him then to keep waking, to stand in watch, to set good guards and sentinels about his received opinions, to walk the round and counter-round with his fellow inspectors, fearing lest any of his flock be seduced, who also then would be better instructed, better exercised and disciplined. And God send that the fear of this diligence which must then be used do not make us affect the laziness of a licensing church.

For if we be sure we are in the right and do not hold the truth guiltily, which becomes not, if we ourselves condemn not our own weak and frivolous teaching, and the people for an untaught and irreligious gadding rout, what can be more fair, than when a man judicious, learned, and of a conscience, for aught we know as good as theirs that taught us what we know, shall not privily from house to house, which is more dangerous, but openly by writing, publish to the world what his opinion is, what his reasons, and wherefore that which is now thought cannot be sound. Christ urged it as wherewith to justify himself that he preached in public;[137] yet writing is more public than preaching and more easy to refutation, if need be, there being so many whose business and profession

133. **topic folio:** commonplace book, notebook.

134. **harmony:** handbook that arranges parallel scriptural passages respecting the same events to show their agreement or consistency; **catena:** chain of connected passages chosen from biblical commentaries, arranged so that each passage is related to the preceding and following ones. The rest of the sentence refers to commonly taught means of organizing a sermon.

135. The Church of St. Thomas, Apostle, had clothiers nearby (see Dekker and Middleton, *Roaring Girl* 3.1.199); St. Martin le Grand, shoemakers. St. Hugh was a patron saint of shoemakers (Dekker, *Shoemakers' Holiday* 5.5.157–60). Milton thus puns on *vestry* and *boot* (apparel and shoes) as he suggests that religion is being regulated and standardized like any commerce.

136. **impaled:** fenced in, protected.

137. John 18.19–20.

merely it is to be the champions of truth, which if they neglect, what can be imputed but their sloth or inability?

Thus much we are hindered and disinured[138] by this course of licensing toward the true knowledge of what we seem to know. For how much it hurts and hinders the licensers themselves in the calling of their ministry, more than any secular employment, if they will discharge that office as they ought, so that of necessity they must neglect either the one duty or the other, I insist not, because it is a particular, but leave it to their own conscience, how they will decide it there.

There is yet behind[139] of what I purposed to lay open the incredible loss and detriment that this plot of licensing puts us to; more than if some enemy at sea should stop up all our havens and ports, and creeks, it hinders and retards the importation of our richest merchandize, truth. Nay, it was first established and put in practice by antichristian malice and mystery on set purpose to extinguish, if it were possible, the light of reformation and to settle falsehood, little differing from that policy wherewith the Turk upholds his Alcoran,[140] by the prohibition of printing. 'Tis not denied, but gladly confessed, we are to send our thanks and vows to heaven louder than most of nations, for that great measure of truth which we enjoy, especially in those main points between us and the Pope, with his appurtenances the prelates. But he who thinks we are to pitch our tent here and have attained the utmost prospect of reformation that the mortal glass[141] wherein we contemplate can show us till we come to beatific vision, that man by this very opinion declares that he is yet far short of truth.

Truth indeed came once into the world with her divine Master and was a perfect shape most glorious to look on. But when he ascended and his apostles after him were laid asleep, then straight arose a wicked race of deceivers, who, as that story goes of the Egyptian Typhon with his conspirators, how they dealt with the good Osiris, took the virgin Truth, hewed her lovely form into a thousand pieces, and scattered them to the four winds.[142] From that time ever since, the sad friends of Truth, such as durst appear, imitating the careful search that Isis made for the mangled body of Osiris, went up and down gathering up limb by limb still as they could find them. We have not yet found them all, Lords and Commons, nor ever shall do, till her Master's second coming. He shall bring together every joint and member, and shall mold them into an immortal feature[143] of loveliness and perfection. Suffer not these licensing prohibitions to stand at every place of opportunity, forbidding and disturbing them that con-

138. **disinured:** rendered unaccustomed or unfamiliar.

139. **yet behind:** still to show.

140. **Alcoran:** sacred writings of Islam; the Koran.

141. **mortal glass:** the mirror of mortal existence (cp. 1 Cor. 13.12: "Now we see through a glass darkly; but then face to face"; see also 2 Cor. 3.17–19).

142. Milton's application of the myth of Osiris and Typhon recalls Plutarch's in "Isis and Osiris."

143. **feature:** shape.

tinue seeking, that continue to do our obsequies to the torn body of our martyred saint.

We boast our light, but if we look not wisely on the sun itself, it smites us into darkness. Who can discern those planets that are oft combust,[144] and those stars of brightest magnitude that rise and set with the sun, until the opposite motion of their orbs bring them to such a place in the firmament where they may be seen evening or morning? The light which we have gained, was given us, not to be ever staring on, but by it to discover onward things more remote from our knowledge. It is not the unfrocking of a priest, the unmitering of a bishop, and the removing him from off the Presbyterian shoulders that will make us a happy nation. No, if other things as great in the church and in the rule of life both economical and political be not looked into and reformed, we have looked so long upon the blaze that Zwinglius and Calvin[145] hath beaconed up to us that we are stark blind.

There be who perpetually complain of schisms and sects, and make it such a calamity that any man dissents from their maxims. 'Tis their own pride and ignorance which causes the disturbing, who neither will hear with meekness, nor can convince, yet all must be suppressed which is not found in their syntagma.[146] They are the troublers, they are the dividers of unity, who neglect and permit not others to unite those dissevered pieces which are yet wanting to the body of Truth. To be still searching what we know not by what we know, still closing up truth to truth as we find it (for all her body is homogeneal and proportional), this is the golden rule[147] in theology as well as in arithmetic and makes up the best harmony in a church, not the forced and outward union of cold and neutral and inwardly divided minds.

Lords and Commons of England, consider what nation it is whereof ye are, and whereof ye are the governors: a nation not slow and dull, but of a quick, ingenious, and piercing spirit, acute to invent, subtle and sinewy to discourse, not beneath the reach of any point the highest that human capacity can soar to. Therefore the studies of learning in her deepest sciences have been so ancient and so eminent among us that writers of good antiquity and ablest judgment have been persuaded that even the school of Pythagoras and the Persian wisdom took beginning from the old philosophy of this island.[148] And that wise and

144. A planet within eight and a half degrees of the sun is said to be *combust,* its light subsumed by the sun's and its astrological influence "burnt up." Mars and Venus are regularly eclipsed by the sun but at other times can be seen morning and evening.

145. Ulrich *Zwingli* (1484–1531) was the principal figure of the Swiss Reformation. John *Calvin* (1509–64), a Frenchman who established a theocracy in Geneva, became the principal theologian of the Reformation.

146. **syntagma:** a systematic collection of doctrines.

147. **golden rule:** also known as the rule of three, a method of finding an unknown number from three given numbers, where the first is in the same proportion to the second as the third is to the unknown fourth.

148. **Persian wisdom:** occult arts, magic; **old philosophy:** that of the Druids, who practiced magic and, like the Pythagoreans, believed in the transmigration of souls.

civil Roman, Julius Agricola, who governed once here for Caesar, preferred the natural wits of Britain before the labored studies of the French.[149] Nor is it for nothing that the grave and frugal Transylvanian sends out yearly from as far as the mountainous borders of Russia and beyond the Hercynian wilderness,[150] not their youth, but their staid men to learn our language and our theologic arts.

Yet that which is above all this, the favor and the love of Heaven, we have great argument to think in a peculiar manner propitious and propending[151] towards us. Why else was this nation chosen before any other, that out of her as out of Sion should be proclaimed and sounded forth the first tidings and trumpet of reformation to all Europe? And had it not been the obstinate perverseness of our prelates against the divine and admirable spirit of Wycliffe, to suppress him as a schismatic and innovator, perhaps neither the Bohemian Huss and Jerome, no, nor the name of Luther or of Calvin, had been ever known; the glory of reforming all our neighbors had been completely ours.[152] But now, as our obdurate clergy have with violence demeaned the matter, we are become hitherto the latest and backwardest scholars of whom God offered to have made us the teachers.

Now once again by all concurrence of signs and by the general instinct of holy and devout men as they daily and solemnly express their thoughts, God is decreeing to begin some new and great period in his church, even to the reforming of reformation itself. What does he then but reveal himself to his servants, and, as his manner is, first to his Englishmen? I say as his manner is, first to us, though we mark not the method of his counsels and are unworthy. Behold now this vast city, a city of refuge, the mansion house of liberty, encompassed and surrounded with his protection. The shop of war hath not there more anvils and hammers waking, to fashion out the plates and instruments of armed justice in defence of beleaguered truth, than there be pens and heads there, sitting by their studious lamps, musing, searching, revolving new notions and ideas wherewith to present, as with their homage and their fealty, the approaching reformation; others as fast reading, trying all things, assenting to the force of reason and convincement. What could a man require more from a nation so pliant and so prone to seek after knowledge? What wants there to such a towardly and pregnant soil but wise and faithful laborers to make a knowing people a nation of prophets, of sages, and of worthies?[153] We reckon more than five months

149. *Agricola* (40–93) was a Roman general and governor of Britain. Tacitus, his son-in-law, records his regard for British ingenuity (*Agricola* 21).

150. **Hercynian wilderness:** forested region in central and southern Germany. Transylvania ("beyond the forest") was an independent state in Milton's era and zealously Protestant.

151. **propending:** inclining.

152. The reformist doctrines of John *Wycliffe* (c. 1330–1384) found supporters in England but were ultimately condemned and proscribed by the Church. John *Huss,* influenced by Wycliffe, was a reformer in Prague burned alive for heresy in 1414. His friend *Jerome* (1370–1416), also of Prague, was likewise influenced by Wycliffe and burned at the stake.

153. I.e., "What does this intellectually and spiritually apt country lack to fulfill its potential but those seekers of religious truth whose reasoned efforts can make it a land of the wise and holy?"

yet to harvest. There need not be five weeks; had we but eyes to lift up, the fields are white already.[154] Where there is much desire to learn, there of necessity will be much arguing, much writing, many opinions: for opinion in good men is but knowledge in the making. Under these fantastic[155] terrors of sect and schism, we wrong the earnest and zealous thirst after knowledge and understanding which God hath stirred up in this city.

What some lament of, we rather should rejoice at, should rather praise this pious forwardness among men to reassume the ill-deputed care of their religion into their own hands again. A little generous prudence, a little forbearance of one another, and some grain of charity might win all these diligences to join and unite into one general and brotherly search after truth, could we but forgo this prelatical tradition of crowding free consciences and Christian liberties into canons and precepts of men. I doubt not, if some great and worthy stranger should come among us, wise to discern the mold and temper of a people and how to govern it, observing the high hopes and aims, the diligent alacrity of our extended thoughts and reasonings in the pursuance of truth and freedom, but that he would cry out as Pyrrhus did, admiring the Roman docility and courage: "if such were my Epirots, I would not despair the greatest design that could be attempted to make a church or kingdom happy."[156]

Yet these are the men cried out against for schismatics and sectaries; as if, while the temple of the Lord was building, some cutting, some squaring the marble, others hewing the cedars, there should be a sort of irrational men who could not consider there must be many schisms and many dissections made in the quarry and in the timber ere the house of God can be built.[157] And when every stone is laid artfully together, it cannot be united into a continuity, it can but be contiguous in this world. Neither can every piece of the building be of one form; nay, rather the perfection consists in this, that out of many moderate varieties and brotherly dissimilitudes that are not vastly disproportional arises the goodly and the graceful symmetry that commends the whole pile and structure.

Let us therefore be more considerate builders, more wise in spiritual architecture, when great reformation is expected. For now the time seems come, wherein Moses, the great prophet, may sit in Heaven rejoicing to see that memorable and glorious wish of his fulfilled, when, not only our seventy elders, but all the Lord's people are become prophets. No marvel then though some men—and some good men too, perhaps, but young in goodness, as Joshua then was—envy them.[158] They fret and out of their own weakness are in agony lest

154. See John 4.35: "Say not ye, There are yet four months, and then cometh harvest? Behold, I say unto you, Lift up your eyes, and look on the fields; for they are white already to harvest."

155. **fantastic:** imaginary.

156. After a costly victory, King *Pyrrhus* of Epirus (319–272 B.C.E.) said that with soldiers like those of Rome, he could conquer the world.

157. On the hewing and cutting for Solomon's Temple, see 1 Kings 5–7 and 2 Chron. 2–4.

158. The young *Joshua* bid Moses to forbid other Hebrews from prophesying, but Moses replied, "Enviest thou for my sake? Would God that all the Lord's people were prophets" (Num. 11.29).

these divisions and subdivisions will undo us. The adversary again applauds and waits the hour. "When they have branched themselves out," sayeth he, "small enough into parties and partitions, then will be our time." Fool! He sees not the firm root out of which we all grow, though into branches; nor will beware until he see our small-divided maniples cutting through at every angle of his ill-united and unwieldy brigade.[159] And that we are to hope better of all these supposed sects and schisms, and that we shall not need that solicitude—honest, perhaps, though over-timorous—of them that vex in this behalf, but shall laugh in the end at those malicious applauders of our differences, I have these reasons to persuade me.

First, when a city shall be as it were besieged and blocked about, her navigable river infested, inroads and incursions round, defiance and battle oft rumored to be marching up even to her walls and suburb trenches, that then the people, or the greater part, more than at other times, wholly taken up with the study of highest and most important matters to be reformed, should be disputing, reasoning, reading, inventing, discoursing, even to a rarity and admiration, things not before discoursed or written of, argues first a singular goodwill, contentedness, and confidence in your prudent foresight and safe government, Lords and Commons.[160] And from thence derives itself to a gallant bravery and well-grounded contempt of their enemies, as if there were no small number of as great spirits among us as his was, who, when Rome was nigh besieged by Hannibal, being in the city, bought that piece of ground at no cheap rate whereon Hannibal himself encamped his own regiment.[161]

Next, it is a lively and cheerful presage of our happy success and victory. For as in a body, when the blood is fresh, the spirits pure and vigorous, not only to vital but to rational faculties, and those in the acutest and the pertest operations of wit and subtlety, it argues in what good plight and constitution the body is, so when the cheerfulness of the people is so sprightly up as that it has not only wherewith to guard well its own freedom and safety, but to spare, and to bestow upon the solidest and sublimest points of controversy and new invention, it betokens us not degenerated nor drooping to a fatal decay, but casting off the old and wrinkled skin of corruption to outlive these pangs and wax young again, entering the glorious ways of truth and prosperous virtue destined to become great and honorable in these latter ages.

Methinks I see in my mind a noble and puissant nation rousing herself like a strong man after sleep and shaking her invincible locks. Methinks I see her as an eagle mewing[162] her mighty youth and kindling her undazzled eyes at the full midday beam, purging and unscaling her long-abused sight at the fountain

159. **maniples:** small units (literally "handfuls") of soldiers. A *brigade* is a much larger unit.

160. This sentence recalls the situation in October 1642, when the Royalist army was poised to attack London. Cp. *Sonnet 8*. The threat of attack continued intermittently.

161. The story of a Roman citizen who paid full price for land then occupied by Hannibal's besieging troops appears in Livy's *History* (26.11).

162. **mewing:** molting, though some editors amend to "newing" (renewing).

itself of heavenly radiance, while the whole noise of timorous and flocking birds, with those also that love the twilight, flutter about, amazed at what she means, and in their envious gabble would prognosticate a year of sects and schisms.

What would ye do then; should ye suppress all this flowery crop of knowledge and new light sprung up and yet springing daily in this city? Should ye set an oligarchy of twenty engrossers[163] over it to bring a famine upon our minds again, when we shall know nothing but what is measured to us by their bushel? Believe it, Lords and Commons, they who counsel ye to such a suppressing do as good as bid ye suppress yourselves, and I will soon show how.

If it be desired to know the immediate cause of all this free writing and free speaking, there cannot be assigned a truer than your own mild and free and human government. It is the liberty, Lords and Commons, which your own valorous and happy counsels have purchased us, liberty which is the nurse of all great wits. This is that which hath rarified and enlightened our spirits like the influence of heaven; this is that which hath enfranchised, enlarged, and lifted up our apprehensions degrees above themselves. Ye cannot make us now less capable, less knowing, less eagerly pursuing of the truth, unless ye first make yourselves, that made us so, less the lovers, less the founders of our true liberty. We can grow ignorant again, brutish, formal, and slavish, as ye found us; but you then must first become that which ye cannot be, oppressive, arbitrary, and tyrannous, as they were from whom ye have freed us. That our hearts are now more capacious, our thoughts more erected to the search and expectation of greatest and exactest things, is the issue of your own virtue propagated in us; ye cannot suppress that unless ye reinforce an abrogated and merciless law that fathers may dispatch at will their own children.[164] And who shall then stick closest to ye and excite others? Not he who takes up arms for coat and conduct, and his four nobles of Danegelt. Although I dispraise not the defense of just immunities, yet love my peace better, if that were all.[165] Give me the liberty to know, to utter, and to argue freely according to conscience, above all liberties.

What would be best advised then, if it be found so hurtful and so unequal[166] to suppress opinions for the newness or the unsuitableness to a customary acceptance, will not be my task to say. I only shall repeat what I have learned from one of your own honorable number, a right noble and pious lord, who, had he not sacrificed his life and fortunes to the church and commonwealth, we had

163. **engrossers:** those who obtain sole possession; monopolizers.

164. The Roman law giving fathers the power of life and death over children was abolished in 318.

165. **coat and conduct:** tax levied on counties to pay for the equipment and transport of troops; **danegelt:** a tax imposed originally to fend off the Danes from English shores, and subsequently for other ends, such as the defense of the coast. Charles's attempt to revive and extend it without consent of Parliament was challenged as a violation of *just immunities* from such impositions. The sense of this passage seems to be that those who stood by Parliament against the Royalists did so not for money but to establish freedom of inquiry and expression.

166. **unequal:** unjust.

not now missed and bewailed a worthy and undoubted patron of this argument. Ye know him I am sure; yet I for honor's sake (and may it be eternal to him) shall name him, the Lord Brooke.[167] He, writing of episcopacy and by the way treating of sects and schisms, left ye his vote, or rather now the last words of his dying charge (which I know will ever be of dear and honored regard with ye) so full of meekness and breathing charity, that, next to his last testament who bequeathed love and peace to his disciples,[168] I cannot call to mind where I have read or heard words more mild and peaceful. He there exhorts us to hear with patience and humility those, however they be miscalled, that desire to live purely, in such a use of God's ordinances as the best guidance of their conscience gives them, and to tolerate them, though in some disconformity to ourselves. The book itself will tell us more at large, being published to the world and dedicated to the Parliament by him who, both for his life and for his death, deserves that what advice he left be not laid by without perusal.

And now the time in special is by privilege[169] to write and speak what may help to the further discussing of matters in agitation. The temple of Janus with his two controversial faces might now not unsignificantly be set open.[170] And though all the winds of doctrine were let loose to play upon the earth, so Truth be in the field, we do injuriously by licensing and prohibiting to misdoubt her strength.[171] Let her and Falsehood grapple; who ever knew Truth put to the worse in a free and open encounter? Her confuting is the best and surest suppressing. He who hears what praying there is for light and clearer knowledge to be sent down among us would think of other matters to be constituted beyond the discipline of Geneva, framed and fabricked already to our hands.[172]

Yet when the new light which we beg for shines in upon us, there be who envy and oppose if it come not first in at their casements. What a collusion is this, whenas we are exhorted by the wise man to use diligence, "to seek for wisdom as for hidden treasures early and late,"[173] that another order shall enjoin us to know nothing but by statute? When a man hath been laboring the hardest labor in the deep mines of knowledge, hath furnished out his findings in all their equipage, drawn forth his reasons as it were a battle ranged, scattered and defeated all objections in his way, calls out his adversary into the plain, offers him the advantage of wind and sun, if he please, only that he may try the mat-

167. Robert Greville (1608–43), the second *Lord Brooke,* a general of the Parliamentary army, was killed at the attack on Lichfield. Milton refers to his *Discourse Opening the Nature of that Episcopacy, which is Exercised in England* (1641).

168. See John 14.27.

169. **in special:** especially; **by privilege:** an idiom used to signify the right to print or publish a book or the like.

170. **Janus:** Roman god of gates and doorways. His two faces looked *controversially,* that is, in opposed directions. His temple lay open in time of war, closed in time of peace.

171. In opposing the *winds of doctrine* to *Truth,* Milton alludes to Eph. 4.14–15.

172. **discipline of Geneva:** Presbyterianism, which followed Calvin; **fabricked:** fashioned.

173. Though printed as a quotation in the first edition, this imperative combines and paraphrases Prov. 2.4, 8.11, and Matt. 13.44.

ter by dint of argument; for his opponents then to skulk, to lay ambushments, to keep a narrow bridge of licensing where the challenger should pass, though it be valor enough in soldiership, is but weakness and cowardice in the wars of Truth.

For who knows not that Truth is strong next to the Almighty; she needs no policies, nor stratagems, nor licensings to make her victorious—those are the shifts and the defenses that error uses against her power. Give her but room and do not bind her when she sleeps, for then she speaks not true as the old Proteus did, who spake oracles only when he was caught and bound,[174] but then rather she turns herself into all shapes, except her own, and perhaps tunes her voice according to the time, as Micaiah did before Ahab, until she be adjured into her own likeness.[175]

Yet is it not impossible that she may have more shapes than one? What else is all that rank of things indifferent[176] wherein Truth may be on this side or on the other without being unlike herself? What but a vain shadow else is the abolition of "those ordinances, that handwriting nailed to the cross"?[177] What great purchase is this Christian liberty which Paul so often boasts of?[178] His doctrine is that he who eats or eats not, regards a day or regards it not, may do either to the Lord.[179] How many other things might be tolerated in peace and left to conscience, had we but charity, and were it not the chief stronghold of our hypocrisy to be ever judging one another? I fear yet this iron yoke of outward conformity hath left a slavish print upon our necks; the ghost of a linen decency[180] yet haunts us. We stumble and are impatient at the least dividing of one visible congregation from another, though it be not in fundamentals. And through our forwardness to suppress and our backwardness to recover any enthralled piece of truth out of the grip of custom,[181] we care not to keep truth separated from truth, which is the fiercest rent and disunion of all. We do not see that while we still affect by all means a rigid external formality, we may as soon fall again into a gross conforming stupidity, a stark and dead congealment of "wood and hay and stubble" [1 Cor. 3.12][182] forced and frozen together, which is more to the sudden degenerating of a church than many subdichotomies of petty schisms.

Not that I can think well of every light separation, or that all in a Church is

174. On oracular *Proteus*, the shape-changing sea god, see Homer, *Od.* 4.384–93.

175. For *Ahab* and *Micaiah*, see 1 Kings 22.1–38.

176. **things indifferent:** points of religion not explicitly set out in Scripture, a much debated category in Milton's era.

177. **those . . . cross:** the old law, superseded through the sacrifice of Christ, as expressed by St. Paul (Col. 2.14).

178. See, e.g., Gal. 5.1, Rom. 8.21.

179. See Rom. 14.1–13.

180. **linen decency:** The phrase evokes priestly vestments dictated by Archbishop Laud and condemned by the Puritans.

181. See the preface to *DDD* on the opposition of truth and custom.

182. Another part of the same verse is quoted in the next sentence.

to be expected "gold and silver and precious stones." It is not possible for man to sever the wheat from the tares, the good fish from the other fry; that must be the angels' ministry at the end of mortal things.[183] Yet if all cannot be of one mind (as who looks they should be?), this doubtless is more wholesome, more prudent, and more Christian that many be tolerated, rather than all compelled. I mean not tolerated popery and open superstition, which as it extirpates all religions and civil supremacies, so itself should be extirpate, provided first that all charitable and compassionate means be used to win and regain the weak and the misled; that also which is impious or evil absolutely either against faith or manners no law can possibly permit, that intends not to unlaw itself. But those neighboring differences, or rather indifferences, are what I speak of, whether in some point of doctrine or of discipline, which though they may be many, yet need not interrupt "the unity of spirit," if we could but find among us "the bond of peace."[184]

In the meanwhile, if any one would write and bring his helpful hand to the slow-moving reformation which we labor under, if Truth have spoken to him before others, or but seemed at least to speak, who hath so bejesuited[185] us that we should trouble that man with asking license to do so worthy a deed?—and not consider this, that if it come to prohibiting, there is not aught more likely to be prohibited than truth itself, whose first appearance to our eyes, bleared and dimmed with prejudice and custom, is more unsightly and unplausible than many errors, even as the person[186] is of many a great man slight and contemptible to see to. And what do they tell us vainly of new opinions, when this very opinion of theirs, that none must be heard but whom they like, is the worst and newest opinion of all others and is the chief cause why sects and schisms do so much abound, and true knowledge is kept at distance from us; besides yet a greater danger which is in it. For when God shakes a kingdom with strong and healthful commotions to a general reforming, 'tis not untrue that many sectaries and false teachers are then busiest in seducing. But yet more true it is that God then raises to his own work men of rare abilities and more than common industry, not only to look back and revise what hath been taught heretofore, but to gain further and go on some new enlightened steps in the discovery of truth.

For such is the order of God's enlightening his church, to dispense and deal out by degrees his beam so as our earthly eyes may best sustain it. Neither is God appointed[187] and confined where and out of what place these his chosen shall be first heard to speak. For he sees not as man sees,[188] chooses not as man

183. Milton alludes to the parable of the wheat and the tares (Matt. 13.24–30, 36–43).

184. See Eph. 4.3.

185. **bejesuited:** initiated to Jesuitism.

186. **person:** bodily form.

187. **appointed:** fixed by agreement; settled beforehand.

188. Before choosing the shepherd David as King of Israel, God informs the prophet Samuel that "the Lord seeth not as man seeth" (1 Sam. 16.7).

chooses, lest we should devote ourselves again to set places, and assemblies, and outward callings of men, planting our faith one while in the old convocation house and another while in the chapel at Westminster;[189] when all the faith and religion that shall be there canonized is not sufficient without plain convincement,[190] and the charity of patient instruction to supple[191] the least bruise of conscience, to edify the meanest Christian who desires to walk in the spirit and not in the letter of human trust, for all the number of voices that can be there made; no, though Harry the Seventh himself there, with all his liege tombs about him, should lend them voices from the dead to swell their number.

And if the men be erroneous who appear to be the leading schismatics, what withholds us but our sloth, our self-will, and distrust in the right cause, that we do not give them gentle meeting and gentle dismissions, that we debate not and examine the matter thoroughly with liberal and frequent audience, if not for their sakes yet for our own? Seeing no man who hath tasted learning but will confess the many ways of profiting by those who, not contented with stale receipts, are able to manage and set forth new positions to the world. And were they but as the dust and cinders of our feet, so long as in that notion they may yet serve to polish and brighten the armory of truth, even for that respect they were not utterly to be cast away. But if they be of those whom God hath fitted for the special use of these times with eminent and ample gifts—and those perhaps neither among the priests nor among the pharisees—and we in the haste of a precipitant zeal shall make no distinction but resolve to stop their mouths because we fear they come with new and dangerous opinions (as we commonly forejudge them ere we understand them), no less than woe to us while, thinking thus to defend the Gospel, we are found the persecutors.

There have been not a few since the beginning of this Parliament, both of the presbytery and others, who, by their unlicensed books to the contempt of an *imprimatur*, first broke that triple ice clung about our hearts and taught the people to see day. I hope that none of those were the persuaders to renew upon us this bondage which they themselves have wrought so much good by contemning. But if neither the check that Moses gave to young Joshua, nor the countermand which our Savior gave to young John,[192] who was so ready to prohibit those whom he thought unlicensed, be not enough to admonish our elders how unacceptable to God their testy mood of prohibiting is; if neither their own remembrance what evil hath abounded in the church by this let of licensing, and

189. The bishops who until the 1640s set church policy in England met in the Jerusalem Chamber at Westminster. Once the episcopacy was undone, the *Westminster* Assembly of Divines met in the chapel of Henry VII (named at the end of the paragraph) to establish a new church discipline.

190. **convincement:** conviction of conscience.

191. **supple:** soften or mollify.

192. When *Joshua* wanted to forbid others from prophesying, *Moses* checked him (Num. 11.29). See note 156. Jesus tells *John* not to forbid others from acting in Jesus' name: "He that is not against us is for us" (Luke 9.50).

what good they themselves have begun by transgressing it, be not enough but that they will persuade and execute the most Dominican part of the Inquisition over us,[193] and are already with one foot in the stirrup so active at suppressing, it would be no unequal distribution in the first place to suppress the suppressors themselves, whom the change of their condition hath puffed up more than their late experience of harder times hath made wise.

And as for regulating the press, let no man think to have the honor of advising ye better than yourselves have done in that order published next before this, that no book be printed unless the printer's and the author's name, or at least the printer's, be registered.[194] Those which otherwise come forth, if they be found mischievous and libelous, the fire and the executioner will be the timeliest and the most effectual remedy that man's prevention can use. For this authentic Spanish policy of licensing books, if I have said aught, will prove the most unlicensed book itself within a short while, and was the immediate image of a Star Chamber decree to that purpose made in those very times when that court did the rest of those her pious works, for which she is now fallen from the stars with Lucifer.[195] Whereby ye may guess what kind of state prudence, what love of the people, what care of religion or good manners there was at the contriving, although with singular hypocrisy it pretended to bind books to their good behavior. And how it got the upper hand of your precedent order so well constituted before, if we may believe those men whose profession gives them cause to inquire most, it may be doubted[196] there was in it the fraud of some old patentees and monopolizers in the trade of bookselling; who, under pretence of the poor in their company not to be defrauded, and the just retaining of each man his several copy[197] (which God forbid should be gainsaid), brought diverse glossing colors[198] to the House, which were indeed but colors and serving to no end except it be to exercise a superiority over their neighbors, men who do not therefore labor in an honest profession to which learning is indebted that they should be made other men's vassals. Another end is thought was aimed at by some of them in procuring by petition this order,[199] that having power in their hands, malignant books might the easier scape abroad, as the event shows.

But of these sophisms and elenchs of merchandise I skill not.[200] This I know, that errors in a good government and in a bad are equally almost incident,[201] for

193. *Dominican* friars often served as licensers and were strict enforcers of doctrine.
194. Milton cites the Order of Parliament regulating printing that was made in January 1642.
195. The Court of the Star Chamber on July 11, 1637, gave control of the press to the Church. In July 1641, the Court was abolished. Milton compares its demise to the fall of Lucifer, the "morning star" (see Isa. 14.12, Rev. 12.4).
196. **doubted:** suspected.
197. **copy:** copyright.
198. **glossing colors:** explanations intended to disguise the truth.
199. In April 1643, the Stationers' Company petitioned Parliament to reinstitute control of the press.
200. I.e., "But of such fallacious arguments born of commercial interest, I profess ignorance."
201. **incident:** likely to occur.

what magistrate may not be misinformed, and much the sooner if liberty of printing be reduced into the power of a few. But to redress willingly and speedily what hath been erred, and in highest authority to esteem a plain advertisement[202] more than others have done a sumptuous bribe, is a virtue, honored Lords and Commons, answerable to your highest actions, and whereof none can participate but greatest and wisest men.

The End.

202. **advertisement:** warning.

Introduction to *Of Education*

Today *humanism* has become a slippery term. But for scholars of the early modern period it refers to an educational program based on the extant writings of Greek and Latin antiquity. The program can be traced to the thirteenth century, in Italy, and its rise has often been thought to be the defining feature of the Renaissance itself as a period in Western culture. Milton's essay *Of Education,* though in crucial ways a defense of traditional humanism, nonetheless owes its genesis to a movement in seventeenth-century European education dedicated to ending once and for all the cultural reign of humanism, and thus to ending, in some views at least, the Renaissance.

A new pedagogy had come into being. Most of its adherents were Protestants, though its leading figure, the Czech educator Johann Amos Comenius (1592–1670), was not. Gradually, over several centuries, and after undergoing numerous historical transformations, the new pedagogy carried the field. Most of its proposed changes are now firmly instituted in educational systems around the world.

Here are some of its tenets. Scientific empiricism should dominate the curriculum. The work of Francis Bacon, especially the assault on traditional logic and rhetoric in his *Novum Organum* (1620), was much admired by these reformers, and presented as a shining alternative to the arid culture of Greek and Latin studies. Literature, the humanities in general, amounted to a tyranny of words, occasioning a pedantic, snobbish, elitist pseudo-learning confined to its own word-world, not the world God created and Bacon taught us to number, weigh, and measure. Comenius favored state-sponsored schools offering an empirical, vocational education to all children, male and female. In a humanistic curriculum students would read Herodotus to learn about the conflicts between Greece and Asia, Donatus to discover the laws of drama, Quintilian and Cicero to discern the techniques and ethics of public speaking, and so on, through a whole host of ever-relevant originators, the *fontes* (springs) of civilized culture. Education meant having read and understood them. But Comenius hoped to subvert this reliance on great and seminal writers by collecting "Pansophy" (all truth) in a single book, a précis of knowledge in its entirety, or as Samuel Hartlib put it, "a true anatomy of the universe" (Comenius 13). Latin would still be taught, but in a vastly streamlined fashion. The new emphasis would fall on the twin virtues of the shortcut and the simplification.

Hartlib was a main champion of the new pedagogy in the England of Milton's day. Adopting the role of unofficial adviser to the mid-century Protestant Parliaments, Hartlib championed a wide variety of causes, from better use of farmland in England to utopian social schemes in the Virginia colony. He brought Comenius himself to England in 1641. He promoted a stable of like-minded authors, and it was no doubt this lifelong urge to proselytize that led him, at some point in the early 1640s, to invite Milton, then earning his living as a schoolmaster, to write about education. Perhaps Hartlib already knew or strongly suspected what the nation would find out in the decades ahead: that John Milton, graduate of St. Paul's, a grammar school designed by the formidable sixteenth-century humanist John Colet, and of Trinity College, Cambridge, was the supreme living product of humanistic learning. What a victory that would be! A Milton endorsing a Comenius!

Milton did agree wholeheartedly with certain of the Comenian indictments of Renaissance pedagogy. He thought his education wasteful, inefficient, and dispiriting. He detested the barren brambles of logic. He deplored the absence of Baconian subjects in the traditional curriculum. Like proponents of vocational instruction, he considered it wise to learn from actual practitioners. But Milton was also humanist-trained and Renaissance-inspired. Hartlib and Comenius had little or nothing to say about the power of art and literature to enrich and elevate, whereas that power was the central truth of Milton's existence. He also detested the idea of handbooks and compendiums. When Milton assures Hartlib that he has not looked into "what many modern *Januas* and *Didactics,* more than ever I shall read, have projected," he is alluding to two of the best-known books by Comenius, the *Janua Linguarum Reserata* (The Door of Languages Unlocked) and the *Didactica Magna* (Great Instruction), joking with evident contempt that even in the work of Comenius himself the dream of one Pansophic book had turned plural, and there were already too many of these supposedly time-saving digests to waste his time reading.

In the ideal school Milton envisions, there is time for the venerable humanistic authors as well as Baconian practicality, for Christian education with its imperative "to repair the ruins of our first parents by regaining to know God aright," as well as classical education, with its goal of preparing men "to perform justly, skilfully, and magnanimously all the offices both private and public of peace and war." There is time for Scripture and epic, music and martial exercise—time, magically, for *everything.* As the historian Charles Webster put it, "Milton is perhaps the only leading writer to embody a compromise between the old and new pedagogies" (113).

A telling feature of Milton's pedagogical scheme is the postponement of original composition until the entire curriculum has been mastered. Then, as education's crowning act, "will be the season of forming them to be able writers and composers." He clearly resented having been forced to write prematurely of various subjects through the course of his studies. The belief that composition should be the supreme act of maturity, and the anxious fear that this maturity, this readiness, may not yet have been attained, became part of the drama of his poetic compositions. A concern with the spiritual discipline of "inward ripeness" marks *Sonnet 7*, the 1633 "Letter to a Friend" that contains a draft of *Sonnet 7*, and the opening lines of *Lycidas*, where the premature death of a shepherd forces an unready author to begin his eulogy "before the mellowing year." *Of Education* was published in 1644. It would not be long before the publication of the 1645 *Poems*, whose dated works announce that the author has finally reached a first stage in artistic maturity and can now, at long last, submit his labors to public scrutiny. That the author himself felt a deep affinity between the pedagogical ideals expressed in *Of Education* and the fulfillment of his poetic ambitions is suggested by the fact that the 1673 edition of his *Poems Upon Several Occasions*, which appeared a year before Milton's death, reprints the "small tractate Of Education to Mr. Hartlib" after the early verse. This is the sole instance of Milton publishing his poetry and one of his prose works between the same covers.

Our text is based on the copy of the first edition in the Carl H. Pforzheimer Library in the Harry Ransom Humanities Research Center, Austin, Texas.

OF EDUCATION. TO MASTER SAMUEL HARTLIB.

Master Hartlib,

I am long since persuaded that to say or do aught worth memory and imitation, no purpose or respect should sooner move us than simply the love of God and of mankind. Nevertheless, to write now the reforming of education, though it be one of the greatest and noblest designs that can be thought on, and for the want whereof this nation perishes, I had not yet at this time been induced but by your earnest entreaties and serious conjurements; as having my mind, for the present, half-diverted in the pursuance of some other assertions, the knowledge and the use of which cannot but be a great furtherance both to the enlargement of truth and honest living with much more peace.

Nor should the laws of any private friendship have prevailed with me to divide thus or transpose my former thoughts, but that I see those aims, those actions which have won you with me the esteem of a person sent hither by some good providence from a far country to be the occasion and the incitement of great good to this island.[1] And, as I hear, you have obtained the same repute with men of most approved wisdom, and some of highest authority among us. Not to mention the learned correspondence which you hold in foreign parts, and the extraordinary pains and diligence which you have used in this matter both here and beyond the seas, either by the definite will of God so ruling or the peculiar sway of nature,[2] which also is God's working. Neither can I think that, so reputed and so valued as you are, you would, to the forfeit of your own discerning ability, impose upon me an unfit and over-ponderous argument, but that the satisfaction which you profess to have received from those incidental discourses which we have wandered into hath pressed and almost constrained you into a persuasion that what you require from me in this point I neither ought nor can in conscience defer beyond this time both of so much need at once and so much opportunity to try what God hath determined.[3]

I will not resist, therefore, whatever it is either of divine or human obligement that you lay upon me, but will forthwith set down in writing, as you re-

1. A native of Prussia, Hartlib (1600–62) attended Cambridge briefly around 1625. By 1628 he returned to England, where he maintained a voluminous international correspondence and tirelessly advocated educational and other reforms.

2. **peculiar sway of nature:** i.e., Hartlib's own natural bent.

3. In 1641 Parliament dedicated land taken from prelates to the advancement of learning, providing the resources, in Milton's view, to attempt to fulfill God's will.

quest me, that voluntary[4] idea, which hath long in silence presented itself to me, of a better education—in extent and comprehension far more large, and yet of time far shorter and of attainment far more certain—than hath been yet in practice. Brief I shall endeavor to be: for that which I have to say, assuredly this nation hath extreme need should be done sooner than spoken. To tell you, therefore, what I have benefited herein among old renowned authors, I shall spare; and to search what many modern *Januas* and *Didactics*[5] (more than ever I shall read) have projected, my inclination leads me not. But if you can accept of these few observations which have flowered off and are, as it were, the burnishing of many studious and contemplative years altogether spent in the search of religious and civil knowledge, and such as pleased you so well in the relating, I here give you them to dispose of.

The end then of learning is to repair the ruins of our first parents[6] by regaining to know God aright, and out of that knowledge to love him, to imitate him, to be like him as we may the nearest by possessing our souls of true virtue, which, being united to the heavenly grace of faith, makes up the highest perfection. But, because our understanding cannot in this body found itself but on sensible things, nor arrive so clearly to the knowledge of God and things invisible as by orderly conning over the visible and inferior creature,[7] the same method is necessarily to be followed in all discreet teaching. And, seeing every nation affords not experience and tradition enough for all kind of learning, therefore we are chiefly taught the languages of those people who have at any time been most industrious after wisdom; so that language is but the instrument conveying to us things useful to be known. And though a linguist should pride himself to have all the tongues that Babel cleft the world into, yet if he have not studied the solid things in them, as well as the words and lexicons, he were nothing so much to be esteemed a learned man as any yeoman or tradesman competently wise in his mother dialect only.

Hence appear the many mistakes which have made learning generally so unpleasing and so unsuccessful. First, we do amiss to spend seven or eight years merely in scraping together so much miserable Latin and Greek as might be learnt otherwise easily and delightfully in one year.[8] And that which casts our proficiency therein so much behind is our time lost, partly in too oft idle vacancies[9] given both to schools and universities, partly in a preposterous[10] exaction forcing the empty wits of children to compose themes, verses, and orations,

4. **voluntary:** spontaneous, unbidden.

5. Works by Johann Amos Comenius (1592–1670), Moravian pedagogical theorist who inspired Hartlib's project in England. He held that the end of education is the development of Christian virtue and that learning begins in the sensible realm.

6. In Christian teaching, the fall of Adam and Eve devastated human understanding.

7. **visible and inferior creature:** visible creation; the world we perceive.

8. In his *Minutes on the Life of Mr. John Milton,* John Aubrey records that Milton taught his nephews to sight-read Latin within a year.

9. **vacancies:** vacations; holidays.

10. **preposterous:** literally, putting the last thing first; backward.

which are the acts of ripest judgment and the final work of a head filled, by long reading and observing, with elegant maxims and copious invention.[11] These are not matters to be wrung from poor striplings like blood out of the nose or the plucking of untimely fruit—besides the ill habit which they get of wretched barbarizing against the Latin and Greek idiom with their untutored Anglicisms,[12] odious to be read, yet not to be avoided without a well-continued and judicious conversing among pure authors digested, which they scarce taste; whereas, if after some preparatory grounds of speech by their certain forms got into memory, they were led to the praxis[13] thereof in some chosen short book, lessoned thoroughly to them, they might then forthwith proceed to learn the substance of good things and arts in due order, which would bring the whole language quickly into their power. This I take to be the most rational and most profitable way of learning languages, and whereby we may best hope to give account to God of our youth spent herein.

And for the usual method of teaching arts, I deem it to be an old error of universities not yet well recovered from the scholastic grossness of barbarous ages that, instead of beginning with arts most easy (and those be such as are most obvious to the sense), they present their young, unmatriculated[14] novices at first coming with the most intellective abstractions of logic and metaphysics.[15] So that they, having but newly left those grammatic flats and shallows where they stuck unreasonably to learn a few words with lamentable construction, and now on the sudden transported under another climate to be tossed and turmoiled with their unballasted wits in fathomless and unquiet deeps of controversy,[16] do for the most part grow into hatred and contempt of learning, mocked and deluded all this while with ragged notions and babblements while they expected worthy and delightful knowledge; till poverty or youthful years call them importunately their several ways and hasten them with the sway of friends[17] either to an ambitious and mercenary or ignorantly zealous divinity;[18] some allured to the trade of law, grounding their purposes not on the prudent and heavenly contemplation of justice and equity, which was never taught them, but on the promising and pleasing thoughts of litigious terms,[19] fat contentions,[20] and flowing fees; others betake them to state affairs, with souls so unprincipled in virtue

11. In classical rhetoric, *inventio* refers to research, finding out all materials relevant to a given topic. *Copia* refers to the full use of these materials to address the topic fruitfully.
12. **Anglicisms:** expressions in Latin or Greek that follow English usage.
13. **praxis:** practice.
14. **unmatriculated:** not yet enrolled in a college or university.
15. In *Prolusion 7*, Milton laments that logic, "the queen of the Arts," is mistaught and scorns metaphysics as a "bog of fallacies" (1827).
16. As may be seen from Milton's *Prolusions*, school exercises typically took the form of disputations, often on metaphysical topics.
17. **sway of friends:** influence of relatives.
18. **divinity:** career in the clergy.
19. **litigious terms:** periods when courts were in session and dockets full.
20. **fat contentions:** lucrative legal disputes.

and true generous breeding that flattery and court shifts[21] and tyrannous aphorisms[22] appear to them the highest points of wisdom, instilling their barren hearts with a conscientious slavery if, as I rather think, it be not feigned. Others, lastly, of a more delicious[23] and airy[24] spirit, retire themselves, knowing no better, to the enjoyments of ease and luxury, living out their days in feast and jollity—which indeed is the wisest and the safest course of all these, unless they were with more integrity undertaken. And these are the errors, and these are the fruits of misspending our prime youth at the schools and universities as we do, either in learning mere words or such things chiefly as were better unlearnt.

I shall detain you no longer in the demonstration of what we should not do, but straight conduct ye to a hillside, where I will point ye out the right path of a virtuous and noble education—laborious indeed at the first ascent, but else so smooth, so green, so full of goodly prospect and melodious sounds on every side that the harp of Orpheus was not more charming.[25] I doubt not but ye shall have more ado to drive our dullest and laziest youth, our stocks and stubs,[26] from the infinite desire of such a happy nurture, than we have now to haul and drag our choicest and hopefullest wits to that asinine feast of sow-thistles and brambles which is commonly set before them as all the food and entertainment of their tenderest and most docible[27] age. I call therefore a complete and generous[28] education that which fits a man to perform justly, skillfully, and magnanimously all the offices both private and public of peace and war. And how all this may be done between twelve and one and twenty (less time than is now bestowed in pure trifling at grammar and sophistry) is to be thus ordered.

First, to find out a spacious house and ground about it fit for an academy, and big enough to lodge a hundred and fifty persons, whereof twenty or thereabout may be attendants, all under the government of one who shall be thought of desert sufficient and ability either to do all or wisely to direct and oversee it done. This place should be at once both school and university, not needing a remove to any other house of scholarship, except it be some peculiar college of law or physic[29] where they mean to be practitioners; but as for those general studies which take up all our time from Lily[30] to the commencing, as they term it, Master of Art, it should be absolute.[31] After this pattern, as many edifices may

21. **shifts:** subterfuges; sophistries.
22. **aphorisms:** customary maxims; *tyrannous* because untested by reason.
23. **delicious:** prone to sensuous indulgence.
24. **airy:** unsubstantial, vain. The sentence echoes parts of Comus's first speech (*Masque* 102–12).
25. In Greek myth, Orpheus was a poet-musician whose song enraptured and civilized listeners, even beasts, rocks, and trees—or in this case stocks and stubs.
26. **stocks and stubs:** tree stumps, here signifying "blockheads."
27. **docible:** teachable.
28. **generous:** appropriate for one of noble lineage.
29. **peculiar college of law or physic:** specialized school of law or medicine.
30. The standard Latin grammar used in English schools for over two centuries was written by the eponymous William Lily (c. 1468–1522). John Colet made him the first headmaster of St. Paul's School, Milton's alma mater.
31. **absolute:** complete, entire.

be converted to this use as shall be needful in every city throughout this land, which would tend much to the increase of learning and civility[32] everywhere. This number, less or more, thus collected to the convenience of a foot company,[33] or interchangeably two troops of cavalry, should divide their days' work into three parts as it lies orderly: their studies, their exercise, and their diet.

For their studies: first, they should begin with the chief and necessary rules of some good grammar, either that now used or any better; and while this is doing, their speech is to be fashioned to a distinct and clear pronunciation, as near as may be to the Italian, especially in the vowels. For we Englishmen, being far northerly, do not open our mouths in the cold air wide enough to grace a southern tongue, but are observed by all other nations to speak exceeding close and inward—so that to smatter[34] Latin with an English mouth is as ill a-hearing as law-French.[35]

Next, to make them expert in the usefullest points of grammar, and withal to season them and win them early to the love of virtue and true labor ere any flattering seducement or vain principle seize them wandering, some easy and delightful book of education would be read to them, whereof the Greeks have store, as Cebes, Plutarch, and other Socratic discourses.[36] But in Latin we have none of classic authority extant except the two or three first books of Quintilian[37] and some select pieces elsewhere. But here the main skill and groundwork will be to temper[38] them such lectures and explanations, upon every opportunity, as may lead and draw them in willing obedience, inflamed with the study of[39] learning and the admiration of virtue, stirred up with high hopes of living to be brave men and worthy patriots, dear to God and famous to all ages. That they may despise and scorn all their childish and ill-taught qualities to delight in manly and liberal[40] exercises; which he who hath the art and proper eloquence to catch them with—what with mild and effectual persuasions, and what with the intimation of some fear if need be, but chiefly by his own example—might in a short space gain them to an incredible diligence and courage, infusing into their young breasts such an ingenuous[41] and noble ardor as would not fail to make many of them renowned and matchless men.

At the same time, some other hour of the day might be taught them the rules of arithmetic and soon after the elements of geometry, even playing as the old

32. **civility:** good citizenship.
33. **convenience of a foot company:** number of soldiers in an infantry company (about one hundred).
34. **smatter:** both "to besmirch" and "to speak ignorantly."
35. **law-French:** corrupt variety of French used in English legal books.
36. Among the Greek works to which Milton refers are Cebes' *Table,* Plutarch's *On the Education of Children* and *Moralia,* and Plato's *Republic* and *Laws.* There were Latin translations of these texts that could pull the double duty Milton envisions, teaching grammar and inculcating high ideals at one stroke.
37. The first three books of Quintilian's *Institutes* concern pedagogy and rhetoric.
38. **temper:** adapt for.
39. **study of:** devotion to.
40. **liberal:** befitting a gentleman.
41. **ingenous:** high-minded.

manner was.[42] After evening repast till bedtime, their thoughts will be best taken up in the easy[43] grounds of religion and the story of scripture. The next step would be to the authors of agriculture—Cato, Varro, and Columella[44]—for the matter is most easy; and if the language be difficult, so much the better: it is not a difficulty above their years. And here will be an occasion of inciting and enabling them hereafter to improve the tillage of their country, to recover the bad soil, and to remedy the waste that is made of good, for this was one of Hercules' praises.[45] Ere half these authors be read, which will soon be with plying hard and daily, they cannot choose but be masters of any ordinary prose. So that it will be then seasonable for them to learn in any modern author the use of the globes and all the maps, first with the old names and then with the new;[46] or they might be then capable to read any compendious method of natural philosophy.

And at the same time might be entering into the Greek tongue, after the same manner as was before prescribed in the Latin, whereby the difficulties of grammar being soon overcome, all the historical physiology of Aristotle and Theophrastus are open before them, and, as I may say, under contribution.[47] The like access will be to Vitruvius, to Seneca's *Natural Questions*, to Mela, Celsus, Pliny, or Solinus.[48] And having thus passed the principles of arithmetic, geometry, astronomy, and geography, with a general compact of physics, they may descend in mathematics to the instrumental science of trigonometry and from thence to fortification, architecture, enginery,[49] or navigation. And in natural philosophy they may proceed leisurely from the history of meteors, minerals, plants, and living creatures as far as anatomy. Then also in course might be read to them out of some not tedious writer the institution of physic, that they may know the tempers, the humors, the seasons, and how to manage a crudity;[50]

42. The use of games to teach mathematics was recommended by Plato and Quintilian in *Laws* and *Institutes*, respectively. "The prominence given to mathematics in Milton's educational plan, here and later, is progressive if not indeed unique for his time" (Sirluck; Yale 2:386).

43. **easy:** advantageous, comforting.

44. All three Romans wrote standard agricultural tracts entitled *De Re Rustica* (On Rural Concerns).

45. The cleansing of the Augean stables, one of Hercules' twelve labors, was commonly allegorized as the first manuring of Italian soil.

46. Both classical and vernacular place names appeared on maps of Milton's era.

47. The zoological works of Aristotle and the botanical works of his pupil Theophrastus. **under contribution:** rendered tributary.

48. *Vitruvius*, first-century B.C.E. Roman authority on architecture, was highly regarded in the Renaissance. In *Natural Questions*, *Seneca* (4 B.C.E.–65 C.E.) summarizes classical knowledge about the natural world. Pomponius *Mela* wrote the earliest surviving Latin geography (c. 43 C.E.); Anlus Cornelius *Celsus* was a first-century Roman encyclopedist whose surviving volumes concern medicine; *Pliny* the Elder (c. 23–79 C.E.) produced a thirty-seven-volume *Natural History*; the geographer Julius *Solinus* (fl. c. 200 C.E.) compiled a digest of Mela and Pliny.

49. **enginery:** military engineering.

50. **institution of physic:** fundamentals of medicine. Ancient physiology identified four personality types or *tempers* (choleric, melancholic, sanguine, and phlegmatic) that varied according to the four *seasons* of the year as well as to the proportions of the four basic bodily fluids or *humors* (yellow bile, black bile, blood, and phlegm). **crudity:** an imperfect "concoction" of the humors, indigestion.

which he who can wisely and timely do is not only a great physician to himself and to his friends but also may at some time or other save an army by this frugal and expenseless means only and not let the healthy and stout bodies of young men rot away under him for want of this discipline, which is a great pity and no less a shame to the commander.

To set forward all these proceedings in nature and mathematics, what hinders but that they may procure, as oft as shall be needful, the helpful experiences of hunters, fowlers, fishermen, shepherds, gardeners, apothecaries, and, in the other sciences, architects, engineers, mariners, anatomists, who doubtless would be ready, some for reward and some to favor such a hopeful seminary. And this will give them such a real tincture of natural knowledge as they shall never forget but daily augment with delight. Then also those poets which are now counted most hard will be both facile and pleasant: Orpheus, Hesiod, Theocritus, Aratus, Nicander, Oppian, Dionysius, and in Latin Lucretius, Manilius, and the rural part of Vergil.[51]

By this time, years and good general precepts will have furnished them more distinctly with that act of reason which in ethics is called *proairesis*,[52] that they may with some judgment contemplate upon moral good and evil. Then will be required a special reinforcement of constant and sound indoctrinating to set them right and firm, instructing them more amply in the knowledge of virtue and the hatred of vice while their young and pliant affections are led through all the moral works of Plato, Xenophon, Cicero, Plutarch, Laertius, and those Locrian remnants[53]—but still to be reduced in their nightward studies, wherewith they close the day's work, under the determinate sentence of David or Solomon or the evangels and apostolic scriptures.[54]

Being perfect in the knowledge of personal duty, they may then begin the study of economics.[55] And either now, or before this, they may have easily learnt at any odd hour the Italian tongue. And soon after, but with wariness and good antidote, it would be wholesome enough to let them taste some choice comedies, Greek, Latin, or Italian; those tragedies also that treat of household matters, as *Trachiniae, Alcestis*, and the like.[56]

The next remove must be to the study of politics—to know the beginning, end, and reasons of political societies—that they may not in a dangerous fit of the commonwealth be such poor, shaken, uncertain reeds of such a tottering

51. Milton lists Greek and Roman poets whose writings on the natural world would be easily understood by students versed in the "visible creature." (The didactic poem *Lithica*, on the magical properties of stones, had long been attributed to the legendary Orpheus.).

52. **proairesis:** Aristotle's widely adopted term for the power of individual moral choice.

53. Timaeus of Locri (fifth century B.C.E.), namesake of Plato's *Timaeus*, was long deemed the author of *On the Soul of the World and Nature*.

54. I.e., pagan ethical philosophy must always be subjected to the definitive judgment of David, Solomon, the Gospels, and apostolic writings.

55. **economics:** the science or art of household management.

56. Classical comedy is more likely than tragedy to treat household affairs, though there are exceptions, such as Sophocles' *Trachiniae* and Euripides' *Alcestis* (cp. *Sonnet 23*).

conscience as many of our great counselors have lately shown themselves, but steadfast pillars of the state. After this they are to dive into the grounds of law and legal justice, delivered first and with best warrant by Moses and, as far as human prudence can be trusted, in those extolled remains of Grecian lawgivers, Lycurgus, Solon, Zaleucus, Charondas,[57] and thence to all the Roman edicts and tables with their Justinian,[58] and so down to the Saxon and common laws of England and the statutes. Sundays also and every evening may be now understandingly spent in the highest matters of theology and church history ancient and modern; and ere this time the Hebrew tongue at a set hour might have been gained, that the Scriptures may be now read in their own original, whereto it would be no impossibility to add the Chaldee and the Syrian dialect.[59] When all these employments are well conquered, then will the choice histories, heroic poems, and Attic tragedies of stateliest and most regal argument, with all the famous political orations, offer themselves, which if they were not only read but some of them got by memory and solemnly pronounced with right accent and grace, as might be taught, would endue them even with the spirit and vigor of Demosthenes or Cicero, Euripides or Sophocles.[60]

And now lastly will be the time to read with them those organic arts[61] which enable men to discourse and write perspicuously, elegantly, and according to the fitted style of lofty, mean, or lowly. Logic, therefore, so much as is useful, is to be referred to this due place with all her well-couched heads[62] and topics until it be time to open her contracted palm[63] into a graceful and ornate rhetoric taught out of the rule of Plato, Aristotle, Phalereus, Cicero, Hermogenes, Longinus.[64]

To which poetry would be made subsequent, or indeed, rather precedent, as being less subtle[65] and fine but more simple, sensuous and passionate. I mean not here the prosody of a verse, which they could not but have hit on before among the rudiments of grammar, but that sublime art which in Aristotle's *Poetics*, in Horace, and the Italian commentaries of Castelvetro, Tasso, Mazzoni,[66] and others, teaches what the laws are of a true epic poem, what of a dramatic,

57. Ancient lawgivers who helped form or reform early constitutions in Greece and its Italian colonies.

58. **Justinian:** sixth-century emperor who codified and rationalized the Roman legal system.

59. Aramaic dialects in which parts of the Bible had been preserved.

60. Milton's contemporaries looked for examples of persuasive speaking to the Athenian statesman Demosthenes, the Roman statesman Cicero, and the plays of Euripides and Sophocles.

61. **organic arts:** instrumental disciplines, such as logic, rhetoric, and poetry.

62. **well-couched heads:** strategically arranged points.

63. **contracted palm:** The closed fist symbolizes logic; the open palm, rhetoric.

64. Classical authors, actual or reputed, of standard works on rhetoric. See, e.g., Plato's *Gorgias* and *Phaedrus*, and Aristotle's *Rhetoric*. Cicero was the most influential of those Milton lists; see especially *De Oratore*. The Athenian statesman Demetrius *Phalereus* was traditionally but mistakenly identified as the author of *On Style*, and the Greek rhetorician Cassius *Longinus* as the author of *On the Sublime*. *Hermogenes* of Tarsus, a Greek grammarian who wrote on style and rhetoric, is the least known of those Milton names.

65. **precedent:** could mean both "earlier" in time and "superior or prime in value"; **subtle:** analytical.

66. Ludovico *Castelvetro* (1505–71) translated Aristotle's *Poetics* into Italian; his rigorous conception of the dramatic unities fostered neoclassical theory. Torquato *Tasso* (1544–95) profoundly influenced Milton's understanding of heroic poetry. Giacomo *Mazzoni* (1548–98) championed Dante.

what of a lyric, what decorum[67] is, which is the grand masterpiece to observe. This would make them soon perceive what despicable creatures our common rhymers and playwrights be, and show them what religious, what glorious and magnificent use might be made of poetry both in divine and human things. From hence, and not till now, will be the right season of forming them to be able writers and composers in every excellent matter, when they shall be thus fraught[68] with an universal insight into things. Or whether they be to speak in parliament or counsel, honor and attention would be waiting on their lips. There would then also appear in pulpits other visages, other gestures, and stuff otherwise wrought than what we now sit under, oft-times to as great a trial of our patience as any other that they preach to us.

These are the studies wherein our noble and our gentle youth ought to bestow their time in a disciplinary way from twelve to one-and-twenty—unless they rely more upon their ancestors dead than upon themselves living. In which methodical course it is so supposed they must proceed, by the steady pace of learning, onward, as at convenient times for memory's sake to retire back into the middleward,[69] and sometimes into the rear of what they have been taught, until they have confirmed and solidly united the whole body of their perfected knowledge, like the last embattling[70] of a Roman legion. Now will be worth the seeing what exercises and recreations may best agree and become these studies.

THEIR EXERCISE

The course of study hitherto briefly described is, what I can guess by reading, likest to those ancient and famous schools of Pythagoras, Plato, Isocrates, Aristotle, and such others, out of which were bred up[71] such a number of renowned philosophers, orators, historians, poets, and princes all over Greece, Italy, and Asia, besides the flourishing studies of Cyrene and Alexandria.[72] But herein it shall exceed them and supply a defect as great as that which Plato noted in the commonwealth of Sparta: whereas that city trained up their youth most for war and these, in their academies and Lyceum, all for the gown,[73] this institution of breeding which I here delineate shall be equally good both for peace and war. Therefore about an hour and a half ere they eat at noon should be allowed them

67. **decorum:** that which is proper to the nature, unity, or harmony of a literary composition.
68. **fraught:** laden, supplied.
69. **middleward:** middle part of an army.
70. **embattling:** arrangement of troops in battle order.
71. Aristotle, for example, was *bred up* or educated in Plato's Academy and later founded his own school, the Lyceum.
72. **Cyrene and Alexandria:** third-century centers of medicine and physical sciences.
73. **gown:** peacetime careers (Roman usage).

for exercise and due rest afterwards—but the time for this may be enlarged at pleasure, according as their rising in the morning shall be early.

The exercise which I commend first is the exact use of their weapon,[74] to guard and to strike safely with edge or point. This will keep them healthy, nimble, strong, and well in breath; is also the likeliest means to make them grow large and tall and to inspire them with a gallant and fearless courage, which, being tempered with seasonable lectures and precepts to them of true fortitude and patience, will turn into a native and heroic valor and make them hate the cowardice of doing wrong. They must be also practiced in all the locks and grips of wrestling, wherein Englishmen were wont to excel, as need may often be in fight to tug or grapple, and to close. And this perhaps will be enough wherein to prove and heat their single strength.[75]

The interim of unsweating themselves regularly and convenient rest before meat may both with profit and delight be taken up in recreating and composing their travailed spirits with the solemn and divine harmonies of music heard or learnt; either while the skillful organist plies his grave and fancied descant in lofty fugues, or the whole symphony with artful and unimaginable touches adorn and grace the well-studied chords of some choice composer; sometimes the lute or soft organ-stop waiting on elegant voices either to religious, martial, or civil ditties; which, if wise men and prophets be not extremely out,[76] have a great power over dispositions and manners to smooth and make them gentle from rustic harshness and distempered passions. The like also would not be unexpedient after meat to assist and cherish nature in her first concoction[77] and send their minds back to study in good tune and satisfaction.

Where, having followed it close under vigilant eyes till about two hours before supper, they are by a sudden alarum or watchword to be called out to their military motions, under sky or covert according to the season, as was the Roman wont; first on foot, then, as their age permits, on horseback to all the art of cavalry. That having in sport, but with much exactness and daily muster, served out the rudiments of their soldiership in all the skill of embattling, marching, encamping, fortifying, besieging, and battering, with all the helps of ancient and modern stratagems, tactics, and warlike maxims, they may, as it were out of a long war, come forth renowned and perfect commanders in the service of their country. They would not then, if they were trusted with fair and hopeful armies, suffer them, for want of just and wise discipline, to shed away from about them like sick feathers, though they be never so oft supplied; they would not suffer their empty and unrecruitable[78] colonels of twenty men in a

74. **weapon:** sword (cp. *2Def,* p. 331).
75. **prove . . . strength:** test and arouse their individual fortitude.
76. **out:** mistaken.
77. **cherish . . . concoction:** encourage vital functioning as the digestive process begins.
78. **unrecruitable:** incapable of getting recruits.

company to quaff out or convey into secret hoards the wages of a delusive list and a miserable remnant[79]—yet in the meanwhile to be overmastered with a score or two of drunkards, the only soldiery left about them, or else to comply with all rapines and violences. No, certainly, if they knew aught of that knowledge that belongs to good men or good governors, they would not suffer these things.

But to return to our own institute: besides these constant exercises at home, there is another opportunity of gaining experience to be won from pleasure itself abroad;[80] in those vernal seasons of the year when the air is calm and pleasant, it were an injury and sullenness against nature not to go out and see her riches and partake in her rejoicing with heaven and earth. I should not therefore be a persuader to them of studying much then, after two or three years that they have well laid their grounds, but to ride out in companies with prudent and staid guides to all the quarters of the land: learning and observing all places of strength, all commodities[81] of building and of soil for towns and tillage, harbors and ports for trade. Sometimes taking sea as far as to our navy, to learn there also what they can in the practical knowledge of sailing and of sea-fight.

These ways would try all their peculiar[82] gifts of nature, and if there were any secret excellence among them, would fetch it out and give it fair opportunities to advance itself by, which could not but mightily redound to the good of this nation, and bring into fashion again those old admired virtues and excellencies with far more advantage now in this purity of Christian knowledge. Nor shall we then need the monsieurs of Paris to take our hopeful youth into their slight and prodigal custodies and send them over back again transformed into mimics, apes, and kickshaws.[83] But if they desire to see other countries at three or four and twenty years of age, not to learn principles, but to enlarge experience and make wise observation, they will by that time be such as shall deserve the regard and honor of all men where they pass and the society and friendship of those in all places who are best and most eminent. And perhaps then other nations will be glad to visit us for their breeding, or else to imitate us in their own country.

Now lastly for their diet there cannot be much to say, save only that it would be best in the same house—for much time else would be lost abroad, and many ill habits got—and that it should be plain, healthful, and moderate, I suppose is out of controversy.

Thus, Mr. Hartlib, you have a general view in writing, as your desire was, of that which at several times I had discoursed with you concerning the best and

79. **colonels . . . remnant:** Unable to recruit soldiers, the colonel commands a small company depleted by desertion and illness but submits a deceptive list of his troops, padded with false names, then embezzles the wages of both his real and his imaginary soldiers.

80. **abroad:** outdoors.

81. **commodities:** material advantages.

82. **peculiar:** special, individual.

83. **kickshaws:** fantastical, frivolous persons (Fr. *quelques choses*).

noblest way of education; not beginning, as some have done, from the cradle, which yet might be worth many considerations; if brevity had not been my scope, many other circumstances also I could have mentioned, but this,[84] to such as have the worth in them to make trial, for light and direction may be enough. Only I believe that this is not a bow for every man to shoot in that counts himself a teacher, but will require sinews almost equal to those which Homer gave Ulysses;[85] yet I am withal persuaded that it may prove much more easy in the assay than it now seems at distance, and much more illustrious, how-beit not more difficult than I imagine, and that imagination presents me with nothing but very happy and very possible according to best wishes,[86] if God have so decreed, and this age have spirit and capacity enough to apprehend.

The End

84. **this:** what I have here proposed.
85. In Book 21 of Homer's *Odyssey*, Odysseus (*Ulysses*) alone can string his famed bow, much to the chagrin of his wife's suitors.
86. I.e., the actual attempt to establish such an academy may prove easier than it might now appear, and much more obviously beneficial (*illustrious*) although no more difficult than Milton imagines, and his imagination presents only happy and manageable prospects in line with the best intentions.

Introduction to Selections from *Tetrachordon*

In March 1645 appeared *Tetrachordon: Expositions upon the four chief Places in Scripture which treat of Marriage or nullities in Marriage. On Gen. 1:27, 28. compared and explained by Gen. 2:18, 23, 24; Deut. 24:1, 2; Matt. 5:31, 32 with Matt. 19, from verse 3 to 11; 1 Cor. 7, from verse 10 to 16. Wherein the Doctrine and Discipline of Divorce, as was late published, is confirmed by explanation of Scripture, by testimony of ancient Fathers, of civil laws in the Primitive Church, of famousest Reformed Divines, and lastly, by an intended Act of the Parliament and Church of England in the last year of Edward the sixth. By the former Author J. M.* The title, which means "four-stringed," points to the four main biblical texts that Milton hopes to harmonize in his argument for divorce. The main challenge, as in *The Doctrine and Discipline*, was reconciling Christ's apparent prohibition of divorce in the Gospel of Matthew with the Mosaic allowance of divorce in Deuteronomy.

Milton again argues that God would contradict himself were the Mosaic permission to be overturned by a Gospel prohibition. The most important new element in *Tetrachordon* is a reinterpretation of Matthew 19:8: "He saith unto them, Moses because of the hardness of your hearts suffered you to put away your wives: but from the beginning it was not so." Earlier Milton, taking hard-heartedness as characterizing a subset of the Jews, argued that God allowed divorce for the relief of the conscientious despite knowing that the hard-hearted would abuse the law by divorcing for trivial reasons. Now, by identifying another meaning of *hard-heartedness*—the imperfection or weakness among even the good after the Fall—Milton salvages for virtuous Christians (such as himself) the Mosaic allowance of divorce as glossed by Christ in Matthew 19:8, without having to evoke a complex and ironical interpretive setting (Yale 2:153–55). When Christ adds "from the beginning it was not so," he refers not to the time before Moses but to Paradise, before the Fall resulted in the kinds of temperamental differences that can make marital union impossible. Given that the Mosaic Law is adapted to our weakness after the Fall, it is inconceivable to Milton that the Gospel Law would be harsher and less merciful. Not only the lawfulness of divorce but the rest of "the secondary law of nature and of nations" is adapted to our fallen condition (p. 263); the implication is that the Mosaic (and by extension Christian) authorization of divorce is a universal law.

The new reading of "hardness of heart" seems to promise a firmer foundation for the no-fault divorce advanced in the *Doctrine and Discipline.* The earlier argument, however, all but disappears from *Tetrachordon,* in which marriages fail almost invariably owing to the wife's willfulness and hostility (Fallon 2007).

As in the *Doctrine and Discipline,* Milton holds out an ideal of companionate marriage that should resonate today. The differences between the sexes can make for a happy meeting of "most resembling unlikeness, and most unlike resemblance" (p. 246), and Milton explicitly takes Augustine to task for his "crabbed opinion" that, were woman not required for procreation, Adam would have been better off with a man as his companion (p. 246).

Tetrachordon fared no better with its audience than did the *Doctrine and Discipline.* Milton turns the tables on his attackers among the Scottish Presbyterians with his sharply satirical *Sonnet 11,* "A book was writ of late called *Tetrachordon.*" In his related *Sonnet 12,* "I did but prompt the age to quit their clogs," Milton rebukes those who have pronounced his idealistic argument on marriage and divorce licentious: they "bawl for freedom in their senseless mood, / And still revolt when truth would set them free. / License they mean when they cry libertie; / For who loves that, must first be wise and good."

Our text follows the copy of the first edition in the British Library's Thomason Collection (E. 271[12]).

Selections from TETRACHORDON

Σκαιοῖσι καινὰ προσφέρων σοφὰ
Δόξεις ἀρχεῖος, κοὐ σοφὸς πεφυκέναι.
Τῶν δ' αὖ δοκαύντων εἰδέναι τι ποικίλον,
Κρείσσων νομισθεὶς ἐν πόλει, λυπρὸς φανῇ.[1]
Euripid[es], *Medea*

TO THE PARLIAMENT

That which I knew to be the part of a good magistrate, aiming at true liberty through the right information of religious and civil life, and that which I saw, and was partaker of, your vows and solemn covenants,[2] Parliament of England, your actions also manifestly tending to exalt the truth and to depress the tyranny of error and ill custom with more constancy and prowess than ever yet any, since that Parliament which put the first scepter of this kingdom into his hand whom God and extraordinary virtue made their monarch,[3] were the causes that moved me, one else not placing much in the eminence of a dedication, to present your high notice with a discourse, conscious to itself of nothing more than of diligence and firm affection to the public good. And that ye took it so as wise and impartial men, obtaining so great power and dignity, are wont to accept, in matters both doubtful and important, what they think offered them well meant, and from a rational ability, I had no less than to persuade me.

And on that persuasion am returned as to a famous and free port, myself also bound by more than a maritime Law, to expose as freely what freightage I conceive to bring of no trifles. For although it be generally known, how and by whom ye have been instigated to a hard censure of that former book,[4] entitled

1. Euripides, *Medea* 298–301: "If you put new ideas before the eyes of fools/They'll think you foolish and worthless into the bargain;/And if you are thought to be superior to those who have/Some reputation for learning, you will become hated" (tr. Rex Warner).

2. **solemn covenants:** An allusion to the Solemn Covenant of 1643, by which Parliament and the Westminster Assembly agreed to bring the churches of England, Scotland, and Wales into uniformity of doctrine, worship, and church government, under the model of the Presbyterian national church of Scotland.

3. Most likely a reference to Parliament's 1534 Act of Supremacy, which placed Henry VIII at the head of the English Church.

4. A reference to the Presbyterian clergy, and particularly to Herbert Palmer, who denounced the author of the *Doctrine and Discipline* in a sermon preached to Parliament on August 13, 1644, a special Day of Humiliation.

The Doctrine and Discipline of Divorce, an opinion held by some of the best among reformed writers without scandal or confutement, though now thought new and dangerous by some of our severe Gnostics[5] (whose little reading and less meditating holds ever with hardest obstinacy that which it took up with easiest credulity), I do not find yet that aught, for the furious incitements which have been used, hath issued by your appointment that might give the least interruption or disrepute either to the author, or to the book. Which he who will be better advised than to call your neglect or connivance at a thing imagined so perilous, can attribute it to nothing more justly than to the deep and quiet stream of your direct and calm deliberations, that gave not way either to the fervent rashness or the immaterial gravity of those who ceased not to exasperate without cause. For which uprightness and incorrupt refusal of what ye were incensed to, Lords and Commons, (though it were done to justice, not to me, and was a peculiar demonstration how far your ways are different from the rash vulgar) besides those allegiances of oath and duty, which are my public debt to your public labors, I have yet a store of gratitude laid up which cannot be exhausted; and such thanks perhaps they may live to be, as shall more than whisper to the next ages.

Yet that the author may be known to ground himself upon his own innocence and the merit of his cause, not upon the favor of a diversion or a delay to any just censure, but wishes rather he might see those his detractors at any fair meeting, as learned debatements are privileged with a due freedom under equal moderators, I shall here briefly single one of them[6] (because he hath obliged me to it), who I persuade me having scarce read the book nor knowing him who writ it, or at least feigning the latter, hath not forborne to scandalize him, unconferred with, unadmonished, undealt with by any pastorly or brotherly convincement, in the most open and invective manner, and at the most bitter opportunity that drift or set design could have invented. And this, whenas the canon Law, though commonly most favoring the boldness of their priests, punishes the naming or traducing of any person in the Pulpit, was by him made no scruple. If I shall therefore take license by the right of nature, and that liberty wherein I was born, to defend my self publicly against a printed calumny, and do willingly appeal to those judges to whom I am accused, it can be no immoderate or unallowable course of seeking so just and needful reparations. Which I had done long since, had not these employments, which are now visible, deferred me.

It was preached before ye, Lords and Commons, in August last upon a special Day of Humiliation, that "there was a wicked book abroad," and ye were taxed of sin that it was yet "uncensured, the book deserving to be burnt"; and

5. By calling his opponents *Gnostics,* Milton implies that to oppose divorce for incompatibility is to condone hateful, loathsome sexuality (the sex of people who hate each other), and in that sense to show a gnostic contempt for physical life.

6. Herbert Palmer (see note 4).

"impudence" also was charged upon the author, who durst "set his name to it, and dedicate it to yourselves." First, Lords and Commons, I pray to that God, before whom ye then were prostrate, so to forgive ye those omissions and trespasses which ye desire most should find forgiveness, as I shall soon show to the world how easily ye absolve yourselves of that which this man calls your sin, and is indeed your wisdom and your nobleness, whereof to this day ye have done well not to repent. He terms it "a wicked book" and (why but "for allowing other causes of divorce, than Christ and his Apostles mention"?); and with the same censure condemns of wickedness not only Martin Bucer, that elect instrument of reformation, highly honored and had in reverence by Edward the Sixth, and his whole Parliament, whom also I had published in English by a good providence about a week before this calumnious digression was preached,[7] so that if he knew not Bucer then, as he ought to have known, he might at least have known him some months after, ere the sermon came in print; wherein notwithstanding he persists in his former sentence, and condemns again of wickedness, either ignorantly or willfully, not only Martin Bucer and all the choicest and holiest of our reformers, but the whole Parliament and church of England in those best and purest times of Edward the Sixth. All which I shall prove with good evidence at the end of these explanations. And then let it be judged and seriously considered with what hope the affairs of our religion are committed to one among others,[8] who hath now only left him which of the twain he will choose, whether this shall be his palpable ignorance, or the same wickedness of his own book, which he so lavishly imputes to the writings of other men: and whether this of his, that thus peremptorily defames and attaints of wickedness unspotted churches, unblemished Parliaments, and the most eminent restorers of Christian doctrine, deserve not to be burnt first.

And if his heat had burst out only against the opinion, his wonted passion had no doubt been silently borne with wonted patience. But since, against the charity of that solemn place and meeting, it served him further to inveigh opprobriously against the person, branding him with no less than impudence only for setting his name to what he had written, I must be excused not to be so wanting to the defense of an honest name, or to the reputation of those good men who afford me their society, but to be sensible of such a foul endeavored disgrace; not knowing aught either in mine own deserts or the laws of this land why I should be subject, in such a notorious and illegal manner, to the intemperancies of this man's preaching choler. And indeed to be so prompt and ready, in the midst of his humbleness, to toss reproaches of this bulk and size, argues as if they were the weapons of his exercise, I am sure not of his ministry, or of that day's work. Certainly to subscribe my name at what I was to own, was what the state had ordered and requires. And he who lists not to be malicious would

7. Milton published his translation of Bucer as *The Judgement of Martin Bucer concerning Divorce* in early August 1644.

8. Palmer chaired the committee charged with revising the doctrine of marriage.

call it ingenuity,[9] clear conscience, willingness to avouch what might be questioned, or to be better instructed. And if God were so displeased with those (Isa. 58[.4]) who "on the solemn fast were wont to smite with the fist of wickedness," it could be no sign of his own humiliation accepted, which disposed him to smite so keenly with a reviling tongue.

But if only to have writ my name must be counted "impudence," how doth this but justify another who might affirm, with as good warrant, that the late discourse of *Scripture and Reason,* which is certain to be chiefly his own draught, was published without a name, out of base fear and the sly avoidance of what might follow to his detriment if the party at court should hap to reach him?[10] And I, to have set my name where he accuses me to have set it, am so far from recanting that I offer my hand also, if need be, to make good the same opinion which I there maintain by inevitable consequences drawn parallel from his own principal arguments in that of *Scripture and Reason,* which I shall pardon him if he can deny without shaking his own composition to pieces. The "impudence" therefore, since he weighed so little what a gross revile that was to give his equal, I send him back again for a phylactery[11] to stitch upon his arrogance, that censures not only before conviction, so bitterly without so much as one reason given, but censures the congregation of his governors to their faces, for not being so hasty as himself to censure.

And wheras my other crime is that I addressed the dedication of what I had studied to the Parliament, how could I better declare the loyalty which I owe to that supreme and majestic tribunal, and the opinion which I have of the high-entrusted judgment, and personal worth assembled in that place? With the same affeetions therefore, and the same addicted fidelity, Parliament of England, I here again have brought to your perusal on the same argument these following expositions of scripture. The former book, as pleased some to think who were thought judicious, had of reason in it to a sufficiency; what they required was that the scriptures there alleged might be discussed more fully. To their desires thus much further hath been labored in the scriptures. Another sort also, who wanted more authorities and citations, have not been here unthought of. If all this attain not to satisfy them, as I am confident that none of those our great controversies at this day hath had a more demonstrative explaining, I must confess to admire what it is; for doubtless it is not reason nowadays that satisfies or suborns the common credence of men, to yield so easily and grow so vehement in matters much more disputable and far less conducing to the daily good and peace of life.

Some whose necessary shifts have long inured them to cloak the defects of

9. **ingenuity:** frankness, ingenuousness.

10. In *Scripture and Reason Pleaded for Defensive Arms* (1643), Palmer and his coauthors argued against the divine right of kings.

11. **phylactery:** Leather prayer box containing excerpts of Deuteronomy and Exodus, worn by Jews during morning prayer as a sign of obedience to the law. Milton uses the term figuratively to mean an ostentatious or hypocritical show of piety or rectitude.

their unstudied years and hatred now to learn, under the appearance of a grave solidity (which estimation they have gained among weak perceivers), find the ease of slighting what they cannot refute, and are determined, as I hear, to hold it not worth the answering. In which number I must be forced to reckon that doctor,[12] who in a late equivocating treatise plausibly set afloat against the Dippers, diving the while himself with a more deep prelatical malignance against the present state and church government, mentions with ignominy "the Tractate of Divorce"; yet answers nothing, but instead thereof (for which I do not commend his marshalling) sets Moses also among the crew of his Anabaptists, as one who to a holy nation, the commonwealth of Israel, gave laws "breaking the bonds of marriage to inordinate lust." These are no mean surges of blasphemy, not only dipping Moses the divine lawgiver, but dashing with a high hand against the justice and purity of God himself, as these ensuing scriptures plainly and freely handled shall verify to the lancing of that old apostemated[13] error. Him therefore I leave now to his repentance.

Others, which is their courtesy, confess that wit and parts may do much to make that seem true which is not (as was objected to Socrates by them who could not resist his efficacy, that he ever made the worse cause seem the better),[14] and thus, thinking themselves discharged of the difficulty, love not to wade further into the fear of a convincement. These will be their excuses to decline the full examining of this serious point. So much the more I press it and repeat it, Lords and Commons, that ye beware while time is, ere this grand secret and only art of ignorance affecting tyranny grow powerful and rule among us. For if sound argument and reason shall be thus put off, either by an undervaluing silence, or the masterly censure of a railing word or two in the pulpit, or by rejecting the force of truth as the mere cunning of eloquence and sophistry, what can be the end of this, but that all good learning and knowledge will suddenly decay? Ignorance and illiterate presumption, which is yet but our disease, will turn at length into our very constitution, and prove the hectic evil of this age, worse to be feared, if it get once to reign over us, than any Fifth Monarchy.[15]

If this shall be the course, that what was wont to be a chief commendation and the ground of other men's confidence in an author, his diligence, his learning, his elocution, whether by right or by ill meaning granted him, shall be turned now to a disadvantage and suspicion against him, that what he writes,

12. Daniel Featley, who in *The Dippers Dipt* (1645) attacked the Anabaptists for, among other things, permitting divorce. In this sentence, which ends by quoting Featley's attack on his own *Doctrine and Discipline,* Milton, as elsewhere, both implicitly associates himself with fringe sectarians and adroitly positions his opponents as enemies to the mainstream.

13. **apostemated:** abscessed.

14. See Plato's *Apology* 18b.

15. The *Fifth Monarchy,* the last of the succession of kingdoms foretold in the apocalyptic Book of Daniel (2.44), was interpreted in Milton's time as the reign of Christ after the Second Coming. Fifth Monarchy Men hoped to usher in that reign by force.

though unconfuted, must therefore be mistrusted, therefore not received for the industry, the exactness, the labor in it, confessed to be more than ordinary; as if wisdom had now forsaken the thirsty and laborious inquirer, to dwell against her nature with the arrogant and shallow babbler. To what purpose all those pains and that continual searching required of us by Solomon to the attainment of understanding?[16] Why are men bred up with such care and expense to a life of perpetual studies? Why do yourselves with such endeavor seek to wipe off the imputation of intending to discourage the progress and advance of learning?

He, therefore, whose heart can bear him to the high pitch of your noble enterprises, may easily assure himself that the prudence and far-judging circumspectness of so grave a magistracy sitting in Parliament, who have before them the prepared and purposed act of their most religious predecessors to imitate in this question, cannot reject the clearness of these reasons and these allegations both here and formerly offered them; nor can overlook the necessity of ordaining more wholesomely and more humanely in the casualties of divorce than our laws have yet established, if the most urgent and excessive grievances happening in domestic life be worth the laying to heart, which, unless charity be far from us, cannot be neglected. And that these things, both in the right constitution and in the right reformation of a commonwealth, call for speediest redress and ought to be the first considered, enough was urged in what was prefaced to that monument of Bucer which I brought to your remembrance, and the other time before.

Henceforth, except new cause be given, I shall say less and less. For if the law make not timely provision, let the law, as reason is, bear the censure of those consequences which her own default now more evidently produces. And if men want manliness to expostulate the right of their due ransom, and to second their own occasions, they may sit hereafter and bemoan themselves to have neglected through faintness the only remedy of their sufferings, which a seasonable and well-grounded speaking might have purchased them. And perhaps in time to come, others will know how to esteem what is not every day put into their hands, when they have marked events, and better weighed how hurtful and unwise it is to hide a secret and pernicious rupture under the ill counsel of a bashful silence. But who would distrust aught, or not be ample in his hopes of your wise and Christian determinations? Who have the prudence to consider, and should have the goodness, like gods as ye are called,[17] to find out readily, and by just law to administer, those redresses which have of old, not without God ordaining, been granted to the adversities of mankind, ere they who needed were put to ask. Certainly, if any other have enlarged his thoughts to expect from this government, so justly undertaken and by frequent assistances

16. See, e.g., Prov. 2.4.

17. Milton plays on a Hebrew word for God, *elohim*, which literally means "powers" and was also used for rulers and judges.

from Heaven so apparently upheld, glorious changes and renovations both in church and state, he among the foremost might be named, who prays that the fate of England may tarry for no other deliverers.

John Milton

TETRACHORDON,

Expositions upon the four chief places in scripture which treat of marriage or nullities in marriage.

GEN. 1.27.

"So God created man in his own image, in the image of God created he him; male and female created he them.

28. "And God blessed them, and God said unto them, Be fruitful," etc.

GEN. 2.18.

"And the Lord God said, It is not good that man should be alone, I will make him a help meet for him.

23. "And Adam said, This is now bone of my bones, and flesh of my flesh; she shall be called woman, because she was taken out of man.
24. "Therefore shall a man leave his father and his mother, and shall cleave unto his wife, and they shall be one flesh."

GEN. 1.27.

["So God created Man in his own image."][18] To be informed aright in the whole history of marriage, that we may know for certain, not by a forced yoke but by an impartial definition, what marriage is and what is not marriage, it will undoubtedly be safest, fairest, and most with our obedience, to inquire, as our Savior's direction is, how it was in the beginning. And that we begin so high as man created after God's own image, there want not earnest causes. For nothing nowadays is more degenerately forgotten than the true dignity of man, almost in every respect, but especially in this prime institution of matrimony, wherein his native preeminence ought most to shine. Although if we consider that just and natural privileges men neither can rightly seek, nor dare fully claim, unless they be allied to inward goodness and steadfast knowledge, and that the want of

18. Here and throughout, the bracketed paragraph-heading quotations are Milton's.

this quells them to a servile sense of their own conscious unworthiness, it may save the wondering why in this age many are so opposite both to human and to Christian liberty,[19] either while they understand not or envy others that do; contenting or rather priding themselves in a specious humility and strictness bred out of low ignorance, that never yet conceived the freedom of the Gospel; and is therefore by the Apostle to the Colossians ranked with no better company than will-worship and the mere show of wisdom.[20] And how injurious herein they are, if not to themselves yet to their neighbors, and not to them only but to the all-wise and bounteous grace offered us in our redemption, will orderly appear.

["In the image of God created he him."] It is enough determined that this image of God wherein man was created, is meant wisdom, purity, justice, and rule over all creatures. All which, being lost in Adam, was recovered with gain by the merits of Christ. For albeit our first parent had lordship over sea, and land, and air, yet there was a law without him, as a guard set over him. But Christ having cancelled the handwriting of ordinances which was against us (Coloss. 2.14) and interpreted the fulfilling of all through charity, hath in that respect set us over law, in the free custody of his love, and left us victorious under the guidance of his living Spirit, not under the dead letter; to follow that which most edifies, most aids and furthers a religious life, makes us holiest and likest to his immortal image, not that which makes us most conformable and captive to civil and subordinate precepts; whereof the strictest observance may ofttimes prove the destruction not only of many innocent persons and families, but of whole nations. Although indeed no ordinance, human or from heaven, can bind against the good of man, so that to keep them strictly against that end is all one with to break them. Men of most renowned virtue have sometimes by transgressing most truly kept the law, and wisest magistrates have permitted and dispensed it, while they looked not peevishly at the letter, but with a greater spirit at the good of mankind, if always not written in the characters of law, yet engraven in the heart of man by a divine impression.

This heathens could see, as the well-read in story can recount of Solon and Epaminondas, whom Cicero in his first book of *Invention*[21] nobly defends. "All law," saith he, "we ought refer to the common good, and interpret by that, not by the scroll of letters. No man observes law for law's sake, but for the good of them for whom it was made." The rest might serve well to lecture these times, deluded through belly doctrines[22] into a devout slavery. The scripture also af-

19. *Human liberty* denotes external freedom from burdensome and inappropriate laws; *Christian liberty* denotes the internal freedom of the regenerate Christian to follow God's law willingly, made possible because Christ, as Milton phrases it later, "redeemed us to a state above prescriptions by dissolving the whole law into charity."

20. Col. 2.23: "Which things have indeed a show of wisdom in will worship, and humility."

21. Cicero, *On Invention* 1.38.

22. See Rom. 16.18.

fords us David in the shewbread, Hezekiah in the Passover,[23] sound and safe transgressors of the literal command, which also dispensed not seldom with itself; and taught us on what just occasions to do so: until our Savior, for whom that great and Godlike work was reserved, redeemed us to a state above prescriptions by dissolving the whole law into charity. And have we not the soul to understand this, and must we against this glory of God's transcendent love towards us be still the servants of literal indictment?

["Created he him."] It might be doubted why he saith, "In the image of God created he him," not them, as well as "male and female" them; especially since that image might be common to them both, but male and female could not, however the Jews fable and please themselves with the accidental concurrence of Plato's wit, as if man at first had been created hermaphrodite[24] (but then it must have been male and female created he him). So had the image of God been equally common to them both, it had no doubt been said, 'In the image of God created he them.' But St. Paul ends the controversy, by explaining that the woman is not primarily and immediately the image of God, but in reference to the man: "The head of the woman," saith he (1 Cor. 11[.3,7]), "is the man"; "he the image and glory of God, she the glory of the man"; he not for her, but she for him.[25] Therefore his precept is, "Wives be subject to your husbands as is fit in the Lord" (Coloss. 3.18). "In everything" (Eph. 5.24). Nevertheless man is not to hold her as a servant, but receives her into a part of that empire which God proclaims him to, though not equally, yet largely, as his own image and glory. For it is no small glory to him, that a creature so like him should be made subject to him. Not but that particular exceptions may have place, if she exceed her husband in prudence and dexterity, and he contentedly yield; for then a superior and more natural law comes in, that the wiser should govern the less wise, whether male or female.

But that which far more easily and obediently follows from this verse is that, seeing woman was purposely made for man, and he her head, it cannot stand before the breath of this divine utterance that man, the portraiture of God, joining to himself for his intended good and solace an inferior sex, should so become her thrall, whose willfulness or inability to be a wife frustrates the occasional end[26] of her creation, but that he may acquit himself to freedom by his natural birthright and that indelible character of priority which God crowned him with. If it be urged that sin hath lost him this, the answer is not far to seek, that from her the sin first proceeded, which keeps her justly in the same proportion still beneath. She is not to gain by being first in the transgression, that man

23. For David, see 1 Sam. 21.2–6; for Hezekiah, see 2 Chron. 30.18–19.

24. The notion that human beings were originally hermaphroditic appears both in Plato's *Symposium* and in Jewish sources.

25. Cp. *PL* 4.299: "He for God only, she for God in him."

26. Milton agrees with the tradition that woman was made for a purpose or *occasional end,* though he viewed that purpose as companionship for the man rather than, as commonly thought, procreation.

should further lose to her, because already he hath lost by her means. Oft it happens that in this matter he is without fault, so that his punishment herein is causeless; and God hath the praise in our speeches of him, to sort his punishment in the same kind with the offence. Suppose he erred; it is not the intent of God or man to hunt an error so to the death with a revenge beyond all measure and proportion.

But if we argue thus, this affliction is befallen him for his sin, therefore he must bear it without seeking the only remedy: first, it will be false that all affliction comes for sin, as in the case of Job and of the man born blind (John 9.3) was evident; next, by that reason, all miseries coming for sin, we must let them all lie upon us like the vermin of an Indian Catharist,[27] which his fond religion forbids him to molest. Were it a particular punishment inflicted through the anger of God upon a person or upon a land, no law hinders us in that regard, no law but bids us remove it if we can; much more if it be a dangerous temptation withal, much more yet, if it be certainly a temptation, and not certainly a punishment, though a pain. As for what they say we must bear with patience, to bear with patience and to seek effectual remedies implies no contradiction. It may no less be for our disobedience, our unfaithfulness, and other sins against God, that wives become adulterous to the bed, and questionless we ought to take the affliction as patiently as Christian prudence would wish; yet hereby is not lost the right of divorcing for adultery. No, you say, because our Savior excepted that only. But why, if he were so bent to punish our sins and try our patience in binding on us a disastrous marriage, why did he except adultery? Certainly to have been bound from divorce in that case also had been as plentiful a punishment to our sins, and not too little work for the patientest. Nay, perhaps they will say it was too great a sufferance. And with as slight a reason, for no wise man but would sooner pardon the act of adultery once and again committed by a person worth pity and forgiveness, than to lead a wearisome life of unloving and unquiet conversation with one who neither affects nor is affected, much less with one who exercises all bitterness, and would commit adultery too, but for envy lest the persecuted condition should thereby get the benefit of his freedom. 'Tis plain therefore that God enjoins not this supposed strictness of not divorcing either to punish us or to try our patience.

Moreover, if man be the image of God, which consists in holiness, and woman ought in the same respect to be the image and companion of man, in such wise to be loved as the Church is beloved of Christ; and if, as God is the head of Christ, and Christ the head of man, so man is the head of woman; I cannot see by this golden dependence of headship and subjection, but that piety and religion is the main tie of Christian matrimony. So as if there be found between the pair a notorious disparity either of wickedness or heresy, the husband by all manner of right is disengaged from a creature not made and inflicted on

27. The *Cathars* were an ascetic sect in medieval Europe.

him to the vexation of his righteousness. The wife also, as her subjection is terminated in the Lord, being herself the redeemed of Christ, is not still bound to be the vassal of him who is the bond-slave of Satan; she being now neither the image nor the glory of such a person, nor made for him, nor left in bondage to him, but hath recourse to the wing of charity and protection of the church, unless there be a hope on either side. Yet such a hope must be meant, as may be a rational hope and not an endless servitude. Of which hereafter.

But usually it is objected that, if it be thus, then there can be no true marriage between misbelievers and irreligious persons. I might answer, let them see to that who are such; the church hath no commission to judge those without (1 Cor. 5). But this they will say, perhaps, is but penuriously to resolve a doubt. I answer therefore, that where they are both irreligious, the marriage may be yet true enough to them in a civil relation. For there are left some remains of God's image in man, as he is merely man; which reason God gives against the shedding of man's blood (Gen. 9.[5–6]), as being made in God's image, without expression whether he were a good man or a bad, to exempt the slayer from punishment. So that in those marriages where the parties are alike void of religion, the wife owes a civil homage and subjection, the husband owes a civil loyalty. But where the yoke is misyoked, heretic with faithful, godly with ungodly, to the grievance and manifest endangering of a brother or sister, reasons of a higher strain than matrimonial bear sway; unless the Gospel, instead of freeing us, debase itself to make us bondmen, and suffer evil to control good.

["Male and female created he them."] This contains another end of matching man and woman, being the right and lawfulness of the marriage-bed, though much inferior to the former end of her being his image and help in religious society. And who of weakest insight may not see that this creating of them male and female cannot in any order of reason, or Christianity, be of such moment against the better and higher purposes of their creation, as to enthrall husband or wife to duties or to sufferings, unworthy and unbeseeming the image of God in them? Now whenas not only men, but good men, do stand upon their right, their estimation, their dignity, in all other actions and deportments with warrant enough and good conscience, as having the image of God in them, it will not be difficult to determine what is unworthy and unseemly for a man to do or suffer in wedlock (and the like proportionally may be found for woman), if we love not to stand disputing below the principles of humanity. He that said, "Male and female created he them," immediately before that said also in the same verse, "In the image of God created he him," and redoubled it, that our thoughts might not be so full of dregs as to urge this poor consideration of "male and female," without remembering the nobleness of that former repetition; lest when God sends a wise eye to examine our trivial glosses, they be found extremely to creep upon the ground. Especially since they confess that what here concerns marriage is but a brief touch, only preparative to the institution which follows more expressly in the next chapter. And that Christ so took it, as desiring to be briefest with them who came to tempt him, account shall be given in due place.

> Ver. 28. "And God blessed them, and God said unto them, be fruitful and multiply, and replenish the earth," etc.

This declares another end of matrimony, the propagation of mankind, and is again repeated to Noah and his sons.[28] Many things might be noted on this place not ordinary, nor unworth the noting, but I undertook not a general comment. Hence therefore we see the desire of children is honest and pious; if we be not less zealous in our Christianity than Plato was in his heathenism, who, in the sixth of his *Laws*,[29] counts offspring therefore desirable, that we may leave in our stead sons of our sons, continual servants of God; a religious and prudent desire, if people knew as well what were required to breeding as to begetting; which desire perhaps was a cause why the Jews hardly could endure a barren wedlock, and Philo in his book of special laws esteems him only worth pardon that sends not barrenness away.[30] Carvilius, the first recorded in Rome to have sought divorce, had it granted him for the barrenness of his wife, upon his oath that he married to the end he might have children, as Dionysius and Gellius are authors.[31] But to dismiss a wife only for barrenness is hard; and yet in some the desire of children is so great, and so just, yea sometime so necessary, that to condemn such a one to a childless age, the fault apparently not being in him, might seem perhaps more strict than needed. Sometimes inheritances, crowns, and dignities are so interested and annexed in their common peace and good to such or such lineal descent, that it may prove a great moment both in the affairs of men and of religion, to consider thoroughly what might be done herein, notwithstanding the waywardness of our school doctors.

GEN. 2.18.

> "And the Lord said, It is not good that man should be alone; I will make him a help meet for him."
>
> V 23. "And Adam said," etc. V 24. "Therefore shall a man leave," etc.

This second chapter is granted to be a commentary on the first; and these verses granted to be an exposition of that former verse, "Male and female created he them," and yet when this male and female is by the explicit words of

28. See Gen. 9.1.
29. *Laws* 6 (774a).
30. In his *Special Laws* (3.35), Philo, condemning men who marry barren women as moved only by lust, insists that barren wives be divorced; he recognizes the dilemma of men who, not aware at first of their wives' barrenness, develop affection for them.
31. Dionysius of Helicarnassus, *Roman Antiquities* 2.25; Aulus Gellius, *Noctes Aticae* 4.3.

God himself here declared to be not meant other than a fit help, and meet society, some, who would engross to themselves the whole trade of interpreting, will not suffer the clear text of God to do the office of explaining itself.

["And the Lord God said it is not good."] A man would think that the consideration of who spake should raise up the attention of our minds to inquire better, and obey the purpose of so great a Speaker. For as we order the business of marriage, that which he here speaks is all made vain, and in the decision of matrimony, or not matrimony, nothing at all regarded. Our presumption hath utterly changed the state and condition of this ordinance. God ordained it in love and helpfulness to be indissoluble, and we in outward act and formality to be a forced bondage; so that being subject to a thousand errors in the best men, if it prove a blessing to any, it is of mere accident, as man's law hath handled it, and not of institution.

["It is not good for man to be alone."] Hitherto all things that have been named were approved of God to be very good. Loneliness is the first thing which God's eye named not good (whether it be a thing, or the want of something, I labor not; let it be their tendance, who have the art to be industriously idle). And here "alone" is meant alone without woman; otherwise Adam had the company of God himself and angels to converse with, all creatures to delight him seriously, or to make him sport. God could have created him out of the same mold a thousand friends and brother Adams to have been his consorts, yet for all this, till Eve was given him, God reckoned him to be alone.

["It is not good."] God here presents himself like to a man deliberating; both to show us that the matter is of high consequence, and that he intended to found it according to natural reason, not impulsive command; but that the duty should arise from the reason of it, not the reason be swallowed up in a reasonless duty. "Not good" was as much to Adam before his fall as not pleasing, not expedient; but since the coming of sin into the world, to him who hath not received the continence, it is not only not expedient to be alone, but plainly sinful. And therefore he who willfully abstains from marriage, not being supernaturally gifted, and he who by making the yoke of marriage unjust and intolerable causes men to abhor it, are both in a diabolical sin, equal to that of Antichrist, who forbids to marry.[32] For what difference at all whether he abstain men from marrying, or restrain them in a marriage happening totally discommodious, distasteful, dishonest and pernicious to him, without the appearance of his fault? For God does not here precisely say, I make a female to this male, as he did before, but expounding himself here on purpose, he saith, because it is not good for man to be alone, I make him therefore a meet help. God supplies the privation of not good, with the perfect gift of a real and positive good; it is man's perverse cooking who hath turned this bounty of God into a scorpion, either by weak and shallow constructions or by proud arrogance and cruelty to them who neither in their purposes nor in their actions have offended against the due honor of wedlock.

32. A reference to the Roman Catholic prescription of priestly celibacy.

Now whereas the apostle speaking in the Spirit (1 Cor. 7[.1]) pronounces quite contrary to this word of God, "It is good for a man not to touch a woman," and God cannot contradict himself, it instructs us that his commands and words, especially such as bear the manifest title of some good to man, are not to be so strictly wrung as to command without regard to the most natural and miserable necessities of mankind. Therefore the apostle adds a limitation in the 26th verse of that chapter, for the present necessity it is good; which he gives us doubtless as a pattern how to reconcile other places by the general rule of charity.

["*For man to be alone.*"] Some would have the sense hereof to be in respect of procreation only; and Austin contests that manly friendship in all other regards had been a more becoming solace for Adam, than to spend so many secret years in an empty world with one woman.[33] But our writers deservedly reject this crabbed opinion, and defend that there is a peculiar comfort in the married state besides the genial bed,[34] which no other society affords. No mortal nature can endure, either in the actions of religion or study of wisdom, without sometime slackening the cords of intense thought and labor, which, lest we should think faulty, God himself conceals us not his own recreations before the world was built: "I was," saith the eternal Wisdom, "daily his delight, playing always before him" [Prov. 8.30]. And to him indeed wisdom is as a high tower of pleasure, but to us a steep hill, and we toiling ever about the bottom. He executes with ease the exploits of his omnipotence, as easy as with us it is to will, but no worthy enterprise can be done by us without continual plodding and wearisomeness to our faint and sensitive abilities. We cannot therefore always be contemplative, or pragmatical abroad, but have need of some delightful intermissions, wherein the enlarged soul may leave off a while her severe schooling, and, like a glad youth in wandering vacancy, may keep her holidays to joy and harmless pastime; which as she cannot well do without company, so in no company so well as where the different sex in most resembling unlikeness, and most unlike resemblance, cannot but please best and be pleased in the aptitude of that variety.

Whereof lest we should be too timorous, in the awe that our flat sages would form us and dress us, wisest Solomon among his gravest Proverbs[35] countenances a kind of ravishment and erring fondness in the entertainment of wedded leisures; and in the Song of Songs, which is generally believed, even in the jolliest expressions, to figure the spousals of the church with Christ, sings of a thousand raptures between those two lovely ones far on the hither side of carnal enjoyment. By these instances, and more which might be brought, we may imagine how indulgently God provided against man's loneliness; that he approved it not, as by himself declared not good; that he approved the remedy

33. Milton accurately paraphrases the sense of Augustine in *De Genesi ad Litteram* 9.5.

34. **genial:** related to procreation; cp. Adam's parallel discussion of the "genial bed" in *PL* 8.596–606.

35. See Prov. 5.18–19.

thereof, as of his own ordaining, consequently good; and as he ordained it, so doubtless proportionably to our fallen estate he gives it; else were his ordinance at least in vain, and we for all his gift still empty-handed. Nay, such an unbounteous giver we should make him, as in the fables Jupiter was to Ixion, giving him a cloud instead of Juno; giving him a monstrous issue by her, the breed of Centaurs, a neglected and unloved race, the fruits of a delusive marriage; and, lastly, giving him her with a damnation to that wheel in hell, from a life thrown into the midst of temptations and disorders.[36] But God is no deceitful giver, to bestow that on us for a remedy of loneliness, which if it bring not a sociable mind as well as a conjunctive body, leaves us no less alone than before; and, if it bring a mind perpetually averse and disagreeable, betrays us to a worse condition than the most deserted loneliness. God cannot in the justice of his own promise and institution so unexpectedly mock us by forcing that upon us as the remedy of solitude, which wraps us in a misery worse than any wilderness, as the Spirit of God himself judges (Prov. 19);[37] especially knowing that the best and wisest men amidst the sincere and most cordial designs of their heart do daily err in choosing.

We may conclude therefore, seeing orthodoxal expositors confess to our hands, that by loneliness is not only meant the want of copulation, and that man is not less alone by turning in a body to him, unless there be within it a mind answerable; that it is a work more worthy the care and consultation of God to provide for the worthiest part of man, which is his mind, and not unnaturally to set it beneath the formalities and respects of the body, to make it a servant of its own vassal. I say we may conclude that such a marriage, wherein the mind is so disgraced and vilified below the body's interest, and can have no just or tolerable contentment, is not of God's institution, and therefore no marriage. Nay, in concluding this, I say we conclude no more than what the common expositors themselves give us, both in that which I have recited and much more hereafter. But the truth is, they give us in such a manner as they who leave their own mature positions like the eggs of an ostrich in the dust. I do but lay them in the sun; their own pregnancies hatch the truth. And I am taxed of novelties and strange producements, while they, like that inconsiderate bird, know not that these are their own natural breed.

["I will make him a help meet for him."] Here the heavenly institutor, as if he labored not to be mistaken by the supercilious hypocrisy of those that love to master their brethren, and to make us sure that he gave us not now a servile yoke, but an amiable knot, contents not himself to say, I will make him a wife; but resolving to give us first the meaning before the name of a wife, saith graciously, "I will make him a help meet for him." And here again, as before, I do not require more full and fair deductions than the whole consent of our divines usually raise from this text, that in matrimony there must be first a mutual help

36. Pindar recounts this story in *Pythian Odes* 2.20–48.

37. Prov. 19.13: "The contentions of a wife are a continual dropping."

to piety, next to civil fellowship of love and amity, then to generation, so to household affairs, lastly the remedy of incontinence. And commonly they reckon them in such order as leaves generation and incontinence to be last considered. This I amaze me at, that though all the superior and nobler ends both of marriage and of the married persons be absolutely frustrate, the matrimony stirs not, loses no hold, remains as rooted as the center. But if the body bring but in a complaint of frigidity, by that cold application only this adamantine Alp of wedlock has leave to dissolve, which else all the machinations of religious or civil reason at the suit of a distressed mind, either for divine worship or human conversation violated, cannot unfasten. What courts of concupiscence are these, wherein fleshly appetite is heard before right reason, lust before love or devotion? They may be pious Christians together, they may be loving and friendly, they may be helpful to each other in the family, but they cannot couple—that shall divorce them, though either party would not. They can neither serve God together, nor one be at peace with the other, nor be good in the family one to other, but live as they were dead, or live as they were deadly enemies in a cage together—'tis all one, they can couple, they shall not divorce till death, no, though this sentence be their death.

What is this besides tyranny, but to turn nature upside down, to make both religion and the mind of man wait upon the slavish errands of the body, and not the body to follow either the sanctity or the sovereignty of the mind, unspeakably wronged and with all equity complaining? What is this but to abuse the sacred and mysterious bed of marriage to be the compulsive sty of an ingrateful and malignant lust, stirred up only from a carnal acrimony,[38] without either love or peace, or regard to any other thing holy or human. This I admire, how possibly it should inhabit thus long in the sense of so many disputing theologians, unless it be the lowest lees of a canonical infection liver-grown to their sides, which perhaps will never uncling without the strong abstersive[39] of some heroic magistrate, whose mind equal to his high office dares lead him both to know and to do without their frivolous case-putting. For certain he shall have God and this institution plainly on his side. And if it be true both in divinity and law, that consent alone, though copulation never follow, makes a marriage, how can they dissolve it for the want of that which made it not, and not dissolve it for that not continuing which made it, and should preserve it in love and reason, and difference it from a brute conjugality?

["*Meet for him.*"] The original here is more expressive than other languages word for word can render it, but all agree effectual conformity of disposition and affection to be hereby signified; which God, as it were, not satisfied with the naming of a help, goes on describing "another self," "a second self," "a very self itself." Yet now there is nothing in the life of man, through our misconstruction, made more uncertain, more hazardous and full of chance, than this divine

38. **acrimony:** sharpness. Milton refers to the sting of lust.
39. **abstersive:** having the quality of purging and washing away impurities.

blessing with such favorable significance here conferred upon us; which if we do but err in our choice, the most unblamable error that can be, err but one minute, one moment after those mighty syllables pronounced, which take upon them to join heaven and hell together unpardonably till death pardon, this divine blessing that looked but now with such a humane smile upon us, and spoke such gentle reason, straight vanishes like a fair sky, and brings on such a scene of cloud and tempest as turns all to shipwreck without haven or shore, but to a ransomless captivity. And then they tell us it is our sin; but let them be told again, that sin through the mercy of God hath not made such waste upon us as to make utterly void to our use any temporal benefit, much less any so much availing to a peaceful and sanctified life, merely for a most incident error which no wariness can certainly shun. And wherefore serves our happy redemption, and the liberty we have in Christ, but to deliver us from calamitous yokes not to be lived under without the endangerment of our souls, and to restore us in some competent measure to a right in every good thing both of this life and the other? Thus we see how treatably and distinctly God hath here taught us what the prime ends of marriage are: mutual solace and help. That we are now, upon the most irreprehensible mistake in choosing, defeated and defrauded of all this original benignity was begun first through the snare of anti-Christian canons long since obtruded upon the church of Rome, and not yet scoured off by reformation, out of a lingering vainglory that abides among us to make fair shows in formal ordinances, and to enjoin continence and bearing of crosses in such a garb as no scripture binds us, under the thickest arrows of temptation, where we need not stand. Now we shall see with what acknowledgment and assent Adam received this new associate which God brought him. . . .

[*In an omitted section on Genesis 2.23, Milton argues that, except in the case of Adam and Eve, who were literally "flesh of flesh," marriage is a civil rather than a natural relation.*]

> V. 24. "Therefore shall a man leave his father and his mother, and shall cleave unto his wife; and they shall be one flesh."

This verse, as our common heed expounds it, is the great knot-tier, which hath undone by tying, and by tangling, millions of guiltless consciences. This is that grisly porter, who having drawn men—and wisest men—by subtle allurement within the train of an unhappy matrimony, claps the dungeon-gate upon them, as irrecoverable as the grave. But if we view him well, and hear him with not too hasty and prejudicant[40] ears, we shall find no such terror in him. For, first, it is not here said absolutely without all reason he shall cleave to his wife, be it to his weal or to his destruction as it happens, but he shall do this upon the premises and considerations of that meet help and society before mentioned: "Therefore he shall cleave to his wife," no otherwise a wife, than a fit help. He

40. **prejudicant:** prejudging.

is not bid to leave the dear cohabitation of his father, mother, brothers and sisters, to link himself inseparably with the mere carcass of a marriage, perhaps an enemy. This joining particle "therefore" is in all equity, nay in all necessity of construction, to comprehend first and most principally what God spake concerning the inward essence of marriage in his institution, that we may learn how far to attend what Adam spake of the outward materials thereof in his approbation. For if we shall bind these words of Adam only to a corporal meaning, and that the force of this injunction upon all us his sons to live individually with any woman which hath befallen us in the most mistaken wedlock, shall consist not in[41] those moral and relative causes of Eve's creation, but in the mere anatomy of a rib, and that Adam's insight concerning wedlock reached no further, we shall make him as very an idiot as the Socinians[42] make him (which would not be reverently done of us). Let us be content to allow our great forefather so much wisdom as to take the instituting words of God along with him into this sentence, which, if they be well-minded,[43] will assure us that flesh and ribs are but of a weak and dead efficacy to keep marriage united where there is no other fitness.

The rib of marriage, to all since Adam, is a relation much rather than a bone. The nerves and sinews thereof are love and meet help; they knit not every couple that marries, and where they knit they seldom break. But where they break, which for the most part is where they never truly joined, to such at the same instant both flesh and rib cease to be in common; so that here they argue nothing to the continuance of a false or violated marriage, but must be led back to receive their meaning from those institutive words of God which give them all the life and vigor they have.

["Therefore shall a man leave his father," etc.] What to a man's thinking more plain by this appointment, that the fatherly power should give place to conjugal prerogative? Yet it is generally held by reformed writers against the papist, that though in persons at discretion the marriage in itself be never so fit, though it be fully accomplished with benediction, board and bed, yet the father not consenting, his main will without dispute shall dissolve all. And this they affirm only from collective reason, not any direct law. For that in Exod. 22.17, which is most particular, speaks that a father may refuse to marry his daughter to one who hath deflowered her, not that he may take her away from one who hath soberly married her. Yet because the general honor due to parents is great, they hold he may, and perhaps hold not amiss. But again when the question is of harsh and rugged parents, who defer to bestow their children seasonably, they agree jointly that the church or magistrate may bestow them, though without the father's consent; and for this they have no express authority in scripture. So that they may see by their own handling of this very place, that it is not the

41. **shall not consist in:** will not be consistent with.
42. The *Socinians* were thought to hold that Adam was created ignorant.
43. **well-minded:** i.e., kept in mind by the reader.

stubborn letter must govern us, but the divine and softening breath of charity, which turns and winds the dictate of every positive command, and shapes it to the good of mankind.

Shall the outward accessory of a father's will wanting rend the fittest and most affectionate marriage in twain, after all nuptial consummations, and shall not the want of love and the privation of all civil and religious concord, which is the inward essence of wedlock, do as much to part those who were never truly wedded? Shall a father have this power to vindicate his own willful honor and authority to the utter breach of a most dearly united marriage, and shall not a man in his own power have the permission to free his soul, his life, and all his comfort of life from the disaster of a no-marriage? Shall fatherhood, which is but man, for his own pleasure dissolve matrimony, and shall not matrimony, which is God's ordinance, for its own honor and better conservation dissolve itself, when it is wrong, and not fitted to any of the chief ends which it owes us?

["And they shall be one flesh."] These words also infer that there ought to be an individuality[44] in marriage, but without all question presuppose the joining causes. Not a rule yet that we have met with, so universal in this whole institution, but hath admitted limitations and conditions according to human necessity. The very foundation of matrimony, though God laid it so deliberately, "that it is not good for man to be alone," holds not always, if the apostle can secure us. Soon after we are bid leave father and mother, and cleave to a wife, but must understand the father's consent withal, else not. "Cleave to a wife," but let her be a wife, let her be a meet help, a solace, not a nothing, not an adversary, not a desertrice. Can any law or command be so unreasonable as to make men cleave to calamity, to ruin, to perdition?

In like manner here, "They shall be one flesh"; but let the causes hold, and be made really good, which only have the possibility to make them one flesh. We know that flesh can neither join, nor keep together two bodies of itself. What is it then must make them one flesh, but likeness, but fitness of mind and disposition, which may breed the spirit of concord and union between them? If that be not in the nature of either, and that there has been a remediless mistake, as vain we go about to compel them into one flesh as if we undertook to weave a garment of dry sand. It were more easy to compel the vegetable and nutritive power of nature to assimilations and mixtures which are not alterable each by other, or force the concoctive stomach to turn that into flesh which is so totally unlike that substance as not to be wrought on.

For as the unity of mind is nearer and greater than the union of bodies, so doubtless is the dissimilitude greater and more dividual, as that which makes between bodies all difference and distinction. Especially whenas besides the singular and substantial differences of every soul, there is an intimate quality of good or evil, through the whole progeny of Adam, which like a radical heat or

44. **individuality:** indivisibility. Milton acknowledges the inseparability of a married couple, but a couple is truly married only if the ends of God's original institution are fulfilled.

mortal chillness joins them or disjoins them irresistibly. In whom therefore either the will, or the faculty is found to have never joined, or now not to continue so, 'tis not to say, they shall be one flesh, for they cannot be one flesh. God commands not impossibilities, and all the ecclesiastical glue that liturgy or laymen can compound is not able to solder up two such incongruous natures into the one flesh of a true beseeming marriage.

Why did Moses then set down their uniting into one flesh? And I again ask, why the Gospel so oft repeats the eating of our Savior's flesh, the drinking of his blood? "That we are one body with him, the members of his body, flesh of his flesh and bone of his bone" (Ephes. 5[.30]). Yet lest we should be Capernaitans,[45] as we are told there that the flesh profiteth nothing, so we are told here, if we be not as deaf as adders, that this union of the flesh proceeds from the union of a fit help and solace. We know that there was never a more spiritual mystery than this Gospel taught us under the terms of body and flesh, yet nothing less intended than that we should stick there. What a stupidness then is it, that in marriage, which is the nearest resemblance of our union with Christ, we should deject ourselves to such a sluggish and underfoot philosophy, as to esteem the validity of marriage merely by the flesh, though never so broken and disjointed from love and peace, which only can give a human qualification to that act of the flesh and distinguish it from bestial. The text therefore uses this phrase, that "they shall be one flesh," to justify and make legitimate the rites of marriage-bed; which was not unneedful, if for all this warrant they were suspected of pollution by some sects of philosophy and religions of old, and latelier among the papists, and other heretics elder than they.

Some think there is a high mystery in those words, from that which Paul saith of them (Ephes. 5[.32]), "This is a great mystery, but I speak of Christ and the Church," and thence they would conclude marriage to be inseparable. For me I dispute not now whether matrimony be a mystery or no; if it be of Christ and his church, certainly it is not meant of every ungodly and miswedded marriage, but then only mysterious, when it is a holy, happy, and peaceful match. But when a saint is joined with a reprobate, or both alike wicked with wicked, fool with fool, a he-drunkard with a she, when the bed hath been nothing else for twenty years or more but an old haunt of lust and malice mixed together, no love, no goodness, no loyalty, but counterplotting and secret wishing one another's dissolution, this is to me the greatest mystery in the world, if such a marriage as this can be the mystery of aught, unless it be the mystery of iniquity: according to that which Paræus cites out of Chrysostom, that a bad wife is a help for the devil,[46] and the like may be said of a bad husband. Since therefore none but a fit and pious Matrimony can signify the union of Christ and his church, there cannot hence be any hindrance of divorce to that wedlock wherein there can be no good mystery. Rather it might to a Christian con-

45. In Matt. 11.23 and Luke 10.15, Jesus denounces the residents of Capernaum for their lack of faith.
46. Paraeus, *In Genesin* (1614), col. 420.

science be matter of finding itself so much less satisfied than before, in the continuance of an unhappy yoke, wherein there can be no representation either of Christ, or of his Church....

[*In the remainder of this section, Milton defines the Aristotelian causes of marriage (material: man and woman; efficient: God and the couple's consent; formal: conjugal love; and final: help and society) and defines marriage as "a divine institution joining man and woman in a love fitly disposed to the helps and comforts of domestic life."*]

DEUT. 24. 1, 2.

1. "When a man hath taken a wife, and married her, and it come to pass that she find no favor in his eyes, because he hath found some uncleanness in her, then let him write her a bill of divorcement, and give it in her hand, and send her out of his house.
2. "And when she is departed out of his house, she may go and be another man's wife."

[*In an omitted section, Milton argues that if divorce among the Jews had been merely an evil custom, Mosaic Law would have forbidden it and that the "uncleanness" of Deuteronomy 24.1, though usually read as adultery, refers instead to "any defect, annoyance, or ill quality in nature, which to be joined with, makes life tedious, and such company worse than solitude."*]

Now although Moses needed not to add other reason of this law than that one there expressed, yet to these ages wherein canons, and Scotisms, and Lombard laws[47] have dulled and almost obliterated the lively sculpture of ancient reason and humanity, it will be requisite to heap reason upon reason, and all little enough to vindicate the whiteness and the innocence of this divine law from the calumny it finds at this day of being a door to license and confusion. Whenas indeed there is not a judicial point in all Moses consisting of more true equity, high wisdom, and God-like pity than this law; not derogating, but preserving the honor and peace of marriage, and exactly agreeing with the sense and mind of that institution in Genesis.

For first, if marriage be but an ordained relation, as it seems not more, it cannot take place above the prime dictates of nature; and if it be of natural right, yet it must yield to that which is more natural, and before it by eldership and precedence in nature. Now it is not natural that Hugh marries Beatrice, or Thomas, Rebecca, being only a civil contract, and full of many chances; but that these men seek them meet helps, that only is natural; and that they espouse them such, that only is marriage. But if they find them neither fit helps nor tolerable society, what thing more natural, more original, and first in nature than

47. Milton alludes scornfully to Canon Law and the writings of the scholastic theologians John Duns Scotus (c. 1265–1308) and Peter Lombard (c. 1100–1160).

to depart from that which is irksome, grievous, actively hateful, and injurious even to hostility, especially in a conjugal respect, wherein antipathies are invincible, and where the forced abiding of the one can be no true good, no real comfort to the other? For if he find no contentment from the other, how can he return it from himself; or no acceptance, how can he mutually accept? What more equal, more pious, than to untie a civil knot for a natural enmity held by violence from parting, to dissolve an accidental conjunction of this or that man and woman, for the most natural and most necessary disagreement of meet from unmeet, guilty from guiltless, contrary from contrary? It being certain that the mystical and blessed unity of marriage can be no way more unhallowed and profaned than by the forcible uniting of such disunions and separations. Which if we see ofttimes they cannot join or piece up to a common friendship, or to a willing conversation in the same house, how should they possibly agree to the most familiar and united amity of wedlock?

Abraham and Lot, though dear friends and brethren in a strange country, chose rather to part asunder than to infect their friendship with the strife of their servants.[48] Paul and Barnabas, joined together by the Holy Ghost to a spiritual work, thought it better to separate when once they grew at variance.[49] If these great saints, joined by nature, friendship, religion, high providence, and revelation, could not so govern a casual difference, a sudden passion, but must in wisdom divide from the outward duties of a friendship, or a colleagueship in the same family, or in the same journey, lest it should grow to a worse division, can anything be more absurd and barbarous than that they, whom only error, casualty, art, or plot hath joined, should be compelled, not against a sudden passion but against the permanent and radical discords of nature, to the most intimate and incorporating duties of love and embracement, therein only rational and human as they are free and voluntary, being else an abject and servile yoke, scarce not brutish? And that there is in man such a peculiar sway of liking or disliking in the affairs of matrimony is evidently seen before marriage among those who can be friendly, can respect each other, yet to marry each other would not for any persuasion. If then this unfitness and disparity be not till after marriage discovered, through many causes and colors and concealments that may overshadow, undoubtedly it will produce the same effects, and perhaps with more vehemence, that such a mistaken pair would give the world to be unmarried again. And their condition Solomon to the plain justification of divorce expresses (Prov. 30.21, 23), where he tells us of his own accord that a "hated" or a "hateful woman when she is married is a thing for which the earth is disquieted and cannot bear it"; thus giving divine testimony to this divine law, which bids us nothing more than is the first and most innocent lesson of nature, to turn away peaceably from what afflicts and hazards our destruction; especially when our staying can do no good, and is exposed to all evil....

48. Gen. 13.6–12.
49. Acts 15.37–40.

[*In an omitted section, Milton argues again that no law or covenant can bind against the welfare, properly understood, of those governed by the law or party to the covenant.*]

Fourthly, the law is not to neglect men under greatest sufferances, but to see covenants of greatest moment faithfullest performed. And what injury comparable to that sustained in a frustrate and false-dealing marriage, to lose, for another's fault against him, the best portion of his temporal comforts, and of his spiritual too, as it may fall out? It was the law that, for man's good and quiet, reduced things to propriety, which were at first in common.[50] How much more lawlike were it to assist nature in disappropriating that evil which by continuing proper becomes destructive? But he might have bewared. So he might in any other covenant, wherein the law does not constrain error to so dear a forfeit. And yet in these matters wherein the wisest are apt to err, all the wariness that can be ofttimes nothing avails. But the law can compel the offending party to be more duteous. Yes, if all these kind of offences were fit in public to be complained on, or being compelled were any satisfaction to a mate not sottish or malicious. And these injuries work so vehemently, that if the law remedy them not by separating the cause when no way else will pacify, the person not relieved betakes him either to such disorderly courses, or to such a dull dejection, as renders him either infamous or useless to the service of God and his country. Which the law ought to prevent as a thing pernicious to the commonwealth; and what better prevention than this which Moses used?

Fifthly, the law is to tender the liberty and the human dignity of them that live under the law, whether it be the man's right above the woman or the woman's just appeal against wrong and servitude. But the duties of marriage contain in them a duty of benevolence,[51] which to do by compulsion against the soul, where there can be neither peace, nor joy, nor love, but an enthrallment to one who either cannot or will not be mutual in the godliest and the civilest ends of that society, is the ignoblest and the lowest slavery that a human shape can be put to. This law therefore justly and piously provides against such an unmanly task of bondage as this. The civil law, though it favored the setting free of a slave, yet if he proved ungrateful to his patron, reduced him to a servile condition. If that law did well to reduce from liberty to bondage for an ingratitude not the greatest, much more became it the law of God to enact the restorement of a freeborn man from an unpurposed and unworthy bondage to a rightful liberty for the most unnatural fraud and ingratitude that can be committed against him. And if the civilian emperor, in his title of *Donations*, permit the giver to recall his gift from him who proves unthankful towards him (yea, though he had subscribed and signed in the deed of his gift not to recall it, though for this very cause of ingratitude),[52] with much more equity doth Moses permit here the

50. **reduced . . . in common:** i.e., assigned things held communally to private ownership.
51. **duty of benevolence:** obligation to participate in sexual relations with one's spouse.
52. The Yale editor points to the *Juris Civilis, Code,* book 8, title 56, ¶s 1, 10.

giver to recall no petty gift, but the gift of himself, from one who most injuriously and deceitfully uses him against the main ends and conditions of his giving himself, expressed in God's institution.

Sixthly, although there be nothing in the plain words of this law that seems to regard the afflictions of a wife, how great soever, yet expositors determine, and doubtless determine rightly, that God was not uncompassionate of them also in the framing of this law. For should the rescript of Antoninus in the civil law give release to servants flying for refuge to the emperor's statue, by giving leave to change their cruel masters,[53] and should God, who in his law also is good to injured servants by granting them their freedom in diverse cases, not consider the wrongs and miseries of a wife, which is no servant? Though herein the countersense of our divines, to me, I must confess, seems admirable; who teach that God gave this as a merciful law, not for man whom he here names, and to whom by name he gives this power, but for the wife whom he names not, and to whom by name he gives no power at all. For certainly if man be liable to injuries in marriage, as well as woman, and man be the worthier person, it were a preposterous law to respect only the less worthy, her whom God made for marriage, and not him at all for whom marriage was made. . . .

[*In the omitted section, Milton cites prescriptions in Jewish law that implicitly confirm the right of divorce.*]

Ninthly, suppose it might be imputed to a man that he was too rash in his choice, and why he took not better heed, let him now smart, and bear his folly as he may; although the law of God, that terrible law, do not thus upbraid the infirmities and unwilling mistakes of man in his integrity. But suppose these and the like proud aggravations of some stern hypocrite, more merciless in his mercies than any literal law in the vigor of severity, must be patiently heard; yet all law, and God's law especially, grants everywhere to error easy remitments, even where the utmost penalty exacted were no undoing. With great reason therefore and mercy doth it here not torment an error, if it be so, with the endurance of a whole life lost to all household comfort and society, a punishment of too vast and huge dimension for an error, and the more unreasonable for that the like objection may be opposed against the plea of divorcing for adultery: he might have looked better before to her breeding under religious parents. Why did he not then more diligently inquire into her manners, into what company she kept? Every glance of her eye, every step of her gait, would have prophesied adultery, if the quick scent of these discerners had been took along; they had the divination to have foretold you all this, as they have now the divinity to punish an error inhumanly. As good reason to be content, and forced to be con-

53. The Yale editor points here to the *Juris Civilis, Institutes,* book 1, title 8, ¶ 2.

tent with your adulteress, if these objectors might be the judges of human frailty.

But God, more mild and good to man than man to his brother, in all this liberty given to divorcement, mentions not a word of our past errors and mistakes, if any were, which these men objecting from their own inventions prosecute with all violence and iniquity. For if the one be to look so narrowly what he takes, at the peril of ever keeping, why should not the other be made as wary what is promised, by the peril of losing? For without those promises the treaty of marriage had not proceeded. Why should his own error bind him, rather than the other's fraud acquit him? Let the buyer beware, saith the old law-beaten termer. Belike then there is no more honesty nor ingenuity in the bargain of a wedlock than in the buying of a colt. We must, it seems, drive it on as craftily with those whose affinity we seek, as if they were a pack of sale-men and complotters. But the deceiver deceives himself in the unprosperous marriage, and therein is sufficiently punished. I answer that the most of those who deceive are such as either understand not or value not the true purposes of marriage; they have the prey they seek, not the punishment. Yet say it prove to them some cross, it is not equal that error and fraud should be linked in the same degree of forfeiture, but rather that error should be acquitted, and fraud bereaved his morsel, if the mistake were not on both sides; for then on both sides the acquitment will be reasonable, if the bondage be intolerable; which this law graciously determines, not unmindful of the wife, as was granted willingly to the common expositors, though beyond the letter of this law, yet not beyond the spirit of charity.

Tenthly, marriage is a solemn thing, some say a holy, the resemblance of Christ and his Church; and so indeed it is where the persons are truly religious. And we know all sacred things not performed sincerely as they ought are no way acceptable to God in their outward formality. And that wherein it differs from personal duties, if they be not truly done, the fault is in ourselves; but marriage, to be a true and pious marriage, is not in the single power of any person; the essence whereof, as of all other covenants, is in relation to another, the making and maintaining causes thereof are all mutual, and must be a communion of spiritual and temporal comforts. If then either of them cannot, or obstinately will not, be answerable in these duties, so as that the other can have no peaceful living, or enduring the want of what he justly seeks, and sees no hope, then straight from that dwelling love, which is the soul of wedlock, takes his flight, leaving only some cold performances of civil and common respects; but the true bond of marriage, if there were ever any there, is already burst like a rotten thread. Then follows dissimulation, suspicion, false colors, false pretences, and, worse than these, disturbance, annoyance, vexation, sorrow, temptation even in the faultless person, weary of himself and of all action, public or domestic; then comes disorder, neglect, hatred, and perpetual strife, all these the enemies of holiness and Christianity, and every one of these, persisted in, a remediless violation to matrimony. Therefore God, who hates all feigning and formality where there should be all faith and sincereness, and abhors to see the inevitable discord where there should be greatest concord, when through another's default faith and concord cannot be, counts it neither just to punish the innocent with the transgressor, nor holy, nor honorable for the sanctity of marriage, that should be the union of peace and love, to be made the commitment, and close fight of enmity and hate. And therefore doth in this law what best agrees with his goodness, loosening a sacred thing to peace and charity, rather than binding it to hatred and contention; loosening only the outward and formal tie of that which is already inwardly and really broken, or else was really never joined.

Eleventhly, one of the chief matrimonial ends is said to seek a holy seed, but where an unfit marriage administers continual cause of hatred and distemper, there, as was heard before, cannot choose but much unholiness abide. Nothing more unhallows a man, more unprepares him to the service of God in any duty, than a habit of wrath and perturbation, arising from the importunity of troublous causes never absent. And where the household stands in this plight, what love can there be to the unfortunate issue, what care of their breeding, which is of main conducement to their being holy? God therefore knowing how unhappy it would be for children to be born in such a family, gives this law either as a prevention, that, being an unhappy pair, they should not add to be unhappy parents, or else as a remedy that if there be children, while they are fewest, they may follow either parent, as shall be agreed or judged, from the house of hatred and discord to a place of more holy and peaceable education.

Twelfthly, all law is available to some good end, but the final prohibition of divorce avails to no good end, causing only the endless aggravation of evil. And therefore this permission of divorce was given to the Jews by the wisdom and fatherly providence of God, who knew that law cannot command love, without which matrimony hath no true being, no good, no solace, nothing of God's instituting, nothing but so sordid and so low as to be disdained of any generous person. Law cannot enable natural inability either of body or mind, which gives the grievance; it cannot make equal those inequalities; it cannot make fit those unfitnesses; and where there is malice more than defect of nature, it cannot hinder ten thousand injuries and bitter actions of despite too subtle and too unapparent for law to deal with. And while it seeks to remedy more outward wrongs, it exposes the injured person to other more inward and more cutting. All these evils unavoidably will redound upon the children, if any be, and the whole family.

It degenerates and disorders the best spirits, leaves them to unsettled imaginations and degraded hopes, careless of themselves, their households, and their friends, unactive to all public service, dead to the commonwealth; wherein they are by one mishap, and no willing trespass of theirs, outlawed from all the benefits and comforts of married life and posterity. It confers as little to the honor and inviolable keeping of matrimony, but sooner stirs up temptations and occasions to secret adulteries and unchaste roving. But it maintains public honesty.[54] Public folly, rather; who shall judge of public honesty? The law of God and of ancientest Christians, and all civil nations, or the illegitimate law of monks and canonists, the most malevolent, most unexperienced, and incompetent judges of matrimony?

These reasons, and many more that might be alleged, afford us plainly to perceive both what good cause this law had to do for good men in mischances, and what necessity it had to suffer accidentally the hard-heartedness of bad men, which it could not certainly discover, or discovering could not subdue, no nor endeavor to restrain without multiplying sorrow to them, for whom all was endeavored. The guiltless therefore were not deprived their needful redresses, and the hard hearts of others, unchastisable in those judicial courts, were so remitted there, as bound over to the higher session of conscience.

Notwithstanding all this, there is a loud exception against this law of God, nor can the holy author save his law from this exception, that it opens a door to all license and confusion. But this is the rudest, I was almost saying the most graceless objection, and with the least reverence to God and Moses, that could be devised. This is to cite God before man's tribunal, to arrogate a wisdom and holiness above him. Did not God then foresee what event of license or confusion could follow? Did not he know how to ponder these abuses with more prevailing respects, in the most even balance of his justice and pureness, till these correctors came up to show him better? The law is, if it stir up sin any way, to stir it up by forbidding, as one contrary excites another (Rom. 7).[55] But if it once come to provoke sin by granting license to sin, according to laws that have no other honest end but only to permit the fulfilling of obstinate lust, how is God not made the contradicter of himself?

No man denies that best things may be abused, but it is a rule resulting from many pregnant experiences, that what doth most harm in the abusing, used rightly doth most good. And such a good to take away from honest men, for being abused by such as abuse all things, is the greatest abuse of all. That the whole law is no further useful than as a man uses it lawfully, St. Paul teaches (1 Tim. 1).[56] And that Christian liberty may be used for an occasion to the flesh, the same Apostle confesses (Galat. 5),[57] yet thinks not of removing it for that, but bids us rather "stand fast in the liberty wherewith Christ hath freed us, and not be held again in the yoke of bondage" [Galat. 5.1]. The very permission which Christ gave to divorce for adultery may be foully abused by any whose hardness of heart can either feign adultery or dares commit, that he may divorce. And for this cause the pope and hitherto the church of England forbid all divorce from

54. Milton voices, in order to answer, the argument of his opponents.

55. Rom. 7.7: "I had not known sin, but by the law; for I had not known lust, except the law had said, Thou shalt not covet."

56. 1 Tim. 1.8: "But we know that the law is good, if a man use it lawfully."

57. Galat. 5.13: "Ye have been called unto liberty; only use not liberty for an occasion to the flesh."

the bond of marriage, though for openest adultery. If then it be righteous to hinder, for the fear of abuse, that which God's law, notwithstanding that caution, hath warranted to be done, doth not our righteousness come short of Antichrist, or do we not rather herein conform ourselves to his unrighteousness in this undue and unwise fear? For God regards more to relieve by this law the just complaints of good men, than to curb the license of wicked men, to the crushing withal and the overwhelming of his afflicted servants. He loves more that his law should look with pity upon the difficulties of his own, than with rigor upon the boundless riots of them who serve another master, and, hindered here by strictness, will break another way to worse enormities.

If this law therefore have many good reasons for which God gave it, and no intention of giving scope to lewdness, but as abuse by accident comes in with every good law and every good thing, it cannot be wisdom in us, while we can content us with God's wisdom, nor can be purity, if his purity will suffice us, to except against this law as if it fostered license. But if they affirm this law had no other end but to permit obdurate lust because it would be obdurate, making the law of God intentionally to proclaim and enact sin lawful, as if the will of God were become sinful, or sin stronger than his direct and law-giving will, the men would be admonished to look well to it, that while they are so eager to shut the door against license, they do not open a worse door to blasphemy.

And yet they shall be here further shown their iniquity. What more foul and common sin among us than drunkenness? And who can be ignorant that, if the importation of wine and the use of all strong drink were forbid, it would both clean rid the possibility of committing that odious vice, and men might afterwards live happily and healthfully without the use of those intoxicating liquors. Yet who is there, the severest of them all, that ever propounded to lose his sack, his ale, toward the certain abolishing of so great a sin? Who is there of them, the holiest, that less loves his rich canary[58] at meals, though it be fetched from places that hazard the religion of them who fetch it, and though it make his neighbor drunk out of the same tune? While they forbid not therefore the use of that liquid merchandise, which forbidden would utterly remove a most loathsome sin, and not impair either the health or the refreshment of mankind, supplied many other ways, why do they forbid a law of God, the forbidding whereof brings into excessive bondage ofttimes the best of men, and betters not the worse? He, to remove a national vice, will not pardon his cups, nor think it concerns him to forbear the quaffing of that outlandish grape, in his unnecessary fullness, though other men abuse it never so much, nor is he so abstemious as to intercede with the magistrate that all matter of drunkenness be banished the commonwealth; and yet for the fear of a less inconvenience unpardonably requires of his brethren, in their extreme necessity, to debar themselves the use of God's permissive law, though it might be their saving, and no man's endan-

58. **canary:** sweet wine from the Canary Islands. Cp. Jonson, "Inviting a Friend to Supper," l. 29: "a pure cup of rich canary wine."

gering the more. Thus this peremptory strictness we may discern of what sort it is, how unequal, and how unjust.

But it will breed confusion.[59] What confusion it would breed, God himself took the care to prevent in the fourth verse of this chapter [Deut. 24.4], that the divorced, being married to another, might not return to her former husband. And Justinian's law counsels the same in his title of *Nuptials.* And what confusion else can there be in separation, to separate upon extreme urgency the religious from the irreligious, the fit from the unfit, the willing from the willful, the abused from the abuser? Such a separation is quite contrary to confusion. But to bind and mix together holy with atheist, heavenly with hellish, fitness with unfitness, light with darkness, antipathy with antipathy, the injured with the injurer, and force them into the most inward nearness of a detested union, this doubtless is the most horrid, the most unnatural mixture, the greatest confusion that can be confused![60]

Thus by this plain and Christian Talmud[61] vindicating the law of God from irreverent and unwary expositions, I trust, where it shall meet with intelligible perusers, some stay at least of men's thoughts will be obtained, to consider these many prudent and righteous ends of this divorcing permission. That it may have, for the great author's sake, hereafter some competent allowance to be counted a little purer than the prerogative of a legal and public ribaldry granted to that holy seed. So that from hence we shall hope to find the way still more open to the reconciling of those places which treat this matter in the Gospel. And thither now without interruption the course of method brings us.

MATT. 5.31, 32.

31. "It hath been said, Whosoever shall put away his wife, let him give her a writing of divorcement.
32. "But I say unto you that whosoever shall put away his wife," etc.

MATT. 19.3, 4 &C.

3. "And the Pharisees also came unto him tempting him," etc.

. . .

[*In a lengthy omitted section, Milton acknowledges that his argument will not seem to fit the letter of Matthew but argues that Christ would have us read the Gospel in the light of charity, not literal rigor. Because marriage and divorce fall under the moral law as opposed to the merely positive ceremonial and judical laws, to assume, as orthodox opinion did in his day, that Christ's teaching on divorce diverged from Mosaic Law on divorce amounts to a*

59. Once again Milton articulates an objection before countering it.
60. Despite the argument elsewhere in the tract for divorce for mutually blameless incompatibility, Milton's binaries in these sentences assign blame, with the single exception of *antipathy with antipathy.*
61. **Talmud:** ancient Jewish writings interpreting Scripture.

kind of Manichaeanism, with one God in the Old Testament and another in the New. Christ's apparent prohibition of divorce in Matthew 19, Milton argues, is in fact a response to the Pharisees' attempt to trap him; it is "not so much a teaching [for us], but an entangling [of the Pharisees]." Because they had abused the Mosaic permission of divorce, and because they had treated marriage as merely the carnal work of male and female, Christ answers them according to their degraded capacity. At the same time, Christ implies that marriage is marriage only when the purposes of the original institution are fulfilled.]

> Ver. 7. "They say unto him, Why did Moses then command to give a writing of divorcement, and to put her away?
> Ver. 8. "He saith unto them, Moses because of the hardness of your hearts suffered you to put away your wives, but from the beginning it was not so."

. . .

[*In another lengthy section, Milton argues, as he had in the* Doctrine and Discipline *(see Book 2, chapter 3), that to insist that Christ overturns the Mosaic permission of divorce is to imply that God lured the Jews into a sinful practice, and that God is thus the author of their sins. The argument that the Mosaic Law is designed to limit rather than to encourage sin is fallacious, for sin by its nature is chaotic and boundless, and it cannot be limited.*]

["Moses suffered you to put away," etc.] Not commanded you, says the common observer, and therefore cared not how soon it were abolished, being but suffered; herein declaring his annotation to be slight and nothing law-prudent. For in this place "commanded" and "suffered" are interchangeably used in the same sense both by our Savior and the Pharisees. Our Savior, who here saith, "Moses suffered you," in the 10th of Mark saith, "Moses wrote you this command." And the Pharisees who here say, "Moses commanded," and would mainly have it a command, in that place of Mark say, "Moses suffered," which had made against them in their own mouths if the word of "suffering" had weakened the command. So that "suffered" and "commanded" is here taken for the same thing on both sides of the controversy, as Cameron[62] also and others on this place acknowledge. And lawyers know that all the precepts of law are divided into obligatory and permissive, containing either what we must do, or what we may do; and of this latter sort are as many precepts as of the former, and all as lawful. Tutelage, an ordainment than which nothing more just, being for the defense of orphans, the *Institutes* of Justinian say, "is given and permitted by the civil law," and "to parents it is permitted to choose and appoint by will the guardians of their children."[63] What more equal? And yet the civil law calls this "permission." So likewise to "manumise," to adopt, to make a will, and to be

62. Johannes Cameron makes this point in his *Myrothecium Evangelicum* (1632, 98).
63. *Juris Civiles, Institutes,* book 1, title 13, ¶s 1, 3.

made an heir is called "permission" by law. Marriage itself, and this which is already granted, to divorce for adultery, obliges no man, is but a permission by law, is but suffered. By this we may see how weakly it hath been thought that all divorce is utterly unlawful, because the law is said to suffer it: whenas to "suffer" is but the legal phrase denoting what by law a man may do or not do.

["Because of the hardness of your hearts."] Hence they argue that therefore he allowed it not, and therefore it must be abolished. But the contrary to this will sooner follow, that because he suffered it for a cause, therefore in relation to that cause he allowed it. Next, if he in his wisdom and in the midst of his severity allowed it for hardness of heart, it can be nothing better than arrogance and presumption to take stricter courses against hardness of heart than God ever set an example, and that under the Gospel,[64] which warrants them to no judicial act of compulsion in this matter, much less to be more severe against hardness of extremity, than God thought good to be against hardness of heart. He suffered it rather than worse inconveniences; these men wiser, as they make themselves, will suffer the worst and heinousest inconveniences to follow rather than they will suffer what God suffered. Although they can know, when they please, that Christ spake only to the conscience, did not judge on the civil bench, but always disavowed it. What can be more contrary to the ways of God than these their doings?

If they be such enemies to hardness of heart, although this groundless rigor proclaims it to be in themselves, they may yet learn or consider that hardness of heart hath a twofold acceptation in the Gospel. One, when it is in a good man taken for infirmity and imperfection, which was in all the apostles, whose weakness only, not utter want of belief, is called hardness of heart (Mark 16).[65] Partly for this hardness of heart, the imperfection and decay of man from original righteousness, it was that God suffered not divorce only, but all that which by civilians[66] is termed the "secondary law of nature and of nations." He suffered his own people to waste and spoil and slay by war, to lead captives, to be some masters, some servants, some to be princes, others to be subjects; he suffered propriety to divide all things by several possession, trade, and commerce, not without usury; in his commonwealth some to be undeservedly rich, others to be undeservingly poor. All which, till hardness of heart came in, was most unjust; whenas prime nature made us all equal, made us equal coheirs by common right and dominion over all creatures. In the same manner and for the same cause, he suffered divorce as well as marriage, our imperfect and degenerate condition of necessity requiring this law among the rest, as a remedy against

64. **and that under the Gospel:** i.e., it would be particularly arrogant and presumptuous to act so under the new law.

65. Mark 16.14: "Afterward he appeared unto the eleven as they sat at meat, and upbraided them with their unbelief and hardness of heart, because they believed not them which had seen him after he was raised."

66. **civilians:** students of civil law.

intolerable wrong and servitude above the patience of man to bear. Nor was it given only because our infirmity or (if it must be so called) hardness of heart could not endure all things, but because the hardness of another's heart might not inflict all things upon an innocent person, whom far other ends brought into a league of love and not of bondage and indignity.

If therefore we abolish divorce as only suffered for hardness of heart, we may as well abolish the whole law of nations, as only suffered for the same cause; it being shown us by Saint Paul (1 Cor. 6[.7]) that the very seeking of a man's right by law, and at the hands of a worldly magistrate, is not without the hardness of our hearts: "For why do ye not rather take wrong," saith he, "why suffer ye not rather yourselves to be defrauded?" If nothing now must be suffered for hardness of heart, I say the very prosecution of our right by way of civil justice can no more be suffered among Christians, for the hardness of heart wherewith most men pursue it. And that would next remove all our judicial laws, and this restraint of divorce also in the number, which would more than half end the controversy. But if it be plain that the whole juridical law and civil power is only suffered under the Gospel for the hardness of our hearts, then wherefore should not that which Moses suffered be suffered still by the same reason?

In a second signification, hardness of heart is taken for a stubborn resolution to do evil. And that God ever makes any law purposely to such, I deny. For he vouchsafes not to enter covenant with them but as they fortune to be mixed with good men and pass undiscovered, much less that he should decree an unlawful thing only to serve their licentiousness. But that God "suffers" this reprobate hardness of heart I affirm, not only in this law of divorce but throughout all his best and purest commandments. He commands all to worship in singleness of heart according to all his ordinances; and yet suffers the wicked man to perform all the rites of religion hypocritically and in the hardness of his heart. He gives us general statutes and privileges in all civil matters, just and good of themselves, yet suffers unworthiest men to use them, and by them to prosecute their own right, or any color of right, though for the most part maliciously, covetously, rigorously, revengefully. He allowed by law the discreet father and husband to forbid, if he thought fit, the religious vows of his wife or daughter (Num. 30[.3-8]), and in the same law suffered the hardheartedness of impious and covetous fathers or husbands abusing this law to forbid their wives or daughters in their offerings and devotions of greatest zeal. If then God suffer hardness of heart equally in the best laws, as in this of divorce, there can be no reason that for this cause this law should be abolished.

But other laws, they object, may be well used, this never. How often shall I answer, both from the institution of marriage and from other general rules in scripture, that this law of divorce hath many wise and charitable ends besides the being suffered for hardness of heart (which is indeed no end, but an accident happening through the whole law), which gives to good men right, and to bad men (who abuse right under false pretences) gives only sufferance. Now although Christ express no other reasons here, but only what was suffered, it nothing follows that this law had no other reason to be permitted but for hardness of heart. The scripture seldom or never in one place sets down all the reasons of what it grants or commands, especially when it talks to enemies and tempters. St. Paul permitting marriage (1 Cor. 7[.2]) seems to permit even that also for hardness of heart only, lest we should run into fornication; yet no intelligent man thence concludes marriage allowed in the Gospel only to avoid an evil, because no other end is there expressed. Thus Moses of necessity suffered many to put away their wives for hardness of heart, but enacted the law of divorce doubtless for other good causes, not for this only sufferance. He permitted not divorce by law as an evil, for that was impossible to divine law, but permitted by accident the evil of them who divorced against the law's intention undiscoverably.

This also may be thought not improbably, that Christ, stirred up in his spirit against these tempting Pharisees, answered them in a certain form of indignation usual among good authors; whereby the question or the truth is not directly answered, but something which is fitter for them who ask to hear. So in the ecclesiastical stories, one demanding how God employed himself before the world was made, had answer, that he was making hell for curious questioners.[67] Another (and Libanius the Sophist, as I remember) asking in derision some Christian what the carpenter, meaning our Savior, was doing, now that Julian so prevailed, had it returned him, that the carpenter was making a coffin for the apostate.[68] So Christ, being demanded maliciously why Moses made the law of divorce, answers them in a vehement scheme, not telling them the cause why he made it, but what was fittest to be told them, that "for the hardness of their hearts" he suffered them to abuse it. And albeit Mark say not "he suffered you," but "to you he wrote this precept," Mark may be warrantably expounded by Matthew the larger. And whether he suffered or gave precept (being all one, as was heard), it changes not the trope of indignation, fittest account for such askers. Next, "for the hardness of your hearts to you he wrote this precept" infers not therefore for this cause only he wrote it, as was paralleled by other scriptures.

Lastly, it may be worth the observing that Christ, speaking to the Pharisees, does not say in general that for hardness of heart he gave this precept, but "you he suffered, and to you he gave this precept for your hardness of heart." It cannot be easily thought that Christ here included all the children of Israel under the person of these tempting Pharisees, but that he conceals wherefore he gave the better sort of them this law, and expresses by saying emphatically "To you" how he gave it to the worser, such as the Pharisees best represented, that is to

67. See, e.g., Augustine's *Confessions* 11.12.

68. See Theodoret, *Ecclesiasticae Historiae* 3.18.

say, for the hardness of your hearts (as indeed to wicked men and hardened hearts he gives the whole law and the Gospel also, to harden them the more). Thus many ways it may orthodoxally be understood how God or Moses suffered such as the demanders were, to divorce for hardness of heart. Whereas the vulgar expositor beset with contradictions and absurdities round, and resolving at any peril to make an exposition of it (as there is nothing more violent and boisterous than a reverend ignorance in fear to be convicted), rushes brutely and impetuously against all the principles both of nature, piety, and moral goodness; and in the fury of his literal expounding overturns them all.

["But from the beginning it was not so."] Not how from the beginning? Do they suppose that men might not divorce at all, not necessarily, not deliberately, except for adultery, but that some law (like canon law presently) attached them both before and after the flood, till stricter Moses came and with law brought license into the world? That were a fancy indeed to smile at. Undoubtedly as to point of judicial law, divorce was more permissive from the beginning before Moses than under Moses. But from the beginning (that is to say, by the institution in Paradise) it was not intended that matrimony should dissolve for every trivial cause, as you Pharisees accustom. But that it was not thus suffered from the beginning ever since the race of men corrupted and laws were made, he who will affirm must have found out other antiquities than are yet known. Besides we must consider now, what can be so as from the beginning, not only what should be so. In the beginning, had men continued perfect, it had been just that all things should have remained as they began to Adam and Eve. But after that the sons of men grew violent and injurious, it altered the lore of justice and put the government of things into a new frame. While man and woman were both perfect each to other, there needed no divorce; but when they both degenerated to imperfection, and ofttimes grew to be an intolerable evil each to other, then law more justly did permit the alienating of that evil which mistake made proper, than it did the appropriating of that good which nature at first made common. For if the absence of outward good be not so bad as the presence of a close evil, and that propriety, whether by covenant or possession, be but the attainment of some outward good, it is more natural and righteous that the law should sever us from an intimate evil than appropriate any outward good to us from the community of nature. The Gospel indeed, tending ever to that which is perfectest, aimed at the restorement of all things as they were in the beginning. And therefore all things were in common to those primitive Christians in the Acts, which Ananias and Sapphira dearly felt.[69] That custom also continued more or less till the time of Justin Martyr, as may be read in his second *Apology*, which might be writ after that act of communion perhaps some forty years above a hundred.[70] But who will be the man shall introduce this kind

69. See Acts 5.1–10.
70. See *Apologia I, Pro Christianis* 15.

of commonwealth, as Christianity now goes? If then marriage must be as in the beginning, the persons that marry must be such as then were; the institution must make good, in some tolerable sort, what it promises to either party. If not, it is but madness to drag this one ordinance back to the beginning, and draw down all other to the present necessity and condition, far from the beginning, even to the tolerating of extortions and oppressions. Christ only told us that from the beginning it was not so; that is to say, not so as the Pharisees manured[71] the business; did not command us that it should be forcibly so again in all points as at the beginning; or so at least in our intentions and desires, but so in execution, as reason and present nature can bear. Although we are not to seek, that the institution itself from the first beginning was never but conditional, as all covenants are: because thus and thus, therefore so and so; if not thus, then not so. Then moreover was perfectest to fulfill each law in itself; now is perfectest in this estate of things to ask of charity how much law may be fulfilled, else the fulfilling ofttimes is the greatest breaking. If any therefore demand which is now most perfection, to ease an extremity by divorce or to enrage and fester it by the grievous observance of a miserable wedlock, I am not destitute to say which is most perfection (although some who believe they think favorably of divorce, esteem it only venial to infirmity). Him I hold more in the way to perfection who forgoes an unfit, ungodly, and discordant wedlock, to live according to peace and love and God's institution in a fitter choice, than he who debars himself the happy experience of all godly, which is peaceful conversation in his family, to live a contentious and unchristian life not to be avoided, in temptations not to be lived in, only for the false keeping of a most unreal nullity, a marriage that hath no affinity with God's intention, a daring phantasm, a mere toy of terror awing weak senses, to the lamentable superstition of ruining themselves, the remedy whereof God in his law vouchsafes us. Which not to dare use, he warranting, is not our perfection, is our infirmity, our little faith, our timorous and low conceit of charity; and in them who force us, it is their masking pride and vanity, to seem holier and more circumspect than God. So far is it that we need impute to him infirmity, who thus divorces: since the rule of perfection is not so much that which was done in the beginning, as that which now is nearest to the rule of charity. This is the greatest, the perfectest, the highest commandment. . . .

[*In the rest of this section, Milton distinguishes between those who wish to divorce for fleeting or contingent causes and those who find themselves deprived of the ends of the institution of marriage for immutable causes. As in the* Doctrine and Discipline, *he argues that "fornication" is not limited to sexual infidelity but that it signifies a "constant alienation and disaffection of mind" between husband and wife.*]

71. **manured:** handled.

I COR. 7.10, ETC.

10. "And unto the married I command," etc.
11. "And let not the husband put away his wife."

[*Milton examines Paul's teaching on a Christian's divorcing an unbelieving spouse, and he argues that life with one unable or unwilling to fulfill the ends of marriage is worse than marriage to an infidel. In a coda at the end of the work, Milton, while deprecating "the weaker sort" of readers and teachers who rely on authority, supplies for their benefit arguments supporting his own from church fathers and reformers.*]

Introduction to *The Tenure of Kings and Magistrates*

The path of Milton's life in relation to English public affairs from the 1630s to the 1660s might be compared to the orbit of a comet that comes out of nowhere and completes a turn of compelling brilliance and apparent sway before receding into the interstellar distance. *Tenure of Kings and Magistrates* was published at the pivotal moment of Milton's eccentric orbit of civic pertinence, and if comets are indeed malignant to monarchs, his first regicide tract would seem to justify the celestial analogy. Biographers have assumed that its argument brought Milton to the attention of Oliver Cromwell and the Council of State because shortly after its publication he was appointed Secretary for Foreign Tongues and asked to reply to Charles's posthumous *Eikon Basilike.* Thereafter, "John Milton Englishman" became the brand author of the English Commonwealth, his name and nationality appearing above the titles of his works defending it. The increasing prominence of this public persona profoundly influenced Milton's conception of himself until the Restoration and continued to do so afterward, if we judge by his later masterpieces.

Politically, *Tenure* is Milton's most radical work. David Masson singles it out as unequivocal evidence of his complicity in "compassing or imagining" the death of Charles I and insists that it would certainly have cost Milton his life upon the return of Charles II had the public eye not been averted, or intentionally distracted, at the proper moment (6:170–92). One scarcely need read the pamphlet's full title to see Masson's point: *The Tenure of Kings and Magistrates: proving that it is lawful, and hath been held so through all ages, for any, who have the power, to call to account a tyrant or wicked king, and after due conviction, to depose and put him to death if the ordinary magistrate have neglected or denied to do it.* . . . Not until the nineteenth century did British editors begin including *Tenure* with Milton's collected works, and then they introduced it with an apology or condemned the pamphlet outright: "Enunciation of this elaborate and wicked title is quite enough to deter any from wasting time in the perusal of the treatise itself," said the Reverend James Graham in his 1870 edition of Milton's prose (230). One hundred years earlier, on the other side of the Atlantic, it had made a much different impression on John Adams and Thomas Jefferson, and along with other of Milton's works figured in the revolutionary transformation of the American colonies into the United States of America. Indeed, the proposition on which Milton's entire argument depends—that "all men naturally were born free" (p. 276)—is one embraced and developed in the Declaration of Independence.

Milton's radical insistence that governmental authority derives from the people recapitulates a major development in his thought, one that originated in the divorce tracts' conception of marriage as society's most fundamental institution. His advocacy of divorce in 1643 invoked concepts new to his writings, of individual rights, equity, natural law, and the contingency of social bonds. It was written, after all, in the midst of an intense political debate on the propriety of violating one's allegiance to a bad king: "He who marries, intends as little to conspire his own ruin, as he that swears allegiance: and as a whole people is in proportion to an ill government, so is one man to an ill marriage" (*DDD*, p. 110). By comparing marriage to the bond between subject and ruler, Milton aimed to win over influential Presbyterians who in 1643 were intent on justifying Parliament's militant defiance of Charles I. The choice of rhetorical strategy was questionable at best, and Milton was publicly and harshly condemned by his former allies. He evidently bore this embarrassing episode in mind. The same Herbert Palmer who in August 1644 lashed Milton the divorcer in a sermon before Parliament had a year earlier published *Scripture and Reason.* In it, he supported the right to bear "defensive" arms against the king. Milton singles out *Scripture and Reason* in *Tenure* to illustrate the inconsistency and hypocrisy of the Presbyterians' position in 1649 by comparing it with more bellicose arguments they had made earlier in the decade.

On one crucial point, however, Presbyterian criticism of the effort to put Charles on trial seemed to make good sense. In the early 1640s, the full and frequent Long Parliament opposed Charles. Now, however, it was the Rump, that is, the Long Parliament purged (as of December 1648) of those who advocated compromise with Charles. According to Presbyterian arguments, the soldiers who purged Parliament were a group of private citizens lacking governmental authority, and the Rump, being the consequence of that illegal action, similarly lacked authority. It therefore could not bring Charles to account. But Milton in the first edition of *Tenure* argues that to remove a tyrant is an imperative of natural law and an inalienable right of every man, as the title to which the Reverend Graham so vehemently objected insists: "It is lawful for any, who have the power, to call to account a tyrant or a wicked king." The position is subject to abuse, obviously, and the second edition, published probably eight months after the first, retreats from it by addition. By then the political situation had changed greatly. A new government of dubious legitimacy and with many opponents was in place. It needed to shore up its support or at least undermine its opposition. The radical argument of the first edition remains intact, but the additions to it, as Martin Dzelzainis argues (xi–xix), especially the concluding list of quotations culled from the writings of revered reformers, support the more conservative conclusion that resistance to the magistrate properly comes only from within a duly elected government: "to do justice on a lawless king is to a private man unlawful, to an inferior magistrate lawful" (p. 306). Perhaps after due consideration Milton wanted to back away from a position that he himself had come to see as too extreme. More likely he wanted to remind the Presbyterians to restrain their own opposition by citing the opinion of the authorities they most honored. Although our text follows the second edition, we indicate its additions to the first with brackets.

Our text is based on the copy of the second edition held in the Wrenn Library of the Harry Ransom Humanities Research Center, University of Texas, Austin, with reference to the copy of the first edition held in the Carl H. Pforzheimer Library in the Harry Ransom Humanities Research Center, Austin, Texas.

THE TENURE OF KINGS AND MAGISTRATES

If men within themselves would be governed by reason and not generally give up their understanding to a double tyranny of custom[1] from without and blind affections within, they would discern better what it is to favor and uphold the tyrant of a nation. But being slaves within doors, no wonder that they strive so much to have the public state conformably governed to the inward vicious rule by which they govern themselves. For indeed none can love freedom heartily but good men; the rest love not freedom but license, which never hath more scope or more indulgence than under tyrants. Hence is it that tyrants are not often offended, nor stand much in doubt of bad men, as being all naturally servile. But in whom[2] virtue and true worth most is eminent, them they fear in earnest, as by right their masters; against them lies all their hatred and suspicion. Consequently, neither do bad men hate tyrants, but have been always readiest with the falsified names of *loyalty* and *obedience* to color over their base compliances.[3]

And although sometimes for shame, and when it comes to their own grievances, of purse especially, they would seem good patriots and side with the better cause, yet when others for the deliverance of their country, endued with fortitude and heroic virtue to fear nothing but the curse written against those "that do the work of the Lord negligently,"[4] would go on to remove not only the calamities and thraldoms of a people but the roots and causes whence they spring, straight these men and sure helpers at need, as if they hated only the miseries but not the mischiefs, after they have juggled and paltered with the world, bandied and borne arms against their king, divested him, disanointed him, nay, cursed him all over in their pulpits and their pamphlets to the engaging of sincere and real men beyond what is possible or honest to retreat from,

1. For similar attacks on custom, see *DDD* (pp. 105–106) and *Eikon* (pp. 311, 312).
2. **in whom:** those in whom. Milton claims that tyrants do not doubt the allegiance of bad men, however vicious, because bad men are intrinsically servile. Tyrants fear good men, because the virtuous are intrinsically self-governing.
3. The distinction between liberty and license, and its political application, is common in Milton's poetry and prose (e.g., *Sonnet 12*; *DDD*, pp. 107–108). His views reflect arguments developed in Aristotle's *Politics* and *Nichomachean Ethics* on the servility of those who lack virtue; conversely, the self-rule of the virtuous fits them for political sovereignty (Hawkes). Cp. *PL* 12.82–96.
4. Jer. 48.10. The marginal gloss in the second edition erroneously cites Jer. 48.19.

not only turn revolters from those principles which only could at first move them, but lay the stain of disloyalty and worse on those proceedings which are the necessary consequences of their own former actions, nor disliked by themselves, were they managed to the entire advantages of their own faction; not considering the while that he toward whom they boasted their new fidelity counted them accessory and, by those statutes and laws which they so impotently brandish against others, would have doomed them to a traitor's death for what they have done already.[5] 'Tis true, that most men are apt enough to civil wars and commotions as a novelty, and for a flash[6] hot and active; but through sloth or inconstancy and weakness of spirit, either fainting ere their own pretenses,[7] though never so just, be half attained, or through an inbred falsehood and wickedness, betray ofttimes to destruction with themselves men of noblest temper joined with them for causes whereof they in their rash undertakings were not capable.

If God and a good cause give them victory, the prosecution whereof for the most part inevitably draws after it the alteration of laws, change of government, downfall of princes with their families, then comes the task to those worthies which are the soul of that enterprise, to be sweat and labored out amidst the throng and noises of vulgar and irrational men. Some contesting for privileges, customs, forms, and that old entanglement of iniquity, their gibberish laws, though the badge of their ancient slavery.[8] Others who have been fiercest against their prince under the notion of a tyrant, and no mean incendiaries of the war against him, when God out of his providence and high disposal hath delivered him into the hand of their brethren, on a sudden and in a new garb of allegiance, which their doings have long since canceled, they plead for him, pity him, extol him, protest against those that talk of bringing him to the trial of justice, which is the sword of God, superior to all mortal things, in whose hand soever by apparent signs his testified will is to put it. But certainly if we consider who and what they are, on a sudden grown so pitiful,[9] we may conclude their pity can be no true and Christian commiseration but either levity and shallowness of mind or else a carnal admiring of that worldly pomp and greatness from whence they see him fallen; or rather lastly a dissembled and seditious pity, feigned of industry[10] to beget new discord. As for mercy, if it be to a tyrant, under which name they themselves have cited him so oft in the hearing of God, of angels, and the holy church assembled, and there charged him with the

5. The former allies of Parliament described in this paragraph are the Presbyterians. Milton insists that Charles would have had them drawn and quartered for their early opposition, regardless of their late change of course.

6. **for a flash:** for brief moment.

7. **pretenses:** assertions or claims of rights.

8. Milton refers to the Levellers, who, though they objected to the Norman influence over English law and the class system since the Conquest, nevertheless deemed Charles's trial illegal.

9. **pitiful:** i.e., full of pity.

10. **of industry:** on purpose, intentionally.

spilling of more innocent blood by far than ever Nero[11] did, undoubtedly the mercy which they pretend is the mercy of wicked men. And "their mercies," we read, "are cruelties,"[12] hazarding the welfare of a whole nation to have saved one whom so oft they have termed Agag,[13] and vilifying the blood of many Jonathans that have saved Israel;[14] insisting with much niceness on the unnecessariest clause of their Covenant[15] [wrested], wherein the fear of change and the absurd contradiction of a flattering hostility had hampered them, but not scrupling to give away for compliments, to an implacable revenge, the heads of many thousand Christians more.

Another sort there is who (coming in the course of these affairs to have their share in great actions above the form of law or custom, at least to give their voice and approbation) begin to swerve and almost shiver at the majesty and grandeur of some noble deed, as if they were newly entered into a great sin; disputing precedents, forms, and circumstances, when the commonwealth nigh perishes for want of deeds in substance, done with just and faithful expedition. To these I wish better instruction, and virtue equal to their calling; the former of which, that is to say instruction, I shall endeavor, as my duty is, to bestow on them; and exhort them not to startle from the just and pious resolution of adhering with all their strength and assistance to the present Parliament and army, in the glorious way wherein justice and victory hath set them—the only warrants through all ages, next under immediate revelation, to exercise supreme power—in those proceedings which hitherto appear equal to what hath been done in any age or nation heretofore justly or magnanimously.

Nor let them be discouraged or deterred by any new apostate scarecrows, who, under show of giving counsel, send out their barking monitories and *mementoes*, empty of aught else but the spleen of a frustrated faction.[16] For how can that pretended counsel be either sound or faithful, when they that give it see not, for madness and vexation of their ends lost, that those statutes and scriptures which both falsely and scandalously they wrest against their friends and associates, would, by sentence of the common adversary, fall first and heaviest upon their own heads. Neither let mild and tender dispositions be foolishly

11. Protestant social theorists typically construed civil obedience as a religious duty. The limiting case was whether the Christian subject owed obedience even to a tyrant such as *Nero*.

12. Milton here refers to Prov. 12.10.

13. **Agag:** impious Amalekite king "hewn to pieces" by Samuel (1 Sam. 15.33–34). The biblical books of Samuel and Kings, particularly as they concern the origin and early course of kingship in Israel, were often cited in early modern debates over monarchy.

14. *Jonathan*, after battling heroically against the Philistine enemy, remained unscathed upon his return despite orders from his father, King Saul, to have him killed on account of a ceremonial infraction (1 Sam. 14.1–45).

15. The Solemn League and Covenant (1643) was an agreement meant to uphold Parliament's rights. Its third article demanded that the sovereign's personal safety and authority be defended while Parliament sought civil liberty and the establishment of true religion.

16. William Prynne wrote *A Brief Memento to the Present Unparliamentary Junto* (1649); John Gauden, the self-proclaimed "faithful monitor," wrote *The Religious and Loyal Protestation* (1649).

softened from their duty and perseverance with the unmasculine rhetoric of any puling priest or chaplain—sent as a friendly letter of advice, for fashion sake in private, and forthwith published by the sender himself (that we may know how much of friend there was in it) to cast an odious envy upon them to whom it was pretended to be sent in charity.[17] Nor let any man be deluded by either the ignorance or the notorious hypocrisy and self-repugnance of our dancing divines, who have the conscience and the boldness to come with scripture in their mouths, glossed and fitted for their turns with a double contradictory sense, transforming the sacred verity of God to an idol with two faces, looking at once two several ways, and with the same quotations to charge others, which in the same case they made serve to justify themselves. For while the hope to be made classic and provincial lords led them on, while pluralities greased them thick and deep to the shame and scandal of religion more than all the sects and heresies they exclaim against[18]—then to fight against the king's person and no less a party of his Lords and Commons or to put force upon both the Houses, was good, was lawful, was no resisting of superior powers; they only were powers not to be resisted who countenanced the good and punished the evil.

But now that their censorious domineering is not suffered to be universal, truth and conscience to be freed, tithes and pluralities to be no more, though competent allowance provided and the warm experience of large gifts, and they so good at taking them—yet now to exclude and seize upon impeached members,[19] to bring delinquents without exemption to a fair tribunal by the common national law against murder, is now to be no less than Corah, Dathan, and Abiram.[20] He who but erewhile in the pulpits was a cursed tyrant, an enemy to God and saints, laden with all the innocent blood spilt in three kingdoms, and so to be fought against, is now, though nothing penitent or altered from his first principles, a lawful magistrate, a sovereign lord, the Lord's anointed, not to be touched, though by themselves imprisoned. As if this only were obedience, to preserve the mere useless bulk of his person, and that only in prison, not in the field, and to disobey his commands, deny him his dignity and office, everywhere to resist his power but where they think it only surviving in their own faction.

But who in particular is a tyrant cannot be determined in a general discourse, otherwise than by supposition. His particular charge and the sufficient proof of it must determine that; which I leave to magistrates, at least to the

17. Gauden (see previous note) appealed to the army to demonstrate masculine and Christian heroism by taking pity on Charles.

18. In Presbyterian church organization, parishes were grouped in "classes," and representative divines met in provincial assemblies. **pluralities:** multiple church livings held by a single, privileged cleric.

19. The army in 1647 impeached eleven members of Parliament suspected of conspiring with the queen.

20. These men rebelled against Moses; two of them were swallowed up by the earth, making them traditional examples of justly punished rebels (Num. 16.1–33).

uprighter sort of them and of the people, though in number less by many, in whom faction least hath prevailed above the law of nature and right reason, to judge as they find cause. But this I dare own as part of my faith, that if such a one there be, by whose commission whole massacres have been committed on his faithful subjects,[21] his provinces offered to pawn or alienation as the hire of those whom he had solicited to come in and destroy whole cities and countries[22]—be he king, or tyrant, or emperor, the sword of justice is above him, in whose hand soever is found sufficient power to avenge the effusion and so great a deluge of innocent blood. For if all human power to execute not accidentally but intendedly the wrath of God upon evildoers without exception be of God, then that power—whether ordinary or, if that fail, extraordinary so executing that intent of God—is lawful and not to be resisted.[23]

But to unfold more at large this whole question, though with all expedient brevity, I shall here set down from first beginning the original of kings, how and wherefore exalted to that dignity above their brethren; and from thence shall prove that, turning to tyranny, they may be as lawfully deposed and punished, as they were at first elected. This I shall do by authorities and reasons not learnt in corners among schisms and heresies, as our doubling divines are ready to calumniate, but fetched out of the midst of choicest and most authentic learning, and no prohibited authors, nor many heathen, but Mosaical, Christian, orthodoxal, and, which must needs be more convincing to our adversaries, presbyterial.

No man who knows aught can be so stupid to deny that all men naturally were born free, being the image and resemblance of God himself, and were by privilege above all the creatures born to command and not to obey; and that they lived so till from the root of Adam's transgression falling among themselves to do wrong and violence, and foreseeing that such courses must needs tend to the destruction of them all, they agreed by common league to bind each other from mutual injury and jointly to defend themselves against any that gave disturbance or opposition to such agreement. Hence came cities, towns, and commonwealths. And because no faith in all was found sufficiently binding, they saw it needful to ordain some authority that might restrain by force and punishment what was violated against peace and common right. This authority and power of self-defense and preservation being originally and naturally in every one of them and unitedly in them all, for ease, for order, and, lest each man should be his own partial judge, they communicated and derived either to one, whom for the eminence of his wisdom and integrity they chose above the rest, or to more than one whom they thought of equal deserving. The first was

21. Milton alludes to the Irish rebellion against English rule under the Long Parliament and the subsequent massacre of Protestants in Ulster (1641).

22. In exchange for military aid, Charles had offered to cede counties to the Irish and Scots.

23. As his introductory remarks draw to an end, Milton alludes to Rom. 12.2, which had been interpreted to vindicate those who take it upon themselves to execute justice when magistrates fail to perform that divinely appointed duty.

called a king, the other, magistrates: not to be their lords and masters (though afterward those names in some places were given voluntarily to such as had been authors of inestimable good to the people) but to be their deputies and commissioners, to execute, by virtue of their entrusted power, that justice which else every man by the bond of nature and of covenant must have executed for himself and for one another. And to him that shall consider well why among free persons one man by civil right should bear authority and jurisdiction over another, no other end or reason can be imaginable.

These for a while governed well and with much equity decided all things at their own arbitrement,[24] till the temptation of such a power left absolute in their hands, perverted them at length to injustice and partiality. Then did they, who now by trial had found the danger and inconveniences of committing arbitrary power to any, invent laws either framed or consented to by all, that should confine and limit the authority of whom they chose to govern them: that so[25] man, of whose failing they had proof, might no more rule over them, but law and reason abstracted as much as might be from personal errors and frailties: [while, as the magistrate was set above the people, so the law was set above the magistrate].[26] When this would not serve, but that the law was either not executed, or misapplied, they were constrained from that time, the only remedy left them, to put conditions and take oaths from all kings and magistrates at their first installment to do impartial justice by law: who, upon those terms and no other, received allegiance from the people, that is to say, bond or covenant to obey them in execution of those laws which they the people had themselves made or assented to. And this ofttimes with express warning, that if the king or magistrate proved unfaithful to his trust, the people would be disengaged.

They added also counselors and parliaments, nor to be only at his beck, but with him or without him, at set times, or at all times when any danger threatened, to have care of the public safety. Therefore saith Claudius Sesell, a French statesman, "The parliament was set as a bridle to the king";[27] which I instance rather, [not because our English lawyers have not said the same long before, but] because that [French] monarchy is granted by all to be a far more absolute than ours. That this and the rest of what hath hitherto been spoken is most true, might be copiously made appear throughout all stories heathen and Christian, even of those nations where kings and emperors have sought means to abolish all ancient memory of the people's right by their encroachments and usurpations. But I spare long insertions, appealing to the [known constitutions of both the latest Christian empires in Europe, the Greek and] German, [besides the] French, Italian, Aragonian, English, and not least the Scottish histories: not forgetting this only by the way, that William the Norman, though a conqueror,

24. **arbitrement:** free choice, the right or capacity to decide for oneself.
25. **that so:** i.e., they legislated these limitations on arbitrary power so that . . .
26. Cp. Cicero, *On the Laws* 3.1.
27. Claude de Seissel, *La Grand Monarchie de France* (1519).

and not unsworn at his coronation, was compelled the second time to take oath at St. Albans, ere the people would be brought to yield obedience.

It being thus manifest that the power of kings and magistrates is nothing else but what is only derivative, transferred and committed to them in trust from the people to the common good of them all, in whom the power yet remains fundamentally and cannot be taken from them without a violation of their natural birthright, and seeing that from hence Aristotle and the best of political writers have defined a king, him[28] who governs to the good and profit of his people and not for his own ends, it follows from necessary causes that the titles of sovereign lord, natural lord, and the like, are either arrogancies, or flatteries, not admitted by emperors and kings of best note, and disliked by the church both of Jews (Isa. 26.13) and ancient Christians, as appears by Tertullian and others. Although generally the people of Asia, and with them the Jews also, especially since the time they chose a king against the advice and counsel of God, are noted by wise authors much inclinable to slavery.[29]

Secondly, that to say, as is usual, the king hath as good right to his crown and dignity as any man to his inheritance, is to make the subject no better than the king's slave, his chattel, or his possession that may be bought and sold. And doubtless if hereditary title were sufficiently inquired, the best foundation of it would be found either but in courtesy or convenience. But suppose it to be of right hereditary, what can be more just and legal, if a subject for certain crimes be to forfeit by law from himself and posterity all his inheritance to the king, than that a king for crimes proportional should forfeit all his title and inheritance to the people? Unless the people must be thought created all for him, he not for them, and they all in one body inferior to him single, which were a kind of treason against the dignity of mankind to affirm.

Thirdly, it follows that to say kings are accountable to none but God, is the overturning of all law and government. For if they may refuse to give account, then all covenants made with them at coronation, all oaths are in vain and mere mockeries, all laws which they swear to keep made to no purpose. For if the king fear not God (as how many of them do not?), we hold then our lives and estates by the tenure of his mere grace and mercy, as from a God, not a mortal magistrate, a position that none but court parasites or men besotted would maintain. [Aristotle, therefore, whom we commonly allow for one of the best interpreters of nature and morality, writes in the fourth of his *Politics*, chap. 10, that "monarchy unaccountable is the worst sort of tyranny, and least of all to be endured by freeborn men."]

And [surely] no Christian prince, not drunk with high mind and prouder than those pagan Caesars that deified themselves, would arrogate so unreasonably above human condition, or derogate so basely from a whole nation of men

28. I.e., defined a king *as* him who governs . . .

29. E.g., Aristotle, *Politics* (7.7), John Calvin, *Institutes* (4.20.8).

his brethren, as if for him only subsisting, and to serve his glory; valuing them in comparison of his own brute will and pleasure, no more than so many beasts or vermin under his feet, not to be reasoned with, but to be trod on; among whom there might be found so many thousand men for wisdom, virtue, nobleness of mind, and all other respects but the fortune of his dignity, far above him. Yet some would persuade us that this absurd opinion was King David's because in the 51 Psalm he cries out to God, "Against thee only have I sinned"; as if David had imagined that to murder Uriah and adulterate his wife had been no sin against his neighbor, when as that law of Moses was to the king expressly not to think so highly of himself above his brethren.[30] David therefore by those words could mean no other than either that the depth of his guiltiness was known to God only or to so few as had not the will or power to question him, or that the sin against God was greater beyond compare than against Uriah. Whatever his meaning were, any wise man will see that the pathetical words of a psalm can be no certain decision to a point that hath abundantly more certain rules to go by.

How much more rationally spake the heathen king Demophoön, in a tragedy of Euripides, than these interpreters would put upon King David: "I rule not my people by tyranny, as if they were barbarians, but am myself liable, if I do unjustly, to suffer justly."[31] Not unlike was the speech of Trajan, the worthy emperor, to one whom he made general of his praetorian forces: "Take this drawn sword," saith he, "to use for me, if I reign well; if not, to use against me."[32] Thus Dion[33] relates. And not Trajan only, but Theodosius the younger,[34] a Christian emperor and one of the best, caused it to be enacted as a rule undeniable and fit to be acknowledged by all kings and emperors, that a prince is bound to the laws, that on the authority of law the authority of a prince depends, and to the laws ought submit. Which edict of his remains yet in the Code of Justinian (Bk. 1, title 24) as a sacred constitution to all the succeeding emperors.[35] How then can any king in Europe maintain and write himself accountable to none but God, when emperors in their own imperial statutes have written and decreed themselves accountable to law. And indeed where such account is not feared, he that bids a man reign over him above law, may bid as well a savage beast.

It follows, lastly, that since the king or magistrate holds his authority of the

30. Ps. 51.4; 2 Sam. 11.22–27; Deut. 17.20.

31. Euripides, *Heraclidae* 423–24.

32. *Trajan* was a Roman emperor (98–117 C.E.) who, along with Theodosius, was lauded for respecting the rule of law. The *praetorian* guard were the emperor's bodyguards.

33. **Dion:** also known as Dio Cassius (150–235), Roman historian. Only fragments of his eighty-volume history of Rome survive, though subsequent historians relay some of what is missing. This account of Trajan was widely reported.

34. Theodosius II, Byzantine emperor whose edict at Ravenna (429) declared the ruler's authority to be dependent upon the law.

35. *Justinian* was Roman emperor at Constantinople (527–65); he issued his law code in 529.

people, both originally and naturally for their good in the first place, and not his own, then may the people, as oft as they shall judge it for the best, either choose him or reject him, retain him or depose him, though no tyrant, merely by the liberty and right of freeborn men to be governed as seems to them best. This, though it cannot but stand with plain reason, shall be made good also by scripture (Deut. 17.14): "When thou art come into the land which the Lord thy God giveth thee, and shalt say I will set a king over me, like as all the nations about me." These words confirm us that the right of choosing, yea of changing their own government, is by the grant of God himself in the people. And therefore when they desired a king, though then under another form of government, and though their changing displeased him, yet he that was himself their king and rejected by them would not be a hindrance to what they intended, further than by persuasion, but that they might do therein as they saw good (1 Sam. 8). Only he reserved to himself the nomination of who should reign over them. Neither did that exempt the king, as if he were to God only accountable, though by his especial command anointed. Therefore "David first made a covenant with the Elders of Israel, and so was by them anointed king" [2 Sam 5.3]; 1 Chron. 11. And Jehoiada the priest, making Jehoash king, made a covenant between him and the people (2 Kings 11.17). Therefore when Roboam at his coming to the crown rejected those conditions which the Israelites brought him, hear what they answer him, "What portion have we in David, or inheritance in the son of Jesse? See to thine own house, David."[36] And for the like conditions not performed, all Israel before that time deposed Samuel, not for his own default but for the misgovernment of his sons.

But some will say to both these examples, it was evilly done. I answer that not the latter, because it was expressly allowed them in the law to set up a king if they pleased; and God himself joined with them in the work, though in some sort it was at that time displeasing to him, in respect of old Samuel who had governed them uprightly. As Livy praises the Romans who took occasion from Tarquinius, a wicked prince, to gain their liberty, which to have extorted, saith he, from Numa, or any of the good kings before, had not been seasonable. Nor was it in the former example done unlawfully; for, when Roboam had prepared a huge army to reduce the Israelites, he was forbidden by the prophet, 1 Kings 12.24: "Thus saith the Lord: 'Ye shall not go up, nor fight against your brethren, for this thing is from me.' " He calls them their brethren, not rebels, and forbids to be proceeded against them, owning the thing himself, not by single providence but by approbation, and that not only of the act, as in the former example, but of the fit season also. He had not otherwise forbid to molest them. And those grave and wise counselors, whom Rehoboam[37] first advised with, spake no such thing as our old gray-headed flatterers now are wont: "Stand upon your

36. See 1 Kings 12.16. The northern kingdom rejected his government.

37. **Rehoboam:** the more common spelling of the name of the tyrannical king of Judah (previously spelled *Roboam*).

birthright, scorn to capitulate, you hold of God, not of them." For they knew no such matter, unless conditionally, but gave him politic counsel, as in a civil transaction.

Therefore kingdom and magistracy, whether supreme or subordinate, is [without difference] called a "human ordinance," 1 Pet. 2.13 etc., which we are there taught is the will of God we should [alike] submit to, so far as for the punishment of evildoers and the encouragement of them that do well. "Submit," saith he, "as free men." [But to any civil power unaccountable, unquestionable, and not to be resisted, no, not in wickedness and violent actions, how can we submit as free men?] "There is no power but of God," saith Paul, Rom. 13,[38] as much as to say, God put it into man's heart to find out that way at first for common peace and preservation, approving the exercise thereof; else it contradicts Peter, who calls the same authority an ordinance of man. It must be also understood of lawful and just power, else we read of great power in the affairs and kingdoms of the world permitted to the devil: for saith he to Christ, Luke 4.6, "All this power will I give thee and the glory of them, for it is delivered to me, and to whomsoever I will, I give it." Neither did he lie, or Christ gainsay what he affirmed, for in the thirteenth of the Revelation we read how the dragon gave to the beast "his power, his seat, and great authority," which beast so authorized most expound to be the tyrannical powers and kingdoms of the earth. Therefore Saint Paul in the fore-cited chapter tells us that such magistrates he means as are not a terror to the good but to the evil, such as bear not the sword in vain but to punish offenders and to encourage the good.[39]

If such only be mentioned here as powers to be obeyed, and our submission to them only required, then doubtless those powers that do the contrary are no powers ordained of God, and by consequence no obligation laid upon us to obey or not to resist them. And it may be well observed that both these apostles, whenever they give this precept, express it in terms not concrete but abstract, as logicians are wont to speak; that is, they mention the ordinance, the power, the authority before the persons that execute it; and what that power is, lest we should be deceived, they describe exactly. So that if the power be not such, or the person execute not such power, neither the one nor the other is of God, but of the devil, and by consequence to be resisted. From this exposition Chrysostom[40] also on the same place dissents not, explaining that these words were not written in behalf of a tyrant. And this is verified by David, himself a king, and likeliest to be author of the Psalm 94.20, which saith, "Shall the throne of iniquity have fellowship with thee?" And it were worth the knowing, since kings [in these days,] and that by scripture, boast the justness of their title by holding it immediately of God yet cannot show the time when God ever set on the throne

38. Along with 1 Pet. 2, Rom. 13.1–2 was often cited by Royalist apologists as scriptural authority for royal prerogative.

39. Rom. 13.4.

40. St. John Chrysostom, archbishop of Constantinople (c. 400) and prolific exegete.

them or their forefathers, but only when the people chose them; why by the same reason, since God ascribes as oft to himself the casting down of princes from the throne, it should not be thought as lawful and as much from God when none are seen to do it but the people, and that for just causes. For if it needs must be a sin in them to depose, it may as likely be a sin to have elected. And contrary, if the people's act in election be pleaded by a king as the act of God and the most just title to enthrone him, why may not the people's act of rejection be as well pleaded by the people as the act of God and the most just reason to depose him? So that we see the title and just right of reigning or deposing, in reference to God, is found in scripture to be all one, visible only in the people, and depending merely upon justice and demerit. Thus far hath been considered briefly the power of kings and magistrates, how it was and is originally the people's, and by them conferred in trust only to be employed to the common peace and benefit; with liberty therefore and right remaining in them to reassume it to themselves if by kings or magistrates it be abused, or to dispose of it by any alteration as they shall judge most conducing to the public good.[41]

We may from hence with more ease and force of argument determine what a tyrant is, and what the people may do against him. A tyrant, whether by wrong or by right coming to the crown, is he who, regarding neither law nor the common good, reigns only for himself and his faction. Thus St. Basil among others defines him.[42] And because his power is great, his will boundless and exorbitant, the fulfilling whereof is for the most part accompanied with innumerable wrongs and oppressions of the people—murders, massacres, rapes, adulteries, desolation, and subversion of cities and whole provinces, look how great a good and happiness a just king is, so great a mischief is a tyrant; as he the public father of his country, so this the common enemy. Against whom what the people lawfully may do, as against a common pest and destroyer of mankind, I suppose no man of clear judgment need go further to be guided than by the very principles of nature in him.

But because it is the vulgar folly of men to desert their own reason and shutting their eyes to think they see best with other men's, I shall show by such examples as ought to have most weight with us, what hath been done in this case heretofore. The Greeks and Romans, as their prime authors witness, held it not only lawful, but a glorious and heroic deed, rewarded publicly with statues and garlands, to kill an infamous tyrant at any time without trial. And but reason, that he who trod down all law, should not be vouchsafed the benefit of law. Insomuch that Seneca the tragedian brings in Hercules the grand suppressor of tyrants, thus speaking,

41. This concludes the general statement of Milton's case: that it belongs to the people to choose or depose their king for the common good. He now proceeds to elaborate on what makes a king a tyrant and thus subject to be deposed justly.

42. *St. Basil* the Great, bishop of Cappadocia (370–79). His definition of a tyrant also appears in Milton's *Commonplace Book* (Yale 1:453).

——— *Victima haud ulla amplior*
Potest, magisque opima mactari Jovi
Quam Rex iniquus ——— ———
——— ——— There can be slain
No sacrifice to God more acceptable
Than an unjust and wicked king.[43] ——— ———

But of these I name no more, lest it be objected they were heathen, and come to produce another sort of men that had the knowledge of true religion. Among the Jews this custom of tyrant-killing was not unusual. First Ehud, a man whom God had raised to deliver Israel from Eglon, king of Moab, who had conquered and ruled over them eighteen years, being sent to him as an ambassador with a present, slew him in his own house.[44] But he was a foreign prince, an enemy, and Ehud besides had special warrant from God. To the first I answer, it imports not whether foreign or native. For no prince so native but professes to hold by law; which when he himself overturns, breaking all the covenants and oaths that gave him title to his dignity and were the bond and alliance between him and his people, what differs he from an outlandish king or from an enemy?[45]

For look how much right the king of Spain hath to govern us at all, so much right hath the king of England to govern us tyrannically. If he, though not bound to us by any league, coming from Spain in person to subdue us or to destroy us, might lawfully by the people of England either be slain in fight or put to death in captivity, what hath a native king to plead, bound by so many covenants, benefits, and honors to the welfare of his people; why he through the contempt of all laws and parliaments, the only tie of our obedience to him, for his own will's sake and a boasted prerogative unaccountable, after seven years warring and destroying of his best subjects, overcome, and yielded prisoner, should think to scape unquestionable as a thing divine, in respect of whom so many thousand Christians destroyed should lie unaccounted for, polluting with their slaughtered carcasses all the land over and crying for vengeance against the living that should have righted them? Who knows not that there is a mutual bond of amity and brotherhood between man and man over all the world?[46] Neither is it the English Sea that can sever us from that duty and relation: a

43. Seneca, *Hercules Furens* 2.922–24.

44. Judg. 3.12–23. Royalist authors knew that Ehud could be construed as a precedent and objected to it for reasons that Milton rehearses in the next sentence.

45. Milton questions the distinction drawn by constitutional theorists between two kinds of tyrants: tyrants by practice (duly appointed rulers who proceed to act tyrannically) and tyrants without title (usurpers or foreign conquerors). It was generally agreed that the first sort could be removed only by governmental authority, not by the common people or an inspired individual like Ehud. Theorists could not agree over which sort of tyrants the oppressors of Israel had been. Dzelzainis argues that Milton chose the story of Ehud as an example "precisely because of the pivotal place it occupied in the controversy over who may lawfully resist a tyrant" (xiii).

46. Cicero regularly argues for a general brotherhood among men on the basis of reason. See, e.g., *On the Nature of the Gods* 1.2.4, where he asserts that the only division in human society should be between rational men and tyrants.

straiter bond yet there is between fellow-subjects, neighbors, and friends. But when any of these do one to another so as hostility could do no worse, what doth the law decree less against them than open enemies and invaders? Or if the law be not present, or too weak, what doth it warrant us to less than single defense or civil war? And from that time forward the law of civil defensive war differs nothing from the law of foreign hostility. Nor is it distance of place that makes enmity, but enmity that makes distance. He therefore that keeps peace with me, near or remote, of whatsoever nation, is to me as far as all civil and human offices an Englishman and a neighbor. But if an Englishman, forgetting all laws, human, civil and religious, offend against life and liberty, to him offended and to the law in his behalf, though born in the same womb, he is no better than a Turk, a Saracen,[47] a heathen.

This is gospel, and this was ever law among equals; how much rather then in force against any king whatever, who in respect of the people is confessed inferior and not equal. To distinguish therefore of a tyrant by outlandish, or domestic, is a weak evasion. To the second that he was an enemy, I answer, "What tyrant is not?" Yet Eglon by the Jews had been acknowledged as their sovereign. They had served him eighteen years, as long almost as we our William the Conqueror, in all which time he could not be so unwise a statesman but to have taken of them oaths of fealty and allegiance, by which they made themselves his proper subjects, as their homage and present sent by Ehud testified. To the third, that he had special warrant to kill Eglon in that manner, it cannot be granted, because not expressed. 'Tis plain that he was raised by God to be a deliverer, and went on just principles such as were then and ever held allowable to deal so by a tyrant that could no[48] otherwise be dealt with.

Neither did Samuel, though a prophet, with his own hand abstain from Agag, a foreign enemy no doubt. But mark the reason: "As thy sword hath made women childless,"[49] a cause that by the sentence of law itself nullifies all relations. And as the law is between brother and brother, father and son, master and servant, wherefore not between king, or rather tyrant, and people? And whereas Jehu had special command to slay Jehoram, a successive and hereditary tyrant, it seems not the less imitable for that.[50] For where a thing grounded so much on natural reason hath the addition of a command from God, what does it but establish the lawfulness of such an act?[51] Nor is it likely that God, who had so many ways of punishing the house of Ahab, would have sent a subject against his prince, if the fact in itself, as done to a tyrant, had been of bad example. And

47. **Saracen:** archaic term for "Arab," often used simply to mean a nonbeliever.
48. The first edition reads "not."
49. 1 Sam. 15.33.
50. 2 Kings 9.1–2.
51. The position that reason alone can provide grounds enough for tyrannicide represents a sharp turn from Puritan voluntarism: "The individualistic, even anarchic nature of this claim should not be underestimated—nor should its secularism" (Dzelzainis xv).

if David refused to lift his hand against the Lord's anointed, the matter between them was not tyranny but private enmity, and David as a private person had been his own revenger, not so much the people's.[52] But when any tyrant at this day can show to be the Lord's anointed, the only mentioned reason why David withheld his hand, he may then but not till then presume on the same privilege.

We may pass therefore hence to Christian times. And first our Savior himself, how much he favored tyrants, and how much intended they should be found or honored among Christians, declares his mind not obscurely: accounting their absolute authority no better than Gentilism, yea, though they flourished it over with the splendid name of benefactors;[53] charging those that would be his disciples to usurp no such dominion, but that they who were to be of most authority among them should esteem themselves ministers and servants to the public. Matt. 20.25, "The princes of the Gentiles exercise lordship over them," and Mark 10.42, "They that seem to rule," saith he, either slighting or accounting them no lawful rulers, "but ye shall not be so, but the greatest among you shall be your servant." And although he himself were the meekest and came on earth to be so, yet to a tyrant we hear him not vouchsafe an humble word, but, "Tell that fox" (Luke 13).[54] [So far we ought to be from thinking that Christ and his gospel should be made a sanctuary for tyrants from justice, to whom his law before never gave such protection.] And wherefore did his mother, the Virgin Mary, give such praise to God in her prophetic song, that he had now by the coming of Christ cut down *dynastas*[55] or proud monarchs from the throne, if the church, when God manifests his power in them to do so, should rather choose all misery and vassalage to serve them, and let them still sit on their potent seats to be adored for doing mischief?

Surely it is not for nothing that tyrants by a kind of natural instinct both hate and fear none more than the true church and saints of God, as the most dangerous enemies and subverters of monarchy, though indeed of tyranny. Hath not this been the perpetual cry of courtiers and court prelates? Whereof no likelier cause can be alleged but that they well discerned the mind and principles of most devout and zealous men, and indeed the very discipline of church, tending to the dissolution of all tyranny. No marvel then if since the faith of Christ received, in purer or impurer times, to depose a king and put him to death for tyranny hath been accounted so just and requisite that neighbor kings have both upheld and taken part with subjects in the action. And Ludovicus Pius,[56] himself an emperor, and son of Charles the Great, being made judge (du Haillan

52. David's refusal to harm Saul (1 Sam. 24.5) was a mainstay of Royalist arguments that the people should be submissive to their rulers, however vicious.

53. Luke 22.25.

54. Luke 13.32. Jesus is referring to Herod.

55. **dynastas:** Milton is translating Luke 1.52, where Mary prophesies that her son will cast down great powers (Gk. *dynastas*) from their thrones.

56. **Ludovicus Pius:** Louis the Pious, Holy Roman emperor (814–40).

is my author) between Milegast, king of the Vultzes, and his subjects who had deposed him, gave his verdict for the subjects and for him whom they had chosen in his room. Note here that the right of electing whom they please is by the impartial testimony of an emperor in the people. For, said he, "A just prince ought to be preferred before an unjust, and the end of government before the prerogative."[57] And Constantinus Leo, another emperor, in the Byzantine Laws saith "that the end of a king is for the general good, which, he not performing, is but the counterfeit of a king."[58]

And to prove that some of our own monarchs have acknowledged that their high office exempted them not from punishment, they had the sword of St. Edward borne before them by an officer who was called Earl of the Palace, even at the times of their highest pomp and solemnities, to mind them, saith Matthew Paris, the best of our historians, that if they erred the sword had power to restrain them.[59] And what restraint the sword comes to at length, having both edge and point, if any skeptic will doubt, let him feel. It is also affirmed from diligent search made in our ancient books of law that the peers and barons of England had a legal right to judge the king, which was the cause most likely, for it could be no slight cause, that they were called his peers or equals. This however may stand immovable, so long as man hath to deal with no better than man, that if our law judge all men to the lowest by their peers, it should in all equity ascend also and judge the highest.

And so much I find both in our own and foreign story, that dukes, earls, and marquises were at first not hereditary, not empty and vain titles, but names of trust and office,[60] and with the office ceasing, as induces me to be of opinion, that every worthy man in Parliament (for the word baron imports no more) might for the public good be thought a fit peer and judge of the king, without regard had to petty caveats and circumstances, the chief impediment in high affairs and ever stood upon most by circumstantial men.[61] Whence doubtless our ancestors who were not ignorant with what rights either nature or ancient constitution had endowed them, when oaths both at coronation and renewed in Parliament would not serve, thought it no way illegal to depose and put to death their tyrannous kings. Insomuch that the Parliament drew up a charge against Richard the Second, and the Commons requested to have judgment decreed against him that the realm might not be endangered.[62] And Peter Martyr,

57. See Du Haillan, Bernard de Girard (1535–1610), *Histoire Générale des Rois de France* (Paris, 1576), 248.
58. Quoting from the *Eclogue* of Johann Leunclavius, *Juris Graeco-Romani,* issued in 740, toward the end of the reign of Leo III.
59. Matthew Paris (1200–1259), *Historia Maior* (London, 1644), 421, relates that the Earl of Chester carried the sword of King Edward the Confessor (1042–66) as a symbolic gesture of monarchical self-restraint.
60. Cp. Du Haillan, 163, 316.
61. **circumstantial men:** distinguished merely by the "pomp and circumstance" of their position (*OED*).
62. Cp. Holinshed, 3.512.

a divine of foremost rank, on the third of Judges approves their doings.[63] Sir Thomas Smith, also a Protestant and a statesman, in his *Commonwealth of England,* putting the question whether it be lawful to rise against a tyrant, answers that the vulgar judge of it according to the event and the learned according to the purpose of them that do it.[64]

But far before these days, Gildas, the most ancient of all our historians, speaking of those times wherein the Roman Empire, decaying, quitted and relinquished what right they had by conquest to this island and resigned it all into the people's hands, testifies that the people thus re-invested with their own original right, about the year 446, both elected them kings whom they thought best (the first Christian British kings that ever reigned here since the Romans) and by the same right, when they apprehended cause, usually deposed and put them to death. This is the most fundamental and ancient tenure that any king of England can produce or pretend to, in comparison of which all other titles and pleas are but of yesterday. If any object that Gildas condemns the Britons for so doing, the answer is as ready, that he condemns them no more for so doing than he did before for choosing such; for saith he, "They anointed them kings, not of God, but such as were more bloody than the rest."[65] Next he condemns them not at all for deposing or putting them to death, but for doing it over hastily, without trial or well examining the cause, and for electing others worse in their room.

Thus we have here both domestic and most ancient examples that the people of Britain have deposed and put to death their kings in those primitive Christian times. And to couple reason with example, if the Church in all ages, primitive, Romish, or Protestant, held it ever no less their duty than the power of their keys, though without express warrant of scripture, to bring indifferently both king and peasant under the utmost rigor of their canons and censures ecclesiastical, even to the smiting him with a final excommunion, if he persist impenitent; what hinders but that the temporal law both may and ought, though without a special text or precedent, extend with like indifference the civil sword, to the cutting off without exemption him that capitally offends, seeing that justice and religion are from the same God, and works of justice ofttimes more acceptable? Yet because that some lately with the tongues and arguments of malignant backsliders have written that the proceedings now in Parliament against the king are without precedent from any Protestant state or kingdom, the examples which follow shall be all Protestant and chiefly Presbyterian.[66]

63. *Peter Martyr,* or Pietro Martire Vermigli (1499–1562), Augustinian monk turned Reformation theologian. Milton refers to his commentary on Judges, chapter 3.

64. Smith, 1.5.

65. Cp. Habingdon's translation (1638) of the same passage: "Kings were anointed, not as God appointed, but such as in cruelty excelled others" (43).

66. Concluding the portion of his argument devoted to asserting the propriety of bringing tyrants to justice, Milton will now cite Presbyterian authorities to refute the claim that it is wrong to subject a king to lawful judgment.

In the year 1546, The Duke of Saxony, Landgrave of Hessen, and the whole Protestant league raised open war against Charles the Fifth, their emperor, sent him a defiance, renounced all faith and allegiance towards him, and debated long in council whether they should give him so much as the title of Caesar. Sleidan, Bk. 17.[67] Let all men judge what this wanted of deposing or of killing but the power to do it.

In the year 1559, the Scotch Protestants claiming promise of their Queen Regent for liberty of conscience, she answering that promises were not to be claimed of princes beyond what was commodious for them to grant, told her to her face in the Parliament then at Stirling that if it were so they renounced their obedience; and soon after betook them to arms (Buchanan, *Hist.*, Bk. 16).[68] Certainly, when allegiance is renounced, that very hour the king or queen is in effect deposed.

In the year 1564, John Knox, a most famous divine and the reformer of Scotland to the Presbyterian discipline, at a general assembly maintained openly in a dispute against Lethington,[69] the Secretary of State, that subjects might and ought execute God's judgments upon their king; that the fact of Jehu and others against their king, having the ground of God's ordinary command to put such and such offenders to death, was not extraordinary, but to be imitated of all that preferred the honor of God to the affection of flesh and wicked princes; that kings, if they offend, have no privilege to be exempted from the punishments of law more than any other subject: so that if the king be a murderer, adulterer, or idolater, he should suffer, not as a king, but as an offender; and this position he repeats again and again before them. Answerable was the opinion of John Craig, another learned divine, and that laws made by the tyranny of princes or the negligence of people, their posterity might abrogate, and reform all things according to the original institution of commonwealths. And Knox, being commanded by the nobility to write to Calvin and other learned men for their judgment in that question, refused, alleging that both himself was fully resolved in conscience and had heard their judgments and had the same opinion under handwriting of many the most godly and most learned that he knew in Europe, that if he should move the question to them again, what should he do but show his own forgetfulness or inconstancy? All this is far more largely in the *Ecclesiastic History Of Scotland*, Bk. 4,[70] with many other passages to this effect all

67. Milton cites Johann Philippson [Sleidan], *De Statu Religionis et Reipublicae Carolo V Caesare, Commentarii XXV Libris Comprehensi* (Strasburg, 1555).

68. Milton here and in subsequent citations refers to George Buchanan, *Rerum Scoticarum Historia* (Edinburgh, 1582). As sixteenth-century reformers venerated by the Presbyterians, Knox and Buchanan "could not be disowned," though their "radicalism was now likely to embarrass their seventeenth-century descendents" (Dzelzainis, xii).

69. William Maitland of Lethington (1528–73); what follows is an account of the debate between Maitland and Knox, in which Lethington defended Queen Mary's controversial decision to marry Henry Stuart Darnley.

70. John Knox, *History of the Reformation of the Church of Scotland* (London, 1644), which Milton paraphrases, more or less, throughout his account of the debate.

the book over, set out with diligence by Scotchmen of best repute among them at the beginning of these troubles, as if they labored to inform us what we were to do, and what they intended upon the like occasion.

And to let the world know that the whole church and Protestant state of Scotland in those purest times of reformation were of the same belief, three years after, they met in the field, Mary, their lawful and hereditary queen, took her prisoner yielding before fight, kept her in prison, and the same year deposed her. Buchan. *Hist.* Bk. 18.

And four years after that, the Scots, in justification of their deposing Queen Mary, sent ambassadors to Queen Elizabeth, and in a written declaration alleged that they had used toward her more lenity than she deserved; that their ancestors had heretofore punished their kings by death or banishment; that the Scots were a free nation, made king whom they freely chose, and with the same freedom unkinged him if they saw cause, by right of ancient laws and ceremonies yet remaining, and old customs yet among the Highlanders in choosing the head of their clans, or families; all which, with many other arguments, bore witness that regal power was nothing else but a mutual covenant or stipulation between king and people. Buch. *Hist.*, Bk. 20. These were Scotchmen and Presbyterians: but what measure then have they lately offered to think such liberty less beseeming us than themselves, presuming to put him upon us for a master whom their law scarce allows to be their own equal? If now then we hear them in another strain than heretofore in the purest times of their church, we may be confident it is the voice of faction speaking in them, not of truth and reformation. [Which no less in England than in Scotland, by the mouths of those faithful witnesses commonly called puritans and non-conformists, spake as clearly for the putting down, yea, the utmost punishing of kings, as in their several treatises may be read even from the first reign of Elizabeth to these times. Insomuch that one of them, whose name was Gibson,[71] foretold King James he should be rooted out and conclude his race if he persisted to uphold bishops. And that very inscription stamped upon the first coins at his coronation, a naked sword in a hand with these words, *Si mereor in me*, "Against me, if I deserve," not only manifested the judgment of that State, but seemed also to presage the sentence of divine justice in this event upon his son.[72]]

In the year 1581, the states of Holland in a general assembly at the Hague abjured all obedience and subjection to Philip, king of Spain, and in a declaration justify their so doing, for that by his tyrannous government, against faith so many times given and broken, he had lost his right to all the Belgic provinces; that therefore they deposed him and declared it lawful to choose another in his stead. Thuan. Bk. 74.[73] From that time to this, no state or kingdom in the world

71. James Gibson reportedly warned James in 1586 that he would share the fate of Jeroboam if he upheld bishops (Dzelzainis 25).

72. **his son:** Charles I.

73. Jacques-Auguste de Thou [Thuanus], *History of His Own Times* [*Historiarum sui Temporis*] (Geneva, 1620).

hath equally prospered. But let them remember not to look with an evil and prejudicial eye upon their neighbors walking by the same rule.[74]

But what need these examples to Presbyterians, I mean to those who now of late would seem so much to abhor deposing, whenas they to all Christendom have given the latest and the liveliest example of doing it themselves. I question not the lawfulness of raising war against a tyrant in defense of religion or civil liberty, for no Protestant church from the first Waldenses of Lyons and Languedoc[75] to this day but have done it round and maintained it lawful. But this I doubt not to affirm, that the Presbyterians, who now so much condemn deposing, were the men themselves that deposed the king, and cannot with all their shifting and relapsing wash off the guiltiness from their own hands. For they themselves by these their late doings have made it guiltiness and turned their own warrantable actions into rebellion. There is nothing that so actually makes a king of England as rightful possession and supremacy "in all causes both civil and ecclesiastical," and nothing that so actually makes a subject of England as those two oaths of allegiance and supremacy "observed without equivocating or any mental reservation."[76] Out of doubt then, when the king shall command things already constituted in church or state, obedience is the true essence of a subject, either to do, if it be lawful, or, if he hold the thing unlawful, to submit to that penalty which the law imposes, so long as he intends to remain a subject. Therefore when the people or any part of them shall rise against the king and his authority, executing the law in any thing established, civil or ecclesiastical, I do not say it is rebellion, if the thing commanded though established be unlawful, and that they sought first all due means of redress (and no man is further bound to law). But I say it is an absolute renouncing both of supremacy and allegiance, which in one word is an actual and total deposing of the king and the setting up of another supreme authority over them.

And whether the Presbyterians have not done all this and much more, they will not put me, I suppose, to reckon up a seven years' story fresh in the memory of all men. Have they not utterly broke the oath of allegiance, rejecting the king's command and authority sent them from any part of the kingdom whether in things lawful or unlawful? Have they not abjured the oath of supremacy by setting up the Parliament without the king, supreme to all their obedience, and though their vow and Covenant bound them in general to the Parliament, yet sometimes adhering to the lesser part of Lords and Commons

74. Having listed Presbyterian authorities who refuted the claim that monarchy was above the law, Milton moves to conclude his argument with persuasive force.

75. Milton's source of information about the Waldensians, a sect founded in the twelfth century by Peter Waldo of Lyons, was Pierre Gilles, *Histoire Ecclesiastique des Eglises Reformees* [*Ecclesiastical History of the Reformed Churches*] (Geneva, 1644). Cp. *Sonnet 18.* **Languedoc:** region of south-central France.

76. Milton quotes from "An act for the better discovering and repressing of popish recusants" (1606), drafted by James I. The Oaths of Supremacy and Allegiance acknowledging the supremacy of the king were originally instituted by Henry VIII for the detection and suppression of closet Catholicism.

that remained faithful, as they term it, and even of them, one while to the Commons without the Lords, another while to the Lords without the Commons? Have they not still declared their meaning, whatever their oath were, to hold them only for supreme whom they found at any time most yielding to what they petitioned? Both these oaths which were the straightest bond of an English subject in reference to the king, being thus broke and made void, it follows undeniably that the king from that time was by them in fact absolutely deposed, and they no longer in reality to be thought his subjects, notwithstanding their fine clause in the Covenant to preserve his person, crown, and dignity,[77] set there by some dodging casuist with more craft than sincerity to mitigate the matter in case of ill success and not taken, I suppose, by any honest man, but as a condition subordinate to every the least particle that might more concern religion, liberty, or the public peace.

To prove it yet more plainly that they are the men who have deposed the king, I thus argue. We know that king and subject are relatives, and relatives have no longer being than in the relation. The relation between king and subject can be no other than regal authority and subjection. Hence I infer, past their defending, that if the subject, who is one relative, take away the relation, of force he takes away also the other relative.[78] But the Presbyterians who were one relative, that is to say subjects, have for this seven years taken away the relation, that is to say the king's authority and their subjection to it. Therefore the Presbyterians for these seven years have removed and extinguished the other relative, that is to say the king, or to speak more in brief have deposed him; not only by depriving him the execution of his authority, but by conferring it upon others.

If then their oaths of subjection broken, new supremacy obeyed, new oaths and covenants taken, notwithstanding frivolous evasions, have in plain terms unkinged the king, much more than hath their seven years war not deposed him only, but outlawed him and defied him as an alien, a rebel to law, and enemy to the state—it must needs be clear to any man not averse from reason, that hostility and subjection are two direct and positive contraries, and can no more in one subject stand together in respect of the same king, than one person at the same time can be in two remote places. Against whom therefore the subject is in act of hostility, we may be confident that to him he is in no subjection; and in whom hostility takes place of subjection, for they can by no means consist together, to him the king can be not only no king, but an enemy.

So that from hence we shall not need dispute whether they have deposed him, or what they have defaulted towards him as no king, but show manifestly how much they have done toward the killing him. Have they not levied all these

77. See note 15.

78. Milton's position on relation differs from Satan's in *PR* (4.518–19): "The son of God I also am or was, / And if I was, I am; relation stands."

wars against him whether offensive or defensive (for defense in war equally offends, and most prudently beforehand)[79] and given commission to slay where they knew his person could not be exempt from danger? And if chance or flight had not saved him, how often had they killed him, directing their artillery without blame or prohibition to the very place where they saw him stand? Have they not [sequestered him, judged or unjudged, and] converted his revenue to other uses, detaining from him [as a grand delinquent] all means of livelihood, so that for them long since he might have perished or have starved? Have they not hunted and pursued him round about the kingdom with sword and fire? Have they not formerly denied to treat with him,[80] and their now recanting ministers preached against him as a reprobate incurable, an enemy to God and his church, marked for destruction, and therefore not to be treated with? Have they not besieged him and to their power forbidden him water and fire, save what they shot against him to the hazard of his life? Yet while they thus assaulted and endangered it with hostile deeds, they swore in words to defend it with his crown and dignity; not in order, as it seems now, to a firm and lasting peace or to his repentance after all this blood, but simply, without regard, without remorse, or any comparable value of all the miseries and calamities suffered by the poor people, or to suffer hereafter through his obstinacy or impenitence.

No understanding man can be ignorant that covenants are ever made according to the present state of persons and of things, and have ever the more general laws of nature and of reason included in them, though not expressed. If I make a voluntary covenant as with a man to do him good, and he prove afterward a monster to me, I should conceive a disobligement. If I covenant not to hurt an enemy, in favor of him and forbearance and hope of his amendment, and he after that shall do me tenfold injury and mischief to what he had done when I so covenanted and still be plotting what may tend to my destruction, I question not but that his after actions release me; nor know I covenant so sacred that withholds me from demanding justice on him.

Howbeit, had not their distrust in a good cause and the fast and loose of our prevaricating divines overswayed, it had been doubtless better not to have inserted in a covenant unnecessary obligations and words not works of a supererogating[81] allegiance to their enemy; no way advantageous to themselves had the king prevailed, as to their cost many would have felt, but full of snare and distraction to our friends; useful only, as we now find, to our adversaries, who under such a latitude and shelter of ambiguous interpretation have ever since been plotting and contriving new opportunities to trouble all again. How

79. The Presbyterians in Parliament had insisted that their campaign against Charles had been defensive. See note 89.

80. In January 1648, frustrated by the king's maneuvering, Parliament passed a resolution of "No More Addresses." By September, it reversed itself under political pressure and resumed negotiations. See note 86.

81. **supererogating:** beyond what is required or expected.

much better had it been and more becoming an undaunted virtue, to have declared openly and boldly whom and what power the people were to hold supreme; as on the like occasion Protestants have done before, and many conscientious men now in these times have more than once besought the Parliament to do, that they might go on upon a sure foundation and not with a riddling Covenant in their mouths, seeming to swear counter, almost in the same breath, allegiance and no allegiance; which doubtless had drawn off all the minds of sincere men from siding with them had they not discerned their actions far more deposing him than their words upholding him; which words made now the subject of cavillous[82] interpretations, stood ever in the Covenant, by judgment of the more discerning sort, an evidence of their fear, not of their fidelity.

What should I return to speak on, of those attempts for which the king himself hath often charged the Presbyterians of seeking his life, whenas in the due estimation of things they might without a fallacy be said to have done the deed outright? Who knows not that the king is a name of dignity and office, not of person? Who therefore kills a king, must kill him while he is a king. Then they certainly who by deposing him have long since taken from him the life of a king, his office, and his dignity, they in the truest sense may be said to have killed the king, nor only by their deposing and waging war against him (which besides the danger to his personal life, set him in the farthest opposite point from any vital function of a king) but by their holding him in prison, vanquished and yielded into their absolute and despotic power, which brought him to the lowest degradement and incapacity of the regal name.[83] I say not by whose matchless valor[84] next under God, lest the story of their ingratitude thereupon carry me from the purpose in hand, which is to convince them that they, which I repeat again, were the men who in the truest sense killed the king, not only as is proved before, but by depressing him their king far below the rank of a subject to the condition of a captive, without intention to restore him (as the Chancellor of Scotland[85] in a speech told him plainly at Newcastle) unless he granted fully all their demands, which they knew he never meant. Nor did they treat or think of treating with him, till their hatred to the army that delivered them, not their love or duty to the king, joined them secretly with men sentenced so oft for reprobates in their own mouths, by whose subtle inspiring they grew mad upon a most tardy and improper treaty.[86] Whereas if the whole bent of their actions had not been against the king himself, but [only] against

82. **cavillous:** hairsplitting. Milton's references here and elsewhere to equivocation in relation to regicide evoke Shakespeare's *Macbeth* (Foran).

83. In May 1646, Charles I surrendered to the Scots, who a year later released him to agents for Parliament, then controlled by Presbyterians.

84. Presumably Cromwell and the New Model Army.

85. In 1646, John Campbell, Earl of Loudon and Scottish Chancellor, negotiated with Charles, then confined at Newcastle-on-Tyne.

86. Negotiations for the Treaty of Newport took place between Parliamentary representatives and the king in 1648, from September to November, while Charles was held on the Isle of Wight. See note 80.

his evil counselors, as they feigned and published, wherefore did they not restore him all that while to the true life of a king, his office, crown, and dignity, when he was in their power and they themselves his nearest counselors. The truth, therefore, is both that they would not, and that indeed they could not without their own certain destruction, having reduced him to such a final pass as was the very death and burial of all in him that was regal, and from whence never king of England yet revived, but by the new reinforcement of his own party, which was a kind of resurrection to him.

Thus having quite extinguished all that could be in him of a king, and from a total privation clad him over, like another specifical thing,[87] with forms and habitudes destructive to the former, they left in his person, dead as to law and all the civil right either of king or subject, the life only of a prisoner, a captive, and a malefactor. Whom the equal and impartial hand of justice finding, was no more to spare than another ordinary man; not only made obnoxious[88] to the doom of law by a charge more than once drawn up against him and his own confession to the first article at Newport,[89] but summoned and arraigned in the sight of God and his people, cursed and devoted to perdition worse than any Ahab, or Antiochus,[90] with exhortation to curse all those in the name of God that made not war against him, as bitterly as Meroz was to be cursed that went not out against a Canaanitish king,[91] almost in all the sermons, prayers, and fulminations that have been uttered this seven years by those cloven tongues of falsehood and dissention, who now, to the stirring up of new discord, acquit him; and against their own discipline, which they boast to be the throne and scepter of Christ, absolve him, unconfound him—though unconverted, unrepentant, unsensible of all their precious saints and martyrs whose blood they have so oft laid upon his head. And now again with a new sovereign anointment can wash it all off, as if it were as vile and no more to be reckoned for than the blood of so many dogs in a time of pestilence, giving the most opprobrious lie to all the acted zeal that for these many years hath filled their bellies and fed

87. **specifical thing:** i.e., a different species or kind of thing. The terminology used in this sentence—*privation, specifical, forms, habitudes*—is scholastic. Milton claims that Charles has been deprived of the essence of kingship and all that remains of the former king is a prisoner devoid of his previous identity.

88. **obnoxious:** liable or subject.

89. "Whereas both Houses of the Parliament of England have been necessitated to undertake a war in their just and lawful defense." So read the preamble to the articles presented to Charles at Newport (see note 86). Charles agreed to it provisionally, on the condition that all other issues were completely settled.

90. **Ahab:** king of Israel (c. 869–850 B.C.E.) condemned by the prophet Elijah for permitting his wife's idolatry and the murder of Naboth for his vineyard (1 Kings 16–22). **Antiochus:** a Greek who ruled over the Jews (175–64 B.C.E.) and strove to wipe out their religion. A heroic resistance eventually defeated him and restored the Hebrew religion. Cp. the apocryphal book 1 Maccabees. Presbyterian preachers had once compared Charles to both Ahab and Antiochus.

91. The Song of Deborah says that Meroz's inhabitants are cursed "because they came not to the help of the Lord against the mighty" (Judg. 5.23), specifically Jabin the Canaanite king.

them fat upon the foolish people. Ministers of sedition, not of the gospel, who, while they saw it manifestly tend to civil war and bloodshed, never ceased exasperating the people against him; and now that they see it likely to breed new commotion, cease not to incite others against the people that have saved them from him, as if sedition were their only aim, whether against him or for him.

But God, as we have cause to trust, will put other thoughts into the people and turn them from giving ear or heed to these mercenary noisemakers of whose fury and false prophecies we have enough experience, and from the murmurs of new discord will incline them to hearken rather with erected minds to the voice of our supreme magistracy, calling us to liberty and the flourishing deeds of a reformed commonwealth; with this hope, that as God was heretofore angry with the Jews who rejected him and his form of government to choose a king,[92] so that he will bless us and be propitious to us who reject a king to make him only our leader and supreme governor, in the conformity, as near as may be, of his own ancient government; if we have at least but so much worth in us to entertain the sense of our future happiness, and the courage to receive what God vouchsafes us wherein we have the honor to precede other nations who are now laboring to be our followers.

For as to this question in hand what the people by their just right may do in change of government or of governor, we see it cleared sufficiently, besides other ample authority, even from the mouths of princes themselves. And surely they that shall boast, as we do, to be a free nation, and not have in themselves the power to remove or to abolish any governor supreme or subordinate, with the government itself upon urgent causes, may please their fancy with a ridiculous and painted freedom, fit to cozen babies; but are indeed under tyranny and servitude, as wanting that power which is the root and source of all liberty, to dispose and economize[93] in the land which God hath given them, as masters of family in their own house and free inheritance. Without which natural and essential power of a free nation, though bearing high their heads, they can in due esteem be thought no better than slaves and vassals born, in the tenure and occupation of another inheriting lord, whose government, though not illegal, or intolerable, hangs over them as a lordly scourge, not as a free government, and therefore to be abrogated.

How much more justly then may they fling off tyranny or tyrants, who being once deposed can be no more than private men, as subject to the reach of justice and arraignment as any other transgressors. And certainly if men, not to speak of heathen, both wise and religious, have done justice upon tyrants what way they could soonest, how much more mild and humane then is it, to give them fair and open trial? To teach lawless kings, and all who so much adore them, that not mortal man, or his imperious will, but justice is the only true

92. 1 Sam. 8.

93. **economize:** to act as the governor of a household (*OED,* citing this passage as the sole example).

sovereign and supreme majesty upon earth? Let men cease therefore out of faction and hypocrisy to make outcries and horrid things of things so just and honorable.

[Though perhaps till now no Protestant state or kingdom can be alleged to have openly put to death their king, which lately some have written and imputed to their great glory, much mistaking the matter: it is not, neither ought to be, the glory of a Protestant state never to have put their king to death; it is the glory of a Protestant king never to have deserved death.][94] And if the Parliament and Military Council do what they do without precedent, if it appear their duty, it argues the more wisdom, virtue, and magnanimity, that they know themselves able to be a precedent to others, who perhaps in future ages, if they prove not too degenerate, will look up with honor and aspire toward these exemplary and matchless deeds of their ancestors, as to the highest top of their civil glory and emulation. Which, heretofore, in the pursuance of fame and foreign dominion, spent itself vaingloriously abroad, but henceforth may learn a better fortitude—to dare execute highest justice on them that shall by force of arms endeavor the oppressing and bereaving of religion and their liberty at home, that no unbridled potentate or tyrant, but to his sorrow, for the future may presume such high and irresponsible license over mankind, to havoc and turn upside-down whole kingdoms of men as though they were no more in respect of his perverse will than a nation of pismires.[95]

As for the party called Presbyterian, of whom I believe very many to be good and faithful Christians though misled by some of turbulent spirit, I wish them earnestly and calmly not to fall off from their first principles nor to affect rigor and superiority over men not under them; not to compel unforcible things, in religion especially, which, if not voluntary, becomes a sin; nor to assist the clamor and malicious drifts of men whom they themselves have judged to be the worst of men, the obdurate enemies of God and his church: nor to dart against the actions of their brethren, for want of other argument, those wrested laws and scriptures thrown by prelates and malignants against their own sides, which though they hurt not otherwise, yet taken up by them to the condemnation of their own doings, give scandal to all men and discover[96] in themselves either extreme passion or apostasy. Let them not oppose their best friends and associates, who molest them not at all, infringe not the least of their liberties (unless they call it their liberty to bind other men's consciences), but are still seeking to live at peace with them and brotherly accord. Let them beware an old and perfect enemy, who, though he hope by sowing discord to make them his instruments, yet cannot forbear a minute the open threatening of his destined revenge upon them, when they have served his purposes. Let them fear therefore, if they be wise, rather what they have done already, than what re-

94. Dzelzainis sees in this passage a possible reference to Salmasius's *Defensio Regia*.
95. **pismires:** ants.
96. **discover:** reveal.

mains to do, and be warned in time they put no confidence in princes whom they have provoked, lest they be added to the examples of those that miserably have tasted the event.

Stories[97] can inform them how Christiern the Second, king of Denmark, not much above a hundred years past, driven out by his subjects and received again upon new oaths and conditions, broke through them all to his most bloody revenge, slaying his chief opposers when he saw his time, both them and their children invited to a feast for that purpose. How Maximilian dealt with those of Bruges,[98] though by mediation of the German princes reconciled to them by solemn and public writings drawn and sealed. How the massacre at Paris[99] was the effect of that credulous peace which the French Protestants made with Charles the Ninth, their king. And that the main visible cause which to this day hath saved the Netherlands from utter ruin was their final not believing the perfidious cruelty which, as a constant maxim of state, hath been used by the Spanish kings on their subjects that have taken arms and after trusted them, as no later age but can testify, heretofore in Belgia[100] itself and this very year in Naples.[101] And to conclude with one past exception though far more ancient, David[, whose sanctified prudence might be alone sufficient, not to warrant us only but to instruct us,] when once he had taken arms never after that trusted Saul, though with tears and much relenting he twice promised not to hurt him. These instances, few of many, might admonish them both English and Scotch not to let their own ends and the driving on of a faction betray them blindly into the snare of those enemies whose revenge looks on them as the men who first begun, fomented, and carried on, beyond the cure of any sound or safe accommodation, all the evil which hath since unavoidably befallen them and their king.

I have something also to the divines, though brief to what were needful; not to be disturbers of the civil affairs, being in hands better able and more belonging to manage them; but to study harder and to attend the office of good pastors, knowing that he whose flock is least among them hath a dreadful charge, not performed by mounting twice into the chair[102] with a formal preachment huddled up at the odd hours of a whole lazy week, but by incessant pains and watching, "in season and out of season," "from house to house" over the souls of whom they have to feed.[103] Which if they ever well considered, how little leisure would they find to be the most pragmatical sidesmen[104] of every popular

97. **Stories:** histories. Dzelzainis notes that most of the examples listed in this paragraph appear in de Thou, *History of His Own Times* 3.423–24. See note 73.

98. Maximilian I, Holy Roman emperor, cruelly put down an uprising by inhabitants of the city of Bruges in 1490.

99. The 1572 slaughter of Huguenots on St. Bartholomew's Eve.

100. **Belgia:** the Netherlands.

101. Despite a formal pledge not to, the Spaniards crushed a Neapolitan revolt in 1648.

102. **chair:** pulpit.

103. Milton quotes 2 Tim. 4.2 and Acts 20:20.

104. **sidesmen:** officious partisans.

tumult and sedition? And all this while are[105] to learn what the true end and reason is of the gospel which they teach, and what a world it differs from the censorious and supercilious lording over conscience. It would be good also they lived so as might persuade the people they hated covetousness, which, worse than heresy, is idolatry; hated pluralities and all kind of simony; left rambling from benefice to benefice like ravenous wolves seeking where they may devour the biggest. Of which if some well and warmly seated from the beginning be not guilty, 'twere good they held not conversation with such as are. Let them be sorry that being called to assemble about reforming the church, they fell to progging[106] and soliciting the Parliament, though they had renounced the name of priests, for a new settling of their tithes and oblations, and double lined[107] themselves with spiritual places of commodity beyond the possible discharge of their duty. Let them assemble in consistory with their elders and deacons, according to ancient ecclesiastical rule, to the preserving of church discipline, each in his several charge, and not a pack of clergymen by themselves to belly-cheer[108] in their presumptuous Sion, or to promote designs, abuse and gull the simple laity, and stir up tumult, as the prelates did, for the maintenance of their pride and avarice.

These things if they observe and wait with patience, no doubt but all things will go well without their importunities or exclamations; and the printed letters which they send subscribed with the ostentation of great characters and little moment[109] would be more considerable than now they are. But if they be the ministers of Mammon instead of Christ and scandalize his church with the filthy love of gain—aspiring also to sit the closest and the heaviest of all tyrants upon the conscience—and fall notoriously into the same sins whereof so lately and so loud they accused the prelates, as God rooted out those [wicked ones] immediately before, so will he root out them their imitators; and, to vindicate his own glory and religion, will uncover their hypocrisy to the open world and visit upon their own heads that "Curse ye Meroz," the very motto of their pulpits, wherewith so frequently, not as Meroz but more like atheists, they have blasphemed the vengeance of God and [traduced] the zeal of his people. [And that they be not what they go for, true ministers of the Protestant doctrine, taught by those abroad, famous and religious men who first reformed the church, or by those no less zealous who withstood corruption and the bishops here at home, branded with the name of Puritans and Nonconformists, we shall abound with testimonies to make appear: that men may yet more fully know the difference between Protestant divines and these pulpit-firebrands.

105. **are:** have yet.

106. **progging:** prodding.

107. **double lined:** crammed or stuffed.

108. **belly-cheer:** feast luxuriously, in this case at Sion College, the seat of the Presbyterian provincial assembly.

109. Milton contrasts the abundance of capital letters and poverty of substance in books published by Presbyterian divines.

LUTHER.

Lib. contra Rusticos apud Sleidan.[110] *Bk. 5.*

Is est hodie rerum status, &c.[111] "Such is the state of things at this day, that men neither can, nor will, nor indeed ought to endure longer the domination of you princes."[112]

Neque vero Cæsarem, &c. "Neither is Cæsar to make war as head of Christendom, Protector of the Church, Defender of the Faith; these titles being false and windy, and most kings being the greatest enemies to religion." *Liber de bello contra Turcas apud Sleid.* Bk 14.[113] What hinders then, but that we may dispose or punish them?

These also are recited by Cochlæus[114] in his *Miscellanies* to be the words of Luther, or some other eminent divine then in Germany, when the Protestants there entered into solemn covenant at Smalcaldia. *Ut ore ijs obturem &c.* "That I may stop their mouths, the Pope and Emperor are not born but elected, and may also be deposed as hath bin often done." If Luther, or whoever else thought so, he could not stay there; for the right of birth or succession can be no privilege in nature to let a tyrant sit irremovable over a nation free born, without transforming that nation from the nature and condition of men born free into natural, hereditary, and successive slaves. Therefore he saith further: "To displace and throw down this exactor, this Phalaris,[115] this Nero, is a work well pleasing to God." Namely, for being such a one, which is a moral reason. Shall then so slight a consideration as his hap to be not elective simply but by birth, which was a mere accident, overthrow that which is moral, and make unpleasing to God that which otherwise had so well pleased him? Certainly not, for if the matter be rightly argued, election much rather than chance binds a man to content himself with what he suffers by his own bad election. Though indeed neither the one nor other binds any man, much less any people, to a necessary sufferance of those wrongs and evils which they have ability and strength enough given them to remove.

110. Milton includes in his *Commonplace Book* many extracts from Johannes Sleidan's *Commentaries on the State of Religion under Charles V* (555), where he found accounts of Reformers' assertion of religious and political rights against princes.

111. In the following list of quotations from Reformed authors, Latin phrases are the beginnings of passages immediately translated by Milton.

112. In Book 5, "Against the Peasants," Sleidan presents Luther as critical both of peasants' crimes against their landlords and injustices born by peasants.

113. From Book 14, "Against the Turks."

114. Milton draws the two quotations below from Johannes Dobneck, known as *Cochlæus,* a Catholic polemicist and court chaplain to Duke George of Saxony, who painted Luther as an anarchist in his *Miscellaneorum Libri Primi Tractatus Quartus* (1545); the quotations below, taken from pp. 49^{v} and 49^{r}, ascribe to Luther attacks on impious authority and a denial of rulers' rights to tax subjects.

115. **Phalaris:** tyrant of Agrigentum (570–554 BCE), remembered for roasting enemies inside a bronze bull.

Zwinglius.[116] *Vol. 1. articul. 42.*

Quando vero perfidè, &c. "When Kings reign perfidiously and against the rule of Christ, they may according to the word of God be deposed."

Mihi ergo compertum non est, &c. "I know not how it comes to pass that kings reign by succession, unless it be with consent of the whole people. *Ibid.*

Quum vero consensu, &c. "But when by suffrage and consent of the whole people, or the better part of them, a tyrant is deposed or put to death, God is the chief leader in that action." *Ibid.*

Nunc cum tam tepidi sumus, &c. "Now that we are so lukewarm in upholding public justice, we endure the vices of tyrants to reign nowadays with impunity; justly therefore by them we are trod underfoot, and shall at length with them be punished. Yet ways are not wanting by which tyrants may be removed, but there wants public justice." *Ibid.*

Cavete vobis ô tyranni. "Beware ye tyrants, for now the Gospel of Jesus Christ spreading far and wide will renew the lives of many to love innocence and justice; which if ye also shall do, ye shall be honored. But if ye shall go on to rage and do violence, ye shall be trampled on by all men." *Ibid.*

Romanum imperium imò quodq; &c. "When the Roman Empire or any other shall begin to oppress religion, and we negligently suffer it, we are as much guilty of religion so violated as the oppressors themselves. *Idem Epist. ad Conrad. Somium.*

Calvin[117] *on Daniel. chap. 4. verse. 25.*

Hodie Monarchae semper in suis titulis, &c. "Nowadays monarchs pretend always in their titles to be kings by the grace of God: but how many of them to this end only pretend it, that they may reign without control? For to what purpose is the grace of God mentioned in the title of kings, but that they may acknowledge no superior? In the meanwhile God, whose name they use to support themselves, they willingly would tread under their feet. It is therefore a mere cheat when they boast to reign by the grace of God.

Abdicant se terreni principes, &c. "Earthly princes depose themselves while they rise against God, yea they are unworthy to be numbered among men; rather it behooves us to spit upon their heads than to obey them." *On Daniel,* chap. 6. verse 22.

116. **Huldrich Zwingli,** a Swiss Reformer, argued for congregational government of the church and republican government in Switzerland. Milton takes the first five of six Zwingli passages from Article 42 of *Opus Articulorum sive Conclusionum Huldrichi Zwingli,* in *Opera D. Huldrychi Zwinglii,* 4 vols. (Zurich, 1545), 1:84^{r}–85^{r}; the sixth passage is taken from his letter to Conrado Somio and Simperto Memmingensi, in *Opera* 8:493.

117. Whatever his thoughts on Milton's argument would have been, **John Calvin** does attack the pride of monarchs in his *Prælectiones in Librum Prophetiarum Danielis* (Geneva, 1551); the quotations below appear on pp. 60, 91.

Bucer[118] *on Matthew, chap. 5.*

Si princeps superior, &c. "If a sovereign prince endeavor by arms to defend transgressors, to subvert those things which are taught in the word of God, they who are in authority under him ought first to dissuade him; if they prevail not, and that he now bears himself not as a prince but as an enemy, and seeks to violate privileges and rights granted to inferior magistrates or commonalities, it is the part of pious magistrates, imploring first the assistance of God, rather to try all ways and means than to betray the flock of Christ to such an enemy of God. For they also are to this end ordained, that they may defend the people of God and maintain those things which are good and just. For to have supreme power lessens not the evil committed by that power, but makes it the less tolerable, by how much the more generally hurtful. Then certainly the less tolerable, the more unpardonably to be punished.

Of Peter Martyr we have spoke before.

Paraeus[119] *in*[120] *Romans 13.*

Quorum est constituere magistratus, &c. "They whose part it is to set up magistrates may restrain them also from outrageous deeds, or pull them down; but all magistrates are set up either by parliament, or by electors, or by other magistrates; they therefore who exalted them may lawfully degrade and punish them."

Of the Scotch divines I need not mention others than the famousest among them, Knox, and his fellow laborers in the reformation of Scotland whose large treatises on this subject defend the same opinion. To cite them sufficiently were to insert their whole books, written purposely on this argument. Knox' *Appeal*[121] and *To the Reader,* where he promises in a postscript that the book which he intended to set forth, called *The Second Blast of the Trumpet,* should maintain more at large that the same men most justly may depose and punish him whom unadvisedly they have elected, notwithstanding birth, succession, or any oath of

118. **Martin Bucer** was Luther's friend, an important early Reformer, and author of *De Regno Christi* (1550), part of which Milton had translated as *The Judgment of Martin Bucer on Divorce* (1644). The passage that Milton quotes below can be found in Bucer's commentary on the four evangelists, *In Sacra Quatuor Evangelia, Ennarationes* (Basel, 1536), p. 145.

119. **David Paraeus,** professor at Heidelberg, was author of an important Calvinist commentary on Romans. The passage below can be found in his *In Divinam ad Romanos Epistolam Commentarius* (Geneva, 1617), p. 1064. As Hughes notes, Paraeus was attacked in David Owen's 1642 royalist treatise *Anti-Paraeus,* or, *A Treatise in the efence of the Royal Right of Kings.*

120. I.e., on.

121. Milton refers to **John Knox**'s *The appellation of Iohn Knoxe from the cruell and most iniust sentence pronounced against him by the false bishoppes and clergie of Scotland* (Geneva, 1558) and his *To the Reader,* bound in the same volume.

allegiance. Among our own divines, Cartwright[122] and Fenner,[123] two of the learnedest, may in reason satisfy us what was held by the rest. Fenner in his book of *Theology* maintaining that "they who have power, that is to say a parliament, may either by fair means or by force depose a tyrant," whom he defines to be him that willfully breaks all, or the principal, conditions made between him and the commonwealth. Fenner *Sacra Theologia,* chap. 13 (and Cartwright in a prefixed epistle testifies his approbation of the whole book).

Gilby,[124] *de Obedientia. pp. 25 and 105.*

"Kings have their authority of the people, who may upon occasion reassume it to themselves."

England's Complaint against the Canons.

"The people may kill wicked princes as monsters and cruel beasts."

Christopher Goodman,[125] *Of Obedience.*

"When kings or rulers become blasphemers of God, oppressors and murderers of their subjects, they ought no more to be accounted kings or lawful magistrates, but as private men to be examined, accused, condemned, and punished by the law of God, and being convicted and punished by that law, it is not man's but God's doing" (chap. 10, p. 139).

"By the civil laws a fool or idiot born, and so proved, shall lose the lands and inheritance whereto he is born, because he is not able to use them aright. And especially ought in no case be suffered to have the government of a whole nation; but there is no such evil can come to the commonwealth by fools and idiots as doth by the rage and fury of ungodly rulers. Such therefore being without God ought to have no authority over God's people, who by his word requireth the contrary" (chap. 11, pp. 143, 144).

"No person is exempt by any law of God from this punishment; be he king, queen, or emperor, he must die the death, for God hath not placed them above others to transgress his laws as they list, but to be subject to them as well as others, and if they be subject to his laws, then to the punishment also, so much the more as their example is more dangerous" (chap. 13, p. 184).

122. **Thomas Cartwright,** one of the founders of English Presbyterianism, was Lady Margaret Professor of Divinity at Cambridge, and author of the 1572 *Admonition to Parliament.*

123. **Dudley Fenner** was Cartwright's associate and successor as pastor of the English church in Middelburg in the Netherlands. Milton draws the passage below from the *Sacra Theologia, sive Veritas quae est secundum Pietatem* (1585), p. 186, where Fenner cites 2 Kings 11:4–7 in support of his position.

124. Milton, following Sir Thomas Aston's *A Remonstrance, against Presbitery* (1641), misattributes the following two passages from John Ponet's 1556 *A shorte treatise of politike pouuer and of the true obedience which subiectes owe to kynges and other ciuile gouernours* to **Anthony Gilby,** Ponet's fellow Marian exile, and to *England's Complaint to Jesus Christ against the Bishops Canons* (1640), as Sonia Miller has shown ("Two References in Milton's *Tenure of Kings,*" *JEGP* 50 [1951]: 320–25).

125. **Christopher Goodman,** who lost his Oxford chair in divinity for his religious views, was co-pastor with John Knox of Geneva's English congregation. Milton quotes below, with some variations, from the indicated chapters and pages of Goodman's *How superior powers oght to be obeyd of their subiects and wherin they may lawfully by Gods Worde be disobeyed and resisted* (Geneva, 1558).

"When magistrates cease to do their duty, the people are as it were without magistrates, yea worse, and then God giveth the sword into the people's hand, and he himself is become immediately their head" (p. 185).

"If princes do right and keep promise with you, then do you owe to them all humble obedience. If not, ye are discharged, and your study ought to be in this case how ye may depose and punish according to the law such rebels against God and oppressors of their country" (p. 190).

This Goodman was a minister of the English Church at Geneva, as Dudley Fenner was at Middleburrough [i.e., Middleburg, the Netherlands], or some other place in that country. These were the pastors of those saints and confessors who, flying from the bloody persecution of Queen Mary, gathered up at length their scattered members into many congregations; whereof some in upper, some in lower Germany, part of them settled at Geneva, where this author, having preached on this subject to the great liking of certain learned and godly men who heard him, was by them sundry times & with much instance required to write more fully on that point. Who thereupon took it in hand, and conferring with the best learned in those parts (among whom Calvin was then living in the same city) with their special approbation he published this treatise, aiming principally, as is testified by Whittingham[126] in the preface, that his brethren of England, the Protestants, might be persuaded in the truth of that doctrine concerning obedience to magistrates (Whittingham in Prefat.).

These were the true Protestant divines of England, our fathers in the faith we hold. This was their sense, who for so many years laboring under prelacy, through all storms and persecutions kept religion from extinguishing and delivered it pure to us till there arose a covetous and ambitious generation of divines (for divines they call themselves) who, feigning on a sudden to be new converts and proselytes from episcopacy, under which they had long temporized, opened their mouths at length, in show against pluralities and prelacy, but with intent to swallow them down both; gorging themselves like harpies on those simonious places and preferments of their outed[127] predecessors, as the quarry for which they hunted, not to plurality only but to multiplicity; for possessing which they had accused them their brethren, and aspiring under another title to the same authority and usurpation over the consciences of all men.

Of this faction, diverse reverend and learned divines (as they are styled in the phylactery[128] of their own title page) pleading the lawfulness of defensive arms against this king in a treatise called *Scripture and Reason,* seem in words to

126. **William Whittingham,** like Ponet and Goodman a Marian exile, wrote a preface to Goodman's *Superior Powers,* upon which Milton draws in this paragraph.

127. **harpies:** mythical monsters, rapacious plunderers; **simonious:** tainted by the practice of using religion for profit; **outed:** expelled.

128. **phylactery:** See *Tetrachordon,* note 11.

disclaim utterly the deposing of a king.[129] But both the scripture and the reasons which they use draw consequences after them which, without their bidding, conclude it lawful. For if by scripture, and by that especially to the Romans,[130] which they most insist upon, kings, doing that which is contrary to St. Paul's definition of a magistrate, may be resisted, they may altogether with as much force of consequence be deposed or punished. And if by reason the unjust authority of kings "may be forfeited in part, and his power be reassumed in part, either by the parliament or people, for the case in hazard and the present necessity," as they affirm, p. 34, there can no scripture be alleged, no imaginable reason given that necessity continuing—as it may always, and they in all prudence and their duty may take upon them to foresee it—why in such a case they may not finally amerce him with the loss of his kingdom, of whose amendment they have no hope. And if one wicked action persisted in against religion, laws, and liberties may warrant us to thus much in part, why may not forty times as many tyrannies by him committed warrant us to proceed on restraining him till the restraint become total? For the ways of justice are exactest proportion. If for one trespass of a king it require so much remedy or satisfaction, then for twenty more as heinous crimes, it requires of him twenty-fold, and so proportionably, till it come to what is utmost among men. If in these proceedings against their king they may not finish by the usual course of justice what they have begun, they could not lawfully begin at all. For this golden rule of justice and morality as well as of arithmetic, out of three terms which they admit, will as certainly and unavoidably bring out the fourth, as any problem that ever Euclid or Apollonius made good by demonstration.[131]

And if the Parliament, being undeposable but by themselves, as is affirmed, (pp. 37, 38), might for his whole life, if they saw cause, take all power, authority, and the sword out of his hand, which in effect is to unmagistrate him, why might they not, being then themselves the sole magistrates in force, proceed to punish him who being lawfully deprived of all things that define a magistrate, can be now no magistrate to be degraded lower but an offender to be punished? Lastly, whom they may defy and meet in battle, why may they not as well prosecute by justice? For lawful war is but the execution of justice against them who refuse law. Among whom if it be lawful, as they deny not (pp. 19, 20), to slay the king himself coming in front at his own peril, wherefore may not justice do that intendedly, which the chance of a defensive war might without blame have done casually, nay, purposely, if there it find him among the rest. They ask (p. 19), "By what rule of conscience or God a state is bound to sacrifice religion,

129. Herbert Palmer, *Scripture and Reason Pleaded for Defensive Arms* (London, 1643). Milton cites this text by page number later in the paragraph.

130. Rom. 13.1–2.

131. In arithmetic, *golden rule* refers to a method of finding an unknown number from three given numbers, where the first is in the same proportion to the second as the third is to the unknown fourth. Milton repeatedly presents the mathematical golden rule as an expression of proportion analogous to the golden rule of morality and justice. Cp. *Areop*, p. 204. *Euclid* (328–283 B.C.E.) and *Apollonius* of Perga (262?–190 B.C.E.) were pioneers in geometry.

laws, and liberties, rather than a prince, defending such as subvert them, should come in hazard of his life." And I ask by what conscience, or divinity, or law, or reason, a state is bound to leave all these sacred concernments under a perpetual hazard and extremity of danger, rather than cut off a wicked prince, who sits plotting day and night to subvert them.

They tell us that the law of nature justifies any man to defend himself, even against the king in person. Let them show us then why the same law may not justify much more a state or whole people to do justice upon him against whom each private man may lawfully defend himself; seeing all kind of justice done is a defense to good men, as well as a punishment to bad, and justice done upon a tyrant is no more but the necessary self-defense of a whole commonwealth. To war upon a king that his instruments may be brought to condign[132] punishment and thereafter to punish them the instruments, and not to spare only but to defend and honor him the author, is the strangest piece of justice to be called Christian, and the strangest piece of reason to be called human, that by men of reverence and learning, as their style imports them, ever yet was vented. They maintain in the third and fourth section[133] that a judge or inferior magistrate is anointed of God, is his minister, hath the sword in his hand, is to be obeyed by St. Peter's rule[134] as well as the supreme and without difference anywhere expressed: and yet will have us fight against the supreme till he remove and punish the inferior magistrate (for such were greatest delinquents) when as by scripture and by reason there can no more authority be shown to resist the one than the other; and altogether as much, to punish or depose the supreme himself, as to make war upon him till he punish or deliver up his inferior magistrates, whom in the same terms we are commanded to obey and not to resist.

Thus while they, in a cautious line or two here and there stuffed in, are only verbal against the pulling down or punishing of tyrants, all the scripture and the reason which they bring is in every leaf direct and rational to infer it altogether as lawful as to resist them. And yet in all their sermons, as hath by others been well noted, they went much further. For divines, if ye observe them, have their postures and their motions no less expertly and with no less variety than they that practice feats in the artillery-ground. Sometimes they seem furiously to march on, and presently march counter. By and by they stand, and then retreat, or if need be can face about, or wheel in a whole body with that cunning and dexterity as is almost unperceivable, to wind themselves by shifting ground into places of more advantage. And "Providence" only must be the drum, "Providence" the word of command that calls them from above, but always to some larger benefice, or acts[135] them into such or such figures and promotions. At their turns and doublings no men readier, to the right, or to the

132. **condign:** well deserved, completely appropriate.

133. Palmer, *Scripture and Reason*, 33–37.

134. 1 Pet. 2.13–14.

135. **acts:** impels, moves to action.

left; for it is their turns which they serve chiefly; herein only singular, that with them there is no certain hand right or left, but as their own commodity[136] thinks best to call it. But if there come a truth to be defended which to them and their interest of this world seems not so profitable, straight these nimble motionists can find no even legs to stand upon and are no more of use to reformation thoroughly performed and not superficially, or to the advancement of Truth (which among mortal men is always in her progress),[137] than if on a sudden they were struck maim and crippled. Which the better to conceal, or the more to countenance by a general conformity to their own limping, they would have scripture, they would have reason also, made to halt with them for company, and would put us off with impotent conclusions, lame and shorter than the premises.[138]

In this posture they seem to stand with great zeal and confidence on the wall of Sion, but like Jebusites, not like Israelites or Levites. Blind also as well as lame, they discern not David from Adonibezek,[139] but cry him up for the Lord's anointed whose thumbs and great toes not long before they had cut off upon their pulpit cushions. Therefore he who is our only King, the Root of David, and whose Kingdom is eternal righteousness, with all those that war under him, whose happiness and final hopes are laid up in that only just and rightful Kingdom (which we pray incessantly may come soon, and in so praying wish hasty ruin and destruction to all tyrants), even he our immortal King and all that love him, must of necessity have in abomination these blind and lame defenders of Jerusalem, as the soul of David hated them, and forbid them entrance into God's house and his own.[140] But as to those before them which I cited first (and with an easy search, for many more might be added), as they there stand, without more in number, being the best and chief of Protestant divines, we may follow them for faithful guides and without doubting may receive them as witnesses abundant of what we here affirm concerning tyrants. And indeed I find it generally the clear and positive determination of them all (not prelatical, or of this late faction subprelatical) who have written on this argument, that to do justice on a lawless king is to a private man unlawful, to an inferior magistrate lawful.[141] Or if they were divided in opinion, yet greater than these here alleged, or of more authority in the church, there can be none produced.

136. **commodity:** advantage, profit.

137. **progress:** onward march, journey.

138. Like Shakespeare before him (cp. *OTH* 2.1.161), Milton may have had in mind Quintilian, whose *Institutes of Oratory* were a staple of English schools: "The conclusions of clauses sometimes seem to halt or hang" (9.4.70).

139. **Adonibezek:** Lord of Bezek, leader of the Canaanite tribe known in scripture as the Jebusites; they inhabited Jerusalem before its conquest by David. After his defeat, the Israelites cut off his thumbs and big toes, the punishment he had inflicted on his prisoners. See Judg. 1.5–7.

140. See 2 Sam. 5.6–8.

141. Dzelzainis finds this conclusion, based on the second edition's citations from the greatest reformers, to be a departure from Milton's effort in the first edition to undermine the distinction between private citizen and public official. That is, Milton's original, more radical, and even anarchic position was that any individual citizen has the inalienable right to remove a tyrant from power.

If anyone shall go about by bringing other testimonies to disable these, or by bringing these against themselves in other cited passages of their books, he will not only fail to make good that false and impudent assertion of those mutinous ministers—that the deposing and punishing of a king or tyrant "is against the constant judgment of all Protestant divines" (it being quite the contrary),[142] but will prove rather what perhaps he intended not, that the judgment of divines, if it be so various and inconstant to itself, is not considerable or to be esteemed at all. Ere which be yielded, as I hope it never will, these ignorant asserters in their own art will have proved themselves more and more not to be Protestant divines (whose constant judgment in this point they have so audaciously belied) but rather to be a pack of hungry church-wolves, who in the steps of Simon Magus[143] their father, following the hot scent of double livings and pluralities, advowsons, donatives, inductions, and augmentations (though uncalled to the flock of Christ but by the mere suggestion of their bellies, like those priests of Bel, whose pranks Daniel found out),[144] have got possession or rather seized upon the pulpit as the stronghold and fortress of their sedition and rebellion against the civil magistrate. Whose friendly and victorious hand having rescued them from the bishops, their insulting lords, fed them plenteously, both in public and in private, raised them to be high and rich of poor and base, only suffered not their covetousness and fierce ambition (which as the pit that sent out their fellow locusts hath been ever bottomless and boundless)[145] to interpose in all things, and over all persons, their impetuous ignorance and importunity.]

142. Milton's quotation condenses a passage in Palmer, *Scripture and Reason*, 11.

143. Simon the magician (*Magus*) was rebuked by Peter for attempting to traffic in spiritual power (Acts 8). The offense of simony derives from his name.

144. **advowsons:** rights to appoint clergy to an endowed position; **donatives:** endowed positions that patrons can present on their own authority; **inductions:** formal introductions of clergymen to church offices and incomes; **augmentations:** increases in clerical stipends obtained through legal action. In the apocryphal *Bel and the Dragon*, Daniel exposes corrupt priests who hoard sacrifices that worshipers intended for their gods.

145. Rev. 9.1–3 describes "smoke like the smoke of a great furnace" rising from the "bottomless pit." Out of the smoke come locusts to torment humanity.

Frontispiece to *Eikon Basilike* (1644), engraving by William Marshall
(cp. Milton's Greek poem *In Effigiei eius sculptor*).

Introduction to Selections from *Eikonoklastes*

Eikonoklastes, published in October 1649, is the first of several works that Milton wrote in his role as Secretary for Foreign Tongues of the interregnum Council of State. The Greek title positions the author as an iconoclast, or "image or idol breaker." Barbara Lewalski observes that among the idols Milton attempts to smash are "rote prayers, liturgical forms, the Solemn League and Covenant, kings, bishops, and the church of Rome" (2000, 270). The main idol, and the immediate occasion of the Council's command, is Charles I's posthumous and wildly popular *Eikon Basilike* (or "image of the king"), which followed hard upon Charles's execution on January 30, 1649, and which boasted an astounding thirty-five editions in English printed in England by the end of the year, not to mention numerous editions in Latin, Dutch, French, and German. In the *Eikon*, Charles presents himself (or rather the ghostwriter John Gauden presents him) as a saint and martyr, roles captured in William Marshall's famous frontispiece (see opposite). This strategy's resounding success, like the shocked response to the public execution, complicated matters for the nascent interregnum government. Turning to Milton, no doubt impressed by the persuasive power of *The Tenure of Kings and Magistrates*, the Council hoped to blunt the force of *Eikon Basilike* and mold public opinion in its favor.

Milton was in the unenviable position of not merely arguing against but impugning the character of a dead man (to say nothing of a martyr). His response, as he writes, is to treat Charles "as in his book alive" (p. 315) Milton labors to replace *Eikon*'s image of the king with his own image of Charles (see Loewenstein 1990), who now appears as a selfish, prevaricating, treasonous tyrant and vassal of Rome. The book's method is point-by-point, chapter-by-chapter refutation of Charles's, or Gauden's, work. The selections included here, the Preface and the peroration (or rhetorically charged conclusion), betray Milton's frustration and sense of injured merit as he observes what he calls "an inconstant, irrational, and image-doting rabble" (p. 320) enchanted and deluded by the display of the king's name and image, turning against the "truth and wisdom" of Milton's party, which is already in danger of becoming, even at the beginning of the interregnum experiment, the "sole remainder" (p. 318) of the faithful. Whatever the later verdict of history, and particularly of literary scholars, *Eikonoklastes* proved no match for the *Eikon Basilike,* seeing only two editions in the author's lifetime.

The text of our selection is based on a copy of the enlarged second edition in the British Library (1507/1350).

Selections from

EIKONOKLASTES

IN ANSWER TO A BOOK ENTITLED *EIKON BASILIKE, THE PORTRAITURE OF HIS SACRED MAJESTY IN HIS SOLITUDES AND SUFFERINGS*

The Preface

To descant on the misfortunes of a person fallen from so high a dignity, who hath also paid his final debt both to nature and his faults, is neither of itself a thing commendable nor the intention of this discourse. Neither was it fond ambition or the vanity to get a name, present or with posterity, by writing against a king: I never was so thirsty after fame nor so destitute of other hopes and means better and more certain to attain it. For kings have gained glorious titles from their favorers by writing against private men, as Henry the Eighth did against Luther,[1] but no man ever gained much honor by writing against a king, as not usually meeting with that force of argument in such courtly antagonists which to convince might add to his reputation. Kings most commonly, though strong in legions, are but weak at arguments; as they who ever have accustomed from the cradle to use their will only as their right hand, their reason always as their left. Whence, unexpectedly constrained to that kind of combat, they prove but weak and puny adversaries. Nevertheless, for their sakes who through custom, simplicity, or want of better teaching have not more seriously considered kings than in the gaudy name of majesty, and admire them and their doings as if they breathed not the same breath with other mortal men, I shall make no scruple to take up (for it seems to be the challenge both of him and all his party) to take up this gauntlet, though a king's, in the behalf of liberty, and the commonwealth.

And further, since it appears manifestly the cunning drift of a factious and defeated party[2] to make the same advantage of his book which they did before

1. Milton refers to Henry's *Assertio Septem Sacramentorum adversus Martinum Lutherum* (1521).

2. Milton refers not only to the Royalists but also to the Presbyterian party, which had earlier opposed Charles but which had late in the 1640s attempted to enter a treaty separately with him to the disadvantage of the Independent party represented by Cromwell's New Model Army. Excluded from the

of his regal name and authority, and intend it not so much the defense of his former actions as the promoting of their own future designs (making thereby the book their own rather than the king's, as the benefit now must be their own more than his), now the third time to corrupt and disorder the minds of weaker men by new suggestions and narrations, either falsely or fallaciously representing the state of things to the dishonor of this present government and the retarding of a general peace (so needful to this afflicted nation and so nigh obtained), I suppose it no injury to the dead, but a good deed rather to the living, if by better information given them or, which is enough, by only remembering them the truth of what they themselves know to be here[3] misaffirmed, they may be kept from entering the third time unadvisedly into war and bloodshed. For as to any moment[4] of solidity in the book itself, save only that a king is said to be the author, a name than which there needs no more among the blockish vulgar to make it wise, and excellent, and admired, nay to set it next the Bible, though otherwise containing little else but the common grounds of tyranny and popery dressed up, the better to deceive, in a new Protestant guise, and trimly garnished over, or as to any need of answering, in respect of staid and well-principled men, I take it on me as a work assigned rather than by me chosen or affected,[5] which was the cause both of beginning it so late, and finishing it so leisurely in the midst of other employments and diversions.

And though well it might have seemed in vain to write at all, considering the envy and almost infinite prejudice likely to be stirred up among the common sort against whatever can be written or gainsaid to the king's book, so advantageous to a book it is only to be a king's, and though it be an irksome labor to write with industry and judicious pains that which, neither weighed nor well read, shall be judged without industry or the pains of well-judging by faction and the easy literature of custom and opinion, it shall be ventured yet, and the truth not smothered but sent abroad in the native confidence of her single self, to earn, how she can, her entertainment in the world, and to find out her own readers; few perhaps, but those few of such[6] value and substantial worth, as truth and wisdom, not respecting numbers and big names, have been ever wont in all ages to be contented with.

And if the late king had thought sufficient those answers and defenses made

---

Long Parliament in Pride's Purge of December 1648, the Presbyterian party denounced the execution of the king. In *The Tenure of Kings and Magistrates,* Milton warns the Presbyterians that their rediscovered allegiance to Charles will do them no good.

3. **here:** in Charles's *Eikon Basilike.*

4. **moment:** particle.

5. In the *Second Defense* (p. 348), Milton will claim that he was assigned the task of writing *Eikonoklastes*: "Not long afterwards there appeared a book attributed to the king, and plainly written with great malice against Parliament. Bidden to reply to this, I opposed to the *Eikon* the *Eikonoklastes,* not, as I am falsely charged, 'insulting the departed spirit of the king,' but thinking that Queen Truth should be preferred to King Charles."

6. **of such:** Although the 1650 edition prints "such of," the phrase has in our copy text been transposed by hand to read "of such," an emendation we have adopted.

for him in his lifetime, they who on the other side accused his evil government, judging that on their behalf enough also hath been replied, the heat of this controversy was in likelihood drawing to an end; and the further mention of his deeds, not so much unfortunate as faulty, had in tenderness to his late sufferings been willingly forborne, and perhaps for the present age might have slept with him unrepeated, while his adversaries, calmed and assuaged with the success of their cause, had been the less unfavorable to his memory. But since he himself, making new appeal to truth and the world, hath left behind him this book as the best advocate and interpreter of his own actions, and that his friends by publishing, dispersing, commending, and almost adoring it, seem to place therein the chief strength and nerves of their cause, it would argue doubtless in the other party great deficience and distrust of themselves not to meet the force of his reason in any field whatsoever, the force and equipage of whose arms they have so often met victoriously. And he who at the bar stood excepting against the form and manner of his judicature and complained that he was not heard,[7] neither he nor his friends shall have that cause now to find fault, being met and debated with in this open and monumental court of his own erecting; and not only heard uttering his whole mind at large, but answered—which to do effectually, if it be necessary that to his book nothing the more respect be had for being his, they of his own party can have no just reason to exclaim.

For it were too unreasonable that he, because dead, should have the liberty in his book to speak all evil of the Parliament; and they, because living, should be expected to have less freedom, or any for them, to speak home the plain truth of a full and pertinent reply. As he, to acquit himself, hath not spared his adversaries to load them with all sorts of blame and accusation, so to him, as in his book alive, there will be used no more courtship than he uses; but what is properly his own guilt, not imputed any more to his evil counselors (a ceremony used longer by the Parliament than he himself desired)[8] shall be laid here without circumlocutions at his own door. That they who from the first beginning or but now of late, by what unhappiness I know not, are so much affatuated[9] not with his person only but with his palpable faults, and dote upon his deformities, may have none to blame but their own folly if they live and die in such a strucken blindness, as next to that of Sodom[10] hath not happened to any sort of men more gross or more misleading. Yet neither let his enemies expect to find recorded here all that hath been whispered in the court or alleged openly of the king's bad actions, it being the proper scope of this work in hand

7. During his trial, Charles repeatedly denied the authority of his Parliamentary judges and claimed that a king was not subject to any earthly court.

8. In Chapter 15, not included in this edition, Milton quotes Charles's rejection in *Eikon Basilike* of the conventional pretense that opposition to a king's policies is opposition not to the king but to evil counselors.

9. **affatuated:** infatuated.

10. Destroyed with fire after failing to reform in response to repeated warnings (Gen. 19.24), *Sodom* was a common figure for spiritual blindness.

not to rip up and relate the misdoings of his whole life, but to answer only and refute the missayings of his book.

First, then, that some men (whether this were by him intended, or by his friends) have by policy accomplished after death that revenge upon their enemies which in life they were not able, hath been oft related. And among other examples we find that the last will of Caesar being read to the people, and what bounteous legacies he had bequeathed them, wrought more in that vulgar audience to the avenging of his death than all the art he could ever use to win their favor in his lifetime.[11] And how much their intent who published these over-late apologies and meditations of the dead king, drives to the same end of stirring up the people to bring him that honor, that affection, and by consequence that revenge to his dead corpse which he himself living could never gain to his person, it appears both by the conceited portraiture before his book,[12] drawn out to the full measure of a masking scene[13] and set there to catch fools and silly gazers, and by those Latin words after the end, *"Vota dabunt quæ bella negarunt,"* intimating that "what he could not compass by war, he should achieve by his meditations." For in words which admit of various sense the liberty is ours to choose that interpretation which may best mind us of what our restless enemies endeavor and what we are timely to prevent.

And here may be well observed the loose and negligent curiosity of those who took upon them to adorn the setting out of this book. For though the picture set in front would martyr him and saint him to befool the people, yet the Latin motto in the end, which they understand not, leaves him as it were a politic contriver to bring about that interest by fair and plausible words which the force of arms denied him. But quaint emblems and devices, begged from the old pageantry of some Twelfth-night's entertainment at Whitehall,[14] will do but ill to make a saint or martyr. And if the people resolve to take him sainted at the rate of such a canonizing, I shall suspect their calendar more than the Gregorian.[15] In one thing I must commend his openness who gave the title to this book, Εικὼν Βασιλικὴ, that is to say, *The King's Image;* and by the shrine

11. See Suetonius's *Lives of the Caesars* 83, for Caesar's generosity even to those who would murder him, an episode dramatized in Shakespeare's *Julius Caesar,* in which Mark Antony states that Caesar's will would lead the Romans to "go kiss dead Caesar's wounds" (3.2.140).

12. Milton refers here, and at the beginning of the next paragraph, to *Eikon Basilike*'s elaborate frontispiece, which depicts Charles as a saint and martyr at prayer (p. 308).

13. **masking scene:** a tableau in a mask, or masque, an elaborate courtly entertainment typically celebrating the royal family as guarantors of universal order. Milton's own masques, *Arcades* and especially *A Masque Presented at Ludlow Castle,* stayed at arm's length from the usual ideology of the genre. In the body of his work, Milton accuses Charles of being a mere poet, one who trades in fiction: "I begun to think that the whole Book might perhaps be intended a peece of Poetrie. The words are good, the fiction smooth and cleanly; there wanted only Rime" (Yale 3:406).

14. Entertainments customarily marked the end of the Christmas season at court; Shakespeare's *Twelfth Night* is an example.

15. The *Gregorian* calendar, proclaimed by Pope Gregory XIII in 1582 and the standard today, was suspect in part because of its Roman Catholic association; England would continue to use the Julian calendar until 1752.

he dresses out for him certainly would have the people come and worship him. For which reason this answer also is entitled *Eikonoklastes*, the famous surname of many Greek emperors who, in their zeal to the command of God, after long tradition of idolatry in the church, took courage and broke all superstitious images to pieces.[16]

But the people, exorbitant and excessive in all their motions, are prone ofttimes not to a religious only, but to a civil kind of idolatry in idolizing their kings, though never more mistaken in the object of their worship; heretofore being wont to repute for saints those faithful and courageous barons who lost their lives in the field making glorious war against tyrants for the common liberty: as Simon de Montfort, Earl of Leicester, against Henry the Third; Thomas Plantagenet, Earl of Lancaster, against Edward the Second.[17] But now, with a besotted and degenerate baseness of spirit, except some few who yet retain in them the old English fortitude and love of freedom and have testified it by their matchless deeds, the rest, imbastardized from the ancient nobleness of their ancestors, are ready to fall flat and give adoration to the image and memory of this man, who hath offered at more cunning fetches to undermine our liberties, and put tyranny into an art, than any British king before him. Which low dejection and debasement of mind in the people, I must confess, I cannot willingly ascribe to the natural disposition of an Englishman, but rather to two other causes. First, to the prelates and their fellow-teachers, though of another name and sect,[18] whose pulpit stuff, both first and last, hath been the doctrine and perpetual infusion of servility and wretchedness to all their hearers; whose lives the type of worldliness and hypocrisy, without the least true pattern of virtue, righteousness, or self-denial in their whole practice. I attribute it next to the factious inclination of most men divided from the public by several ends and humors of their own.

At first no man less beloved, no man more generally condemned, than was the king; from the time that it became his custom to break Parliaments at home and either willfully or weakly to betray Protestants abroad, to the beginning of these combustions. All men inveighed against him; all men except court-vassals opposed him and his tyrannical proceedings; the cry was universal; and this full Parliament was at first unanimous in their dislike and protestation against his evil government. But when they who sought themselves and not the public began to doubt that all of them could not by one and the same way attain to

16. The name had been given to Leo III, who in 726 outlawed the use of images and image worship, in opposition to Pope Gregory II.

17. Polemicists during the Civil War replayed the thirteenth-century struggle between Simon de Montfort, Earl of Leicester, and Henry the Third. Royalists, such as Edward Chamberlayne in his *The Present War Parallel'd. Or, a briefe Relation of the five yeares Civil Warres of Henry the Third* (1647), painted Montfort and the barons as traitors. Parliamentary polemicists, such as George Walker in his *Anglo-Tyrannus, Represented in the parallel Reignes of Henry the Third and Charles King of England* (1650), portrayed the same figures as defenders of liberty.

18. Another shot at the Presbyterians (see note 2), branded by association with the Laudian high church party.

their ambitious purposes, then was the king, or his name at least, as a fit property, first made use of, his doings made the best of, and by degrees justified. Which begot him such a party as, after many wiles and strugglings with his inward fears, emboldened him at length to set up his standard against the Parliament. Whenas before that time all his adherents, consisting most of dissolute swordmen and suburb roisterers, hardly amounted to the making up of one ragged regiment strong enough to assault the unarmed House of Commons. After which attempt, seconded by a tedious and bloody war on his subjects, wherein he hath so far exceeded those his arbitrary violences in time of peace, they who before hated him for his high misgovernment, nay, fought against him with displayed banners in the field, now applaud him and extol him for the wisest and most religious prince that lived. By so strange a method amongst the mad multitude is a sudden reputation won, of wisdom by willfulness and subtle shifts, of goodness by multiplying evil, of piety by endeavoring to root out true religion.

But it is evident that the chief of his adherents never loved him, never honored either him or his cause, but as they took him to set a face upon their own malignant designs; nor bemoan his loss at all, but the loss of their own aspiring hopes, like those captive women whom the poet notes in his *Iliad* to have bewailed the death of Patroclus in outward show, but indeed their own condition:

Πάτροκλον πρόφασιν, σφῶν δ'αὐτων κήδε' ἑκάστη.

Hom[er] *Iliad* 19.[302][19]

And it needs must be ridiculous to any judgment unenthralled, that they who in other matters express so little fear either of God or man should in this one particular outstrip all precisianism[20] with their scruples and cases and fill men's ears continually with the noise of their conscientious loyalty and allegiance to the king, rebels in the meanwhile to God in all their actions beside; much less that they whose professed loyalty and allegiance led them to direct arms against the king's person and thought him nothing violated by the sword of hostility drawn by them against him, should now in earnest think him violated by the unsparing sword of justice,[21] which undoubtedly so much the less in vain she bears among men, by how much greater and in highest place the offender. Else justice, whether moral or political, were not justice, but a false counterfeit of that impartial and godlike virtue. The only grief is that the head was not struck off to the best advantage and commodity of them that held it by

19. Milton quotes the narrator's comment, following Briseis's grief-stricken speech in Book 19, that she and her companions bewailed "Patroclus' fortunes in pretext, but in sad truth their own" (George Chapman's translation).

20. **precisianism:** a derogatory term for Puritanism.

21. Here, as in the *Tenure,* Milton ridicules Presbyterians for protesting the trial of Charles after they had taken up arms against him.

the hair—an ingrateful and perverse generation,[22] who having first cried to God to be delivered from their king, now murmur against God that heard their prayers, and cry as loud for their king against those that delivered them.

But as to the author of these soliloquies, whether it were undoubtedly the late king, as is vulgarly believed, or any secret coadjutor (and some stick not to name him),[23] it can add nothing, nor shall take from the weight, if any be, of reason which he brings. But allegations, not reasons, are the main contents of this book, and need no more than other contrary allegations to lay the question before all men in an even balance; though it were supposed that the testimony of one man in his own cause affirming, could be of any moment to bring in doubt the authority of a Parliament denying. But if these his fair-spoken words shall be here fairly confronted and laid parallel to his own far differing deeds, manifest and visible to the whole nation, then surely we may look on them who notwithstanding shall persist to give to bare words more credit than to open deeds, as men whose judgment was not rationally evinced and persuaded, but fatally stupefied and bewitched into such a blind and obstinate belief. For whose cure it may be doubted, not whether any charm, though never so wisely murmured, but whether any prayer can be available.

This however would be remembered and well noted, that while the king, instead of that repentance which was in reason and in conscience to be expected from him, without which we could not lawfully readmit him, persists here to maintain and justify the most apparent of his evil doings, and washes over with a court-fucus[24] the worst and foulest of his actions, disables and uncreates the Parliament itself, with all our laws and native liberties that ask not his leave, dishonors and attaints all Protestant churches not prelatical,[25] and what they piously reformed, with the slander of rebellion, sacrilege, and hypocrisy. They who seemed of late to stand up hottest for the Covenant,[26] can now sit mute and much pleased to hear all these opprobrious things uttered against their faith, their freedom, and themselves in their own doings made traitors to boot. The divines also, their wizards, can be so brazen as to cry "hosanna" to this his book,

22. Cp. Matt. 17.17.

23. John Gauden was Charles's ghostwriter and *secret coadjutor*; he was to be rewarded with the bishoprics of Exeter and Worcester.

24. **fucus:** a liquid cosmetic.

25. In the *Tenure*, Milton praises the nonprelatical churches (i.e., churches without bishops) of the continent for resisting tyranny and labels his backsliding Presbyterian contemporaries "subprelatical."

26. In 1643 the Scots and the English Parliament entered into the Solemn League and Covenant, agreeing to reform religion in England and Ireland on the Presbyterian model. Though motivated by shared opposition to Charles's attempts to impose episcopal church government on Scotland, the covenanters pledged to preserve not only "the Rights and Priviledges of the Parliament" but also "the Kings Majesties Person and Authority." After the Presbyterians' political influence was eclipsed by the Independents under Oliver Cromwell, they attempted to negotiate with the defeated king to advance their agenda. Although they had once fought against him, now they emphasized the clause concerning the preservation of the king's person.

which cries louder against them for no disciples of Christ, but of Iscariot;[27] and to seem now convinced with these withered arguments and reasons here, the same which in some other writings of that party and in his own former declarations and expresses,[28] they have so often heretofore endeavored to confute and to explode—none appearing all this while to vindicate church or state from these calumnies and reproaches but a small handful of men whom they defame and spit at with all the odious names of schism and sectarism. I never knew that time in England when men of truest religion were not counted sectaries.[29] But wisdom now, valor, justice, constancy, prudence—united and embodied to defend religion and our liberties both by word and deed against tyranny—is counted schism and faction.

Thus in a graceless age things of highest praise and imitation under a right name, to make them infamous and hateful to the people, are miscalled. Certainly, if ignorance and perverseness will needs be national and universal, then they who adhere to wisdom and to truth are not therefore to be blamed for being so few as to seem a sect or faction. But in my opinion it goes not ill with that people where these virtues grow so numerous and well joined together as to resist and make head against the rage and torrent of that boisterous folly and superstition that possesses and hurries on the vulgar sort. This therefore we may conclude to be a high honor done us from God and a special mark of his favor, whom he hath selected as the sole remainder,[30] after all these changes and commotions, to stand upright and steadfast in his cause, dignified with the defense of truth and public liberty; while others, who aspired to be the top of zealots[31] and had almost brought religion to a kind of trading monopoly, have not only by their late silence and neutrality belied their profession, but foundered themselves and their consciences to comply with enemies in that wicked cause and interest which they have too often cursed in others, to prosper now in the same themselves.

[*In twenty-eight long chapters, Milton answers the* Eikon Basilike *point for point, ridiculing Charles's pretensions to piety and love for his subjects. The selection here is the peroration that concludes Chapter 28 and the book. Quotation marks indicate passages from the* Eikon Basilike.]

27. The followers of Judas *Iscariot* are traitors.
28. **expresses:** royal communications less formal than *declarations.*
29. From the mid-1640s, Milton was increasingly sympathetic to the sects. Cp. Abdiel's defiant vaunt to Satan at the beginning of the War in Heaven: "My sect thou seest, now learn too late / How few sometimes may know, when thousands err" (*PL* 6.147–48).
30. Milton compares those remaining faithful to Parliament with the faithful "remnant" of Israel (Isa. 11.16).
31. Milton's use of the term *zealots* alludes to the faction of Jews who betrayed the chief priest during the siege of Titus in 70 C.E. (Josephus, *Wars of the Jews*).

He[32] would fain bring us out of conceit with the good "success" which God hath vouchsafed us. We measure not our cause by our success, but our success by our cause. Yet certainly in a good cause success is a good confirmation, for God hath promised it to good men almost in every leaf of scripture.[33] If it argue not for us, we are sure it argues not against us; but as much or more for us than ill success argues for them, for to the wicked God hath denounced ill success in all that they take in hand.[34]

He hopes much of those "softer tempers," as he calls them, and "less advantaged by his ruin, that their consciences do already" gripe them. 'Tis true, there be a sort of moody, hot-brained, and always unedified consciences, apt to engage their leaders into great and dangerous affairs past retirement, and then, upon a sudden qualm and swimming of their conscience, to betray them basely in the midst of what was chiefly undertaken for their sakes. Let such men never meet with any faithful Parliament to hazard for them; never with any noble spirit to conduct and lead them out; but let them live and die in servile condition and their scrupulous queasiness, if no instruction will confirm them. Others there be in whose consciences the loss of gain and those advantages they hoped for hath sprung a sudden leak. These are they that cry out the Covenant broken,[35] and to keep it better slide back into neutrality or join actually with incendiaries and malignants.[36] But God hath eminently begun to punish those, first in Scotland,[37] then in Ulster,[38] who have provoked him with the most hateful kind of mockery to break his Covenant under pretense of strictest keeping it; and hath subjected them to those malignants with whom they scrupled not to be associates. In God therefore we shall not fear what their false fraternity can do against us.

He seeks again with cunning words to turn our success into our sin, but might call to mind that the scripture speaks of those also who, "when God slew them, then sought him," yet did but "flatter him with their mouth, and lied to him with their tongues; for their heart was not right with him."[39] And there was one, who in the time of his affliction trespassed more against God: "This was that King Ahaz."[40]

32. **He:** Charles.

33. See, e.g., Ps. 1.1–3.

34. Ps. 1.6: "The way of the ungodly shall perish."

35. The London Presbyterian clergy had appealed against Parliament on January 24, 1649, to the "Covenant-keeping Citizens," and on February 24 the Scottish Commissioners in London had declared that they "detested the execution of the late King" and had charged Parliament with "breach of the Solemn League and Covenant" (Hughes's note).

36. **malignants:** Royalists.

37. A reference to the defeat of the Marquis of Montrose, Charles II's supporter, in April 1650.

38. The *Ulster* Scots, from Milton's perspective, shared in the August 1649 defeat of the Duke of Ormond by Parliamentary forces. Ormond had attempted to establish Charles II's authority in Ireland.

39. Milton here paraphrases Ps. 78.34–37, in response to Charles's invoking of Ps. 5.9: "For there is no faithfulness in their mouth; . . . they flatter with their tongue").

40. 2 Chron. 28.22.

He glories much in the forgiveness of his enemies. So did his grandmother at her death.[41] Wise men would sooner have believed him had he not so often told us so. But he hopes to erect "the trophies of his charity over us." And trophies of charity no doubt will be as "glorious" as trumpets before the alms of hypocrites, and more especially the trophies of such an aspiring charity as offers in his prayer to share victory with God's "compassion," which is over all his works. Such prayers as these may haply catch the people, as was intended. But how they please God is to be much doubted, though prayed in secret, much less written to be divulged. Which perhaps may gain him after death a short, contemptible, and soon fading reward; not what he aims at, to stir the constancy and solid firmness of any wise man or to unsettle the conscience of any knowing Christian (if he could ever aim at a thing so hopeless and above the genius of his "cleric" elocution),[42] but to catch the worthless approbation of an inconstant, irrational, and image-doting rabble; that like a credulous and hapless herd, begotten to servility and enchanted with these popular institutes of tyranny (subscribed with a new device of the king's picture at his prayers),[43] hold out both their ears with such delight and ravishment to be stigmatized and bored through in witness of their own voluntary and beloved baseness. The rest, whom perhaps ignorance without malice, or some error less than fatal, hath for the time misled, on this side sorcery or obduration, may find the grace and good guidance to bethink themselves and recover.

41. Like her grandson, Mary Queen of Scots had denied the jurisdiction of the court that tried her. Before her execution in 1587, she prayed for Elizabeth and her other enemies.

42. Milton surmised correctly that the *Eikon Basilike* was ghostwritten by a cleric (see n. 23).

43. Another reference to the frontispiece of Charles as a martyr at prayer.

Introduction to Selections from *Second Defense of the English People*

Milton was ordered by the Council of State to compose two major works of controversy before the *Second Defense.* In September 1649 came *Eikonoklastes* ("The Image Breaker"), aimed at discrediting *Eikon Basilike* (The King's Image), which appeared about a week after the execution of King Charles, its putative author, on January 30, 1649. Charles's maudlin self-portrait as a saintly martyr succeeded better with the home audience than Milton's fierce if factually accurate exposure of the late king's ill doing. Not only did the royal image remain unbroken but, by telling hard truths about the dead king, Milton incurred centuries of Royalist abuse—for having "bespatter[ed] the white robes of [Charles's] spotless life . . . with the dirty filth of his satirical pen" (G.S., *Epistle Dedicatory*).

Milton's second major effort on behalf of the Commonwealth was better received. *A Defense of the English People* appeared in February 1651, little more than a year after *A Defense of Kingship,* a massive tome by the renowned French scholar Claude de Saumaise. Writing in Latin for an elite European audience, Saumaise (Salmasius, his Latin pen name) ponderously asserted the divine right of kings and the odious impiety of regicide. Milton, relatively unknown, efficiently rebutted his charges and, mixing invective with argument in a manner reminiscent of Cicero's *Philippics,* attacked his opponent's integrity and mocked his manhood. "All Europe took part in the paper-war of these two great men," Isaac D'Israeli observed, adding that Milton "perfectly massacred Salmasius" (237).

More than three years separated Milton's first two major secretarial efforts from the *Second Defense of the English People,* which came out in May 1654. The attack it answered, *The Cry of the Royal Blood to Heaven, against the English Parricides* (hereafter, *The Cry*), was published in the summer of 1652 by Adriaan Vlacq, who also signed the prefatory epistle dedicating the book to Charles II. Although Milton was made aware of the fresh attack and asked to rebut it, he could not have read it himself, since earlier that year his blindness had become total. Compounding that trauma, his wife and fifteen-month-old son died in quick succession over the next few months. Under these circumstances it would have been surprising had Milton managed to produce a third major polemical work more quickly than he did. Yet he offers no personal excuses for the delay, claiming instead that it was owing to the promise of a renewed assault by the infuriated giant Salmasius: "I thought it better to wait, so that I might keep my strength intact for the more formidable adversary." A smarting Salmasius seemed a worthier opponent than the reputed author of *The Cry*, that "fornicating priest" Alexander More (Parker 1968, 1:423).

Published anonymously, as Salmasius's *Defense of Kingship* had been, *The Cry* was attributed to More soon after its publication. His authorship was confirmed in 1653 and early 1654 by usually reliable government spies and by Milton's own continental correspondents (Parker 2:1026, n. 54). Yet it was Peter Du Moulin, an Anglican divine residing in Oxford, who composed *The Cry* and sent it to Salmasius to use as he saw fit. Though not the author, More was Salmasius's protégé and an intimate of his household. The mistaken attribution occurred because it was More, at Salmasius's behest, who saw to its publication. After penning the dedication and lacing it with threats of Salmasius's imminent revenge, More delivered the manuscript to Vlacq, arranging for the printer to take responsibility for the dedication. Ironically, that last dodge was easily ferreted out (the merely mercenary Vlacq had no reason to keep silent) and led to the misidentification of More as author of the entire work. Only after Milton had completed the *Second Defense* was he informed of the error and entreated not to publish his work. He refused and has long been blamed for stubbornness and unjustified cruelty to More. Yet it is difficult to sympathize with More, or to wish Milton's chastisement undone, given More's sniping dedication and servile instrumentality in publishing *The Cry*.

We also find it difficult to blame Milton for wishing to publish the entire work, complete with its attacks on the man who arranged for its publication and wrote but would not sign its dedication. As it happens, More in Latin is *Morus*, which also means "mulberry tree" and "fool," and invites puns with other near homonyms. Milton took full advantage. The rumors that had More seducing and impregnating Salmasius's serving girl (also fortunately named) were true, as had been those concerning Salmasius's domineering wife, which Milton exploited in the *First Defense*. Although not known for his sense of humor, as a satirist Milton could be wickedly funny, never more brilliantly than in this tract. Some may deem the humor low and obscene, but it is nonetheless marvelously inventive.

Still, there is more to the *Second Defense* than More, and he could have been left out had Milton wished. Indeed, because most of the virtuoso wit is lost in translation, the excerpts printed here largely omit Milton's rapid-fire slaps at More. Balancing the invective and sexual innuendo are noble panegyrics on Cromwell, Fairfax, Overton, Fleetwood, and Bradshaw, among others, which we have included for their abiding historical interest. The people Milton chooses to praise and the reasons for which he praises them have often been understood as a submerged petition to Cromwell, now Lord Protector, to protect freedom of conscience and reconcile with those who opposed his recent assumption of kinglike power. Robert Fallon has skeptically and we think properly questioned the claim that these laudatory portraits amount to a Miltonic critique of Cromwell. Yet readers have long recognized that worries about the future direction of the commonwealth haunt the panegyrics of this nonetheless undoubted loyalist "ready to place high hopes in Cromwell's semi-royal government" (Norbrook 18).

Overall, as with other of his tracts advocating political liberty (e.g., *Areopagitica, Tenure of Kings and Magistrates*), the *Second Defense* takes the form of a classical oration, a genre that, as Milton well knew, originated and flourished in free states, precisely in the face of threats to their liberty. It is Demosthenes of Athens and Cicero of "free Rome" that he emulates (*PL* 9.671), but through the power of print he imagines himself addressing not the citizens of Athens or the Roman Senate but "virtually all of Europe," indeed, "the entire assembly and council of all the most influential men, cities, and nations everywhere." David Loewenstein has suggested that the *Second Defense* "succeeds brilliantly" in its effective merger of "personal drama with its epic vision of history" (1990, 171). Yet this merger, however successful, left Milton open to the criticism that he was following the precedent of Charles in establishing an exaggerated, self-serving image of his own virtue (S. Fallon 2002, 119). Isolated by blindness and deaths in his immediate family, Milton may well have compensated by exaggerating the significance of his accomplishment. His accounts of his triumph over Salmasius, in both *Second Defense* and *Sonnet 22*, clearly reveal that he took solace in the reputation he had won as a champion of liberty. Also, the extended autobiographical passages in *Second Defense* that are the kernel of all subsequent Milton biographies suggest a powerful retrospective effort to shape his past as if it had found its culmination in his present triumph.

Leaving aside the question of whether, or to what degree, Milton overstates the righteous coherence of his life and the heroic sacrifice of his eyesight in opposing Salmasius, we must at least recognize that he nursed false hopes about the subsequent willingness of his countrymen to heed their champion. By the end of the 1650s, Milton had become a prophet without honor in his own country. The once celebrated defender of the English people was rejected as a "blind guide" and ridiculed for having "scribbled [his] eyes out" for "little or no purpose" (*No Blind Guides; Censure of the Rota* 4). Some who wrote against him were explicit and eager in their desire to see him drawn and quartered when Charles II took his father's throne.

Yet Milton survived to write his greatest work in the crucible of a defeat so crushing that we find it difficult to imagine him strong enough to persevere. Although he did not suffer public execution, the image he had created of himself as a prophet of liberty came under an iconoclastic attack more severe and sustained than any he had mounted against Charles. Still, by 1688, events in England vindicated his opposition to divine right monarchy, and in the following century his political orations would inspire republican revolutionaries in North America and France. His image and reputation survived the desertion of his countrymen, as he anticipated it would: "It will seem to posterity that a mighty harvest of glory was at hand, together with the opportunity for doing the greatest deeds, but that to this opportunity men were wanting. Yet there was not one wanting who could rightly counsel, encourage, and inspire, who could honor both the noble deeds and those who had done them, and make both deeds and doers illustrious with praises that will never die" (p. 362).

Our text follows the translation in volume four, part one of the Yale edition of Milton's prose works.

Selections from

John Milton
ENGLISHMAN
Second Defense
of
The English People
Against the Base Anonymous Libel, Entitled
The Cry of the Royal Blood to Heaven, against the English Parricides.[1]

BY JOHN MILTON, ENGLISHMAN[2]

In the whole life and estate of man the first duty is to be grateful to God and mindful of his blessings, and to offer particular and solemn thanks without delay when his benefits have exceeded hope and prayer. Now, on the very threshold of my speech, I see three most weighty reasons for my discharge of this duty.[3] First that I was born at a time in the history of my country when her citizens, with preeminent virtue and a nobility and steadfastness surpassing all the glory of their ancestors, invoked the Lord, followed his manifest guidance, and after accomplishing the most heroic and exemplary achievements since the foundation of the world, freed the state from grievous tyranny and the church from unworthy servitude. Secondly, that when a multitude had sprung up which in the wonted manner of a mob venomously attacked these noble achievements, and when one man above all, swollen and complacent with his empty grammarian's conceit and the esteem of his confederates, had in a book of unparalleled baseness attacked us and wickedly assumed the defense of all tyrants, it was I and no other who was deemed equal to a foe of such repute and

1. The original Latin title of the tract to which Milton replies is *Regii Sanguinis Clamor ad Coelum, Adversus Parricidas Anglicanos,* published by Adriaan Vlacq, at The Hague (1652).
2. Milton regularly adjoins his nationality to his name in works intended for a foreign readership.
3. The rhetorical structure of *Second Defense,* like those of *Areopagitica* and the *Tenure of Kings and Magistrates,* is that of a classical oration. The political orators he names as models in *Of Education* are Demosthenes and Cicero, both of whom spoke in opposition to tyranny.

to the task of speaking on so great a theme, and who received from the very liberators of my country this role, which was offered spontaneously with universal consent, the task of publicly defending (if anyone ever did) the cause of the English people and thus of Liberty herself.[4] Lastly, I thank God that in an affair so arduous and so charged with expectation, I did not disappoint the hope or the judgment of my countrymen about me, nor fail to satisfy a host of foreigners, men of learning and experience, for by God's grace I so routed my audacious foe that he fled, broken in spirit and reputation.[5] For the last three years of his life, he did in his rage utter frequent threats, but gave us no further trouble, save that he sought the secret help of certain rogues and persuaded some bungling and immoderate panegyrists to repair, if they could, his fresh and unlooked-for disgrace. All this will shortly be made clear.

In the belief that such great blessings come from on high and that they should properly be recognized both out of gratitude to God and in order to secure favorable auspices for the work in hand, I held that they should be reverently proclaimed, as they are, at the outset. For who does not consider the glorious achievements of his country as his own? But what can tend more to the honor and glory of any country than the restoration of liberty both to civil life and to divine worship? What nation, what state has displayed superior fortune or stouter courage in securing for itself such liberty in either sphere? In truth, it is not in warfare and arms alone that courage shines forth, but she pours out her dauntless strength against all terrors alike, and thus those illustrious Greeks and Romans whom we particularly admire expelled the tyrants from their cities without other virtues than the zeal for freedom, accompanied by ready weapons and eager hands. All else they easily accomplished amid universal praise, applause, and joyful omens. Nor did they hasten so much towards danger and doubtful issues as towards the fair and glorious trial of virtue, towards distinctions, in short, and garlands, and the sure hope of immortality. For not yet was tyranny a sacred institution. Not yet had tyrants, suddenly become viceroys, indeed, and vicars of Christ, sheltered themselves behind the blind superstition of the mob, when they could not fortify themselves with their good will.[6] Not yet had the common people, maddened by priestly machinations, sunk to a barbarism fouler than that which stains the Indians, themselves the most stupid of mortals. The Indians indeed worship as gods malevolent demons whom they cannot exorcize, but this mob of ours, to avoid driving out its

4. The renowned French scholar Claude de Saumaise (1588–1653) or, in Latin, Claudius Salmasius, authored *Defensio Regia pro Carolo I* (*Defense of Kingship on behalf of Charles I*), published in November 1649. Though he studied philosophy and law, Salmasius was best known in the field of literary studies. He published numerous editions of classical authors and was especially celebrated for his discovery in 1606 of the unique Palatine manuscript of *The Greek Anthology*. The Council of State in January 1650 ordered Milton to pen a reply to his defense of monarchy.

5. Ill health occasioned Salmasius's departure from Stockholm. He died before finishing a reply to Milton's *Defense*.

6. Milton thus characterizes divine right polity, in which monarchs such as Charles I claimed that their right to rule derived directly from God.

tyrants, even when it could, has set up as gods over it the most impotent of mortals and to its own destruction has consecrated the enemies of mankind.[7] And against all this close array of long-held opinions, superstitions, slanders, and fears, more dreadful to other men than the enemy[8] himself, the English people had to contend. Being better instructed and doubtless inspired by heaven, they overcame all these obstacles with such confidence in their cause and such strength of mind and courage that although they were indeed a multitude in numbers, yet the lofty exaltation of their minds kept them from being a mob. Britain herself, which was once called a land teeming with tyrants, shall hereafter deserve the everlasting praise of all the ages as a country where liberators flourish. The English people were not driven to unbridled license by scorn for the laws or desecration of them. They were not inflamed with the empty name of liberty by a false notion of virtue and glory, or senseless emulation of the ancients. It was their purity of life and their blameless character which showed them the one direct road to true liberty, and it was the most righteous defense of law and religion that of necessity gave them arms. And so, trusting completely in God, with honorable weapons, they put slavery to flight.

Although I claim for myself no share in this glory, yet it is easy to defend myself from the charge of timidity or cowardice, should such a charge be leveled. For I did not avoid the toils and dangers of military service without rendering to my fellow citizens another kind of service that was much more useful and no less perilous. In time of trial I was neither cast down in spirit nor unduly fearful of envy or death itself. Having from early youth been especially devoted to the liberal arts, with greater strength of mind than of body, I exchanged the toils of war, in which any stout trooper might outdo me, for those labors which I better understood, that with such wisdom as I owned I might add as much weight as possible to the counsels of my country and to this excellent cause, using not my lower but my higher and stronger powers. And so I concluded that if God wished those men to achieve such noble deeds, He also wished that there be other men by whom these deeds, once done, might be worthily praised and extolled, and that truth defended by arms be also defended by reason—the only defense truly appropriate to man.[9] Hence it is that while I admire the heroes victorious in battle, I nevertheless do not complain about my own role. Indeed I congratulate myself and once again offer most fervent thanks to the heavenly bestower of gifts that such a lot has befallen me—a lot that seems much more a source of envy to others than of regret to myself. And yet, to no

7. Milton scorned the religious practices of Indians as reported in travel literature of his time, particularly the worship of deities that inflict misery. Cp. *DDD* (p. 134): "worshipped like some Indian deity, when it can confer no blessing"; *Tetrachordon* (p. 242): "the vermin of an Indian Catharist, which his fond religion forbids him to molest."

8. **enemy:** The Latin original is *hostis,* which means an enemy met in open battle, as opposed to the "close array" of customary bias and social pressure tactics.

9. Cp. *PL* 6.121–23: "Nor is it aught but just,/That he who in debate of truth hath won,/Should win in arms."

one, even the humblest, do I willingly compare myself, nor do I say one word about myself in arrogance, but whenever I allow my mind to dwell upon this cause, the noblest and most renowned of all, and upon the glorious task of defending the very defenders, a task assigned me by their own vote and decision,[10] I confess that I can scarcely restrain myself from loftier and bolder flights than are permissible in this exordium,[11] and from the search for a more exalted manner of expression. Indeed, in the degree that the distinguished orators of ancient times undoubtedly surpass me, both in their eloquence and in their style (especially in a foreign tongue, which I must of necessity use, and often to my own dissatisfaction),[12] in that same degree shall I outstrip all the orators of every age in the grandeur of my subject and my theme. This circumstance has aroused so much anticipation and notoriety that I do not now feel that I am surrounded, in the Forum or on the Rostra, by one people alone, whether Roman or Athenian, but that, with virtually all of Europe attentive, in session, and passing judgment, I have in the *First Defense* spoken out and shall in the *Second* speak again to the entire assembly and council of all the most influential men, cities, and nations everywhere. I seem now to have embarked on a journey and to be surveying from on high far-flung regions and territories across the sea, faces numberless and unknown, sentiments in complete agreement with mine. Here the manly strength of the Germans, hostile to slavery, meets my eye; there the lively and generous ardor of the Franks, worthy of their name; here the well-considered courage of the Spaniards; there the serene and self-controlled magnanimity of the Italians. Wherever liberal sentiment, wherever freedom, or wherever magnanimity either prudently conceals or openly proclaims itself, there some in silence approve, others openly cast their votes, some make haste to applaud, others, conquered at last by the truth, acknowledge themselves my captives.

Now, surrounded by such great throngs, from the Pillars of Hercules all the way to the farthest boundaries of Father Liber,[13] I seem to be leading home again everywhere in the world, after a vast space of time, Liberty herself, so long expelled and exiled. And, like Triptolemus of old, I seem to introduce to the nations of the earth a product from my own country, but one far more excellent than that of Ceres.[14] In short, it is the renewed cultivation of freedom

10. Milton refers here to his 1649 appointment as Secretary for Foreign Tongues, a position whose duties included replying to foreign censure of the new republic.

11. **exordium:** the opening of the five-part classical oration.

12. Milton writes in Latin, because it was the international language of his intended audience. The claim of dissatisfaction may seem disingenuous, given Milton's polish as a Latinist, but it comes in a comparison with the greatest classical orators speaking in their native tongues.

13. The imagined crowd stretches from the conventional western limit of Europe, Gibraltar (*the Pillars of Hercules*) to India as its eastern limit, the realm of Dionysus, identified as *Father Liber* by the Romans. Milton may resort to this less familiar name so that he can pun on *liberty*.

14. In Greek myth, Ceres sent Triptolemus to introduce the arts of agriculture to the world once the golden age had ended, so that humanity might sustain itself. In his final paragraph, Milton will claim that he has spread the word successfully and that "a mighty harvest of glory" is at hand if only the English will rise to the occasion.

and civic life that I disseminate throughout cities, kingdoms, and nations. But not entirely unknown, nor perhaps unwelcome, shall I return if I am he who disposed of the contentious satellite of tyrants, hitherto deemed unconquerable, both in the view of most men and in his own opinion.[15] When he with insults was attacking us and our battle array, and our leaders looked first of all to me, I met him in single combat and plunged into his reviling throat this pen,[16] the weapon of his own choice. And (unless I wish to reject outright and disparage the views and opinions of so many intelligent readers everywhere, in no way bound or indebted to me) I bore off the spoils of honor. That this is actually the truth and no empty boast finds ready proof in the following event—which I believe did not occur without the will of God—namely, that when Salmasius (or Salmasia,[17] for which of the two he was, the open domination of his wife, both in public and in private, had made it quite difficult to determine), when Salmasius had been courteously summoned by Her Most Serene Majesty, the Queen of the Swedes (whose devotion to the liberal arts and to men of learning has never been surpassed) and had gone thither, there in the very place where he was living as a highly honored guest, he was overtaken by my *Defence*, while he was expecting nothing of the kind. Nearly everyone read it immediately, and the Queen herself, who had been among the first to do so, having regard only for what was worthy of her, omitted nothing of her earlier kindness and generosity towards her guest. But for the rest, if I may report what is frequently mentioned and is no secret, so great a reversal of opinion suddenly took place that he who the day before yesterday had flourished in the highest favor now all but withered away. When he departed, not much later, with good leave, there was but one doubt in many minds, namely, whether he came more honored or went more despised. Nor in other places, it is certain, did less harm befall his reputation.

Yet I have not referred to all these matters with the intention of ingratiating myself with anyone (for there is no need), but only to show more copiously that which I undertook at the outset, for what reasons—and what weighty ones—I began by offering my most fervent thanks to almighty God. I would show that this proem,[18] in which I offer so many convincing proofs that, although by no means exempt from the disasters common to humanity, I and my interests are nevertheless under the protection of God—this proem, I say, will be a source of honor and credit to me. I would show that with respect to matters of well-nigh primary importance, relating to the immediate needs of my country and destined to be of the greatest service to civil life and religion, when I speak, not on behalf of one people nor yet one defendant, but rather for the entire human

15. The reference is to Salmasius, whose accomplishments and reputation were indeed formidable.

16. **pen:** The Latin original is *stilo*, which literally refers to a long, sharply pointed piece of metal for inscribing letters on a wax tablet. Milton also knew it as an Italian word for "dagger."

17. The feminine form of the name. Rumor had it that Salmasius's wife lorded it over him; Milton in the *First Defense* repeatedly mocked him for his effeminate slackness.

18. **proem:** introduction, preamble.

race against the foes of human liberty, amid the common and well-frequented assembly (so to speak) of all nations, I have been aided and enriched by the favor and assistance of God. Anything greater or more glorious than this I neither can, nor wish to, claim. Accordingly, I beg the same immortal God that, just as, depending on his familiar help and grace alone, I lately defended deeds of supreme courage and justice, so with the same or greater honesty, industry, fidelity, and even good fortune, I may be able to defend from undeserved insults and slanders both the doers of those deeds and myself, who have been linked with these great men for the purpose of ignominy, rather than honor. And if there is anyone who thinks that these attacks might better have been ignored, I for my part agree, provided that they were circulated among men who had an accurate knowledge of us. But how in the world will everyone else be convinced that the lies our enemy has told are not the truth? Yet when I shall have seen to it (as is proper) that Truth the avenger shall follow wherever calumny has gone before, I believe that men will cease to think wrongly of us, and that that creature will perhaps be ashamed of his lies. If he feel no shame, then at last we may properly ignore him.

Meanwhile I should more quickly have sped him a reply in accord with his merits, had he not protected himself up until now with false reports, announcing again and again that Salmasius was sweating at the anvil, forging new charges against us, always on the very point of publishing them. By these tactics he achieved but one result—that of postponing for a little while the payment of the penalty for slander, for I thought it better to wait, so that I might keep my strength intact for the more formidable adversary.[19] But with Salmasius, since he is dead, I think my war is over. How he died, I shall not say, for I shall not impute his death as a crime to him, as he imputed my blindness to me.[20] Yet there are those who even place the responsibility for his death on me and on those barbs of mine, too keenly sharpened.[21] While he fixed them more deeply in himself by his resistance, while he saw that the work which he had in hand was proceeding too slowly, that the time for reply had passed and the welcome accorded his work had died, when he realized that his reputation was gone, along with his good name, and finally that the favor of princes was diminished, so far as he was concerned, because of his poor defense of the royal cause,[22] they say that at last, after a three-year illness, worn away by mental distress rather than by bodily disease, he died. However that may be, if I must wage a posthumous war as well, and with a familiar enemy whose attacks I easily sustained when

19. Nearly two years had passed since *The Cry* was published, in the summer of 1652; here Milton explains the delay.

20. Salmasius had not impugned his blindness, but the preface to *The Cry* claimed that, when Salmasius did reply, he would give Milton "the castigation he deserves, a monster horrible, deformed, huge, and sightless."

21. "Salmasius died at the Spa, September 3, 1653; and, as controvertists are commonly said to be killed by their last dispute, Milton was flattered with the credit of destroying him" (Johnson 1905, 1:115).

22. Actually, the *Defense of Kingship* was favorably received by European royalty.

they were fierce and vigorous, there is no reason for me to fear his efforts when feeble and dying.

[*Milton distinguishes between kingship and tyranny, derides the authors of* Defense of Kingship *and* The Cry *for their anonymity, and names Alexander More as the author of the latter. He mocks him as a philanderer with a penchant for servant girls, particularly Pontia, a maid in the employ of Salmasius's wife. He characterizes Vlacq, the tract's printer and ostensible author of the prefatory letter addressed to Charles, as a profligate opportunist and a shill of Salmasius and More. He ridicules the letter for being of uncertain authorship and for its empty threats of a forthcoming reply by Salmasius. In the excerpt that follows, Milton responds to the attacks that have been made on him.*]

Let us now come to the charges against me. Is there anything in my life or character which he could criticize? Nothing, certainly. What then? He does what no one but a brute and barbarian would have done—casts up to me my appearance and my blindness.

"A monster, dreadful, ugly, huge, deprived of sight." Never did I think that I should rival the Cyclops in appearance.[23] But at once he corrects himself. "Yet not huge, for there is nothing more feeble, bloodless, and pinched." Although it ill befits a man to speak of his own appearance, yet speak I shall, since here too there is reason for me to thank God and refute liars, lest anyone think me to be perhaps a dog-headed ape or a rhinoceros, as the rabble in Spain, too credulous of their priests, believe to be true of heretics, as they call them.[24] Ugly I have never been thought by anyone, to my knowledge, who has laid eyes on me. Whether I am handsome or not, I am less concerned. I admit that I am not tall, but my stature is closer to the medium than to the small. Yet what if it were small, as is the case with so many men of the greatest worth in both peace and war? (Although why is that stature called small which is great enough for virtue?) But neither am I especially feeble, having indeed such spirit and such strength that when my age and manner of life required it, I was not ignorant of how to handle or unsheathe a sword, nor unpracticed in using it each day. Girded with my sword, as I generally was, I thought myself equal to anyone, though he was far more sturdy, and I was fearless of any injury that one man could inflict on another.[25] Today I possess the same spirit, the same strength, but not the same eyes. And yet they have as much the appearance of being uninjured, and are as clear and bright, without a cloud, as the eyes of men who see most keenly. In this respect alone, against my will, do I deceive. In my face, than which he says there is "nothing more bloodless," still lingers a color exactly

23. The insulting description of Milton derives from Vergil's account of Polyphemus, the Cyclops blinded by Odysseus (*Aen.* 3.658).

24. Heretics in Spanish writing and theater were often portrayed as monsters. Such representations were not unknown in England. English Protestants credulously repeated accounts of monstrous births delivered to heretic mothers in New England (Rumrich 1996, 103–4).

25. Milton practiced fencing as exercise and in *Of Education* included it as part of the curriculum.

opposite to the bloodless and pale, so that although I am past forty, there is scarcely anyone to whom I do not seem younger by about ten years. Nor is it true that either my body or my skin is shriveled. If I am in any way deceitful in respect to these matters, I should deserve the mockery of many thousands of my fellow-citizens, who know me by sight, and of not a few foreigners as well. But if this fellow is proved such a bold and gratuitous liar in a matter by no means calling for deceit, you will be able to draw the same conclusion as to the rest.

So much have I been forced to say about my appearance. Concerning yours, although I have heard that it is utterly despicable and the living image of the falseness and malice that dwell within you, I do not care to speak nor does anyone care to hear.[26] Would that it were equally possible to refute this brutish adversary on the subject of my blindness, but it is not possible. Let me bear it then. Not blindness but the inability to endure blindness is a source of misery. Why should I not bear that which every man ought to prepare himself to bear with equanimity, if it befall him—that which I know may humanly befall any mortal and has indeed befallen certain men who are the most eminent and virtuous in all history? Or shall I recall those ancient bards and wise men of the most distant past, whose misfortune the gods, it is said, recompensed with far more potent gifts, and whom men treated with such respect that they preferred to blame the very gods than to impute their blindness to them as a crime? The tradition about the seer Tiresias is well known. Concerning Phineus,[27] Apollonius sang as follows in the *Argonautica:*

> Nor did he fear Jupiter himself,
> Revealing truly to men the divine purpose.
> Wherefore he gave him a prolonged old age,
> But deprived him of the sweet light of his eyes.[28]

But God himself is truth! The more veracious a man is in teaching truth to men, the more like must he be to God and the more acceptable to him. It is impious to believe that God is grudging of truth or does not wish it to be shared with men as freely as possible. Because of no offence, therefore, does it seem that this man who was godlike and eager to enlighten the human race was deprived of his eyesight, as were a great number of philosophers. Or should I

26. The underlying premise, that outward appearance reflects intrinsic value, is Platonic (see *Phaedo* 81; *Timaeus* 90). It informs Adam and Raphael's discussion in *PL* 8 concerning the problematic beauty of Eve as well as their discussion of celestial dynamics.
27. In one tradition, Hera struck Tiresias blind when he affirmed Zeus's claim that women take more pleasure in sex than men. Zeus then compensated him with prophetic vision. Explanations for the blindness of Phineus are also multiple. In one version, Zeus blinds the legendary King of Salmydessus because he revealed divine secrets, but Milton resists the inference that he was punished for teaching the truth, suggesting that prophetic insight richly compensates for loss of vision.
28. In the original text, Milton quotes Apollonius's Greek (*Argonautica* 2.181–84) and provides a Latin translation.

mention those men of old who were renowned for statecraft and military achievements? First, Timoleon of Corinth, who freed his own city and all Sicily, than whom no age has borne a man greater or more venerated in his state.[29] Next, Appius Claudius, whose vote, nobly expressed in the Senate, delivered Italy from Pyrrhus, her mortal enemy, but not himself from blindness.[30] Thirdly, Caecilius Metellus, the Pontifex, who, while he saved from fire not the city alone but also the Palladium, the symbol of its destiny, and its innermost mysteries, lost his own eyes, although on other occasions certainly God has given proof that he favors such remarkable piety, even among the heathen.[31] Therefore what has befallen such a man should scarcely, I think, be regarded as an evil.

Why should I add to the list other men of later times, such as the famous Doge of Venice, Dandolo,[32] by far the most eminent of all, or Zizka, the brave leader of the Bohemians and the bulwark of the orthodox faith[33]? Why should I add theologians of the highest repute, Hieronymus Zanchius[34] and some others, when it is established that even Isaac[35] the patriarch himself—and no mortal was ever dearer to God—lived in blindness for many years, as did also (for a few years perhaps) Jacob,[36] his son, who was no less beloved by God. When, finally, it is perfectly certain from the divine testimony of Christ our Savior that the man who was healed by Him had been blind from the very womb, through no sin of his own or of his parents.[37]

For my part, I call upon Thee, my God, who knowest my inmost mind and all my thoughts, to witness that (although I have repeatedly examined myself on this point as earnestly as I could, and have searched all the corners of my life) I am conscious of nothing, or of no deed, either recent or remote, whose wickedness could justly occasion or invite upon me this supreme misfortune.

29. The Corinthian statesman and soldier was sent with a small force to Syracuse to help the natives resist the tyrant Dionysius II. Triumphant, he retired into venerated private life in Syracuse, losing his vision as he grew old.

30. In his old age, when blind, the former censor (312–8 B.C.E.) in a celebrated speech successfully attacked the proposals of Pyrrhus for peace (279/8 B.C.E.).

31. Lucius *Caecilius Metellus*, consul 251 B.C.E., pontifex maximus 243, died in 221. Hero of the First Punic War, in 241 he rescued the Palladium when the temple of Vesta was on fire and lost his sight as a result. A sacred image of Athena that legend traced back to Troy, the Palladium was thought to protect Rome from danger so long as it remained safe.

32. Milton includes the famed Doge of Venice Enrico Dandolo (c. 1108–1205) in his list of blind statesmen. Dandolo, who personally directed the Fourth Crusade in the sack of Constantinople, had poor sight but was not blind. Milton apparently accepted the spurious rumor that he was blinded by the Emperor of Byzantium.

33. John Zizka (1376–1424), Bohemian military leader and head of the Hussite forces during Catholic crusades against them. He lost his eyes in battle. As elsewhere, by "orthodox faith" (*orthodoxae fidei*) Milton means "Protestant." The Hussites followed John Huss (1373–1415), Bohemian supporter of the early reformer John Wyclifffe (1329–84).

34. In *Christian Doctrine*, Milton repeatedly cites the monk turned Calvinist theologian Jerome Zanchius (1516–90), though usually in disagreement (see, e.g., 1.14). He lost the power of sight in his old age.

35. For the blindness of Isaac, see Gen. 27.1.

36. For the blindness of Jacob, see Gen. 48.10.

37. John 9.1–41.

As for what I have at any time written (since the royalists think that I am now undergoing this suffering as a penance, and they accordingly rejoice), I likewise call God to witness that I have written nothing of such kind that I was not then and am not now convinced that it was right and true and pleasing to God. And I swear that my conduct was not influenced by ambition, gain, or glory, but solely by considerations of duty, honor, and devotion to my country. I did my utmost not only to free my country, but also to free the church. Hence, when the business of replying to the royal defense had been officially assigned to me, and at that same time I was afflicted at once by ill health[38] and the virtual loss of my remaining eye, and the doctors were making learned predictions that if I should undertake this task, I would shortly lose both eyes, I was not in the least deterred by the warning. I seemed to hear, not the voice of the doctor (even that of Aesculapius, issuing from the shrine at Epidaurus), but the sound of a certain more divine monitor within.[39] And I thought that two lots had now been set before me by a certain command of fate: the one, blindness, the other, duty. Either I must necessarily endure the loss of my eyes, or I must abandon my most solemn duty. And there came into my mind those two fates which, the son of Thetis[40] relates, his mother brought back from Delphi, where she inquired concerning him:

> Two destinies lead me to the end, which is death:
> If staying here I fight around the city of Troy,
> Return is denied me, but immortal will be my fame.
> If homeward I return to my dear native land,
> Lost is fair fame, but long will be my life.

Then I reflected that many men have bought with greater evil smaller good; with death, glory. To me, on the contrary, was offered a greater good at the price of a smaller evil: that I could at the cost of blindness alone fulfill the most honorable requirement of my duty. As duty is of itself more substantial than glory, so it ought to be for every man more desirable and illustrious. I resolved therefore that I must employ this brief use of my eyes while yet I could for the greatest possible benefit to the state. You see what I chose, what I rejected, and why.

Then let those who slander the judgments of God cease to speak evil and invent empty tales about me. Let them be sure that I feel neither regret nor shame for my lot, that I stand unmoved and steady in my resolution, that I nei-

38. Milton reports in a letter to Leonard Philaras of Athens that the deterioration of his eyesight over several years was accompanied by intestinal distress and intense ocular pain.

39. **Aesculapius:** Latin for Asclepius, Apollo's son and the Greek god of healing. The ancient Greek city of *Epidaurus* was the center of his cult. By *more divine monitor,* Milton seems to mean the voice of conscience.

40. Achilles in the *Iliad,* from which Milton took the following excerpt (9.411–16). He quotes the original Greek and adds a Latin translation.

ther discern nor endure the anger of God, that in fact I know and recognize in the most momentous affairs his fatherly mercy and kindness towards me, and especially in this fact, that with his consolation strengthening my spirit I bow to his divine will, dwelling more often on what he has bestowed on me than on what he has denied. Finally, let them rest assured that I would not exchange the consciousness of my achievement for any deed of theirs, be it ever so righteous, nor would I be deprived of the recollection of my deeds, ever a source of gratitude and repose.

Finally, as to my blindness, I would rather have mine, if it be necessary, than either theirs, More, or yours. Your blindness, deeply implanted in the inmost faculties, obscures the mind, so that you may see nothing whole or real. Mine, which you make a reproach, merely deprives things of color and superficial appearance. What is true and essential in them is not lost to my intellectual vision. How many things there are, moreover, which I have no desire to see, how many things that I should be glad not to see, how few remain that I should like to see.[41] Nor do I feel pain at being classed with the blind, the afflicted, the suffering, and the weak (although you hold this to be wretched), since there is hope that in this way I may approach more closely the mercy and protection of the Father Almighty.[42] There is a certain road which leads through weakness, as the apostle teaches, to the greatest strength.[43] May I be entirely helpless, provided that in my weakness there may arise all the more powerfully this immortal and more perfect strength; provided that in my shadows the light of the divine countenance may shine forth all the more clearly. For then I shall be at once the weakest and the strongest, at the same time blind and most keen in vision. By this infirmity may I be perfected, by this completed. So in this darkness, may I be clothed in light.

To be sure, we blind men are not the least of God's concerns, for the less able we are to perceive anything other than himself, the more mercifully and graciously does he deign to look upon us. Woe to him who mocks us, woe to him who injures us. He deserves to be cursed with a public malediction. Divine law[44] and divine favor have rendered us not only safe from the injuries of men, but almost sacred, nor do these shadows around us seem to have been created so much by the dullness of our eyes as by the shade of angels' wings. And divine favor not infrequently is wont to lighten these shadows again, once made, by an inner and far more enduring light. To this circumstance I refer the fact that my friends now visit, esteem, and attend me more diligently even than before, and

41. Milton here distinguishes between the world of Platonic forms containing the essence of things, which he can still see with "intellectual vision," and the everyday world of objects, which contains little that he still wishes to see even if he were able. Cp. *Phaedrus* 247.

42. Cp. *PL* 1.157–58: "To be weak is miserable/Doing or suffering."

43. Here and in the rest of the paragraph, Milton alludes to 2 Cor. 12, especially verse 9: "My strength is made perfect in weakness." His inscription of verse 9 in several autograph albums during the 1650s indicates that it became his motto (Kerrigan 1983, 134).

44. See, e.g., Deut. 27.18.

that there are some with whom I might as with true friends exchange the conversation of Pylades [with Orestes] and Theseus [with Heracles]:

ORESTES: Go slowly as the rudder of my feet.
PYLADES: A precious care is this to me.

And elsewhere:

THESEUS: Give your hand to your friend and helper.
Put your arm around my neck, and I will be your guide.[45]

For my friends do not think that by this calamity I have been rendered altogether worthless, nor that whatever is characteristic of an honest and prudent man resides in his eyes. In fact, since the loss of my eyesight has not left me sluggish from inactivity but tireless and ready among the first to risk the greatest dangers for the sake of liberty, the chief men in the state do not desert me either, but, considering within themselves what human life is like, they gladly favor and indulge me, and grant to me rest and leisure, as to one who well deserves it. If I have any distinction, they do not remove it, if any public office, they do not take it away, if any advantage from that office, they do not diminish it, and although I am no longer as useful as I was, they think that they should reward me no less graciously.[46] They pay me the same honor as if, according to the custom of ancient Athens, they had decreed that I take my meals in the Prytaneum.[47]

So long as I find in God and man such consolation for my blindness, let no one mourn for my eyes, which were lost in the cause of honor. Far be it from me either to mourn. Far be it from me to have so little spirit that I cannot easily despise the revilers of my blindness, or so little charity that I cannot even more easily pardon them. To you, whoever you are, I return, who with but little consistency regard me now as a dwarf, now as Antaeus.[48] You have (finally) no more ardent desire "for the United Provinces of Holland than that they should dispose of this war as easily and successfully as Salmasius will dispose of Milton."[49] If I give glad assent to this prayer, I think that I express no bad omen or evil wish against our success and the cause of England.

But listen! Another Cry, something strange and hissing. I take it that geese are flying in from somewhere or other. Now I realize what it is. I remember that

45. The quotations are from plays by Euripides: the first, *Orestes* (795); the second, *Heracles* (1398, 1402). His devoted friend Pylades helps Orestes endure the madness that visits him after he kills his mother. After madness so deludes Hercules that he kills his family, his friend Theseus comforts him. Both quotations appear in the original Greek followed by Latin translations.

46. Although Milton stopped attending conferences with ambassadors after blindness set in, his appointment as Latin Secretary was not affected.

47. **Prytaneum:** state house where distinguished Athenians were rewarded with free meals.

48. **Antaeus:** a giant, the son of the sea god Poseidon and Gaia (Earth).

49. Holland and England had been engaged in a naval war since May 1652.

this is the Tragedy of a Cry.[50] The Chorus appears. Behold, two poetasters[51]—either two or a single one, twofold in appearance and of two colors. Should I call it a sphinx, or that monster which Horace describes in the *Ars Poetica*, with the head of a woman, the neck of an ass, clad in varied plumage, with limbs assembled from every source?[52] Yes, this is that very monster. It must be some rhapsode or other, strewn with centos and patches.[53] Whether it is one or two is uncertain, for it also is anonymous.

Now, poets who deserve the name, I love and cherish, and I delight in hearing them frequently. Most of them, I know, are bitterly hostile to tyrants, if I should list them from the first down to our own Buchanan.[54] But these peddlers of effeminate little verses—who would not despise them? Nothing could be more foolish, more idle, more corrupt, or more false than such as they. They praise, they censure, without choice, without discrimination, judgment, or measure, now princes, now commoners, the learned as well as the ignorant, whether honest or wicked, it makes no difference, according as they are puffed up and swept away by the bottle, by the hope of a halfpenny, or by that empty frenzy of theirs. From every source they accumulate their absurdities of diction and matter, so many, so inconsistent, so disgusting, that it is far better for the object of their praise to suffer their neglect and live, as the saying is, with a crooked nose,[55] than to receive such praise. But he whom they attack should consider it no small honor that he finds no favor with such absurd and paltry fools.[56]

It is doubtful whether the first[57] (if there really are two of them) should be called a poet or a plasterer, to such a degree does he whitewash the façade of Salmasius, or rather whiten and plaster him entirely, as if he were a wall. He brings on in a "triumphal" chariot, no less, the giant-fighting hero, brandishing his "javelins and boxing-gloves" and all manner of trifling weapons, with all the scholars following the chariot on foot, but a tremendous distance to the rear, since he is the one "whom divine providence has raised up in evil times for the salvation of the world. At last, therefore, the time was at hand for kings to be protected by such a shield—the parent [no less] of law and empire." Salmasius must have been mad and in his second childhood not only to have been so

50. With *Cry,* Milton mocks the title of the tract for which he holds both More and Vlacq responsible as if they were a hybrid author.

51. **poetasters:** writers of poor or trashy verse.

52. The description of the monster paraphrases the first three lines of *Epistula ad Pisones* [Letters to Piso], usually known as *Ars Poetica* [The Art of Poetry].

53. In ancient Greece, *rhapsodes* recited epic poetry, particularly Homer's, and often improvised, including pieces by other poets in their performances. In Milton's time, collectors of literary pieces were also known as rhapsodists. **centos:** pieces of patchwork; patched garments.

54. The Scottish author George Buchanan (1506–82) wrote prose tracts regarding monarchy that anticipated Milton's. Most of his efforts in poetry were translations.

55. **with a crooked nose:** i.e., with his nose out of joint (indignant at their neglect).

56. Cp. *PR* 3.56: "Of whom to be dispraised were no small praise."

57. Vlacq.

hugely gratified by such praises but also to have taken such pains to have them printed with all possible haste. Wretched too and ignorant of propriety was the poet if he thought a mere schoolmaster worthy of such immoderate eulogy, since that breed of men has always been at the service of poets and inferior to them.[58]

The other, however, does not write verses, but simply raves, himself the most insane of all the possessed whom he so rabidly assails. As if he were an executioner for Salmasius, a son of Syrian Dama,[59] he calls for the floggers and Cadmus;[60] then drunk with hellebore,[61] he vomits up out of the index to Plautus[62] all the filthy language of slaves and scoundrels that can be found anywhere. You would suppose that he was speaking Oscan,[63] not Latin, or was croaking like a frog from the hellish swamps in which he swims. Then, to show you how great is his mastery of iambics, he is guilty of two false quantities in a single word, one syllable incorrectly prolonged, the other shortened:

Hi trucidate rege per horrendum nefas.[64]

Take away, you ass, those saddlebags filled with your "emptinesses" and bring us at last just three words, if you can, like a sane and sober man, provided that that pumpkinhead of yours, that "blockhead," can be sensible even for a second. Meanwhile I hand you over, an Orbilius, to be executed by the "harvest of rods" of your pupils.[65]

Continue to curse me as being "worse than Cromwell" in your estimation—the highest praise you could bestow on me. But should I call you a friend, a fool, or a crafty foe? A friend you surely are not, for your words prove you a foe. Why then have you been so inept in your slander that it occurred to you to exalt me above so great a man? Is it possible that you do not understand, or think that I do not understand, that the greater the hatred you show towards me, the greater is your advertisement of my merits with respect to the Commonwealth, and that your insults amount to so many eulogies of me among my own people? For

58. Milton calls Salmasius a schoolmaster or grammarian [*grammaticum*], but Salmasius was a professor and eminent scholar. Milton himself instructed students but scoffs at the idea that teachers merit such praise as Vlacq lavishes on Salmasius. In the passage quoted, Salmasius is depicted in a manner that oddly anticipates Milton's epic account of Messiah's single-handed assault on the rebel angels (*PL* 6.760–843).

59. **Dama:** in Horace's *Satires* (1.6.38–39), a slave who threatens a freeborn man with death.

60. Mentioned in the same passage from Horace's *Satires, Cadmus* was an infamously cruel executioner.

61. **hellebore:** a plant used as poison but also as a treatment for mental disease.

62. Titus Maccius *Plautus* (c. 250–184 B.C.E.), Roman dramatist particularly known for his comic representations of slaves and other low characters.

63. **Oscan:** a primitive dialect of southern Italy.

64. The iambic meter used by the author of the ode in *The Cry* mangles the pronunciation of *trucidate* in two of its syllables, making the short *u* long and the long *i* short.

65. *Orbilius* was Horace's schoolmaster, notoriously liberal with the cane. Milton suggests that, for More's mistakes in prosody, the roles should be reversed, and More should take a beating from his students.

if you hate me most of all, surely I am the one who has injured you most of all, hurt you most of all, and damaged your cause. If such is the case, I am also the one who has deserved most highly of my fellow-citizens, for the testimony or judgment of an enemy, even if in other circumstances somewhat unreliable, is nevertheless by far the most weighty when it concerns his own suffering. Or do you not remember that when Ajax and Ulysses vied for the weapons of the dead Achilles, the poet chose as judges, on the advice of Nestor, not Greeks, their fellow-countrymen, but Trojans, their enemies?

> Therefore let the prudent Trojans decide this quarrel.

And a little later:

> Who will give just judgment concerning these men
> Partial to neither party, since all the Achaeans with equal bitterness
> They hate, mindful of their grievous loss.

These are the words of the poet of Smyrna or Calabria.[66]

Hence it follows that you are a crafty foe and take pains to cast infamy on me, when with malicious intent and the purpose of inflicting still deeper injury you pervert and debase that judgment which is wont in the case of an enemy to be impartial and honest. So perverted are you, not just as a man, but even as an enemy. Yet, my fine fellow, I shall without difficulty circumvent you. For although I should like to be Ulysses—should like, that is, to have deserved as well as possible of my country—yet I do not covet the arms of Achilles. I do not seek to bear before me heaven painted on a shield,[67] for others, not myself to see in battle, while I carry on my shoulders a burden, not painted, but real, for myself, and not for others to perceive.

Since I bear no grudge whatever nor harbor private quarrels against any man, nor does any man, so far as I know, bear any grudge against me, I endure with the greater equanimity all the curses that are uttered against me, all the insults that are hurled, so long as they are suffered for the sake of the state, not for myself. Nor do I complain that to me has fallen the tiniest share of the rewards and benefits which thus accrue, but the greatest share of ignominy. I am content to have sought for their own sake alone, and to accomplish without recompense, those deeds which honor bade me do. Let others look to that, and do you rest assured that I have not touched these "abundances" and "riches" of which you accuse me, nor have I become a penny richer by reason of that renown with which especially you charge me.

66. Quintus of Smyrna, whose epic *Posthomerica* was found in Calabria. Milton quotes the original Greek and provides a Latin translation.

67. The famous shield wrought for Achilles by Hephaestus depicts the entire cosmos. Ulysses, not Ajax, was awarded the arms of Achilles as the most deserving of the Greeks.

[*Milton continues his attacks on More, charging him with blasphemy for comparing Charles's execution to Christ's Crucifixion, then turns again to Salmasius, whom he brands a lowly pedant undeserving of his high reputation. He lavishly praises the Queen of Sweden, whom he claims admired his* Defense *and reviled the defeated Salmasius, and sets her up as an example of a just monarch to further distinguish between kings and tyrants.*]

Now I must return to the work from which I digressed, a very different matter. We "became frantic," you say, "at the news of the *Defensio Regia* and therefore" we "hunted out some starveling little schoolmaster,[68] who would consent to lend his corrupt pen to the defense of parricide." This tale you have maliciously invented out of your recollection that the royalists, when they were seeking a herald for their own lies and abuse, approached a grammarian, who was, if not hungry, at least more than a little thirsty for gold—Salmasius. He gladly sold them, not only his services at that time, but also his intellectual powers, if any were his before. The tale springs also from your recollection that Salmasius, his reputation now lost and ruined, when he was casting about for some one who might be able in some way to repair his good name, thus damaged and disgraced, found you, by the just judgment of God, not the minister of Geneva (whence you had been expelled) but the bishop of Lampsacus, that is, a Priapus from the garden, the defiler of his own home.[69] Thereafter, revolted by your insipid praises, which he had purchased with such dishonor, he was converted from a friend into the bitterest enemy and uttered many curses against you, his eulogist, as he died.

"Only one man was found, most assuredly a great hero, whom they could oppose to Salmasius, a certain John Milton." I did not realize that I was a hero, although you may, so far as I am concerned, be the son, perhaps, of some hero or other, since you are totally noxious.[70] And that I alone was found to defend the cause of the people of England, certainly I regret, if I consider the interests of the Commonwealth, but if I consider the glory involved, I am perfectly content that I have no one with whom to share it. Who I am and whence I come is uncertain, you say; so once it was uncertain who Homer was, and who Demosthenes.[71] But in fact, I had learned to hold my peace, I had mastered the art of not writing,[72] a lesson that Salmasius could never learn. And I carried silently in my breast that which, if I had then wished to publish it, would long since have made me as famous as I am today. But I was not greedy for fame, whose gait is slow, nor did I ever intend to publish even this, unless a fitting opportunity presented itself. It made no difference to me even if others did not realize

68. *Grammaticastum,* i.e., petty grammarian.

69. *Priapus,* a god of fertility represented in garden statues as a grotesque figure with an incongruously swollen phallus, had a cult in Lampsacus, a city in Asia Minor.

70. A Latin proverb, *Heroum filii nexae,* holds that the sons of heroes are nothing.

71. Demosthenes was seven when his father died. His guardians mismanaged the estate, and the boy grew up in obscurity and neglect.

72. *Posse non scribere,* or, literally, the power not to write.

that I knew whatever I knew, for it was not fame, but the opportune moment for each thing that I awaited. Hence it happened that I was known to a good many, long before Salmasius was known to himself. Now he is better known than the nag Andraemon.[73]

"Is he a man or a worm?" Indeed I should prefer to be a worm, which even King David confesses that he is, rather than hide in my breast your worm that dieth not.[74] "They say," you continue, "that this fellow, expelled from the University of Cambridge, because of his offences, fled his disgrace and his country and traveled to Italy." Even from this statement one can infer how truthful were your sources of information, for on this point everyone who knows me knows that both you and your informants lie most shamelessly, and I shall at once make this fact clear. If I had actually been expelled from Cambridge, why should I travel to Italy, rather than to France or Holland, where you, enveloped in so many offenses, a minister of the Gospel, not only live in safety, but preach, and even defile with your unclean hands the sacred offices, to the extreme scandal of your church? But why to Italy, More? Another Saturn, I presume, I fled to Latium that I might find a place to lurk.[75] Yet I knew beforehand that Italy was not, as you think, a refuge or asylum for criminals, but rather the lodging-place of *humanitas*[76] and of all the arts of civilization, and so I found it.

"Returning, he wrote his book on divorce." I wrote nothing different from what Bucer had written before me—and copiously—about the kingdom of Christ, nothing different from what Fagius had written on Deuteronomy, Erasmus on the first Epistle to the Corinthians (a commentary intended for the benefit of the English people), nothing different from what many other illustrious men wrote for the common good. No one blamed them for so doing, and I fail to understand why it should be to me above all a source of reproach. One thing only could I wish, that I had not written it in the vernacular, for then I would not have met with vernacular readers, who are usually ignorant of their own good, and laugh at the misfortunes of others. But do you, vilest of men, protest about divorce, you who procured the most brutal of all divorces from Pontia, the maidservant engaged to you, after you seduced her under cover of that engagement? Moreover, she was a servant of Salmasius, an English woman it is said, warmly devoted to the royalist cause. It is beyond question that you wickedly courted her as royal property and left her as public property. Take care lest you yourself prove to have been the author of the very conversion which you profess to find so distasteful. Take care, I repeat, lest with the rule of Salmasius utterly overthrown you may yourself have converted Pontia into a "republic."[77]

73. *Andraemon,* a horse driven by the famous charioteer Scorpus, probably was, as Martial insisted, better known than the celebrated poet (*Epigrams* 10.9).

74. In Ps. 22.6, David confesses he is "a worm and no man, scorned by men and despised by the people"; in Mark 9.48, Jesus describes "hell, where their worm dieth not."

75. According to Vergil (*Aen.* 8.314–23), Saturn took refuge in Latium after being deposed by Jupiter.

76. ***humanitas:*** civility, culture.

77. Milton is punning on the Latin for "republic," *res publica,* literally, "public thing."

And take care lest in this way, you, though a royalist, may be said to have founded many "republics" in a single city, or as minister of state to have served them after their foundation by other men. These are your divorces, or, if you prefer, diversions, from which you emerge against me as a veritable Curius.[78]

Now you continue with your lies. "When the conspirators were agitating the decapitation of the king, Milton wrote to them, and when they were wavering urged them to the wicked course." But I did not write to them, nor did it rest with me to urge men who had already without me determined on precisely this course. Yet I shall describe hereafter what I did write on this subject, and I shall also speak of *Eikonoklastes.* Now since this fellow (I am uncertain whether to call him a man or the dregs of manhood), progressing from adultery with servant girls to the adulteration of all truth, has tried to render me infamous among foreigners, by piling up a whole series of lies against me, I ask that no one take it amiss or make it a source of reproach, or resent it, if I have said previously and shall say hereafter more about myself than I would wish, so that if I cannot rescue my eyes from blindness or my name from oblivion or slander, I can at least bring my life into the light out of that darkness which accompanies disgrace. And I must do this for more reasons than one. First, in order that the many good and learned men in all the neighboring countries who are now reading my works and thinking rather well of me, may not despise me on account of this man's abuse, but may persuade themselves that I am incapable of ever disgracing honorable speech by dishonorable conduct, or free utterances by slavish deeds, and that my life, by the grace of God, has ever been far removed from all vice and crime. Next, in order that those distinguished and praiseworthy men whom I undertake to extol may know that I should consider nothing more shameful than to approach the task of praising them while myself deserving blame and censure. Finally, in order that the English people whose defense their own virtue has impelled me to undertake (whether it be my fate or my duty) may know that if I have always led a pure and honorable life, my *Defense* (whether it will be to their honor or dignity I know not) will certainly never be for them a source of shame or disgrace.

Who I am, then, and whence I come, I shall now disclose.[79] I was born in London, of an honorable family. My father was a man of supreme integrity, my mother a woman of purest reputation, celebrated throughout the neighborhood for her acts of charity.[80] My father destined me in early childhood for the study of literature, for which I had so keen an appetite that from my twelfth year scarcely ever did I leave my studies for my bed before the hour of midnight. This was the first cause of injury to my eyes, whose natural weakness was augmented by frequent headaches. Since none of these defects slackened my

78. Manius *Curius* Dentatus (d. 270 B.C.E.), Roman general and exemplar of simple and severe republican virtues. The philanderer More, Milton says, postures as such a model of rectitude.

79. The narrative that follows underlies all subsequent accounts of Milton's life.

80. *Eleemosynis* ["for her acts of charity"] is more precisely translated as "for almsgiving."

assault upon knowledge, my father took care that I should be instructed daily both in school and under other masters at home.[81] When I had thus become proficient in various languages and had tasted by no means superficially the sweetness of philosophy, he sent me to Cambridge, one of our two universities. There, untouched by any reproach, in the good graces of all upright men, for seven years I devoted myself to the traditional disciplines and liberal arts, until I had attained the degree of Master, as it is called, *cum laude.* Then, far from fleeing to Italy, as that filthy rascal alleges, of my own free will I returned home, to the regret of most of the fellows of the college, who bestowed on me no little honor.[82] At my father's country place, whither he had retired to spend his declining years, I devoted myself entirely to the study of Greek and Latin writers, completely at leisure, not, however, without sometimes exchanging the country for the city, either to purchase books or to become acquainted with some new discovery in mathematics or music, in which I then took the keenest pleasure.[83]

When I had occupied five years in this fashion, I became desirous, my mother having died, of seeing foreign parts,[84] especially Italy, and with my father's consent I set forth, accompanied by a single attendant. On my departure Henry Wotton, a most distinguished gentleman, who had long served as King James' ambassador to the Venetians, gave signal proof of his esteem for me, writing a graceful letter which contained good wishes and precepts of no little value to one going abroad.[85] On the recommendation of others I was warmly received in Paris by the noble Thomas Scudamore, Viscount Sligo, legate of King Charles.[86] He on his own initiative introduced me, in company with several of his suite, to Hugo Grotius, a most learned man (then ambassador from the Queen of Sweden to the King of France) whom I ardently desired to meet.[87] When I set out for Italy some days thereafter, Scudamore gave me letters to English merchants along my projected route, that they might assist me as they could. Sailing from Nice, I reached Genoa, then Leghorn and Pisa, and after that Florence. In that city, which I have always admired above all others because of the elegance, not just of its tongue, but also of its wit, I lingered for about two months. There I at once became the friend of many gentlemen eminent in rank

81. Cp. Milton's poem *To His Father,* where Milton thanks his father for supporting his education.
82. Actually, Milton was not eligible for a fellowship that became available in 1630; it was awarded instead to Edward King, whose subsequent death occasioned *Lycidas.* Milton's repudiation of the priesthood and indeed all other traditional career paths rendered moot any possibility of formal retention by the university, however much its fellows may have esteemed him.
83. These years "at leisure" were also devoted to poetry; some of Milton's most celebrated early works date from this period, including *Arcades, A Masque,* and *Lycidas.*
84. What Sara Milton's death had to do with Milton's wanderlust remains a subject of critical conjecture. See, e.g., Kerrigan 1983, 56; Boesky.
85. Sir Henry Wotton (1568–1639) was a favorite of James I, who knighted him and made him ambassador to Venice. He was provost of Eton (near Milton's country retreat in Horton) from 1624 until his death. In *Poems* (1645) Milton prefaces his *Masque* with the letter from Wotton.
86. The legate of King Charles in Paris was John, not Thomas, Scudamore, Viscount Sligo.
87. Grotius, well-known for his works on international law, also wrote Latin poetry that was an early source of inspiration for Milton. He is cited as an authority in the divorce tracts.

and learning, whose private academies I frequented—a Florentine institution which deserves great praise not only for promoting humane studies but also for encouraging friendly intercourse. Time will never destroy my recollection—ever welcome and delightful—of you, Jacopo Gaddi, Carlo Dati, Frescobaldi, Coltellini, Buonmattei, Chimentelli, Francini, and many others.[88]

From Florence I traveled to Siena and thence to Rome. When the antiquity and venerable repute of that city had detained me for almost two months and I had been graciously entertained there by Lukas Holste[89] and other men endowed with both learning and wit, I proceeded to Naples. Here I was introduced by a certain Eremite Friar, with whom I had made the journey from Rome, to Giovanni Battista Manso, Marquis of Villa, a man of high rank and influence, to whom the famous Italian poet, Torquato Tasso, dedicated his work on friendship.[90] As long as I was there I found him a very true friend. He personally conducted me through the various quarters of the city and the Viceregal Court, and more than once came to my lodgings to call. When I was leaving he gravely apologized because even though he had especially wished to show me many more attentions, he could not do so in that city, since I was unwilling to be circumspect in regard to religion.[91] Although I desired also to cross to Sicily and Greece, the sad tidings of civil war from England summoned me back. For I thought it base that I should travel abroad at my ease for the cultivation of my mind, while my fellow-citizens at home were fighting for liberty. As I was on the point of returning to Rome, I was warned by merchants that they had learned through letters of plots laid against me by the English Jesuits, should I return to Rome, because of the freedom with which I had spoken about religion. For I had determined within myself that in those parts I would not indeed begin a conversation about religion, but if questioned about my faith would hide nothing, whatever the consequences. And so, I nonetheless returned to Rome. What I was, if any man inquired, I concealed from no one. For almost two more months, in the very stronghold of the Pope, if anyone attacked the orthodox religion, I openly, as before, defended it. Thus, by the will of God, I returned again in safety to Florence, revisiting friends who were as anxious to see me as if it were my native land to which I had returned. After gladly lingering there for as many months as before (except for an excursion of a few days to Lucca)[92] I crossed the Apennines and hastened to Venice by way of Bologna and

88. Among these Italian friends were lawyers, priests, poets, and aristocratic patrons of the arts. Dati, then only nineteen, seems to have been the closest friend Milton made while in Italy. Correspondence between them is extant; Milton mentions him in *Damon* (137–38); and a tribute from him appears in *Poems* (1645).

89. A German scholar and librarian to Cardinal Barberini, Holste (Holstenius) showed Milton books and manuscripts in the Vatican Library. See Milton's letter to him (1784–87).

90. Cp. *Manso.*

91. One of Henry Wotton's "precepts of no little value to one going abroad" had been to maintain a politic discretion, advice that Milton evidently ignored when it came to religious matters.

92. **Lucca:** the ancestral home of the family of Milton's dearest friend, Charles Diodati. News of Diodati's death may have reached Milton in Naples and spurred his return home (Rumrich 1999).

Ferrara. When I had spent one month exploring that city and had seen to the shipping of the books which I had acquired throughout Italy, I proceeded to Geneva by way of Verona, Milan, and the Pennine Alps, and then along Lake Leman. Geneva, since it reminds me of the slanderer More, impels me once again to call God to witness that in all these places, where so much license exists, I lived free and untouched by the slightest sin or reproach, reflecting constantly that although I might hide from the gaze of men, I could not elude the sight of God. In Geneva I conversed daily with John Diodati,[93] the learned professor of theology. Then by the same route as before, through France, I returned home after a year and three months, more or less, at almost the same time as Charles broke the peace and renewed the war with the Scots, which is known as the second Bishops' War.

The royalist troops were routed in the first engagement of this war, and Charles, when he perceived that all the English, as well as the Scots, were extremely—and justly—ill disposed towards him, soon convened Parliament, not of his own free will but compelled by disaster. I myself, seeking a place to become established, could I but find one anywhere in such upset and tumultuous times, rented a house in town,[94] sufficiently commodious for myself and my books, and there, blissfully enough, devoted myself to my interrupted studies, willingly leaving the outcome of these events, first of all to God, and then to those whom the people had entrusted with this office. Meanwhile, as Parliament acted with vigor, the haughtiness of the bishops began to deflate. As soon as freedom of speech (at the very least) became possible, all mouths were opened against them. Some complained of the personal defects of the bishops, others of the defectiveness of the episcopal rank itself. It was wrong, they said, that their church alone should differ from all other reformed churches. It was proper for the church to be governed by the example of the brethren, but first of all by the word of God.[95] Now, thoroughly aroused to these concerns, I perceived that men were following the true path to liberty and that from these beginnings, these first steps, they were making the most direct progress towards the liberation of all human life from slavery—provided that the discipline arising from religion should overflow into the morals and institutions of the state. Since, moreover, I had so practiced myself from youth that I was above all things unable to disregard the laws of God and man, and since I had asked myself whether I should be of any future use if I now failed my country (or rather the church and so many of my brothers who were exposing themselves to danger for the sake of the Gospel) I decided, although at that time occupied with

93. Charles Diodati's uncle, expatriated from Lucca for his conversion to Protestantism.

94. The house was in St. Bride's Churchyard. In it Milton began the private school in which he instructed John and Edward Phillips. "I cannot but remark a kind of respect, perhaps unconsciously paid to this great man by his biographers: every house in which he resided is historically mentioned, as if it were an injury to neglect naming any place that he honored by his presence" (Johnson 1905, 1:127).

95. In Milton's view, there was no scriptural justification for the clerical hierarchy found in Catholicism and retained by the Church of England.

certain other matters,[96] to devote to this conflict all my talents and all my active powers.

First, therefore, I addressed to a certain friend two books on the reformation of the English church.[97] Then, since two bishops of particularly high repute were asserting their prerogatives against certain eminent ministers,[98] and I concluded that on those subjects which I had mastered solely for love of truth and out of regard for Christian duty, I could express myself at least as well as those who were wrangling for their own profit and unjust authority, I replied to one of the bishops in two books, of which the first was entitled *Of Prelatical Episcopacy* and the second *The Reason of Church-Government,* while to the other bishop I made reply in certain *Animadversions* and later in an *Apology.* I brought succor to the ministers, who were, as it was said, scarcely able to withstand the eloquence of this bishop, and from that time onward, if the bishops made any response, I took a hand. When they, having become a target for the weapons of all men, had at last fallen and troubled us no more, I directed my attention elsewhere, asking myself whether I could in any way advance the cause of true and substantial liberty, which must be sought, not without, but within, and which is best achieved, not by the sword, but by a life rightly undertaken and rightly conducted. Since, then, I observed that there are, in all, three varieties of liberty without which civilized life is scarcely possible, namely ecclesiastical liberty, domestic or personal liberty, and civil liberty, and since I had already written about the first, while I saw that the magistrates were vigorously attending to the third, I took as my province the remaining one, the second or domestic kind. This too seemed to be concerned with three problems: the nature of marriage itself, the education of the children, and finally the existence of freedom to express oneself. Hence I set forth my views on marriage, not only its proper contraction, but also, if need be, its dissolution. My explanation was in accordance with divine law, which Christ did not revoke; much less did He give approval in civil life to any other law more weighty than the law of Moses. Concerning the view which should be held on the single exception, that of fornication, I also expressed both my own opinion and that of others. Our distinguished countryman Selden still more fully explained this point in his *Hebrew Wife,* published about two years later.[99] For in vain does he prattle about liberty in assembly and market-place who at home endures the slavery most unworthy of man, slavery to an inferior. Concerning this matter then I published several books,[100] at the

96. Presumably, these *other matters* include the schooling of his nephews and plans to pen an epic on British history.

97. *Of Reformation* comprises two books.

98. Milton attacked the two bishops, James Ussher and Joseph Hall, on behalf of the five antiprelatical clergymen whose initials formed the pen name Smectymnuus, including his former tutor, Thomas Young.

99. Milton also cites this work by the eminent jurist John Selden in *CD* (1.10).

100. *The Doctrine and Discipline of Divorce* (1643, 1st ed.; 1644, 2nd ed.), *The Judgment of Martin Bucer Concerning Divorce* (1644), *Tetrachordon* (1645), and *Colasterion* (1645).

very time when man and wife were often bitter foes, he dwelling at home with their children, she, the mother of the family, in the camp of the enemy, threatening her husband with death and disaster. Next, in one small volume, I discussed the education of children,[101] a brief treatment, to be sure, but sufficient, as I thought, for those who devote to the subject the attention it deserves. For nothing can be more efficacious than education in molding the minds of men to virtue (whence arises true and internal liberty), in governing the state effectively, and preserving it for the longest possible space of time.

Lastly I wrote, on the model of a genuine speech, the *Areopagitica,* concerning freedom of the press, that the judgment of truth and falsehood, what should be printed and what suppressed, ought not to be in the hands of a few men (and these mostly ignorant and of vulgar discernment) charged with the inspection of books, at whose will or whim virtually everyone is prevented from publishing aught that surpasses the understanding of the mob. Civil liberty, which was the last variety, I had not touched upon, for I saw that it was being adequately dealt with by the magistrates, nor did I write anything about the right of kings, until the king, having been declared an enemy by Parliament and vanquished in the field, was pleading his cause as a prisoner before the judges and was condemned to death. Then at last, when certain Presbyterian ministers, formerly bitter enemies of Charles, but now resentful that the Independent parties were preferred to theirs and carried more weight in Parliament, persisted in attacking the decree which Parliament had passed concerning the king (wroth, not because of the fact, but because their own faction had not performed it) and caused as much tumult as they could, even daring to assert that the doctrines of Protestants and all reformed churches shrank from such an outrageous sentence against kings, I concluded that I must openly oppose so open a lie. Not even then, however, did I write or advise anything concerning Charles, but demonstrated what was in general permissible against tyrants, adducing not a few testimonies from the foremost theologians. And I attacked, almost as if I were haranguing an assembly, the pre-eminent ignorance or insolence of these ministers, who had given promise of better things. This book did not appear until after the death of the king, having been written to reconcile men's minds, rather than to determine anything about Charles (which was not my affair, but that of the magistrates, and which had by then been effected).[102] This service of mine, between private walls, I freely gave, now to the church and now to the state. To me, in return, neither the one nor the other offered more than protection, but the deeds themselves undoubtedly bestowed on me a good conscience, good repute among good men, and this honorable freedom of speech. Other men gained for themselves advantages, other men secured offices at no cost to themselves. As for me, no man has ever seen me seeking office, no man has ever seen me soliciting aught through my friends, clinging with suppliant expression

101. *Of Education* (1644).
102. *The Tenure of Kings and Magistrates* (1649).

to the doors of Parliament, or loitering in the hallways of the lower assemblies. I kept myself at home for the most part, and from my own revenues, though often they were in large part withheld because of the civil disturbance, I endured the tax—by no means entirely just—that was laid on me and maintained my frugal way of life.

When these works had been completed and I thought that I could look forward to an abundance of leisure, I turned to the task of tracing in unbroken sequence, if I could, the history of my country, from the earliest origins even to the present day.[103] I had already finished four books when the kingdom of Charles was transformed into a republic, and the so-called Council of State, which was then for the first time established by the authority of Parliament, summoned me, though I was expecting no such event, and desired to employ my services, especially in connection with foreign affairs. Not long afterwards there appeared a book attributed to the king, and plainly written with great malice against Parliament. Bidden to reply to this, I opposed to the *Eikon* the *Eikonoklastes,* not, as I am falsely charged, "insulting the departed spirit of the king," but thinking that Queen Truth should be preferred to King Charles. Indeed, since I saw that this slander would be at hand for any calumniator, in the very introduction (and as often as I could elsewhere) I averted this reproach from myself. Then Salmasius appeared. So far were they from spending a long time (as More alleges) seeking one who would reply to him, that all, of their own accord, at once named me, then present in the Council. I have given an account of myself to this extent in order to stop your mouth, More, and refute your lies, chiefly for the sake of those good men who otherwise would know me not. Do you then, I bid you, unclean More, be silent. Hold your tongue, I say![104] For the more you abuse me, the more copiously will you compel me to account for my conduct. From such accounting you can gain nothing save the reproach, already most severe, of telling lies, while for me you open the door to still higher praise of my own integrity.

[*Returning to his favorite theme—More's lechery—Milton also derides his opponent for using anecdotal rather than theoretical arguments. He then answers the charges that the regicides lacked popular support, judicial legitimacy, and ecclesiastical backing by citing the incompetence and riotousness of the masses, extolling John Bradshaw* (*the judge who presided over Charles's trial*), *and alleging the hypocrisy of the Church of England. He ridicules the idealization of Charles as a martyr, praises the behavior of the British troops, and defends the seizure of church assets.*]

You now presume to deal with political considerations, you slave of the chair (or rather the easy-chair), namely our offences against all kings and peoples.

103. *The History of Britain* (1670).

104. In Mark 1.23–25, Jesus heals a supplicant possessed by an unclean spirit by ordering the spirit to be silent. Milton wrote the command in the Greek of the New Testament, [φιμώσητι], which literally means "be muzzled."

What offences? For we had no such design. We merely attended to our own affairs and dismissed the affairs of others. If any good has redounded to our neighbors from our example, we do not begrudge it; if any evil, we hold that it occurs through the fault, not of ourselves, but of those who abuse our principles. And pray, what kings or peoples established you, a mere buffoon, as the spokesman of their wrongs? Certainly other men in Parliament, and I myself in the Council, have often heard their ambassadors and legates, when they were given an audience, so far from complaining about their grievances, actually asking of their own free will for our friendship and alliance, even, in fact, congratulating us on our affairs in the names of their own kings and princes, wishing us well indeed and invoking eternal peace and security and the continuance of the same auspicious success. These are not the words of enemies nor of those who hate us, as you allege. Either you must be condemned for lying (in you a trifle) or the kings themselves for fraud and wicked designs (which to them would be a great disgrace). But you reproach us with our writings, in which we admit, "We have given an example beneficial to all people, dreadful to all tyrants." It is a monstrous crime that you describe, to be sure; almost the same as if someone had said, "Take warning, learn to practice justice and respect the gods."[105] Could any utterance be more baleful?

"Cromwell wrote this message to the Scots after the battle of Dunbar." And it was worthy of him and of that noble victory. "The unspeakable pages of Milton are sprinkled with this kind of sesame and poppy."[106] Illustrious indeed is the comrade whom you always associate with me, and in this crime you clearly make me his equal and sometimes his superior. With this title I should think myself most highly honored by you, if from you could proceed anything honorable. "Those pages have been burned," you assert, "by the public hangman in Paris, at the instance of the supreme Parliament."[107] In no wise, I have learned, was this done by Parliament, but by some city official, a *locum tenens*,[108] whether civil or uncivil I do not know, at the instigation of certain clergymen, lazy beasts, who foresaw from a distance and at a great remove what I pray may someday befall their own paunch. Do you not perceive that we too could in turn have burned Salmasius' *Royal Defense*? Even I myself could easily have obtained this request from our magistrates, if I had not thought the insult better avenged by contempt. You, hastening to put out one fire with another, built a Herculean pyre, whence I might rise to greater fame. We more sensibly decided that the frigidity of the *Royal Defense* should not be kindled into flame. I marvel that the people of Toulouse (for I have heard that I was burned also at Toulouse)

105. The quotation is a paraphrase of Vergil (*Aen.* 6.620).

106. *Sesame* was used to induce vomiting; the *poppy*, sleep.

107. Milton's *Defense* was condemned and ordered to be burned by the hangman at Paris, June 26, 1651. Contemporary correspondence from the Dutch scholar Isaac Vossius to Nicholas Heinsius observes that "men come under the executioner's hands for the most part for their crimes and depravity, but books for their worth and excellence" (quoted in Masson 4:342).

108. ***locum tenens:*** a place holder; one who holds office temporarily, as a substitute.

have become so unlike their ancestors that in the city where under the counts Raimond both liberty and religion were once so nobly defended, the Defense of liberty and religion has now been burned. "Would that the writer had been burned as well," you say. So, you slave? But you have taken extraordinary care that I should not return a similar greeting to you, More, for you have long since been consumed by far darker flames—the flames of your adulteries, the flames of your foul deeds, the flames of your prejudices, with the help of which you faithlessly discarded the woman who was betrothed to you by her own seduction. You are consumed by your fits of desperate madness, which drove you to lust after the holiest of rites, foul wretch that you are. They drove you as a priest to defile with incestuous[109] hands the unperceived body of the Lord, and, even as you feigned holiness, to threaten with this Cry of yours all dreadful consequences to those who feign holiness. The flames of madness drove you to untangle your own infamous head, condemned by your own pronouncement. With these crimes and infamies you are all afire, with these raging flames you are scorched night and day, and you pay us a penalty more severe than that which any foe could invoke against you. Meanwhile these burnings of yours do not injure, do not touch me, and I have a great many consolations that delight and gratify my mind, with which to counter those insults of yours. One court, one Parisian hangman, impelled by evil auspices, has perhaps burned me, but a very great many good and learned men throughout all France nonetheless read, approve, and embrace me, as do great numbers throughout the boundless reaches of all Germany, the very home of liberty, and throughout all other countries as well, wherever any of her footprints still remain. And even Greece herself, Athens herself in Attica, as if come to life again, has applauded me in the voice of Philaras,[110] her most illustrious nursling. Indeed, I can truthfully assert that from the time when my *Defense* was first published, and kindled the enthusiasm of its readers, no ambassador from any prince or state who was then in the city failed to congratulate me, if we chanced to meet, or omitted to seek an interview with me at his own house, or to visit me at mine. It would be a sacrilege to omit mention of your departed spirit, Adrian Pauw, glory and ornament of the Netherlands, you who were sent to us with the highest dignity as Ambassador and took care that, although we chanced never to meet, many messages should often assure me of your great and singular good will towards me.[111] Even more often is it a pleasure to recall what I think could never have happened without the favor of God—that on me, whose writings seemed to have attacked kings, the royal majesty itself benignly smiled and bore witness to my integrity and the superior truth of my judgment, with a testimony neighboring on the divine. For why should I shrink from such an epithet, when I contem-

109. **incestuous:** adulterous.

110. Leonard *Philaras*, ambassador to France who, when he visited England and learned of Milton's blindness, recommended a Paris specialist to him. Cp. letter *To Leonard Philaras.*

111. Adrian de Pauw visited London on a diplomatic mission in 1652.

plate that most august queen and the high praise with which she is celebrated on the lips of all men? Indeed, I should not regard the wisest of Athenians (to whom, however, I do not compare myself) as more honored even by the oracle of the Pythian himself, than I by the judgment of that queen.[112] But if it had been my fate to write these words in my youth, and if orators were allowed the same license as poets, I should not have hesitated to exalt my lot above that of certain gods, for they, being gods, contended before a human judge concerning beauty alone, or music, while I, a human being, with a goddess for judge, have come off victorious in by far the noblest contest of all. When I had been so honored, no one would dare to treat me with contempt, save only a public hangman, whether he who gave the orders or he who carried them out.

[*Milton defends the English Church and invokes the support of other European Protestants, specifically the French and Dutch. He cites precedents for aggression against tyrants in European and classical history, and celebrates England for being the first to execute a tyrant. More, he argues, is also destined for the gallows for his adulterous crimes. After defending Cromwell from charges made against him, Milton proceeds with the following laudatory history.*]

But I shall have accomplished nothing if I merely prove that this great man, who has deserved so well of the state, has done no wrong. For it is to the interest not only of the state, but of myself as well (since I have been so deeply involved in the same slanderous accusations) to show to all peoples and all ages, so far as I can, how supremely excellent he is, how worthy of all praise.

Oliver Cromwell is sprung of renowned and illustrious stock. The name was celebrated in former times for good administration under the monarchy and became more glorious as soon as the orthodox religion was reformed, or rather established among us for the first time. He had grown up in the seclusion of his own home, until he reached an age mature and settled, and this too he passed as a private citizen, known for nothing so much as his devotion to the Puritan religion and his upright life. For an occasion of supreme importance he had nourished in his silent heart a faith dependent on God and a mighty spirit. When Parliament was for the last time convened by the king, Cromwell was chosen by his town's electorate and won a seat.[113] There he at once became known for his upright sentiments and steadfast counsels. When war broke out, he offered his services and was put in command of a squadron of horse, but because of the concourse of good men who flocked to his standards from all sides, his force was greatly increased and he soon surpassed well-nigh the greatest generals both in the magnitude of his accomplishments and in the speed with

112. In Plato's *Apology* (21a), the oracle of Apollo (*the Pythian*) at Delphi declares Socrates the wisest of all men.

113. Cromwell first served in Parliament in 1628 for his hometown of Huntingdon; at the 1640 initiation of the last session convened by Charles, the Long Parliament, he was a member for Cambridge.

which he achieved them. Nor was this remarkable, for he was a soldier well-versed in self-knowledge, and whatever enemy lay within—vain hopes, fears, desires—he had either previously destroyed within himself or had long since reduced to subjection. Commander first over himself, victor over himself, he had learned to achieve over himself the most effective triumph, and so, on the very first day that he took service against an external foe, he entered camp a veteran and past-master in all that concerned the soldier's life.

It is impossible for me within the confines of this discourse to describe with fitting dignity the capture of the many cities, to list the many battles, and indeed such great ones, in which he was never conquered nor put to flight, but traversed the entire realm of Britain with uninterrupted victory. Such deeds require the grand scope of a true history, a second battlefield, so to speak, on which they may be recounted, and a space for narration equal to the deeds themselves. The following single proof of his rare and all-but-divine excellence suffices—that there flourished in him so great a power, whether of intellect and genius or of discipline (established not merely according to military standards, but rather according to the code of Christian virtue) that to his camp, as to the foremost school, not just of military science, but of religion and piety, he attracted from every side all men who were already good and brave, or else he made them such, chiefly by his own example. Throughout the entire war, and sometimes even in the intervening periods of peace, amid the many shifts of opinion and circumstance, in spite of opposition, he kept them at their duty, and does so still, not by bribes and the licentiousness typical of the military, but by his authority and their wages alone. No greater praise is wont to be attributed to Cyrus or Epaminondas[114] or any other pre-eminent general among the ancients. And so no one has ever raised a larger or better-disciplined army in a shorter space of time than did Cromwell, an army obedient to his command in all things, welcomed and cherished by their fellow-citizens, formidable indeed to the enemy in the field, but wonderfully merciful to them once they had surrendered. On the estates and under the roofs of the enemy this army proved so mild and innocent of all offence that when the royalists considered the violence of their own soldiery, their drunkenness, impiety, and lust, they rejoiced in their altered lot and believed that Cromwell's men had come, not as enemies, but as guests, a bulwark to all good men, a terror to the wicked, and in fact an inspiration to all virtue and piety.[115]

Nor should I pass you by, Fairfax, in whom nature and divine favor have joined with supreme courage supreme modesty and supreme holiness. By your own right and merit you deserve to be called upon to share these praises, al-

114. *Cyrus* the Great (d. 530 B.C.E.) founded the Persian Empire, vastly expanded its territories, and ruled it with unprecedented tolerance. *Epaminondas* (d. 362 B.C.E.), Theban general and statesman, made his city the most powerful in Greece.

115. Even the Royalists conceded that Cromwell's New Model Army surpassed their own in moral conduct. Troops were forbidden to plunder, abuse prisoners, or harm noncombatants.

though in your present retreat you conceal yourself as well as you can, like Scipio Africanus of old in Liternum.[116] You have defeated, not only the enemy, but ambition as well, and the thirst for glory which conquers all the most eminent men, and you are reaping the reward of your virtues and noble deeds amid that most delightful and glorious retirement which is the end of all labors and human action, even the greatest. When the heroes of old, after wars and honors no greater than yours, enjoyed such repose, the poets who sought to praise them despaired of being able fittingly to describe its nature in any other way than by creating a myth to the effect that they had been received into heaven and were sharing the banquets of the gods. But whether ill health, as I suspect, or some other reason has withdrawn you from public life, I am firmly convinced that nothing could have torn you from the needs of the State had you not seen how great a defender of liberty, how strong and faithful a pillar and support of English interests you were leaving in your successor.[117] For while you, Cromwell, are safe, he does not have sufficient faith even in God himself who would fear for the safety of England, when he sees God everywhere so favorable to you, so unmistakably at your side. But you were now left alone to fight upon another battleground.

Yet why go on at length? The greatest events I shall relate, if I can, with brevity comparable to the speed with which you are wont to achieve them. When all Ireland was lost, but for a single city, you transported the army and in one battle instantly broke the power of Hibernia. You were completing the task day by day, when suddenly you were recalled to the Scottish War. Then, tireless, you proceeded against the Scots who with their king were preparing an invasion of England, and in about one year you completely subdued and added to the wealth of England that realm which all our kings for eight hundred years had been unable to master. When the remnant of their forces, still powerful and marching swiftly with no encumbrances, set out in utter desperation for England, which was then almost stripped of defenses, and, making an unforeseen attack, got as far as Worcester, you pursued them with forced marches and in one battle destroyed them, capturing almost all their noblemen. Afterwards peace was maintained at home.

Then, but not for the first time, we perceived that you were as mighty in deliberation as in the arts of war. Daily you toiled in Parliament, that the treaty made with the enemy might be honored, or that decrees in the interest of the State might at once be passed. When you saw delays being contrived and every man more attentive to his private interest than to that of the state, when you saw the people complaining that they had been deluded of their hopes and circumvented by the power of the few, you put an end to the domination of these few

116. Publius Cornelius Scipio, or *Scipio Africanus* Major (c. 200 B.C.E.), was the greatest Roman general of the Second Punic War. He retired to his country home in Liternum following a political controversy in which he was charged with misconduct.

117. Milton neglects to mention that Fairfax withdrew because he disapproved of the regicide.

men, since they, although so often warned, had refused to do so. Another Parliament was convened anew, and the suffrage granted only to those who deserved it.[118] The elected members came together. They did nothing. When they in turn had at length exhausted themselves with disputes and quarrels, most of them considering themselves inadequate and unfit for executing such great tasks, they of their own accord dissolved the Parliament.

Cromwell, we are deserted! You alone remain.[119] On you has fallen the whole burden of our affairs. On you alone they depend. In unison we acknowledge your unexcelled virtue. No one protests save such as seek equal honors, though inferior themselves, or begrudge the honors assigned to one more worthy, or do not understand that there is nothing in human society more pleasing to God, or more agreeable to reason, nothing in the state more just, nothing more expedient, than the rule of the man most fit to rule. All know you to be that man, Cromwell! Such have been your achievements as the greatest and most illustrious citizen, the director of public counsels, the commander of the bravest armies, the father of your country. It is thus that you are greeted by the spontaneous and heartfelt cries of all upright men. Your deeds recognize no other name as worthy of you; no other do they allow, and the haughty titles which seem so great in the opinion of the mob, they properly reject. For what is a title, except a certain limited degree of dignity? Your deeds surpass all degrees, not only of admiration, but surely of titles too, and like the tops of pyramids, bury themselves in the sky, towering above the popular favor of titles. But since it is, not indeed worthy, but expedient for even the greatest capacities to be bounded and confined by some sort of human dignity, which is considered an honor, you assumed a certain title very like that of father of your country. You suffered and allowed yourself, not indeed to be borne aloft, but to come down so many degrees from the heights and be forced into a definite rank, so to speak, for the public good.[120] The name of king you spurned from your far greater eminence, and rightly so.[121] For if, when you became so great a figure, you were captivated by the title which as a private citizen you were able to send under the yoke and reduce to nothing, you would be doing almost the same thing as if, when you had subjugated some tribe of idolaters with the help of the true God, you were to worship the gods that you had conquered. May you then, O Cromwell, increase in your magnanimity, for it becomes you. You, the liberator of your country, the author of liberty, and likewise its guardian and savior,

118. After Cromwell dissolved the Rump Parliament in April 1653, he convened a new one, the Barebones Parliament, its members chosen by the officers of the army from among those nominated by the Independent churches of each county.

119. Cromwell accepted the abdication of the Barebones Parliament and assumed sovereign power under the title Lord Protector in December 1653.

120. Milton's interpretation of Cromwell's assumption of the title Lord Protector bears comparison with Abdiel's interpretation of the Son's installation as head of the angels (*PL* 5.831–45).

121. Led by General Lambert, a group of army officers had indeed urged Cromwell to accept the title of king in the last days of the Barebones Parliament.

can undertake no more distinguished role and none more august. By your deeds you have outstripped not only the achievements of our kings, but even the legends of our heroes.

Consider again and again how precious a thing is this liberty which you hold, committed to your care, entrusted and commended to you by how dear a mother, your native land. That which she once sought from the most distinguished men of the entire nation, she now seeks from you alone and through you alone hopes to achieve. Honor this great confidence reposed in you, honor your country's singular hope in you. Honor the faces and the wounds of the many brave men, all those who under your leadership have striven so vigorously for liberty. Honor the shades of those who have fallen in that very struggle. Honor too what foreign nations think and say of us, the high hopes which they have for themselves as a result of our liberty, so bravely won, and our republic, so gloriously born. If the republic should miscarry, so to speak, and as quickly vanish, surely no greater shame and disgrace could befall this country. Finally, honor yourself, so that, having achieved that liberty in pursuit of which you endured so many hardships and encountered so many perils, you may not permit it to be violated by yourself or in any degree diminished by others. Certainly you yourself cannot be free without us, for it has so been arranged by nature that he who attacks the liberty of others is himself the first of all to lose his own liberty and learns that he is the first of all to become a slave. And he deserves this fate. For if the very patron and tutelary god of liberty, as it were, if that man than whom no one has been considered more just, more holy, more excellent, shall afterwards attack that liberty which he himself has defended, such an act must necessarily be dangerous and well-nigh fatal not only to liberty itself but also to the cause of all virtue and piety. Honor itself, virtue itself will seem to have melted away, religious faith will be circumscribed, reputation will hereafter be a meager thing. A deeper wound than this, after that first wound,[122] can never be inflicted on the human race. You have taken upon yourself by far the heaviest burden, one that will put to the test your inmost capacities, that will search you out wholly and intimately, and reveal what spirit, what strength, what authority are in you, whether there truly live in you that piety, faith, justice, and moderation of soul which convince us that you have been raised by the power of God beyond all other men to this most exalted rank. To rule with wisdom three powerful nations, to desire to lead their peoples from base customs to a better standard of morality and discipline than before, to direct your solicitous mind and thoughts into the most distant regions, to be vigilant, to exercise foresight, to refuse no toil, to yield to no allurements of pleasure, to flee from the pomp of wealth and power, these are arduous tasks compared to which war is a mere game. These trials will buffet you and shake you; they require a man supported by divine help, advised and instructed by all-but-divine inspiration.

122. **first wound:** i.e., Original Sin.

Such matters and still others I have no doubt that you consider and reflect upon, times without number, and also the following concern—by what means you can best, can not only accomplish these momentous ends, but also restore to us our liberty, unharmed and even enhanced. In my judgment you can do this in no better way than by admitting those men whom you first cherished as comrades in your toils and dangers to the first share in your counsels—as indeed you do—men who are eminently modest, upright, and brave, men who from the sight of so much death and slaughter before their very eyes have learned, not cruelty or hardness of heart, but justice, the fear of God, and compassion for the lot of mankind, have learned finally that liberty is to be cherished the more dearly in proportion to the gravity of the dangers to which they have exposed themselves for her sake. These men come not from the off-scourings of the mob or of foreign countries. They are no random throng, but most of them citizens of the better stamp, of birth either noble or at least not dishonorable, of ample or moderate means. What if some are more highly valued because of their very poverty? It was not booty that attracted them, but the most troubled times, when our situation was beyond question dubious and often desperate, inspired them to free the state by killing the tyrant. And they were ready, not merely to bandy speeches and views with one another in a place of safety or in Parliament, but to join battle with the enemy. Therefore, unless we are for ever to pursue vague and empty hopes, I see not in what men faith can finally be reposed if not in them, or in their like. Of their loyalty we have the surest and most indubitable pledge in that they were willing to meet death itself for their country, if such had been their destiny. Of their piety in that, after humbly imploring God's assistance and so often receiving notable help from him, they were accustomed to assign the whole glory of their successful enterprises to him from whom they were wont to seek aid. Of their justice in that they brought even the king to trial, and, when he was condemned, refused to spare him. Of their moderation, in that we have now for a long time tasted it, and also in that if the peace which they themselves have secured should be broken through their own fault, they would themselves be the first to feel the evils that would then ensue. They would themselves receive in their own bodies the first wounds and must fight again for all those fortunes and distinctions which they had just now so gloriously secured. Of their courage, at last, in that other men have never recovered their liberty with better fortune or greater bravery. Let us not suppose that any others can preserve it with greater care.

My discourse is on fire to commemorate the names of these illustrious men: first you, Fleetwood, whom I know to have shown the same civility, gentleness, and courtesy from your earliest days in the army even to those military commands which you now hold, next to the very highest.[123] The enemy found you brave and fearless, but also merciful in victory. You, Lambert, who as a mere youth and the leader of a bare handful of men checked the advance of the Duke

123. Charles *Fleetwood* was then commander in chief of Ireland.

of Hamilton and kept him in check, though around him was the flower and strength of all Scotland's young manhood.[124] You, Desborough, and you, Whalley, whom, when I heard or read about the most violent battles of this war, I always sought and found where the enemy was thickest.[125] You, Overton, who for many years have been linked to me with a more than fraternal harmony, by reason of the likeness of our tastes and the sweetness of your disposition.[126] At the unforgettable Battle of Marston Moor, when our left wing had been routed, the leaders, looking behind them in flight, beheld you making a stand with your infantry and repelling the attacks of the enemy amid dense slaughter on both sides. Then, in the war in Scotland, once the shores of Fife had been seized by your efforts under the leadership of Cromwell and a way laid open beyond Stirling, the Scots of the West and the North admit that you were a most humane foe, and the farthest Orkneys confess you a merciful conqueror. I shall name others too, whom you summoned to share your counsels, men famous in private life and the arts of peace, and known to me either through friendship or by report. Whitelocke, Pickering, Strickland, Sydenham, and Sidney (which glorious name I rejoice has ever been loyal to our side), Montague, Lawrence,[127] both of them men of supreme genius, cultivated in the liberal arts, and a great many other citizens of pre-eminent merits, some already famed for service in Parliament, some for military distinction. To these most illustrious men and honored citizens it would beyond doubt be appropriate for you to entrust our liberty. Indeed, it would be hard to say to whom that liberty could more safely be committed.

Next, I would have you leave the church to the church and shrewdly relieve yourself and the government of half your burden (one that is at the same time completely alien to you), and not permit two powers, utterly diverse, the civil and the ecclesiastical, to make harlots of each other and while appearing to strengthen, by their mingled and spurious riches, actually to undermine and at length destroy each other. I would have you remove all power from the church (but power will never be absent so long as money, the poison of the church, the quinsy[128] of truth, extorted by force even from those who are unwilling, remains

124. John *Lambert* was only twenty-nine when he defeated the invading Scottish forces led by Hamilton, and had already achieved a rank second only to Fairfax and Cromwell.

125. John *Desborough* almost captured Charles II in the battle at Worcester, and Edmund *Whalley* commanded the regiment responsible for Charles I while he was at Hampton Court.

126. Robert *Overton,* the governor of Hull, played a prominent part in the battle of Marston Moor but openly criticized the new Protectorate.

127. Bulstrode Whitelocke and Gilbert *Pickering* served in Parliament from 1640 until its dissolution in 1653. Walter *Strickland* and William *Sydenham* both served in the Barebones Parliament, the latter after a distinguished career as a colonel. Algernon *Sidney,* a captain of horse who sustained serious injury at Marston Moor, was nevertheless twice suspected of Royalist sympathies but proved loyal to the Parliamentarians. Edward *Montague* and Henry *Lawrence* were both expelled from the Long Parliament in the 1648 purge, but the former later served in the Council of State, and the latter ascended to the position of Lord President of Cromwell's Supreme Council. Milton wrote *Sonnet 20* for Henry's son, Edward.

128. **quinsy:** tonsillitis.

the price of preaching the Gospel). I would have you drive from the temple the money-changers, who buy and sell, not doves, but the Dove, the Holy Spirit Himself. Then may you propose fewer new laws than you repeal old ones, for there are often men in the state who itch with a kind of lust to promulgate many laws, as versifiers itch to pour forth many poems. But the greater the number, the worse in general is the quality of the laws, which become, not precautions, but pitfalls. You should keep only those laws that are essential and pass others—not such as subject good men with bad to the same yoke, nor, while they take precautions against the wiles of the wicked, forbid also that which should be free for good men—but rather such laws as appertain only to crimes and do not forbid actions of themselves licit, merely because of the guilt of those who abuse them. For laws are made only to curb wickedness, but nothing can so effectively mould and create virtue as liberty.

Next, would that you might take more thought for the education and morality of the young than has yet been done, nor feel it right for the teachable and the unteachable, the diligent and the slothful to be instructed side by side at public expense. Rather should you keep the rewards of the learned for those who have already acquired learning, those who already deserve the reward. Next, may you permit those who wish to engage in free inquiry to publish their findings at their own peril without the private inspection of any petty magistrate, for so will truth especially flourish, nor will the censure, the envy, the narrow-mindedness, or the superstition of the half-educated always mete out the discoveries of other men, and indeed knowledge in general, according to their own measure and bestow it on us according to their whim.[129] Lastly, may you yourself never be afraid to listen to truth or falsehood, whichever it is, but may you least of all listen to those who do not believe themselves free unless they deny freedom to others, and who do nothing with greater enthusiasm or vigor than cast into chains, not just the bodies, but also the consciences of their brothers, and impose on the state and the church the worst of all tyrannies, that of their own base customs or opinions. May you always take the side of those who think that not just their own party or faction, but all citizens equally have an equal right to freedom in the state. If there be any man for whom such liberty, which can be maintained by the magistrates, does not suffice, he is, I judge, more in love with self-seeking and mob-rule than with genuine liberty, for a people torn by so many factions (as after a storm, when the waves have not yet subsided) does not itself permit that condition in public affairs which is ideal and perfect.

For, my fellow countrymen, your own character is a mighty factor in the acquisition or retention of liberty. Unless your liberty is such as can neither be won nor lost by arms, but is of that kind alone which, sprung from piety, justice, temperance, in short, true virtue, has put down the deepest and most far-reaching roots in your souls, there will not be lacking one who will shortly

129. Here Milton restates the gist of *Areopagitica*.

wrench from you, even without weapons, that liberty which you boast of having sought by force of arms. Many men has war made great whom peace makes small. If, having done with war, you neglect the arts of peace, if warfare is your peace and liberty, war your only virtue, your supreme glory, you will find, believe me, that peace itself is your greatest enemy. Peace itself will be by far your hardest war, and what you thought liberty will prove to be your servitude. Unless with true and sincere devotion to God and men—not empty and verbose, but effective and fruitful devotion—you drive from your minds the superstitions that are sprung from ignorance of real and genuine religion, you will have those who will perch upon your back and shoulders as if on beasts of burden, who will sell you at public auction, though you be victors in the war, as if you were their own booty, and will reap rich reward from your ignorance and superstition. Unless you expel avarice, ambition, and luxury from your minds, yes, and extravagance from your families as well, you will find at home and within that tyrant who, you believed, was to be sought abroad and in the field—now even more stubborn. In fact, many tyrants, impossible to endure, will from day to day hatch out from your very vitals. Conquer them first. This is the warfare of peace, these are its victories, hard indeed, but bloodless, and far more noble than the gory victories of war. Unless you be victors here as well, that enemy and tyrant whom you have just now defeated in the field has either not been conquered at all or has been conquered in vain. For if the ability to devise the cleverest means of putting vast sums of money into the treasury, the power readily to equip land and sea forces, to deal shrewdly with ambassadors from abroad, and to contract judicious alliances and treaties has seemed to any of you greater, wiser, and more useful to the state than to administer incorrupt justice to the people, to help those cruelly harassed and oppressed, and to render to every man promptly his own deserts, too late will you discover how mistaken you have been, when those great affairs have suddenly betrayed you and what now seems to you small and trifling shall then have turned against you and become a source of ruin. Nay, the loyalty of the armies and allies in whom you trust is fleeting, unless it be maintained by the power of justice alone. Wealth and honors, which most men pursue, easily change masters; they desert to the side which excels in virtue, industry, and endurance of toil, and they abandon the slothful. Thus nation presses upon nation, or the sounder part of a nation overthrows the more corrupt. Thus did you drive out the royalists. If you begin to slip into the same vices, to imitate those men, to seek the same goals, to clutch at the same vanities, you actually are royalists yourselves, at the mercy either of the same men who up to now have been your enemies, or of others in turn, who, depending on the same prayers to God, the same patience, integrity, and shrewdness which were at first your strength, will justly subdue you, who have now become so base and slipped into royalist excess and folly. Then in truth, as if God had become utterly disgusted with you—a horrid state—will you seem to have passed through the fire only to perish in the smoke. Then will you be as much despised by all men as you are now admired and will leave behind you only this salutary lesson (which could in the future perhaps be of assistance to others, though not to you), how great might have been the achievements of genuine virtue and piety, when the mere counterfeit and shadow of these qualities—cleverly feigned, no more—could embark upon such noble undertakings and through you progress so far towards execution.

For if through your want of experience, of constancy, or of honesty such glorious deeds have issued in failure, it will yet be possible for better men to do as much hereafter, and no less must be expected of them. But no one, not even Cromwell himself, nor a whole tribe of liberating Brutuses, if Brutus[130] were to come to life again, either could if they would, or would if they could, free you a second time, once you had been so easily corrupted. For why should anyone then claim for you freedom to vote or the power of sending to Parliament whomever you prefer? So that each of you could elect in the cities men of his own faction, or in the country towns choose that man, however unworthy, who has entertained you more lavishly at banquets and supplied farmers and peasants with more abundant drink? Under such circumstances, not wisdom or authority, but faction and gluttony would elect to Parliament in our name either inn-keepers and hucksters of the state from city taverns or from country districts ploughboys and veritable herdsmen. Who would commit the state to men whom no one would trust with his private affairs? the treasury and revenues to men who have shamefully wasted their own substance? Who would hand over to them the public income, to steal and convert from public to private? Or how could they suddenly become legislators for the whole nation who themselves have never known what law is, what reason, what right or justice, straight or crooked, licit or illicit; who think that all power resides in violence, all grandeur in pride and arrogance; who in Parliament give priority to showing illegitimate favor to their friends and persistent hostility to their foes; who establish their relatives and friends in every section of the country to levy taxes and confiscate property—men for the most part mean and corrupt, who by bidding at their own auctions collect therefrom great sums of money, embezzle what they have collected, defraud the state, ravage the provinces, enrich themselves, and suddenly emerge into opulence and pride from the beggary and rags of yesterday? Who could endure such thieving servants, the deputies of their masters? Who could believe the masters and patrons of such thieves to be fit guardians of liberty, or think his own liberty enlarged one iota by such caretakers of the state (though the customary number of five hundred be thus elected from all the towns), since there would then be so few among the guardians and watchdogs of liberty who either knew how to enjoy, or deserved to possess, it?

Lastly (a reflection not to be neglected), men who are unworthy of liberty most often prove ungrateful to their very liberators. Who would now be willing to fight, or even encounter the smallest danger for the liberty of such men? It is

130. Lucius Junius Brutus (c. 500 B.C.E.), legendary founder of the Roman republic, liberated Rome from the Tarquins.

not fitting, it is not meet, for such men to be free. However loudly they shout and boast about liberty, slaves they are at home and abroad, although they know it not. When at last they do perceive it and like wild horses fretting at the bit try to shake off the yoke, driven not by the love of true liberty (to which the good man alone can rightly aspire), but by pride and base desires, even though they take arms in repeated attempts, they will accomplish naught.[131] They can perhaps change their servitude; they cannot cast it off.[132] This often happened even to the ancient Romans, once they had been corrupted and dissipated by luxury; still more often to the modern Romans; when after a long interval they sought under the auspices of Crescentius Nomentanus and later under the leadership of Cola di Rienzo, self-styled Tribune of the People, to renew the ancient glory of Rome and restore the Republic.[133] For rest assured (that you may not be vexed, or seek to blame someone other than yourselves), rest assured, I say, that to be free is precisely the same as to be pious, wise, just, and temperate and just, careful of one's property, aloof from another's, and thus finally to be magnanimous and brave, so to be the opposite to these qualities is the same as to be a slave. And by the customary judgment and, so to speak, just retaliation of God, it happens that a nation which cannot rule and govern itself, but has delivered itself into slavery to its own lusts, is enslaved also to other master whom it does not choose, and serves not only voluntarily but also against its will. Such is the decree of law and of nature herself, that he who cannot control himself, who through poverty of intellect or madness cannot properly administer his own affairs, should not be his own master, but like a ward be given over to the power of another.[134] Much less should he be put in charge of the affairs of other men, or of the state. You, therefore, who wish to remain free, either be wise at the outset or recover your senses as soon as possible. If to be a slave is hard, and you do not wish it, learn to obey right reason, to master yourselves. Lastly refrain from factions, hatreds, superstitions, injustices, lusts, and rapine against one another. Unless you do this with all your strength you cannot seem either to God

131. According to Masson (4:547–52), the Protectorate was opposed both by those who wanted a republican form of government, not single-person rule, and by those loyal to the Stuarts. Both factions actively plotted against Cromwell.

132. Cp. *Sonnet 12* 8–12: "But this is got by casting pearl to hogs,/That bawl for freedom in their senseless mood,/And still revolt when truth would set them free./License they mean when they cry libertie;/ For who loves that, must first be wise and good"; also, *TKM:* "None can love freedom heartily but good men. The rest love not freedom, but license; which never hath more scope, or more indulgence, than under tyrants."

133. *Crescentius Nomentanus* (c. 950–98), who like the rest of his powerful clan (the Crescentii) affected the ways of classical Rome, actively opposed the dominion of Saxon rulers over Rome's affairs. Otto III besieged, captured, and had him beheaded. *Cola di Rienzo* (1313–54) took the title of tribune and sought fiscal, political, and judicial reform in Rome. Ultimately successful in enlisting papal support, he returned to Rome from exile and was killed by the mob.

134. The theological application of this classical principle of ethics and political theory pervades Milton's late masterpieces. See *PL* 12.90–95: "Therefore since he permits/Within himself unworthy powers to reign/Over free reason, God in judgment just/Subjects him from without to violent lords;/ Who oft as undeservedly enthrall/His outward freedom"; also, with specific application to the descent of Rome from republican virtue to imperial servility *PR* 4.132–45.

or to men, or even to your recent liberators, fit to be entrusted with the liberty and guidance of the state and the power of commanding others, which you arrogate to yourselves so greedily. Then indeed, like a nation in wardship, you would rather be in need of some tutor, some brave and faithful guardian of your affairs.

As for me, whatever the issue, I have bestowed my services by no means grudgingly nor, I hope, in vain, where I judged that they would be most useful to the state. I have not borne arms for liberty merely on my own doorstep, but have also wielded them so far afield that the reason and justification of these by no means commonplace events, having been explained and defended both at home and abroad, and having surely won the approval of all good men, are made splendidly manifest to the supreme glory of my countrymen and as an example to posterity. If the most recent deeds of my fellow countrymen should not correspond sufficiently to their earliest, let them look to it themselves. I have borne witness, I might almost say I have erected a monument that will not soon pass away, to those deeds that were illustrious, that were glorious, that were almost beyond any praise, and if I have done nothing else, I have surely redeemed my pledge. Moreover, just as the epic poet, if he is scrupulous and disinclined to break the rules, undertakes to extol, not the whole life of the hero whom he proposes to celebrate in his verse, but usually one event of his life (the exploits of Achilles at Troy, let us say, or the return of Ulysses, or the arrival of Aeneas in Italy) and passes over the rest, so let it suffice me too, as my duty or my excuse, to have celebrated at least one heroic achievement of my countrymen. The rest I omit. Who could extol all the achievements of an entire nation? If after such brave deeds you ignobly fail, if you do aught unworthy of yourselves, be sure that posterity will speak out and pass judgment: the foundations were soundly laid, the beginnings, in fact more than the beginnings, were splendid, but posterity will look in vain, not without a certain distress, for those who were to complete the work, who were to put the pediment in place. It will be a source of grief that to such great undertakings, such great virtues, perseverance was lacking. It will seem to posterity that a mighty harvest of glory was at hand, together with the opportunity for doing the greatest deeds, but that to this opportunity men were wanting. Yet there was not one wanting who could rightly counsel, encourage, and inspire, who could honor both the noble deeds and those who had done them, and make both deeds and doers illustrious with praises that will never die.[135]

135. In defining his historical role in the last two sentences, Milton returns to the agricultural myth invoked early in this work, when he compared himself to "Triptolemus of old" disseminating "the renewed cultivation of freedom and civic life." The *mighty harvest of glory* waiting to be reaped owes much to his oratorical efforts. See note 14.

Introduction to *The Ready and Easy Way to Establish a Free Commonwealth*

The Ready and Easy Way to Establish a Free Commonwealth; and the Excellence Thereof Compared with the Inconveniences and Dangers of Readmitting Kingship in this Nation appeared in two editions in late February and early April 1660, amid conditions that were from Milton's perspective rapidly deteriorating (Norbrook 1999; Lewalski 2000; Knoppers 2001). Although Milton wrote both versions in great haste in order to keep pace with events, *The Ready and Easy Way* is at once a grimly and gloriously eloquent work. The immediate political context was the unpopular rule of the Rump Parliament, agitation by Republication army leaders, and the arrival in London of General George Monck's army. In January and early February, Monck reiterated his support of the Commonwealth and his opposition to the restoration of monarchy, but his true intentions were as much a subject of debate and speculation among his contemporaries as they are among scholars today.

It is clear from the first edition of *The Ready and Easy Way* that Milton placed in Monck his hopes for the continuation of republican government. On February 21, however, before Milton could see the first edition through the press, Monck reinstated the Presbyterian MPs excluded in Pride's Purge of 1648, making the return of Charles II all but inevitable. In the greatly expanded second edition, reprinted here, Milton by turns adjusts to and pointedly ignores Monck's ominous about-face. While Milton refers in the opening lines to the "resolution of those who are in power tending to the establishment of a free commonwealth," the end had come for the Good Old Cause of antimonarchic republicanism. The Rump's "writs for new elections," in which eligibility depended on opposition to a rule by a "single person," had been recalled, and public sentiment was gathering for the restoration of Charles II. By the time of the second edition, the restored Long Parliament had called its own new elections, and it was clear that the new body, elected without the Rump's qualifications, would restore monarchy. Milton's thinly veiled plea that Monck thwart pro-monarchist sentiment by force underlines the bleakness of anti-monarchism prospects: "More just it is, doubtless, if it come to force, that a less number compel a greater to retain (which can be no wrong to them) their liberty, than that a greater number, for the pleasure of their baseness, compel a less most injuriously to be their fellow slaves" (pp. 383–84).

If there was an element of bandwagon jumping in the publication of the antiprelatical tracts (see the introduction to *Of Reformation*), the circumstances surrounding *The Ready and Easy Way* could not have been more different. Milton was the last republican to put his name to a work opposing monarchy before the Restoration. His claim that "with all hazard I have ventured what I thought my duty to speak" (p. 388) is no exaggeration. Publishing the work at a time of growing public opposition to the Rump and growing support for the restoration of monarchy took remarkable physical courage. Within months, the new House of Commons had successfully called for the burning of several of Milton's books, and Milton was imprisoned. It is not altogether clear how the author escaped the punishment for treason: hanging until half-dead, disembowelment while alive, and quartering.

The title refers to Milton's plan for a grand council (a national assembly perpetuating the Long Parliament, with members granted life tenure) and for regional assemblies. Members of the grand council are to be chosen by a series of nominations and elections that gradually sift and refine candidate lists, a process superior in Milton's eyes to "committing all to the noise and shouting of a rude multitude" (p. 378). Milton may have seen his model as "ready and easy," but he must have also recognized by late February that popular sentiment made its implementation impossible. It may be significant in this connection that Milton in his later poetry was critical of ready ways and of ease (see, e.g., *PL* 2.81 and 12.214–26 and *SA* 268–71).

The Ready and Easy Way is simultaneously a groundbreaking work of political theory and the last gasp of the Good Old Cause. Blair Hoxby (2002) argues persuasively that Milton invents here the federalist republican balance between central and local authority. At the same time, Milton in his prophetic mode unleashes a jeremiad against the backsliding English, who like the Israelites are an elect nation but who have, again like the Israelites, chosen "a captain back for Egypt" (p. 388; Knoppers 1990). After years in which the spokesperson of the party in power had moderated his style (Corns 1982), Milton returns in the rhetoric of *The Ready and Easy Way* to the fiery incandescence of his early prose works, as he articulates a principle close to his heart: external tyranny, though an apt punishment for those who are slaves within, is an insupportable outrage when imposed on those endowed with inward freedom. Milton's passionate conviction fuels the tract's language, culminating in a peroration justly celebrated as one of the high points of Milton's prose.

Our copy text for the second edition of April 1660 is a Harvard University Library copy (14496.17.2*).

THE READY AND EASY WAY TO ESTABLISH A FREE COMMONWEALTH

Et nos
Consilium dedimus Syllae, demus populo nunc.[1]

Although since the writing of this treatise the face of things hath had some change, writs for new elections have been recalled, and the members at first chosen readmitted from exclusion,[2] yet not a little rejoicing to hear declared the resolution of those who are in power tending to the establishment of a free commonwealth,[3] and to remove, if it be possible, this noxious humor of returning to bondage (instilled of late by some deceivers, and nourished from bad principles and false apprehensions among too many of the people), I thought best not to suppress what I had written, hoping that it may now be of much more use and concernment to be freely published in the midst of our elections to a free parliament, or their sitting to consider freely of the government, whom it behooves to have all things represented to them that may direct their judgment therein. And I never read of any state, scarce of any tyrant, grown so incurable as to refuse counsel from any in a time of public deliberation, much less to be offended. If their absolute determination be to enthrall us, before so long a Lent of servitude they may permit us a little shroving time[4] first, wherein to speak freely and take our leaves of liberty. And because in the former edition, through haste, many faults escaped, and many books were suddenly dispersed ere the note to mend them could be sent, I took the opportunity from this occasion to revise and somewhat to enlarge the whole discourse, especially that

1. Juvenal's *Satires* 1 ("And we have given advice to Sulla, now let us give it to the people"). Under the name of the Roman ruler Lucius Cornelius Sulla (138–78 B.C.E.), who paved the way for the monarchy of Julius Caesar, Milton points to General George Monck, to whom he had recently addressed proposals for preventing the restoration of monarchy; having in the meantime lost confidence in Monck, he turns now to the people.
2. In the days before the publication of the first edition, *new elections* for Parliament, in which Royalists would be ineligible, were called off after the Presbyterian and largely Royalist members purged in 1648 (see n. 13) had been *readmitted from exclusion* as a result of Monck's intervention. With this change, the restoration of monarchy became inevitable. By the time of the second edition, things looked even bleaker from Milton's perspective.
3. The Rump emphatically and Monck and the army officers at least nominally were opposed to the *returning to bondage,* i.e., the restoration of monarchy; Milton is grasping at straws.
4. **shroving time:** Shrovetide, which precedes Ash Wednesday and Lent, was set aside for confession and carnivals (Shrove Tuesday is the English *Mardi Gras*).

part which argues for a perpetual senate. The treatise thus revised and enlarged is as follows.

The parliament of England, assisted by a great number of the people who appeared and stuck to them faithfulest in defense of religion and their civil liberties, judging kingship by long experience a government unnecessary, burdensome, and dangerous, justly and magnanimously abolished it,[5] turning regal bondage into a free commonwealth, to the admiration and terror of our emulous neighbors. They took themselves not bound by the light of nature or religion to any former covenant,[6] from which the king himself, by many forfeitures of a latter date or discovery, and our own longer consideration thereon, had more and more unbound us, both to himself and his posterity, as hath been ever the justice and the prudence of all wise nations that have ejected tyranny. They covenanted "to preserve the king's person and authority in the preservation of the true religion and our liberties," not in his endeavoring to bring in upon our consciences a popish religion, upon our liberties thraldom, upon our lives destruction, by his occasioning (if not complotting, as was after discovered) the Irish massacre,[7] his fomenting and arming the rebellion, his covert leaguing with the rebels against us, his refusing, more than seven times, propositions[8] most just and necessary to the true religion and our liberties, tendered him by the parliament both of England and Scotland. They made not their covenant concerning him with no difference between a king and a god, or promised him, as Job did to the Almighty, "to trust in him, though he slay us."[9] They understood that the solemn engagement[10] wherein we all forswore kingship was no more a breach of the covenant than the covenant was of the protestation[11] before, but a faithful and prudent going on both in the words, well weighed, and in the true sense of the covenant, "without respect of persons,"[12] when we could not serve two contrary masters, God and the king, or the king and that more supreme law sworn in the first place to maintain our safety and our liberty.

They knew the people of England to be a free people, themselves the representers of that freedom. And although many were excluded,[13] and as many fled

5. In February 1649, shortly after the execution of Charles I, the Rump Parliament abolished monarchy.

6. **covenant:** the Solemn League and Covenant of 1643, quoted several lines later.

7. Although Charles was not behind the massacre of English Protestants by Irish Catholics in 1641, he did attempt to secure the military help of Irish Catholic armies during the Civil War.

8. **propositions:** In the seven years preceding his execution, Charles received seven or more sets of proposals from the English and Scottish Parliaments.

9. Milton paraphrases Job 13.15.

10. **engagement:** oath of loyalty to the Commonwealth mandatory for Members of Parliament following October 1649.

11. **protestation:** In a formal protest in May 1641, Parliament tied the duties of defending the king and defending the Church of England; Milton believed that the first duty lapsed when Charles sought alliance with Irish Catholics.

12. Milton again quotes from the Solemn League and Covenant.

13. **excluded:** Presbyterian M.P.'s with Royalist sympathies were expelled by Pride's Purge in 1648.

(so they pretended) from tumults to Oxford,[14] yet they were left a sufficient number to act in parliament: therefore not bound by any statute of preceding parliaments but by the law of nature only, which is the only law of laws truly and properly to all mankind fundamental, the beginning and the end of all government, to which no parliament or people that will thoroughly reform but may and must have recourse—as they had and must yet have in church reformation (if they thoroughly intend it) to evangelic rules, not to ecclesiastical canons, though never so ancient, so ratified and established in the land by statutes, which for the most part are mere positive laws,[15] neither natural nor moral—and so by any parliament, for just and serious considerations, without scruple to be at any time repealed.

If others of their number in these things were under force, they were not, but under free conscience; if others were excluded by a power which they could not resist, they were not therefore to leave the helm of government in no hands, to discontinue their care of the public peace and safety, to desert the people in anarchy and confusion, no more than when so many of their members left them as made up in outward formality a more legal parliament of three estates against them.[16] The best affected also and best principled of the people stood not numbering or computing on which side were most voices in parliament, but on which side appeared to them most reason, most safety, when the house divided upon main matters. What was well motioned and advised, they examined not whether fear or persuasion carried it in the vote. Neither did they measure votes and counsels by the intentions of them that voted, knowing that intentions either are but guessed at or not soon enough known, and, although good, can neither make the deed such nor prevent the consequence from being bad. Suppose bad intentions in things otherwise well done; what was well done was, by them who so thought, not the less obeyed or followed in the state, since in the church who had not rather follow Iscariot[17] or Simon the magician,[18] though to covetous ends preaching, than Saul, though in the uprightness of his heart persecuting the gospel?

Safer they therefore judged what they thought the better counsels, though carried on by some perhaps to bad ends, than the worse by others, though endeavored with best intentions. And yet they were not to learn[19] that a greater

14. In 1644, Royalist members of Parliament had answered Charles's call for an alternative Parliament in Oxford.

15. **positive laws:** laws not entailed by the law of nature, and therefore merely conventional.

16. **three estates:** king, lords, and commons; Milton's strained argument is that, just as the Long Parliament, without the king, was more legitimate than the Royalist Oxford Parliament, so the Rump Parliament gained rather than lost legitimacy with the exclusion by military force of elected members in Pride's Purge.

17. **Iscariot:** Judas, who before betraying Christ for silver preached the good news.

18. Simon Magus offered money to Peter and John for the power of the Holy Spirit (Acts 8.9–25).

19. **were not to learn:** did not need to be taught.

number might be corrupt within the walls of a parliament as well as of a city,[20] whereof in matters of nearest concernment all men will be judges; nor easily permit that the odds of voices in their greatest council shall more endanger them by corrupt or credulous votes than the odds of enemies by open assaults, judging that most voices ought not always to prevail where main matters are in question. If others hence will pretend to disturb all counsels, what is that to them who pretend not, but are in real danger?—not they only so judging, but a great, though not the greatest, number of their chosen patriots, who might be more in weight than the others in number, there being in number little virtue, but by weight and measure wisdom working all things. And the dangers on either side they seriously thus weighed: from the treaty, short fruits of long labors and seven years war—security for twenty years, if we can hold it; reformation in the church for three years[21]—then put to shift again with our vanquished master. His justice, his honor, his conscience declared quite contrary to ours, which would have furnished him with many such evasions, as in a book entitled *An Inquisition for Blood*[22] soon after were not concealed: bishops not totally removed but left, as it were, in ambush, a reserve, with ordination in their sole power; their lands already sold, not to be alienated but rented, and the sale of them called "sacrilege"; delinquents,[23] few of many brought to condign[24] punishment; accessories punished, the chief author[25] above pardon, though after utmost resistance vanquished, not to give but to receive laws; yet besought, treated with, and to be thanked for his gracious concessions, to be honored, worshiped, glorified.

If this we swore to do, with what righteousness in the sight of God, with what assurance that we bring not by such an oath the whole sea of blood-guiltiness upon our own heads?[26] If on the other side we prefer a free government, though for the present not obtained, yet all those suggested fears and difficulties, as the event will prove, easily overcome, we remain finally secure from the exasperated regal power and out of snares; shall retain the best part of our liberty, which is our religion; and the civil part will be from these who defer[27] us much more easily recovered, being neither so subtle nor so awful as a king reenthroned. Nor were their actions less both at home and abroad than might become the hopes of a glorious, rising commonwealth; nor were the expressions

20. Presbyterians now sympathetic to Charles formed the majority in Parliament (before their expulsion) and in London.

21. Milton refers dismissively to terms of the 1648 Treaty of Newport between Parliament and Charles, *our vanquished master,* at the end of *seven years* of civil war.

22. James Howell's Royalist pamphlet (July 1649) argued that Charles, having acted only in his public capacity, was not bound personally by his concessions in the Treaty of Newport.

23. **delinquents:** those who opposed Parliamentary forces in the Civil War.

24. **condign:** deserved.

25. **chief author:** Charles I.

26. I.e., if in the Solemn League and Covenant we swore to be loyal to the king even in his crimes against his people, then we share his guilt for those killed in the Civil War.

27. **defer:** delay.

both of army and people, whether in their public declarations or several writings, other than such as testified a spirit in this nation no less noble and well fitted to the liberty of a commonwealth than in the ancient Greeks or Romans. Nor was the heroic cause unsuccessfully defended to all Christendom against the tongue of a famous and thought invincible adversary,[28] nor the constancy and fortitude that so nobly vindicated our liberty, our victory at once against two the most prevailing usurpers over mankind, superstition and tyranny, unpraised or uncelebrated in a written monument likely to outlive detraction, as it hath hitherto convinced or silenced not a few of our detractors, especially in parts abroad.

After our liberty and religion thus prosperously fought for, gained, and many years possessed (except in those unhappy interruptions which God hath removed), now that nothing remains but in all reason the certain hopes of a speedy and immediate settlement forever in a firm and free commonwealth for this extolled and magnified nation, regardless both of honor won or deliverances vouchsafed from heaven, to fall back, or rather to creep back so poorly, as it seems the multitude would, to their once abjured and detested thraldom of kingship, to be ourselves the slanderers of our own just and religious deeds (though done by some to covetous and ambitious ends, yet not therefore to be stained with their infamy, or they to asperse the integrity of others); and yet these now by revolting from the conscience of deeds well done both in church and state, to throw away and forsake or rather to betray a just and noble cause for the mixture of bad men who have ill managed and abused it (which had our fathers done heretofore, and on the same pretence deserted true religion, what had long ere this become of our gospel and all Protestant reformation so much intermixed with the avarice and ambition of some reformers?), and by thus relapsing to verify all the bitter predictions of our triumphing enemies—who will now think they wisely discerned and justly censured both us and all our actions as rash, rebellious, hypocritical and impious—not only argues a strange, degenerate contagion suddenly spread among us, fitted and prepared for new slavery, but will render us a scorn and derision to all our neighbors.

And what will they at best say of us and of the whole English name but scoffingly, as of that foolish builder, mentioned by our savior, who began to build a tower and was not able to finish it?[29] Where is this goodly tower of a commonwealth, which the English boasted they would build to overshadow kings and be another Rome in the west? The foundation indeed they laid gallantly, but fell into a worse confusion, not of tongues but of factions, than those at the tower of Babel, and have left no memorial of their work behind them remaining but in the common laughter of Europe. Which must needs redound the more to our

28. **adversary:** Salmasius, the eminent French scholar whose defense of Charles I Milton answered in a *written monument,* his Latin *First Defense of the English People* (1651). Heroic self-portraits are frequent in Milton's polemical prose.

29. Luke 14.28–30.

shame if we but look on our neighbors the United Provinces,[30] to us inferior in all outward advantages, who notwithstanding, in the midst of greater difficulties, courageously, wisely, constantly went through with the same work and are settled in all the happy enjoyments of a potent and flourishing republic to this day.

Besides this, if we return to kingship and soon repent, as undoubtedly we shall when we begin to find the old encroachments coming on by little and little upon our consciences, which must necessarily proceed from king and bishop united inseparably in one interest, we may be forced perhaps to fight over again all that we have fought, and spend over again all that we have spent, but are never like to attain thus far as we are now advanced to the recovery of our freedom, never to have it in possession as we now have it, never to be vouchsafed hereafter the like mercies and signal assistances from heaven in our cause, if by our ingrateful backsliding we make these fruitless; flying now to regal concessions from his divine condescensions and gracious answers to our once importuning prayers against the tyranny which we then groaned under; making vain and viler than dirt the blood of so many thousand faithful and valiant Englishmen, who left us in this liberty bought with their lives; losing by a strange aftergame of folly all the battles we have won, together with all Scotland as to our conquest,[31] hereby lost, which never any of our kings could conquer, all the treasure we have spent, not that corruptible treasure only, but that far more precious of all our late miraculous deliverances, treading back again with lost labor all our happy steps in the progress of reformation and most pitifully depriving ourselves the instant fruition of that free government which we have so dearly purchased, a free commonwealth, not only held by wisest men in all ages the noblest, the manliest, the equallest, the justest government, the most agreeable to all due liberty and proportioned equality, both human, civil, and Christian, most cherishing to virtue and true religion, but also (I may say it with greatest probability) plainly commended, or rather enjoined, by our Savior himself to all Christians, not without remarkable disallowance and the brand of gentilism upon kingship.[32]

God in much displeasure gave a king to the Israelites, and imputed it a sin to them that they sought one,[33] but Christ apparently forbids his disciples to admit of any such heathenish government. "The kings of the gentiles," saith he, "exercise lordship over them," and they that "exercise authority upon them are called benefactors: but ye shall not be so; but he that is greatest among you, let him be as the younger, and he that is chief, as he that serveth" [Luke 22.25–27]. The occasion of these his words was the ambitious desire of Zebedee's two

30. **United Provinces:** the Netherlands, a Protestant republic.

31. Cromwell had defeated the Scots at Dunbar and Worcester.

32. "Ye know that they which are accounted to rule over the Gentiles exercise lordship over them. . . . But so shall it not be among you" (Mark 10.42–43).

33. 1 Sam. 8.11–18.

sons[34] to be exalted above their brethren in his kingdom, which they thought was to be ere long upon earth. That he speaks of civil government is manifest by the former part of the comparison, which infers the other part to be always in the same kind. And what government comes nearer to this precept of Christ than a free commonwealth, wherein they who are greatest are perpetual servants and drudges to the public at their own cost and charges, neglect their own affairs, yet are not elevated above their brethren, live soberly in their families, walk the streets as other men, may be spoken to freely, familiarly, friendly, without adoration? Whereas a king must be adored like a demigod, with a dissolute and haughty court about him of vast expense and luxury, masks and revels, to the debauching of our prime gentry both male and female; not in their pastimes only, but in earnest, by the loose employments of court service, which will be then thought honorable. There will be a queen also of no less charge, in most likelihood outlandish and a papist, besides a queen mother such already, together with both their courts and numerous train;[35] then a royal issue, and ere long severally their sumptuous courts, to the multiplying of a servile crew not of servants only but of nobility and gentry, bred up then to the hopes not of public, but of court offices, to be stewards, chamberlains, ushers, grooms, even of the close-stool;[36] and the lower their minds debased with court opinions, contrary to all virtue and reformation, the haughtier will be their pride and profuseness. We may well remember this not long since at home, or need but look at present into the French court, where enticements and preferments daily draw away and pervert the Protestant nobility.

As to the burden of expense, to our cost we shall soon know it; for any good to us deserving to be termed no better than the vast and lavish price of our subjection and their debauchery, which we are now so greedily cheapening,[37] and would so fain by paying most inconsiderately to a single person, who, for anything wherein the public really needs him, will have little else to do but to bestow the eating and drinking of excessive dainties, to set a pompous face upon the superficial actings of state, to pageant himself up and down in progress among the perpetual bowings and cringings of an abject people, on either side deifying and adoring him for nothing done that can deserve it. For what can he more than another man, who, even in the expression of a late court poet, sits only like a great cipher[38] set to no purpose before a long row of other significant figures? Nay, it is well and happy for the people if their king be but a cipher, being ofttimes a mischief, a pest, a scourge of the nation, and, which is worse,

34. **Zebedee's two sons:** James and John, who asked to sit next to Christ in glory (Mark 10.37).

35. **outlandish:** foreign; the *queen mother*, Henrietta Maria, was a French Catholic; following the Restoration, Charles II would marry a Portuguese Catholic princess, Catherine of Braganza.

36. **close-stool:** chamber pot.

37. **cheapening:** bargaining over.

38. **cipher:** arithmetical 0, which multiplies figures placed before it; Milton slyly places the 0 before the other numbers, thus rendering it worthless (his source is unknown, though Sir William Davenant and George Chapman have been suggested).

not to be removed, not to be controlled—much less accused or brought to punishment—without the danger of a common ruin, without the shaking and almost subversion of the whole land; whereas in a free commonwealth, any governor or chief counselor offending may be removed and punished without the least commotion.

Certainly then that people must needs be mad or strangely infatuated that build the chief hope of their common happiness or safety on a single person, who, if he happen to be good, can do no more than another man, if to be bad, hath in his hands to do more evil without check than millions of other men. The happiness of a nation must needs be firmest and certainest in a full and free council of their own electing, where no single person, but reason only, sways. And what madness is it for them who might manage nobly their own affairs themselves, sluggishly and weakly to devolve all on a single person, and, more like boys under age than men, to commit all to his patronage and disposal who neither can perform what he undertakes, and yet for undertaking it, though royally paid, will not be their servant, but their lord? How unmanly must it needs be to count such a one the breath of our nostrils, to hang all our felicity on him, all our safety, our well-being, for which, if we were aught else but sluggards or babies, we need depend on none but God and our own counsels, our own active virtue and industry. "Go to the ant, thou sluggard," saith Solomon, "consider her ways, and be wise; which, having no prince, ruler, or lord, provides her meat in the summer and gathers her food in the harvest" [Prov. 6.6–8]:[39] which evidently shows us that they who think the nation undone without a king, though they look grave or haughty, have not so much true spirit and understanding in them as a pismire.[40] Neither are these diligent creatures hence concluded to live in lawless anarchy, or that commended, but are set the examples to imprudent and ungoverned men of a frugal and self-governing democraty or commonwealth, safer and more thriving in the joint providence and counsel of many industrious equals than under the single domination of one imperious Lord.

It may be well wondered that any nation styling themselves free can suffer any man to pretend hereditary right over them as their lord, whenas, by acknowledging that right, they conclude themselves his servants and his vassals, and so renounce their own freedom. Which how a people and their leaders especially can do, who have fought so gloriously for liberty, how they can change their noble words and actions, heretofore so becoming the majesty of a free people, into the base necessity of court flatteries and prostrations, is not only strange and admirable,[41] but lamentable to think on. That a nation should be so valorous and courageous to win their liberty in the field, and, when they have

39. The ant colony and beehive were often cited to support the natural legitimacy and strength of, respectively, republican and monarchic governments.
40. **pismire:** ant.
41. **admirable:** astonishing, to be wondered at.

won it, should be so heartless[42] and unwise in their counsels as not to know how to use it, value it, what to do with it or with themselves, but, after ten or twelve years' prosperous war and contestation with tyranny, basely and besottedly to run their necks again into the yoke which they have broken and prostrate all the fruits of their victory for naught at the feet of the vanquished, besides our loss of glory and such an example as kings or tyrants never yet had the like to boast of, will be an ignominy—if it befall us—that never yet befell any nation possessed of their liberty; worthy indeed themselves, whatsoever they be, to be forever slaves—but that part of the nation which consents not with them, as I persuade me of a great number, far worthier than by their means to be brought into the same bondage.

Considering these things so plain, so rational, I cannot but yet further admire on the other side how any man who hath the true principles of justice and religion in him can presume or take upon him to be a king and lord over his brethren, whom he cannot but know, whether as men or Christians, to be for the most part every way equal or superior to himself; how he can display with such vanity and ostentation his regal splendor so supereminently above other mortal men, or, being a Christian, can assume such extraordinary honor and worship to himself while the kingdom of Christ, our common King and Lord, is hid to this world, and such gentilish[43] imitation forbid in express words by himself to all his disciples. All Protestants hold that Christ in his church hath left no vicegerent[44] of his power, but himself without deputy is the only head thereof, governing it from heaven. How then can any Christian man derive his kingship from Christ, but with worse usurpation than the pope his headship over the church, since Christ not only hath not left the least shadow of a command for any such vicegerence from him in the state as the pope pretends for his in the Church, but hath expressly declared that such regal dominion is from the gentiles, not from him, and hath strictly charged us not to imitate them therein?

I doubt not but all ingenuous and knowing men will easily agree with me that a free commonwealth without single person or House of Lords is by far the best government, if it can be had.[45] "But we have all this while," say they, "been expecting[46] it, and cannot yet attain it." 'Tis true indeed, when monarchy was dissolved, the form of a commonwealth should have forthwith been framed, and the practice thereof immediately begun, that the people might have soon been satisfied and delighted with the decent order, ease, and benefit thereof. We had been then by this time firmly rooted, past fear of commotions or mutations, and now flourishing. This care of timely settling a new government instead of the old, too much neglected, hath been our mischief. Yet the cause thereof may

42. **heartless:** cowardly.

43. **gentilish:** see note 32.

44. **vicegerent:** one appointed to act in the place of a ruler.

45. The bland assertion of a highly contested opinion as self-evident is a Miltonic signature.

46. **expecting:** awaiting.

be ascribed with most reason to the frequent disturbances, interruptions, and dissolutions which the parliament hath had, partly from the impatient or disaffected people, partly from some ambitious leaders in the army;[47] much contrary, I believe, to the mind and approbation of the army itself and their other commanders, once undeceived or in their own power.

Now is the opportunity, now the very season, wherein we may obtain a free commonwealth and establish it forever in the land without difficulty or much delay. Writs are sent out for elections, and, which is worth observing, in the name not of any king but of the keepers of our liberty, to summon a free parliament,[48] which then only will indeed be free, and deserve the true honor of that supreme title, if they preserve us a free people; which never parliament was more free to do, being now called not as heretofore by the summons of a king, but by the voice of liberty. And if the people, laying aside prejudice and impatience, will seriously and calmly now consider their own good both religious and civil, their own liberty, and the only means thereof, as shall be here laid before them, and will elect their knights and burgesses[49] able men, and according to the just and necessary qualifications (which for aught I hear remain yet in force unrepealed, as they were formerly decreed in parliament),[50] men not addicted to a single person or house of lords, the work is done; at least the foundation firmly laid of a free commonwealth, and good part also erected of the main structure. For the ground and basis of every just and free government (since men have smarted so oft for committing all to one person) is a general council of ablest men, chosen by the people to consult of public affairs from time to time for the common good. In this grand council must the sovereignty (not transferred but delegated only, and as it were deposited) reside, with this caution: they must have the forces by sea and land committed to them for preservation of the common peace and liberty; must raise and manage the public revenue, at least with some inspectors deputed for satisfaction of the people, how it is employed; must make or propose, as more expressly shall be said anon, civil laws, treat of commerce, peace, or war with foreign nations; and, for the carrying on some particular affairs with more secrecy and expedition, must elect, as they have already out of their own number and others, a council of state.[51]

And, although it may seem strange at first hearing, by reason that men's

47. Milton certainly refers to two dissolutions of Parliament under pressure from army leaders in 1659; he may also refer to Oliver Cromwell's expulsion of the Rump and dissolution of the Barebones Parliament.

48. In March 1660, the Long Parliament, elected in 1640 and having gone through many permutations as a result of defections, expulsions, and reinstatements, issued writs for new election and dissolved itself.

49. **knights and burgesses:** Knights represented counties and shires; burgesses represented cities, towns, and the universities of Oxford and Cambridge.

50. The measures Milton describes, while passed by the Rump at the beginning of 1660, were repealed after excluded members were readmitted in late February.

51. Milton refers to both the executive councils attempted by the Rump in 1659–60 and the perpetual *grand or general council* that he is about to propose.

minds are prepossessed with the notion of successive parliaments, I affirm that the grand or general council, being well chosen, should be perpetual; for so their business is or may be, and ofttimes urgent, the opportunity of affairs gained or lost in a moment. The day of council cannot be set as the day of a festival, but must be ready always to prevent or answer all occasions.[52] By this continuance they will become every way skilfullest, best provided of intelligence from abroad, best acquainted with the people at home, and the people with them. The ship of the commonwealth is always under sail. They sit at the stern, and if they steer well, what need is there to change them, it being rather dangerous? Add to this that the grand council is both foundation and main pillar of the whole state, and to move pillars and foundations not faulty cannot be safe for the building.

I see not, therefore, how we can be advantaged by successive and transitory parliaments; but that they are much likelier continually to unsettle rather than to settle a free government, to breed commotions, changes, novelties, and uncertainties, to bring neglect upon present affairs and opportunities, while all minds are suspense[53] with expectation of a new assembly, and the assembly, for a good space, taken up with the new settling of itself. After which, if they find no great work to do, they will make it by altering or repealing former acts or making and multiplying new, that they may seem to see what their predecessors saw not and not to have assembled for nothing, till all law be lost in the multitude of clashing statutes.

But if the ambition of such as think themselves injured that they also partake not of the government, and are impatient till they be chosen, cannot brook the perpetuity of others chosen before them, or if it be feared that long continuance of power may corrupt sincerest men, the known expedient is, and by some lately propounded, that annually (or if the space be longer, so much perhaps the better) the third part of senators may go out according to the precedence of their election, and the like number be chosen in their places, to prevent the settling of too absolute a power, if it should be perpetual: and this they call "partial rotation."[54] But I could wish that this wheel or partial wheel in state, if it be possible, might be avoided as having too much affinity with the wheel of fortune. For it appears not how this can be done without danger and mischance of putting out a great number of the best and ablest, in whose stead new elections may bring in as many raw, unexperienced, and otherwise affected, to the weakening and much altering for the worse of public transactions. Neither do I think a perpetual senate, especially chosen and entrusted by the people, much in this land to be feared, where the well-affected[55] either in a standing army or in a

52. I.e., anticipate and address all emergencies.

53. **suspense:** in suspense.

54. The *lately propounded* proposal for a rotating senate is James Harrington's, in *Oceana* (1656); it is associated with the republican Rota Club. The *wheel* in the next sentence is a play on the proposal and the club's name (Lat. *rota* = wheel).

55. **well-affected:** loyal and right thinking.

settled militia have their arms in their own hands. Safest therefore to me it seems, and of least hazard or interruption to affairs, that none of the grand council be moved unless by death or just conviction of some crime: for what can be expected firm or steadfast from a floating foundation? However, I forejudge not any probable expedient, any temperament that can be found in things of this nature so disputable on either side.

Yet lest this which I affirm be thought my single opinion, I shall add sufficient testimony. Kingship itself is therefore counted the more safe and durable because the king, and for the most part his council, is not changed during life. But a commonwealth is held immortal, and therein firmest, safest, and most above fortune. For the death of a king causeth ofttimes many dangerous alterations, but the death now and then of a senator is not felt, the main body of them still continuing permanent in greatest and noblest commonwealths, and as it were eternal. Therefore among the Jews the supreme council of seventy, called the Sanhedrim, founded by Moses, in Athens that of Areopagus, in Sparta that of the ancients,[56] in Rome the senate, consisted of members chosen for term of life; and by that means remained as it were still the same to generations. In Venice they change indeed ofter than every year some particular councils of state, as that of six, or such other; but the true senate, which upholds and sustains the government, is the whole aristocracy immovable.[57] So in the United Provinces, the States-General, which are indeed but a council of state deputed by the whole union, are not usually the same persons for above three or six years; but the states of every city, in whom the sovereignty hath been placed time out of mind, are a standing senate, without succession, and accounted chiefly in that regard the main prop of their liberty. And why they should be so in every well-ordered commonwealth, they who write of policy[58] give these reasons: "That to make the senate successive not only impairs the dignity and luster of the senate but weakens the whole commonwealth and brings it into manifest danger, while by this means the secrets of state are frequently divulged, and matters of greatest consequence committed to inexpert and novice counselors, utterly to seek[59] in the full and intimate knowledge of affairs past."[60] I know not therefore what should be peculiar in England to make successive parliaments thought safest, or convenient here more than in other nations, unless it be the fickleness which is attributed to us as we are islanders. But good education and acquisite[61]

56. The *Sanhedrim,* or Sanhedrin, which Milton later calls "great senate" (*PL* 12.225), was Israel's legislative and judicial assembly, established by Moses (Num. 11.16–17); the *Areopagus* was the seat of the Athenian Council of State and, after Solon's reforms, its judicial tribunal; Lycurgus established the assembly of *ancients* in Sparta. Milton's reference to the legendary founders of these assemblies is calculated to flatter and persuade Parliament.

57. As Milton indicates, the Doge of Venice and his advisory Council of Six served brief terms, while members of the Grand Council served for life.

58. **policy:** politics, government.

59. **to seek:** lacking.

60. Milton adapts this passage from Jean Bodin's *De Republica* (1576).

61. **acquisite:** acquired.

wisdom ought to correct the fluxible[62] fault, if any such be, of our watery situation.

It will be objected that in those places where they had perpetual senates, they had also popular remedies against their growing too imperious: as in Athens, besides Areopagus, another senate of four or five hundred; in Sparta, the Ephori; in Rome, the tribunes of the people.[63] But the event tells us that these remedies either little availed the people, or brought them to such a licentious and unbridled democraty[64] as in fine[65] ruined themselves with their own excessive power. So that the main reason urged why popular assemblies are to be trusted with the people's liberty, rather than a senate of principal men—because great men will be still endeavoring to enlarge their power, but the common sort will be contented to maintain their own liberty—is by experience found false, none being more immoderate and ambitious to amplify their power than such popularities; which was seen in the people of Rome, who, at first contented to have their tribunes, at length contended with the senate that one consul, then both, soon after that the censors and praetors also, should be created plebeian, and the whole empire put into their hands; adoring lastly those who most were adverse to the senate, till Marius, by fulfilling their inordinate desires, quite lost them all the power for which they had so long been striving, and left them under the tyranny of Sylla.[66]

The balance therefore must be exactly so set as to preserve and keep up due authority on either side, as well in the senate as in the people. And this annual rotation of a senate to consist of three hundred, as is lately propounded, requires also another popular assembly upward of a thousand, with an answerable rotation. Which, besides that it will be liable to all those inconveniences found in the foresaid remedies, cannot but be troublesome and chargeable,[67] both in their motion[68] and their session, to the whole land, unwieldy with their own bulk, unable in so great a number to mature their consultations as they ought, if any be allotted them, and that they meet not from so many parts remote to sit a whole year lieger[69] in one place, only now and then to hold up a forest of fingers, or to convey each man his bean or ballot into the box, without reason shown or common deliberation; incontinent of secrets, if any be imparted to

62. **fluxible:** fluid, and therefore changeable.

63. The office of Spartan *Ephors,* like that of Roman *Tribunes,* was established as a check on the power of ancients and senators who served for life; in each case the office established as a curb on arbitrary power itself became subject to abuse.

64. In Milton's time, *democraty,* or democracy, was as often as not a pejorative term; two paragraphs later, Milton cautions against trusting elections to "the noise and shouting of a rude multitude."

65. **in fine:** in the end.

66. Gaius *Marius,* of plebeian or common birth, amassed power by military victories, alliance with demagogues, and the massacre of patricians; after his death in 86 B.C.E., he was succeeded by the patrician Lucius Cornelius *Sulla* (see epigraph and note 1).

67. **chargeable:** expensive.

68. **motion:** travel.

69. **lieger:** residing, particularly as an agent or ambassador.

them, emulous and always jarring with the other senate.[70] The much better way doubtless will be, in this wavering condition of our affairs, to defer the changing or circumscribing of our senate more than may be done with ease, till the commonwealth be thoroughly settled in peace and safety, and they themselves give us the occasion.

Military men hold it dangerous to change the form of battle in view of an enemy; neither did the people of Rome bandy with their senate while any of the Tarquins[71] lived, the enemies of their liberty, nor sought by creating tribunes to defend themselves against the fear of their patricians, till, sixteen years after the expulsion of their kings and in full security of their state, they had or thought they had just cause given them by the senate. Another way will be to well qualify and refine elections: not committing all to the noise and shouting of a rude multitude, but permitting only those of them who are rightly qualified to nominate as many as they will, and out of that number others of a better breeding to choose a less number more judiciously, till after a third or fourth sifting and refining of exactest choice, they only be left chosen who are the due number and seem by most voices the worthiest.

To make the people fittest to choose, and the chosen fittest to govern, will be to mend our corrupt and faulty education, to teach the people faith not without virtue, temperance, modesty, sobriety, parsimony, justice; not to admire wealth or honor; to hate turbulence and ambition; to place everyone his private welfare and happiness in the public peace, liberty, and safety. They shall not then need to be much mistrustful of their chosen patriots in the grand council, who will be then rightly called the true keepers of our liberty, though the most of their business will be in foreign affairs. But to prevent all mistrust, the people then will have their several ordinary assemblies (which will henceforth quite annihilate the odious power and name of committees)[72] in the chief towns of every county—without the trouble, charge, or time lost of summoning and assembling from far in so great a number, and so long residing from their own houses, or removing of their families—to do as much at home in their several shires, entire or subdivided, toward the securing of their liberty, as a numerous assembly of them all formed and convened on purpose with the wariest rotation. Whereof I shall speak more ere the end of this discourse, for it may be referred to time,[73] so we be still[74] going on by degrees to perfection. The people well weighing and performing these things, I suppose would have no cause to fear, though the parliament, abolishing that name as originally signifying but the "parley" of our lords and commons with their Norman king when he pleased to call them, should,

70. Milton criticizes Harrington's proposal for a bicameral parliament, with a 300-member senate to debate and propose laws, and a second chamber of 1,050 that would simply vote the senate's proposals up or down.

71. The Roman republic was founded after the expulsion of the final Tarquin king, in 510 B.C.E.

72. **committees:** local governing bodies that enforced loyalty to Cromwell.

73. **it may be referred to time:** discussed later.

74. **still:** always.

with certain limitations of their power, sit perpetual, if their ends be faithful and for a free commonwealth, under the name of a grand or general council.

Till this be done, I am in doubt whether our state will be ever certainly and thoroughly settled, never likely till then to see an end of our troubles and continual changes, or at least never the true settlement and assurance of our liberty. The grand council being thus firmly constituted to perpetuity, and still, upon the death or default of any member, supplied and kept in full number, there can be no cause alleged why peace, justice, plentiful trade, and all prosperity should not thereupon ensue throughout the whole land, with as much assurance as can be of human things that they shall so continue (if God favor us, and our willful sins provoke him not) even to the coming of our true and rightful and only to be expected king, only worthy as he is our only Savior, the Messiah, the Christ, the only heir of his eternal father, the only by him anointed and ordained since the work of our redemption finished, universal Lord of all mankind.[75]

The way propounded is plain, easy, and open before us, without intricacies, without the introducement of new or obsolete forms, or terms, or exotic models—ideas that would effect nothing but with a number of new injunctions to manacle the native liberty of mankind, turning all virtue into prescription, servitude, and necessity, to the great impairing and frustrating of Christian liberty. I say again, this way lies free and smooth before us, is not tangled with inconveniences, invents no new encumbrances, requires no perilous, no injurious alteration or circumscription of men's lands and proprieties;[76] secure that in this commonwealth, temporal and spiritual lords removed, no man or number of men can attain to such wealth or vast possession as will need the hedge of an agrarian law[77] (never successful, but the cause rather of sedition, save only where it began seasonably with first possession) to confine them from endangering our public liberty. To conclude, it can have no considerable objection made against it that it is not practicable, lest it be said hereafter that we gave up our liberty for want of a ready way or distinct form proposed of a free commonwealth. And this facility we shall have above our next neighboring commonwealth (if we can keep us from the fond conceit[78] of something like a duke of Venice, put lately into many men's heads by some one or other subtly driving on under that notion his own ambitious ends to lurch[79] a crown) that our liberty shall not be hampered or hovered over by any engagement to such a potent family as the house of Nassau,[80] of whom to stand in perpetual doubt and suspicion, but we shall live the clearest and absolutest free nation in the world.

75. Milton, believing that only the Son of God is worthy to be a king, voices a millenarian vision of the reign of Christ on Earth.

76. **proprieties:** properties.

77. In *Oceana*, Harrington proposed a law limiting the size of landed estates.

78. **fond conceit:** foolish idea; apparently a suggestion that Richard Cromwell, who had succeeded his father as Protector, be returned to power as something like the Doge of Venice (see note 57).

79. **lurch:** steal.

80. **house of Nassau:** The heirs of William of Orange inherited the powers he had gained as Stadtholder in the Dutch republic.

On the contrary, if there be a king, which the inconsiderate multitude are now so mad upon, mark how far short we are like to come of all those happinesses which in a free state we shall immediately be possessed of. First, the grand council, which, as I showed before, should sit perpetually (unless their leisure give them now and then some intermissions or vacations, easily manageable by the council of state left sitting), shall be called, by the king's good will and utmost endeavor, as seldom as may be. For it is only the king's right, he will say, to call a parliament, and this he will do most commonly about his own affairs rather than the kingdom's, as will appear plainly so soon as they are called. For what will their business then be, and the chief expense of their time, but an endless tugging between petition of right and royal prerogative,[81] especially about the negative voice,[82] militia, or subsidies, demanded and ofttimes extorted without reasonable cause appearing to the commons, who are the only true representatives of the people and their liberty, but will be then mingled with a court faction. Besides which, within their own walls, the sincere part of them who stand faithful to the people will again have to deal with two troublesome counterworking adversaries from without, mere creatures of the king, spiritual, and the greater part, as is likeliest, of temporal lords, nothing concerned with the people's liberty.[83]

If these prevail not in what they please, though never so much against the people's interest, the parliament shall be soon dissolved, or sit and do nothing, not suffered to remedy the least grievance or enact aught advantageous to the people. Next, the council of state shall not be chosen by the parliament, but by the king, still his own creatures, courtiers and favorites, who will be sure in all their counsels to set their master's grandeur and absolute power, in what they are able, far above the people's liberty. I deny not but that there may be such a king who may regard the common good before his own, may have no vicious favorite, may hearken only to the wisest and incorruptest of his parliament. But this rarely happens in a monarchy not elective, and it behooves not a wise nation to commit the sum of their well-being, the whole state of their safety, to fortune. What need they? And how absurd would it be, whenas they themselves, to whom his[84] chief virtue will be but to hearken, may with much better management and dispatch, with much more commendation of their own worth and magnanimity, govern without a master? Can the folly be paralleled, to adore and be the slaves of a single person for doing that which it is ten thousand to one whether he can or will do, and we without him might do more easily, more effectually, more laudably ourselves? Shall we never grow old enough to be wise to make seasonable use of gravest authorities, experiences, examples? Is it such an unspeakable joy to serve, such felicity to wear a yoke, to clink our shackles locked

81. In 1628, Parliament, resisting Charles I's assertion of *royal prerogative*, forced him to agree to the Petition of Right.

82. **negative voice:** royal veto.

83. I.e., a restored king would recall the House of Lords, abolished in 1649.

84. **his:** the king's.

on by pretended law of subjection, more intolerable and hopeless to be ever shaken off than those which are knocked on by illegal injury and violence?[85]

Aristotle, our chief instructor in the universities (lest this doctrine be thought sectarian, as the royalist would have it thought), tells us in the third of his *Politics* that certain men at first, for the matchless excellence of their virtue above others, or some great public benefit, were created kings by the people, in small cities and territories, and in the scarcity of others to be found like them; but when they abused their power and governments grew larger and the number of prudent men increased, that then the people, soon deposing their tyrants, betook them in all civilest places to the form of a free commonwealth.[86] And why should we thus disparage and prejudicate[87] our own nation as to fear a scarcity of able and worthy men united in counsel to govern us, if we will but use diligence and impartiality to find them out and choose them, rather yoking ourselves to a single person, the natural adversary and oppressor of liberty; though good, yet far easier corruptible by the excess of his singular power and exaltation, or at best not comparably sufficient to bear the weight of government, nor equally disposed to make us happy in the enjoyment of our liberty under him?

But admit that monarchy of itself may be convenient to some nations, yet to us who have thrown it out, received back again it cannot but prove pernicious. For kings to come, never forgetting their former ejection, will be sure to fortify and arm themselves sufficiently for the future against all such attempts hereafter from the people, who shall be then so narrowly watched and kept so low that, though they would never so fain (and at the same rate of their blood and treasure), they never shall be able to regain what they now have purchased and may enjoy, or to free themselves from any yoke imposed upon them. Nor will they dare to go about it, utterly disheartened for the future, if these their highest attempts prove unsuccessful; which will be the triumph of all tyrants hereafter over any people that shall resist oppression. And their[88] song will then be to others, "how sped the rebellious English?" to our posterity, "how sped the rebels your fathers?"

This is not my conjecture, but drawn from God's known denouncement against the gentilizing[89] Israelites, who, though they were governed in a commonwealth of God's own ordaining, he only their king,[90] they his peculiar[91] people, yet affecting rather to resemble heathen, but pretending the misgovernment of Samuel's sons (no more a reason to dislike their commonwealth than the violence of Eli's sons was imputable to that priesthood or religion) clamored

85. I.e., is subservience so attractive that we will place manacles on ourselves worse than any placed upon us by force?

86. Milton paraphrases Aristotle's *Politics* III.15 (1286b).

87. **prejudicate:** prejudge unfairly.

88. **their:** the tyrants'.

89. **gentilizing:** imitating the Gentiles in their desire for a king (1 Sam. 8.4–22); see notes 32 and 33.

90. See note 75.

91. **peculiar:** chosen, particular.

for a king. They had their longing, but with this testimony of God's wrath: "Ye shall cry out in that day because of your king whom ye shall have chosen, and the Lord will not hear you in that day" [1 Sam. 8.18]. Us if he shall hear now, how much less will he hear when we cry hereafter, who once delivered by him from a king, and not without wondrous acts of his providence, insensible and unworthy of those high mercies, are returning precipitantly, if he withhold us not, back to the captivity from whence he freed us.

Yet neither shall we obtain or buy at an easy rate this new gilded yoke which thus transports us. A new royal revenue must be found, a new episcopal, for those are individual.[92] Both which being wholly dissipated, or bought by private persons, or assigned for service done (and especially to the army), cannot be recovered without a general detriment and confusion to men's estates or a heavy imposition on all men's purses[93]—benefit to none but to the worst and ignoblest sort of men, whose hope is to be either the ministers of court riot and excess or the gainers by it. But not to speak more of losses and extraordinary levies on our estates, what will then be the revenges and offenses remembered and returned, not only by the chief person but by all his adherents; accounts and reparations that will be required, suits, indictments, inquiries, discoveries, complaints, informations, who knows against whom or how many, though perhaps neuters,[94] if not to utmost infliction, yet to imprisonment, fines, banishment, or molestation? if not these, yet disfavor, discountenance, disregard, and contempt on all but the known royalist, or whom he favors, will be plenteous.

Nor let the new royalized Presbyterians[95] persuade themselves that their old doings, though now recanted, will be forgotten, whatever conditions be contrived or trusted on. Will they not believe this, nor remember the pacification, how it was kept to the Scots,[96] how other solemn promises many a time to us? Let them now but read the diabolical forerunning libels, the faces, the gestures that now appear foremost and briskest in all public places, as the harbingers of those that are in expectation to reign over us. Let them but hear the insolencies, the menaces, the insultings of our newly animated common enemies crept lately out of their holes, their hell I might say by the language of their infernal pamphlets, the spew of every drunkard, every ribald; nameless, yet not for want of license, but for very shame of their own vile persons, not daring to name themselves while they traduce others by name.[97] And give us to foresee that

92. **individual:** both inseparable and distinct.

93. In the event, those who purchased or who had been awarded lands confiscated from the bishops and from Charles I's supporters were not compensated when the lands were returned after the Restoration.

94. **neuters:** neutrals.

95. In *The Tenure of Kings and Magistrates,* Milton castigates the Presbyterians for supporting the imprisoned Charles after working to bring down the monarchy.

96. There are several broken agreements between Charles and the Scottish Presbyterians to which Milton could refer here.

97. Milton was among those attacked *by name* in the *forerunning libels,* e.g., in Sir Roger L'Estrange's *No Blinde Guides* (1660).

they intend to second their wicked words, if ever they have power, with more wicked deeds.

Let our zealous backsliders forethink now with themselves how their necks yoked with these tigers of Bacchus,[98] these new fanatics of not the preaching- but the sweating-tub, inspired with nothing holier than the venereal pox,[99] can draw one way under monarchy to the establishing of church discipline with these new-disgorged atheisms. Yet shall they not have the honor to yoke with these, but shall be yoked under them. These shall plow on their backs. And do they among them who are so forward to bring in the single person think to be by him trusted or long regarded? So trusted they shall be and so regarded as by kings are wont reconciled enemies: neglected and soon after discarded, if not prosecuted for old traitors; the first inciters, beginners, and more than to the third part actors of all that followed.

It will be found also that there must be then, as necessarily as now (for the contrary part will be still feared), a standing army, which for certain shall not be this, but of the fiercest cavaliers, of no less expense, and perhaps again under Rupert.[100] But let this army[101] be sure they shall be soon disbanded, and likeliest without arrear or pay, and, being disbanded, not be sure but they may as soon be questioned for being in arms against their king. The same let them fear who have contributed money, which will amount to no small number that must then take their turn to be made delinquents and compounders.[102]

They who past reason and recovery are devoted to kingship perhaps will answer that a greater part by far of the nation will have it so, the rest therefore must yield. Not so much to convince these, which I little hope, as to confirm them who yield not, I reply that this greatest part[103] have both in reason and the trial of just battle lost the right of their election what the government shall be. Of them who have not lost that right, whether they for kingship be the greater number, who can certainly determine? Suppose they be, yet of freedom they partake all alike, one main end of government; which if the greater part value not, but will degenerately forgo, is it just or reasonable that most voices against the main end of government should enslave the less number that would be free? More just it is, doubtless, if it come to force, that a less number compel a greater to retain (which can be no wrong to them) their liberty, than that a greater number, for the pleasure of their baseness, compel a less most injuriously to be

98. **tigers of Bacchus:** tigers pulled the chariot of the god of wine; Milton associated the monarchist Cavaliers with Bacchus, for their devotion to pleasure.

99. The *preaching-tub* was the improvised pulpit of street preachers; the *sweating-tub* was used to treat *venereal pox,* or syphilis.

100. Prince *Rupert,* nephew of Charles I, commanded the Royalist army, and afterward the navy, during the Civil War.

101. **this army:** the current, republican army.

102. **delinquents and compounders:** Royalist *delinquents,* who had their estates confiscated during the Civil War, were allowed to keep them if they *compounded,* or made a specified payment; Milton assumes that the Royalists would do the same to commonwealth supporters at the Restoration.

103. **this greatest part:** the Royalists, having lost the war, have lost the right to vote.

their fellow slaves. They who seek nothing but their own just liberty have always right to win it and to keep it whenever they have power, be the voices never so numerous that oppose it. And how much we above others are concerned to defend it from kingship, and from them who in pursuance thereof so perniciously would betray us and themselves to most certain misery and thraldom, will be needless to repeat.

Having thus far shown with what ease we may now obtain a free commonwealth, and by it, with as much ease, all the freedom, peace, justice, plenty that we can desire, on the other side the difficulties, troubles, uncertainties, nay, rather impossibilities, to enjoy these things constantly under a monarch, I will now proceed to show more particularly wherein our freedom and flourishing condition will be more ample and secure to us under a free commonwealth than under kingship.

The whole freedom of man consists either in spiritual or civil liberty. As for spiritual, who can be at rest, who can enjoy anything in this world with contentment, who hath not liberty to serve God and to save his own soul according to the best light which God hath planted in him to that purpose, by the reading of his revealed will and the guidance of his holy spirit? That this is best pleasing to God, and that the whole Protestant church allows no supreme judge or rule in matters of religion but the scriptures, and these to be interpreted by the scriptures themselves, which necessarily infers liberty of conscience, I have heretofore proved at large in another treatise,[104] and might yet further by the public declarations, confessions, and admonitions of whole churches and states, obvious in all history since the Reformation.

This liberty of conscience, which above all other things ought to be to all men dearest and most precious, no government more inclinable not to favor only, but to protect, than a free commonwealth, as being most magnanimous, most fearless, and confident of its own fair proceedings. Whereas kingship, though looking big, yet indeed most pusillanimous, full of fears, full of jealousies, startled at every umbrage,[105] as it hath been observed of old to have ever suspected most and mistrusted them who were in most esteem for virtue and generosity of mind, so it is now known to have most in doubt and suspicion them who are most reputed to be religious. Queen Elizabeth, though herself accounted so good a Protestant, so moderate, so confident of her subjects' love, would never give way so much as to Presbyterian reformation in this land, though once and again besought, as Camden[106] relates; but imprisoned and persecuted the very proposers thereof, alleging it as her mind and maxim unalterable that such reformation would diminish regal authority.

What liberty of conscience can we then expect of others, far worse principled from the cradle, trained up and governed by popish and Spanish coun-

104. *A Treatise of Civil Power in Ecclesiastical Causes* (1659).
105. **umbrage:** shadow.
106. Milton refers to William Camden's *History of the Most Renowned and Victorious Princess Elizabeth.*

sels,[107] and on such depending hitherto for subsistence? Especially what can this last parliament expect, who, having revived lately and published the covenant,[108] have re-engaged themselves never to readmit episcopacy? Which no son of Charles returning but will most certainly bring back with him, if he regard the last and strictest charge of his father, "to persevere in not the doctrine only but government of the church of England, not to neglect the speedy and effectual suppressing of errors and schisms,"[109] among which he accounted presbytery one of the chief. Or if, notwithstanding that charge of his father, he submit to the covenant, how will he keep faith to us with disobedience to him, or regard that faith given which must be founded on the breach of that last and solemnest paternal charge, and the reluctance, I may say the antipathy, which is in all kings against Presbyterian and Independent discipline?[110] For they hear the gospel speaking much of liberty, a word which monarchy and her bishops both fear and hate, but a free commonwealth both favors and promotes, and not the word only, but the thing itself. But let our governors beware in time lest their hard measure to liberty of conscience be found the rock whereon they shipwreck themselves, as others have now done before them in the course wherein God was directing their steerage to a free commonwealth; and the abandoning of all those whom they call "sectaries," for the detected falsehood and ambition of some, be a willful rejection of their own chief strength and interest in the freedom of all Protestant religion, under what abusive name soever calumniated.

The other part of our freedom consists in the civil rights and advancements of every person according to his merit: the enjoyment of those never more certain, and the access to these never more open, than in a free commonwealth. Both which, in my opinion, may be best and soonest obtained if every county in the land were made a kind of subordinate commonalty or commonwealth, and one chief town or more, according as the shire is in circuit,[111] made cities, if they be not so called already; where the nobility and chief gentry, from a proportionable compass of territory annexed to each city, may build houses or palaces befitting their quality, may bear part in the government, make their own judicial laws, or use these that are, and execute them by their own elected judicatures and judges without appeal, in all things of civil government between man and man. So they shall have justice in their own hands, law executed fully and finally in their own counties and precincts, long wished and spoken of, but

107. Charles II, the son of a French Catholic mother, allied himself with the Spanish against Cromwell in the Battle of Flanders (1658).

108. The 1643 Solemn League and Covenant pledging loyalty to the king had been reinstated in March 1660.

109. Milton conflates two passages from Charles I's *Eikon Basilike*, chap. 27; he paraphrases the same passages in his own *Eikonoklastes* (Yale 3:571, 573).

110. **Independent discipline:** Milton's preferred system, under which individual churches govern themselves, as opposed to subordination to a hierarchy of bishops or Presbyterian synods.

111. **in circuit:** in size.

never yet obtained. They shall have none then to blame but themselves if it be not well administered, and fewer laws to expect or fear from the supreme authority. Or to those that shall be made of any great concernment to public liberty, they may, without much trouble in these commonalties or in more general assemblies called to their cities from the whole territory on such occasion, declare and publish their assent or dissent by deputies within a time limited sent to the grand council; yet so as this their judgment declared shall submit to the greater number of other counties or commonalties, and not avail them to any exemption of themselves, or refusal of agreement with the rest, as it may in any of the United Provinces, being sovereign within itself, ofttimes to the great disadvantage of that union.

In these employments they may, much better than they do now, exercise and fit themselves till their lot fall to be chosen into the grand council, according as their worth and merit shall be taken notice of by the people. As for controversies that shall happen between men of several counties, they may repair, as they do now, to the capital city, or any other more commodious, indifferent[112] place, and equal[113] judges. And this I find to have been practiced in the old Athenian commonwealth, reputed the first and ancientest place of civility in all Greece: that they had in their several cities a peculiar,[114] in Athens a common, government;[115] and their right, as it befell them, to the administration of both.

They should have here also schools and academies at their own choice, wherein their children may be bred up in their own sight to all learning and noble education, not in grammar only, but in all liberal arts and exercises. This would soon spread much more knowledge and civility, yea religion, through all parts of the land, by communicating the natural heat of government and culture more distributively to all extreme parts which now lie numb and neglected; would soon make the whole nation more industrious, more ingenuous at home, more potent, more honorable abroad. To this a free commonwealth will easily assent (nay, the parliament hath had already some such thing in design), for of all governments a commonwealth aims most to make the people flourishing, virtuous, noble, and high spirited. Monarchs will never permit, whose aim is to make the people wealthy indeed perhaps and well fleeced for their own shearing and the supply of regal prodigality, but otherwise softest, basest, viciousest, servilest, easiest to be kept under. And not only in fleece, but in mind also sheepishest, and will have all the benches of judicature annexed to the throne, as a gift of royal grace that we have justice done us, whenas nothing can be more essential to the freedom of a people than to have the administration of justice and all public ornaments[116] in

112. **indifferent:** impartial.

113. **equal:** fair.

114. **peculiar:** separate.

115. Milton's proposal for a federal constitution follows Aristotle's description of Athenian reform (*Athenian Constitution* 21.3–22).

116. **ornaments:** a usage not recorded in the *OED;* Milton may refer to judgeships, which bring honor to those chosen.

their own election and within their own bounds, without long traveling or depending on remote places to obtain their right or any civil accomplishment; so it be not supreme, but subordinate to the general power and union of the whole republic.

In which happy firmness, as in the particular above mentioned, we shall also far exceed the United Provinces by having, not as they (to the retarding and distracting ofttimes of their counsels or urgentest occasions), many sovereignties united in one commonwealth, but many commonwealths under one united and entrusted sovereignty. And when we have our forces by sea and land, either of a faithful army or a settled militia, in our own hands to the firm establishing of a free commonwealth, public accounts under our own inspection, general laws and taxes, with their causes, in our own domestic suffrages, judicial laws, offices, and ornaments at home in our own ordering and administration, all distinction of lords and commoners that may any way divide or sever the public interest removed, what can a perpetual senate have then wherein to grow corrupt, wherein to encroach upon us or usurp? Or if they do, wherein to be formidable? Yet if all this avail not to remove the fear or envy of a perpetual sitting, it may be easily provided to change a third part of them yearly or every two or three years, as was above mentioned; or that it be at those times in the people's choice whether they will change them or renew their power, as they shall find cause.

I have no more to say at present. Few words will save us, well considered; few and easy things, now seasonably done. But if the people be so affected as to prostitute religion and liberty to the vain and groundless apprehension that nothing but kingship can restore trade, not remembering the frequent plagues[117] and pestilences that then wasted this city, such as through God's mercy we never have felt since, and that trade flourishes nowhere more than in the free commonwealths of Italy, Germany, and the Low Countries before their eyes at this day; yet if trade be grown so craving and importunate through the profuse living of tradesmen that nothing can support it but the luxurious expenses of a nation upon trifles or superfluities, so as if the people generally should betake themselves to frugality, it might prove a dangerous matter, lest tradesmen should mutiny for want of trading, and that therefore we must forgo and set to sale religion, liberty, honor, safety, all concernments divine or human to keep up trading; if, lastly, after all this light among us, the same reason shall pass for current to put our necks again under kingship, as was made use of by the Jews to return back to Egypt and to the worship of their idol queen,[118] because they falsely imagined that they then lived in more plenty and prosperity, our condition is not sound, but rotten,[119] both in religion and all civil prudence,

117. There had not been a plague in England since 1625, in James I's reign; there would not be another until 1665, during the reign of Charles II.

118. See Num. 11 for the story of Moses' displeasure with his followers' desire to return to Egypt; Milton may be alluding to God's instructions to Moses to call a council of elders to address the crisis (Num. 11.16–18) as a model for his own grand council.

119. Milton comes finally to the main clause, after three long dependent clauses.

and will bring us soon, the way we are marching, to those calamities which attend always and unavoidably on luxury, all national judgments under foreign or domestic slavery. So far we shall be from mending our condition by monarchizing our government, whatever new conceit now possesses us.

However, with all hazard I have ventured what I thought my duty to speak in season, and to forewarn my country in time, wherein I doubt not but there be many wise men in all places and degrees, but am sorry the effects of wisdom are so little seen among us. Many circumstances and particulars I could have added in those things whereof I have spoken, but a few main matters now put speedily in execution will suffice to recover us and set all right. And there will want at no time who are good at circumstances,[120] but men who set their minds on main matters and sufficiently urge them, in these most difficult times I find not many.

What I have spoken is the language of that which is not called amiss "the good old cause."[121] If it seem strange to any, it will not seem more strange, I hope, than convincing to backsliders. Thus much I should perhaps have said though I were sure I should have spoken only to trees and stones, and had none to cry to, but with the prophet, "O earth, earth, earth!" [Jer. 22.29] to tell the very soil itself what her perverse inhabitants are deaf to. Nay, though what I have spoke should happen (which Thou suffer not, who didst create mankind free, nor Thou next, who didst redeem us from being servants of men!) to be the last words of our expiring liberty. But I trust I shall have spoken persuasion to abundance of sensible and ingenuous men; to some perhaps whom God may raise of these stones to become children of reviving liberty,[122] and may reclaim, though they seem now choosing them a captain back for Egypt, to bethink themselves a little and consider whither they are rushing; to exhort this torrent also of the people not to be so impetuous, but to keep their due channel; and at length recovering and uniting their better resolutions, now that they see already how open and unbounded the insolence and rage is of our common enemies, to stay these ruinous proceedings, justly and timely fearing to what a precipice of destruction the deluge of this epidemic madness would hurry us, through the general defection of a misguided and abused multitude.

120. **who are good at circumstances:** people who can work out the details.

121. **"the good old cause":** Milton reclaims the republican rallying cry; Royalist adversaries were using it ironically against Milton's party as the Restoration approached.

122. Milton echoes another voice crying in the wilderness, John the Baptist: "I say unto you, That God is able of these stones to raise up children unto Abraham" (Matt. 3.9, Luke 3.8).

Introduction to Selections from *Christian Doctrine*

The heavily and repeatedly revised Latin manuscript of Milton's *Christian Doctrine* was found in 1823, in a storage compartment in London's Old State Paper Office. It had Milton's name on it, was bundled with copies of his State Papers, and appeared to be the final product of his lifelong study of Scripture, scriptural commentaries, and precedent theological systems. The prefatory epistle to the treatise describes its genesis and growth, and this account dovetails neatly with references in Milton's *Commonplace Book* to a "theological index" and Edward Phillips's mention of his uncle's theological "tractate" (Darbishire 1932, 61). Since discovery of the manuscript, scholars have gradually pieced together a documentary record that with the evidence of the manuscript itself establishes the following: (1) Though it was the evolving product of a lifetime of devotional searching, work on the treatise proceeded most intensively from 1658 to 1660, about the time *Paradise Lost* began to be composed. (2) After Milton's death a young man named Daniel Skinner had possession of the manuscripts of both the treatise and Milton's State Papers. (3) In 1675, Skinner tried to have both published in Amsterdam, but even there, where freedom of the press flourished by comparison with Restoration England, the prospective publisher decided to suppress the treatise because of its heresies. (4) By 1677, Skinner, ignorant of the publisher's decision, came under pressure from the British government, specifically its Secretary of State, Sir Joseph Williamson, to prevent publication. (5) Williamson successfully intimidated and manipulated Skinner, confiscated the manuscripts, and put them in storage, where they remained until 1823. The most thorough and up-to-date account of the documentary evidence establishing these circumstances appears in Campbell et al. (2007).

Had Milton himself attempted to publish the treatise during the Restoration, its heretical contents would likely have caused him serious trouble, especially on account of his Arian rejection of the Trinity. That *Arian* is the correct theological category for Milton's views has been definitively demonstrated (Bauman 1987, Stoll), and it is precisely the label that was applied to them in the seventeenth century. The Dutch professor of theology consulted by the Amsterdam publisher advised against publication of the treatise specifically "because the strongest Arianism was to be found throughout it" (Campbell et al. 2007, 7). Even without the treatise, various early readers of *Paradise Lost* suspected Milton of holding just such views (Bauman 1986).

In the seventeenth century, denial of Christ's full divinity was among the gravest heresies. Bartholomew Legate and Edward Wightman were burned to death during the reign of James I for maintaining such opinions. Even after the recovery of the treatise in the nineteenth century, its Arianism provoked strong reaction, both from disappointed Christian readers (except, of course, Unitarians) and, during the last half of the twentieth century, from scholars inclined to see Milton as being "closer to the great traditions of Christianity, no longer associated with a merely eccentric fringe" (Hunter et al. 1992, 166). The result has been a long and varied history of erudite evasion, culminating in an effort to deny Milton's original authorship of the treatise through statistical analysis of its style (Corns et al. 1998). Although this long-running dispute has made scholars more attentive to the history of Milton's treatise and the exact nature of his theological opinions, the effort to uncouple Milton from authorship of a work its prefatory epistle calls his "dearest and best possession" has proven unconvincing. For rebuttal of that effort, see S. Fallon (1998, 1999), Hill (1994), Kelley (1994), Lewalski (Hunter et al. 1992, 1998), and Rumrich (Dobranski and Rumrich 1998, 2004).

Space does not permit characterization of all Milton's deviations from orthodox Protestant dogma of his time—Arminianism, antinomianism, vitalist materialism, and polygamy prominent among them. Some of these heterodoxies are at least as pertinent to Milton's poetry as his Arianism, and it is unfortunate that sensitivity to this particular heresy should have drawn critical attention away from the others. Interested readers should begin with Maurice Kelley's edition of the treatise, and particularly the relevant section of his introduction (Yale 6:43–99). Rather than list here the heresies detailed by Kelley, we would stress that the treatise took shape as Milton was composing *Paradise Lost* and that his epic narrative developed in dialogue with his ongoing attempt to make a systematic account of his faith (cp. introduction to our Modern Library edition of *Paradise Lost*). Not surprisingly, the mutual pertinence of Milton's theological treatise and his epic is the implicit premise of some of the most useful recent scholarship.

Telling precedent informs Milton's effort as a systematic theologian of Protestantism. Among those closest to *Christian Doctrine* in structure, in many points of theology, and even in the expression of some of these points are *Compendium Theologiae Christianae* (1626) by Johannes Wollebius and *Medulla Theologica* (1623) by the Englishman Guilielmus Amesius (William Ames), whom Milton quotes in book 2, chapter 7. Ames's work was soon translated into English as *The Marrow of Sacred Divinity* (1650) and became highly influential in the North American colonies. The most distinctive characteristic of the treatise and of Milton as a theologian is his unremitting reliance on Scripture. According to Bauman (1989, 178), the treatise includes a staggering 9,346 citations of canonical Scripture and apocrypha, and many of these accompany generous quotation. As Milton himself puts it in the prefatory epistle, he strove "to cram [his] pages even to overflowing, with quotations drawn from all part of the Bible and to leave as little space as possible for my own words." The primary interest of the present volume nevertheless lies in Milton's own words. Although we have retained the scriptural citations, many quotations have been deleted for reasons of space. We have indicated our deletions with ellipses in brackets. All other ellipses are Milton's own.

Our text is based on John Carey's translation for the Yale edition of Milton's prose works. Some chapters and sections of chapters have been omitted, but where possible we have kept discussion of doctrine that seems to us relevant to Milton's other writings. Our notes point to some of these connections and where necessary summarize what has been omitted. But because this work is a systematic treatise in discrete chapters, bridging summaries of the sort provided for other selected prose works in this edition do not appear. The cross-references in our notes sometimes repeat without specific acknowledgment connections made by Maurice Kelley before us, as indeed Kelley himself sometimes repeated cross-references put forward by the treatise's first translator, Charles Sumner.

Selections from

CHRISTIAN DOCTRINE

John Milton

ENGLISHMAN

To All the Churches of Christ and to All in any part of the world who profess the Christian Faith, Peace, Knowledge of the Truth, and Eternal Salvation in God the Father and in our Lord Jesus Christ.[1]

The process of restoring religion to something of its pure original state, after it had been defiled with impurities for more than thirteen hundred years,[2] dates from the beginning of the last century. Since that time many theological systems have been propounded, aiming at further purification, and providing sometimes brief, sometimes more lengthy and methodical expositions of almost all the chief points of Christian doctrine. This being so, I think I should explain straight away why, if any work has yet been published on this subject which is as exhaustive as possible, I have been dissatisfied with it, and why, on the other hand, if all previous writers have failed in this attempt, I have not been discouraged from making the same attempt myself.

If I were to say that I had focused my studies principally upon Christian doctrine because nothing else can so effectually wipe away those two repulsive afflictions, tyranny and superstition,[3] from human life and the human mind, I should show that I had been concerned not for religion but for life's well-being.

But in fact I decided not to depend upon the belief or judgment of others in religious questions for this reason: God has revealed the way of eternal salva-

1. "Renaissance theologians tended to address their works to noblemen, patrons, friends, or to the reader; and I have not noted another Renaissance systematic theology directed, like Milton's, to the combined churches of Christ and all Christians" (Kelley's note, Yale 6:117).
2. That is, from the early fourth century, when Constantine (306–37) legalized Christianity and the Council of Nicaea (325) formulated the doctrine of the Trinity.
3. Cp. *1Def* (Yale 4:535): "the two greatest evils in human life, the most fatal to virtue, namely, tyranny and superstition"; *REW*: "the two most prevailing usurpers over mankind, superstition and tyranny" (p. 369).

tion only to the individual faith of each man, and demands of us that any man who wishes to be saved should work out his beliefs for himself. So I made up my mind to puzzle out a religious creed for myself by my own exertions, and to acquaint myself with it thoroughly. In this the only authority I accepted was God's self-revelation, and accordingly I read and pondered the Holy Scriptures themselves with all possible diligence, never sparing myself in any way.

I shall mention those methods that proved profitable for me, in case desire for similar profit should, perhaps, lead someone else to start out upon the same path in the future. I began by devoting myself when I was a boy to an earnest study of the Old and New Testaments in their original languages, and then proceeded to go carefully through some of the shorter systems of theologians. I also started, following the example of these writers, to list under general headings[4] all passages from the scriptures which suggested themselves for quotation, so that I might have them ready at hand when necessary. At length, gaining confidence, I transferred my attention to more diffuse volumes of divinity, and to the conflicting arguments in controversies over certain heads of faith. But, to be frank, I was very sorry to find, in these works, that the authors frequently evaded an opponent's point in a thoroughly dishonest way, or countered it, in appearance rather than in reality, by an affected display of logical ingenuity or by constant linguistic quibbles. Such writers, moreover, often defended their prejudices tooth and nail, though with more fervor than force, by misinterpretations of biblical texts or by the false conclusions which they wrung from these. Hence, they sometimes violently attacked the truth as error and heresy, while calling error and heresy truth and upholding them not upon the authority of the Bible but as a result of habit and partisanship.

So I considered that I could not properly entrust either my creed or my hope of salvation to such guides. But I still thought that it was absolutely necessary to possess a systematic exposition of Christian teaching, or at any rate a written investigation of it, which could assist my faith or my memory or both. It seemed, then, safest and most advisable for me to make a fresh start and compile for myself, by my own exertion and long hours of study, some work of this kind which might be always at hand. I should derive this from the word of God and from that alone, and should be scrupulously faithful to the text, for to do otherwise would be merely to cheat myself. After I had painstakingly persevered in this work for several years, I saw that the citadel of reformed religion was adequately fortified against the Papists. Through neglect, however, it was open to attack in many other places where defenses and defenders were alike wanting to make it safe. In religion as in other things, I discerned, God offers all

4. The phrase *general headings* translates *locos communes,* more literally rendered "common places." "Authorship within a commonplace tradition implies readily observable stylistic consequences. The point is straightforward enough. Where *De Doctrina Christiana* does *not* disagree with the exegetical tradition . . . , it simply restates it, though—and the import of this authorial contribution should not be underestimated—it often supplements the tradition with scriptural citations and fresh or altered arguments" (Rumrich 2004, 223). Kelley's introduction to the treatise (Yale 6:16–22) discusses Milton's composition of the work and identifies precursors consulted by Milton.

his rewards not to those who are thoughtless and credulous, but to those who labor constantly and seek tirelessly after truth.[5] Thus I concluded that there was more than I realized which still needed to be measured with greater strictness against the yardstick of the Bible, and reformed with greater care. I pursued my studies, and so far satisfied myself that eventually I had no doubt about my ability to distinguish correctly in religion between matters of faith and matters of opinion. It was, furthermore, my greatest comfort that I had constructed, with God's help, a powerful support for my faith, or rather that I had laid up provision for the future in that I should not thenceforth be unprepared or hesitant when I needed to give an account of my beliefs.

God is my witness that it is with feelings of universal brotherhood and good will that I make this account public. By so doing I am sharing, and that most willingly, my dearest and best possession with as many people as possible. I hope, then, that all my readers will be sympathetic, and will avoid prejudice and malice, even though they see at once that many of the views I have published are at odds with certain conventional opinions. I implore all friends of truth not to start shouting that the church is being thrown into confusion by free discussion and inquiry. These are allowed in academic circles, and should certainly be denied to no believer. For we are ordered to find out the truth about all things, and the daily increase of the light of truth fills the church much rather with brightness and strength than with confusion. I do not see how anyone should be able or is able to throw the church into confusion by searching after truth, any more than the heathen were thrown into confusion when the gospel was first preached. For assuredly I do not urge or enforce anything upon my own authority. On the contrary, I advise every reader, and set him an example by doing the same myself, to withold his consent from those opinions about which he does not feel fully convinced, until the evidence of the Bible convinces him and induces his reason to assent and to believe. I do not seek to conceal any part of my meaning. Indeed I address myself with much more confidence to learned than to untutored readers or, if the very learned are not always the best judges and critics of such matters, at any rate to mature, strong-minded men who thoroughly understand the teaching of the gospel. Most authors who have dealt with this subject at the greatest length in the past have been in the habit of filling their pages almost entirely with expositions of their own ideas. They have relegated to the margin, with brief reference to chapter and verse, the scriptural texts upon which all that they teach is utterly dependent. I, on the other hand, have striven to cram my pages even to overflowing, with quotations drawn from all parts of the Bible and to leave as little space as possible for my own words, even when they arise from the putting together of actual scriptural texts.[6]

5. Cp. *Areop*, p. 200ff.

6. "I have discovered no systematic theology, Protestant or other, that is even remotely as biblically grounded as Milton's. For page after page, the range and number of his biblical references easily outstrip those of every other comparable text" (Bauman 1989, 9).

I intend also to make people understand how much it is in the interests of the Christian religion that men should be free not only to sift and winnow any doctrine, but also openly to give their opinions of it and even to write about it, according to what each believes. This I aim to achieve not only by virtue of the intrinsic soundness and power of the arguments, new or old, which my readers will find me bringing forward, but much more by virtue of the authority of the Bible, upon very frequent citations of which these arguments are based. Without this freedom to which I refer, there is no religion and no gospel. Violence alone prevails; and it is disgraceful and disgusting that the Christian religion should be supported by violence. Without this freedom, we are still enslaved: not, as once, by the law of God but, what is vilest of all, by human law, or rather, to be more exact, by an inhuman tyranny. There are some irrational bigots who, by a perversion of justice, condemn anything they consider inconsistent with conventional beliefs and give it an invidious title—"heretic" or "heresy"—without consulting the evidence of the Bible upon the point. To their way of thinking, by branding anyone out of hand with this hateful name, they silence him with one word and need take no further trouble. They imagine that they have struck their opponent to the ground, as with a single blow, by the impact of the name heretic alone. I do not expect that my unprejudiced and intelligent readers will behave in this way: such conduct would be utterly unworthy of them. But to these bigots I retort that, in apostolic times, before the New Testament was written, the word heresy, whenever it was used as an accusation, was applied only to something which contradicted the teaching of the apostles as it passed from mouth to mouth. Heretics were then, according to Rom. 16.17, 18, only those people who *caused divisions of opinion and offences contrary to the teaching of the apostles: serving not our Lord Jesus Christ but their own belly.* On the same grounds I hold that, since the compilation of the New Testament, nothing can correctly be called heresy unless it contradicts that.[7] For my own part, I devote my attention to the Holy Scriptures alone. I follow no other heresy or sect. I had not even studied any of the so-called heretical writers, when the blunders of those who are styled orthodox, and their unthinking distortions of the sense of scripture, first taught me to agree with their opponents whenever these agreed with the Bible. If this is heresy, I confess, as does Paul in Acts 24.14, that *following the way which is called heresy I worship the God of my fathers, believing all things that are written in the law and the prophets* and, I add, whatever is written in the New Testament as well.[8] In common with the whole Protestant Church I refuse to recognize any other arbiters of or any other supreme authorities for Christian belief, or any faith not independently arrived at but "implicit," as it is termed. For the rest, brethren, cherish the truth with love for your fellow men. Assess this work as God's spirit shall direct you. Do not accept or reject what I

7. Hunter observes the close correspondence of this view of heresy with Milton's position in *Civil Power* and in *True Religion* (Yale 7:247, n. 23).

8. On Milton's understanding of the term *heresy,* see Mueller.

say unless you are absolutely convinced by the clear evidence of the Bible. Lastly, live in the spirit of our Lord and Savior Jesus Christ, and so I bid you farewell.

J.M.

BOOK 1

CHAPTER I

WHAT CHRISTIAN DOCTRINE IS, AND HOW MANY ITS PARTS

Christian doctrine is the doctrine which, in all ages, CHRIST (though he was not known by that name from the beginning) taught by divine communication, for the glory of God and the salvation of mankind, about God and about worshipping him.

[. . .][9]

I do not teach anything new in this work. I aim only to assist the reader's memory by collecting together, as it were, into a single book texts which are scattered here and there throughout the Bible, and by systematizing them under definite headings, in order to make reference easy. This procedure might well be defended on grounds of Christian prudence, but in fact a more powerful argument in its favor is that apparently it fulfils God's own command: Matt. 13.52: *every scribe who has been instructed in the kingdom of heaven, is like a householder who brings out of his treasure new and old possessions.* So also the apostle says to Timothy, 2 Tim. 1.13: ὑποτύπωσιν ἔχε, "Hold fast the pattern," which the author of the epistle to the Hebrews seems to have been determined to do, so as to teach the main points of Christian doctrine methodically: Heb. 6.1–3: *of repentance, faith, the doctrine of Baptisms, and of the laying on of hands, the resurrection of the dead and eternal judgment: and this we will do if God permit.* This was a very convenient way of instructing catechumens when they were making their first profession of faith in the Church. The same method is indicated in Rom. 6.17: *You have listened from the heart to that pattern of doctrine which you were taught.* In this quotation the Greek word τύπος, like ὑποτύπωσις in 2 Tim. 1.13, seems to mean either those parts of the gospels that were actually written at the time (as in Rom. 2.20 the word μόρφωσις, meaning "form" or "semblance", signifies the law itself in the phrase "the *form* of knowledge and of truth in the law"), or else some systematic course of instruction derived from those parts or from the whole doctrine of the gospel. It appears from Acts 20.27: *I have not avoided making known to you God's whole counsel,* that there is a complete corpus of doctrine, conceived in terms

9. The deleted passage cites Scripture to elaborate the definition of Christian doctrine.

of a definite course of instruction. This was of no great length, however, since the whole course was completed, and perhaps even repeated several times, in about three years, while Paul was at Ephesus.

The PARTS of CHRISTIAN DOCTRINE are two: FAITH, or KNOWLEDGE OF GOD, and LOVE, or THE WORSHIP OF GOD.[10] Gen. 17.1: *walk in sight of me and be perfect;* Ps. 37.3: *have faith in God, and do good;* Luke 11.28: *blessed are those who hear and obey;* Acts 24.14; *I, as one who believes,* and 24.16: *I train myself;* 2 Tim. 1.13: *hold fast the pattern of words with faith and love, which is in Christ Jesus;* 1 Tim. 1.19 [. . .]; Titus 3.8 [. . .]; 1 John 3.23 [. . .].

Although these two parts are distinguished in kind, and are divided for the purpose of instruction, in practice they are inseparable. Rom. 2.13: *not hearers but doers;* James 1.22 [. . .]. Besides, obedience and love are always the best guides to knowledge, and often cause it to increase and flourish, though very small at first. Ps. 25.14: *the secret of Jehovah is with those who reverence him;* John 7.17: *if any man wants what he wills, he shall know about the doctrine,* and 8.31, 32: *if you remain, you will know, and the truth will make you free;* 1 John 2.3: *if we keep his commandments we know, by this, that we know him.*

Faith, however, in this section, does not mean the habit of believing, but the things which must habitually be believed. Acts 6.7: *was obedient to the faith;* Gal. 1.23: *he preaches the faith.*

CHAPTER 2

OF GOD

That there is a God, many deny: *for the fool says in his heart, There is no God,* Ps. 14.1.[11] But he has left so many signs of himself in the human mind, so many traces of his presence through the whole of nature, that no sane person can fail to realize that he exists. Job 12.9: *who does not know from all these things?;* Ps. 19.2: *the heavens declare the glory of God;* Acts 14.17: *he did not allow himself to exist without evidence,* and 17.27, 28: *he is not far from every one of us;* Rom. 1.19, 20: *that which can be known about God is obvious,* and 2.14, 15 [. . .]; 1 Cor. 1.21 [. . .]. It is indisputable that all the things which exist in the world, created in perfection of beauty and order for some definite purpose, and that a good one, provide proof that a supreme creative being existed before the world, and had a definite purpose of his own in all created things.

There are some who prattle about nature or fate, as if they were to be identified with this supreme being. But nature or *natura* implies by its very name that it was *natam,* born. Strictly speaking it means nothing except the specific character of a thing, or that general law in accordance with which everything

10. Cp. *Of Civil Power* (Yale 7:255): "What evangelic religion is, is told in two words, faith and charity; or belief and practice." Hunter's note explains that these "traditional divisions" underlie "Milton's arrangement of the *Christian Doctrine* into two books." See also *PL* 3.103–4; 12.583–85.

11. Cp. *SA* 295–99.

comes into existence and behaves.[12] Surely, too, fate or *fatum* is only what is *fatum*, spoken, by some almighty power. [13]

Moreover, those who want to prove that all things are created by nature, have to introduce the concept of chance as well, to share godhead with nature. What, then, do they gain by their theory? In place of one God, whom they find intolerable, they are forced to set up as universal rulers two goddesses who are almost always at odds with each other. In fact, then, many visible proofs, the fulfillment of many prophecies and the narration of many marvels have driven every nation to the belief that either God or some supreme evil power of unknown name presides over the affairs of men. But it is intolerable and incredible that evil should be stronger than good and should prove the true supreme power. Therefore God exists.

Further evidence for the existence of God is provided by the phenomenon of conscience, or right reason. This cannot be altogether asleep, even in the most evil men. If there were no God, there would be no dividing line between right and wrong. What was to be called virtue, and what vice, would depend upon mere arbitrary opinion. No one would try to be virtuous, no one would refrain from sin because he felt ashamed of it or feared the law, if the voice of conscience or right reason did not speak from time to time in the heart of every man, reminding him, however unwilling he may be to remember it, that a God does exist, that he rules and governs all things, and that everyone must one day render to him an account of his actions, good and bad alike.

The whole of scripture proves the same point, and it is absolutely requisite that those who wish to learn Christian doctrine should be convinced of this fact from the outset. This is stated in Heb. 11.6: *he who comes to God must believe that he is God.* The fact that the Jews, an extremely ancient nation, are now dispersed all over the world, demonstrates the same thing. God often warned them that this would be the outcome of their sins. Amidst the constant flux of history they have been preserved in this state, scattered among the other nations, right up to the present day. This has been done not only to make them pay the penalty of their sins but much rather to give the whole world a perpetual, living proof of the existence of God and the truth of the scriptures.

No one, however, can form correct ideas about God guided by nature or reason alone, without the word or message of God: Rom. 10.14: *how shall they believe in him about whom they have not heard?*

We know God, in so far as we are permitted to know him, from either his nature or his efficiency.

When we talk about knowing God, it must be understood in terms of man's limited powers of comprehension. God, as he really is, is far beyond man's

12. Cp. *PL* 11.48–49: "But longer in that Paradise to dwell,/The law I gave to nature him forbids"; 10.804–7: "that were to extend/His sentence beyond dust and nature's law,/By which all causes else according still/To the reception of their matter act."
13. Cp. *PL* 7.173: "and what I will is Fate"; *Art of Logic* (Yale 8:229): "fate or divine decree."

imagination, let alone his understanding: 1 Tim. 6.16: *dwelling in unapproachable light.* God has revealed only so much of himself as our minds can conceive and the weakness of our nature can bear: Ex. 33.20, 23: *no one can see me and live: but you will see my back parts;* Isa. 6.1: [. . .]; John 1.18: [. . .] and 6.46: [. . .] and 5.37: [. . .]; 1 Cor. 13.12: [. . .].

It is safest for us to form an image of God in our minds which corresponds to his representation and description of himself in the sacred writings. Admittedly, God is always described or outlined not as he really is but in such a way as will make him conceivable to us. Nevertheless, we ought to form just such a mental image of him as he, in bringing himself within the limits of our understanding, wishes us to form. Indeed he has brought himself down to our level expressly to prevent our being carried beyond the reach of human comprehension, and outside the written authority of scripture, into vague subtleties of speculation.[14]

In my opinion, then, theologians do not need to employ anthropopathy, or the ascription of human feelings to God. This is a rhetorical device thought up by grammarians to explain the nonsense poets write about Jove. Sufficient care has been taken, without any doubt, to ensure that the holy scriptures contain nothing unfitting to God or unworthy of him. This applies equally to those passages in scripture where God speaks about his own nature. So it is better not to think about God or form an image of him in anthropopathetic terms, for to do so would be to follow the example of men, who are always inventing more and more subtle theories about him. Rather we should form our ideas with scripture as a model, for that is the way in which he has offered himself to our contemplation. We ought not to imagine that God would have said anything or caused anything to be written about himself unless he intended that it should be a part of our conception of him. On the question of what is or what is not suitable for God, let us ask for no more dependable authority than God himself. If *Jehovah repented that he had created man,* Gen. 6.6, *and repented because of their groanings,* Judges 2.18, let us believe that he did repent. But let us not imagine that God's repentance arises from lack of foresight, as man's does, for he has warned us not to think about him in this way: Num. 23.19: *God is not a man that he should lie, nor the son of man that he should repent.* The same point is made in 1 Sam. 15.29. If *he grieved in his heart* Gen. 6.6, and if, similarly, *his soul was grieved,* Judges 10.16, let us believe that he did feel grief. For those states of mind which are good in a good man, and count as virtues, are holy in God. If it is said that God, after working for six days, *rested and was refreshed,* Ex. 31.17, and if he *feared his enemy's displeasure,* Deut. 32.27, let us believe that it is not beneath God to feel what grief he does feel, to be refreshed by what refreshes him, and to fear what he does

14. Milton recommends acquiescence to scriptural metaphor in terms similar to those that Raphael uses in warning Adam against abstruse astronomical investigations (8.119–22): "God to remove his ways from human sense,/Placed heav'n from Earth so far, that earthly sight,/If it presume, might err in things too high,/And no advantage gain."

fear. For however you may try to tone down these and similar texts about God by an elaborate show of interpretative glosses, it comes to the same thing in the end. After all, if *God is said to have created man in his own image, after his own likeness,* Gen. 1.26, and not only his mind but also his external appearance (unless the same words mean something different when they are used again in Gen. 5.3: *Adam begot his son after his own likeness, in his own image*), and if God attributes to himself again and again a human shape and form, why should we be afraid of assigning to him something he assigns to himself, provided we believe that what is imperfect and weak in us is, when ascribed to God, utterly perfect and utterly beautiful? We may be certain that God's majesty and glory were so dear to him that he could never say anything about himself which was lower or meaner than his real nature, nor would he ever ascribe to himself any property if he did not wish us to ascribe it to him. Let there be no question about it: they understand best what God is like who adjust their understanding to the word of God, for he has adjusted his word to our understanding, and has shown what kind of an idea of him he wishes us to have. In short, God either is or is not really like he says he is. If he really is like this, why should we think otherwise? If he is not really like this, on what authority do we contradict God? If, at any rate, he wants us to imagine him in this way, why does our imagination go off on some other tack? Why does our imagination shy away from a notion of God which he himself does not hesitate to promulgate in unambiguous terms? For God in his goodness has revealed to us in ample quantity those things which we need to understand about him for our salvation: Deut. 29.29: *hidden things are in the power of Jehovah, but the things which are revealed are revealed to us that we may do them.* We do not imply by this argument that God, in all his parts and members, is of human form, but that, so far as it concerns us to know, he has that form which he attributes to himself in Holy Writ. God, then, has disclosed just such an idea of himself to our understanding as he wishes us to possess. If we form some other idea of him, we are not acting according to his will, but are frustrating him of his purpose, as if, indeed, we wished to show that our concept of God was not too debased, but that his concept of us was.[15]

Since it has no causes, we cannot define the "divine nature." However, this is the name given to it in 2 Pet. 1.4: *that you might be made sharers of the divine nature* (though "nature" here does not mean the essence but the image of God) and in Gal. 4.8: *which by nature are not Gods,* while θεοτῆς in Col. 2.9, θειοτῆς in Rom. 1.20, and τό θεῖον in Acts 17.29 are all translated "godhead." But though God, by his very nature, transcends everything, including definition, some description of him may be gathered from his names and attributes, as in Isa. 28.29.

[. . . .][16]

15. Calvin proposed an interpretive theory of accommodation that attributes theologically embarrassing scriptural moments, e.g., when God "repents," to divine condescension (*Institutes* 1.13.1). Milton concedes that scriptural accounts of God's emotions may not be accurate but insists that readers of Scripture should think of the deity as he has chosen to depict himself rather than judge the accuracy of Scripture on the basis of doctrine.

16. The deleted passage discusses the implied meanings of three Hebrew names for God.

The ATTRIBUTES which show the essential nature of God are, first, that he is the TRUE GOD: Jer. 10.10: *Jehovah the true God;* John 17.3 [. . .]; 1 Thess. 1.9 [. . .]; 1 John 5.20 [. . .].

Secondly, that God in his most simple nature is a SPIRIT. Ex. 3.14, 15: *I am who I am;* Rom. 11.35, 36: *from him and through him are all things;* John 4.24: *God is a spirit.* Moreover, it is shown what a spirit is, or rather, what it is not: Isa. 31.3: *flesh, not spirit;* Luke 24.39: *a spirit does not have flesh and bones.* From this it may be understood that the essence of God, since it is utterly simple, allows nothing to be compounded with it, and that the word *hypostasis,* Heb. 1.3, which is variously translated *substance, subsistence,* or *person,* is nothing but that most perfect essence by which God exists from himself, in himself, and through himself. For neither *substance* nor *subsistence* can add anything to an utterly complete essence, and the word *person,* in its more recent use, means any individual thing gifted with intelligence, while *hypostasis* means not the thing itself but the essence of the thing in the abstract. *Hypostasis,* therefore, is clearly the same as essence, and in the passage cited above many translate it by the Latin word *essentia.*[17] Therefore, just as God is an utterly simple essence, so he is an utterly simple subsistence.

Thirdly, he is IMMENSE and INFINITE:[18] 1 Kings 8.27: *the heaven of heavens cannot contain you;* Job 11.8: *higher than the highest heavens, deeper than the lowest depth,* and 36.26: so *great that we do not know.*

Fourthly, that he is ETERNAL: everyone agrees that nothing can properly be called eternal unless it has no beginning and no end. It can be seen that both these are true of God from the following passages; not, indeed from each of them separately, but from a comparison of the several texts. [. . . .][19]

The fifth attribute, derived from the fourth, is that God is IMMUTABLE.[20] Ps. 102.28: *but you are the same;* Mal. 3.6: *I, Jehovah, am not changed;* James 1.17: *with whom there is no variation or shadow caused by change.*

The sixth, also derived from the fourth attribute, is that he is INCORRUPTIBLE:[21] Ps. 102.26, 27: you *remain;* Rom. 1.23: *of God, who is not corrupted;* 1 Tim. 1.17 [. . .].

The seventh attribute, which is a consequence of his infinity, is that God is PRESENT EVERYWHERE.[22] Ps. 139.8, 9: *if I climb up to the heavens you are there,* etc.; Prov. 15.3: *Jehovah's eyes are in every place;* Jer. 23.24 [. . .]; Eph. 4.6 [. . .]. Our ideas about the omnipresence of God, as it is called, should be only such as appear most reconcilable with the reverence we ought to have for him.

17. The terms addressed by Milton in this paragraph have a vexed history in Christian theology. See Prestige; also Rumrich 1982.

18. Cp. *PL* 7.168–69: "Boundless the deep, because I am who fill/Infinitude."

19. The rest of the paragraph cites verses that together imply the eternity of God and concludes with the observation that "the concept of what is, strictly speaking, eternity, is expressed in the Hebrew language by inference rather than by distinct words."

20. Cp. *PL* 3.372–73: "Thee Father first they sung omnipotent,/Immutable."

21. Cp. *PL* 2.137–38: "our great enemy/All incorruptible."

22. Cp. *PL* 11.336–37: "his omnipresence fills/Land, sea, and air, and every kind that lives."

The eighth attribute, that God is OMNIPOTENT: 2 Chron. 20.6: *might and power are in your hand;* Job 42.2: *I know that you can do everything;* Ps. 33.9 [. . .] and 115.3 [. . .], and similarly 135.6. Matt. 19.26 [. . .]. Luke 1.37 [. . .]. Because of this attribute the name El Shaddai is applied to God. Gen. 17.1: *I am the omnipotent God,* literally, *the sufficiently powerful God* [. . .]. Hence it appears that God cannot rightly be called Actus Purus, or pure actuality, as is customary in Aristotle, for thus he could do nothing except what he does do, and he would do that of necessity, although in fact he is omnipotent and utterly free in his actions.[23] It should be noted, however, that the power of God is not exerted in those kinds of things which, as the term goes, imply a contradiction: 2 Tim. 2.13: *he cannot deny himself;* Tit. 1.2 [. . .]; Heb. 6.18 [. . .].[24]

The ninth attribute, that God is ONE,[25] proceeds from the eight previous attributes and is, as it were, the logical conclusion of them all. Still further proof of it is to be found, however: Deut. 4.35: *that Jehovah is God and that there is no God except him,* 4.39 [. . .], 6.4: *Hear, Israel, Jehovah our God is one Jehovah,* and 32.39 [. . .]; 1 Kings 8.60: *that all the peoples of the earth may know that Jehovah is God and that there is no one else except him;* 2 Kings 19.15 [. . .]; Isa. 44.1 [. . .], and 44.8 [. . .]; and 45.5 [. . .]; and 45.21 [. . .]; 45.22: *I am God and there is none besides,* that is, no spirit, no person, no being besides him is God, for "none" is a negative of general application: Isa. 46.9: *that I am God and that there is no God besides me, and that no one is like me.* What could be more plain and straightforward? What could be better adapted to the average intelligence, what more in keeping with everyday speech, so that God's people should understand that there is numerically one God and one spirit, just as they understand that there is numerically one of anything else. It was indeed fitting, and thoroughly in accordance with reason, that God should communicate his first and therefore greatest commandment, which he wanted all people, even the lowest, scrupulously to obey, in terms like these which contain nothing ambiguous or obscure that might mislead his worshippers or leave them in doubt. Certainly the Israelites under the law and the prophets always understood that God was without question numerically one, and that there was no other besides him, let alone any equal to him.[26] The schoolmen, to be sure, had not yet appeared on the scene. When they did, by relying upon subtleties,

23. St. Thomas Aquinas used Aristotle's concept of pure actuality to characterize the divine nature and distinguish God from his creatures. Milton's heterodox claim that God's essence includes potentiality is motivated not only by his insistence on divine immunity from necessity but also on God's containing the matter (and thus the material potency) that he shaped in creating the world (see Chapter 7).

24. Cp. *PL* 10.798–801: "Can he make deathless Death? That were to make/Strange contradiction, which to God himself/Impossible is held; as argument/Of weakness, not of power."

25. "Milton is laying groundwork for his antitrinitarian doctrine. To the attribute of unity, he pauses to devote more than a manuscript page, citing proof texts first from the Old Testament and then from the New, and establishing in his exegesis of Mark 12.28–32 the concord of the two. This authority of the scripture he buttresses with appeals to reason: the simplicity of the Bible, the mathematical concept on oneness, and the axiom that God cannot be involved in anything that implies a contradiction—three points that Milton will again urge in chapter 5" (Kelley's note, Yale 6:146–47).

26. Cp. *PL* 8.406–7: "for none I know/Second to me or like, equal much less."

or rather upon utterly contradictory arguments, they threw doubt upon the unity of God, which they ostensibly asserted. But, as I pointed out earlier, everyone agrees that an exception must be made to God's omnipotence, namely that he cannot do things which, as it is put, imply a contradiction. Accordingly we must remember here that nothing can be said of the one God that is inconsistent with his unity, and which makes him both one and not one. Now let us look at the evidence of the New Testament. It is no less clear upon the points already dealt with, and in this respect even clearer: it asserts that this one God is the Father of Our Lord Jesus Christ. When Christ was asked, in Mark 12.28–29, what was the first commandment of all, he replied, quoting from Deut. 6.4, a passage already cited, and understood here in no other sense than the customary one: *Hear, Israel, the Lord our God is one Lord.* The lawyer agreed with this reply, Mark 12.42: *Master, he said, you have spoken well and truthfully, for there is one God and there is no other except him;* John 17.3: *this is eternal life, that they may know that you are the only true God;* Rom. 3.30: *there is one God;* 1 Cor. 8.4 [. . .], 8.6 [. . .]; Gal. 3.20: *an intermediary however is not needed for one person acting alone, but God is one;* Eph. 4.6 [. . .]; 1 Tim. 2.5 [. . .].[27]

CHAPTER 3

OF DIVINE DECREE

Up to now I have examined God from the point of view of his nature: now we must learn more about him by investigating his efficiency.

God's EFFICIENCY is either INTERNAL or EXTERNAL.

God's INTERNAL EFFICIENCY is that which begins and ends within God himself. His decrees come into this category: Eph. 1.9: *which he had determined beforehand in his own mind.*

A DECREE of God is either GENERAL or SPECIAL.

God's GENERAL DECREE is that by which HE DECREED FROM ETERNITY, WITH ABSOLUTE FREEDOM, WITH ABSOLUTE WISDOM AND WITH ABSOLUTE HOLINESS, ALL THOSE THINGS WHICH HE PROPOSED OR WHICH HE WAS GOING TO PERFORM.

ALL THOSE THINGS WHICH, etc.: Eph. 1.11: *who does all things according to the resolution of his own will.* This does not mean the things which others perform, or which God performs in co-operation with others, to whom he has granted, by nature, freedom of action, but rather the things he performs or purposes singly and by himself. For example, he decreed by himself to create the world, and he decreed by himself that he would not curse the earth any longer, Gen. 8.21.

27. Three deleted sentences at the end of this paragraph concern the singular application of plural Hebrew terms for God. The chapter closes by detailing the attributes that convey God's life, intellect, and will.

FROM ETERNITY. Acts 15.18: *all God's works are known to him from the beginning* of *the world;* 1 Cor. 2.7 [. . .].

WITH ABSOLUTE FREEDOM: that is, not forced, not impelled by any necessity,[28] but just as he wished: Eph. 1.11, as above.

WITH ABSOLUTE WISDOM: that is, according to his perfect foreknowledge of all things that were to be created. Acts 2.23: *by the deliberate counsel and foreknowledge of God,* and 4.28: *to do whatever your power and counsel foreordained,* 15.18: *all God's works are known to him from the beginning of the world;* 1 Cor. 2.7 [. . .]; Eph. 3.10, 11 [. . .].

It is absurd, then, to separate God's decree or intention from his eternal resolution and foreknowledge and give the former chronological priority. For God's foreknowledge is simply his wisdom under another name, or that idea of all things which, to speak in human terms, he had in mind before he decreed anything.[29]

So we must conclude that God made no absolute decrees about anything which he left in the power of men, for men have freedom of action. The whole course of scripture shows this: [. . .]. In 2 Kings 20.1, though God said that Hezekiah would die straight away, this did not happen: therefore God had not decreed it without reservation. The death of Josiah was not positively decreed, but he did not listen to Necho's speech, which was derived from the word of God, warning him not to march out, 2 Chron. 35.22. Again, Jer. 18.9, 10: *at that moment when I speak about a nation or a kingdom, saying that I will build or plant it, if, through not paying attention to my voice, it do something that seems evil in my sight, I shall, in turn, repent of the good which I said I should do for it.* In other words, I shall reverse my decree because that nation did not keep the condition upon which the decree depended. Here we have a rule given by God himself! He wishes us always to understand his decrees in the light of this agreement, and always clearly to appreciate the condition upon which the decree depends. Jer. 26.3: *if it should happen that they are obedient and that each man turn from his evil path, so that I repent the harm I intend to do them because of the depravity of their behavior.* So, too, God had not decreed absolutely even upon the destruction of Jerusalem: Jer. 38.17, etc. [. . .]; Jonah 3.4: *yet forty days and Nineveh will be overthrown,* but, at 3.10, when he saw they had reformed God repented, although Jonah was angry and thought it did not become God in the least.[30] Acts 27.24, 31: *I have given you all as a gift. But unless these men stay on board . . . ;* here Paul revokes the divinely inspired statement which he had made: God takes back the gift given to Paul unless they all take care of themselves to the utmost of their ability.

28. The Latin of the manuscript reads *"nulla necessitate impulsus."* Cp. *PL* 3.120: "So without least impulse or shadow of fate."

29. Cp. *PL* 7.554–57: "Thence to behold this new created world/Th' addition of his empire, how it showed/In prospect from his throne, how good, how fair/Answering his great idea."

30. On divine repentance and its implications, see previous chapter, note 15.

Judging from these passages of scripture then, and from many others of the same kind, which we are immediately bound to acknowledge as authoritative, it is beyond dispute that the supreme God has not absolutely decreed all things.

Each side of this controversy has hosts of adherents, all arguing at great length and with altogether more subtlety than weight. However, if it is allowable to apply the standards of mortal reason to divine decrees, this method of making decrees in a non-absolute way can be readily defended, even with regard to human considerations, as supremely wise and in no way unworthy of God. For if the decrees of God quoted above, and others of the same kind which frequently occur, were interpreted in an absolute sense without any implied conditions, God would seem to contradict himself and be changeable. [. . .][31]

It is no good replying that this necessity is not the result of compulsion but that it springs from God's immutability, by virtue of which everything is decreed, or from his infallibility of foreknowledge, by virtue of which everything is foreknown. I shall give a full exposure of these two purely academic types of necessity later. Meanwhile I recognize no other type of necessity than the one which Logic, that is, reason teaches:[32] namely, when a given cause produces some single unalterable effect either as a result of its own inherent propensity, as when fire burns, which is called natural necessity, or as the result of the compulsion of some external force, which is called compulsory necessity. In the latter case, whatever effect the given cause produces is said to be produced *per accidens.*[33] Now any necessity operating externally upon a given cause either makes it produce a certain effect or limits it from producing other effects. In either case it is clear that the cause loses all freedom of action. In God a certain immutable internal necessity to do good, independent of all outside influence, can be consistent with absolute freedom of action. For in the same divine nature each tends to the same result. However, it does not follow from this that I must allow the same possibility where two different natures are concerned, namely the nature of God and the nature of man. For in this case the external immutability of the one and the internal liberty of the other may not have the same aim at all but point in opposite directions. Nor, incidentally, do I concede

31. In the deleted paragraph, Milton considers and rejects the claim that God predestines not only the end but the means to the end of his decree. Milton revisits the point in chapter 4.

32. Cp. *Art of Logic* (Yale 8:211): "For the theologians produce rules about God, about divine substances, and about sacraments purportedly out of the middle of logic, as though these rules had been furnished simply for their own convenience, although nothing is more foreign to logic, or indeed to reason itself, than the grounds for these rules as formulated by them."

33. Cp. *Art of Logic* (Yale 8:226–27): "An efficient cause is such either *per se* or *per accidens*. . . . A *per se* efficient cause is one which causes efficiently through its own power, that is, one which produces an effect from an intrinsic principle. . . . A *per accidens* efficient cause is one which causes through an eternal power, that is, one not its own."

the point that there is in God any necessity to act. I grant only that he is necessarily God. For scripture itself bears witness to the fact that his decrees and still more his actions, whatever they may be, are absolutely free.[34]

But it is said that divine necessity, or the necessity of a first cause, does not bring any compulsion to bear upon the liberty of free agents. I reply that, if it does not compel, then either it restricts liberty within certain limits, or assists it, or does nothing. If it restricts or assists then it is either the only or the joint and principal cause of every action,[35] good and bad, of the free agent. If it does nothing, it is not a cause at all, still less should it be called necessity.

We imagine nothing unworthy of God if we maintain that those results, those conditions which God himself has chosen to place within man's free power, depend upon man's free will. In fact, God made his decrees conditional in this way for the very purpose of allowing free causes to put into effect that freedom which he himself gave them.[36] It would be much more unworthy of God to announce that man is free but really deprive him of freedom; and freedom is destroyed or at least obscured if we admit any such sophistical concept of necessity as that which, we are asked to believe, results not from compulsion but from immutability or infallibility. This concept has misled and continues to mislead a lot of people.

However, I affirm that, strictly speaking, the divine plan depends only upon God's own wisdom. By this wisdom he had perfect foreknowledge of all things in his own mind, and knew what they would be like and what their consequence would be when it eventually occurred.

But, you ask, how can these consequences which, on account of man's free will, are uncertain, be reconciled with God's absolutely firm decree? For it is written, Ps. 33.11: *Jehovah's intention will be stable for ever,* similarly Prov. 19.21; Isa. 46.10; Heb. 6.17: *the immutability of his plan.* My reply is that, in the first place, these consequences are not uncertain from God's point of view, but known with absolute certainty. They are not, however, inevitable, as we shall see later. Secondly, in all the passages quoted the divine plan is said to stand in the face of all human power and intention. It is not said to stand in opposition to the freedom of the will in matters where God himself has made man his own master, and decreed to make him so from all eternity. If it were otherwise, one of God's decrees would contradict another. This would lead to the result you object to in the arguments of others, that is, God becomes mutable so long as you make those things which by his command are matters of free will, appear inevitabilities.

34. Cp. *Art of Logic* (Yale 8:227): "Only God does all things with absolute freedom, that is, He does whatever he wills; and He can act or not act. This is attested to throughout Sacred Scripture." See S. Fallon 1988.

35. Cp. *Art of Logic* (Yale 8:224): "An efficient cause works either by itself or along with other efficient causes, and of all these often one will be the principal cause, while another is less principal, or an assisting and helping cause."

36. Cp. *Art of Logic* (Yale 8:227): "Only those causes act freely *ex hypothesi* which do things through reason and deliberation, as angels and men—on the hypothesis, to be sure, of the divine will, which in the beginning gave them the power to act freely. For freedom is the power to do or not to do this or that, unless of course God wills otherwise or some other force violently interferes."

But God is not mutable if he makes no positive decree about anything which, through the freedom he decided to give man, could turn out otherwise. He would be mutable, and his intention would not be stable, if, by a second decree, he thwarted the freedom he had once decided upon, or cast the least shadow of necessity over it.

From the concept of freedom, then, all idea of necessity must be removed. No place must be given even to that shadowy and peripheral idea of necessity based on God's immutability and foreknowledge. If any idea of necessity remains, as I have said before, it either restricts free agents to a single course, or compels them against their will, or assists them when they are willing, or does nothing at all. If it restricts free agents to a single course, this makes man the natural cause of all his actions and therefore of his sins, just as if he were created with an inherent propensity towards committing sins. If it compels free agents against their will, this means that man is subject to the force of another's decree, and is thus the cause of sins only *per accidens,* God being the cause of the sin *per se.* If it assists free agents when they are willing, this makes God either the principal or the joint cause of sins. Lastly, if it does nothing at all, no necessity exists. By doing nothing it reduces itself to nothingness. For it is quite impossible that God should have made an inflexible decree about something which we know man is still at liberty to do or not to do. It is also impossible that a thing should be immutable which afterwards might or might not take place.

Whatever was a matter of free will for the first created man, could not then have been immutably or absolutely decreed from all eternity. Obviously, either nothing ever was in the power of man, or if anything was, God cannot be said to have made a firm decree about it.[37]

The absurdities which are said to ensue from this argument are either not absurdities or do not ensue from it. For it is neither absurd nor impious to say that the idea of certain things or events might come to God from some other source. Since God has decreed from eternity that man should have free will to enable him either to fall or not to fall, the idea of that evil event, the fall, was clearly present in God from some other source: everyone admits this.

It cannot be deduced from this that something temporal may cause or limit something eternal; for nothing temporal, but rather eternal wisdom supplied a cause for the divine plan.

The matter or object of the divine plan was that angels and men alike should be endowed with free will, so that they could either fall or not fall. Doubtless God's actual decree bore a close resemblance to this, so that all the evils which have since happened as a result of the fall could either happen or not: if you stand firm, you will stay; if you do not, you will be thrown out: if you do not eat it, you will live; if you do, you will die.

37. This statement opposes Calvinist orthodoxy. Cp. Calvin, *Institutes* (3.23.7): "The decree is dreadful, I confess. Yet no one can deny that God foreknew what end man was to have before he created him, and consequently foreknew because he so ordained by his decree."

Those, then, who argue that man's freedom of action is subordinate to an absolute decree by God, wrongly conclude that God's decree is the cause of his foreknowledge and antecedent to it. But really, if we must discuss God in terms of our own habits and understandings, it seems more consonant with reason to foresee first and then decree, and indeed this is more in keeping with scripture, and with the nature of God himself, since, as I have just proved, he decreed everything with supreme wisdom in accordance with his foreknowledge.

I do not deny that God's will is the first cause of everything. But neither do I divorce his foreknowledge and wisdom from his will, much less pretend that the latter is antecedent. In short, God's will is no less the first cause of everything if he decrees that certain things shall depend upon the will of man, than if he had decreed to make all things inevitable.

To sum up these numerous arguments in a few words, this is briefly how the matter stands, looked at from a thoroughly reasonable angle. By virtue of his wisdom God decreed the creation of angels and men as beings gifted with reason and thus with free will.[38] At the same time he foresaw the direction in which they would tend when they used this absolutely unimpaired freedom. What then? Shall we say that God's providence or foreknowledge imposes any necessity upon them? Certainly not: no more than if some human being possessed the same foresight. For an occurrence foreseen with absolute certainty by a human being will no less certainly take place than one foretold by God. For example, Elisha foresaw what evils King Hazael would bring upon the Israelites in a few years' time: 2 Kings 8.12. But no one would claim that these happened inevitably as a result of Elisha's foreknowledge: for these events, no less than any others, clearly arose from man's will, which is always free.[39] Similarly, nothing happens because God has foreseen it, but rather he has foreseen each event because each is the result of particular causes which, by his decree, work quite freely and with which he is thoroughly familiar. So the outcome does not rest with God who foresees it, but only with the man whose action God foresees. As I have demonstrated above, there can be no absolute divine decree about the action of free agents. Moreover, divine foreknowledge can no more affect the action of free agents than can human foreknowledge, that is, not at all, because in both cases the foreknowledge is within the mind of the foreknower and has no external effect.[40] Divine foreknowledge definitely cannot itself impose any necessity, nor can it be set up as a cause, in any sense, of free actions. If it is set up in this way, then liberty will be an empty word, and will have to be banished utterly not only from religion but also from morality and even from indifferent matters. Nothing will happen except by necessity, since there is nothing God does not foresee.

38. Cp. *PL* 3.108: "reason also is choice"; also 9.351–52: "But God left free the will, for what obeys/Reason, is free."

39. *"arbitrio semper libro."* In classical usage, *arbitrio libro* denotes discretionary power.

40. Cp. *Art of Logic* (Yale 8:236): "While [an end] is still only in the mind . . . and has not been achieved, it does not yet truly exist; and since it does not yet exist, how can it be a cause?"

To conclude, we should feel certain that God has not decreed that everything must happen inevitably. Otherwise we should make him responsible for all the sins ever committed, and should make demons and wicked men blameless. But we should feel certain also that God really does foreknow everything that is going to happen. My opponent, of course, snatches up this last remark and thinks I have conceded enough for him to prove either that God does not foreknow everything, or that all future events must happen by necessity because God has foreknown them. But though future events will certainly happen, because divine foreknowledge cannot be mistaken, they will not happen by necessity, because foreknowledge, since it exists only in the mind of the foreknower, has no effect on its object.[41] A thing which is going to happen quite freely in the course of events is not then produced as a result of God's foreknowledge, but arises from the free action of its own causes, and God knows in what direction these will, of their own accord, tend. In this way he knew that Adam would, of his own accord, fall. Thus it was certain that he would fall, but it was not necessary, because he fell of his own accord and that is irreconcilable with necessity.[42] [. . .]. From all that has been said it is sufficiently clear that neither God's decree nor his foreknowledge can shackle free causes with any kind of necessity. There are some people, however, who, struggling to oppose this doctrine through thick and thin, do not hesitate to assert that God is, in himself, the cause and author of sin.[43] If I did not believe that they said such a thing from error rather than wickedness, I should consider them of all blasphemers the most utterly damned. If I should attempt to refute them, it would be like inventing a long argument to prove that God is not the Devil. So much for God's GENERAL DECREE.

God's first and most excellent SPECIAL DECREE of all concerns HIS SON: primarily by virtue of this he is called FATHER:[44] Ps. 2.7: *I shall declare the decree: Jehovah said to me, You are my son I have begotten you today;* Heb. 1.5 [. . .]. And again *"I shall be a Father to him and he shall be a son to me"*; 1 Pet. 1.19, 20 [. . .]; Isa. 42.1 [. . .]; 1 Pet. 2.14 [. . .]. From all these quotations it appears that the Son of God was begotten by a decree of the Father.

41. Cp. *Art of Logic* (Yale 8:229): "Theology will discuss providence better than logic will. But in passing let this much be said: fate or divine decree does not force anyone to do evil, and on the hypothesis of divine foreknowledge all things are certain, to be sure, but not necessary."

42. Cp. *PL* 3.111–23.

43. Arminius, whose theology of free will and predestination anticipates Milton's, writes that the doctrine that God by eternal decree determines our choice or inclines us in one direction or another "makes God to be the author of sin, and man to be exempt from blame. . . . It constitutes God as the real, proper, and only sinner" (*Apology or Defense,* art. 7, in *The Writings of James Arminius,* trans. James Nichols and W. R. Bagnall, 3 vols. [Baker Book House, 1956], 1.298). See Danielson.

44. "Milton is here laying the foundation for his argument against the eternal generation of the Son: the Son was begotten in consequence of a decree; the decree preceded the execution of the decree; therefore the Son was begotten within the limits of time" (Kelley's note, Yale 6:166). On the prominence of Psalm 2 in contexts concerning the generation of the Son, see chapter 5, note 74.

Distinct mention is nowhere made of a SPECIAL DECREE of God about THE ANGELS: but it is implied in 1 Tim. 5.21: *of the elect angels;* Eph. 1.9, 10: *the mystery of his will* etc. *that he might collect together under a single head in Christ, all things in heaven,* etc.

CHAPTER 4

OF PREDESTINATION

The principal SPECIAL DECREE of God which concerns men is called PREDESTINATION: by which GOD, BEFORE THE FOUNDATIONS OF THE WORLD WERE LAID, HAD MERCY ON THE HUMAN RACE, ALTHOUGH IT WAS GOING TO FALL OF ITS OWN ACCORD, AND, TO SHOW THE GLORY OF HIS MERCY, GRACE AND WISDOM, PREDESTINED TO ETERNAL SALVATION, ACCORDING TO HIS PURPOSE or plan IN CHRIST, THOSE WHO WOULD IN THE FUTURE BELIEVE AND CONTINUE IN THE FAITH.

In academic circles the word "predestination" is habitually used to refer to reprobation as well as to election. For the discussion of such an exacting problem, however, this usage is too slapdash. Whenever the subject is mentioned in scripture, specific reference is made only to election: Rom. 8.29, 30: *he predestined that they should be shaped to the likeness of his son: and those whom he has predestined he has also called, justified and made glorious;* 1 Cor. 2.7 [...]; Eph. 1.5 [...], and 1.11 [...]; Acts 2.23: *when he had been given to you by the deliberate counsel and foreknowledge of God,* compared with 4.28: *that they might do everything which your power and your counsel predestined would be done*—in order, that is, to procure the salvation of man.

When other terms are used to signify predestination, the reference is always to election alone: Rom. 8.28: *who are called according to his purpose,* or plan, and 9.23, 24: *vessels of mercy which he prepared for glory beforehand; even those whom he has called;* Eph. 3.11 [...]; 2 Tim. 1.9 [...]; 1 Thess. 5.9: *God has not appointed us to anger, but to obtain salvation through our Lord Jesus Christ.* It does not follow from the negative part of this last quotation that others are appointed to anger. Nor does the clause in 1 Pet. 2.8: *to which they had been appointed,* mean that they were predestined from eternity, but rather from some time after they rebelled, just as the apostles are said to be "elected" in time and "appointed" by Christ to their employment, John 15.16.

If, in such a controversial question, any importance can be attached to metaphor and allegory, it is worth noting that mention is often made of "enrollment among the living" and of "the book of life," but never of the "book of death": Isa. 4.3: *enrolled among the living;* Dan. 12.1: *at that time the people will be set free, each one that will be found written in that book;* Luke 10.20 [...]; Phillip. 4.3 [...]. However this metaphor from writing does not seem to signify predestination from eternity, which is general, but rather some particular decree made by God within the bounds of time, and referring to certain men, on account of their works. Ps. 69.28: *let them be blotted out from the book of life, and not enrolled with the righteous:* it follows they were not enrolled from eternity. Isa. 65.6 [. . .]; Rev. 20.12: *the dead were judged in accordance with the things which had been written in these books, in accordance with the things they had done*—clearly, then, this was not the book of eternal predestination, but of their deeds.[45] Similarly those people were not marked down from eternity who are described in Jude 4 as *marked down for this doom long ago.* Why should we extend the sense of *long ago* so much, and not interpret it rather as "from the time when they became inveterate and hardened sinners"? Why, I repeat, should we extend the meaning of *long ago* so far into the past, either in this quotation or in the passage from which it seems to be taken, 2 Pet. 2.3: *the judgment long ago decreed for them has not been idle; destruction waits for them with unsleeping eyes?* Here it clearly means "from the time of their apostasy," however long they concealed it.

Another text which is quoted against me is Prov. 16.4: *Jehovah has made all things for himself, even the wicked man for the day of evil.* But God did not make man wicked, much less did he make him so "for himself." What did he do? He threatened the wicked man with the punishment he deserved, as was just, but did not predestine to punishment the man who did not deserve it. The point is clearer in Eccles. 7.29: *that God has made man upright, but they have thought up numerous devices.* The day of evil follows as certainly from this as if the wicked man had been made for it.

PREDESTINATION, then, must always be taken to refer to election, and seems often to be used instead of that term. What Paul says, Rom. 8.29: *those whom he foreknew, he also predestined* has the same meaning as 1 Pet. 1.2: *elect according to foreknowledge;* Rom. 9.11 [. . .] and 11.5 [. . .]; Eph. 1.4 [. . .]; Col. 3.12 [. . .]; 2 Thess. 2.13 [. . .]. There could, then, be nothing of reprobation in predestination: 1 Tim. 2.4: *who wishes that all men should be saved and should come to a knowledge of the truth;* 2 Pet. 3.9: *he is patiently disposed towards us, not wishing that any should perish but that all should come to repentance. Towards us,* that is, all men: not only the elect, as some propose, but particularly towards the wicked; thus Rom. 9.22: *tolerated the vessels of wrath.* If, as some object, Peter would hardly have numbered himself among the unbelievers, then surely neither would he have numbered himself, in the previous quotation, among the elect who had not yet repented. Besides, God does not delay on account of the elect, but hurries rather: Matt. 24.22: *those days shall be shortened.*

I do not understand by the term election that general or, so to speak, national election by which God chose the whole nation of Israel as his own people, Deut. 4.37: *because he loved your forefathers and elected their seed after them,* and 7.6–8: *Jehovah selected you to be a people peculiar to him,* and elsewhere, Isa. 45.4 [. . .].[46] Nor do I mean the election by which, after rejecting the Jews, God chose the Gentiles to whom he wished the gospel should be preached. This is spoken of

45. Cp. *PL* 1.362–63: "blotted out and razed/By their rebellion, from the Books of Life."

46. Cp. *PL* 12.111–12: "And one peculiar nation to select/From all the rest"; also 12.214–15.

particularly in Rom. 9 and 11. Nor do I mean the election by which he chooses an individual for some employment, 1 Sam. 10.24: *do you see whom Jehovah has chosen?*; John 6.70: *have I not chosen you twelve, and one of you is a devil*; whence they are sometimes called elect who are superior to the rest for any reason, as 2 John 1: *to the elect Lady*, which means, as it were, most excellent, and 2 John 13: *of your elect sister*; 1 Pet. 2.6: *the elect stone, precious*; 1 Tim. 5. 21: *of the elect angels.* I mean, rather, that special election which is almost the same as eternal predestination. Election, then, is not a part of predestination; much less is reprobation. Predestination, strictly speaking, includes a concept of aim, namely the salvation at least of believers, a thing in itself desirable. The aim of reprobation, on the other hand, is the destruction of unbelievers, a thing in itself repulsive and hateful. Clearly, then, God did not predestine reprobation at all, or make it his aim. Ezek. 18.32: *I have no pleasure in the death of a man who dies*, and 33.11: *may I not live*, etc. *if I have pleasure in the death of the wicked, but* etc. If God wished neither for sin nor for the death of the sinner, that is neither for the cause nor for the effect of reprobation, then certainly he did not wish for reprobation itself. Reprobation, therefore, is no part of divine predestination.

BY WHICH GOD: meaning, of course, the Father.[47] Luke 12.32: *it was your father's pleasure*; similarly whenever mention is made of the divine decree or plan: John 17.2: *as many as you have given him*; 17.6 [. . .]; similarly 11.24. Eph. 1.4 [. . .], 1.5 [. . .], 1.11: *predestined according to his purpose.*

BEFORE THE FOUNDATIONS OF THE WORLD WERE LAID: Eph. 1.4; 2 Tim. 1.9: *before the world began*; similarly Tit. 1.2.

HAD MERCY ON THE HUMAN RACE, ALTHOUGH IT WAS GOING TO FALL OF ITS OWN ACCORD. The matter or object of predestination was not simply man who was to be created, but man who was going to fall of his own free will. For the demonstration of divine mercy and grace which God purposed as the final end of predestination necessarily presupposes man's sin and misery, originating in man alone. Everyone agrees that man could have avoided falling.[48] But if, because of God's decree, man could not help but fall (and the two contradictory opinions are sometimes voiced by the same people), then God's restoration of fallen man was a matter of justice not grace. For once it is granted that man fell, though not unwillingly, yet by necessity, it will always seem that that necessity either prevailed upon his will by some secret influence, or else guided his will in some way. But if God foresaw that man would fall of his own accord, then there was no need for him to make a decree about the fall, but only about what would become of man who was going to fall. Since, then, God's supreme wisdom foreknew the first man's falling away, but did not decree

47. As the next chapter makes clear, in Milton's view, the Father alone is truly God.

48. In fact, not everyone agreed that man could have avoided falling. For the argument that God not only foresaw but necessitated the Fall of Adam and Eve, see Calvin's *Institutes* 2.12.5 and 3.23.7–8. Blithe assertion of a contested opinion is characteristic of Milton; cp. *TKM* (p. 276): "No man who knows aught can be so stupid to deny that all men naturally were born free."

it, it follows that, before the fall of man, predestination was not absolutely decreed either. Predestination, even after the fall, should always be considered and defined not so much as the result of an actual decree but as arising from the immutable condition of a decree.[49]

PREDESTINED: that is designated, elected. He made the salvation of man the goal and end, as it were, of his purpose. Hence may be refuted those false theories about preterition from eternity and the abandonment of the non-elect. For in opposition to these God has clearly and frequently declared, as I have quoted above, that he desires the salvation of all and the death of none, that he hates nothing he has made, and has omitted nothing which might provide salvation for everyone.

TO SHOW THE GLORY OF HIS MERCY, GRACE AND WISDOM. This is the supreme end of predestination: Rom. 9.23: *that he might make known the riches of his glory towards the vessels of mercy;* Eph. 1.6 [. . .]; 1 Cor. 2.7 [. . .].

ACCORDING TO HIS PURPOSE or plan IN CHRIST: Eph. 3.10, 11: *the wisdom of God in all its forms; according to his eternal purpose, which he appointed in Jesus Christ our Lord;* 1.4 [. . .]; and 1.5 [. . .]; 1.11: *in him, in whom indeed we have been given our share, as we were predestined according to his purpose.* Hence that love of God shown to us in Christ: John 3.16: *God loved the world so much that he gave his only begotten Son;* Eph. 2.4, 5 [. . .]; 1 John 4.9, 10 [. . .], etc. Except for Christ, then, who was foreknown, no grace was decided upon, no reconciliation between God and man who was going to fall.[50] Since God has so openly declared that predestination is the effect of his mercy, love, grace, and wisdom in Christ, we ought not attribute it, as is usually done, to his absolute and inscrutable will, even in those passages which mention will alone: Ex. 33.19: *I shall be gracious to him to whom I shall be gracious,* that is, not to elaborate further upon the causes of my graciousness at present. Rom. 9.18: *he has mercy on whom he will,* that is to say, by the method he determined upon in Christ: and in passages of this kind God is, in fact, usually speaking of his extraordinary grace and mercy, as will be evident when we examine particular texts. Thus Luke 12.32: *it was your father's pleasure;* Eph. 1.5: *by himself through Jesus Christ, according to the good pleasure of his will,* 1.11 [. . .]; James 1.18: *because he wished it he has begotten us by the word of truth,* that is, through Christ, who is the word and truth of God.

THOSE WHO WOULD IN THE FUTURE BELIEVE AND CONTINUE IN THE FAITH. This is the immutable condition of his decree. It does not attribute any mutability to God or his decrees. *This, God's solid foundation, stands sure and bears this inscription,* 2 Tim. 2.19: *the Lord knows his own, and these are all who leave wickedness and name the name of Christ,* that is, all who believe. The

49. Cp. *PL* 3.124–34.

50. Cp. *PL* 3.274–75: "O thou in Heav'n and Earth the only peace / Found out for mankind under wrath." Arminian soteriology tends to stress the Son's unique role in effecting God's decision to show mercy. This emphasis is even more pronounced in Milton's works because his Arianism also renders the Son's self-sacrifice voluntary; see chapter 14.

mutability is all on the side of those who renounce their faith: thus in 2 Tim. 2.13: *if we do not believe, nevertheless he remains faithful, he cannot deny himself.* It seems, then, that predestination and election are not particular but only general: that is, they belong to all who believe in their hearts and persist in their belief. Peter is not predestined or elected as Peter, or John as John, but each only insofar as he believes and persists in his belief. Thus the general decree of election is individually applicable to each believer, and is firmly established for those who persevere.[51]

The whole of scripture makes this very clear. It offers salvation and eternal life to all equally, on condition of obedience to the Old Testament and faith in the New. Without doubt the decree as it was made public was consistent with the decree itself. Otherwise we should have to pretend that God was insincere, and said one thing but kept another hidden in his heart. This is, indeed, the effect of that academic distinction which ascribes a twofold will to God: the revealed will, by which he instructs us what he wants us to do, and the will of his good pleasure, by which he decrees that we will never do it.[52] As good split the will in two and say: will in God is twofold—a will by which he wishes, and a will by which he contradicts that wish! But, my opponents reply, we find in scripture these two statements about the same matter: God wishes Pharaoh to let the people go, because he orders it: he does not wish it, because he hardens Pharaoh's heart. But, in fact, God wished it only. Pharaoh did not wish it, and to make him more unwilling God hardened his heart. He postponed the accomplishment of his will, which was the opposite of Pharaoh's, so that he might punish the latter all the more severely for his prolonged unwillingness. To order us to do right but decree that we shall do wrong!—this is not the way God dealt with our forefather, Adam, nor is it the way he deals with those he calls and invites to grace. Could anything be imagined more absurd than such a theory? To make it work, you have to invent a necessity which does not necessitate and a will which does not will.

The other point which must be proved is that the decree, as it was made public, is everywhere conditional: Gen. 2.17: *do not eat of this, for on the day you eat it you will die.* This is clearly as if God had said: I do not wish you to eat of this, and therefore I have certainly not decreed that you will eat it; for if you eat it you will die, if you do not you will live. Thus the decree itself was conditional before the fall, and it is evident from numerous other passages that it was conditional after the fall as well: Gen. 4.7: *surely, if you do well, lenity awaits you? but if you do not do well, sin is at the door,* or rather, sin's penalty, ever watchful. Ex. 32.32, 33: *blot me out now from your book which you have written. I shall blot out from my book the man who sins against me.* Here Moses, on account of his love for his people, forgot that the faithful cannot be blotted out so long as they remain faithful: or

51. Cp. *PL* 3.185–97.

52. Cp. *DDD* (p. 139), where Milton similarly rejects the Calvinist tenet of God's twofold will.

perhaps his speech should be modified by reference to Rom. 9.1, etc.: *indeed I should wish, if it were possible* . . . But God's reply, though metaphorical, shows quite clearly that the principle of predestination has a conditional basis: *I shall blot out the man who sins.* This is shown at greater length when the compact of the law is laid down, Deut. 7.6, 7, 8. [. . .][53]

Two difficult texts remain, which must be explained by reference to many clearer passages which resemble them; for clear things are not elucidated by obscure things, but obscure by clear.[54] The first passage is Acts 13.48, the second Rom. 8.28–30. I shall deal first with the latter as in my opinion it is less difficult. The words are as follows: *but we know that with those who love God all things work together for good; with those who are called according to his purpose. For those whom he foreknew he also predestined that they should be shaped to the likeness of his Son,* etc. *and those whom he has predestined he has also called; those he has called, he has also justified, and those he has justified he has also made glorious.*[55]

First it must be noticed that, in 8.28, *those who love God* and *those who are called according to his purpose* are the same, and that they are identical with *those whom he foreknew* and *those whom he has predestined* and *those he has called* in 8.30. Hence it is evident that the method and order of general election is being outlined here, not of the election of certain individuals in preference to others. It is just as if Paul had said: We know that with those who love God, that is, those who believe (for those who love, believe) all things work together for good: and the order of events is as follows. First, God foreknew those who would believe; that is, he decided or approved that it should be those alone upon whom, through Christ, he would look kindly: in fact, then, that it should be all men, if they believed. He predestined these to salvation, and, in various ways, he called all men to believe, that is, truly to acknowledge God. He justified those who believed in this way, and finally glorified those who persevered in their belief. But to make it clearer who they are whom God has foreknown, it must be realized that there are three different ways in which God is said to know a person or thing. First, by universal knowledge, as in Acts 15.8: *all God's works are known to him from the beginning of time.* Secondly, by knowledge which implies approval or grace, which is a Hebraic idiom, and must therefore be explained more fully: Ex. 33.12: *I know you by name, and also you have found grace in my eyes;* Ps. 1.6 [. . .]; Matt. 7.23 [. . .]. Thirdly, by knowledge which implies displeasure: Deut. 31.21: *I know the product of their imagination* etc.; 2 Kings 19.27 [. . .]; Rev. 3.1: *I know all your works, that you have*

53. In the deleted passage, Milton cites various examples of divine decree conditional on the law in the Old and on faith in the New Testament.

54. Cp. *Areop* (p. 204): "To be still searching what we know not by what we know, still closing up truth to truth as we find it . . . , this is the golden rule in theology as well as in arithmetic"; also, *Art of Logic* (Yale 8:391).

55. Cp. *Art of Logic* (Yale 8:388), where Milton quotes these verses to exemplify *sorites:* "propositions proceeding in a continuous series in such a way that the predicate of the preceding proposition is invariably the subject of the following, until finally the consequent of the last proposition is concluded of the antecedent of the first." (The final clause of Rom. 8.30 reads, "Therefore, those whom he has foreknown, he has glorified.")

a name for being alive, but are dead. It is clear that, in our passage, the knowledge which implies approval can alone be intended. [...].[56] God has predestined and elected each person who believes and persists in his belief. What is the point of knowing whether God had prescience about who in the future would believe or not believe? For no man believes because God had prescience about it, but rather God had prescience about it because the man was going to believe.[57] It is hard to see what purpose is served by introducing God's prescience or foreknowledge about particular individuals into the doctrine of predestination, except that of raising useless and utterly unanswerable questions. For why should God foreknow particular individuals? What could he foreknow in them which might induce him to predestine them in particular, rather than all in general, once the general condition of belief had been laid down? Suffice it to know, without investigating the matter any further, that God, out of his supreme mercy and grace in Christ, has predestined to salvation all who shall believe.

The other passage is Acts 13.48: *when the Gentiles heard this they were glad and glorified the word of the Lord; and as many as were ordained to eternal life, believed.* The difficulty lies in the author's sudden introduction of an idea which is at first sight quite inconsistent with the rest of scripture, including the part he wrote himself. For he had just recorded Peter's speech, Acts 10.34, 35: *truly I perceive that God is no respecter of the person* or, of the appearance, *but anyone in any nation who fears him and follows righteousness is acceptable to him.* "Acceptable" here certainly means elect. Moreover, in case it should be objected that Cornelius was already a proselyte, Paul says the same even of those who are ignorant of the law: Rom. 2.10, 11, 14: *with God there is no respect of persons. He who has not the law,* etc.; 1 Pet. 1.17: *who, without respect of persons, judges according to each man's work.* But those who teach that each man believes because he was ordained, not that he was ordained because he was going to believe, cannot avoid the conclusion that God is a respecter of persons which, as he so often asserts, he does not wish to be thought. Again, if the Gentiles believed because they were ordained to do so, this same reason will account for the Jews' failure to believe, Acts 13.46, which excuses them to a large extent, for it would appear that eternal life was not offered them but merely shown them. If this were so, moreover, it would not be likely to encourage other nations, for they would immediately draw the conclusion that what was necessary for eternal life was not any will or exertion of their own, but some sort of fatal decree. But on the contrary, scripture is absolutely clear on this point throughout: all who have been ordained to eternal life believe, not simply because they have been ordained, but because they were ordained on condition that they believed. For this reason interpreters who are, in my opinion, more acute, think there is some ambiguity in the Greek word τεταγμένοι, normally translated *ordained.* They consider it equivalent to "well or

56. The deleted sentences discuss intricacies of divine foreknowledge, causes of a believer's faith, and predestination.

57. Cp. *PL* 3.102–22.

moderately disposed or affected," that is, of a composed, attentive, upright and not disorderly mind, and, with reference to eternal life, unlike those Jews who had rejected God's word and shown themselves unworthy of it. A similar sense of this word "ordained" is not unknown among the Greek writers: it is found in Plutarch's *Pompey*. In 2 Thess. 3.6, 11 we find *those who behaved in a disorderly way,* meaning, undoubtedly, disorderly from the point of view of attaining eternal life. This meaning, and the very application which we wish to give it, is not uncommonly found in the scriptures, expressed in other words: Luke 9.62: *well disposed* or *fit for the kingdom of God;* Mark 12.34: *not far from the kingdom of God;* 2 Tim. 2.21: *a vessel fit to grace his Lord's use, and prepared for every good work.* For, as we shall show later, some traces of the divine image remain in man,[58] and when they combine in an individual he becomes more suitable, and as it were, more properly disposed for the kingdom of God than another. Since we are not mere puppets, some cause at least should be sought in human nature itself why some men embrace and others reject this divine grace. One thing may be established at the outset: although all men are dead in sin and children of wrath, nevertheless some are worse than others. This may be observed every day, in the nature, disposition, and habits of those who are most estranged from God's grace. It may also be inferred from that parable in Matt. 13 where, before any seed had been sown, there were four, or at any rate three kinds of soil, some stony, some covered with thorns, and some, compared at least with the rest, quite good. See also Matt, 10.11, etc.: *inquire who is worthy in it,* etc. *and if the house is worthy let your peace come upon it.* How could anyone be worthy before hearing the gospel preached, unless he were ordained, in the sense of being well inclined or disposed to eternal life? Christ teaches that others will be made to feel the truth of this by the punishment which they suffer after death: Matt. 11.22: *it will be more tolerable for Tyre and Sidon,* etc.; Luke 12.47, 48: *he shall be beaten with many stripes, he with few.* Lastly, everyone is provided with a sufficient degree of innate reason for him to be able to resist evil desires by his own effort; so no one can add strength to his excuse by complaining that his own nature is peculiarly depraved. But, you will object, God does not aim to pick out the less wicked from among the wicked, but prefers more often the inferior, Deut. 9.5: *it is not on account of your righteousness or your upright mind that you are going to march in and possess their land,* and Luke 10.13: *if the miracles that were performed in you had been performed in Tyre and Sidon, they would have repented long ago, sitting in sackcloth and ashes.* My answer is that we cannot be sure from these passages what it is God looks for in those he chooses. [. . .].[59] Finally, you will quote at me: *it does not depend on him that wills or on him that runs but on God who is merciful,* Rom. 9.16. But I reply, I am not talking about anyone willing or running, but about someone being less unwilling, less backward, less opposed, and I grant that God is still merciful, and is, at the same time, supremely wise and just. On the other hand,

58. Cp. *PL* 11.512–13: "Retaining still divine similitude / In part."

59. The deleted sentences reply to two minor objections to Milton's account of human responsibility.

those that say *it does not depend on him that wills or on him that runs,* do presuppose a man willing and running, only they deny him any praise or merit. However, when God determined to restore mankind, he also decided unquestionably (and what could be more just?) to restore some part at least of man's lost freedom of will. So he gave a greater power of willing or running (that is, of believing) to those whom he saw willing or running already by virtue of the fact that their wills had been freed either before or at the actual time of their call. These, probably, represent here the "ordained." Thus we find: 1 Sam. 16.7: *Jehovah looks on the heart,* that is, either on the natural disposition as it is in itself, or as it is after receiving grace from God, who calls to it. The famous quotation, *to him that has shall be given,* illustrates the same point. [. . .].[60]

But the following objection may, perhaps be made: if you decide that God has predestined men only on condition that they believe and persist in their belief, then predestination will not be entirely a matter of grace but will depend upon human will and faith, so that the esteem in which divine grace is held will not, in fact, be consistent with its real importance. I insist, on the contrary, that it will be absolutely consistent, not less so in any way, but indeed much more so, and far more clearly so than if we were to accept the theory of those who raise this objection. For God's grace is acknowledged supreme, firstly, because when we were going to fall through our own fault, he had any pity for us at all; secondly, because he loved the world so much that he gave his only begotten Son for it; lastly, because he granted that we should once again be able to use our wills, that is, to act freely, when we had recovered liberty of the will through renewing of the Spirit. In this way he opened Lydia's heart, Acts 16.14. The condition upon which God's decision depends, then, entails the action of a will which he himself has freed and a belief which he himself demands from men. If this condition is left in the power of men who are free to act, it is absolutely in keeping with justice and does not detract at all from the importance of divine grace. For the power to will and believe is either the gift of God or, insofar as it is inherent in man at all, has no relation to good work or merit but only to the natural faculties. God does not then, by my argument, depend upon the will of man, but accomplishes his own will, and in doing so has willed that in the love and worship of God, and thus in their own salvation, men should always use their free will. If we do not, whatever worship or love we men offer to God is worthless and of no account. The will which is threatened or overshadowed by any external decree cannot be free, and once force is imposed, all esteem for services rendered grows faint and vanishes altogether.[61]

Many people decry this theory and violently attack it. They say that, since

60. The deleted sentences cite more scriptural examples of those more or less naturally suitable for eternal life.

61. Cp. *PL* 3.103–6: "Not free, what proof could they have giv'n sincere/Of true allegiance, constant faith or love,/Where only what they needs must do, appeared,/Not what they would? What praise could they receive?"

repentance and faith have been foreseen already, predestination is made subsequent to man's works. Thus, they say, this predestination depends upon human will. They say this deprives God of some of the glory of our salvation. They say that man is thus swollen with pride, that Christian consolation in life and death is shaken, and that gratuitous justification is denied. None of these objections can be allowed. On the contrary, this theory makes the method and consequently the glory not only of divine grace, but also of divine wisdom and justice considerably more apparent, and to show this was God's principal aim in predestination.

It is quite clear, then, that God has predestined from eternity all who would believe and persist in their belief. It follows, therefore, that there is no reprobation except for those who do not believe or do not persist, and that this is rather a matter of consequence than of an express decree by God. Thus there is no reprobation from eternity of particular men. For God has predestined to salvation all who use their free will, on one condition, which applies to all. None are predestined to destruction except through their own fault and, in a sense, *per accidens.* Thus, for example, even the gospel is said to be a stumbling-block and a bane to many. [. . .].

If God decreed unconditionally that some people must be condemned, and there is no scriptural authority for such a belief, it follows from this theory of unconditionally decreed reprobation that God also decided upon the means without which he could not fulfill his decree. But the means are sin, and that alone. It is no use evading the issue in the conventional way by saying that God did not decree sin but decreed that he would permit sin, for there is this objection: if he decreed that he would permit, then he does not merely permit, because he who permits a thing does not decree anything, but leaves it free.

[. . .].[62]

If, then, God rejects none except the disobedient and the unbeliever, he undoubtedly bestows grace on all, and if not equally upon each, at least sufficient to enable everyone to attain knowledge of the truth and salvation.[63] I say not equally upon each, because he has not distributed grace equally, even among the reprobate, as they are called: Matt. 11.21, 23: *woe to you* etc. *For if the miracles which were performed in you had been performed in Tyre and Sidon,* similarly Luke 10.13. For like anyone else, where his own possessions are concerned, God claims for himself the right of making decrees about them as he thinks fit, without being obliged to give a reason for his decree, though he could give a very good one if he wished: Rom. 9.20, 21: *indeed, who are you, man, to answer God back? Shall the statue say to the sculptor, Why have you made me like this? Has not the potter power over his clay?* So God does not consider everyone worthy of equal grace, and the

62. The deleted paragraph insists that even if Scripture admitted the possibility of divine reprobation, repentance on the part of the reprobate would undo it.

63. Cp. *PL* 3.185–90: "The rest shall hear me call, and oft be warned/Their sinful state, and to appease betimes/Th' incensèd Deity, while offered grace/Invites; for I will clear their senses dark,/What may suffice, and soften stony hearts/To pray, repent, and bring obedience due."

cause of this is his supreme will.[64] But he considers all worthy of sufficient grace, and the cause is his justice. [. . .]. Clearly he wishes only that sinners should turn from their wickedness, Ezek. 33.11, as above, if he wishes that everyone should be saved, 1 Tim. 2.4, and that none should perish, 2 Pet. 3.9, he must also wish that no one should lack sufficient grace for salvation. Otherwise it is not clear how he can demonstrate his truthfulness to mankind. It is not enough that the grace in question should be sufficient only to deprive us of any excuse: we should perish without excuse even if we had no grace at all. But once grace has been revealed and offered, surely those who perish will always have some excuse, and will perish unjustly, unless it is quite clear that that grace is really adequate for salvation. So what Moses said, Deut. 29.4, in his address to the Israelites, *Jehovah has not given you a mind to understand, eyes to see and ears to hear until today,* must be explained by reference to Moses' kindness and tenderness. These made him avoid the accusations of severity or harshness which he would have incurred had he openly, before so large an assembly of the people, reproved the hardness of their hearts at that particular time, when they were about to enter into covenant with God. Their impenitence might be ascribed to two causes: either God, who was free to turn their minds to penitence whenever he wished, had not yet done so, or they had not yet obeyed him. Accordingly Moses mentioned only the first, God's free will, and left the second, their obstinacy, to be understood. For indeed no one can fail to understand that, in the first place, if God had not turned their minds to penitence until that day, their own obstinacy was the chief cause, and, secondly, that God who had performed so many miracles for their sake, had in fact given them mind, eyes and ears in ample measure, though they had refused to make use of his gifts.

Of one thing, then, we may be absolutely positive: God, to show the glory of his long-suffering and justice, excludes no man from the way of penitence and eternal salvation, unless that man has continued to reject and despise the offer of grace, and of grace sufficient for salvation, until it is too late.[65] For God has nowhere declared, unambiguously and directly, that his will is the cause of reprobation. On the contrary he has frequently explained the considerations which influence his will in the matter of reprobation: namely, the heinous sins of the reprobate, either already committed or foreseen by God; the absence of penitence; the contempt for grace; and the refusal to listen to God's repeated call. Unlike the election of grace, then, reprobation must not be attributed to the divine will alone: Deut. 9.5: *it is not on account of your righteousness or your upright mind that you are going to march in; but Jehovah is expelling those nations on account of their wickedness.* It is unnecessary to give any cause or reason for the exercise of mercy, other than God's own merciful will. On the other hand, the

64. Cp. *PL* 3.183–84: "Some I have chosen of peculiar grace/Elect above the rest; so is my will."

65. Cp. *PL* 3.198–202: "This my long sufferance and my day of grace/They who neglect and scorn, shall never taste;/But hard be hardened, blind be blinded more,/That they may stumble on, and deeper fall;/And none but such from mercy I exclude."

cause of reprobation, which is followed by punishment, must, if it is to be just, be man's sin alone, not God's will. I say sin, meaning sin either committed or foreseen, and when the sinner has either spurned grace right to the end, or has looked for it too late, and then only because he fears punishment, when the time-limit for grace has already passed. God does not reprobate for one reason, and condemn and assign to death for another, though this distinction is commonly made. Rather, those whom he has condemned for their sin, he has also reprobated for their sin, as in time, so from eternity. This reprobation lies not so much in God's will as in their own obstinate minds, and is not so much God's decree as theirs, resulting from their refusal to repent while they have an opportunity: Acts 13.46: *since you reject it and consider yourselves unworthy of eternal life;* Matt. 21.43: *the stone they rejected,* etc. *therefore the kingdom of God shall be taken away from you.* Similarly 1 Peter 2.7, 8. Matt. 23.37: *how often have I wished,* etc. *and you would not?* It would be no less unjust to decree reprobation for any cause other than sin than it would be to condemn for any cause other than sin. Condemnation does not occur except because of unbelief or sin, John 3.18, 19: *he who does not believe is already condemned because he has not believed,* etc. *this is the condemnation: light came into the world, but men loved darkness rather than light,* and 7.48 [. . .] 2 Thess. 2.12 [. . .]. Similarly all the texts which are produced to prove a decree of reprobation will be seen to point to the fact that no one is excluded by a decree of God from the way of penitence and eternal salvation unless he has rejected and despised the offer of grace until it is too late. [. . .][66]

[. . .] That is, it was appointed that they should be disobedient. Why? Because they had rejected the stone and stumbled over it: they rejected it themselves, before they were rejected. Attention to these points will quickly reveal the fact that, in discussion of this doctrine, difficulty mostly arises when no distinction is made between a decree of reprobation and that punishment which involves the hardening of a sinner's heart. Prov. 19.3 has an apt comment: *man's foolishness leads him astray, and his spirit is roused in indignation against Jehovah.* For those who believe in a decree of reprobation do, in fact, accuse God, however strongly they may deny it. Even a heathen like Homer emphatically reproves such people in *Odyssey* 1.7:[67]

They perished by their own impieties.

—and again, through the mouth of Jupiter, 1.32:

66. The deleted passage continues the discussion of election owing to God's good will and reprobation owing to the sinner's perverse will, particularly with respect to "the undeserved calling of the Gentiles after the Jews' merited rejection" (Yale 6:196). We resume the excerpt in the midst of the chapter's final paragraph.

67. Cp. *DDD* (p. 140): "Man's own free will corrupted is the adequate and sufficient cause of his disobedience besides fate; as Homer also wanted not to express both in his *Iliad* and *Odyssey*."

O how falsely men
Accuse us gods as authors of their ill,
Where by the bane their own bad lives instill
They suffer all the miseries of their states—
Past our inflictions and beyond their fates.

CHAPTER 5

PREFACE

I am now going to talk about the Son of God and the Holy Spirit, and I do not think I should broach such a difficult subject without some fresh preliminary remarks. The Roman Church demands implicit obedience on all points of faith. If I professed myself a member of it, I should be so indoctrinated, or at any rate so besotted by habit, that I should yield to its authority and to its mere decree even if it were to assert that the doctrine of the Trinity, as accepted at present, could not be proved from any passage of scripture. As it happens, however, I am one of those who recognize God's word alone as the rule of faith; so I shall state quite openly what seems to me much more clearly deducible from the text of scripture than the currently accepted doctrine. I do not see how anyone who calls himself a Protestant or a member of the Reformed Church, and who acknowledges the same rule of faith as myself, could be offended with me for this, especially as I am not trying to browbeat anyone, but am merely pointing out what I consider the more credible doctrine. This one thing I beg of my reader: that he will weigh each statement and evaluate it with a mind innocent of prejudice and eager only for the truth. For I take it upon myself to refute, whenever necessary, not scriptural authority, which is inviolable, but human interpretations. That is my right, and indeed my duty as a human being. Of course, if my opponents could show that the doctrine they defend was revealed to them by a voice from heaven, he would be an impious wretch who dared to raise so much as a murmur against it, let alone a sustained protest.[68] But in fact they can lay claim to nothing more than human powers and that spiritual illumination which is common to all men.[69] What is more just, then, than that they should allow someone else to play his part in the business of research and discussion: someone else who is hunting the same truth, following the same track, and using the same methods as they, and who is equally anxious to benefit his fellow men? Now, relying on God's help, let us come to grips with the subject itself.

68. Milton alludes to 2 Pet. 1.16–18, where "cleverly devised myths" about the Son are set against the revelation received by Peter when Jesus was transfigured: "We were eyewitnesses of his majesty. For when he received honor and glory from God the Father and the voice was borne to him by the Majestic Glory, 'This is my beloved Son, with whom I am well pleased,' we heard this voice borne from heaven, for we were with him on the holy mountain."

69. That all men receive spiritual illumination sufficient to effect salvation is an Arminian tenet. See 1.4, p. 419: "God . . . undoubtedly bestows grace on all, and if not equally upon each, at least sufficient to enable everyone to attain knowledge of the truth and salvation"; cp. *PL* 3.185–90.

OF THE SON OF GOD

So far the efficiency of God has been treated as INTERNAL, residing in his decrees.

His EXTERNAL efficiency takes the form of the execution of these decrees. By this he effects outside himself something he has decreed within himself.

EXTERNAL efficiency subdivides into GENERATION, CREATION, and THE GOVERNMENT OF THE UNIVERSE.[70]

By GENERATION God begot his only Son, in accordance with his decree. That is the chief reason why he is called Father.

Generation must be an example of external efficiency, since the Son is a different person from the Father. Theologians themselves admit as much when they say that there is a certain emanation of the Son from the Father. This point will appear more clearly in the discussion of the Holy Spirit, for although they maintain that the Spirit is of the same essence as the Father, they admit that it emanates and issues and proceeds and is breathed from the Father, and all these expressions denote external efficiency. They also hold that the Son is of the same essence as the Father, and generated from all eternity. So this question, which is quite difficult enough in itself, becomes very complicated indeed if you follow the orthodox line. In scripture there are two senses in which the Father is said to have begotten the Son: one literal, with reference to production; the other metaphorical, with reference to exaltation. Many commentators have cited those passages which allude to the exaltation of the Son, and to his function as mediator, as evidence of his generation from eternity. As a matter of fact they have some excuse, if there is any room for excuse at all, because not a scrap of real evidence for the eternal generation of the Son can be found in the whole of scripture. Whatever certain modern scholars may say to the contrary, it is certain that the Son existed in the beginning, under the title of the Word or Logos, that he was the first of created things,[71] and that through him all other things, both in heaven and earth, were afterwards made.[72] John 1.1–3: *in the beginning was the Word, and the Word was with God and the Word was God,* etc., and 17.5: *now therefore glorify me, Father, with your own self, with the glory which I had with you before the world was;* Col. 1.15, 18 [. . .]; Rev. 3.14 [. . .]; 1 Cor. 8.6 [. . .]; Eph. 3.9 [. . .]; Col. 1.16 [. . .], etc.; Heb. 1.2: *through whom also he made the world*—hence 1.10: *you have created.* For more on this subject see below, chapter 7 (On the Creation). All these passages prove that the Son existed before the creation of the world, but not that his generation was from eternity. The other texts which are cited

70. Orthodox doctrine deemed generation an internal efficiency essential to the deity. Milton instead makes divine generation external, contingent, and, like any other of God's acts, voluntary, not necessary.

71. Cp. *PL* 3.383: "Thee next they sang of all creation first." In orthodox doctrine, the Son is not created but eternally and continuously generated by the Father.

72. Cp. *PL* 5.835–37: "begotten Son, by whom/As by his Word the mighty Father made/All things."

indicate only metaphorical generation, that is resurrection from the dead or appointment to the functions of mediator, according to St. Paul's own interpretation of the second Psalm: Ps. 2.7: *I will declare the decree: Jehovah has said to me, You are my Son, I have begotten you today,* which Paul interprets thus, Acts 13.32, 33: *having raised up Jesus, as indeed it is written in the second Psalm, You are my Son, I have begotten you today.* Rom. 1.4: *powerfully defined as the Son of God, according to the Spirit of holiness, by the resurrection from the dead;* hence Col. 1.18; Rev. 1.4: *the firstborn from the dead.* Then, again, we have Heb. 1.5, where it is written of the Son's exaltation above the angels: *for to which of the angels did he ever say, You are my Son, I have begotten you today? And again, I will be to him a Father, and he shall be to me a Son.* And 5.5, 6, with reference to the priesthood of Christ: so *also Christ did not confer upon himself the glory of becoming high priest, but he who said to him, You are my Son, I have begotten you today.* As also in another Psalm he says, *You are a priest for ever,* etc. From the second Psalm it will also be seen that God begot the Son in the sense of making him a king, Ps. 2.6, 7: *anointing my king, I have set him upon my holy hill of Sion.* Then, in the next verse, having anointed his king, from which process the name "Christ" is derived, he says: *I have begotten you today.*[73] Similarly Heb. 1.4, 5: *made as superior to the angels as the name he has obtained as his lot is more excellent than theirs.* What name, if not "Son"? The next verse drives the point home: *for to which of the angels did he ever say, You are my Son, I have begotten you today?* The Son declares the same of himself, John 10.35, 36: *do you say that I, whom the Father has sanctified and sent into the world, blaspheme, because I have said, I am the Son of God?* By the same figure of speech, though in a much less exalted sense, the saints also are said to have been begotten by God.

When all the above passages, especially the second Psalm, have been compared and digested carefully, it will be apparent that, however the Son was begotten, it did not arise from natural necessity, as is usually maintained, but was just as much a result of the Father's decree and will as the Son's priesthood, kingship, and resurrection from the dead.[74] The fact that he is called "begotten," whatever that means, and God's *own Son,* Rom. 8.32, does not stand in the way of this at all. He is called God's own Son simply because he had no other Father but God, and this is why he himself said that God was his Father, John 5.18. For to Adam, formed out of the dust, God was creator rather than Father; but he was in a real sense Father of the Son, whom he made of his own substance. It does not follow, however, that the Son is of the same essence as the Father. Indeed, if he were, it would be quite incorrect to call him Son. For a real son is not of the same age as his father, still less of the same numerical essence: otherwise

73. Cp. *PL* 5.602–6: "Hear my decree, which unrevoked shall stand./This day I have begot whom I declare/My only Son, and on this holy hill/Him have anointed, whom ye now behold/At my right hand"; 6.708–9: "to be heir and to be King/By sacred unction, thy deservèd right"; 5.776–77: "and us eclipsed under the name/Of King anointed."

74. The Father's exaltation of the Son in Book 5 of *PL* (600–615) echoes Psalm 2, which, according to the 1673 *Poems,* Milton translated on August 8, 1653. Orthodox theologians inferred the necessity of the Son's begetting from the premise of a triune Godhead.

father and son would be one person. This particular Father begot his Son not from any natural necessity but of his own free will: a method more excellent and more in keeping with paternal dignity, especially as this Father is God.[75] For it has already been demonstrated from the text of scripture that God always acts with absolute freedom, working out his own purpose and volition. Therefore he must have begotten his Son with absolute freedom.

God could certainly have refrained from the act of generation and yet remained true to his own essence, for he stands in no need of propagation.[76] So generation has nothing to do with the essence of deity. And if a thing has nothing to do with his essence or nature, he does not do it from natural necessity like a natural agent.[77] Moreover, if natural necessity was the deciding factor, then God violated his own essence by begetting, through the force of nature, an equal. He could no more do this than deny himself. Therefore he could not have begotten the Son except of his own free will and as a result of his own decree.

So God begot the Son as a result of his own decree. Therefore it took place within the bounds of time, for the decree itself must have preceded its execution (the insertion of the word *today* makes this quite clear). As for those who maintain that the Son's generation was from eternity, I cannot discover on what passage in the scriptures they ground their belief. Micah 5.2 refers to his works, not his generation, and states only that these were from the beginning of the world—but more of this later. The Son is also called *only begotten,* John 1.14: *and we saw his glory, a glory indeed as of the only begotten having proceeded from the Father,* and 1.18 [. . .]; 3.16: *that he gave his only begotten Son,* similarly 3.18. 1 John 4.9: *he sent his only begotten Son.* Notice that it is not said that he is of the same essence as the Father but, on the contrary, that he is visible and given by, sent from, and proceeding from the Father. He is called *only begotten* to distinguish him from the numerous other people who are likewise said to be begotten by God, John 1.13: *begotten by God;* 1 John 3.9: *whoever is born of God,* etc.; James 1.18 [. . .]; 1 John 5.1 [. . .]; 1 Pet. 1.3 [. . .], etc. But since nowhere in the scriptures is the Son said to be begotten except, as above, in a metaphorical sense, it is probable that he is called *only begotten* chiefly because he is the only mediator between God and man.

Then, again, the Son is called *the first born,* Rom. 8.29: *that he might be the first born among many brothers;* Col. 1.15: *the first born of all created things;* 1.18: *the first born from the dead;* Heb. 1.6: *when he brings in the first born.* All these passages preclude the possibility of his being co-essential with the Father, and of his generation from eternity. Furthermore, the same thing is said of Israel, Ex. 4.22: *thus says*

75. Cp. *PL* 10.760–65: "what if thy son/Prove disobedient, and reproved, retort,/'Wherefore didst thou beget me? I sought it not':/Wouldst thou admit for his contempt of thee/That proud excuse? Yet him not thy election,/But natural necessity begot."

76. Cp. *PL* 8.419–20: "No need that thou/Shouldst propagate, already infinite."

77. Cp. *Art of Logic* (Yale 8:227): "Causes which act through nature do so out of necessity."

Jehovah, Israel is my Son, my first born, and of Ephraim, Jer. 31.9: *he is my first born,* and of all the blessed, Heb. 12.23: *to the assembly of the first born.*

Up to now all mention of generation has been entirely metaphorical. But if one in fact begets another being, who did not previously exist, one brings him into existence. And if God begets as a result of physical necessity, he can beget only a God equal to himself (though really a God cannot be begotten at all). It would follow from the first hypothesis that there are two infinite Gods, and from the second that a first cause can become an effect, which no sane man will allow. So it is necessary to inquire how and in what sense God the Father begot the Son. Once again, we can quickly find the answer in scripture. When the Son is said to be *the first born of every creature* and, Rev. 3.14, *the beginning of God's creation,* it is as plain as it could possibly be that God voluntarily created or generated or produced the Son before all things: the Son, who was endowed with divine nature and whom, similarly, when the time was ripe, God miraculously brought forth in his human nature from the Virgin Mary. The generation of the divine nature is by no one more sublimely or more fully explained than by the apostle to the Hebrews, 1.2, 3: *whom he has appointed heir of all things, through whom also he made the world. Who, since he is the brightness of his glory and the image of his substance,* etc. What can this imply but that God imparted to the Son as much as he wished of the divine nature, and indeed of the divine substance also? But do not take *substance* to mean total essence. If it did, it would mean that the Father gave his essence to his Son and at the same time retained it, numerically unaltered, himself. That is not a means of generation but a contradiction of terms. What I have quoted is all that is revealed from heaven about the generation of the Son of God. Anyone who wants to be wiser than this is really not wise at all. Lured on by empty philosophy or sophistry, he becomes hopelessly entangled and loses himself in the dark.

In spite of the fact that we all know there is only one God, Christ in scripture is called not merely *the only begotten Son of God* but also, frequently, *God.* Many people, pretty intelligent people in their own estimation, felt sure that this was inconsistent. So they hit upon the bizarre and senseless idea that the Son, although personally and numerically distinct, was nevertheless essentially one with the Father, and so there was still only one God.

The numerical significance of "one" and of "two" must be unalterable and the same for God as for man. It would have been a waste of time for God to thunder forth so repeatedly that first commandment which said that he was the one and only God, if it could nevertheless be maintained that another God existed as well, who ought himself to be thought of as the only God. Two distinct things cannot be of the same essence. God is one being, not two. One being has one essence, and also one subsistence—by which is meant simply a substantial essence. If you were to ascribe two subsistences or two persons to one essence, it would be a contradiction in terms. You would be saying that the essence was at once one and not one. If one divine essence is common to two components, then that essence or divinity will be in the position of a whole in relation to its parts, or of a genus in relation to its several species, or lastly of a common subject, in relation to its non-essential qualities.[78] If you should grant none of these, there would be no escaping the absurdities which follow, as that one essence can be one third of two or more components of an essence.

If my opponents had paid attention to God's own words when he was addressing kings and magnates, Ps. 82.6: *I say, you are Gods, and all of you sons of the Most High,* and to the words of Christ, John 10.35: *if he called those to whom the word of God came, Gods; and the scripture cannot be blotted out,* and to the words of Paul, 1 Cor. 8.5, 6: *although there are those that are called Gods, both in heaven and earth, (for there are many Gods and many Lords), nevertheless for us there is one God, the Father, from whom all things,* etc., and lastly to the words of Peter 2. 1.4: *that through these things you might be made partakers or sharers of the divine nature* (which implies much more than the title *gods* in the sense in which kings are said to be gods, and yet no one would conclude from this text that the saints were of one essence with God)—if, I say, my opponents had paid attention to these words, they would not have found it necessary to fly in the face of reason or, indeed, of so much glaring scriptural evidence.

But let us disregard reason when discussing sacred matters and follow exclusively what the Bible teaches. Accordingly let no one expect me to preface what I have to say with a long metaphysical introduction, or bring into my argument all that play-acting of the persons of the godhead. For a start, it is absolutely clear from innumerable passages of scripture that there is in reality one true and independent supreme God. Since he is called "one"; since human reason and the conventions of language and God's people, the Jews, have always interpreted the term "only one person" to mean one in number, let us examine the sacred books to discover who this one, true, supreme God is. Let us look first at the gospel. This should provide the clearest evidence, for here we find the plain and exhaustive doctrine of the one God which Christ expounded to his apostles and they to their followers. It is very unlikely that the gospel should be ambiguous or obscure on this point. For it was given not for the purpose of spreading new or incredible ideas about God's nature, ideas that his people had never heard of before, but to announce the salvation of the Gentiles through Messiah, the Son of God, which God had promised to Abraham: *no one has ever seen God: the only begotten Son who is in the bosom of the Father, he has revealed him to us,* John 1.18. So first of all let us consult the Son on the subject of God.

According to the Son's clearest possible testimony, the Father is that one true God from whom are all things. Mark 12.28, 29, 32, Christ, asked by the lawyer which was the first commandment of all, replied by quoting Deut. 6.4: *the first commandment of all is: hear, Israel, the Lord our God is one Lord* or, as it is in the Hebrew, *Jehovah our God is one Jehovah.* The lawyer agreed: *there is one God and there is no other except him.* Christ approved of him for agreeing, Mark 12.34.

78. These categories of distributive relation are discussed in *Art of Logic* (Yale 8:299–308).

Now it is absolutely clear that this lawyer and all the Jews understood that there was one God in the sense that he was one person, as that phrase is commonly understood. That this God was none other than the Father is proved by John 8.41–54: *we have one Father, God. It is my Father who glorifies me, whom you say is your God,* and 4.21: *neither on this mountain nor in Jerusalem shall you worship the Father.* Christ therefore agrees with all God's people that the Father is that one and only God. Who can believe that the very first of the commandments was so obscure that it was utterly misunderstood by the Church for so many centuries? Who can believe that these two other persons could have gone without their divine honors and remained wholly unknown to God's people right down to the time of the gospel? Indeed God, teaching his people about their worship under the gospel, warns them that they will have for their God the one Jehovah that they have always had, and David, that is, Christ, for their king and their Lord. Jer. 30.9: *they shall serve Jehovah their God and David their king, whom I will raise up for them.*[79] In this passage Christ, as God wished him to be known and worshipped by his people under the gospel, is firmly distinguished, both by nature and title, from the one God Jehovah. Christ himself, then, the Son of God, teaches us nothing in the gospel about the one God other than what the law had taught us already. He asserts everywhere, quite clearly, that it is the Father. John 17.3: *this is eternal life, that they may know you, the only true God, and Jesus Christ whom you have sent,* 20.17: *I ascend to my Father and your Father, and to my God and your God.* If the Father is Christ's God and our God, and if there is only one God, who can be God except the Father?

Paul, the apostle and interpreter of Christ, makes this same point very clearly and distinctly, almost as if it were the sum of his teaching. So much so, that no instructor in the church could have taught a novice under his care more skillfully or more plainly about the one God—one, that is, in the numerical sense in which human reason always understands it. 1 Cor. 8.4–6: *we know that an idol is nothing in the world, and that there is no other God but one: for although there are those that are called Gods both in heaven and earth (for there are many Gods and many Lords), nevertheless for us there is one God, the Father, from whom all things are and in whom we are, and one Lord Jesus Christ, through whom all things are and through whom we are.* Here, *there is no other* or *second* God, *but one,* excludes not only a second essence but any second person whatsoever. For it is expressly stated, 8.6: *the Father is that one God;* therefore there is no *other* person, but one only. There is no other person, that is, in the sense in which Church divines usually argue that there is when they use John 14.16 as proof of the existence of the Holy Spirit as a person. Again, the single *God, the Father, from whom all things are* is numerically opposed to *those that are called Gods both in heaven and earth,* and *one* is numerically opposed to *many.* Though the Son be another God, here he is called only *Lord.*

79. Like other interpreters, Milton understands Jeremiah's promise of a Davidic king as a prophecy of Christ.

He *from whom all things are* is clearly distinguished from him *through whom all things are,* and since a difference in method of causation proves a difference in essence, the two are distinguished from the point of view of essence as well. Besides, since a numerical difference is the result of a difference in essence, if two things are two numerically, they must also be two essentially.[80] [. . .].

All this is so obvious in itself that it really needs no explanation. It is quite clear that the Father alone is a self-existent God: clear, too, that a being who is not self-existent cannot be a God. But it is amazing what nauseating subtlety, not to say trickery, some people have employed in their attempts to evade the plain meaning of these scriptural texts. They have left no stone unturned; they have followed every red herring they could find; they have tried everything. Indeed they have made it apparent that, instead of preaching the plain, straightforward truth of the gospel to poor and simple men, they are engaged in maintaining an extremely absurd paradox with the maximum of obstinacy and argumentativeness. To save this paradox from utter collapse they have availed themselves of the specious assistance of certain strange terms and sophistries borrowed from the stupidity of the schools.

Their excuse, however, is that though these opinions may seem inconsistent with reason they are, on account of some other scriptural passages, to be countenanced; otherwise there will appear to be inconsistencies in scripture. So let us, again, disregard reason and concentrate on the text of scripture.

Only two passages are relevant. The first is John 10.30: *I and the Father are one,* that is, as it is commonly interpreted, one in essence. But for God's sake let us not come to any rash conclusions about God! There is more than one way in which two things can be called one. Scripture says and the Son says *I and the Father are one.* I agree. Someone or other guesses that this means one in essence. I reject it as man's invention. For whoever it was in the Church who first took it upon himself to guess about it, the Son has not left the question of how he is one with the Father to our conjecture. On the contrary, he explains the doctrine very clearly himself, insofar as it concerns us to know it. The Father and the Son are certainly not one in essence, for the Son had himself asserted the contrary in the preceding verse, *my Father, who gave me them, is greater than all,* (indeed, he also says, 14.28: *he is greater than I*), and in the following verses he expressly denies that by saying *I and the Father are one* he was setting himself up as God. He claims that what he said was only what follows in the next quotation, which amounts to much less, 10.36: *do you say that I whom the Father has sanctified and sent into the world, blaspheme because I have said, I am the Son of God?* It must be that this is said of two persons, distinct in essence and, moreover, not equal to each other. If the Son is here teaching about the one divine essence of two persons of the

80. The rest of this paragraph and the next cite Scripture to elaborate the numerical and therefore essential distinction between God and the Son. Cp. *Art of Logic* (Yale 8:233): "Number, as Scaliger correctly says, is a property consequent upon essence, and never do things differ in number without also differing in essence. *Here let the Theologians take notice.*" Although Milton takes this passage from an antecedent work, the italicized sentence is an insertion.

Trinity, why does he not rather talk about the one essence of the three persons? Why does he divide the indivisible Trinity? That which is not a whole is not one. So it follows from the convictions of those very people who affirm the truth of the Trinity that the Son and the Father, without the Spirit, are not one in essence. How, then, are they one? The Son alone can tell us this, and he does. Firstly, they are one in that they speak and act as one. He explains himself to this effect in the same chapter, after the Jews have misunderstood his statement: 10.38: *believe in my works so that you may know and believe that the Father is in me and I in him.* Similarly 14.10: *do you not believe that I am in the Father and the Father in me? I myself am not the source of the words which I speak to you; but the Father who dwells in me, he performs the works.* Here it is evident that Christ distinguishes the Father from the whole of his own being. However, he does say that the Father dwells in him, though this does not mean that their essence is one, only that their communion is extremely close. Secondly, he declares that he and the Father are one in the same way as we are one with him: that is, not in essence but in love, in communion, in agreement, in charity, in spirit, and finally in glory.[81] John 15.20, 21: *on that day you will know that I am in my Father, and you in me, and I in you. He who has my commandments and keeps them, he it is that loves me; and he that loves me shall be loved by my Father,* and 17.21 [...] and 17.23 [...] and 17.22 [...]. Since the Son plainly teaches that there are so many ways in which the Father and he are one, shall I pay no attention to all these ways of being one? Shall I put my mind to it and think up some other way of being one, namely that of being one in essence? Shall I give preference to this idea when some other mere man has thought it up beforehand? Who will stand surety for me if I do? The Church? The orthodox Church herself teaches me otherwise, and rightly. She tells me that I should listen to Christ before her.

The second passage, and that which is generally thought the clearest of all, upon which the orthodox view of the essential unity of the three persons of the Trinity is based, is 1 John 5.7: *there are three witnesses in heaven, the Father, the Word and the Holy Spirit, and these three are one.* This verse, however, is not found in the Syriac or the other two Oriental versions, the Arabic and the Ethiopic, nor in the majority of the ancient Greek codices. Moreover, in those manuscripts where it does appear a remarkable variety of readings occurs.[82] Anyway, quite apart from this, the verse does not prove that those who are said to be one in heaven are necessarily one in essence, any more than it proves that about those who, in the next verse, are said to be one on earth. The fact that John is speaking here (if John really wrote the verse) only about unity of consent and testmony, as in the last-quoted passage, was not only realized by Erasmus but even

81. *PL* 11.43–44: "All my redeemed may dwell in joy and bliss,/Made one with me as I with thee am one."

82. Milton's account of 1 John 5.7 as a late variant of suspect textual authority is accurate. The so-called Johannine comma is now generally deemed spurious and omitted in modern critical editions. Isaac Newton in 1690 would likewise critique it in a manuscript he shared with John Locke but withheld from publication, entitled *A Historical Account of Two Notable Corruptions of Scripture.* It was first published in 1841.

admitted by Beza, though reluctantly.[83] (You can go and look at their works to prove it.) Besides, who are these three witnesses? You will admit that there are not three Gods; therefore the *one* in the passage is not a God but the one testimony of the three witnesses; one witnessing. But he who is not essentially one with God the Father cannot be the Father's equal. This text will be discussed more fully, however, in the next chapter.

But it is maintained that, although scripture does not say in so many words that the Father and the Son are essentially one, the fact can be reasonably deduced from these texts and from others. To begin with, granting this to be the case (and I do not, in fact, grant it at all) when the point at issue is so sublime and so far above the reach of our understanding, and involves the very elements and, as it were, the first postulates of our faith, we can really base our belief only on God's word, and God's word at its clearest and most distinct, not on mere reason at all. Anyway, reason is loud in its denunciation of the doctrine in question. I ask you, what can reason do here? Can reason maintain an unreasonable opinion? The product of reason must be reason, not absurd notions which are utterly alien to all human ways of thinking. The conclusion must be, then, that this opinion is consonant neither with reason nor scripture. Of the two alternatives only one can remain: namely, that if God is one God, and the Father, and yet the Son is also called God, then he must have received the divine name and nature from God the Father, in accordance with the Father's decree and will, as I said before. This is in no way opposed to reason, and is supported by innumerable texts from scripture.

But not all those who insist that the Son is one with God the Father rely for proof on the two texts I have quoted above. So although deprived of that evidence, they are still confident that they can prove their point quite clearly if they can show, by frequent scriptural quotation, that the name, attributes and works of God, and the divine office itself, are habitually attributed to the Son. To proceed, therefore, in the same line of argument: I do not ask them to believe that the Father alone, and no one else, is God, unless I demonstrate and prove beyond question the following points. First, that all the above particulars are everywhere expressly attributed, both by the Son himself and by his apostles, only to one God, the Father. Second, that if these particulars are anywhere attributed to the Son, it is in such a way that they are easily understood to be attributable, in their primary and proper sense, to the Father alone, and that the Son admits that he possesses whatever measure of Deity is attributed to him, by virtue of the peculiar gift and kindness of the Father, as the apostles also testify.

83. Desiderius *Erasmus* (1466–1536), Dutch scholar, was the greatest of the Renaissance humanists. His translation of the Greek New Testament into Latin exposed errors in the Vulgate. He influenced Luther and other reformers, though he remained in the Catholic Church and disagreed with the course of the Reformation. Theodore *Beza* (1519–1605), Swiss reformed theologian, followed Calvin as leader in Geneva. In 1565 he published the first critical edition of the Greek New Testament.

Third, that the Son himself and his apostles acknowledge in everything they say and write that the Father is greater than the Son in all things.

[. . .].[84]

However, some will still argue vehemently that the Son is at times called God and even Jehovah, and that all the divine attributes are ascribed to him as well, in many passages in both the Old and the New Testaments.

This, then, is the second of the points that I undertook to prove at the beginning. I have already demonstrated satisfactorily, from the agreement of scriptural texts, that when both Father and Son are mentioned, the name, attributes, and works of God, and also the divine honor, are always ascribed to the one and only God the Father. I will now demonstrate that when these things are ascribed to the Son, it is done in such a way as to make it easily intelligible that they should all be attributed primarily and properly to the Father alone.

We should notice first of all that the name "God" is, by the will and permission of God the Father, not infrequently bestowed even upon angels and men (how much more, then, upon the only begotten Son, the image of the Father!).

Upon angels: Ps. 8.6: *less than gods,* and 97.7, 9, compared with Heb. 1.6. Upon judges: Ex. 21.6: *his Master shall make him stand in the presence of the gods,* that is, of the magistrates; and similarly 22.8, 9, 28; Ps. 82.1, 6: *I have said you are gods and all of you sons of the Highest.* Upon the whole house of David, or upon all the saints: Zech. 12.8: *the house of David shall be as gods as an angel before them.*

[. . .][85]

Even the principal texts which are quoted as proof of the Son's divinity show quite plainly, when they are closely and carefully studied, that he is God in the way I have suggested. John 1.1: *in the beginning was the Word, and the Word was with,* that is, *in company with God, and the Word was God. In the beginning,* it says, not from eternity. *The Word* must be audible, but God is inaudible just as he is invisible, John 5.37; therefore the Word is not of the same essence as God. *In company with God, and was God*—was God, in fact, because he was in company with God, that is, in the Father's bosom, as it is later said in verse 18. Does it follow that the Son is essentially one with someone in whose company, or with whom he is? Surely no more than it follows that the disciple who was reclining against Jesus' breast, John 13.23, was essentially one with Christ. Reason rejects the idea, and scripture nowhere supports it; so let us leave the lies of men behind and follow the evangelist himself, who is his own interpreter. Rev. 19.13: *his name is called the Word of God:* that is, of the one God, he himself being a distinct person. Distinct from

84. The deleted passage develops the first of the three points just introduced, asserting that "those who have not numerically the same understanding and the same will cannot have the same essence. There is no way of evading this conclusion, since the Son himself has revealed this in discussing his own divine nature" (Yale 6:229).

85. In the deleted passage, Milton surveys Hebrew and Greek terms for God and characterizes the application of the plurals of such terms to singular subjects as a mark of "respect or reverence" and not as evidence of multiple persons in God. He then notes that in Scripture angels are often called "God," as are men who speak for or otherwise represent him.

whom? From God, of course, who is one. How, then, is he himself God? The answer must be, through the will of the one God, which is how he is the Word and the only begotten Son as well. For this reason, apparently, John repeats the words in the second verse, *he was in the beginning with,* that is, in company with *God.* Thus he drives home what he wants us to see as his chief point: that Christ was not, in the beginning, God, but that he was with, or in company with God. John does this to show that Christ was God not in essence but only by nearness and love: a fact which he subsequently explains in innumerable passages of his gospel.

A second passage is the speech of Thomas in John 20.28: *my Lord and my God.* Anyone who tries to elicit from this abrupt exclamation a new confession of faith, a confession not recognized as such by the other disciples, must be really exceedingly credulous. In his surprise Thomas calls not only upon Christ, his own Lord, but upon the God of his ancestors as well, that is, God the Father. It is as if he had said, "Lord! What do I see: what do I hear: what do I touch?" Christ, whom Thomas is here supposed to call God, has said of himself just before, 20.17: *I ascend to my God and your God.* Now the God of a God cannot be essentially one with him whose God he is. If Thomas really called Christ his God, whose word will provide a safer model for our faith? Christ's, when Christ is giving quite clear information, or Thomas', when Thomas is a novice who was at first incredulous, and who now cries out suddenly in wonder and amazement? For when he had thrust in his fingers, he called the man whom he had touched God, as if unconscious of what he was saying. It is incredible that he should so quickly have perceived the hypostatic union of a person whose resurrection he had just doubted. Besides, Peter's faith is praised, though he had said only, *you are the Son of the living God. Blessed are you, Simon,* said Christ, Matt. 16.16, 17. Thomas' faith, although far more spectacular, as commonly interpreted, in that it asserts Christ's deity, is not praised but, in fact, belittled and almost reproved in the next verse: *Thomas, because you have seen me you have believed; blessed are those who have not seen and yet have believed.* The slowness of his belief may have deserved blame. But surely the clarity of his attestation of Christ's godhead would have been praised, for, if the usual interpretations of it are correct, it is the clearest attestation to be found anywhere. But it was not praised at all. So nothing stands in the way of the interpretation suggested above, namely, that in the disputed passage *my Lord* is to be taken as referring to Christ, and *my God* as referring to God the Father, who had just proved that Christ was his Son by raising him from the dead in such a miraculous way.

Similarly Heb. 1.8: *to the Son,* or, *of the Son: Your throne, O God, is for all ages:* but 1.9: *you have loved righteousness,* etc. *therefore God, your God, has anointed you with the oil of exultation above your fellows.* Almost every word here shows in what sense Christ is God. In fact these were the words spoken by Jehovah through the mouths of the bridesmaids, Ps. 45. They might have been cited by this writer for any other purpose rather than that of demonstrating the Son's equality with the Father. Why? Because in the Psalm they are applied to Solomon who, in accordance with scriptural usage, could also be called God because he was a king.

These three passages are just about the most convincing of those my opponents adduce. That text in Matt. 1.23: *they shall call* (for that is the reading in most of the Greek codices) *his name Immanuel, which means, if you interpret it, God with us,* does not prove that the person they are going to call Immanuel is necessarily God, but only that he is sent by God, as Zacharias sang, Luke 1.68, 69: *blessed is the Lord God of Israel, for he has visited and redeemed his people, and has raised up,* etc. Nor can anything be proved from the text in Acts 16.31, 34: *believe in the Lord Jesus Christ. He rejoiced with his whole house, because he had believed in God.* It does not follow from this that Christ is God. The apostles have never taught explicitly that Christ is the ultimate object of belief. These are the words of the historian, who is making a brief paraphrase of what the apostles doubtless expounded at greater length, that is, faith in God the Father through Christ. Nothing can be proved from the passage in Acts 20.28, either: *the Church of God, which he has bought with his own blood.* This means, with his own Son, as it is expressed elsewhere; for God, properly speaking, has no blood, and the word *blood* is very frequently used to mean offspring.

[. . .][86]

But why should we worry about the name, when the Son, in the same way, receives his very being from the Father? John 7.29: *I am from him.* The same is implied in John 1.1: *in the beginning,* for the idea of eternity is excluded here by the decree, as I showed above, and also by the name *Son* and by sentences like *I have begotten you today,* and *I will be a Father to him. Beginning* here can only mean "before the creation of the world," as in John 17.5. Col. 1.15–17 shows this: *the firstborn of all created things: for through him all things in the heavens and on the earth were created* etc. *As he is before all things and all things exist through him.* Here the Son is himself called the firstborn of all created things, and not as man, nor as mediator, but as creator. Similarly Heb. 2.11: [. . .] and 3.2 [. . .]. Indisputably the Father can never have begotten a being who was begotten from eternity. What was made from eternity, was never in the process of being made. Any being whom the Father begot from eternity, he must still be begetting, for an action which has no beginning can have no end. If the Father is still begetting him, he is not yet begotten, and is therefore not a Son. It seems, then, utterly impossible that the Son either should be or was begotten from eternity. If he is a son, then either he was once in the Father and proceeded from him, or else he must always have existed, as

86. The deleted passage continues the scrutiny of scriptural verses construed by the orthodox to support the Trinity. Milton's analysis delves into linguistic detail, variant readings, and the possibility of textual corruption: "where the very fundamentals of our faith are at stake, we should not place our confidence in something which has to be forced or wrenched, so to speak, from passages dealing with a quite unrelated topic, in which there are sometimes variant readings, and where the meaning is questionable. Nor should we believe in something which has to be lured out from among articles and particles by some sort of verbal bird-catcher, or which has to be dug out from a mass of ambiguities and obscurities like the answers of an oracle. Rather, we should drink our fill from the clearest fountains of truth. For this open simplicity, this true light, this promised clarity of doctrine is what makes the gospel superior to the law" (Yale 6:245–46). Milton then proceeds to consider scriptural usage of *Jehovah* with reference to the Son (and others) and argues for the Son's complete dependence on the Father.

now, separate from the Father, with a separate and independent identity. If he was once in the Father but now exists separately, then he must once have undergone a change, and is therefore mutable.[87] If he has always been separate from the Father, how is he *from* the Father, how *begotten,* how a *Son* and how, lastly, is he separate in subsistence unless he is separate in essence too? For, leaving aside the nonsense of quibbling metaphysicians, a substantial essence and a subsistence are the same thing. Anyway, no one will deny that the Son is numerically different from the Father. And the fact that things numerically different are also different in their proper essences, as logicians call it, is so obvious that no reasonable being could contradict it.[88] Therefore the Father and Son differ from each other in essence. This is certainly the reasonable conclusion. My opponents still claim that it is not the conclusion reached by scripture: let them prove it! Although they put so much confidence in that property which is prefigured in Melchisedec, it does not really go against my case, Heb. 7.3: *without father, without mother, without descent; having neither beginning of days nor end of life, but made like the Son of God.* Insofar as the Son lacked an earthly father, it is true that he did not have a *beginning of days.* But this does not prove that he had no *beginning of days* from all eternity any more than it proves that he did not have a Father and was therefore not a Son. If he did derive his essence from the Father, let my opponents prove how that essence can be supremely divine or, in other words, one with and the same as the Father's essence. For the divine essence, which is always one, cannot possibly generate or be generated by an essence the same as itself. Nor can any subsistence or person possibly act or be acted upon in this way, without its whole essence also acting or being acted upon in a similar way. Now generation produces something that is and exists apart from its generator. Therefore God cannot generate a God equal to himself, because he is by definition one and infinite. Since therefore the Son derives his essence from the Father, the Son undoubtedly comes after the Father not only in rank but also in essence (a distinction, incidentally, which has no scriptural authority, though a good many people are taken in by it). The name "Son," upon which my opponents chiefly build their theory of his supreme divinity, is in fact itself the best refutation of their theory. For a supreme God is self-existent, but a God who is not self-existent, who did not beget but was begotten, is not a first cause but an effect, and is therefore not a supreme God. Moreover it is obvious that anyone who was begotten from all eternity, has existed from all eternity. But if a being who has existed from all eternity has also been begotten, why should not the Father have been begotten, and have had a father? Anyway "father" and "son" are relative terms and differ both in theory and practice.

87. "Possibly a reference to and rejection of early speculation of stoic origin on a two-stage theory of the Logos: the Logos existed first only internally in God's thought and later was generated as a person when God externalized his thought into an intelligible universe" (Kelley's note, Yale 6:262). Hunter's claim that Milton endorsed an orthodox variation of this "two-stage Logos theory" (1959) has been rejected by Kelley (1961) and Bauman (1987).

88. Milton repeats his earlier point that number follows essence. Cp. note 80.

According to the laws of opposites, the father is not the son, nor the son the father.[89] If Father and Son were of one essence, which, because of their relationship, is impossible, it would follow that the Father was the Son's son and the Son the Father's father. Anyone who is not a lunatic can see what kind of a conclusion this is. For I have said enough already to show that more than one hypostasis cannot be fitted into one essence. Lastly, if the Son is of the same essence as the Father, and if the same Son, after a hypostatical union, coalesces in one person with man, I do not see how to avoid the conclusion that man, also, is the same person as the Father—a conclusion which might produce quite a few paradoxes! But perhaps I shall have more to say about this when I deal with the incarnation of Christ.[90]

CHAPTER 6

OF THE HOLY SPIRIT

So much for the Father and the Son: the next thing to be discussed is the Holy Spirit, for this is called the spirit both of the Father and of the Son. The Bible, however, says nothing about what the Holy Spirit is like, how it exists, or where it comes from—a warning to us not to be too hasty in our conclusions. Granted it is a spirit, in the sense in which that term is correctly applied to the Father and the Son, and granted that Christ, in John 20.22, is said to have given the Holy Spirit to his disciples (or, rather, some symbol or pledge of the spirit) by breathing upon them: who, on this evidence, would dare to maintain, in a discussion of the nature of the Holy Spirit, that it was breathed from the Father and the Son? The terms "emanation" and "procession" are irrelevant to the question of the Holy Spirit's nature. Theologians use them on the authority of John 15.26, where the reference is to the *spirit of truth,* ὁ παρὰ τοῦ πατρὸς 'εκπορέυεται, *which proceeds* or goes out from *the Father.* This one word is a pretty slender basis for our belief in so great a mystery. Anyway it refers to the mission, not the nature of the spirit. In the same sense the Son is often said ἐξελθεῖν, as well, that is either *to go out from* or *to proceed from* the Father, whichever translation you prefer: there is nothing to choose between them as far as I can see. Indeed, we are said to *live by every word,* ἐκπορευομένῳ *that proceeds* or *goes out, through the mouth of God,* Matt 4.4.[91] The spirit, then, is not said to be generated or created, and it

89. Cp. *Art of Logic* (Yale 8:254–55): "Opposites cannot be attributed to one and the same thing by reason of the same thing, with reference to the same thing and at the same time. . . . Thus Socrates cannot be . . . father and son of the same."

90. See chapter 14. The rest of chapter 5 takes up a series of divine traits and activities in which the Son participates according to the Father's wishes: omniscience, authority, omnipotence, works, creation, remission of sins, preservation, renovation, the power of conferring gifts, mediatorial work, bringing back to life, judgment, divine honor, and baptism.

91. In this passage, the Greek phrase or word precedes the italicized translation. Milton's point is that the distinct Greek words meaning "proceed from" and "go out from" could well mean the same thing in the contexts in which he quotes them. Believers have no good textual reason to attach special theological significance to "proceed from."

cannot be decided, from biblical evidence, how else it exists. So we must leave the point open, since the sacred writers are so noncommittal about it.

The name "spirit" is habitually applied to God, to the angels, and even to the minds of men. When the term "spirit of God" or "holy spirit" occurs in the Old Testament, it sometimes means God the Father, as in Gen. 6.3: *my spirit will not always strive.*

Sometimes it means the power and virtue of the Father, especially that divine breath which creates and nourishes everything. In the latter sense many interpreters, both ancient and modern, understand that passage in Gen. 1.2: *the spirit of God brooded.* It seems more likely, however, that we should here interpret the word as a reference to the Son, through whom, as we are constantly told, the Father created all things. Job 26.13: *by his spirit he decked the heavens,* and 27.3: *the spirit of God is in my nostrils,* and 33.4 [. . .]; Ps. 104.30: *when you send your spirit out, they are recreated;* and 139.7 [. . .]; Ezek. 37.14 [. . .]. There are many other passages of the same sort.

Sometimes "spirit" means an angel, Isa. 48.16: *the Lord Jehovah and his spirit has sent me;* Ezek. 3.12: *then the spirit took me up . . . ;* similarly 3.14 and 24 and elsewhere.

Sometimes it means Christ, whom, most people think, the Father sent to lead the Israelites into the land of Canaan. Isa. 43.10, 11: *afflicting with grief the spirit of his holiness. Who placed in their midst the spirit of his holiness*—that is, the angel upon which he bestowed his own name: that is, Christ, whom they tempted, Num. 21.5 etc., compared with 1 Cor. 10.9.

Sometimes it means the force or voice of God, in whatever way it was breathed into the prophets: Neh. 9.30: *since you testified against them by your spirit through your prophets.*

[. . .][92]

Let us assume that, appropriately enough, when God wants us to understand and thus believe in a particular doctrine as a primary point of faith, he teaches it to us not obscurely or confusedly, but simply and clearly, in plain words. Let us also take it for granted that, in religion, we should beware above all of exposing ourselves to the charge which Christ brought against the Samaritans in John 4.22: *you worship something you do not know.* Assume, too, that in matters of faith, that saying of Christ, *we worship something which we know,* should be regarded as axiomatic. If these assumptions are correct, then, as the above passages comprise just about all we are told in express terms about the Holy Spirit, they also represent all we can or ought to know on the subject. What they amount to is this: the Holy Spirit, unlike the Son, is nowhere said to have submitted himself to any mediatorial function. He is nowhere said to be under an obligation, as a son is, to pay obedience to the Father. Nevertheless he is obviously inferior to both the Father and the Son, inasmuch as he is represented as being and is said to be subservient and obedient in all things; to have been promised, sent and

92. In the deleted paragraphs, Milton continues his demonstration that scriptural accounts are variable and obscure in what they imply about the nature of the Holy Spirit.

given; to speak nothing of his own accord; and even to have been given as a pledge. You cannot avoid the issue here by talking about his human nature. [. . .] It remains to be seen, then, on what grounds we are to believe that the Holy Spirit is God, and what arguments there are for it. When the point at issue is as difficult to grasp as the present one, and when, like the present one, it is reckoned to be of primary importance and absolutely indispensable, it is inconsiderate and dangerous to burden believers with the necessity of accepting a doctrine which cannot be deduced from the clear testimony of God's word: a doctrine, moreover, which, although itself contrary to human reason, can only be ascertained by human reason, or rather by dubious logic-chopping.

Thus it is usual to defend the theory that the Holy Spirit is God by saying, first, that the name of God seems to be attributed to the Holy Spirit: Acts 5.3 compared with 5.4: *as you have lied to the Holy Spirit, you have not lied to men but to God.* But if we pay proper attention to what is previously said about the Holy Spirit by the Son, this passage will appear a pretty poor reason for asserting such a mysterious doctrine. For since it is explicitly stated that the Spirit is sent by the Father and in the name of the Son, clearly the man who lies to the Spirit lies to God, just as the man who receives an apostle receives God who sent him, Matt. 10.40; John 13.20. Paul himself puts an end to any argument about this passage, and explains it in the most apposite way, when he expounds what is obviously the same idea in a more developed form; 1 Thess. 4.8: *the man who despises these things despises not man but God, who has placed his Holy Spirit in us.* Besides, it is questionable whether, in the passage from Acts, *Holy Spirit* does not really mean God the Father, for Peter says, 5.9: *why . . . that you might tempt the spirit of the Lord,* that is, God the Father himself and his divine intelligence, which no mortal can deceive or be concealed from. And in Acts 5.32 it is evident that the Holy Spirit is called not God but, like the apostles, a witness to Christ—a witness *whom God has given to those who obey him.* Similarly Acts 2.38: *you will receive the gift of the Holy Spirit*—receive it, that is, from God. But how can the gift of God be God himself—especially the supreme God?

The second passage adduced is Acts 28.25, compared with Isa. 6.8, 9: *the Lord said. The Holy Spirit has said,* and similarly Jer. 31.31, compared with Heb. 10.15. But I demonstrated above[93] that in the Old Testament the names "Lord" and "Jehovah" are frequently attributed to whatever angels God sends on his errands. Moreover, in the New Testament, the Son himself openly gives evidence about the Holy Spirit to this effect, John 16.13: *that he does not speak of his own accord, but speaks the things he hears.* So the Holy Spirit cannot be proved God from this passage either.

The third passage is 1 Cor. 3.16, compared with 6.19 and with 2 Cor. 6.16: *the temple of God. The temple of the Spirit.* But it is not stated here, nor does it in any way follow from this that the Holy Spirit is God. For it is because the Father and the Son, not only the Holy Spirit *live in us,* John 14.23, that we are called *the*

93. In chapter 5, p. 432.

temple of God. So in 1 Cor. 6.19, where we are called *the temple of the Spirit,* Paul has added *which you have from God,* as if he were anxious to prevent us from drawing any false conclusions about the Holy Spirit from the expression he uses. How could anyone deduce from this passage, then, that what we have from God, is God? Paul explains more fully in what sense we are called *the temple of the Spirit* in Eph. 2.22: *you, too, are built together in him to be the home of God through the Spirit.*

[. . .][94]

Although the scriptures do not tell us explicitly who or what the Holy Spirit is, we need not be completely ignorant about it, as this much may be understood from the texts quoted above. The Holy Spirit, since he is a minister of God, and therefore a creature, was created, that is, produced, from the substance of God, not by natural necessity, but by the free will of the agent, maybe before the foundations of the world were laid, but after the Son, to whom he is far inferior, was made. You will say that this does not really distinguish the Holy Spirit from the Son. I reply that, in the same way, the expressions *to go forth from* and *to go out from* and *to proceed from the Father,* which are all the same in the Greek, do not distinguish the Son from the Holy Spirit, since they are used about both and signify the mission not the nature of each. There is sufficient reason for placing the name and also the nature of the Son above that of the Holy Spirit, when discussing matters relative to the Deity, in that the brightness of God's glory and the image of his divine subsistence are said to have been impressed on the Son but not on the Holy Spirit.

CHAPTER 7

OF THE CREATION

The second[95] kind of external efficiency is commonly called CREATION. Anyone who asks what God did before the creation of the world is a fool; and anyone who answers him is not much wiser.[96] Most people think they have given an account of the matter when they have quoted 1 Cor. 2.7: *that he preordained, before the creation of the world, his wisdom, hidden in a mystery,* which they take to mean that he was occupied with election and reprobation, and with deciding

94. The deleted passage argues that the attributes of true deity cannot be properly assigned to the Holy Spirit any more than they could be to the Son. It culminates with further discussion of 1 John 5.7, which asserts that "the Father, the Word and the Holy Spirit . . . are one," a verse whose spuriousness was detailed in note 82.

95. "Milton's antitrinitarianism dictates this numbering. According to orthodox theologians the external efficiency of God manifests itself in creation, by which he governs that which he produces. To these Milton adds an earlier species, the generation of the Son, so that creation and providence become the second and third rather than the standard first and second species of the Father's external efficiency" (Kelley's note, Yale 6:299).

96. Cp. *Tetrachordon,* p. 265: "One demanding how God employed himself before the world was made, had answer: that he was making hell for curious questioners."

other related matters. But it would clearly be disproportionate for God to have been totally occupied from eternity in decreeing things which it was to take him only six days to create: things which were to be governed in various ways for a few thousand years, and then finally either received into an unchanging state with God for ever, or else for ever thrown away.

That the world was created, must be considered an article of faith: Heb. 11.3: *through faith we understand that the world was made by God's word.*

CREATION is the act by which GOD THE FATHER PRODUCED EVERYTHING THAT EXISTS BY HIS WORD AND SPIRIT, that is, BY HIS WILL, IN ORDER TO SHOW THE GLORY OF HIS POWER AND GOODNESS.

BY WHICH GOD THE FATHER: Job 9.8: *who alone spreads out the heavens;* Isa. 44.24: *I, Jehovah, make all things, I alone spread out the heavens, and I stretch forth the earth by myself,* and 45.6, 7 [...]. If such things as common sense and accepted idiom exist at all, then these words preclude the possibility not only of there being any other God, but also of there being any person, of any kind whatever, equal to him.[97] Neh. 9.6 [...]; Mal. 2.10: *have we not all one father? Has not one mighty and unparalleled God created us?* Thus Christ himself says, Matt. 11.25: *Father, Lord of heaven and earth;* and so do all the apostles: Acts 4.24, compared with 4.27: *Lord, you are that God who created the heaven and the earth, the sea and all that is in* them ... against *your Son;* Rom. 11.36: *from him and through him and in him are all things;* 1 Cor. 8.6 [...] and 2 Cor. 4.6 [...]; Heb. 2.10 [...] and 3.4 [...].

BY HIS WORD: Gen. 1. *passim, he said ...;* Ps. 33.6: *by Jehovah's word,* and 33.9: *he speaks;* Ps. 148.5: *he commanded;* 2 Pet. 3.5: *through the word of God,* that is, as we learn from other passages, through the Son, who apparently derives from this his title of the Word.[98] John 1.3, 10: *all things were made through him: through him the world was made;* 1 Cor. 8.6: *one God, the Father, from whom all things are. And one Lord Jesus Christ, through whom all things are;* Eph. 3.9 [...]; Col. 1.16 [...]; Heb. 1.2: *through whom also he made the world,* hence 1.10: *you have created.* The preposition *through* sometimes denotes the principal cause, as in Matt. 12.28: *through the Spirit of God I cast out devils,* 1 Cor. 1.9: *through whom you are called,* and sometimes the instrumental or less important cause, as in the passages quoted above.[99] It does not denote the principal cause in these passages, because if it did the Father himself, by whom all things are, would not be the principal. Nor does it denote a joint cause, because then it would be said not that the Father created *by* the Word and Spirit but *with* the Word and Spirit, or alternatively that the Father, the Word, and the Spirit created. These formulae are nowhere to be found in

97. Cp. *PL* 8.406–7: "for none I know/Second to me or like, equal much less."

98. On the significance of the distinction between the roles of the Word and the Son, see Rumrich 1987, 162–64. Cp. *PL* 5.814–18.

99. Cp. *Art of Logic* (Yale 8:224–25): "Properly speaking, instruments do not act, but are rather acted upon or help. And anyone who has only instruments as helping cause can correctly be called a solitary cause."

scripture. Again, "to be *by* the Father" and "to be *through* the Son" are phrases which do not signify the same kind of efficient cause. If they are not of the same kind, then there can be no question of a joint cause, and if there is no joint cause then "the Father *by* whom all things are" will unquestionably be a more important cause than "the Son *through* whom all things are." For the Father is not only he *by* whom, but also he *from* whom, in whom, *through* whom, and *on account of* whom all things are, as I have shown above, inasmuch as he comprehends within himself all lesser causes. But the Son is only he *through* whom all things are, and is therefore the less principal cause. So we often find it said that the Father created the world through the Son, but nowhere that the Son, in the same sense, created the world through the Father. But some try to prove from Rev. 3.14 that the Son was the joint cause of the creation with the Father, or even the principal cause. The reference there is to *the beginning of God's creation,* and they interpret the word *beginning* as meaning *beginner,* on the authority of Aristotle. But in the first place, the Hebrew language, from which this expression is taken, never allows this use of the word *beginning,* but rather requires a quite contrary sense, as in Gen. 49.3: *Reuben, the beginning of my strength.* Secondly, there are two passages in Paul, referring to Christ himself, which make it absolutely clear that the word *beginning* is here used to mean not an agent but something acted upon: Col. 1.15, 18: *the first born of all created things. The beginning, the first born from the dead.* Here both the Greek accent and the verbal passive πϱοτότοκος, show that the Son of God was *the first born of all created things* in the same sense as the Son of man was the πϱοτότοκος or *first born* of Mary, Matt. 1.25. The second passage is Rom. 8.29: *the first born among many brothers,* where *first born* has, of course, a passive sense. Finally it should be noted that Christ is not called merely the *beginning of creation,* but *the beginning of God's creation,* and that can only mean that he was the first of the things which God created. How, then, can he be God himself? Some of the Fathers have suggested that the reason why he is called *the first born of all created things* in Col. 1.15 is that *through him all things were created,* as it says in the next verse. But this argument cannot be admitted, because if St. Paul had meant this, he would have said "who was before every creature" (which is what these Fathers insist that the words mean, although it is a forced reading), not, *who was the first born of all created things.* The words *first born* here are certainly superlative in sense, but they also, in a way, imply that only part of a collective whole is being spoken of. This last remark is true only because the production of Christ was apparently a kind of "birth" or creation: it is not true where Christ is also called the first born *man.* For he is called *first born* in that phrase not just as a title of dignity, but to distinguish him from other men for the chronological reason that *through him all things which are in the heavens were created,* Col. 1.16.

Prov. 8.22, 23 is no better as a basis for argument, even if we admit that the chapter as a whole should be interpreted as a reference to Christ: *Jehovah possessed me, the beginning of his way; I was anointed before the world.* A thing which was *possessed* and *anointed* could not itself be the primary cause. Besides, even a creature is called the beginning of the ways of God in Job 40.19: *he is the beginning of God's ways.* As for the eighth chapter of Proverbs, I should say that the figure introduced as a speaker there is not the Son of God but a poetical personification of Wisdom, as in Job 28.20–27: *From where, then, is that wisdom . . . ? then he saw her. . . .*

Another argument is based on Isa. 45.12, 23: *I have made the earth . . . ; shall bow to me.* My opponents say that these words are spoken by Christ, and they quote St. Paul in their support: Rom. 14.10, 11: *we shall all stand before the judgment seat of Christ: for it is written, As I live, says the Lord, every knee shall bow to me. . . .* But it is obvious from the parallel passage, Phil. 2.9–11, that this is said by God the Father, who gave that judgment seat, and all judgment, to the Son, *that at the name of Jesus every knee shall bow . . . ; to the glory of God the Father,* or in other words, *every tongue shall confess to God.*

AND SPIRIT. Gen. 1.2: *the Spirit of God brooded,* that is to say, God's divine power, not any particular person, as I showed in Chapter 6, Of the Holy Spirit.[100] For if it was a person, why is the Spirit named and nothing said about the Son, by whose labor, as we so often read, the world was made? (Unless, of course, the Spirit referred to was Christ, who, as I have shown, is sometimes called *the Spirit* in the Old Testament.) Anyway, even if we grant that it was a person, it seems only to have been a subordinate, since, after God had created heaven and earth, the Spirit merely brooded upon the face of the waters which had already been created. Similarly Job 26.13: *by his spirit he decked the heavens;* Ps. 33.6: *the heavens were made by Jehovah's word, and all the host of them by the spirit of his mouth.* The person of the Spirit certainly does not seem to have proceeded more from God's mouth than from Christ's, who *shall consume the antichrist with the spirit of his mouth,* 2 Thess. 2.8, compared with Isa. 11.4: *the rod of his mouth.*

BY HIS WILL. Ps. 135.6: *whatever pleases you;* Rev. 4.11: *as a result of your will.*

IN ORDER TO SHOW. Gen. 1.31: *whatever he had done, it was very good,* similarly 1 Tim. 4.4; Ps. 19.2, 3: *the heavens declare the glory of God;* Prov. 16.4 [. . .]; Acts 14.15 [. . .] and 17.24 [. . .] etc.; Rom. 1.20: *for both his eternal power and his eternal godhead are discerned.*[101] So far I have established that God the Father is the first efficient cause of all things.

There is a good deal of controversy, however, about what the original matter was. On the whole the moderns are of the opinion that everything was formed out of nothing (which is, I fancy, what their own theory is based on!). In the first place it is certain that neither the Hebrew verb בָּרָא nor the Greek κτίζειν, nor the Latin *creare* means "to make out of nothing." On the contrary, each of them always means "to make out of something." Gen. 1.21, 27: *God created . . . which the waters brought forth abundantly, he created them male and female;* Isa. 54.16: *I have*

100. Milton never states decisively whether or not the force brooding was contained in a specific person. He admits no doubt, however, that ultimately it is the power of the Father, regardless of whether it was channeled through a person or not.

101. Cp. *PR* 3.110–14: "he seeks glory,/And for his glory all things made, all things / Orders and governs, nor content in Heaven/By all his Angels glorified, requires/Glory from men, from all men, good or bad."

created the maker, I have created the destroyer. Anyone who says, then, that "to create" means "to produce out of nothing," is, as logicians say, arguing from an unproved premise. The passages of scripture usually quoted in this context do not at all confirm the received opinion, but tend to imply the contrary, namely that all things were not made out of nothing, 2 Cor. 4.6: *God who commanded light to shine out of darkness.* It is clear from Isa. 45.7 that this darkness was far from being a mere nothing: *I am Jehovah,* etc. *I form the light and create the darkness.* If the darkness is nothing, then when God created the darkness he created nothing, that is he both created and did not create, which is a contradiction in terms. Again, Heb. 11.3, all we are required *to understand through faith* about *earthly times,* that is, about the world, is that *the things which are seen were not put together from the things which appear.* Now because things do not appear, they must not be considered synonymous with nothing. For one thing, you cannot have a plural of nothing, and for another, a thing cannot be *put together* from nothing as it can from a number of components. The meaning is, rather, that these things are not as they now appear. I might also mention the apocryphal writers, as closest to the scriptures in authority: Wisdom 11.17: *who created the world out of formless matter;* 2 Macc. 7.28: *out of things that were not.* But it is said of Rachel's children in Matt. 2.18, *they are not,* and this does not mean *they are nothing* but, as frequently in the Hebrew language, they are not among the living.

It is clear, then, that the world was made out of some sort of matter. For since "action" and "passivity" are relative terms, and since no agent can act externally unless there is something, and something material, which can be acted upon, it is apparent that God could not have created this world out of nothing. *Could* not, that is, not because of any defect of power or omnipotence on his part, but because it was necessary that something should have existed previously, so that it could be acted upon by his supremely powerful active efficacy. Since, then, both the Holy Scriptures and reason itself suggest that all these things were made not out of nothing but out of matter, matter must either have always existed, independently of God, or else originated from God at some point in time. That matter should have always existed independently of God is inconceivable. In the first place, it is only a passive principle, dependent upon God and subservient to him; and, in the second place, there is no inherent force or efficacy in time or eternity, any more than there is in the concept of number. But if matter did not exist from eternity, it is not very easy to see where it originally came from. There remains only this solution, especially if we allow ourselves to be guided by scripture, namely, that all things came from God. Rom. 11.36: *from him and through him and in him are all things;* 1 Cor. 8.6: *one God, the Father, from whom all things are,—from,* as the Greek reads in both cases. Heb. 2.11: *for both he who sanctifies and he who is sanctified, are all from one.*

There are, to begin with, as everyone knows, four kinds of causes, efficient, material, formal and final.[102] Since God is the first, absolute and sole cause of all

102. Cp. *Art of Logic* (Yale 8:223).

things, he unquestionably contains and comprehends within himself all these causes. So the material cause must be either God or nothing. But nothing is no cause at all; (though my opponents want to prove that forms and, what is more, human forms were created from nothing). Now matter and form are, as it were, internal causes. These are the things which go to make up the object itself. So either all objects must have had only two causes, external causes that is, or else God was not the perfect and absolute cause of all things. Secondly, it is a demonstration of supreme power and supreme goodness that such heterogeneous, multiform and inexhaustible virtue should exist in God, and exist substantially (for that virtue cannot be accidental which admits various degrees and is, as it were, susceptible to augmentation and remission, according his will). It is, I say, a demonstration of God's supreme power and goodness that he should not shut up this heterogeneous and substantial virtue within himself, but should disperse, propagate and extend it as far as, and in whatever way, he wills. For this original matter was not an evil thing, nor to be thought of as worthless: it was good, and it contained the seeds of all subsequent good. It was a substance, and could only have been derived from the source of all substance. It was in a confused and disordered state at first, but afterwards God made it ordered and beautiful.[103]

Those who object to this theory, on the grounds that matter was apparently imperfect, should also object to the theory that God originally produced it out of nothing in an imperfect and formless state. What does it matter whether God produced this imperfect matter out of nothing or out of himself? To argue that there could have been no imperfection in a substance which God produced out of himself, is only to transfer the imperfection to God's efficiency. For why did he not, starting from nothing, make everything absolutely perfect straight away? But in fact, matter was not, by nature, imperfect. The addition of forms (which, incidentally, are themselves material) did not make it more perfect but only more beautiful. But, you will say, how can something corruptible result from something incorruptible? I might well reply, how can God's virtue and efficiency result from nothing? But in fact matter, like the form and nature of the angels, came from God in an incorruptible state, and even since the fall it is still incorruptible, so far as its essence is concerned.

But the same problem, or an even greater one, still remains. How can anything sinful have come, if I may so speak, from God? My usual reply to this is to ask, how can anything sinful have come from that virtue and efficiency which themselves proceed from God? But really it is not the matter nor the form which sins. When matter or form has gone out from God and become the

103. Here we find the theological justification for Milton's vitalist materialism: that a *multiform and inexhaustible virtue* is intrinsic to God's absolute excellence; it is the substantial power that permits him to produce a materially and formally diverse creation. The claim seems inconsistent with the allegorical representation in *Paradise Lost* of a hostile Chaos. For divergent critical views of this apparent inconsistency, see Schwartz; Rumrich 1995.

property of another, what is there to prevent its being infected and polluted, since it is now in a mutable state, by the calculations of the devil or of man, calculations which proceed from these creatures themselves? But, you will say, body cannot emanate from spirit. My reply is, much less can it emanate from nothing. Moreover spirit, being the more excellent substance, virtually, as they say, and eminently contains within itself what is clearly the inferior substance; in the same way as the spiritual and rational faculty contains the corporeal, that is, the sentient and vegetative faculty. For not even God's virtue and efficiency could have produced bodies out of nothing (as it is vulgarly believed he did) unless there had been some bodily force in his own substance, for no one can give something he has not got.

And indeed, St. Paul himself did not hesitate to attribute something bodily to God, Col. 2.9: *the whole fullness of the Godhead dwells in him bodily.* And it is not any more incredible that a bodily force should be able to issue from a spiritual substance, than that something spiritual should be able to arise from a body; and that is what we trust will happen to our own bodies at the resurrection. Lastly, I do not see how God can truthfully be called infinite if there is anything which might be added to him. And if something did exist, in the nature of things, which had not first been from God and in God, then that might be added to him.

It seems to me that, with the guidance of scripture, I have proved that God produced all things not out of nothing but out of himself. Now I think I ought to go on to consider the necessary consequence of this, which is that, since all things come not only from God but out of God, no created thing can be utterly annihilated. To begin with, there is not a word in the Bible about any such annihilation. That is the very best reason for rejecting the concept of annihilation altogether, but I will also suggest some other reasons. First, because it seems to me that God neither wishes to nor, properly speaking, can altogether annihilate anything.[104] He does not wish to, because he makes everything to some definite end, and nothing cannot be the end either of God or of any created thing. It cannot be the end of God, because he is himself his own end; and it cannot be the end of any created thing, because the end of all created things is some kind of good, whereas nothing is neither good nor any kind of thing at all. All entity is good: nonentity, not good. It is not consistent, then, with the goodness and wisdom of God, to make out of entity, which is good, something which is not good, or nothing. Moreover God cannot annihilate anything, because by making nothing he would both make and not make at the same time, which involves a contradiction. But, you will say, God does make something when he annihilates: he makes something which exists, cease to exist. My reply is that any complete action involves two things, motion, and something brought about by the motion. Here the motion is the act of annihilation, but there is not anything

104. Cp. *PL* 2.151–54; 6.347.

brought about by the motion, that is, nothing is brought about, no effect: and if there is no effect there is no efficient.

CREATION is of THINGS INVISIBLE or of THINGS VISIBLE.

THINGS INVISIBLE, at least to us, are the highest heaven, the throne and dwelling place of God, and the heavenly beings, or angels.

This is the distinction which the apostle makes in Col. 1.16. Things invisible deserve priority by virtue of dignity if not of origin. For the highest heaven is, as it were, God's supreme citadel and dwelling-place (see Deut. 26.15; 1 Kings 8.27, 30: *of the heaven of heavens;* Neh. 9.6; similarly Isa. 63.15): *it is far above all heavens,* Eph. 4.10; where God *dwells in unapproachable light, whom no man can see,* 1 Tim. 6.16. Bliss and glory and a kind of perpetual heaven have, apparently, emanated from this light and exist as a result of it; see Ps. 16.11: *eternal pleasures at your right hand;* Isa. 57.15: *whose name dwells in eternity and is holy; I who live in a high and holy place.*

It is not likely that God built a dwelling-place of this kind for his majesty only the day before yesterday, only, that is, from the beginning of the world. If God really has a dwelling-place where he pours forth his glory and the brightness of his majesty in a particular and extraordinary way, why should I believe that it was made at the same time as the fabric of this world, and not ages before? But it does not follow that heaven is eternal, nor, if it is eternal, that it is God. For God could always produce any effect he pleased both when and how he chose. We cannot imagine light without some source of light, but we do not therefore think that a source of light is the same thing as light, or equal in excellence. Similarly we do not consider that what are called *the back parts* of God in Ex. 33, are, strictly speaking, God, yet we do not deny that they are eternal. I prefer to think in the same way about the heavens of heavens, the throne and dwelling-place of God, rather than believe that God was without a heaven until the first of the six days of creation. I say this not because I dare be at all dogmatic on such a subject, but in order to show that other people have been too rashly dogmatic in affirming that that invisible and supreme heaven was, like the heaven we see above us, made on the first day of creation. Since Moses had set himself the task of writing only about the visible heaven, and this visible universe, why should it have concerned him to say what was above the world?

The heaven of the blessed seems to be a part of this highest heaven. It is sometimes called Paradise, Luke 23.43; 2 Cor. 12.2, 4; and sometimes Abraham's bosom, Luke 16.22 compared with Matt. 8.11. Here God reveals himself to the sight of the angels and saints (insofar as they are capable of seeing him); and after the end of the world he will reveal himself more fully, 1 Cor. 13.12. John 14.2, 3: *in my Father's house there are many mansions;* Heb. 11.10, 16 [. . .].

Most people argue that the angels should be understood as included in and created along with "the heavens" at the creation of the world. We may well believe that the angels were, in fact, created at a particular time, see Num. 16.22: *God of spirits,* and similarly 27.16; Heb. 1.7; Col. 1.16: *through him were invisible things made, whether they be thrones . . .* But that they were created on the first or on any one of the six days is asserted by the general mob of theologians with, as usual, quite unjustifiable confidence, chiefly on the authority of the repetition in Gen. 2.1: *thus the heavens and the earth were finished, and all the army of them:* quite unjustifiable, that is, unless we are supposed to pay more attention to this conclusion than to the preceding narrative, and to interpret this *army* which inhabits the visible heavens as a reference to the angels. The fact that they *shouted for joy* before God at the creation, as we read in Job 38.7, proves that they were then already created, not that they were first created at that time. Certainly many of the Greek Fathers, and some of the Latin, were of the opinion that angels, inasmuch as they were spirits, existed long before this material world. Indeed it seems likely that that apostasy, as a result of which so many myriads of them fled, beaten, to the lowest part of heaven, took place before even the first beginnings of this world.[105] There is certainly no reason why we should conform to the popular belief that motion and time, which is the measure of motion, could not, according to our concepts of "before" and "after," have existed before this world was made. For Aristotle, who taught that motion and time are inherent only in this world, asserted, nevertheless, that this world was eternal.[106]

Angels are spirits, Matt. 8.16 and 12.45. Indeed a whole legion of evil angels was able to get inside one man, Luke 8.30; Heb. 1.14 [. . .]. They are ethereal by nature: 1 Kings 22.21; Ps. 104.4 compared with Matt. 8.31; Heb. 1.7: *like lightning;* Luke 10.18; for which reason they are also called Seraphim.[107] They are immortal, Luke 20.36: *they cannot die.* Remarkable for their wisdom, 2 Sam. 14.20. Extremely strong, Ps. 103.20; 2 Pet. 2.11; 2 Kings 19.35; 2 Thess. 1.7. Extremely swift, as if they had wings, Ezek. 1.6; so numerous that they are almost innumerable, Deut. 33.2; Job 25.3; Dan. 7.10; Matt. 26.53; Heb. 12.22; Rev. 5.11, 12. They were created perfect in holiness and righteousness, Luke 9. 26; John 8.44; 2 Cor. 11.14, 15: *angels of light, ministers of righteousness;* Matt. 6.10 [. . .], and 25.31 [. . .]. So they are also called sons of God,[108] Job 1.6 and 38.7; Dan. 3.25, compared with 3.28; and they are even called Gods, Ps. 8.6 and 97.7. But they are not to be compared with God; Job 4.18: *he will give light to his angels,* and 15.15 [. . .], and 25.5 [. . .]; Isa. 6.2 [. . .]. They are distinguished one from another by their duties and their ranks, Matt. 25.41; Rom. 8.38; Col. 1.16; Eph. 1.21 and 3.10; 1 Pet. 3.22; Rev. 12.7. Cherubim, Gen. 3.24. Seraphim, Isa. 6.22. They are also distinguished by their personal names, Dan. 8.16 and 9.21 and 10.13; Luke 1.19. Michael, Jude 9. Rev. 12.7; 1 Thess. 4.16: *with the voice of an archangel.* Josh. 6.2. See more on the subject of angels in chapter 9, below. Those who tried to say more about the nature of angels earned the apostle's rebuke, Col. 2.18: *intruding into those things which he has not seen, rashly puffed up by his fleshly intelligence.*

105. Cp. *PL* 1, Argument: "for that angels were long before this visible creation, was the opinion of many ancient Fathers"; also 5.577ff.

106. Cp. *PL* 5.580–82: "(For time, though in eternity, applied/To motion, measures all things durable/By present, past, and future)."

107. The name of this angelic order is related to the Hebrew word for "fire."

108. Cp. *PL* 5.447; 11.84; and *PR* 1.368; 4.197.

THINGS VISIBLE are this visible world and whatever it contains, and above all the human race.

The creation of the world and of its individual parts is narrated in Gen. 1. It is described in Job 26.7 etc. and 38, and in various passages of the Psalms and Prophets: Ps. 33.6, 9 and 104 and 148.5; Prov. 8.26, etc.; Amos 4.13; 2 Pet. 3.5. But when God is about to make man he speaks like a person giving careful consideration to something, as if to imply that this is a still greater work; Gen. 1.26: *after this God said, let us make man in our image, after our own likeness.* So it was not only the body but also the soul which he made at that time, for it is in our souls that we are most like God. I say this in case anyone should think that souls, which God created at that time, really existed beforehand. Some people have imagined this, but they are refuted by Gen. 2.7: *God formed man out of the dust of the earth, and breathed the breath of life into his nostrils. Thus man became a living soul;* Job 32.8: *truly this spirit is in man, and the breath of the Almighty makes them intelligent beings.* He did not merely breathe that spirit into man, but shaped it in each individual as a fundamental attribute, and separated its various faculties, making it beautiful and orderly, Zech. 12.1: *forming the spirit of man within him.*

We may, however, be absolutely sure, from other scriptural passages, that when God breathed that breath of life into man, he did not make him a sharer in anything divine, any part of the divine essence, as it were. He imparted to him only something human which was proportionate to divine virtue. For he breathed the breath of life into other living things besides man, as we can see from Ps. 104.29, 30: *you take back their spirit, they die: when you send your spirit out, they are re-created.* We learn, then, that all living creatures receive their life from the same source of life and spirit; and that when God takes back that spirit or breath of life, they die. Eccl. 3.19: *they all have the same spirit.* In Holy Scripture that word *spirit* means nothing but the breath of life, which we breathe; or the vital or sensitive or rational faculty, or some action or affection belonging to them.

When man had been created in this way, it is said, finally: *thus man became a living soul.* Unless we prefer to be instructed about the nature of the soul by heathen authors, we must interpret this as meaning that man is a living being, intrinsically and properly one and individual. He is not double or separable: not, as is commonly thought, produced from and composed of two different and distinct elements, soul and body. On the contrary, the whole man is the soul, and the soul the man: a body, in other words, or individual substance, animated, sensitive, and rational. The breath of life mentioned in Genesis was not a part of the divine essence, nor was it the soul, but a kind of air or breath of divine virtue, fit for the maintenance of life and reason and infused into the organic body. For man himself, the whole man, I say, when finally created, is specifically referred to as *a living soul.* Hence the word soul is interpreted by the apostle, 1 Cor. 15.45, as meaning *animal.* And all properties of the body are attributed to the soul as well: touch, Lev. 5.2: *when the soul has touched any unclean thing,* and elsewhere: the ability to eat, 7.18: *the soul which eats of it,* 7.20: *the soul which eats the flesh,* and frequently elsewhere: hunger, Prov. 13.25 and 27.7: thirst, Prov. 25.25: *as cool waters to a weary soul;* Isa. 29.8: apprehensibility, 1 Sam. 24.11: *although you harass my soul in order to capture it;* Ps. 7.6: *let him pursue my soul and capture it.*

But in a context where "body" means merely physical trunk, "soul" may mean either the spirit or its secondary faculties, such as the vital or sensitive faculty. So, to avoid confusion, "soul" is as frequently distinguished from "spirit" as it is from "body": for example Luke 1.46, 47; 1 Thess. 5.23: *the whole spirit, soul and body;* Heb. 4.12: *to the division of soul and spirit.* The idea that the spirit of man is separate from his body, so that it may exist somewhere in isolation, complete and intelligent, is nowhere to be found in scripture, and is plainly at odds with nature and reason, as I will demonstrate more fully below. For it is said of every kind of animal in Gen. 1.30: *in them is a living soul,* and 7.22: *of all that was on the dry land, everything which had in its nostrils the breath of the spirit of life, died.* But no one believes that beasts have therefore souls which enjoy some kind of separate existence.

On the seventh day God ceased to create, and completed the entire work of creation, Gen. 2.2, 3.

So it would seem that the human soul is generated by the parents in the course of nature, and not created daily by the immediate act of God.[109] Tertullian and Apollinarius saw this as the more probable theory, and it seemed so, too, to Augustine and the whole western church in the time of Jerome, as he himself testifies, Tom. 2, Epist. 82, and Gregory of Nyssa in his treatise on the soul. If God still created every day as many souls as man's frequently unlawful passion creates bodies in every part of the world, then he would have left himself a huge and, in a way, a servile task, even after that sixth day of creation—a task which would still remain to be performed, and from which he would not be able to rest even one day in seven. But in fact the force of the divine blessing, that each creature should reproduce in its own likeness, is as fully applicable to man as it is to all other animals; Gen. 1.21, 28. So God made the mother of all things living out of a simple rib, without having to breathe the breath of life a second time, Gen. 2.22; and Adam himself begot his son in his own image and likeness, Gen. 5.3. 1 Cor. 15.49: *as we have borne the image of the earthly,* and this means not only in the body but in the soul, just as it was chiefly with reference to his soul that Adam was made in God's image. So Gen. 46.26: *all the souls which came out of Jacob's loins;* Heb. 7.10: *Levi was in Abraham's loins.* Hence in scripture an offspring is called "seed," and Christ is said to be *the seed of the woman. I will be your God and the God of your seed,* Gen. 17.7. 1 Cor. 15.44: *it is sown an animal body* and 15.46: *the spiritual is not first but the animal.*

Rational arguments can also be adduced. A man who is born, or formed and conceived in sin (and we all are, not only David, Ps. 51.5), must, if he is able to

109. The belief that the individual soul is generated by the parents along with the body is called "traducianism." The more standard view (creationism) was that God himself creates each individual soul and infuses it into the body during gestation.

receive his soul immediately from God, receive it from God in a sinful state. For what do "to be born" and "to be conceived" mean, except to receive soul with body? But if we receive the soul straight from God, it must be a pure soul: for who would dare to call it impure? And if it is pure, in what way are we "conceived in sin" when we receive a pure soul which might well sanctify our impure bodies? How can a pure soul deserve to be charged with bodily sins? But, my opponents insist, God does not create impure souls but only souls which, from the viewpoint of original righteousness, are weakened and impaired. My answer is that to create pure souls which lack original righteousness, and then to put them into contaminated and vicious bodies, to surrender them to the body as to an enemy, imprisoned, innocent and unarmed, with blinded intellect and with will enchained, quite deprived, in other words, of the strength which is needed to resist the body's vicious tendencies—to do all this would argue injustice just as much as to have created them impure would argue impurity. It would be equally unjust to have created the first man, Adam, with his original righteousness weakened and impaired.

Again, if sin is transmitted from the parents to the child in the act of generation, then the πρῶτον δεκτικόν or original subject of sin, namely the rational soul, must also be propagated by the parents.[110] For no one will deny that all sin proceeds in the first instance from the soul. Lastly, by what sort of law could we make a soul answerable for a crime which Adam committed, when that soul was never in Adam and never came from him? Add to this Aristotle's argument, which I think a very strong one indeed, that if the soul is wholly contained in all the body and wholly in any given part of that body, how can the human seed, that intimate and most noble part of the body, be imagined destitute and devoid of the soul of the parents, or at least of the father, when communicated to the son in the act of generation? Nearly everyone agrees that all form—and the human soul is a kind of form—is produced by the power of matter.[111]

I suppose that it was arguments of this kind which brought Augustine to the point where he admitted he had not been able to discover by reading, praying or reasoning how the doctrine of original sin could be reconciled with that of the creation of souls: Epist. 28 *ad Hieron.* and 157 *ad Optat.* The passages which are usually cited, Eccl. 12.7, Isa. 57.20, Zech. 12.1, certainly indicate the nobility of the soul's origin, in that it was breathed from the mouth of God. However they no

110. Cp. *Art of Logic* (Yale 8:242): "A subject has its various modes. . . . [It] can be divided into *receiving* subject, which the Greeks call δεκτικόν, and *appropriating* subject, which is commonly called *object* because in it the adjuncts are appropriated . . . ; the subject receiving its attributes into itself either sustains and as it were supports them, so that they are called *implanted* or *inhering*, or it contains them."

111. The Latin phrase is *"ex potentia materiae."* Cp. *Art of Logic* (Yale 8:230): "*Matter is the cause out of which a thing is.* . . . We think of matter as common to all beings and non-beings. . . . Of whatever sort the things themselves may be, such, too, should be their matter." Also, *PL* 5.472–74: "one first matter all,/Endued with various forms, various degrees/Of substance, and in things that live, of life." On Milton's understanding of the power of matter, see Hunter 1952.

more prove an immediate and separate creation for each soul, than the following texts prove that each body is directly molded by God in the womb: Job 10.8–10: *your hands have made me; you have poured me like milk;* Ps. 33.15 [. . .]; Job 31.15 [. . .]; Isa. 44.24 [. . .]; Acts 17.26 [. . .]. But it does not follow from these passages that natural causes have not in each case made their usual contribution towards the propagation of the body. Nor does the fact that the soul, on account of its origin, returns again at death to elements different from those of the body, prove that it is not handed on from father to son.

As for that passage in Heb. 12.9 where *fathers of the flesh* are contrasted with *the father of spirits,* my answer to that is that it should be taken in a theological sense, not in a physical sense as if the father of the body were opposed to the father of the soul. For *flesh* does not signify here or anywhere else, as far as I know, the body without the soul; and *the father of spirits* does not refer to the father of the soul, who is concerned in the act of generation. On the contrary, *father of flesh* means here nothing more nor less than the earthly, natural father who begets in sin; and *the father of spirits* means either the heavenly Father, who once created all spirits, angels and men alike, or the spiritual father who, according to John 3.6, regenerates the faithful: *that which is born from flesh is flesh: that born from spirit, spirit.* The argument of the passage in Hebrews runs more smoothly, moreover, if it is understood from the viewpoint of castigation, not generation. For the passage does not tell who generated us or what part of us he generated, but who may more usefully chastise and educate us. The apostle might well have used the same argument to persuade his readers to put up with his censure, since he was their spiritual father. As a matter of fact God is as truly Father of the flesh as he is of the spirits of the flesh, Num. 16.22: but that is not the point at issue here, and conclusions squeezed out from a passage of scripture which really deals with a quite different subject are extremely untrustworthy.

As for the soul of Christ, it is enough to say that its generation was supernatural, so it cannot be used as an argument in this controversy. But even he is called *the seed of the woman, the seed of David from the fleshly point of view,* which means, unquestionably, from the point of view of his human nature.

Since man was formed in the image of God, he must have been endowed with natural wisdom, holiness and righteousness: Gen. 1.27, 31 and 2.25; Eccl. 7.29; Eph. 4.24; Col. 3.10; 2 Cor. 3.18. Moreover he could not have given names to the animals in that extempore way, without very great intelligence: Gen. 2.20. I do not see why anyone should make the human soul into an anomaly. For, as I have shown above, God breathed the breath of life into other living things besides man, and when he had breathed it, he mixed it with matter in a very fundamental way, so that the human form, like all other forms, should be propagated and produced as a result of that power which God had implanted in matter.

CHAPTER 8

OF GOD'S PROVIDENCE OR HIS UNIVERSAL GOVERNMENT OF THINGS

The last kind of external divine efficiency is the GOVERNMENT OF THE UNIVERSE.

This is either GENERAL or SPECIAL.

GENERAL GOVERNMENT is that by which GOD THE FATHER VIEWS AND PRESERVES ALL CREATED THINGS AND GOVERNS THEM WITH SUPREME WISDOM AND HOLINESS, ACCORDING TO THE CONDITIONS OF HIS DECREE.

[...][112]

ACCORDING TO THE CONDITIONS OF HIS DECREE. We must add this qualification because God has not preserved angels or men or anything else absolutely, but only so far as the condition of his decree extends. For ever since man fell of his own free will God has preserved him and all other things with him only in the sense that he has continued their existence, not their original perfection.

[...][113]

ALL THINGS. Gen. 8.1: *God remembered Noah, and all beasts and all cattle,* and 9.9, 10, 12, 15 [...]; Prov. 15.3: *Jehovah's eyes are in every place watching the evil and the good.*

Even the smallest things: Job 34.21: *for his eyes are turned towards each man's ways, and he counts all his steps;* Ps. 104.21 [...], and 147.9 [...]; Matt. 6.26 and 10.29, 30: *a sparrow does not fall to the ground without your Father. The hairs of your head are numbered.*

But God does not consider all things worthy of equal care and providence: 1 Cor. 9.9: *is God concerned about oxen?*—as much, that is, as he is about men? Zech. 2.8: *he who touches you touches the pupil of his own eye;* 1 Tim. 4.10: *savior of all, especially of believers.*

Natural things. Ex. 3.21: *I will make this people pleasing in the sight of the Egyptians*—that is, by altering their natural affections. Jer. 51.16 [...]; Amos 5.8: *calling together the waters of the sea and pouring them out on the face of the earth; Jehovah by name.*

And supernatural as well. Lev. 25.20, 21 [...]; Deut. 8.3, 4: *he fed you with manna... your clothing has not worn out and ceased to be a covering for you, and your foot has not swollen these forty years,* similarly 29.5. 1 Kings 17.4 [...], and 17.14 [...].

112. In the deleted passage Milton cites Scripture to elaborate term by term GOD THE FATHER VIEWS AND PRESERVES from his definition of GENERAL GOVERNMENT.

113. In the deleted passage Milton cites Scripture to elaborate GOVERNS THEM WITH SUPREME WISDOM AND HOLINESS.

Contingencies or chance happenings. Ex. 21.13: *if God delivers him to his hand;* Prov. 16.33: *the arrangement of the lot comes from Jehovah.* Those passages of scripture which do not scruple to use the words "fortune" or "chance," imply nothing derogatory to divine providence by such expressions, but merely rule out the possibility of any human causation.[114] Eccl. 9.11: *but time and chance happen to them all;* Luke 10.31 [. . .].

And voluntary actions. 2 Chron. 10.15: *so when the king did not listen to the people, for the cause came from God;* Prov. 16.9: *man's mind thinks out his own way, but Jehovah lays down his path,* and 20.24 [. . .]; and 21.1 [. . .]; Jer. 10.23 [. . .]. But the freedom of the will always remains uninfringed, otherwise we shall have to deprive man of freedom not only in any good but also in any indifferent or evil act.

Lastly, evil occurrences just as much as good ones. Ex. 21.13: *if God delivers him to his hand;* Isa. 45.7: *making peace and creating evil*—that is, what afterwards became and is now evil, for whatever God created was originally good, as he himself testifies, Gen. 1; Matt. 18.7: *woe to the world and its offences; for it must be that offences shall come: nevertheless, woe to that man;* 1 Cor. 11.19 [. . .].

But God either merely allows evil to happen, by not impeding natural causes and free agents, as in Acts 2.23 [. . .] and 14.16: *he allowed all nations to go their own ways;* and 1 Pet. 3.17: *if he wishes it, that though you act righteously you are afflicted with evils,* and 4.19: *who suffer according to the will of God*—or else he causes evil by administering chastisement, and this is called the evil of punishment. 2 Sam. 12.11: *I shall in justice bring evil upon you, that is, punishment, out of your own house.* Prov. 16.4: *Jehovah has created all things for himself, yes, even the wicked for the day of evil,* that is, the man who later became wicked, by his own fault; as I have already said in connection with Isa. 45.7. Isa. 54.16: *I have created the murderer to destroy;* Lam. 3.38, 39 [. . .]; Amos 3.6 [. . .].

For God, who is supremely good, cannot be the source of wickedness or of the evil of crime: on the contrary, he created good out of man's wickedness; Gen. 45.5: *God sent me before you to provide sustenance,* and 50.20: *you had thought evil, but God thought to turn it to good.*

I am writing not for those who are wholly ignorant of Christian doctrine, but for those who are already fairly well informed. So I may be permitted, while I am on the subject of God's general providence, to anticipate a later stage in my argument and say something about sin, though I have not yet reached the place where I deal with that subject. Even in sin, then, we see God's providence at work, not only in permitting it or withdrawing his grace, but often in inciting sinners to commit sin, hardening their hearts and blinding them.

In inciting: Ex. 9.16: *I have made you oppose me;* Judges 9.23: *God sent an evil spirit between Abimelech and the men of Shechem;* 2 Sam. 12.11, 12: *I shall raise up evil against you; and I will hand over your wives to your neighbor; I shall do this thing,* and

114. *Art of Logic* (Yale 8:229): "For fortune surely is to be placed in heaven, but its name should be changed and it should be called 'divine providence.' "

16.10 [. . .], and 24.1 [. . .]. Compare 1 Chron. 21.1. 1 Kings 22.20 [. . .]; Ps. 105.25 [. . .]; Ezek. 14.9 [. . .].

Hardening their hearts. Ex. 4.21: *I will make his heart stubborn,* similarly 7.6. Deut. 2.30 [. . .]; Josh. 11.20 [. . .]; John 12.39, 40: *they were unable to believe, because Esaias said again, he has hardened their hearts;* Rom. 9.18: *he hardens whom he wishes.*

Blinding them. Deut. 28.28: *Jehovah will strike you with madness and blindness and numbness of heart;* 1 Sam. 16.14 [. . .]; 1 Kings 22.22 [. . .]; Isa. 8.14: *he will be a stumbling block and a rock for them to trip over; a snare and a noose,* and 19.14 [. . .], and 29.10 [. . .]; Matt. 13.13: *I speak to them in parables, because seeing they do not see;* John 12.40: *he has blinded their eyes,* compared with Isa. 6.9. Rom. 1.28: *God gave them up to a mind devoid of all judgment;* 2 Thess. 2.11: *God will send them a powerful delusion, so that they believe a lie.*

Although in these quotations and in many others from both Testaments God openly confesses that it is he who incites the sinner, hardens his heart, blinds him and drives him into error, it must not be concluded that he is the originator even of the very smallest sin, for he is supremely holy. Hos. 14.9: *the ways of Jehovah are straight, and the just shall walk in them; but transgressors shall kick against them;* Ps. 5.5, 6, 7 [. . .]; Rom. 7.8 [. . .]; James 1.13, 14: *let no man say when he is tempted, I am tempted by God: for God cannot be tempted with evil, nor does he tempt anyone; but every man is tempted when he is drawn on and enticed by his own lust,* and 4.1: *where do the wars and fighting among you come from? Do they not come from here, here from your lusts which make war in your members?;* 1 John 2.16 [. . .]. For God does not drive the human heart to sinfulness and deceit when it is innocent and pure and shrinks from sin. But when it has conceived sin, when it is heavy with it, and already giving birth to it, then God as the supreme arbiter of all things turns and points it in this or that direction or towards this or that object. Ps. 94.23: *he turns their own wickedness against them, and destroys them with their own viciousness; Jehovah destroys them*—that is, by his punishment. Neither does God make an evil will out of a good one, but he directs a will which is already evil so that it may produce out of its own wickedness either good for others or punishment for itself, though it does so unknowingly, intending something quite different: Prov. 16.9: *man's mind thinks out his own way, but Jehovah lays down his path.* So when, in Ezek. 21.26, 27, the King of Babylon was in doubt whether to attack the Ammonites or the Jews, God controlled the omens, so that the King chose to set out for Jerusalem. Or, to use the common simile, as a rider who spurs on a lame horse in a chosen direction is the cause of the horse's increased speed but not of its lameness, so God, who is the supreme governor of the whole universe, may urge on a criminal although he is in no sense the cause of his crime. I shall say more about this simile later. Let me give an example: God saw that as a result of his power King David's spirit was so haughty and puffed up that even without anyone inciting him he was on the point of doing something that would unmistakably reveal his pride. This being so, God incited him to number the people. He did not incite him to become vainglorious and swollen with pride, but only to show in this particular way rather than any other that haughtiness of spirit which, though hidden, was on the point of breaking out. So God was the instigator of the deed itself, but David alone was responsible for all the wickedness and pride which it involved. The sinner, then, is nearly always evil or unjust in his aims, but God always produces something good and just out of these and creates, as it were, light out of darkness.[115] To this end he explores a man's innermost thoughts. In other words, he makes a man see clearly the evil which lies hidden in his own heart, so that he may reform or become thoroughly inexcusable in the eyes of the world; or alternatively, so that both the malefactor and his victim may pay the penalty for some previous offence. We should, however, be wary of the common saying, that God punishes sins with sins. He does not do this by forcing or helping anyone to sin, but by taking away his usual light-giving grace and the power to resist sin. There is, to be sure, a proverb which says, he who prevents not when he can, commands.[116] Men are bound by this principle as a moral duty, but not God. God says, speaking like a man, that he incites, when really he only omits to prevent, and this does not mean that he commands, for he is not bound by any moral duty to prevent. Ps. 81.12, 13: *they did not hear me or obey me, so I sent them off to follow their own devices,* and so we find in Rom. 1.24: *because of this he has given them up to filthy lusts,* in other words he left them to be driven by and to follow their own desires. For strictly speaking God does not either incite or hand over someone if he leaves him entirely to himself, that is, to his own desires and devices and to the ceaseless promptings of Satan. It is in the same sense that the Church is said to hand over to Satan a recalcitrant member when really it only excludes him from its communion. As for the business of the numbering of the people by David, it can be explained in a single word, for it is not God but Satan who is said to have incited him, 2 Sam. 24.1, 1 Chron. 21.1. A similar explanation is applicable to that passage in 2 Sam. 12.11, 12: *behold I shall raise up evil against you out of your own house,* the evil, that is, of punishment, and *I will take your wives and hand them over to your neighbor,* that is, I will leave them to your son, for him to debauch, on the advice of Achitophel—for this is what *to hand over* means, as I have just shown. That popular simile of the lame horse is itself a bit lame, because the sinner, unlike the horse, is not simply incited to act, if in fact he is incited at all, but to act badly: in other words, because he is lame he is incited to limp. In both passages cited above God had determined to punish publicly David's secret adultery. He saw Absalom, ready to dash into any kind of wickedness: he saw Achitophel's evil counsels. All he did was to direct their minds, which were already ripe for any atrocity, so that when the opportunity presented itself they should commit one crime rather than another. This is in keeping with the text quoted above,

115. Cp. *PL* 1.211–18: "the will/And high permission of all-ruling Heaven/Left him at large to his own dark designs,/That with reiterated crimes he might/Heap on himself damnation, while he sought/Evil to others, and enraged might see/How all his malice served but to bring forth/Infinite goodness, grace and mercy."

116. Cp. *Tetrachordon* (Yale 2:655): "Where else are all our grave and faithful sayings, that he whose office is to forbid and forbids not, bids, exhorts, encourages."

Prov. 16.9: *man's mind thinks out his own way, but Jehovah lays down his path.* For by offering an opportunity for sin you do not make a sinner, but only reveal one. The fact that God gives a good outcome to every evil deed, contrary to the intentions of the sinner, and overcomes evil with good, is well enough illustrated by the example of the selling of Joseph by his brothers: Gen. 45.8, quoted above.[117] It is the same with Christ's crucifixion. Pilate was anxious not to lose Caesar's favor: the Jews wanted to satisfy their hatred and their thirst for vengeance. But God *whose power and counsel had determined everything that was to be done,* Acts 4.28, redeemed mankind through their cruelty and violence, Rom. 11.11: *through their offence salvation has come to the Gentiles;* 1 Cor. 11.19 [. . .]; Phil. 1.12,14 [. . .].

In the same way, just as when God incites to sin he is nevertheless not the cause of anyone's sinning, so when he hardens the heart of a sinner or blinds him, he is not the cause of sin. For he does not do this by infusing wickedness into the man. The means he uses are just and kindly, and ought rather to soften the hearts of sinners than harden them.[118] They are: first, his long-suffering; Rom. 2.4, 5: *do you despise the wealth of his tolerance, and in your hardness lay up anger for yourself?;* second, his insistence upon his own good and just commandments in opposition to the stubbornness of the wicked. This hardens them in the same way as an anvil or steel is said to be hardened by hammering. Thus Pharaoh became more obstinate and more furious when God's commands ran counter to his will; Ex. 5.2 [. . .] and 7.2, 3 [. . .]; Isa. 6.10: *make the heart of that people grow fat,* that is, by drumming commandments into them, as in 28.13: *but the word of Jehovah gave them command after command, . . . so that they should go on and fall headlong . . . .* Third, correction or punishment, Ezek. 3.20: *but if a righteous man turns away from his righteousness and commits a crime, and I place a stumbling block before him,* etc.; Jer. 5.3: *you strike them but they are not hurt, they have made their faces harder than rock.* Hardening of the heart, then, is usually the last punishment inflicted on inveterate wickedness and unbelief in this life; Sam. 2.25: *they did not listen, because Jehovah wished to kill them.* God often hardens the hearts of powerful and arrogant world-leaders to a remarkable degree so that through their pride and arrogance his glory may be more clearly seen by the nations: Ex. 9.16: *to show my power in you,* and 10.2, also, compared with Rom. 9.17: *I have raised you up for this very purpose, to show my power in you.* Ex. 14.4 [. . .], similarly 14.17. But the hardening of the wicked is not solely God's doing. They themselves do a great deal to bring about God's purpose, though not in the least intending to please him. Thus Pharaoh is said to harden his own heart; Ex. 9.34: *when he saw that the rain had ceased* [. . .] *he continued to sin: for he hardened his heart, he and his servants;* 2 Chron. 36.13 [. . .]; Ps. 95.8 [. . .]; Zech. 7.12 [. . .].

The same applies to blinding: Deut. 28.15 compared with 28: *but it will happen*

117. This verse is *not* quoted previously in the treatise; Milton's claim to the contrary may indicate revision.

118. Cp. *PL* 6.789–91: "But to convince the proud what signs avail,/Or wonders move th' obdurate to relent?/They hardened more by what might most reclaim."

if you do not listen to the voice of Jehovah your God, Jehovah will afflict you with madness and blindness and numbness of heart, that is, by taking away the light of his grace, and by confusing the faculties of the mind or making them dull, or simply by allowing Satan to do this: Rom. 1.28: *just as it did not seem fit to them to acknowledge God, so God gave them up to emptiness of mind;* 2 Cor. 4.4 [...]; Eph. 2.2 [...]; 2 Thess. 2.10, 11 [...]. Lastly, God is said to entice men, but not to sin. He entices them either as punishment, or for the accomplishment of some good end. Ezek. 14.9–11: *but when the prophet himself is enticed into saying something, it will be I, Jehovah, who enticed that prophet: and I will stretch out my hand against* etc. *so they will bear the punishment of their wrongdoing* etc. *so that the house of Israel may not go astray from following me any more.* But God enticed a prophet who was already corrupt and avaricious, and easily misled him into giving the answers which the people wanted. Then he justly destroyed both the questioner, because he had asked his question with an evil intention, and the prophet who had been questioned, because he had answered falsely, without command from God. God did this so that in future others would be afraid to commit the same sin.

To this system of providence must be referred what is called Temptation, by which God either tempts a man or allows him to be tempted by the devil or his agents.

Temptation is either good or evil.

It is evil when God, by the methods outlined above, either withdraws his grace from a man or throws opportunities for sin in his path or hardens his heart or blinds him. This is generally an evil temptation from the point of view of the man tempted, but on God's part it is absolutely just, for the reasons I have given above, as for example when it is used to unmask hypocrisy. For God tempts no one in the sense of enticing or persuading him to sin (see James 1.13 above), although he quite justly allows some men to be tempted by the devil in this way. We are taught to pray against temptations of this kind in the Lord's prayer: Matt. 6.13: *do not lead us into temptation, but deliver us from that evil.*

Good temptations are those which God uses to tempt even righteous men, in order to prove them. He does this not for his own sake—as if he did not know what sort of men they would turn out to be—but either to exercise or demonstrate their faith or patience, as in the case of Abraham and Job, or to lessen their self-confidence and prove them guilty of weakness, so that they may become wiser, and others may be instructed. Thus in 2 Chron. 32.31: *God left* Hezekiah, temporarily or partially, *so that by tempting him he might find out whatever was in his mind.* In the same way he tempted the Israelites in the desert, Deut. 8.2, etc.: *to afflict you, by tempting you to find out what was in your mind, whether you would keep his commandments or not...;* Ps. 66.10, etc. [...]; 1 Pet. 1.7 [...], and 4.12 [...]; Rev. 2.10: *behold, it will happen that the devil will throw some of you into prison, so that you may be tried.*

Good temptation, then, is rather to be desired. Ps. 26.2: *prove me Jehovah and try me, make trial of my reins and my heart;* James 1.2, 3: *esteem it a great joy, my brothers, whenever you fall into various temptations, knowing that the trial of your faith produces patience.*

And God promises a happy outcome. 1 Cor. 10.13: *no temptation has entrapped you, except what is common to man: but God is faithful and will not allow you to be tempted beyond your powers. Along with the temptation he will supply an escape, so that you will be able to bear it;* James 1.12: *blessed is the man who endures temptation; for when he is found righteous, he will receive the crown of life.*

But even the faithful are sometimes insufficiently aware of all these methods of divine providence, until they examine the subject more deeply and become better informed about the word of God. Ps. 73.2, 17: *my feet had almost gone astray, until I went into the sanctuary of God: then I understood their end;* Dan. 12.10 [...]. Since I said in my prefatory definition that the providence of God cares for and governs all created things, it may usefully be asked here whether God has laid down any definite limit to human life, beyond which no one can go. Holy Scripture shows very clearly that this is the case; Job 14.5: *since his days are cut short, the number of his months is in your sight: you have set him limits, which he may not overstep;* Ps. 90.10: *in the days of our years there are seventy years, or (if we are very strong) eighty years, yet the best of them is labor and sorrow; it is quickly cut off and away we fly.* From these and similar passages, and especially from the early history of the world, it is clear that God, at any rate after the fall of man, laid down a certain limit for human life. It is also clear that in the course of the years down to the time of David this limit gradually became smaller. Whether the limit is one and the same for all mortals, or whether it is fixed at a different point for each individual, it is certain that no man can prolong it or exceed it. That is in the power of God alone, as is proved by his promise of long life to his people, and by the fifteen years he added to the life of the dying Hezekiah.[119] As for cutting short or anticipating this term of life, not only does God do it as a reward or punishment, but also any mortal may do it by his guiltiness or vice, and this often happens. Prov. 10.27: *reverence for Jehovah adds to one's days, but the years of the wicked will be cut short;* Ex. 20.12: *honor your father,* etc. *that your days may be prolonged,* etc., and there are many other passages in the Old Testament to the same effect. Ps. 55.24: *bloody and deceitful men shall not live out half their days,* that is, the sum total of days which, by virtue of their strong constitutions, they might otherwise have attained.[120] Suicides, and those who hasten their deaths by a depraved way of life, must also be included in this category.

God's providence is either ordinary or extraordinary.

God's ordinary providence is that by which he maintains and preserves that constant and ordered system of causes which was established by him in the beginning.

This is commonly and indeed too frequently called Nature; for nature cannot mean anything except the wonderful power and efficacy of the divine voice which went forth in the beginning, and which all things have obeyed ever since as a perpetual command. Job 38.12: *have you ever given rules to the morning?,* and 38.33:

119. Cp. *PL* 11.554: "Live well, how long or short permit to Heav'n."
120. Cp. *PL* 11.527–34.

or do you know about the laws of the sky?; Ps. 148.8 [...]; Isa. 45.12 [...]; Jer. 31.36 [...], and 33.20 [...].

The extraordinary providence of God is that by which he produces some effect outside the normal order of nature or gives to some chosen person the power of producing this effect. This is what we call a miracle.

Thus God alone is the primary author of miracles, as he alone is able to invert the order of nature which he has appointed: Ps. 72.18: *who alone works miracles;* John 10.21 [...]; 2 Thess. 2.9 [...].

The purpose of miracles is to demonstrate divine power and strengthen our faith: Ex. 6.6, 7: *with great judgments ..., thus you will find out,* and 8.22: *I will make an exception of the land of Goshen... so that you shall know that I am Jehovah;* 1 Kings 17.24 [...]; Mark 16.20 [...]; Heb. 2.4: *it was confirmed for us, since God bore witness to them with signs and with omens and with various manifestations of power and with gifts of the Holy Ghost, according to his own will.*[121]

Another purpose of miracles is to ensure a weightier condemnation for those who do not believe. Matt. 11.21 [...]; John 15.24: *if I had not performed among them works such as no one else performed, they would not be sinful. But now ....*

CHAPTER 9

OF THE SPECIAL GOVERNMENT OF ANGELS

We have been discussing GENERAL PROVIDENCE. SPECIAL PROVIDENCE is concerned particularly with angels and men, as they are far superior to all other creatures.

There are, however, both good and evil angels. Luke 9.26 and 8.2, for it is well known that a great many of them revolted from God of their own free will before the fall of man: John 8.44: *he did not stand firm in the truth, for there is no truth in him, he speaks like what he is, the father of lies;* 2 Pet. 2.4: *he did not spare the angels who sinned;* Jude 6: *the angels who did not maintain their original position;* 1 John 3.8 [...]; Ps. 106.37 [...].

It seems to some people that the good angels now maintain their position not so much by their own strength as by the grace of God. 1 Tim. 5.21: *of the elect angels,* that is, of those who did not revolt; Eph. 1.10: *that he might collect together all things under a single head in Christ, the things in heaven as well;* Col. 1.20 [...]; Job 4.18 [...], similarly 15.

Hence the angels take great pleasure in examining the mystery of man's salvation: 1 Pet. 1.12: *things which the angels desire to look into;* Eph.3.10 [...]; Luke 2.13, 14: *a multitude of the armies praising God,* that is, on account of the birth of Christ; and 15.10: *there is joy in the presence of the angels over one man who repents.*

As a result, also, they adore Christ: Heb. 1.6: *let all the angels of God adore him;* Matt. 4.11 [...]; Phil. 2.10: *that every knee shall bow, among the heavenly creatures ...;*

121. Cp. *PL* 12.497–504.

2 Thess. 1.7 [. . .]; 1 Pet. 3.22 [. . .]; Rev. 5.11, 12 [. . .]. It seems more reasonable, however, to suppose that the good angels stand by their own strength, no less than man did before his fall, and that they are called "elect" only in the sense that they are beloved or choice:[122] also that they desire to contemplate the mystery of our salvation simply out of love,[123] and not from any interest of their own, that they are not included in any question of reconciliation, and that they are reckoned as being under Christ because he is their head, not their Redeemer.[124] [. . .].

They are absolutely obedient[125] to God in all things: Gen. 28.12: *behold the angels of God ascending and descending on it;* Ps. 103.20: *doing his word;* Zech. 1.10 [. . .].

Their chief ministry concerns believers: Heb. 1.14: *they are all ministering spirits who are sent out to minister for the sake of the heirs of salvation;* Ps. 34.8 [. . .], and 91.11 [. . .]; Isa. 63.9 [. . .]; Matt. 18.10 [. . .], and 13.41 [. . .], and 24.31 [. . .]; Acts 12.15 [. . .]; 1 Cor. 11.10: *on account of the angels,* that is, as some suppose, the angels who guard over the meetings of the faithful. There are innumerable examples available besides these.

And seven of them particularly patrol the earth:[126] Zech. 4.10: *these seven are the eyes of Jehovah which go to and fro over the earth,* compared with Rev. 5.6: *who are those seven spirits of God sent forth into the whole earth,* see also 1.4 and 4.5.

It is probable, too, that angels are put in charge of nations, kingdoms and particular districts:[127] Dan. 4.13, 17: *this word is from the decree of the watchers,* and 12.1: *that prince who stands for your fellow-countrymen,* and 10.13 [. . .]; 2 Pet. 2.11 [. . .]; Gen. 3.24: *to guard the way to the tree of life.*

Sometimes they are ministers of divine vengeance,[128] sent from heaven to punish mortal sins. They destroy cities and peoples: Gen. 19.13; 2 Sam. 24.16; 1 Chron. 21.16: *David saw the angel of Jehovah threatening Jerusalem with a drawn sword.* They strike down whole armies with unexpected calamity: 2 Kings 19.35, and similar passages.

As a result they often appeared looking like soldiers: Gen. 32.1, 2: *God's battle-array;* Josh. 6.2: *leader of Jehovah's soldiery;* 2 Kings 6.17: *with horses and chariots of fire;* Ps. 68.18 [. . .]; Luke 2.13 [. . .].

They are also described in Isa. 6; Hos. 1.7; Matt. 28.2, 3; Rev. 10.1.

There seems to be a leader among the good angels, and he is often called

122. Cp. *PL* 4.66–67: "Hadst thou the same free will and power to stand?/Thou hadst."

123. Cp. *PL* 8.224–26: "Nor less think we in Heav'n of thee on Earth/Than of our fellow servant, and inquire/Gladly into the ways of God with man"; 8:639–40: "I in thy persevering shall rejoice,/And all the blest."

124. Cp. *PL* 5.606: "your head I him appoint"; also 5.830–31: "under one head more near/United."

125. **absolutely obedient:** The Latin original reads *"obsequentissimi."*

126. Cp. *PL* 3.648–61.

127. Cp. *PR* 1.447–48: "his angels president/In every province"; also *PL* 4.561–63: "Gabriel, to thee thy course by lot hath giv'n/Charge and strict watch that to this happy place/No evil thing approach or enter in."

128. Cp. *PL* 1.170: "His ministers of vengeance."

Michael: Josh. 6.2: *I am the leader of Jehovah's soldiery;* Dan. 10.13: *Michael is the first of the chief princes,*[129] and 12.1: *the greatest prince;* Rev. 12.7, 8 [...].

A lot of people are of the opinion that Michael is Christ. But whereas Christ alone vanquished Satan and trod him underfoot, Michael is introduced as leader of the angels and Ἀντίπαλος (antagonist) of the prince of the devils: their respective forces were drawn up in battle array and separated after a fairly even fight,[130] Rev. 12.7, 8. And Jude says of Michael *when disputing about Moses' body he did not dare* [...], whereas it would be quite improper to say this about Christ, especially if he is God. See also 1 Thess. 4.16: *the Lord himself will descend with the voice of an archangel.* Finally, it would be very strange for an apostle of the Gospel to talk in such an obscure way, and to call Christ by another name, when reporting these odd and unheard-of things about him.

The good angels do not see into all God's thoughts, as the Papists pretend. They know by revelation only those things which God sees fit to show them, and they know other things by virtue of their very high intelligence, but there are many things of which they are ignorant.[131] For we find an angel full of curiosity and asking questions: Dan. 8.13: *how long is this vision?,* and 12.6: *how far off is its end?;* Matt. 24.36: *no one knows of that day, not even the angels;* Eph. 3.10 [...]; Rev. 5.3 [...].

Bad angels are kept for punishment: Matt. 8.29: *have you come here to torment us before the appointed time?;* 2 Pet. 2.4: *he thrust them down to hell and chained them in dark chains, to be kept for damnation;* Jude 6: [...]; 1 Cor. 6.3 [...]; Matt. 25.41 [...]; Rev. 20.10 [...].

But sometimes they are able to wander all over the earth, the air, and even heaven, to carry out God's judgments:[132] Job 1.7: *from going to and fro on the earth;* 1 Sam. 16.15: *the spirit of Jehovah had left Saul, and an evil spirit from Jehovah troubled him;* 1 Pet. 5.8: [...]; John 12.31: [...]; 2 Cor. 4.4 [...]; Matt. 12.43 [...]; Eph. 2.2 [...], and 6.12 [...]. They even come into the presence of God:[133] Job 1.6 and 2.1; 1 Kings 22.21 [...]; Zech. 3.1: *he showed me Joshua standing in the presence of the angel of Jehovah, and Satan standing at his right hand to oppose him;* Luke 10.18 [...]; Rev. 12.12 [...].

But their proper place is hell, which they cannot leave without permission:[134] Luke 8.31: *they asked him not to command them to go away to hell;* Matt. 12.43:

129. Cp. *PL* 6.44: "Go Michael of celestial armies prince."

130. Michael was traditionally represented as Satan's vanquisher. But the action of *PL 6* is consistent with the idiosyncratic version of the War in Heaven presented here.

131. Cp. *PL* 3.681–85; 7.112–13; 11.67–69.

132. Cp. *PL* 1.209–13: "the Arch-Fiend lay/Chained on the burning lake, nor ever thence/Had ris'n or heaved his head, but that the will/And high permission of all-ruling Heav'n/Left him at large to his own dark designs." Also 2.1025; 7.233–37; and *PR* 1.362–77.

133. Cp. *PR* 1.366–67: "nor from the Heav'n of Heav'ns/Hath he excluded my resort sometimes."

134. Cp. *PR* 1:494–96: "Thy coming hither, though I know thy scope,/I bid not or forbid; do as thou find'st/Permission from above; thou canst not more."

seeking rest through dry places; Mark 5.10 [...]; Rev. 20.3 [...]. They cannot do anything unless God commands them:[135] Job 1.12: *look, let them be in your power;* Matt. 8.31: *allow us to go away into this herd of swine;* Rev. 20.2: *he seized the dragon and bound him.*

Their knowledge is great, but it is a torment to them rather than a consolation; so that they utterly despair of their salvation:[136] Matt. 8.29: *what have we to do with you, Jesus? Have you come here to torment us before the appointed time?,* similarly Luke 4.34; James 2.19: *the devils believe and are horrified*—because they are kept for punishment, as I said before.

The devils have their prince too: Matt. 12.24: *Beelzebub prince of devils,* similarly Luke 11.15; Matt. 25.41: *for the devil and his angels;* Rev. 12.9: *that great dragon and his angels.*

They also keep their ranks: Col. 2.15: *having plundered principalities and powers;* Eph. 6.12: *against powers and principalities.*

Their chief is the author of all wickedness and hinders all good:[137] Job 1 and 2; Zech. 3.1: *Satan;* John 8.44: *the father of lies;* 1 Thess. 2.18 [...]; Acts 5.3 [...]; Rev. 20.3, 8 [...]; Eph. 2.2 [...].

As a result he has been given a number of titles, which suit his actions. He is frequently called *Satan,* that is, enemy or adversary, Job 1.6, 1 Chron. 21.1: also *the great dragon, the old serpent, the devil,* that is, the calumniator, Rev. 12.9 [...].

CHAPTER 10

OF THE SPECIAL GOVERNMENT OF MAN BEFORE THE FALL: DEALING ALSO WITH THE SABBATH AND MARRIAGE

The providence of God which governs man relates either to man's prelapsarian or to his fallen state.

The providence which relates to his prelapsarian state is that by which God placed man in the garden of Eden and supplied him with every good thing necessary for a happy life. And, so that there might be some way for man to show his obedience, God ordered him to abstain only from the tree of the knowledge of good and evil, and threatened him with death if he disobeyed: Gen. 1.28: *subdue the earth and have dominion,* and 2.15, 16, 17: *he placed him in the garden. You may eat freely the fruit of every tree. On the day you eat the fruit of the tree of the knowledge of good and evil, you will die.*

Some people call this "the covenant of works," though it does not appear

135. Cp. *PR* 1.451–52: "thou with trembling fear,/Or like a fawning parasite obey'st."

136. Cp. *PR* 3.204–15.

137. Cp. *PL* 6.262: "Author of evil"; 2.380–82: "for whence,/But from the author of all ill could spring/ So deep a malice"; 1.159–60: "To do aught good never will be our task,/But ever to do ill our sole delight."

from any passage of scripture to have been either a covenant or of works.[138] Adam was not required to perform any works; he was merely forbidden to do one thing. It was necessary that one thing at least should be either forbidden or commanded, and above all something which was in itself neither good nor evil, so that man's obedience might in this way be made evident. For man was by nature good and holy, and was naturally disposed to do right, so it was certainly not necessary to bind him by the requirements of any covenant to something which he would do of his own accord. And he would not have shown obedience at all by performing good works, since he was in fact drawn to these by his own natural impulses, without being commanded. Besides a command, whether it comes from God or from a magistrate, should not be called a covenant just because rewards and punishments are attached: it is rather a declaration of power.

The tree of the knowledge of good and evil was not a sacrament, as is commonly thought, for sacraments are meant to be used, not abstained from; but it was a kind of pledge or memorial of obedience.[139]

It was called the tree of knowledge of good and evil because of what happened afterwards: for since it was tasted, not only do we know evil, but also we do not even know good except through evil.[140] For where does virtue shine, where is it usually exercised, if not in evil?

I do not know whether the tree of life ought to be called a sacrament, rather than a symbol of eternal life or even perhaps the food of eternal life: Gen. 3.22: *lest he eat and live for ever;* [141] Rev. 2.7: *to the victor I will give food from the tree of life.*

Man was made in the image of God, and the whole law of nature was so implanted and innate in him that he was in need of no command. It follows, then, that if he received any additional commands, whether about the tree of knowledge or about marriage, these had nothing to do with the law of nature, which is itself sufficient to teach whatever is in accord with right reason (i.e., whatever is intrinsically good). These commands, then, were simply a matter of what is called positive right. Positive right comes into play when God, or anyone else invested with lawful power, commands or forbids things which, if he had not commanded or forbidden them, would in themselves have been neither good nor bad, and would therefore have put no one under any obligation.[142] As for the Sabbath, it is clear that God sanctified it as his own, in memory of the

138. According to Calvin (*Institutes* 2.9–11), salvation history may be understood as a series of covenants between God and humanity. In *"the covenant of works,"* God promises life in return for humanity's obedience and establishes death as the penalty for disobedience. In Milton's England, the Independent divine John Owen (1616–83) was a proponent of "Covenant Theology."

139. Cp. *PL* 3.94–95: "the sole command,/Sole pledge of his obedience"; 8.323–25: "the tree whose operation brings/Knowledge of good and ill, which I have set/The pledge of thy obedience and thy faith."

140. Cp. *Areop* (p. 187).

141. Cp. *PL* 11.93–96: "Lest therefore his now bolder hand/Reach also of the Tree of Life, and eat,/And live forever, dream at least to live/Forever"; see also 4.194–201.

142. Cp. *PL* 9.651–54: "But of this tree we may not taste nor touch;/God so commanded, and left that command/Sole daughter of his voice; the rest, we live/Law to ourselves, our reason is our law."

completion of his task, and dedicated it to rest;[143] Gen. 2.2, 3, compared with Ex. 31.17. But it is not known, because there is nothing about it in scripture, whether this was ever disclosed to Adam or whether any commandment about the observance of the Sabbath existed before the giving of the law on Mount Sinai, let alone before the fall of man. Probably Moses, who seems to have written the book of Genesis long after the giving of the law, inserted this sentence from the fourth commandment in what was, as it were, an opportune place. Thus he seized an opportunity of reminding the people about the reason, which was, so to speak, topical at this point in his narrative, but which God had really given many years later to show why he wanted the Sabbath to be observed by his people, with whom he had at long last made a solemn covenant. For an example of a similar insertion see Ex. 16.34, 35: *Moses said to Aaron, take a pot . . . So Aaron set it up . . .*—which, however, happened long afterwards. We read in Ex. 16 that, shortly before the giving of the law, it was commanded that the Sabbath should be observed in the wilderness; for God had said that he would rain manna on every day except the seventh, so that no one should go out to look for it on that day. Judging from a comparison of 16.5 with 16.22–30, it seems that this command was first given to the Israelites at that time, as a kind of groundwork for the law which was going to be promulgated more clearly a little later on, and that they were previously ignorant about the observation of the Sabbath. For the elders, who ought to have known the commandment about the Sabbath better than anyone else, wondered why the people had gathered twice as much manna on the sixth day, and asked Moses, who told them only then, as if it were something new, that tomorrow would be the Sabbath. So he writes, as if he had just narrated how the Sabbath first came to be observed, *thus the people rested on the seventh day,* 16.30.

More than one passage in the prophets seems to confirm that the Israelites had not even heard anything about the Sabbath before that time: Ezek. 20.10–12: *I led them away into the wilderness; where I gave them my statutes and made my laws known to them. Also I gave them my sabbaths, to be a sign between me and them, that they might know that I, Jehovah, sanctify them;* Neh. 9.13, 14 [. . .]. But see Book 2 Chapter 7 for more on the subject of the Sabbath.

Marriage also, if it was not commanded, was at any rate instituted, and consisted in the mutual love, delight, help and society of husband and wife, though with the husband having greater authority:[144] Gen. 2.18: *it is not good for the man to be alone; I will make him a help before his eyes, as it were;* 1 Cor. 11.7–9: *since the man is the image and glory of God, but the woman is the glory of her husband. For the man did not come from the woman, but the woman from the man: so the man was not given for the woman's sake but the woman for the man's.* The husband's authority became still

143. Cp. *PL* 7.591–93: "and from work/Now resting, blessed and hallowed the sev'nth day,/As resting on that day from all his work."

144. Cp. *PL* 4.635–37: "My author and disposer, what thou bidd'st/Unargued I obey; so God ordains,/God is thy Law, thou mine." See also 4.295–309, 440–43; 10.146–51; 11.632–34.

greater after the fall:[145] Gen. 3.16: *your desire or your obedience will be towards your husband.* So in Hebrew the same word, בַּעַל, means both *husband* and *lord.* Thus Sarah is said, 1 Pet. 3.6, to have called her husband Abraham *lord.* 1 Tim. 2.12–14: *I do not allow a woman to teach or to usurp authority over a man; she should be silent. For Adam was made first, then Eve; and Adam was not deceived, but the woman was deceived and was the cause of the transgression.*

Marriage, then, is a very intimate relationship between man and woman instituted by God for the procreation of children or the help and solace of life. As a result it is written, Gen. 2.24: *so a man will leave his father and mother and cling to his wife, and they will be one flesh.* This is neither a law nor a commandment, but an effect or natural consequence of that very intimate relationship which would have existed between Adam and Eve in man's unfallen state. Nothing is being discussed in the passage except the origin of families. In my definition I have not said, as most people do, *between one man and one woman.* I have not done so, in order to avoid accusing the most holy patriarchs and pillars of our faith, Abraham, and others who had more than one wife, of constant fornication and adultery. Otherwise I should be forced to exclude from God's sanctuary as bastards all their most holy offspring, all the children of Israel, in fact, for whom the sanctuary itself was made. For it is written, Deut. 23.2: *a bastard shall not come into the congregation of Jehovah, even to his tenth generation.*

So either polygamy is a true form of marriage, or else all children born in it are bastards: and that means the whole race of Jacob, the twelve holy tribes chosen by God. But it would be absolutely absurd and even downright blasphemous to suggest this. Also it is very unjust, and a very dangerous precedent in religion to consider something a sin when it is not a sin. So I am of the opinion that it is not irrelevant but on the contrary absolutely vital to find out whether polygamy is lawful or not.

Those who deny its lawfulness try to prove their case from Gen. 2.24: *he will cling to his wife and they will be one flesh,* compared with Matt. 19.5: *those two will be one flesh. He will cling* they say *to his wife* not *to his wives;* and *those two* not *those several people.* Brilliant! Let me add also Ex. 20.17: *you shall not covet your neighbor's house nor his manservant nor his maidservant nor his ox nor his ass:* therefore no one has more than one house, manservant, maidservant, ox or ass! How ridiculous it would be to argue like this—it says *house* not *houses, servant* not *servants* and even *neighbor's* not *neighbors'*—and not to realize that in nearly all the commandments the singular of the noun signifies not the number but the species of each thing mentioned. As for the fact that Matt. 19.5 says *those two* and not *those several people,* it must be understood that this passage deals only with one man and with the wife whom he wanted to divorce, and that it is in no way concerned with whether he had one wife or several. Then again, it must be understood that marriage is a kind of relationship and that there are only two sides to any one

145. Cp. *PL* 10.195–96: "and to thy husband's will/Thine shall submit, he over thee shall rule"; also 11.290–91.

relationship. So that in the same way, if anyone has a number of sons, his paternal relationship towards them all will be various, but towards each one it will be single and complete in itself. Similarly, if anyone has several wives, his relationship towards each one will be no less complete, and the husband will be no less *one flesh* with each one of them, than if he had only one wife.[146] So it is correctly said of Abraham, with Sarah and with Hagar respectively, that *these two were one flesh.* And with good reason, for anyone who associates with prostitutes, however many they may be, is still said to be *one flesh* with each of them. 1 Cor. 6.16: *do you not know that he who couples with a prostitute is one body with her? For those two,* he says, *will be one flesh.* So this expression may be used about a husband, even though he has several wives, just as correctly as if he had only one; and may be understood in the same sense as if he had only one. It follows, then, that polygamy is neither forbidden nor opposed by this so-called commandment which, as I have shown above, is not really a commandment at all. Otherwise we must assume either that the Mosaic law contradicts this instruction, or else that though the relevant passage had been frequently studied by innumerable priests, Levites and prophets and by very holy men of all ranks who were most acceptable to God, nevertheless they were so wanting in reason that they were swept by a blind impulse to this passion for constant fornication. This is what we must assume if the effect of the instruction we are considering is to make polygamy an unlawful form of marriage.

The second text quoted to prove polygamy unlawful is Lev. 18.18: *you shall not take a woman to her sister, to make enemies of them and to uncover her nakedness, besides the other in her lifetime.* Here Junius translates *a woman to another woman,* instead of *a woman to her sister,* so that with this interpretation, which is plainly forced and inadmissible, he should have some grounds for proving polygamy unlawful. But in drawing up laws, as in writing definitions, it is necessary to use precise words and to interpret them properly, not in any metaphorical way. He claims, however, that these words are found elsewhere in the sense he gives them. I confess that they are, but in a context where there can be no ambiguity, as in Gen. 26.31: *they swore, each man to his brother,* that is, to the other man. For who would think of arguing from this that Isaac was Abimelich's brother? And who could fail to conclude that the Leviticus passage was clearly about not taking one sister in marriage after another, especially in a chapter where the verses which immediately precede this deal with the degrees of kinship to which marriage is forbidden? Moreover by taking one sister in marriage after another, *nakedness is*

146. *Art of Logic* (Yale 8:259): "Nor do I any more see why in one singular relative there cannot be a multiple relation to many things, provided that there be numerically only one relation between two things and that it be considered as many times as there are relatives; the relation of father certainly as many times as there are children; of child as there are parents, namely father and mother; of brother as there are brothers and sisters."

uncovered, which is what this passage warns against.[147] If it is another woman who is taken, not the sister of nor related to the first, then there is no need for this caution, because in this case no nakedness would be uncovered. Lastly, why is *in her lifetime* added? Because, though there could not be any doubt that it was permissible, after the death of one wife, to marry another who was not her sister nor related to her, there could be some doubt whether it was permissible to marry the first wife's sister. But, my opponent objects, marriage with a wife's sister is already forbidden by analogy in 18.16, so this prohibition is superfluous. I reply, first, that there is no analogy, for by marrying a brother's wife, the brother's nakedness is uncovered, but by marrying a wife's sister it is not a sister's nakedness but only that of a relation by marriage which is uncovered. Secondly, if nothing may be prohibited which has already been prohibited by analogy, why, after marriage with one's father has been forbidden, is marriage with one's mother forbidden as well? Why forbid marriage with one's mother's sister after forbidding it with one's father's sister? If such prohibitions are unnecessary it must be concluded that more than half the laws relating to incest are unnecessary. Moreover if polygamy were really forbidden by this passage, much stronger reasons ought to have been given—reasons affecting the institution itself, as was done in the establishment of the Sabbath—whereas the chief reason suggested here is the prevention of enmity.

The third passage which is adduced, Deut. 17.17, does not condemn polygamy either in a king or in anyone else, indeed it expressly allows it, while merely imposing a limit to it in the same way as it imposes a limit to the keeping of horses or the accumulation of wealth. This is clear from the verse cited and the previous one.

Except for the three passages, which are actually irrelevant, no trace of the censure of polygamy can be seen throughout the whole law. Nor, for that matter, can any be found even in all the writings of the prophets, although they interpreted the law very severely, and were constantly censuring the vices of the people. The one exception is a passage in Malachi, the last of the prophets, which some people think utterly destroys the case for polygamy. It would be a real *volte-face* and a long-delayed one at that if a thing which ought to have been prohibited many centuries before was prohibited at long last only after the Babylonian captivity. If it really had been a sin, how could it have escaped the censure of all the prophets who preceded Malachi? What we can be sure of is

147. Franciscus *Junius* (1545–1602) was a French Huguenot theologian. He and John Immanuel Tremellius (1510–80), an Italian Jewish convert to Christianity, published a Latin translation of the Bible from Syriac and Hebrew (Frankfurt, 1579).The critique of Junius's translation is apt, but Milton's reading of the phrase "nakedness is uncovered" seems oddly figurative after his warning about metaphor. In modern translation (*Revised English Bible*), Lev. 18.18 states: "You must not take a woman who is your wife's sister to make her a rival wife, and to have intercourse with her during her sister's lifetime." The point of the prohibition, it seems, is not to warn against uncovering nakedness but, as Milton recognizes at the end of the paragraph, to prevent enmity between sisters.

that if polygamy is not forbidden in the law then it is not forbidden here either, because Malachi did not write a new law. But let us take a look at the words themselves, as Junius translates them, 2.15: *nonne unum effecit? Quamvis reliqui spiritus ipsi essent: quid autem unum?*—[*did he not make one? although the remains of the spirit were his: but why one?*]. It would certainly be far too rash and dangerous to make up one's mind on such an important point, and to impose an article of faith upon one's fellow men, on the evidence of such an obscure passage as this: a passage which various interpreters twist and turn in so many different ways. But whatever the words *nonne unum effecit* mean, what do they prove? Does *unum* mean "one woman"; and does the passage therefore establish the fact that a man should marry only one woman? No, because the word is the wrong gender; and as a matter of fact it is the wrong case as well, because nearly all the other translators render the passage: *annon unus fecit? et residuum spiritus ipsi? et quid ille unus?*—[*did not one make? and is not the rest of the spirit his? and why that one?*] We cannot, then, force a condemnation of polygamy from this very obscure passage, and no such doctrine is mentioned anywhere else, or only in doubtful terms. What we should derive from the passage, rather, is something which we can find all through the scriptures, and which is the chief subject of this very chapter from verse eleven onwards, namely a condemnation of marriage with the daughter of an alien god. As Ezra and Nehemia show it was very common at that time for the Jews to defile themselves by such marriages.

As for the words of Christ, Matt. 5.32 and 19.5, he repeats the passage from Gen. 2.24 in order to condemn not polygamy but unlicensed divorce, which is a very different matter; and you have to wrench his words if you want to make them fit polygamy. Some people argue from Matt. 5.32 that if a man who marries another wife after rejecting his first commits adultery, then he does so much more certainly if he marries another and keeps his first wife. But this argument is adulterate itself, and ought itself to be rejected. For in the first place, it is the actual precepts that bind us, not the consequences deduced from them by human reasoning: for what seems to be a reasonable deduction to one person may not seem so to another, though equally intelligent. Secondly, a man who rejects his first wife and marries another, is not said to commit adultery because he marries another, but because when he married the second wife he did not keep the first though he ought to have behaved like a dutiful husband to her as well. So Mark 10.11 says quite plainly: *he commits adultery against her.* Moreover God himself teaches that it is possible to behave like a dutiful husband towards the first wife, even after marrying a second, Ex. 21.10: *if he takes another wife he shall not diminish her food, her clothing or her portion of time*—and God did not make his provisions for adulterers.

It is not correct to argue from 1 Cor. 7.2: *let every man have his own wife,* that he should therefore not have more than one. The text says that he should have *his own* wife, meaning that he should keep her for himself, not that she should be the only one. Bishops and priests are explicitly required to have only one wife, 1 Tim. 3.2 and Tit. 1.6: *let them be husbands of one wife;* I suppose this was so that they could carry out the ecclesiastical duties which they had undertaken more diligently. And the requirement itself shows plainly enough that polygamy was not forbidden to other people, and that it was common in the church at that time.

Lastly, as for the argument which is based on 1 Cor. 7.4: *but in the same way the husband does not have power over his own body, but the wife does,* this is quickly answered by pointing out, as before, that the word *wife* here refers to species not number. Furthermore, the wife's power over her husband's body cannot be different now from what it was under the law, and in Hebrew this power is called עוֹנָת, Ex. 21.10, which means *her appointed time.* In the present chapter the same idea is expressed by the phrase *due benevolence,* but the Hebrew word makes it quite clear what *due* means.[148]

On the other hand, the following texts clearly admit polygamy: Ex. 21.10: *if he takes another wife he shall not diminish her food, her clothing, or her portion of time;* Deut. 17.17: *let him not increase his wives, lest his heart turn from me.* Who would have worded this law so loosely, if it were not meant to grant more than one wife? And who would be so bold as to add to this: therefore let him have only one? The previous verse says *let him not increase his horses,* so shall we add to that: therefore he must have only one horse? We know well enough that the first institution of marriage applied to the king as well as his people: if it allows only one wife, then it does not allow more even to the king. Moreover the reason given for the law is *lest his heart turn from me*—a danger which might arise if he were to marry a great many wives, especially foreign ones, as Solomon afterwards did. But if this law was meant as a renewal of the first institution of marriage, what could have been more appropriate than to have cited that institution here, instead of giving only this other reason?

Let us listen to God himself, the author of the law, and his own best interpreter: 2 Sam. 12.8: *I have handed over your master's wives into your breast: and if they were not enough I would have added such and such things.* There is no escape here: God gave wives: he gave them to the man he loved among a number of other great benefits: he would have given more if these had not been enough. Besides, the very argument which God uses against David is more forceful when applied to the gift of wives than to any other: you should at least have abstained from another man's wife, not so much because I had given you your master's house or his kingdom, as because I had given you the royal wives. But, says Beza, therefore David committed incest, with the wives of his father-in-law. Beza forgets, however, a point which is made clear by Esther 2.12, 13, that the kings had two harems, one for virgins and the other for concubines, and it is understood that David was given the former, not the latter. This is evident from 1 Kings 1.4 as well: *the king did not know her;* Song of Solomon 6.8: *eighty concubines and countless virgins.* Although as a matter of fact God could be said to have given

148. Cp. *PL* 10.994: "love's due rites, nuptial embraces sweet." *Due* in the phrase *due benevolence* includes the sense "belonging to by right."

him his master's wives if he had given him not necessarily the same wives, but as many wives as his master had, and similar ones. In the same way he did not give him the actual house and retinue of his master, but a house and retinue equally royal and magnificent.

The law itself, then, and even the authority of God's own voice, wholly approve of this practice. So it is not surprising that the holy prophets should speak of it in their divine hymns as something absolutely honorable: Ps. 45.10, (which is called "A Song of Sweethearts"): *kings' daughters among your dear ones,* and 15, 16: *after her the virgins, her friends, shall be brought to you.* Indeed the words of these sweethearts are quoted by the apostle, Heb. 1.7, etc.: *to the Son, Your throne, O God,* as the words of God himself to his Son; and no words anywhere in scripture attribute godhead to the Son more clearly than these words of theirs. Would it have been proper for God the Father to speak through the mouths of prostitutes and reveal the godhead of his holy Son to men through the love-songs of whores? So, too, in the Song of Solomon, 6.8, 9, 10, both queens and concubines are clearly given honorable mention, and are all considered worthy to sing the praises of the bride: *sixty queens and eighty concubines and countless virgins: the queens will bless that only one and the concubines will praise her, saying . . .* Nor should we forget that passage in 2 Chron. 24.2, 3: *and during the whole lifetime of Jehoiada the priest, Joash did what was right in the sight of the Jehovah, and Jehoiada took two wives for him.* For here the two facts, that he did what was right on the instructions of Jehoiada, and that on Jehoiada's authority he married two wives, are not stated in isolation or in opposition to each other, but in conjunction. In eulogies of kings, if anything which was less admirable than the rest was added on at the end, it was usually explicitly excepted from what went before, contrary to what is done here: thus 1 Kings 15.5: *except in the matter of Uriah,* and 11, 14: *and Asa did what was right . . . though the high places were not removed; nevertheless Asa's heart was perfect.* The fact that Joash's bigamy is mentioned straight after his right conduct, without any exception being made, indicates, then, that it was not considered wrong. For the sacred writer would not have missed such a convenient opportunity for making an exception in the customary way if there had been anything less deserving of commendation than the rest.

Moreover God himself in Ezek. 23.4 says that he has taken two wives, Aholah and Aholibah. He would certainly not have spoken about himself like this at such great length, not even in a parable, nor adopted this character or likeness at all, if the thing itself had been intrinsically dishonorable or base.

But how can anything be dishonorable or base when it is forbidden to no one, even under the gospel (for that dispensation does not annul any of the merely civil regulations which existed previous to its introduction)? The only stipulation made is that priests and deacons should be chosen from among men who had only one wife; see 1 Tim. 3 and Tit. 1.6, cited above. And this is stipulated not because it would be a sin to marry more than one wife, for then it would have been forbidden to everyone else as well, but so that priests and deacons should be less involved in household affairs and therefore more at leisure to attend to the business of the church. Since then polygamy is forbidden here only to ecclesiastics, and even then not because it is a sin, and since neither here nor anywhere else is it forbidden to any other members of the church, it follows that it was permitted to all other members of the church, as I said before, and that it was adopted by many without offence.

Lastly, I argue as follows from Heb. 13.4: polygamy is either marriage or fornication or adultery—for the apostle admits no halfway state between these. Let no one dare to say that it is fornication or adultery: the shame this would bring upon so many patriarchs who were polygamists will, I hope, prevent anyone from doing so. For *God will judge fornicators and adulterers,* whereas he loved the patriarchs above all, and declared that they were very dear to him. If, then, polygamy is nothing but marriage, it must, in the opinion of the same apostle, be lawful and honorable as well: *marriage is honorable for all, and the bed unstained.* [. . .][149]

The form of marriage consists in the mutual goodwill, love, help and solace of husband and wife, as the institution itself, or its definition, shows.

The end of marriage is almost the same as the form. Its proper fruit is the procreation of children. Since the fall of Adam, the relief of sexual desire has become a kind of secondary end: 1 Cor. 7.2.

So not everyone is bound by the command to marry, but only those who cannot live chastely and continently outside marriage: Matt. 19.11: *not all are able.*

Marriage is intrinsically honorable, and it is not forbidden to any order of men. So, the Papists are wrong to prohibit their priests from marrying: it is allowable for anyone to marry:[150] Heb. 13.4: *marriage is honorable in all;* Gen. 2.24; 1 Cor. 9.5 [. . .]; 1 Tim. 3.2 [. . .], and 3.4 [. . .].

Marriage is, by definition, a union of the most intimate kind, but it is not indissoluble or indivisible. Some people argue that it is, on the grounds that in Matt. 19.5 the words *those two will be one flesh* are added. But these words, rightly considered, do not mean that marriage is absolutely indissoluble, only that it should not be easily dissolved. For this mention of the indissolubility of marriage, whether it is given as a command, or to describe a natural consequence, depends upon what has gone before (i.e., the institution of marriage itself and the due observation of each of its parts). So we find it written: *for this reason he will leave . . . and they will be one flesh*—if, in other words, the wife, according to the institution described in the preceding verses, Gen. 2.18, 20, is a *fit help* for the husband: that is, if goodwill, love, help, solace and fidelity are firm on both sides, which, as all admit, is the essential form of marriage. But when the form is dissolved it follows that the marriage must really be dissolved as well.

149. The deleted passage presents a long list of holy men in Scripture with more than one wife and then, in a series of short paragraphs, considers various impediments to marriage, from incest to difference in religion.

150. Cp. *PL* 4.744–49: "Whatever hypocrites austerely talk/Of purity and place and innocence,/ Defaming as impure what God declares/Pure, and commands to some, leaves free to all./Our Maker bids increase; who bids abstain/But our destroyer, foe to God and man?"

My opponents emphasize above all those words in Matt. 19.6: *what God has joined together, let no man separate.* The institution of marriage itself shows clearly what it is that God has joined together. He has joined together things compatible, fit, good and honorable: he has not joined chalk and cheese: he has not joined things base, wretched, ill-omened and disastrous. It is violence or rashness or error or some evil genius which joins things like this, not God.

What is there, then, to prevent us from getting rid of an evil so distressing and so deep-seated?

This will not be to separate those whom God has joined together, by his most holy institution, but those whom he has himself separated by his no less holy law: a law which should carry the same weight now as it did with his people of old. As for my opponents' argument about Christian perfection, perfection is not to be forced upon men by penal laws but only encouraged by Christian admonition. It is certainly only a man who does the separating, when he adds to God's law things which the law does not command, and then under cover of the law separates whom he thinks fit. For it should be remembered that God in his most holy, just and pure law has not only allowed divorce on various grounds, but has even, on some occasions, sanctioned it and on others very firmly insisted upon it: Ex. 21.4, 10, 11; Deut. 21.14 and 24.1; Ezra 10.3; Neh. 13.23, 30.

But, say my opponents, he did this *because of the hardness of their hearts,* Matt. 19.8. My answer is that Christ is here making a reply appropriate to the occasion. The Pharisees were tempting him, and his intention, as usual, was to deflate their arrogance and avoid their snares.[151] But he had no intention of giving an explanation of the question of divorce in general. He is replying only to those who, on the grounds of Deut. 24.1, taught that it was lawful to divorce a wife for any reason at all, so long as a bill of divorce was given. This is clear from the same chapter, Matt. 19.3:[152] *is it lawful for every cause?*—because a lot of people were giving bills of divorce not for the single reason allowed by Moses (i.e., the discovery of some uncleanness in the woman that might turn love into hatred), but merely on the pretext of uncleanness, without any just cause. Since, however, the law was not able to convict these people, Christ considered that they ought to be tolerated, although they were hard-hearted, rather than that earthly marriages should be indissoluble. For in his opinion marriage was of so much importance in life as a source either of happiness or of misery.

151. Cp. *DDD* (p. 136): "The occasion which induced our Savior to speak of divorce, was either to convince the extravagance of the Pharisees in that point, or to give a sharp and vehement answer to a tempting question."

152. Cp. *Tetrachordon* (Yale 2:642): "The manner of these men coming to our Savior, not to learn, but to tempt him, may give us to expect that their answer will be such as is fittest for them, not so much a teaching, as an entangling. No man though never so willing or so well enabled to instruct, but if he discern his willingness and candor made use of to entrap him, will suddenly draw in himself, and laying aside the facile vein of perspicuity, will know his time to utter clouds and riddles. . . . This the Pharisees held, that for every cause they might divorce, for every accidental cause, any quarrel or difference that might happen."

The fact is that if we examine the causes of divorce one by one, we shall find that divorce was always sanctioned for an absolutely just and sufficient reason, and not as a concession to hard-heartedness at all. The first passage is Ex. 21.1–4: *these are the judgments which you shall set before them. When you buy a Hebrew slave . . . in the seventh year he shall go free, without paying anything. If he is married, then his wife shall go with him. If his master has given him a wife, and she has borne him sons or daughters, the wife and her children shall be the master's, and the man shall go by himself.* What could be more just? This law certainly did not make allowances for hardness of heart but, on the contrary, opposed it. For it prevented a Hebrew slave, however much he had cost, from being a slave for more than seven years: at the same time it preferred the right of the master to that of the husband.[153] Again, 21.10, 11: *if he takes another wife, he shall not diminish her food, her clothing or her portion of time. If he does not maintain these three things, then she shall go free without payment.* Who can fail to appreciate the supreme humanity and justice of this law? The husband is not allowed to divorce his wife merely because of his hard heart; but on the other hand the wife is allowed to leave her husband if he is harsh and inhuman, which is a very just reason indeed. Again (Deut. 21.13, 14), it is permissible by the right of war and of property both to marry and to divorce a female captive; but it is not permissible either to sell her after divorcing her, or to keep her for profit, both of which would have been a concession to hard-heartedness.[154] The third passage is Deut. 24.1: *if anyone marries a wife and becomes her husband, and it happens that she does not find favor in his eyes, because he has found some nakedness or shameful thing in her, he shall write her a bill of divorce and give it to her, and send her out of his house.* Here, if the cause is a real one, not a mere fiction, what hardness of heart can there be? For it is clear from the institution of marriage itself that when God originally gave man a wife he intended her to be his help, solace and delight.[155] So if, as often happens, she is found to be a source of grief, shame, deception, ruin and calamity instead, why should we think it displeasing to God if we divorce her?[156] In fact I should be inclined to attribute a thick skin to the man who could keep such a wife, rather than a hard heart to the man who sent her packing. And I am not the only one: Solomon is of the same opinion, or rather the Spirit of God itself is, speaking through the mouth of Solomon, Prov. 30.21, 23: *three things shake the earth; or rather there are four things which it cannot bear: an odious woman when she*

153. Cp. *Tetrachordon* (Yale 2:627–28): "[Marriage] gives place to masterly power, for the master might take away from an Hebrew servant the wife which he gave him, *Ex.* 21."

154. Cp. *Tetrachordon* (Yale 2:628): "Lastly, it gives place to the right of war, for a captive woman lawfully married, and afterward not beloved, might be dismissed, only without ransom, *Deut.* 21."

155. Cp. *PL* 8.449–50: "What next I bring shall please thee, be assured,/Thy likeness, thy fit help, thy other self"; 4.486: "Henceforth an individual solace dear"; 8.576: "Made so adorn for thy delight the more." See also 10.137, 940–41; 11.163–65.

156. Cp. *Tetrachordon* (Yale 2:620): "God permitted divorce for whatever was unalterably distasteful, whether in body or mind."

is married. . . .[157] And on the other hand, Eccles. 9.12: *enjoy your life under the sun, all the days of your fragile life, with the wife whom you love; indeed God has given this to you:* the wife whom you love, notice, not the wife you hate. Thus Mal. 2.16: *whoever hates* or *because he hates, let him send her away;* as everyone before Junius[158] interpreted the passage. So it seems that God enacted this law through Moses, and repeated it through the mouths of the prophets, not in order to make any concessions to the hard-heartedness of husbands, but to rescue the wretched wives from any hard-heartedness which might occur. For where is the hard-heartedness in sending away honorably and freely a woman who, through her own fault, you cannot love? But that a woman who is not loved but justly neglected, a woman who is loathed and hated, should, in obedience to the harshest of laws, be kept beneath the yoke of a crushing slavery (for that is what marriage is without love), by a man who has no love or liking for her: that is a hardship harder than any divorce. So God gave laws of divorce which, if not abused, are absolutely just, equitable and humane. He even extended these laws to those whom he knew would abuse them, because of their hard-heartedness. For he considered it preferable to put up with the hard-heartedness of the wicked, rather than fail to help the righteous in their affliction or save the institution of marriage itself from imminent danger. And this danger was that instead of being a God-given benefit, marriage should become the bitterest misery of all. The fourth and fifth passages, Ezra 10.3 and Neh. 13.23, 30 do not allow divorce, as a concession to hard-heartedness, but rigorously command it for the most sacred religious reasons. But on what authority? These prophets were certainly not bearers of a new law, so what authority could they have except the law of Moses? But the law of Moses nowhere commands the dissolution of this kind of marriage. It does, however, forbid its contraction, Ex. 34.15, 16; Deut. 7.3, 4.[159] From this they argued that a marriage which should not have been contracted, ought to be dissolved. Hence you can see the falsity of the common saying that "What's done can't be undone."

So marriage gives way to religion, and it gives way, as I showed above, to the right of .a master; though it is generally agreed, on the grounds of the scriptural passages cited above, and of numerous provisions in the civil law and the law of nations, that the right of a husband is much the same as the right of a master. Finally, marriage must give way to that natural aversion which anyone may feel for a disgusting object, and also to any really irresistible antipathy. But as for hard-heartedness—if that is really set up as the sole or primary reason for the law's

157. Cp. *Tetrachordon* (p. 254): "Solomon to the plain justification of divorce. . . . Prov. 30.21, 23 . . . tells us of his own accord that a 'hated' or a 'hateful woman when she is married is a thing for which the earth is disquieted and cannot bear it,' thus giving divine testimony to this divine law."

158. Cp. *Tetrachordon* (Yale 2:615): "as if it were to be thus rendered, *The Lord God sayeth that he hateth putting away.* But this new interpretation rests only in the authority of *Junius;* for neither *Calvin* nor *Vatablus* himself, nor any other known divine so interpreted before. And they of best note who have translated the scripture since, and *Diodati* for one, follow not his reading."

159. Cp. *Tetrachordon* (Yale 2:681): "the law of *Moses, Ex.* 34.16. *Deut.* 7.3–6, interpreted by *Ezra* and *Nehemiah* two infallible authors, commands to divorce an infidel not for the fear only of a ceremonious defilement but of an irreligious seducement. . . . *Nehem.* 13.24–26."

enactment—marriage nowhere gives way to that. Deut. 22.19 makes this even clearer: *because he has defamed a virgin of Israel, she shall be his wife: he may not send her away as long as he lives,* and 22.29: *she shall be his wife; because he has ravished her, he may not send her away as long as he lives.* Now in this case the Mosaic law does not yield to the hard-heartedness of the ravisher or the defamer if he wishes to send away the ravished virgin or the defamed wife. Why then should it be imagined that it yields only to the hard-heartedness of that man who has formed an aversion because of some uncleanness?[160] In fact, then, Christ was reproving the hard-heartedness of those who abuse this law, that is the Pharisees and those like them, when he said *on account of your hard-heartedness he allowed you to send away your wives.* He did not abrogate the law itself or its legitimate use, for he says that Moses permitted it on account of their hard-heartedness, not that he permitted it wrongly or unjustly. And in this sense almost all the civil law was given on account of their hard-heartedness. This is why Paul rebukes the brethren, 1 Cor. 6.6, for using it at all; but no one argues from that that the civil law is or ought to be abrogated. How much less can anyone who understands what the gospel is, believe that it denies to man something which the law allowed, whether it allowed it rightly or through an indulgent attitude towards human weakness?

Christ's words in Matt. 19.8: *it was not so from the beginning* are only a repetition of what he had said more plainly in 19.4: *the maker made them from the beginning*. . . ; that is, marriage was first made by God in such a way that it could not be destroyed, even by death. For there was no such thing as death yet, nor was there any sin. But once marriage had been violated by the sin of one of the parties, necessity taught them that death must put an end to it, and reason told them that it must often come to an end, even before death.[161] No age or memorial since the fall of man records any other *beginning* from which *it was not so.* Certainly in the very beginning of our faith Abraham himself, the father of the faithful, sent away his argumentative and quarrelsome wife, Hagar, and had God's authority for it; Gen. 21.10, 12, 14.[162]

Moreover Christ himself, Matt. 19.9, permitted divorce on grounds of fornication. He could not have done this if those whom God had once joined in the bond of matrimony were never afterwards to be separated. Furthermore, as Selden demonstrated particularly well in his *Uxor Hebraea,* with the help of numerous rabbinical texts, the word *fornication,* if it is considered in the light of the

160. Cp. *Tetrachordon* (Yale 2:629) "The absolute forbidding of divorce was in part the punishment of a deflowerer and a defamer. Yet not so but that the wife questionless might depart when she pleased. Otherwise this course had not so much righted her, as delivered her up to more spite and cruel usage. This law therefore doth justly distinguish the privilege of an honest and blameless man in the matter of divorce from the punishment of a notorious offender."

161. Cp. *Tetrachordon* (p. 266): "While man and woman were both perfect each to other, there needed no divorce; but when they both degenerated to imperfection and oft times grew to be an intolerable evil each to other, then law more justly did permit the alienating of that evil which mistake made proper."

162. Cp. *DDD* (Yale 2:263): "while we remember that God commanded *Abraham* to send away his irreligious wife and her son for the offences which they gave in a pious family."

idiom of oriental languages, does not mean only adultery.[163] It can mean also either what is called *some shameful thing* (i.e., the lack of some quality which might reasonably be required in a wife), Deut. 24.1, or it can signify anything which is found to be persistently at variance with love, fidelity, help and society (i.e., with the original institution of marriage).[164] I have proved this elsewhere, basing my argument on several scriptural texts,[165] and Selden has demonstrated the same thing. It would be almost laughable to tell the Pharisees, when they asked whether it was lawful to send away one's wife for every cause, that it was not lawful except in the case of adultery. Because everyone already knew that it was not merely lawful but one's duty to send away an adulteress, and not simply to divorce her but to send her to her death. So the word *fornication* must be interpreted here in a much broader sense than that of adultery. The best text to demonstrate this, and there are many, is Judg. 19.2: *she fornicated against him.* This was not by committing adultery, because then she would not have dared to run home to her father, but by behaving in an obstinate way towards her husband.[166] To take another example, Paul would not have been able to grant divorce on grounds of desertion by an unbeliever, unless this was a kind of fornication as well. And it is, in fact, irrelevant that an unbeliever was concerned in this case, because anyone who deserts his family *is worse than an unbeliever,* 1 Tim. 5.8. For what could be more natural or more in keeping with the original institution of marriage than that a couple whom love, honor and mutual assistance in life have joined together, should be separated if hatred or implacable dislike comes between them, or some dishonorable act for which one of them is responsible? So when human nature was perfect, before the fall, God, in paradise, established marriage as an indissoluble bond. But when man had fallen, he granted by the law of nature and by the Mosaic law, which Christ did not contradict, that it should of necessity be subject to dissolution. In this he intended to prevent the innocent from being exposed to perpetual injury at the hands of the wicked. In the same way practically every treaty and contract is meant to be permanent and indissoluble when it is made, but it is immediately nullified if either party breaks his word. No one has so far been able to produce any good reason why marriage should be an exception to this rule. What is more, the

163. The noted jurist John Selden (1584–1654) won fame as an Orientalist with the treatise *De Diis Syriis* (1617). Milton here refers to a work by Selden published in 1646, after the divorce tracts had been published. Selden's study concerns marriage and divorce among the Jews and, like most of his writing, exhibits extensive knowledge of Rabbinical commentaries. Regarding "fornication," Milton in *Second Defense* (p. 346) had previously noted his anticipation of Selden: "Concerning the view which should be held on the single exception, that of fornication, I also expressed both my own opinion and that of others. Our distinguished countryman Selden still more fully explained this point in his *Hebrew Wife* [*Uxor Hebraica*], published about two years later." See *DDD*, p. 165 n. 242.

164. Cp. *Tetrachordon* (Yale 2:673): "The word fornication is to be understood . . . for a constant alienation and disaffection of the mind, or for the continual practice of disobedience and crossness from the duties of love and peace, that, in sum, when to be a tolerable wife is either naturally not in their power, or obstinately not in their will."

165. I.e., *Tetrachordon.* This is the treatise's only explicit reference to another of Milton's works.

166. Cp. *Tetrachordon* (Yale 2:672) and *DDD* (p. 157), both of which cite Judg. 19.2 in making the same point.

apostle has freed even brothers and sisters from their obligations, not only in cases of desertion, but *in things of that kind,* that is, in any circumstances which result in a shameful subjection: 1 Cor. 7.15: *a brother or sister is not bound to subjection in cases of this kind, for God has called us in peace,* or *to peace.* He has not called us, then, so that we should be tormented by continual wrangling and annoyance. We are called to peace and liberty, not to marriage, and certainly not to the perpetual squabbles and the slavish pounding-mill of unhappy marriage which, if the apostle is right, is particularly shameful for a free Christian man.[167] It is quite unthinkable that Christ should have expunged from the Mosaic law any provision which could sanction the extension of charity towards the wretched and the afflicted. It is unthinkable, too, that he should have sanctioned a measure which was far more severe than the civil law. We must conclude that, having reprimanded the abuse of this law, he proceeded to teach what the perfect line of action would be, not by compulsion but, as elsewhere, simply by admonition: for he always utterly renounced the role of a judge. So it is the most flagrant error to twist these injunctions of Christ in the gospels into civil statutes, enforcible by magistrates.

It may be asked why, if Christ was apparently not laying down anything new about divorce, or anything more severe than the existing law, it gave such little satisfaction to the disciples that they said, Matt. 19.10: *if this is the position of a man with his wife, is it a bad thing to marry?* My reply is that it is not surprising if the disciples, imbued as they were with the doctrines of their time, should have had the same opinions about divorce as the Pharisees. That is why it seemed strange and burdensome to them that it should be unlawful to send away a wife, once she had been given a bill of divorce, for every cause.[168]

Finally, to put the whole thing in a nutshell: everyone admits that marriage may be dissolved if the prime end and form of marriage is violated; and most people say that this is the reason why Christ permitted divorce only on grounds of adultery. But the prime end and form of marriage is not the bed, but conjugal love and mutual assistance in life: nearly everyone admits that this is so. For the prime end and form of marriage can only be what is mentioned in the original institution, and mention is there made of pleasant companionship (a thing which ceases to exist if someone is left by himself), and of the mutual assistance of a married couple (a thing which only thrives where there is love). No mention is made of the bed or of procreation, which can take place even where there is hatred. It follows that wedded love is older and more important than the mere marriage bed, and far more worthy to be considered as the prime end and form of marriage. Who is so base and swinish[169] as to deny that this is so?

167. Cp. *Tetrachordon* (Yale 2:688–89), where Milton also construes 1 Cor. 7.15 as a principle that implies the right of divorce.

168. Cp. *Tetrachordon* (Yale 2:678), which interprets Matt. 19.10 in the same way.

169. *"tam prono tamque porcino animo."* Cp. *Colasterion,* where Milton describes a critic of his divorce tracts as one of "ignoble and swinish mind" (Yale 2:740).

Violation of the marriage bed is only serious because it violates peace and love. Divorce, then, should rather be granted because love and peace are perpetually being violated by quarrels and arguments, than because of adultery. Christ himself admitted this for, as I have proved above, it is absolutely certain that the word *fornication* means not so much adultery as the wife's constant contrariness, faithlessness and disobedience, which all show that her mind is not her husband's even if her body is. Moreover the common, though mistaken interpretation, which makes an exception only in the case of adultery, although it is meant to protect the law, does, in fact, break it. For the Mosaic law did not sanction the divorce of an adulteress, but her trial and execution.

CHAPTER II

OF THE FALL OF OUR FIRST PARENTS, AND OF SIN

The PROVIDENCE of God with regard to the fall of man may be discerned both in man's sin and the misery which followed it, and also in his restoration.

SIN, as defined by the apostle, is ἀνομία or the breaking of the law, 1 John 3.4.

Here the word *law* means primarily that law which is innate and implanted in man's mind; and secondly it means the law which proceeded from the mouth of God; Gen. 2.17: *do not eat of this:* for the law written down by Moses is of a much later date. So it is written, Rom. 2.12: *those who have sinned without law will perish without law.*

SIN is either THE SIN COMMON TO ALL MEN or THE SIN OF EACH INDIVIDUAL.

THE SIN COMMON TO ALL MEN IS THAT WHICH OUR FIRST PARENTS, AND IN THEM ALL THEIR POSTERITY[170] COMMITTED WHEN THEY ABANDONED THEIR OBEDIENCE AND TASTED THE FRUIT OF THE FORBIDDEN TREE.

OUR FIRST PARENTS: Gen. 3.6: *the woman took some of the fruit and ate it, and gave some to her husband, and he ate it.* Hence 1 Tim. 2.14: *Adam was not deceived, but the woman was deceived and was the cause of the transgression.* This sin was instigated first by the devil,[171] as is clear from the course of events, Gen. 3 and 1 John 3.8: *the man who commits sin is of the devil; for the devil sins from the beginning.* Secondly it was instigated by man's own inconstant nature, which meant that he, like the devil before him *did not stand firm in the truth,* John 8.44. He did not keep his original state, but left his home, Jude 6. Anyone who examines this sin carefully will admit, and rightly, that it was a most atrocious offence, and that it broke every part of the law.[172] For what fault is there which man did not commit in commit-

170. Cp. *PL* 10.817–18: "in me all/Posterity stands cursed."
171. Cp. *PL* 1.33–34: "Who first seduced them to that foul revolt?/Th' infernal serpent."
172. Cp. *PL* 10.16: "And manifold in sin, deserved to fall."

ting this sin? He was to be condemned both for trusting Satan and for not trusting God; he was faithless, ungrateful, disobedient, greedy, uxorious; she, negligent of her husband's welfare; both of them committed theft, robbery with violence, murder against their children (i.e., the whole human race); each was sacrilegious and deceitful, cunningly aspiring to divinity although thoroughly unworthy of it, proud and arrogant. And so we find in Eccles. 7.29: *God has made man upright, but they have thought up numerous devices,* and in James 2.10: *whoever keeps the whole law, and yet offends in one point, is guilty of all.*

AND IN THEM ALL THEIR POSTERITY: for they are judged and condemned in them, although not yet born, Gen. 3.16, etc., so they must obviously have sinned in them as well. Rom. 5.12: *sin came into the world through one man,* 5.15: *through the offence of that one man many are dead,* and 5.16 [...], and 5.17 [...], and 5.18 [...], and 5.19 [...]; 1 Cor. 15.22: *in Adam all die:* so it is certain that all sinned in Adam.

For Adam, the parent and head of all men, either stood or fell as a representative of the whole human race: this was true both when the covenant was made, that is, when he received God's commands, and also when he sinned. In the same way *Levi also paid tithes in Abraham ... while he was still in his father's loins,* Heb. 7.9, 10; *for God has made the whole human race from the blood of one man, Adam,* Acts 17.26. If all men did not sin in Adam, why was the condition of all made worse by his fall? Some modern thinkers would say that this deterioration was not moral but physical. But I say that it would be quite as unjust to impair the physical perfection of innocent men, especially as this has so much effect on their morals.

Moreover, it is not only a constant principle of divine justice but also a very ancient law among all races and all religions, that when a man has committed sacrilege (and this tree we are discussing was sacred),[173] not only he but also the whole of his posterity becomes an anathema and a sin-offering.[174]

This was so in the flood, in the burning of Sodom and in the destruction of Korah, Num. 16.27, 32, and in the punishment of Achan, Josh. 7.24, 25. When Jericho was demolished, the children paid for the sins of their fathers, and even the cattle were given up to slaughter along with their masters, Josh. 6.21. So, too, with the posterity of Eli, the priest, 1 Sam. 2.31, 33, 36; and Saul's sons paid the penalty for his slaughter of the Gibeonites, 2 Sam. 21.1, etc.

God declares that this is his justice, Ex. 20.5: *punishing the sin of the fathers in the persons of the children, grandchildren and great-grandchildren of those who pursue me with hatred;* Num. 14.33: *your sons, feeding their flocks in the wilderness for forty years, will pay the penalty for your fornication:* they were not guiltless themselves, however.[175] God himself explains what the method behind this justice is: Lev. 26.39: *pining away because of their iniquity and also because of the iniquity of their fathers;*

173. Cp. *PL* 9.904: "The sacred fruit forbidd'n."

174. Cp. *PL* 3.208: "But to destruction sacred and devote."

175. Cp. *PL* 12.398–400: "and suffering death,/The penalty to thy transgression due,/And due to theirs which out of thine will grow."

2 Kings 17.14: *they had stiffened their necks as their ancestors stiffened theirs;* and Ezek. 18.4 [...]. As for infants, the problem is solved by the consideration that all souls are God's, and that though innocent they were the children of sinful parents, and God saw that they would turn out to be like their parents. With everybody else, the explanation is that no one perishes unless he has himself sinned. Thus Agag and his people paid the penalty for the crime of their ancestors four hundred years after the latter had attacked the Israelite fugitives while they were on the march from Egypt, 1 Sam. 15.2, 3; true, they were themselves far from guiltless, 15.33. Then again, Hosea, king of Israel, was better than his ancestors; but when he was guilty of the idolatry of the Gentiles, he paid the penalty for his own sins and the sins of his ancestors as well by the loss of his kingdom, 2 Kings 17.2–4. Similarly Manasseh's sins overflowed onto his children (though they were hardly innocent themselves), 23.26: *because of all the provocations with which Manasseh had provoked him,* compared with Jer. 25.3, 4, etc.: *from the thirteenth year of Josiah king of Judah, right up to this day, the word of Jehovah has come to me: and I have spoken it to you incessantly from daybreak onwards, but you have not listened;* and 2 Kings 24.5: *on account of sins just like those which Manasseh had committed.* So the good king Josiah, and those who were like him, were exempt from the greater part of the punishment. The Pharisees, however, were not exempt, Matt. 23.34, 35: *you shall kill some of them* etc. *that all righteous blood may come upon you, from the blood of righteous Abel,* etc.

Accordingly penitents are ordered to confess both their own sins and the sins of their fathers: Lev. 26.40: *if they will confess their iniquity and the iniquity of their fathers,* and Neh. 9.2: *they confessed their sins and the iniquities of their ancestors:* and frequently elsewhere.

So even a whole family may become guilty because of the crime committed by its head: Gen. 12.14: *Jehovah afflicted Pharaoh and his family with great plagues,* and 20.7 [...].

Subjects have to pay the penalty, too, for the sins of their king, as all Egypt did for Pharaoh's sins. Even King David, who thought it unjust that subjects should suffer in this way, also thought it quite equitable that sons should be punished for and with their fathers: 2 Sam. 24.17: *look, I have sinned and done wrong: but these, these sheep, what have they done? I beg that your hand may be against me and against my father's house.*

Indeed, sometimes a whole nation is punished for the sin of one citizen, Josh. 7, and the offence of a single person is imputed to all, 7.1, 11.

Furthermore, even the most just men have thought it right that a crime committed against them should be atoned for by the punishment not only of the criminal but also of his children. Thus Noah considered that Ham's offence should be avenged upon Ham's son, Canaan,[176] Gen. 9.25.

This feature of divine justice, the insistence upon propitiatory sacrifices for

176. Cp. *PL* 12.101–4: "witness th' irreverent son/Of him who built the ark, who for the shame/Done to his father, heard this heavy curse,/'Servant of servants,' on his vicious race."

sin, was well known among other nations, and never thought to be unfair. So we find in Thucydides 1:[177] *For this they and their family are held to be accursed and offenders against the goddess.* And Virgil, *Aeneid*, 1:[178]

> Could angry Pallas, with revengeful spleen,
> The Grecian navy burn, and drown the men?
> She for the fault of one offending foe . . .

The same fact could easily be demonstrated by a host of other examples and proofs from the pagan writers.

Again, a man convicted of high treason, which is only an offence against another man, forfeits not only his own estate and civil rights but also those of all his family, and lawyers have decided upon the same sentence in other cases of a similar kind. Everyone knows, too, what the right of war is, and that it extends not only to those who are responsible, but to everyone who is in the enemy's power, women, for example, and even children, and people who have done nothing towards the war nor intended to.[179]

THE SIN OF EACH INDIVIDUAL is THE SIN WHICH EACH MAN COMMITS ON HIS OWN ACCOUNT, QUITE APART FROM THAT SIN WHICH IS COMMON TO ALL. All men commit sin of this kind: Job 9.20: *if I were to call myself righteous, my own mouth would condemn me* . . . , and 10.15 [. . .]; Ps. 143.2: *no living man is righteous in your sight;* Prov. 20.9 [. . .]; Eccles. 7.20 [. . .]; Rom. 3.23 [. . .].

Each type of sin, common and personal, has two subdivisions, whether we call them degrees or parts or modes of sin, or whether they are related to each other as cause and effect. These subdivisions are evil desire, or the will to do evil, and the evil deed itself. James 1.14, 15: *every man is tempted when he is drawn on and enticed by his own lust: then, when lust has conceived, it brings forth sin.* This same point is neatly expressed by the poet:[180]

> Mars sees her; seeing desires her; desiring enjoys her

It was evil desire that our first parents were originally guilty of. Then they implanted it in all their posterity, since their posterity too was guilty of that original sin, in the shape of a certain predisposition towards, or, to use a metaphor, a sort of tinder to kindle sin.

This is called in scripture *the old man* and *the body of sin,* Rom. 6.6, Eph. 4.22, Col. 3.9: or simply *sin,* Rom. 7.8: *sin seized its opportunity by means of that commandment; sin dwelling in me,* Rom. 7.17, 20; *evil which is present,* 7.21; [. . .] 7.23; [. . .] 7.24; [. . .] 8.2.

177. *History of the Peloponnesian War* 1.126.11.
178. Lines 39–41.
179. The right of war gives absolute power over a vanquished enemy. Cp. *PL* 1.149–50n; 2.200–208n.
180. Ovid, *Fast.* 3.21.

Apparently Augustine, in his writings against Pelagius, was the first to call this ORIGINAL SIN. He used the word *original*, I suppose, because in the *origin* or generation of man this sin was transmitted to posterity by our first parents. But if that is what he meant, the term is too narrow, because this evil desire, this law of sin, was not only inbred in us, but also took possession of Adam after his fall,[181] and from his point of view it could not be called *original*.[182]

The depravity which all human minds have in common, and their propensity to sin, are described in Gen. 6.5: *that all the thoughts of his heart were always evil and evil alone;* 8.21: *the devices of a man's heart are evil from childhood;* Jer. 17.9 [. . .]; Matt. 15.19 [. . .]; Rom. 7.14 [. . .]; and 8.7 [. . .]; Gal. 5.17 [. . .]; Eph. 4.22: *the old man who is corrupted by deceitful lusts.*

Our first parents implanted it in us: Job 14.4: *who produces purity from impurity?*, and 15.14 [. . .]; Ps. 51.7: *I was formed in iniquity and my mother nursed me in sin;* and 58.4 [. . .]; Isa. 48.8 [. . .]; John 3.6 [. . .]. Eph. 2.3: *we were by nature children of anger, like the others*—even those who were born of regenerate parents, for although faith removes each man's personal guilt, it does not altogether root out the vice which dwells within us. So it is not man as a regenerate creature, but man as an animal, that begets man: Just as the seed, though cleansed from straw and chaff, produces not only the ear or the grain but also the stalk and the husk. Christ alone was free from this contagion, since he was produced by supernatural generation, although descended from Adam: Heb. 7.26: *holy, spotless.*

Some interpret this term original sin primarily as guiltiness. But guiltiness is not a sin, it is the imputation of sin, called elsewhere *the judgment of God:* Rom. 1.32: *knowing the judgment of God.* As a result of this sinners are held *worthy of death*, and ὑπόδικοι, that is, *liable to condemnation and punishment*, Rom. 3.19, and *are under sin*, 3.9. Thus as soon as the fall occurred, our first parents became guilty, though there could have been no original sin in them. Moreover all Adam's descendants were included in the guilt, though original sin had not yet been implanted in them. Finally, guilt is taken away from the regenerate, but they still have original sin.

Others define original sin as the loss of original righteousness and the corruption of the whole mind. But this loss must be attributed to our first parents before it is attributed to us, and they could not have been subject to original sin, as I said before. Their sin was what is called "actual" sin, which these same theologians, as part of their theory, distinguish from original sin. Anyway their loss was a consequence of sin, rather than a sin itself; or if it was a sin, it was only a sin of ignorance, because they did not expect for a moment that they would lose anything good by eating the fruit, or that they would be worse off in any way at all.[183] So I shall not consider this loss under the heading of sin, but under that of punishment in the next chapter.

181. Cp. *PL* 9.1077–78: "And in our faces evident the signs/Of foul concupiscence."

182. Yet Milton at *PL* 9.1003–4 calls the first disobedience "the mortal sin/Original."

183. Cp. *PL* 10.334–36: "his guileful act/By Eve, though all unwilling, seconded/Upon her husband." Milton represents Adam, however, as fully aware of the fatal impact of eating the fruit (*PL* 9.896–907).

The second subdivision of sin, after evil desire, is the evil action or crime itself, which is commonly called "actual" sin.[184] It can be committed not only through actions, as such, but also through words and thoughts and even through the omission of a good action.

It is called "actual" not because sin is really an action, on the contrary it is a deficiency, but because it usually exists in some action. For every action is intrinsically good; it is only its misdirection or deviation from the set course of law which can properly be called evil. So action is not the material out of which sin is made, but only the ὑποκείμενον, the essence or element in which it exists.

Through words: Matt. 12.36: *for every idle word they will be called to account,* and 15.11: *whatever comes out, defiles a man.*

Through thoughts: Ex. 20.17: *you shall not covet your neighbor's house;* Ps. 7.14: *see, he will bring forth vanity; as he conceived trouble so he will bring forth lies;* Prov. 24.8 [...]; Jer. 17.9 [...], etc.; Matt. 5.28 [...], and 15.19 [...]; 1 John 3.15 [...].

Through omission: Matt. 12.30: *he who is not with me is against me; and he who does not gather with me, scatters,* similarly Luke 11.23 and 6.9, where not to save a man is considered the same as destroying him. Matt. 25.42: *I was hungry and you did not give;* James 4.17: *a man who knows how to do right and does not do it, is in the power of sin.*

But all sins are not, as the Stoics maintained, equally great: Ezek. 5.6: *into wickedness more than the nations,* and 8.15 [...]; John 19.11: *he has the greater sin.*

This inequality arises from many and various circumstances of person, place, time, and the like: Isa. 26.10: *in the land of righteousness he will deal unjustly.*

A discussion of the difference between mortal and venial sin will fit in better elsewhere. Meanwhile it is indisputable that even the least sin renders a man liable to condemnation: Luke 16.10: *he who is unjust in little is also unjust in much.*

CHAPTER 12

OF THE PUNISHMENT OF SIN

So far I have spoken of sin. After sin came death, as its affliction or punishment: Gen. 2.17: *on the day you eat it, you will die;* Rom. 5.12: *through sin is death,* and 6.23: *the wages of sin is death,* and 7.5: *the effects of sin, to bring forth fruit to death.*

But in scripture every evil, and everything which seems to lead to destruction, is indeed under the name of *death.* For physical death, as it is called, did not follow *on the same day as* Adam's sin, as God had threatened.[185]

184. Cp. *PL* 10.586–88: "Sin there in power before,/Once actual, now in body, and to dwell/Habitual habitant."

185. Cp. *PL* 8.329–33: "my sole command/Transgressed, inevitably thou shalt die;/From that day mortal, and this happy state/Shalt lose, expelled from hence into a world/Of woe and sorrow"; 10.49–53: "death denounced that day,/Which he presumes already vain and void,/Because not yet inflicted, as he feared,/By some immediate stroke; but soon shall find/Forbearance no acquittance ere day end."

So four degrees of death may conveniently be distinguished. First, as I said above, come ALL EVILS WHICH TEND TO DEATH AND WHICH, IT IS AGREED, CAME INTO THE WORLD AS SOON AS MAN FELL. I will here set out the most important of these. First: guiltiness, which, although it is a thing imputed to us by God, is nevertheless a sort of partial death or prelude to death in us, by which we are fettered to condemnation and punishment as by some actual bond: Gen. 3.7: *then both their eyes opened, and they knew that they were naked;* Lev. 5.2, etc. [. . .]; Rom. 3.19 [. . .]. As a result guiltiness is either accompanied or followed by terrors of conscience:[186] Gen. 3.8: *they heard the voice of God, and Adam hid himself: he said, I was afraid;* Rom. 8.15 [. . .]; Heb. 2.15: *all those who through fear of death were condemned to slavery all their lives,* and 10.27: *a terrifying expectation of judgment:* also by the loss of divine protection and favor, which results in the lessening of the majesty of the human countenance, and the degradation of the mind:[187] Gen. 3.7: *they knew that they were naked.* Thus the whole man is defiled: Tit. 1.15: *both their mind and their conscience is defiled.* Hence comes shame: Gen. 3.7: *they sewed leaves together and made themselves aprons;* Rom. 6.21: *for which you are now ashamed, for the end of those things is death.*

The second degree of death is called SPIRITUAL DEATH. This is the loss of that divine grace and innate righteousness by which, in the beginning, man lived with God: Eph. 2.1: *since you were dead in trespasses and sins,* and 4.18: *alienated from the life of God;* Col. 2.13 [. . .]; Rev. 3.1 [. . .]. And this death took place at the same moment as the fall of man, not merely on the same day. Those who are delivered from it are said to be regenerated and born again and created anew. As I will show in my chapter on Regeneration,[188] this is not the work of God alone.

This death consists, first, in the loss or at least the extensive darkening of that right reason, whose function it was to discern the chief good, and which was, as it were, the life of the understanding: Eph. 4.18: *having a mind obscured by darkness, and alienated from the life of God on account of the ignorance which is in them,* and 5.8 [. . .]; John 1.5 [. . .]; Jer. 6.10 [. . .]; John 8.43 [. . .]; 1 Cor. 2.14 [. . .]; 2 Cor. 3.5: *not that we are fit to think anything out by ourselves,* and 4.4: *the god of this world has blinded their minds;* Col. 1.13 [. . .]: secondly, in that extinction of righteousness and of the liberty to do good, and in that slavish subjection to sin and the devil which is, as it were, the death of the will.[189] John 8.34: *whoever commits sin is the slave of sin.* We have all committed sin in Adam, therefore we are born slaves; Rom. 7.14: *sold to be subject to sin,* and 8.3 [. . .], and 8.7 [. . .]; Rom. 6.16, 17 [. . .]; Phil. 3.19 [. . .]; Acts 26.18 [. . .]; 2 Tim. 2.26: *out of the snare of the devil, who are made captive by him at his*

186. Cp. *PL* 10.842–43: "O conscience, into what abyss of fears/And horrors hast thou driv'n me."

187. Cp. *PL* 9.1077–78: "And in our faces evident the signs/Of foul concupiscence."

188. Chapter 18 of Book 1, not included in our selection.

189. Cp. *PL* 12.83–90: "Since thy original lapse, true liberty/Is lost, which always with right reason dwells/Twinned, and from her hath no dividual being:/Reason in man obscured, or not obeyed,/Immediately inordinate desires/And upstart passions catch the government/From reason, and to servitude reduce/Man till then free."

will; Eph. 2.2 [. . .]. Lastly sin is its own punishment, and the death of the spiritual life; especially when sins are heaped upon sins: Rom. 1.26: *for this reason he has given them up to filthy desires.* The reason for this is not hard to see. As sins increase so they bind the sinners to death more surely, make them more miserable and constantly more vile, and deprive them more and more of divine help and grace, and of their own former glory. No one should have the least doubt that sin is in itself alone the gravest evil of all, for it is opposed to the chief good, that is, to God. Punishment, on the other hand, seems to be opposed only to the good of the creature, and not always to that.

However, it cannot be denied that some traces of the divine image still remain in us, which are not wholly extinguished by this spiritual death.[190] This is quite clear, not only from the holiness and wisdom in both word and deed of many of the heathens, but also from Gen. 9.2: *every beast shall have fear of you,* and 9.6: *who sheds man's blood . . . because God made man in his image.* These traces remain in our intellect, Ps. 19.2: *the heavens declare . . .*—obviously they do not *declare* it to beings who cannot hear. Rom. 1.19, 20: *that which can be known about God . . . the invisible things are evident from the creation of the world,* and 1.32 [. . .], and 2.15 [. . .]; 7.23, 24: *I see another law in my members battling against the law of my mind . . . I am a wretched man. Who will rescue me from this body of death?* The freedom of the will is not entirely extinct: first of all, in indifferent matters, whether natural or civil: 1 Cor. 7.36, 37, 39: *let him do what he will. He has power over his will. She is free to marry whom she likes.* Secondly, this freedom has clearly not quite disappeared even where good works are concerned, or at least good attempts, at any rate after God has called us and given us grace. But it is so weak and of such little moment, that it only takes away any excuse we might have for doing nothing, and does not give us the slightest reason for being proud of ourselves: Deut. 30.19: *choose life, that you and your seed may live;* Ps. 78.8 [. . .]; Jer. 8.13–16: *because when I speak to you from the dawn onwards, you do not hear, and when I shout at you, you do not answer, therefore . . .*—but why, if he had only been speaking to incapable blockheads? And 31.18: *turn to me and I will be turned;* Zech. 1.3 [. . .]; Mark 9.23, 24 [. . .]; Rom. 2.14: *when the Gentiles who have not the law do by nature the things contained in the law,* and 6.16: *do you not know that when you present yourselves as slaves to obey someone, you are the slaves of him whom you obey, whether slaves of sin, to death, or slaves of obedience, to righteousness,* and 7.18 [. . .], and 7.21 [. . .]. Paul seems to speak these words in the person of a man not yet fully regenerate who, although called by God and given grace, had not yet been subject to his regenerating influence. This is clear from 7.14: *I am carnal, sold to be subject to sin.* As for his words in 7.25: *I thank God through Jesus Christ . . .*, these and similar things could be said and done by a man who had only been called. Rom. 9.31: *by following the law of righteousness they did not attain the law of righteousness,* and 10.2: *they have zeal for God, but not from knowledge;* 1 Cor. 9.17 [. . .]; Philipp. 3.6 [. . .]; 1 Pet. 5.2 [. . .]. As a result nearly all human

190. Cp. *PL* 11.511–13: "man,/Retaining still divine similitude/In part." This claim also distinguishes Milton's views from Calvinist orthodoxy, which insisted on humanity's total depravity.

beings profess some concern for virtue, and have an abhorrence of some of the more atrocious crimes: 1 Cor. 5.1: *fornication of a kind which is not mentioned even among the Gentiles.*

As a vindication of God's justice, especially when he calls man, it is obviously fitting that some measure of free will should be allowed to man, whether this is something left over from his primitive state, or something restored to him as a result of the call of grace. It is also fitting that this will should operate in good works or at least good attempts, rather than in things indifferent. For if God rules all human actions, both natural and civil, by his absolute command, then he is not doing anything more than he is entitled to do, and no one need complain. But if he turns man's will to moral good or evil just as he likes, and then rewards the good and punishes the wicked, it will cause an outcry against divine justice from all sides. It would seem then that God's general government of all things, which is so often referred to, should be understood as operating in natural and civil matters and in things indifferent and in chance happenings—in fact in anything rather than in moral or religious concerns. There are several scriptural texts which corroborate this. 2 Chron. 15.12, 14: *they entered into a covenant to seek Jehovah the God of their ancestors with all their heart and with all their soul: and they swore to Jehovah;* Ps. 119.106: *I have sworn (and I will perform it), to keep your righteous judgments.* Obviously if religious matters were not under our control, or to some extent within our power and choice, God could not enter into a covenant with us, and we could not keep it, let alone swear to keep it.

CHAPTER 13

OF THE DEATH WHICH IS CALLED THE DEATH OF THE BODY

The third degree of death is what is usually called the DEATH OF THE BODY. The body's sufferings and hardships and diseases are nothing but the prelude to this bodily death. Gen. 3.16: *I greatly multiply your grief* and 3.17 [. . .] and 3.19 [. . .]; Job 5.7 [. . .]; Deut. 28.22 [. . .]; Hos. 2.18 [. . .]; Rom. 2.9: *affliction and distress upon every man who instigates evil.* The curse of death extends to the whole of nature,[191] because of man—Gen. 3.17: *because of you, the ground shall be cursed;* Rom. 8.20, 21: *the world is made subject to vanity, but not on its own account*—and even to the beasts, Gen. 3.14 and 6.7; the firstborn in Egypt, Ex. 11.5.

Although some people disagree, this bodily death should really be thought of as a punishment for sin, just as much as the other degrees of death: Rom. 5.13, 14: *sin was in the world until the* law . . . *but death reigned from Adam to Moses;* 1 Cor. 15.21: *since death came through man*—death in this world, that is, as well as eternal death, as the second half of the sentence indicates—*through man came also the*

191. Cp. *PL* 10.846–48, 678–80, 687–91.

resurrection of the dead. Therefore that bodily death which precedes resurrection came about not naturally but through man's sin. This refutes those who attribute death in this world to nature, and eternal death alone to sin.

The death of the body, as it is called, is the loss or extinction of life. For the separation of body and soul, which is the usual definition of death, cannot possibly be death at all. What part of man dies when this separation takes place? The soul? Even those who adhere to the usual definition deny that. The body? But how can that be said to die which never had any life of its own?[192] This separation, then, cannot be called the death of man.

This gives rise to a very important question which, because of the prejudice of theologians, has usually been dismissed out of hand, instead of receiving proper and careful examination. Does the whole man die, or only the body? It is a question which can be debated without detriment to faith or devotion, whichever side we may be on. So I shall put forward quite unreservedly the doctrine which seems to me to be instilled by virtually innumerable passages of scripture. I assume that no one thinks you should look for truth among philosophers and schoolmen rather than in the Bible!

Man is always said to be made up of body, spirit and soul, whatever we may think about where one starts and the other leaves off. So I will first prove that the whole man dies, and then that each separate part dies. First of all, we should consider that God pronounced the sentence of death upon the whole sinful man, without making an exception of any part. For what could be more just than that the whole man should die since the whole man had sinned; and that the part, whether soul or spirit, which was found to have the chief hand in the sin should die above all? Or, to put it another way, what could be more absurd than that the part which sinned most (i.e., the soul) should escape the sentence of death; or that the body, which was just as immortal as the soul before sin brought death into the world, should alone pay the penalty for sin by dying although it had no actual part in the sin?

It is quite obvious that all the saints and believers, patriarchs, prophets and apostles alike, were of this same opinion: Jacob, Gen. 37.35: *I will go down mourning to my son in the grave,* and 42.36 [. . .]; Job 3.12–18 [. . .], similarly Job 10.21. Also Job 14.11: *when man has died, where is he?* and 14.13: *when man has lain down, he does not rise again until the heavens are no more,* and 17.12 [. . .], and 17.14, 15 [. . .], and there are many other passages; David, too, as is evident from the reason he so often gave when praying to be delivered from death, Ps. 6.5: *there is no remembrance of you in death, who shall praise you in the tomb,* and similarly 88.11–13, 115.17 [. . .], and 39.14: *before I go away and am no more,* and 146.2: *I will praise my God while I still exist.* Clearly if he had believed that his soul would survive and would be received into heaven without delay he would not have used this kind of argument, because he would know that he would soon take his flight to a place where he

192. Cp. *PL* 10.789–92: "It was but breath/Of Life that sinned; what dies but what had life/And sin? The body properly hath neither./All of me then shall die."

could praise God unceasingly. What David believed of himself, Peter believed about David, Acts 2.29, 34: *let me speak freely among you about the patriarch David: that he is both dead and buried, and his monument is with us to this very day. for David did not ascend into heaven.* Hezekiah shows clearly how convinced he was that all of him would die, when he complains that he will not be able to praise God in the tomb: Isa. 38.18, 19: *the grave cannot praise you. They that go down to the grave have no hope in your faith: the living, the living shall praise you as I do today.* The voice of God himself bears witness to the same truth: Isa. 57.5, 6: *the just man perishes, and no one takes it to heart: merciful men are taken, and no one considers that the just man is taken away before the arrival of that evil. He shall enter into peace, they shall rest in their beds;* Jer. 31.15 compared with Matt. 2.18 [. . .]; so does Daniel, Dan. 12.2 [. . .]. Christ himself proves that God is the God of the living, Luke 20.37, etc., by arguing that they will be resurrected. If they were alive already, it would not necessarily follow from his argument that there was going to be a resurrection of the body. Thus he says, John 11.25: *I am the resurrection and the life.* So, too, he quite openly declares that, before the resurrection, there is no dwelling place in heaven even for the saints, John 14.2, 3: *I am going to prepare a place for you, and if I go away and prepare a place for you, I shall come again and take you to myself, that where I am, you may be also.* No satisfactory reason can be produced for taking this to refer only to physical bodies. So presumably it was spoken about, and should be understood to refer to the soul and the spirit, as well as the body, and to their reception into heaven, after the second coming of the Lord. So, too, Luke 20.35 and Acts 7.60: *when he had said this, he fell asleep* and 23.6: *of the hope and resurrection*—that is, the hope of resurrection, which was the only hope he said he had. Similarly Luke 24.21 and 26.6–8, and 1 Cor. 15.17–19: *if Christ has not risen* (which was done so that the dead might rise again) *then those who sleep in Christ shall perish.* So we see that there are here two, and only two alternatives: either to rise again or to perish. For *if we have hope in Christ in this life only, we are of all men the most miserable:* again there are two alternatives, either to believe in resurrection or to place all one's hopes in this life alone. Also, 1 Cor. 15.29, 30: *if the dead are not raised, why do we put ourselves in danger* and 15.32: *let us eat and drink, for tomorrow we die,* die altogether, that is, otherwise the argument would be worthless. From 15.42 to 50 the reasoning proceeds from the simply mortal to the simply immortal, from death to resurrection. There is not so much as a word about any intermediate state. Even Paul affirmed that he would not gain his own crown of righteousness before that last day came: 2 Tim. 4.8: *as for the rest, a crown of righteousness is laid up for me, which the Lord, the righteous judge, will give me on that day: but not only to me, but also to all those who have longed for his glorious coming.* A crown is laid up for Paul: therefore it is not to be obtained immediately after death. When is it to be obtained, then? At that time when crowns are to be given to all the others: in other words, not before Christ's *glorious coming.* Philipp. 2.16 [. . .], and 3.11 [. . .], and 3.20, 21: *our city is in heaven, from which place, also, we look for a savior, the Lord Jesus Christ: who shall transform our vile body, so that it may become like his glorious body.* Our citizenship, then, is in the heavens: not in that place where we now live, but in the place from which we expect a savior who will lead us back with him. Luke 20.35, 36: *but those who shall be held worthy to obtain that existence, and the resurrection from the dead,* etc. *for they are equal to the angels,* etc. *being sons of the resurrection:* that is, they will eventually be. It follows that they will not attain that heavenly existence before their resurrection.

So far I have proved that the whole man dies. But in case anyone should start quibbling, and should claim that because the whole man dies it does not mean that the whole *of* man dies, I will now prove the same thing about the three components, body, spirit and soul, which I enumerated above. As for the body, no one has any doubt that it dies.

The same thing will be equally apparent in the case of the spirit, once it is agreed that the spirit is not divine but merely human, as I showed in Chapter 7. It must also be conceded that no cause can be found why, when God sentenced the whole sinful man to death, the spirit alone should have been exempted from the punishment of death. After all, the spirit was the chief offender. So, then, before sin came into the world, all man's component parts were equally immortal, but since the advent of sin they have all become equally subject to death, as a result of God's sentence. But now for the proofs. The Preacher himself, the wisest of all mortals, distinctly says that the spirit is not exempt from death: Eccles. 3.18–20: *that as the beast dies, so the man dies, they all have the same spirit. Each of them goes to the same place;* and 3.21 condemns the ignorance of those who are so bold as to affirm that the spirit of a man and the spirit of a beast go different ways after death: *who knows whether the spirit of man goes upwards?;* Ps. 146.4: *his spirit goes out, the man returns to his earth: in that day his thoughts perish*—but his *thoughts* are in his soul and spirit, not in his body. If they *perish,* then the conclusion must be that the soul and spirit themselves also suffer the same fate as the body. 1 Cor. 5.5: *that the spirit may be saved on the day of the Lord Jesus.* Paul does not say *on the day of death,* but *on the day of the Lord.* Lastly there are plenty of texts which prove that the soul also suffers both natural and violent death, whether we take the term *soul* to mean the whole human make-up, or whether we take it as synonymous with *spirit.* Num. 23.14: *may my soul die the death of the righteous.* True, these words are said by Balaam, not one of the most upright of prophets, but they are words which God put into his mouth, 23.9; Job 33.18: *he may keep back his soul from the pit* and 36.14: *their soul dies in youth;* Ps. 22.21 [. . .], and 78.50 [. . .] and 89.49 [. . .] and 94.17 [. . .]. So, too, man, when dead, is referred to as a *soul:* Lev. 19.28 and 21.1, 11: *nor go to any dead souls,* and elsewhere. Isa. 38.17: *you have delivered my soul from the pit.* But the most convincing explanation I can adduce for the death of the soul is God's own, Ezek. 18.20: *the soul which sins shall itself die.* Thus even Christ's soul succumbed to death for a short time when he died for our sins. The prophet, the apostle and Christ himself corroborate this: Ps. 16.10, compared with Acts 2.27, 28, 31: *that his soul was not left in the sepulcher, nor his flesh;*

Matt. 26.38: *my soul is sad, sad to death.*[193] The souls are never spoken of as being summoned to or assembling for judgment from heaven or hell; they are always said to be called out of the grave, or at least to have been in the state of the dead. John 5.28, 29: *the time will come when all who are in their graves will hear his voice, and they will come forth,* etc. Here those who rise again, those who hear and come forth, whether just or unjust, are in their tombs and nowhere else. 1 Cor. 15.52 [. . .]; 1 Thess. 4.13–17: *but I do not want you to be ignorant, brothers, about those who have gone to sleep, in case you should grieve, like those other people who have no hope. For if we believe that Jesus was dead and rose again, so too God, through Jesus, will bring with him those who have been asleep. For we say this to you by the words of the Lord, that we who shall be left alive when the Lord comes, shall not go before those who have been asleep: for the Lord himself,* etc. *and those who died in Christ shall rise first; then we who are left alive will be snatched up into the clouds along with them, to meet the Lord in the air, and so we shall always be with the Lord.* They *have gone to sleep:* the lifeless body, however, does not sleep, unless, that is, you could say that a piece of stone, for example, sleeps. *In case you should grieve, like those other people who have no hope:* but why should they grieve, why should they have no hope, if they believed that, whatever might happen to the body, the soul would be in a state of salvation and blessedness even before the resurrection? Of course *those other people* who had no hope despaired of the soul as well as of the body, because they did not believe in any resurrection. That is why Paul directs the hope of all believers to the resurrection: *God, through Jesus, will bring with him those who have been asleep,* bring them, that is, into heaven from the grave. *That we who shall be left alive when the Lord comes, shall not go before those who have been asleep:* but there would be no question of *us* going before them if those who had gone to sleep had flown off to heaven long ago. And if they had, they would not now go *to meet the Lord,* but would come back with him. In fact, though, *we who are alive shall be snatched up together with them,* not after them, *and so we shall always be with the Lord:* after the resurrection, that is, not before. And then eventually *the just shall be separated from the wicked,* Matt. 13.49. Dan. 12.2: *many of those sleeping in the dust of the earth shall awake: some to eternal life, some to shame and eternal contempt.* I should say that it was in this same sleep that Lazarus lay, if anyone were to ask where his soul went during those four days of death. Indeed, I should not hesitate to answer that in my opinion his soul was not called down from heaven, to undergo a second time the inconveniences of the body, but was called up from the grave and awakened from the sleep of death. Christ's own words lead me to this conclusion: John 11.11, 13: *our friend Lazarus sleeps, but I am going to awake him from sleep: but Jesus said this of his death:* and if it was really a miracle, then it must really have been death. Christ's behavior when he raised Lazarus points to the same thing, 11.43: *he called*

193. Cp. *PL* 3.245–49: "Though now to Death I yield, and am his due/All that of me can die, yet that debt paid,/Thou wilt not leave me in the loathsome grave/His prey, nor suffer my unspotted soul/Forever with corruption there to dwell."

with a loud voice, Lazarus, come out of there. If Lazarus' soul, that is Lazarus' real self, was not in *there,* why did Christ call to the dead body, for that would not be able to hear. And if he called to the soul, why did he call it from a place where it was not? If he had wanted it to be believed that the soul was separated from the body, then clearly he would have directed his eyes to the place from which the soul of Lazarus ought to return, in other words, to heaven. To call something from the grave which is not in the grave is like seeking the living among the dead, which the angel censured as ignorance in the disciples, Luke 24.5. The same thing is apparent in the raising of the widow's son, Luke 7.14.

On the other hand there are some who insist that the soul is exempt from death. They say that once it has thrown off the body it goes directly to or is led by angels to the place appointed for reward or punishment, and that there it remains in isolation until the end of the world. Their case rests fundamentally on the following texts: Ps. 49.16: *God is going to redeem my soul from the grave.* But this, like the various texts I quoted above, proves rather that the soul goes down into the grave with the body, and therefore stands in need of redemption (i.e., at the resurrection, *when God is going to receive it with power,* as it is said in the same verse). As for the others, *whose redemption is forever wanting,* 49.9, *they are like beasts,* 49.13, 15.

The second text is Eccles. 12.9: *the spirit returning to God, who gave it.* But my opponents cannot prove their point from this either, because *returning to God* must be understood in a very broad sense: after all the wicked do not go to God at death, but far away from him. Moreover, it has already been said in 3.20, that *each of them goes to the same place.* In fact God is referred to as having given spirits to all animals, and as taking them to himself again when the body returns to dust, Job 34.14, 15: if . . . he *takes its spirit and its soul to himself: all flesh will die together, and man will turn back to dust.* Ps. 104.29, 30 says the same. Euripides, in the *Suppliants,* has given a far better interpretation of this passage than my opponents, without knowing it:[194]

> Each various part
> That constitutes the frame of man, returns
> Whence it was taken; to th' ethereal sky
> The soul, the body to its earth

that is, when soul and body part, each component returns to the place it came from, to its own element. This is confirmed by Ezek. 37.9: *come from the four winds, o spirit:* obviously the spirit of man must have first gone to *the four winds* if it is now to return from them. I suppose this is what Matt. 24.31 refers to: *they will collect together his elect from the four winds.* Why should they not collect spirits

194. Milton quotes lines 532–34. He praises Euripides to similar effect in *TKM* (p. 279): "How much more rationally spake the heathen king Demophoön in a tragedy of Euripides than these interpreters would put upon King David."

together just as they do the tiniest particles of bodies, which are often scattered far and wide over the face of the earth? The same goes for 1 Kings 17.21: *I pray that the boy's soul may return.* This, however, is an idiom applied to recovery from any kind of unconsciousness: Judges 15.19: *his spirit returned and he lived,* similarly 1 Sam. 30.12. I have quoted only a few of the very large number of texts which prove that the dead do not have any kind of life. Obviously, however, the passages I have cited above about the death of the spirit are enough to deal with this particular part of my opponents' case.

The third passage they refer to is Matt. 10.28: *they kill the body, they cannot kill the soul.* I reply that strictly speaking the body cannot be killed either, since it is in itself lifeless.[195] So the word *body* here, as usual in scripture, must be taken to stand for the whole human make-up, as it is called, or for the animal and temporal life. The word *soul* must mean that spiritual life which we are to put on after the end of the world. This is clear from the remainder of the verse and from 1 Cor. 15.44.

The fourth passage which they quote is Phil. 1.23: *wishing to be dissolved and to be with Christ.* I will not bother to say anything about the disputed and uncertain translation of the word ἀναλύσαι which means nothing less than *to be dissolved.*[196] What I will say, however, is that it is true Paul wanted to obtain the highest perfection and glory at once. It was, as it were, his ultimate aim: a thing which all men wish to achieve. But that does not prove that when someone's soul leaves his body it is received into heaven or hell without delay. Paul desired to *be with Christ* at Christ's second coming, an event which all believers confidently hoped would take place in the very near future. In the same way, someone who is going on a voyage wants to set sail and to reach port safely, and hardly mentions the intervening journey. And what about the theory that there is no time without motion? Aristotle illustrates this (*Phys.* 4.11) by the story of those men who were said to have gone to sleep in the temple of the heroes and who, on waking, thought that they had gone to sleep one moment and woken up the next, and were not aware of any interim. It is even more likely that, for those who have died, all intervening time will be as nothing, so that to them it will seem that they die and are with Christ at the same moment. But Christ himself indicates very clearly the time at which we shall eventually be with him, John 14.3: *for after I have gone and prepared a place for you, I shall come again and take you to myself, that where I am, you may be also.*

The fifth passage which my opponents quote obviously favors my argument: 1 Pet. 3.19: *to the spirits which are in prison,* literally *under guard,* or, as the Syriac version has it, *in the grave,* which comes to the same thing, for the grave is the common guardian of everyone until the day of judgment.[197] The apostle repeats the

195. See note 206.

196. The usual translation is "to depart" or, more literally, "to unloose," as in a boat unloosed from its moorings, as the subsequent comparison with a voyage suggests.

197. Milton refers to the Tremellius translation of the Syriac, in the Junius-Tremellius Bible. See p. 467, n. 147.

idea more plainly in 4.5, 6: *he is ready to judge the living and the dead; for this reason the gospel was preached to those who are dead as well,* whereas in the first passage he was speaking metaphorically. It follows that *the spirits which are under guard* are dead spirits.

The sixth passage quoted is Rev. 6.9: *I saw the souls beneath the altar.* My answer is that in biblical idiom the word *soul* is regularly used to mean the whole animate body, and that here the reference is to souls not yet born, unless, that is, the fifth seal had already been opened in John's day. Similarly, Christ makes no distinction whatsoever, in the parable about Dives and Lazarus in Luke 16, between the soul and the body. He does, however, for purposes of instruction, speak of things which will not happen until after the day of judgment as if they had already happened, and represents the dead as existing in two different states.

The seventh passage quoted is Luke 23.43: *then Jesus said to him, I tell you truly today you will be with me in paradise.* This text has, for various reasons, worried a lot of people, so much so that they have not hesitated to alter the punctuation, as if it had been written with a comma after *today.* In other words, *although today I seem to everyone to be utterly wretched and contemptible, I give you my word that you will be with me in paradise. In paradise* means *in some pleasant place* (for strictly speaking paradise is not heaven), or *in some delightful spiritual state which both soul and body enjoy.* This is how other commentators read Matt. 27.52, 53. During the earthquake (which was on the same day, not three days after, as is commonly believed) the graves were opened and the dead arose and came out. Then, 27.52 καὶ ἐξελθόντες, *when they had come out,* they eventually entered the holy city, after the resurrection of Christ. According to Erasmus, that is how the ancient Greeks punctuated the passage, and the Syriac quite clearly supports it: *and they came out, and after his resurrection they entered,* etc. The spiritual state of the souls and bodies of those saints, when they rose from their graves, might well be called paradise, and presumably it was in that state that the penitent thief was united with the other saints, without doing them any harm. Moreover, there is no need to take the word *today* in its strict sense. It can mean merely *in a short time,* as it does in 2 Sam. 16.3 and Heb. 3.7. Anyway, such a large amount of quite unequivocal evidence should not be discounted because of one very obscure text, the meaning of which has never been properly understood.

The eighth text cited is from the same chapter, Luke 23, 46: *I give up my spirit into your hands.* But this does not mean that the spirit is necessarily separable from the body, nor that it is not subject to death. David speaks in the same way, though he was not at the time near to death, Ps. 31.6: *into your hand,* he says, *I resign my spirit,* though it is still in and with his body. Stephen, too, says, Acts 7.59: *Lord Jesus, receive my spirit,* but then, *when he had said this, he fell asleep.* What does this mean? It means that it was not the bare spirit, separated from the body, that he commended to Christ but, as 1 Thess. 5.23 puts it, the whole spirit with the body and the soul. And whereas Christ's spirit, body and soul were to be raised again after three days, Stephen's were to be kept until the Lord's coming. Similarly 1 Pet. 4.19: *let them resign their souls to him, as to a faithful creator, with well doing.*

The ninth passage quoted is 2 Cor. 5.1–20. However it is quite obvious that this does not assert the separation of the soul and body, but merely contrasts the earthly and animal life of the whole man with his spiritual and heavenly life. Thus, in the first verse, *the house of this tabernacle* is not contrasted with the soul, but with *a building* and *a home,* that is, with the final renewal of the whole man, as Beza also explains it, which will take place when we are clothed in the heavens (*clothed, not naked,* 5.3). The fourth verse clearly bears this out: *we do not desire to put off that in which we are created, but to put something on over it, so that mortality may be swallowed up by life:* so does the fifth verse: *God has created us for the same thing.* It is quite plain that this does not mean, for separation of the soul from the body, but rather for us to attain perfection of both. So the eighth verse, *to be absent from the body and to be present with the Lord,* must, in fact, be understood as a reference to our final and perfect beatitude. The word *body* must here be taken to mean this frail worldly life, as is common in the sacred writers, and the word ἐκδήμησιν in the ninth verse should be interpreted as an indication of our eternal removal to a heavenly existence. Similarly, *to be present in the body and to live away from the Lord,* in the sixth verse, seems to mean the same as to be entangled in worldly matters, and so have less time for heavenly things. The reason for this state of affairs is given in the seventh verse: *for we walk by faith, not by sight.* This explains the eighth verse: *we are confident and think it right rather to be absent from the body and to be at home with the Lord:* that is, to renounce worldly things as much as possible and concentrate upon heavenly things. The ninth verse shows still more plainly that the terms *to be absent* and *to be at home* both refer to this life. It says that we strive, whether living at home with God or away from him, to be accepted by him. Obviously, we do not strive in any future life to be acceptable to God in heaven at our resurrection. That is the work of this life alone, and its reward is not to be looked for until the second coming of Christ. For Paul says, 5.10: *we must appear at the judgment-seat of Christ, so that everyone may be paid back for the things which he has done in the body, according to what he has done, whether good or evil.* It follows that there is no rewarding of good or evil after death until that day of judgment. Compare 1 Cor. 15, the whole of which throws a good deal of light on this text. 2 Pet. 1.13–15 should also be compared with the same passage: *as long as I am in this tabernacle,* etc., that is, in this life. What more is there to say? There is virtually no scriptural text left which cannot be countered by one or other of the arguments which I have already produced.

The last degree of death is ETERNAL DEATH, THE PUNISHMENT OF THE DAMNED. Chapter 27 deals with this.[198]

198. Actually, this topic is dealt with in chapter 33.

CHAPTER 14

OF MAN'S RESTORATION AND OF CHRIST THE REDEEMER

We have seen how God's providence operated in man's fall: now let us see how it operates in his restoration.

MAN'S RESTORATION is the act by which man, freed from sin and death by God the Father through Jesus Christ, is raised to a far more excellent state of grace and glory than that from which he fell. Rom. 5.15: *but the free gift does not correspond to the offense: for if through the offense of that one man many are dead, much more has God's grace, and the gift through grace, which is of one man Jesus Christ, overflowed to many,* also 5.17 [. . .], and 5.21 says the same. Eph. 1.9, 10 [. . .]; 1 John 3.8: *the man who commits sin is of the* devil . . . *for this purpose the Son of God was made manifest: that he might destroy the works of the devil.*

ITS COMPONENTS ARE REDEMPTION AND RENOVATION.

REDEMPTION IS THAT ACT BY WHICH CHRIST, SENT IN THE FULNESS OF TIME, REDEEMED ALL BELIEVERS AT THE PRICE OF HIS OWN BLOOD, WHICH HE PAID VOLUNTARILY, IN ACCORDANCE WITH THE ETERNAL PLAN AND GRACE OF GOD THE FATHER.[199]

ACCORDING TO THE ETERNAL PLAN OF GOD THE FATHER. 1 Pet. 1.20: *of the lamb foreknown before the foundations of the world were laid.* See the other relevant passages in Chapter 4, Of Predestination.

AND GRACE. For in pronouncing punishment upon the serpent, at a time when man had only grudgingly confessed his guilt, God promised that he would raise up from the seed of the woman a man who would bruise the serpent's head, Gen. 3.15. This was before he got as far as passing sentence on the man. Thus he prefaced man's condemnation with a free redemption:[200] John 3.16 [. . .]; Rom. 3.25: *whom God has set forth as a means of appeasement through faith,* and 5.8 [. . .]; Heb. 2.9 [. . .]; 1 John 4.9, 10 [. . .]. For this reason the Father is frequently called *our Savior,* as it is by his eternal counsel and grace alone that we are saved.[201] Luke 1.47: *my spirit rejoices in God my Savior,* and 1.68, 69 [. . .]; 1 Tim. 1.1 [. . .], and 2.3 [. . .], and 4.10 [. . .]; Tit. 1.3 [. . .], and 2.10 [. . .] and 3.4–6 [. . .]; Jude 25 [. . .].

CHRIST, SENT IN THE FULLNESS OF TIME: Gal. 4.4 [. . .]; Eph. 1.10: *in the dispensation of the fullness of times.*

AT THE PRICE OF HIS OWN BLOOD: Isa. 53.1, etc., Acts 20.28: *the Church of God, which he has bought with his own blood;* Rom. 3.25 [. . .]; 1 Cor. 6.20 [. . .], simi-

199. Cp. *PL* 3.171–72: "All hast thou spoken as my thoughts are, all/As my eternal purpose hath decreed."

200. Cp. *PL* 11.113–17 and 12.232–35.

201. Cp. *PL* 3.173–75: "Man shall not quite be lost, but saved who will,/Yet not of will in him, but grace in me/Freely vouchsafed"; and 3.181–82: "and to me owe/All his deliv'rance, and to none but me."

larly 7.23. Gal. 3.13 [. . .]; Eph. 5.2 [. . .]; Heb. 2.9 [. . .], and 13.20 [. . .]; 1 Pet. 1.19 [. . .], and 3.18 [. . .]; Rev. 1.5 [. . .], and 5.9: *you have redeemed us to God through your blood,* and 3.8 [. . .].

WHICH HE PAID VOLUNTARILY:[202] Isa. 53.10: *he has laid himself bare;* Matt. 20.28 [. . .]; John 10.15, 18: *no one has taken life from me, but I lay it down: I have power to lay it down and to take it up again;* Eph. 5.2 [. . .]; Phil. 2.8 [. . .]; 1 Tim. 2.6 [. . .].

ALL BELIEVERS:[203] Rom. 3.25: *a means of appeasement through faith in his blood.*

Christ is the only redeemer or mediator: Acts 4.12: *nor is there salvation in any other, for there is no other name under the sky which may be given to men, through which we must be saved;*[204] 1 Tim. 2.5: *one mediator, the man Jesus Christ;* John 14.6 [. . .].

Moreover this promise was made to all mankind, more or less distinctly, and the fulfillment of it expected, right from the time of man's fall.[205] Gen. 3.15 [. . .], and 22. 8: *in your seed all the nations of the earth will be blessed,* similarly 26.4 and 28.14, also 49.10 [. . .]; Deut. 18.15 [. . .]; Job 19.25, 26 [. . .]. The point is made even more clearly throughout the Psalms and the prophetic books. Ps. 89.36, 37: *I have sworn once by my holiness that I will not lie to David: his seed shall endure for ever . . .* ; Isa. 11.1, etc. [. . .]; Jer. 30.9 [. . .], and 33.15 [. . .].

He was sent into the world at a pre-ordained time, see Gal. 4.4, above.

Two things must be considered when we think of Christ as a redeemer: his NATURE and his OFFICE.

His NATURE is double, divine and human. Matt. 16.16: *Christ, the Son of the living God;* Gen. 3.15: *the seed of woman;* John 1.1, 14 [. . .] and 3.13 [. . .], and 3.31 [. . .]; Acts 2.30 [. . .], similarly Rom. 1.3. Rom. 8.3 [. . .], and 9.5 [. . .], *God;* 1 Cor. 15.47 [. . .]; Gal. 4.4 [. . .]; Phil. 2.7, 8 [. . .]; Heb. 2.14, 16: *he himself was made a sharer in flesh and blood; he did not choose the angels, but the seed of Abraham,* and 10.5, etc. [. . .]; 1 John 1.7 [. . .], and 4.2 [. . .]; Col. 2.9: *the whole fullness of the godhead dwells in him bodily.* I should deduce from this passage not Christ's divine nature but the absolute and complete virtue of the Father. I prefer to read *fullness* as *fulfillment,* and take it to mean that the entire fulfillment of the Father's promises resides in, but is not hypostatically united with Christ as a man.[206] And I should say that the word *bodily* ought to be interpreted as meaning *in reality*—not, that is to say, merely in the rudimentary ceremonies of this world.[207] This interpretation is in accordance with Isa. 11.1, 2, etc.: *the spirit of Jehovah shall rest upon him, the spirit of wisdom;* and John 3.34: *God does not measure out the spirit to him,* and 1.17: *grace and truth through Jesus Christ.* Similarly 1 Tim. 3.16: *God made manifest in flesh,* that is, in

202. Cp. Argument, *PL* 3: "The Son of God freely offers himself a ransom for man." On Christ's voluntary redemption of humanity and the implications of Milton's theology of atonement, see Chaplin.

203. Cp. *PL* 12.407–8: "Proclaiming life to all who shall believe/In his redemption."

204. Cp. *PL* 3.274–75: "O thou in Heav'n and Earth the only peace/Found out for mankind under wrath."

205. Cp. *PL* 10.1031–35: "Part of our sentence, that thy seed shall bruise/The serpent's head; piteous amends, unless/Be meant, whom I conjecture, our grand foe/Satan, who in the serpent hath contrived/Against us this deceit"; also 10.182–90.

206. Milton also quotes this verse in chapters 2 and 7, construing it differently each time.

207. The phrase *rudimentary ceremonies of the world* alludes to Gal. 4.3; cp. *PR* 1.157.

his incarnate Son, his image. As for Christ's divine nature, the reader should recollect the arguments I presented in my chapter on the Son of God. Through Christ all things were made, both in heaven and earth, even the angels. In the beginning he was the Word. He was God with God, and although he was not supreme, he was the firstborn of all creation. It follows that he must have existed before his incarnation, whatever subtleties may have been invented to provide an escape from this conclusion, by those who argue that Christ was a mere man.[208]

Christ, then, although he was God, put on human nature, and was made flesh, but did not cease to be numerically one Christ. Theologians are of the opinion that this incarnation is by far the greatest mystery of our religion, next to that of the three persons existing in one divine essence. There is, however, not a single word in the Bible about the mystery of the Trinity, whereas the incarnation is frequently spoken of as a mystery: 1 Tim. 3.16: *the mystery of godliness is unquestionably great, God was made manifest in flesh . . .* ; Col. 2.2, 3 [. . .]; Eph. 1.9, 10 [. . .] and 3.4 [. . .]; similarly Col. 4.3. Eph. 3.9 [. . .]; Col. 1.26, 27 [. . .].

As this is such a great mystery, let its very magnitude put us on our guard from the outset, to prevent us from making any rash or hasty assertions or depending upon the trivialities of mere philosophy. Let it prevent us from adding anything of our own, or even from placing weight upon any scriptural text which can be easily invalidated. Instead, let us make do with the most unambiguous of texts, even though these may be few. If we pay attention only to texts of this kind, and are willing to be satisfied with the simple truth, ignoring the glosses of metaphysicians, how many prolix and monstrous controversies we shall put an end to! How many opportunities for heresy we shall remove: how much of the raw material for heresy we shall cut away! How many huge volumes, the works of dabblers in theology, we shall fling out of God's temple as filth and rubbish! If teachers, teachers even of the reformed church, had learned by now to rely on divine authorities alone where divine matters are concerned, and to concentrate upon the contents of the Bible, then nothing would be more straightforward than what the Christian faith propounds as essential for our salvation. Nothing would be more reasonable, or more adapted to the understanding even of the least intelligent. We should easily see the essentials, once they were disentangled from the windings of controversy, and we should let mysteries alone and not tamper with them. We should be afraid to pry into things further than we were meant.

I will now outline the orthodox position, as it stands today and as, indeed, it has stood for a great many years.[209] The assumption which we came across earlier was that there were three persons in one natural entity, the Trinity. This time, however, it is assumed that there are two natures in the one person of

208. Socinians denied the preexistent divinity of Christ.

209. For Milton's view of the Incarnation in relation to orthodox doctrine, see Lewalski 1966 and Rumrich 2003.

Christ. Furthermore it is assumed that Christ has a real and perfect subsistence in one of these natures, without that nature having a subsistence of its own. Thus two natures make one person. This is what is called, by scholastic philosophers, the hypostatic union. Zanchius explains it as follows, Vol. 1, Pt. 2, Bk. 2, Chap. 7. He took upon him not, strictly speaking, man, he writes, but the human nature. *For when the Logos was in the virgin's womb, it took human nature upon itself by forming a body for itself out of the substance of Mary, and at the same time creating a soul for that body. And he assumed this nature in and for himself in such a way that the nature never subsisted by itself, independent of the Logos, but has always subsisted, both at first and ever since, in the Logos alone.*

I will not bother to point out that there is no mention of these curious secrets anywhere in the Bible. Zanchius is rash enough to expound them on his own authority, and does so as confidently as if he had been present in Mary's womb and witnessed the mystery himself. But what an absurd idea, that someone should take human nature upon himself without taking manhood as well! For human nature, that is, the form of man contained in flesh, must, at the very moment when it comes into existence, bring a man into existence too, and a whole man, with no part of his essence or his subsistence (if that word signifies anything) or his personality missing.[210] As a matter of fact subsistence does not really mean anything except substantial existence, and personality is merely a word which has been wrenched from its proper meaning to help patch up the holes in the arguments of theologians. Obviously the Logos became what it assumed, and if it assumed human nature, but not manhood, then it became an example of human nature, not a man. But, of course, the two things are really inseparable.

I will now go on to demonstrate the sheer vacuity of the orthodox view. But first I will explain and differentiate between the meanings of three words which commonly recur in this discussion: *nature, person* and *hypostasis* or, as it is translated in Latin, *substantia* (substance) or *subsistentia* (subsistence). *Nature,* in this context, can only mean either the essence itself or the properties of that essence. But as these properties are inseparable from the essence itself, and as the unity of natures is *hypostatical* not *accidental,* we must conclude that *nature* can mean nothing in this context except the essence itself. *Person* is a theatrical term which has been adopted by scholastic theologians to mean any one individual being, as the logicians put it: any intelligent ens, numerically one whether it be one God or one angel or one man. The Greek word *hypostasis* can, in this context, mean only what is expressed by the Latin words *substantia* or

210. Milton rejects the orthodox doctrine that Christ took on generic human nature. Logicians typically make form generic and matter specific. But for Milton, form is the principle of individuation and numerical difference; matter the principle of commonality (cp. *Art of Logic,* Yale 8:233–34; *PL* 5.472–75). The Son by taking human matter becomes generically human; by assuming the specific form of Jesus he becomes an individual man.

subsistentia (i.e., substance or subsistence). It denotes, then, merely a perfect essence existing *per se,* and is therefore usually used in opposition to *accidents.*

It follows that the union of two natures in Christ was the mutual hypostatic union of two essences. Because where a perfect substantial essence exists, there must also be a hypostasis or subsistence, since they are quite evidently the same thing. So one Christ, one ens, and one person is formed from this mutual hypostatic union of two natures. There is no need to be afraid that two persons will result from the union of two hypostases, any more than from the union of two natures, that is, of two essences. But supposing Christ's human nature never had its own separate subsistence, or supposing the Son did not take that subsistence upon himself: it would follow that he could not have been a real man, and that he could not have taken upon himself the true and perfect substance or essence of man. He could not have done so, that is, any more than he could cause his body to be present in the sacrament without mass or local extension, which is what the Papists maintain.[211] They explain this phenomenon, if you please, by reference to divine power, their usual shift in such cases. But it is no good pleading divine power if you cannot prove it on divine authority. There is, then, in Christ a mutual hypostatic union of two natures or, in other words, of two essences, of two substances and consequently of two persons. And there is nothing to stop the properties of each from remaining individually distinct. It is quite certain that this is so. We do not know how it is so, and it is best for us to be ignorant of things which God wishes to remain secret.[212] After all, if it were legitimate to be definite and dogmatic about mysteries of this kind, why should we not play the philosopher and start asking questions about the external form common to these two natures? Because if the divine nature and the human nature coalesced in one person, that is to say, as my opponents themselves admit, in a rational being numerically one, then they must have coalesced in one external form as well. As a result the divine form, if it were not previously identical with the human, must have been either destroyed or blended with the human, both of which seem absurd. Or else the human form, if it did not precisely resemble the divine, must have been either destroyed or blended with the divine. Or else Christ must have had two forms. How much better for us, then, to know only that the Son of God, our Mediator, was made flesh and that he is called and is in fact both God and man.[213] The Greeks express this concept very neatly by the single word θεάνθρωπος. As God has not revealed to us how this comes about it is much better for us to hold our tongues and be wisely ignorant.[214]

However, the opinion I have advanced here about the hypostatic union cor-

211. Cp. *DDD* (p. 150): "those words . . . are as much against plain equity, and the mercy of religion, as those words of 'Take, eat, this is my body,' elementally understood, are against nature and sense."

212. Cp. *PL* 8.71–78 and 172–74.

213. *PL* 3.238: "Account me man"; and 3.315–16: "Here shalt thou sit incarnate, here shalt reign / Both God and man, Son both of God and man." Also 3.283–85, 303–4; 10.60–62; 12.380–82.

214. *PL* 8.173: "be lowly wise."

roborates further the conclusion of my more lengthy discussion of the Son of God in the fifth chapter (i.e. that the essence of the Son is not the same as the essence of the Father). For if it were the same the Son could not have coalesced in one person with man, unless the Father had also been included in the same union—unless, in fact, man had become one person with the Father as well as with the Son, which is impossible.

So let us get rid of those arguments which are produced to prove that the person who was made flesh must necessarily be the supreme God. First of all there is that text from Heb. 7.26, 27: *such a high priest was fitting for us, holy, removed from all evil, spotless, separate from sinners, and made higher than the heavens.* But these words do not prove even that he is God, let alone that he must have been God. To begin with he was *holy* not only as God but as man, since he was conceived through the Holy Spirit and by the power of the Most High. Furthermore, he is not said to have been higher than the heavens, but to have been *made higher* than them. Again *to last for ever,* 7.24, is common both to angels and to men, and the fact that he *can save those who come to God through him,* 7.25, does not prove that he is God either. Finally, it is said that *the word of the oath, taken since the law, makes the Son perfect for ever,* 7.28, and it certainly does not follow from this that he is God. Besides, the Bible nowhere states that only God can approach God, or take away sin, or fulfil the law, or endure and overcome the anger of God, the power of Satan and temporal and eternal death, or recover the blessings lost by us. What it does state is that he whom God has empowered to do all this can do it: in other words, God's beloved Son with whom God has declared himself pleased.

So since we must believe that Christ, after his incarnation, remained one Christ it is not for us to ask whether he retained a two-fold intellect or a two-fold will, for the Bible says nothing of these things. For he could, with the same intellect, both *increase in wisdom,* Luke 2.52, after he had emptied himself, and *know everything,* John 21.17, that is, after the Father had instructed him, as he himself acknowledges.[215] That single text, Matt. 26.39: *not as I will but as you will,* does not imply a two-fold will, unless he and the Father are the same, and as I have already shown this cannot be so.

The fact that Christ had a body shows that he was a real man, Luke 24.39: *a spirit does not have flesh and bones, as you see I have;* so does the fact that he had a soul,[216] Mark 10.45: *that he might give his soul for many,* and 14.34: *my soul is sad, sad to death;* and a spirit, Luke 23.46: *I give up my spirit into your hands.* True, God also claims that he himself has a soul and a spirit. But the Bible gives some absolutely unambiguous reasons why Christ must have been a man: 1 Cor. 15.21: *for since death came through man, through man came also the resurrection of the dead;* Heb. 2.14: *since children are sharers in flesh and blood, he too, likewise . . . that through death he*

215. Cp. *PR* 1.293: "For what concerns my knowledge God reveals."

216. *PL* 3.247–49: "Thou wilt not leave me in the loathsome grave/His prey, nor suffer my unspotted soul/Forever with corruption there to dwell."

might smash him in whose power the strength of death lies, that is, the devil, and 2.17 [...], and 2.18 [...]; and 4.15 [...], and 5.2 [...]. Moreover, God would not accept any other sacrifice, since any other would have been less worthy. Heb. 10.5: *you did not want a sacrifice, but you have prepared a body for me,* and 8.3 [...], and 9.22 [...].

Since Christ's two natures add up to a single person, there are certain things which seem to be said about him in an unrestricted way which actually have to be applied to one or other of the two natures. This way of speaking is known as *communicatio idiomatum* or *proprietatum.* It means that something which is proper to one of the two natures is, by idiomatic license, transferred to the other. John 3.13: *the Son of man, who is in heaven, came down from heaven,* and 8.58: *before Abraham existed, I am.* So these and similar passages, whenever they occur, are to be understood κατ' ἄλλο καὶ ἄλλο, as theologians put it: ἄλλο καὶ ἄλλο not ἄλλος καὶ ἄλλος because it refers not to Christ's self, but to his *person* (i.e. his office of mediator).[217] As for his natures themselves, they constitute in my opinion too deep a mystery for anyone to say anything definite about them.

But sometimes attributes which belong to Christ as a whole are applied to one or other of his natures. 1 Tim. 2.5: *the mediator between God and men, the man Christ Jesus.* It is not as man, however, that Christ is mediator, but as θεάνθρωπος.

It is more usual for the Bible to distinguish the things which are peculiar to his human nature. Acts 2.30: *from David's loins* τὸ κατὰ σάρκα *insofar as the flesh is concerned;* also Rom. 9.5. 1 Pet. 3.18: *having been put to death in the flesh,* that is principally and more obviously in the flesh than in any other way. This point will be raised again in Chapter 16.

There are two parts to Christ's incarnation: the conception and the nativity. The efficient cause of the former was the Holy Spirit, Matt. 1.20: *that which is conceived in her is of the Holy Spirit;* Luke 1.35: *the Holy Spirit shall come upon you, and the power of the Highest shall overshadow you.* I should say that these words refer to the power and spirit of the Father himself, as I have shown before: compare Ps. 40.7 with Heb. 10.5, 6: *you have prepared a body for me.*

The aim of this miraculous conception was to evade the pollution of Adam's sin. Heb. 7.26: *such a high priest was fitting for us, holy, spotless, separate from sinners.*

Christ's birth is foretold by all the prophets, and more particularly in Mic. 5.2: *but you Bethlehem Ephratah;* Isa. 7.14 [...], and 11.1 [...]. It is narrated in Matt. 1.18 onwards; Luke 1.42: *blessed is the fruit of your womb,* and 2.6, 7 [...], and 2.22 [...].

The following arguments can be used to prove that, in spite of what the Jews believe, the Messiah has already come. First, the cities of Bethlehem and Nazareth are now destroyed. It was in these that the Christ was to be born and educated: Mic. 5.2; Zech. 6.12: *behold a man whose name is Nazer or the offshoot.* Secondly, it was foretold that he would come while the second temple and the

217. Milton distinguishes between the neuter ἄλλο and masculine ἄλλος, forms of the Greek word for "other, another." Christ's *self,* Milton insists, is masculine, though the communicable *office* he fulfills is neuter.

Jewish republic were still in existence. Hag. 2.7, 9 [. . .]; Dan. 9.24 [. . .], and 9.26 [. . .], and 9.27 [. . .]; Zech. 9.9 [. . .]; Gen. 49.10: *the people shall not depart from Judah, nor a lawgiver from between his feet, until Shiloh comes.* The three most ancient Jewish commentators, Onkelos, Jonathan and Hierosolymitanus took this name to mean the Messiah. Dan. 2.44: *in the days of those kings the God of heaven will set up a kingdom.* Thirdly, the Gentiles have long since left off worshipping other gods and have embraced the faith of Christ, and it was foretold that this would not happen before Christ's coming: Gen. 49.10: *and the obedience of the peoples will be to him;* Isa. 2.2: *it will happen in the last days that all the Gentiles will come flocking to him,* similarly Mic. 4.1; Hag. 2.7 [. . .]; Mal. 3.1 [. . .], etc.

CHAPTER 27

OF THE GOSPEL AND CHRISTIAN LIBERTY

[. . .][218]

Once the gospel, the new covenant through faith in Christ, is introduced, then all the old covenant, in other words the entire Mosaic law, is abolished.[219] Jer. 31.31–33, as above; Luke 16.16: *the law and the prophets existed until John;* Acts 15.10 [. . .]; Rom. 3.21, 22: *but now God's righteousness is revealed without the law,* and 6.14: *you are not under the law but under grace,* and 7.4 [. . .], and 7.6 [. . .]. At the beginning of the same chapter Paul shows that we are released from the law in the same way as a wife is released from her dead husband. Also 7.7: *I did not know sin except through the law:* that is, the whole law, *for I should not have known lust if the law had not said, Do not lust . . .* The law referred to here is the decalogue, so it follows that we are released from the decalogue too. See also 8.15: *you have not received the spirit of slavery again in fear,* and 14.20: *indeed all things are pure . . . ,* compared with Tit. 1.15: *to the pure, all things are pure: but to the polluted and the unbelieving nothing is pure, but both their mind and their conscience is defiled;* 1 Cor. 6.12 [. . .] and 10.23 [. . .]; 2 Cor. 3.3 [. . .], and 3.6–8 [. . .], and 11 [. . .], and 13 [. . .], and 5.17 [. . .]; Gal. 3.19: *why, then, the law? It was added because of transgressions, until that seed should come to whom the promise was made,* and 3.25: *but after the faith comes we are no longer under a schoolmaster,* and 4.1, etc. [. . .], also 4.21, spoken to those who desired to be under the law, and 4.24, on the subject of Hagar and Sarah: *these are the two covenants; Agar bringing forth offspring to slavery: the other,* 4.26: *is free.* Hence 4.30: *throw out the bondwoman and her son; for the bondwoman's son shall not be heir with the freewoman's son,* and 5.18: *if you are led by the Spirit, you are not under the law;* Eph. 2.14, 15: *the barrier*

218. The previous chapter makes the transition from Milton's account in chapters 15–25 of various aspects of the process of renovation to its "manifestation or exhibition in the covenant of grace," indistinctly under Hebrew law, and more clearly under the Gospel, the topic of this chapter. The excerpt printed here concerns Christian liberty in relation to Mosaic Law.

219. After making the same assertion briefly in *Of Civil Power,* Milton promises "of these things perhaps more some other time," a statement that Hunter notes for its apparent reference to the extensive treatment in this chapter (Yale 7:271–72).

of the dividing wall, that is *enmity, he has abolished in his flesh; and has annulled that law of commandments, contained in decrees.* Now not only the ceremonial code, but the whole positive law of Moses was a law of commandments and contained in decrees. Moreover, the Jews were distinguished from the Gentiles not only by the ceremonial code, as Zanchius, commenting on this passage, claims, but by the whole Mosaic law. They were *alienated from the state of Israel and excluded from the promise of the covenants,* 2.12, and this *promise* was made with reference to the works of the whole law, not only to ceremonies. [. . .].[220]

The usual retort is that all these passages should be taken to refer to the abolition of the ceremonial code only.[221] This argument can be quickly refuted, firstly, by the definition of the law itself, as given in the previous chapter, which contains all the reasons for the law's enactment. When all the causes of the law, considered as a whole, have been removed or have become obsolete, then the whole law must be annulled too. The principal reasons given for the enactment of the law as a whole, are as follows: to stimulate our depravity, and thus cause anger; to inspire us with slavish fear, as a result of the enmity and the written accusation directed against us; to be a schoolmaster to bring us to the righteousness of Christ, and so on.[222] Now the texts quoted above prove not only that every one of these reasons has now been removed, but also that they have nothing at all to do with ceremonies.

First, then, the law is abolished above all because it is a law of works, and in order that it may give place to a law of grace. Rom. 3.27: *By what law? The law of works? No: but by the law of faith,* and 11.6: *if through grace, then no longer from works; otherwise grace is not grace.* Now the law of works was not only the ceremonial law but the whole law.

2. *the law brings anger: for where there is no law there is no transgression,* 4.15. It is no single part of the law, but the whole law, which causes anger, for a transgression is a transgression of the whole, not only of a part. Moreover the law causes anger but the gospel produces grace, and as anger and grace are incompatible, it follows that the law and the gospel are incompatible too.

3. It was the whole law which promised life and salvation to those who obeyed and carried out the things written in it, Lev. 18.5, Gal. 3.12, and which cursed those who did otherwise, Deut. 27.26, Gal. 3.10. Christ has redeemed us from the curse of that law, Gal. 3.13—the law, that is, whose demands we were unable to fulfill. Now we could have fulfilled the demands of the ceremonial code without any difficulty, so it must have been the entire Mosaic law from which Christ redeemed us. Again, the curse was directed against those who did not fulfill the demands of the whole law, so Christ cannot redeem us from that

220. The deleted passages from Scripture elaborate Milton's claim that the whole law has been superceded.

221. Protestant theologians typically distinguished between Jewish ceremonial law, from which Christians were exempt, and moral law, which they were obliged to obey.

222. Cp. *PL* 12.287–90: "And therefore was law given them to evince/Their natural pravity, by stirring up/Sin against law to fight; that when they see/Law can discover sin, but not remove."

curse unless he has annulled the whole law for us. If he has annulled the whole law, then obviously we cannot be bound by any part of it.

4. We are told that the law *which was written on tablets of stone* was *the ministry of death,* and therefore *transitory,* 2 Cor. 3. But this law was the decalogue itself.

5. It is unquestionably not only the ceremonial code, then, but the whole law that is a law of sin and of death. It is a law of sin because it stimulates sin, and of death because it produces death and is opposed to the law of the spirit of life. But it is this same complete law which is abolished: Rom. 8.2: *the law of the spirit of life, which is in Christ Jesus, has freed me from the law of sin and of death.*

6. It was certainly not merely the ceremonial law through which the desires of sins flourished in our members to bring forth fruit to death, Rom. 7.5. But it is that law to which we are dead, 7.4, and which is dead to us, 7.6, and from which we are therefore freed as a wife from her dead husband, 7.3. It follows that we are freed not only from the ceremonial law but from the whole Mosaic law, 7.7, as above.

7. All believers should undoubtedly be considered righteous, since they are justified by God through faith. But Paul distinctly says that there is no law for the righteous, Gal. 5.22, 23, 1 Tim. 1.9. If there were to be any law for the righteous, it would only be a law which justifies. Now justification is beyond the scope not of the ceremonial law alone, but of the whole Mosaic law: I have already established this fact in my discussion of justification; Gal. 3.11, and so on. Therefore it is the whole law and not only the ceremonial code which is repealed because of its inability to justify.

In addition, this law not only cannot justify, it disturbs believers and makes them waver. It even tempts God, if we try to fulfill it. It contains no promise, in fact it breaks and puts an end to all promises—of inheritance, of adoption, of grace itself and even of the spirit. What is more, it makes us accursed. The law which does all this is surely repealed. Now it was not only the ceremonial law but the whole law, the law of works, which did these things. Therefore the whole law is repealed. There is the clearest scriptural proof that the law really did every one of the things I have specified: Acts 15.24: *we have heard that certain people who went out from us have disturbed you by their words, and made your souls waver, saying that you ought to be circumcised and keep the law* . . . and 15.10: *why do you tempt God to put a yoke* . . . ? The Pharisees who had believed wanted believers to be subject to the whole law, 15.5, therefore it was the whole law which, Peter argued, should be removed from the necks of the disciples. Secondly, the law which contains no promise is not merely the ceremonial law but the whole law. This is evident, because if any part of the law were to contain a promise, that would be enough, but the law about which Paul says so much contains no promise in any part of it. Rom. 4.13, 16: *it was not through the law that the promise was granted to Abraham or to his seed that he would be the heir of the world; but through the righteousness of faith;* Gal. 3.18: *if inheritance is from the law, it is no longer from the promise. But God gave it to Abraham through the promise*—not, therefore, through the law or any part of it. Thus Paul proves that either the whole law or the promise itself must be abolished, Rom. 4.14: *for if those who are of the law are heirs, faith is made vain and the promise an empty one.* Also Gal. 3.18, as above. If the promise is abolished, then inheritance and adoption are abolished too, and fear and slavery, which are incompatible with adoption, are brought back, Rom. 8.15, Gal. 4.1, etc. and 4.21, 24, 26, 30, as above. In that case union and communion with Christ are destroyed as well, Gal. 5.4: *cut off from Christ, you have disappeared, all of you who are justified through the law.* Thus glorification is lost and grace itself is destroyed, unless the whole law is destroyed, Gal. 5.4: *all of you who are justified through the law have fallen from grace.* There are various factors which make it obvious that the whole law is being spoken of here, one of which is the previous verse, where obeying the whole law is mentioned. Finally, the Spirit itself is excluded, unless the whole law is destroyed, Gal. 5.18: *if you are led by the Spirit you are not under the law,* therefore, conversely, if you are under the law, you are not led by the Spirit. What is left, is the curse, Gal. 3.10: *all who are of the works of the law are under a curse, for it is written, cursed is everyone who does not continue to observe all the injunctions which are written in the book of the law.* It follows that all the things which are written in the law, and not only the ceremonial law, make us liable to the curse. Thus Christ, when he redeemed us from the curse, 3.13, redeemed us also from the causes of the curse, that is to say, from the works of the law, or from the whole law of works, which is the same thing, and this, as I showed above, does not mean merely the ceremonial law. Even if these results did not follow, there is obviously no point in obeying a law which contains no promise. If you do no good unless you obey the law in every detail, and if it is absolutely impossible to obey it in every detail, then it is ridiculous to obey it at all, especially if it has been superseded by a better law of faith, which God, in Christ, has given us both the will and the ability to obey.[223]

All these arguments and authorities serve to prove that the whole Mosaic law is abolished by the gospel. But in reality the law, that is the substance of the law, is not broken by this abolition. On the contrary its purpose is attained in that love of God and of our neighbor which is born of faith, through the spirit. Thus Christ quite truthfully asserted the law, Matt. 5.17, etc.: *do not think that I have come to repeal the law and the prophets: I have not come to repeal but to fulfill* etc.; Rom. 3.31: *do we then make the law vain, through faith? God forbid: why, we establish the law!,* and 8.4: *that the righteousness of the law might be fulfilled in us who walk not according to the flesh but according to the spirit.*

The common objection to this doctrine is countered by Paul himself. He firmly maintains that sin is not strengthened, on the contrary, either dispersed altogether or at least diminished by this abrogation of the law: Rom. 6.14, 15: *sin will not govern you: for you are not under the law but under grace. What then? shall we sin because we are not under the law but under grace? God forbid . . .* The substance of the

223. Cp. *PL* 12.295–99: "they may find/Justification towards God, and peace/Of conscience, which the law by ceremonies/Cannot appease, nor man the moral part/Perform, and not performing cannot live."

law, love of God and of our neighbor, should not, I repeat, be thought of as destroyed. We must realize that only the written surface has been changed, and that the law is now inscribed on believers' hearts by the spirit. At the same time, however, it sometimes appears that, where particular commandments are concerned, the spirit is at variance with the letter. This happens when by breaking the letter of the law we behave in a way which conforms better with our love of God and of our neighbor. Thus Christ himself broke the letter of the law, Mark 2.27: look at the fourth commandment, and then compare his words, *the sabbath was made for man, not man for the sabbath.* Paul did the same when he said that marriage with an unbeliever was not to be dissolved, contrary, to the express injunction of the law. 1 Cor. 7.12: *I, not the Lord.* In interpreting both these commandments, the commandment about the Sabbath and that about marriage, attention to the requirements of charity is given precedence over any written law. The other commandments should all be treated in the same way. Matt. 22.37, 39, 40: *on these two commandments,* that is, those which concern love for God and for our neighbor, *all the law and the prophets depend.* Neither of these, however, is found, in so many words, among the ten commandments. The first occurs in Deut. 6.5 and the second in Lev. 19.18, and not before. Nevertheless we are told that they are preeminent and include not only the ten commandments but, what is more, all the law and the prophets. Also Matt. 7.12: *whatever you wish men to do to you, do it to them; for that is the law and the prophets*; Rom. 13.8, 10: *he who loves another has fulfilled the demands of the law. charity is the fulfilling of the demands of the law*; Gal. 5.14: *the whole law can be summed up in one sentence: love your neighbor as yourself;* 1 Tim. 1.5 [. . .]. This is the end of the Mosaic commandment, and the same thing is even more true of the commandment of the gospel. James 2.8: *if you obey the royal law according to the scripture, you will love your neighbor as yourself.* Thus anyone with any sense interprets the precepts of Christ in the Sermon on the Mount not in a literal way but in a way that is in keeping with the spirit of charity. The same applies to Paul's remark in 1 Cor. 11.4: *every man praying or prophesying with his head covered . . . ,* a text which will be dealt with later, in book 2 chapter 4, when I discuss the matter of how those who pray should dress. Hence we find, in Rom. 4.15: *where there is no law there is no transgression,* that is, no transgression of the letter, so long as the substance of the law, love for God and for one's neighbor, is, by the Spirit's guidance, preserved. [. . .].[224]

But all the rest stick to the doctrine propounded by the converted Pharisees, and believe that the law should still be observed even in gospel times. This is a doctrine which did a good deal of harm in the early days of the church. It is maintained that the law has many uses even for us Christians. For example, it forces us to be more aware of sin, and thus to receive grace more eagerly, and to understand God's will better. I should reply that, to begin with, my argument does not apply to people who need to be forced to come to Christ, but to those

224. The deleted paragraph is devoted to noting that two other theologians agree with Milton, most prominently the Italian Protestant Jerome Zanchius (1516–90).

who are already believers and thus already firmly attached to Christ. Secondly, the will of God is best understood from the teaching of the gospel itself, under the promised guidance of the Spirit of truth, and from God's law, written in the hearts of believers. Besides, we are made aware of sin and are forced towards an acceptance of Christ's grace merely by knowing the law, not by obeying it; for as scripture constantly reminds us, we do not draw nearer to Christ by the works of the law but wander further away from him.

Then again, those theologians with whom I disagree, particularly Polanus,[225] make the following distinction: *the fact that one is not under the law does not mean that one does not owe obedience to the law, but that one is free from the curse and constraint of the law and from its provocation to sin.* But if this is so, what do believers gain from the gospel? For believers, even under the law, were exempt from its curse and its provocation to sin. Moreover what, I ask you, can it mean to be free from the constraint of the law, if not to be entirely exempt from the law, as I maintain we are? For so long as the law exists, it constrains, because it is a law of slavery. Constraint and slavery are as inseparable from the law as liberty is from the gospel. I will make this clear presently.

Polanus contends, in his comment on Gal. 4.4, 5: *to redeem those who were subject to the law,* that "to say Christians are redeemed from the subjection of the law, and are not under the law, does not mean simply that they owe no more obedience to the law. The words have, instead, a less absolute meaning, which is that Christians are no longer required to fulfil the law of God perfectly in this life, because Christ has fulfilled it for them." Anyone can see, however, that this is not so at all. It is not a less perfect life that is required from Christians but, in fact, a more perfect life than was required of those who were under the law. The whole tenor of Christ's teaching shows this. There is, however, one difference. Moses imposed the literal or external law even on those who were unwilling to receive it;[226] whereas Christ writes the internal law of God on the hearts of believers through his Spirit, and leads them as willing followers.[227] Under the law men who trusted in God were justified through their faith, but not without the works of the law, Rom. 4.12: *the Father of the circumcised,* etc. But the gospel justifies through faith without the works of the law. So we, freed from the works of the law, follow not the letter but the spirit, not the works of the law but the works of faith. Thus it is not said to us, *whatever is not of the law, is sin,* but *whatever is not of faith.* Faith, not law, is our rule. It follows from this that, as faith cannot be compelled, the works of faith cannot be either. See more on this subject in chapter 15, above, on Christ's kingly office and the internal law of the spirit by which he governs the church. Also Book 2, chapter 1 on the form of good works.

225. Of Czech origin, Amandus Polanus von Polansdorf (1561–1610) was the leader of the conservative Calvinists in Basel. His *Syntagma Theologiae Christianae* was published in Hanover in 1609. He also composed commentaries on the Old Testament and translated the New Testament into German.

226. Cp. *PL* 12.304–5: "From imposition of strict laws, to free/Acceptance of large grace."

227. Cp. *PL* 12.523–24: "what the Spirit within/Shall on the heart engrave."

The law of slavery having been abrogated through the gospel, the result is Christian Liberty. It is true that liberty is primarily the fruit of adoption, and was consequently not unknown in the time of the law, as I said in Chapter 23. However, our liberty could not be perfect or manifest before the advent of Christ, our liberator. Therefore liberty is a matter relevant chiefly to the gospel, and is associated with it. This is so, first, because truth exists chiefly under the gospel, John 1.17: *grace and truth are present through Jesus Christ,* and truth liberates, 8.31, 32: *if you remain in my word, then you will really be my disciples, and you will know the truth, and the truth will make you free,* and 8.36 [. . .]. Secondly, because the peculiar gift of the gospel is the Spirit and: *where the Spirit of the Lord is, there is liberty,* 2 Cor. 3.17.

CHRISTIAN LIBERTY means that CHRIST OUR LIBERATOR FREES US FROM THE SLAVERY OF SIN AND THUS FROM THE RULE OF THE LAW AND OF MEN, AS IF WE WERE EMANCIPATED SLAVES. HE DOES THIS SO THAT, BEING MADE SONS INSTEAD OF SERVANTS[228] AND GROWN MEN INSTEAD OF BOYS, WE MAY SERVE GOD IN CHARITY THROUGH THE GUIDANCE OF THE SPIRIT OF TRUTH. Gal. 5.1: *stand fast, then, in the liberty by which Christ has freed us, and do not be entangled again in the yoke of slavery;* Rom. 8.2 [. . .], and 8.15 [. . .]; Gal. 4.7 [. . .]; Heb. 2.15 [. . .]; 1 Cor. 7.23: *you are bought with a price, do not be slaves of men;* James 1.25: *who looks into that perfect law of liberty,* and 2.12: *speak and act like those who are to be judged by the law of liberty.*

THAT WE MAY SERVE GOD. Matt. 11.29, 30: *take my yoke upon you: for my yoke is good,* or *easy, and my burden is light,* compared with 1 John 5.3–5: *to love God, is to keep his commandments, and his commandments are not burdensome. . .;* Rom. 6.18: *freed from sin, you became servants of righteousness,* and 6.22 [. . .], and 7.6 [. . .]; Rom. 12.1, 2 [. . .]; James 1.25: [. . .]; 1 Pet. 2.16: *as free, and not using your liberty as a veil for malice, but as servants of God.* Thus we are freed from the judgments of men, and especially from coercion and legislation in religious matters, Rom. 14.4 [. . .], and 14.8 [. . .]; Matt. 7.1: *do not judge, so that you may not be judged;* Rom. 14.10: *but why do you condemn your brother, why do you think him worth nothing? For we shall all stand before the judgment seat of Christ.* We are forbidden, then, where matters of conscience and religion are concerned, to *judge* or *condemn* our brothers even in everyday speech. So we are certainly forbidden to judge them in a court of law, which has very plainly nothing to do with such matters. St. Paul refers all cases of conscience or religion to the judgment-seat not of man but of Christ. James 2.12: *speak and act like those who are to be judged by the law of liberty*—judged, that is, in questions of religion by God, not by men.[229] If God is going to judge us in these questions according to the law of liberty, why should man prejudge us according to the law of slavery?

228. Cp. *PL* 12.305–6: "from servile fear/To filial, works of law to works of faith."

229. Cp. *PL* 12.528–30: "for on Earth/Who against faith and conscience can be heard/Infallible?"

IN CHARITY THROUGH THE GUIDANCE OF THE SPIRIT OF TRUTH. Rom. 14, and 15.1–15. In these chapters, however, Paul first warns us to beware of two things. First, that however we employ this liberty of ours, we should act in firm faith, convinced that we are allowed to do so: 14.5: *let every man be fully certain in his own mind,* and 23: *whatever is not of faith, is sin.* Secondly, that we should give no just cause of offence to a weak brother: 14.20, 21: *do not destroy the work of God for the sake of food: all things indeed are pure, but it is evil for a man to give offence when he eats* . . . ; 1 Cor. 8.13 [. . .]. This, however, was the effect of Paul's extraordinary love for his brothers. It does not constitute a duty incumbent upon every believer to abstain from meat for ever in case a weaker brother should think vegetable food alone lawful. See also 9.19–22 [. . .], and 10.23: *all things are lawful for me but not all things are good for me* . . . , as above. Gal. 5.13 [. . .]; 2 Pet. 2.19 [. . .]; 1 Cor. 8.9 [. . .].

This seems to have been the only reason for the command given to the churches, Acts 15.28, 29: *to abstain from blood and from things strangled.* It was, that is to say, in case the Jews who were not yet sufficiently firm in their faith should take offense. It is clear that the prohibition of blood was purely ceremonial, from the reason given in Lev. 17.11: *for the life of all flesh is in the blood, and I* . . . Thus the eating of fat was also forbidden in the law, 7.23, etc., but no one thinks that it is therefore unlawful to eat fat. The prohibition applies only to sacrificial times, Acts 10.13, etc.

No consideration is to be shown, however, to the malicious or the obstinate: Gal. 2.4, 5: *but because of false brothers who had crept in. They had entered secretly to find out about the liberty which we enjoy in Christ Jesus, intending to bring us into slavery. We did not yield to them by subjection even for a moment, so that the truth of the gospel might persist among you.* Christ did not worry about giving offence to the Pharisees; instead he defended his disciples when they did not wash their hands before eating, Matt. 15.2, 3, and also when they plucked ears of corn, which was then considered unlawful on the Sabbath day, Luke 6.1, etc. If it were always necessary to satisfy the malicious and the envious, Christ would not have allowed a woman to anoint his feet with such precious ointment. He would not have allowed the same wealthy woman to wipe them with her soft hair: he would not have defended and praised her action, as, indeed, he did, John 12.3, etc. Nor would he have taken advantage of the services and liberality of the women who accompanied him wherever he went, Luke 8.2–3.

No regard is to be paid even to one's fellow-Christians, if they behave in a disingenuous way. Gal. 2.11, etc.: *but when Peter had come to Antioch I opposed him to his face, because he was culpable* . . .

Moreover the weak should not be over-hasty in judging the freedom of the strong. Rather, they should present themselves for instruction. Rom. 14.13: *so let us not judge one another any more.*

So neither this reason, nor even the reason I mentioned before, that is, consideration for the weak, is enough to necessitate magisterial ordinances which compel believers to uniformity or deprive them of any part of their freedom.

Paul argues along these lines in 1 Cor. 9.19: *although I am free from all men I have made myself a slave to all*—I was not made a slave by anyone else: *free from all men*—and therefore, of course, from the magistrate, at any rate in matters of this kind.[230] If a magistrate takes this freedom away he takes the gospel away too: at least, he deprives the good as well as the bad, contrary to the well-known precept in Matt. 13.29: *in case when gathering the tares you root up the wheat at the same time: let both grow together until harvest.*[231]

CHAPTER 30

OF THE HOLY SCRIPTURE

The writings of the prophets, the apostles and the evangelists, since they were divinely inspired, are called THE HOLY SCRIPTURE; 2 Sam. 23.2: *the Spirit of Jehovah spoke in me, and his word was on my tongue;* Matt. 22.43: *David, through the Spirit, calls him Lord, saying*. . . ; 2 Cor. 13.3 [. . .]; 2 Tim: 3.16 [. . .].

As can be seen from standard editions of the Bible, there is general agreement among the orthodox[232] about which books of the Old and New Testaments may be called CANONICAL, that is to say, accepted as the genuine writings of the prophets, apostles and evangelists.

The books usually added to these, and known as the APOCRYPHAL books, have nothing like the same authority as the canonical, and are not admitted as evidence in deciding points of faith.

The reasons for this are: 1. Because although they were written in Old Testament times, they are not in the Hebrew language. They certainly ought to have been, if genuine, because at that time, before the Gentiles had been called, the church existed only among the Hebrews, Rom. 3.2 and 9.4. It would obviously have been ridiculous to write in the language of a people who had nothing as yet to do with the things written about. 2. Their authority is deservedly called in question because they are never cited in the New Testament. 3. Because they contain many things which contradict the canonical scriptures, and some which are fantastic, low, trifling and quite foreign to real sagacity and religion.

The Holy Scriptures were not written merely for particular occasions, as

230. Cp. *Of Civil Power* (Yale 7.267): "None more cautious of giving scandal than St. Paul. Yet while he made himself *servant to all,* that he *might gain the more,* he made himself so of his own accord, was not made so by outward force, testifying at the same time that he *was free from all men,* 1 Cor. 9.19."

231. Cp. *Of Civil Power* (Yale 7.245): "Seeing that in matters of religion . . . none can judge or determine here on earth, no not church governors themselves, against the consciences of other believers, my inference is, or rather not mine but our Savior's own, that in those matters they neither can command or use constraint; lest they run rashly on a pernicious consequence forewarned in that parable Matt. 13. from the 26 to the 31 verse: *lest while ye gather up the tares, ye root up also the wheat with them. Let both grow together until the harvest* . . ."

232. " '*Orthodoxos,*' i.e., Protestant. This usage appears also in *Second Defense* . . . where Milton speaks of his defense in Italy of '*orthodoxam religionem*' " (Kelley's note; the usage to which he refers appears on p. 344).

the Papists teach. They were written for the use of the church throughout all succeeding ages, not only under the law but also under the gospel. Exod. 34.27: *write for yourself these words, because according to the intent of these words I make a covenant with you and with Israel;* Deut. 31.19 [...]; Isa. 8.20: [...], and 30.8 [...]; Hab. 2.2 [...]; Luke 16.29 [...]; John 5.39 [...]; Rom. 15.4: *the things which were written beforehand were written for our instruction, that through patience and the consolation of the scriptures we might still have hope;* 1 Cor. 10.11: [...].

Almost everything in the New Testament is proved by reference to the Old. The function of the books of the New Testament is made clear in John 20.31: *these things are written that you may believe . . . ;* Eph. 2.20 [...]; Phil. 3.1 [...]; 1 Thess. 5.27 [...]; 1 Tim. 3.15 [...]; 2 Tim. 3.15–17: *that you have known the Holy Scriptures from childhood, and they are able to make you wise and lead you to salvation through the faith which is in Christ Jesus. All scripture is divinely inspired, and useful for teaching, for reproof, for correction, for discipline in right living, so that the man of God may be fully prepared and equipped for every good work.* It is true that the scriptures which Timothy is said to have *known from childhood,* and which *are able to make* one *wise through faith in Christ,* seem to have been only the books of the Old Testament. It is not apparent that any book of the New Testament had been written when Timothy was a child. However, in the next verse the same claim is made for the whole divinely inspired scripture. This claim is that it is *useful for teaching*... even those who are already learned and wise, 1 Cor. 10.15: *as I say this to intelligent men, consider what I say,* and even those who have arrived at full maturity, Phil. 3.15: *let as many of us as are adults think this*—such as Timothy himself and Titus, to whom Paul wrote. Also, that it is useful to the strong, 1 John 2.14: *I have written to you, young men, because you are strong, and the word of God dwells in you;* 2 Pet. 1.12, 15 [...], and 3.15, 16 [...]; Paul addressed his epistle to the Romans, 1.7, 15, but Peter here says that he wrote not only to them but to all believers; 2 Pet. 3.1, 2 [...]; 1 John 2.21: *I have not written to you because you are ignorant of the truth, but because you know it;* Rev. 1.19 [...].

It is clear from all these texts that no one should be forbidden to read the scriptures. On the contrary, it is very proper that all sorts and conditions of men should read them or hear them read regularly. This includes the king, Deut. 17.19; magistrates, Josh. 1.8; and every kind of person, Deut. 31.9–11, etc. [. . .], 11.18–20: *you shall store up these my words in your heart and in your soul, and shall bind them as a sign to your hand . . . and you shall write them on the doorposts of your house and on your gates;* and 29.29 [. . .], and 30.11 [. . .]; 2 Chron. 34.30 [. . .]; Isa. 8.20 [. . .]; Nehem. 9.3: *and they got up in their places and read in the book of the law,* etc., that is, all the people, as the second verse shows. Or again, take a writer whom my opponents consider canonical: 1 Macc. 1.59, 60: *wherever anyone was found with the book of the covenant.*

The evidence is clearer in the New Testament: Luke 10.26: *what is written in the law? How do you read it?* The man whom Christ asked this question was an interpreter of the law. It is generally agreed that there were, at that time, many interpreters, Pharisees and others, who were neither priests nor Levites. Moreover Christ himself, whom they did not consider at all learned, was not forbidden to interpret the law even in the synagogue, so obviously there would have been no objection to his reading the scriptures in his own home. Also 16.29: *they have Moses and the prophets, let them hear them;* John 5.39: *examine the scriptures;* Acts 8.28 [. . .], and 17.11 [. . .], and 18.24 [. . .]; 2 Tim. 3.15 [. . .]; Rev. 1.3: *blessed is he who reads.*

Thus the scriptures are, both in themselves and through God's illumination absolutely clear. If studied carefully and regularly, they are an ideal instrument for educating even unlearned readers in those matters which have most to do with salvation. Ps. 19.8: *the doctrine of Jehovah is perfect, restoring the soul; the testimony of Jehovah is true, making the unlearned wise . . .*, and 119.105 [. . .], 119.130: *the entrance of your words gives light, it gives the simple prudence*—another proof that the scriptures ought to be read by everyone; 119.18 [. . .]; Luke 24.45 [. . .]; Acts 18.28 [. . .]; 2 Pet. 1.20, 21: *that no prophecy of the scriptures is susceptible of particular interpretation: for, at the time when it came, the prophecy was not brought by the will of man . . .* The prophecy, then, must not be interpreted by the intellect of a particular individual, that is to say, not by his merely human intellect, but with the help of the Holy Spirit, promised to each individual believer.[233] Hence the gift of prophecy, 1 Cor. 14.

The scriptures, then, are plain and sufficient in themselves. Thus they *can make a man wise and fit for salvation through faith,* and *through them the man of God may be fully prepared and fully provided for every good work.* Through what madness is it, then, that even members of the reformed church persist in explaining and illustrating and interpreting the most holy truths of religion, as if they were conveyed obscurely in the Holy Scriptures? Why do they shroud them in the thick darkness of metaphysics? Why do they employ all their useless technicalities and meaningless distinctions and barbarous jargon in their attempt to make the scriptures plainer and easier to understand, when they themselves are continually claiming how supremely clear they are already? As if scripture did not contain the clearest of all lights in itself: as if it were not in itself sufficient, especially in matters of faith and holiness: as if the sense of the divine truth, itself absolutely plain, needed to be brought out more clearly or more fully, or otherwise explained, by means of terms imported from the most abstruse of human sciences—which does not, in fact, deserve the name of a science at all!

The scriptures are difficult or obscure, at any rate in matters where salvation is concerned, only to those who perish: Luke 8.10: *to you it is given to know the mysteries of the kingdom of God, but to others I speak through parables; so that they may look but not see, and hear but not understand;* 1 Cor. 1.18 [. . .], also 2.14 [. . .], also 2 Cor. 4.2, 3 [. . .]; 2 Pet. 3.16, speaking of the epistles of St. Paul: *in which some things are*

233. Cp. *PL* 12.511–14: "the truth, .../Left only in those written records pure,/Though not but by the Spirit understood."

difficult to understand, which those who are untaught and unstable distort, as they do the other scriptures, to their own destruction.

Each passage of scripture has only a single sense, though in the Old Testament this sense is often a combination of the historical and the typological, take Hosea 11.1, for example, compared with Matt. 2.15: *I have called my son out of Egypt.* This can be read correctly in two senses, as a reference both to the people of Israel and to Christ in his infancy.

The custom of interpreting scripture in the church is mentioned in Neh. 8.9, 10: *they read the book of God distinctly, and by explaining the sense gave them understanding through the scripture: then said Nehemiah (he is the king's legate), and Ezra, the priest, well-read in the law, and the Levites who taught the people . . .* ; 2 Chron. 17.9, 10 [. . .]; Luke 4.17 [. . .]; 1 Cor. 14.1, etc. [. . .]

The right method of interpreting the scriptures has been laid down by theologians. This is certainly useful, but no very careful attention is paid to it. The requisites are linguistic ability, knowledge of the original sources, consideration of the overall intent, distinction between literal and figurative language, examination of the causes and circumstances, and of what comes before and after the passage in question, and comparison of one text with another.[234] It must always be asked, too, how far the interpretation is in agreement with faith. Finally, one often has to take into account the anomalies of syntax, as, for example, when a relative does not refer to its immediate antecedent but to the principal word in the sentence, although it is not so near to it. Compare 2 Kings 16.2 with 16.1: *Ahaz was twenty years old when he began to reign.* Here *he* refers to Jotham, Ahaz's father, as is apparent if you consider the age at which Hezekiah began his reign, 18.2. Similarly 2 Chron. 36.9: *when he began to reign,* compared with 2 Kings 24.10. Ps. 99.6 [. . .]; John 8.44 [. . .]. Lastly, no inferences should be made from the text, unless they follow necessarily from what is written. This precaution is necessary, otherwise we may be forced to believe something which is not written instead of something which is, and to accept human reasoning, generally fallacious, instead of divine doctrine, thus mistaking the shadow for the substance. What we are obliged to believe are the things written in the sacred books, not the things debated in academic gatherings.

Every believer is entitled to interpret the scriptures; and by that I mean interpret them for himself. He has the spirit, who guides truth, and he has the mind of Christ.[235] Indeed, no one else can usefully interpret them for him, unless that person's interpretation coincides with the one he makes for himself and his own conscience. There is more on this subject in the next chapter,

234. Cp. *DDD* (p. 136): "All places of scripture wherein just reason of doubt arises from the letter are to be expounded by considering upon what occasion everything is set down and by comparing other texts." For Miltonic hermeneutics, see Haskin.

235. Cp. *Of Civil Power* (Yale 7:244): "Every true Christian able to give a reason of his faith hath the word of God before him, the promised Holy Spirit, and the mind of Christ within him, 1 Cor. 2.16."

where I deal with the people of particular churches. Whoever God has appointed as apostle or prophet or evangelist or pastor or teacher, is entitled to interpret the scriptures for others in public, 1 Cor. 12.8, 9; Eph. 4.11–13: in other words, anyone endowed with the gift of teaching, *every teacher of the law who has been instructed in readiness for the kingdom of heaven,* Matt. 13.52. This does not mean those who are appointed to professional chairs by mere men or by universities: of these it can often be said, as in Luke 11.52: *woe to you, interpreters of the law, for you have taken away the key of knowledge. You did not enter yourselves, and you stopped those who were entering.*

No visible church, then, let alone any magistrate, has the right to impose its own interpretations upon the consciences of men as matters of legal obligation, thus demanding implicit faith.

If there is disagreement about the sense of scripture among apparent believers, they should tolerate each other until God reveals the truth to all: Phil. 3.15, 16: *let as many of us as are adults think this: if you think differently about anything, God will reveal the truth to you also. However, in things which we have already mastered, let us walk by the same rule and share the same opinion.* Similarly Rom. 14.4 [. . .].

The rule and canon of faith, therefore, is scripture alone: Ps. 19.10: *the judgments of Jehovah are truth itself.* In controversies there is no arbitrator except scripture, or rather, each man is his own arbitrator, so long as he follows scripture and the Spirit of God. It is true that Paul says, 1 Tim. 3.15: *the church of the living God is the pillar and ground of the truth.* Some people turn these words into a claim that the visible church, however defined, has the supreme authority of interpretation and of arbitration in controversy. However, once we examine this and the previous verse, it becomes evident that such people are very far from the truth. Paul wrote these words to Timothy, and for him they were meant to have the force of Holy Scripture. The intention was *that he might know,* through these words, *how he ought to behave in the house of God, which is the church*—that is, in any assembly of believers. Therefore it was not the house of God, or the church, which was to be a rule to him *that he might know,* but the Holy Scripture which he had received from Paul. The church is, or at least ought to be, for it is sometimes not, *the pillar and ground,* that is to say the guardian, repository and confirmer *of the truth.* But though it is all these things, it does not follow that it is the rule or arbiter of truth and scripture. For the house of God is not a rule to itself: it receives its rule from the word of God, and it ought, at any rate, to keep very closely to this. Besides, the writings of the prophets and of the apostles, which constitute the scriptures, are the foundations of the church. Eph. 2.20: *built on,* etc. Now if the church is built on a foundation, it cannot itself be the rule or arbiter of that foundation.

Apparently not all the instructions which the apostles gave the churches were written down, or if they were written down they have not survived: see 2 John 12: *although I had many things to write to you, I did not want to put them down in black and white;* similarly 3 John 13. Col. 4.16 [. . .].

We should conclude that these instructions, though useful, were not necessary for salvation. They ought, then, to be supplied either from other passages of scripture or, if it is doubtful whether this is possible, not from the decrees of popes or councils, much less from the edicts of magistrates, but from that same Spirit operating in us through faith and charity: John 16.12, 13: *I still have many things to say to you; but you cannot bear them now. However when he, the Spirit of truth, comes, he will lead you into all truth.* Peter also warns us, in the same way, *that attention must be paid to the prophetic word, until the day dawns, and the day-star arises in our hearts,* 2 Pet. 1.19. The reference here is to the light of the gospel, which is to be sought in our hearts just as much as in written records: 2 Cor. 3.3: *that you are the epistle of Christ, ministered by us, written not with ink but with the Spirit of the living God; not on tablets of stone, but on the fleshly tablets of the heart;* Eph. 6.17 [. . .]; 1 John 2.20 [. . .], and 2.27 [. . .]. So when the Corinthians asked Paul about certain matters on which scripture had not laid down anything definite, he answered them in accordance with the spirit of Christianity, and by means of that spiritual anointing which he had received: 1 Cor. 7.12: *I say this, not the Lord,* 25, 26: *I have no command from the Lord about virgins, but I give my own opinion, as one to whom the Lord through his mercy has granted faith. I think, then* . . . , 40 [. . .]. Thus he reminds them that they are able to supply answers for themselves in questions of this kind, 7.15: *a brother or sister is not bound to subjection in cases of this kind,* and 36 [. . .].

We have, particularly under the gospel, a double scripture. There is the external scripture of the written word and the internal scripture of the Holy Spirit which he, according to God's promise, has engraved upon the hearts of believers, and which is certainly not to be neglected. See above, Chapter 27, on the gospel. Isa. 59.21: *as for me, this will be my covenant with them, says Jehovah; my spirit which is in you, and my words which I have placed in your mouth, shall not leave your mouth or the mouth of your seed or the mouth of your seed's seed, says Jehovah, from this time forward, for ever;* Jer. 31.33, 34; Acts 5.32 [. . .]; 1 Cor. 2.12 [. . .].

Nowadays the external authority for our faith, in other words, the scriptures, is of very considerable importance and, generally speaking, it is the authority of which we first have experience. The pre-eminent and supreme authority, however, is the authority of the Spirit, which is internal, and the individual possession of each man.

I will say nothing about those books which are not a genuine part of scripture. Paul himself has warned us to beware of these, 2 Thess. 2.2 [. . .], and 3.17 [. . .]. But quite apart from these, the external scripture, particularly the New Testament, has often been liable to corruption and is, in fact, corrupt. This has come about because it has been committed to the care of various untrustworthy authorities, has been collected together from an assortment of divergent manuscripts, and has survived in a medley of transcripts and editions. But no one can corrupt the Spirit which guides man to truth, and a spiritual man is not easily deceived; 1 Cor. 2.15, 16: *the spiritual man judges all things discriminatingly but is himself judged by no one. For who knows the mind of the Lord? Who will be his instructor? But we have the mind of Christ,* and 12.10 [. . .]. An example of a corrupt text found in nearly all the manuscripts is Matt. 27.9, where a quotation attributed to

Jeremiah actually occurs only in Zechariah. Innumerable other instances occur on almost every page of Erasmus, Beza and other New-Testament editors.

In early times the ark of the covenant, which was sacrosanct, held the law of Moses. After the Babylonish captivity the law passed into the care of its pledged protectors, the priests and prophets and other divinely instructed men, as, for example, Ezra, Zechariah and Malachi. Unquestionably these men handed down God's holy books in an uncorrupted state, to be preserved in the sanctuary by the priests who succeeded them. In every period the priests considered it a matter of supreme importance that no word should be changed, and they had no theories which might have made them alter anything. It is true that the other books, particularly the historical ones, cannot be certainly ascribed to a particular date or author, and also that the chronological accuracy of their narrative often seems suspect. Few or none, however, have called in doubt their doctrinal part. The New Testament, on the other hand, has been entrusted throughout the ages, as I said before, to a variety of hands, some more corrupt than others. We possess no autograph copy: no exemplar which we can rely on as more trustworthy than the others. Thus Erasmus, Beza, and other learned men have edited from the various manuscripts what seems to them to be the most authentic text. I do not know why God's providence should have committed the contents of the New Testament to such wayward and uncertain guardians, unless it was so that this very fact might convince us that the Spirit which is given to us is a more certain guide than scripture, and that we ought to follow it.

It is certain, too, that it is not the visible church but the hearts of believers which, since Christ's ascension, have continually constituted the *pillar* and *ground of truth.* They are the real *house and church of the living God,* 1 Tim. 3.15.

Clearly the editors and interpreters of the Greek Testament, which is of prime authority, rest all their decisions upon the weight and reliability of the manuscript evidence, not upon the visible church. If the reliability of the manuscripts varies or is uncertain, these editors must be at a loss. They have nothing which they can then follow or establish as the genuine, uncorrupted text, the indisputable word of God. This happens in the story of the woman taken in adultery, and in some other passages.

However, we believe in the scriptures in a general and overall way first of all, and we do so because of the authority either of the visible church or of the manuscripts. Later we believe in the church, in those very manuscripts, and in particular sections of them, because of the authority and internal consistency of the whole scripture. Finally we believe in the whole scripture because of that Spirit which inwardly persuades every believer. Thus the Samaritans believed in Christ first of all because of the words of the woman. Later they believed not so much because of her words as because of Christ's words as he spoke before them, John 4.42. Thus, too, on the evidence of scripture itself, all things are eventually to be referred to the Spirit and the unwritten word.

Each believer is ruled by the Spirit of God. So if anyone imposes any kind of sanction or dogma upon believers against their will, whether he acts in the name of the church or of a Christian magistrate, he is placing a yoke not only upon man but upon the Holy Spirit itself.[236] The apostles themselves, in a council over which the Holy Spirit presided, refused to impose even the divine law upon believers. They considered it an intolerable yoke, Acts 15.10, 19, 28: *why do you tempt God*... Much less can any modern church, which is unable to claim for itself with any real certainty the presence of the Spirit, and least of all can a magistrate impose rigid beliefs upon the faithful, beliefs which are either not found in scripture at all, or only deduced from scripture by a process of human reasoning which does not carry any conviction with it.

Human traditions, written or unwritten, are expressly forbidden, Deut. 4.2: *do not add to the word which I command you, nor subtract from it,* etc.; Prov. 30.6 [...]; Rev. 22.18, 19 [...], etc. [...], etc.; Isa. 29.13, 14 [...]; Matt. 15.3, 9; Gal. 1.8 [...]; 1 Tim. 6.3 [...]; Tit. 1.14 [...]; 1 Tim. 1.4 [...]; Col. 2.8: *look out, lest anyone rob you by means of philosophy and delusive vanities, based on human traditions and worldly principles, and not on Christ.*

In a matter of this sort we should not rely upon our predecessors or upon antiquity, 2 Chron. 29.6, etc.: *for our fathers did not act uprightly* ...; Ps. 78.8, etc. [...]; Ezek. 20.18 [...]; Amos 2.1 [...]; Mal. 3.7 [...]; Eccles. 7.10 [...]. It is true that Jeremiah advises the people to *seek out the old ways,* but only to find *what the good way is,* and to choose that, 6.16—otherwise this would be an argument in favor of idol-worship, and of the Pharisees and Samaritans; Jer. 44.17, etc. [...]; Matt. 15.2, etc.: *why do your disciples act in a way contrary to the tradition of their elders?* Christ opposes to this God's commandment, 15.3: *and why do you act in a way contrary to the commandment of God by your tradition . . . ?* Similarly Mark 7.8, 9., John 4.20 [...].

We should not attribute too much even to the venerable name of our mother the church[237] (Hos. 2.2: *dispute with your mother, dispute with her; tell her that she is not my wife nor I her husband, so that she may get rid of her fornications*) unless by the church we mean exclusively the mystical church in heaven, Gal. 4.26: *Jerusalem, which is above, is free, and is the mother of us all.*

236. Cp. *PL* 12.520–25: "from that pretense,/Spiritual laws by carnal power shall force/On every conscience; laws which none shall find/Left them enrolled, or what the Spirit within/Shall on the heart engrave. What will they then/But force the Spirit of Grace itself."

237. *Cp. Of Civil Power* (Yale 7:248): "Then ought we to believe what in our conscience we apprehend the scripture to say, though the visible church with all her doctors gainsay."

CHAPTER 31

OF PARTICULAR CHURCHES

[. . .][238]

As for the remuneration of ministers, both those of the universal church and those of each particular church, it is true that some remuneration is allowable, since it is both just in itself and also has the sanction of God's law and of the authority of Christ and his apostle: Matt. 10.10 [. . .]; 1 Cor. 9.7–13 [. . .]; Gal. 6.6: *let the catechumen* or *him who is instructed in the word share all good things with him who has instructed him;* 1 Tim. 5.7, 18 [. . .]: thus it is right and proper, and in accordance with God's own provision, 1 Cor. 9.14: *that those who preach the gospel should get their living from the gospel.* But it is better to serve God's church for nothing and, following our Lord's example, to minister and to serve without pay. This is not only more exemplary, but also it is a more likely way to avoid all offence or suspicion, and a more bright and beautiful way of exulting in God: Matt. 20.28 [. . .] and 10.8 [. . .]; Acts 20.35: *remember the words of the Lord Jesus: he said, It is more blessed to give than to receive.* By his own example Paul proposed and recommended the same course of action for the imitation of all ministers of the church: 20.34, 35: *you yourselves know that these hands have ministered to my needs and to those of my companions. I have shown you everything: that you ought to support the weak by laboring in this way . . . ;* 2 Thess. 3.7–9 [. . .]; 1 Cor. 9.15, 18 [. . .]; and 2 Cor. 11.8 [. . .], and 11.9 [. . .], and 11.10 [. . .], and 11.12 [. . .], and 12.14 [. . .], and 12.17 [. . .] and 12.18: *did Titus make a profit in any transaction with you? Have we not been guided by the same Spirit?,* and 12.19: *but all these things, beloved, are for your edification.* And if at any time, he was compelled by dire necessity to accept any aid from the churches, even though it was freely and spontaneously given, it worried and annoyed him so much that he seems to consider himself guilty of robbery, 2 Cor. 11.8: *I robbed other churches, taking wages from them, so that to you . . .*

If ministers nowadays cannot attain to this high degree of virtue, the next best thing is that they should rely on the providence of God who calls them, and should look to the church, the willing flock of willing shepherds, for the necessaries of life, rather than to any edicts of the civil power. Matt. 10.11 [. . .]; Luke 10.7, 8 [. . .], and 22.35 [. . .]; 2 Cor. 11.9: *the brothers supplied my wants when they came from Macedonia;* Philipp. 4.15, etc. [. . .].

But because a thing is right in itself, and because there are the best of reasons why it should be done, and because it is sanctioned by the word of God, it does not follow that the civil law and the magistracy ought to demand or enforce it. Paul uses the same argument and almost the same words to prove that the ministers of the church should be fed and maintained as he does to prove that alms should be given to the Jews by the Gentiles, 1 Cor. 9.11, compared with Rom.

238. The deleted passage concerns "ordinary ministers" of a particular church, their titles, functions, qualifications, and succession. What follows is Milton's account of their proper remuneration.

15.27: *they have decided to do so, as I say, and indeed they are their debtors: for if they have shared their spiritual goods with the Gentiles, it is the Gentiles' duty to supply their material needs:* yet no one concludes that alms should be demanded or extracted by force. If, then, mere moral and civil gratitude is not to be enforced, how much more ought gratitude for the gospel be freed from every trace of force or constraint? Similarly, monetary considerations should weigh least of all with anyone who preaches the gospel; Acts 8.20: *may your money perish with you, because you thought that you could buy God's gift with money.* If it is wicked to buy the gospel, it must be much more wicked to sell it. O you of little faith, whose incredulous voices I have often heard exclaiming "If you take away ecclesiastical revenues, you destroy the gospel"[239]—what I say is that if the Christian religion is based upon and supported by violence and money, why should it be thought any more worthy of respect than Mohammedanism?[240]

To bargain for or exact tithes or gospel-taxes, to extort a subsidy from the flock by force or by the intervention of the magistrates, to invoke the civil law in order to secure church revenue, and to take such matters into the courts—these are the actions of wolves, not ministers of the gospel; Acts 20.29 [...], and 20.33 [...].[241] Paul, then, did not exact such things himself, and did not think that any minister of the gospel should do so: 1 Tim. 3.3: *not desiring shameful profit or money*—certainly not exacting it, then. Similarly 3.8 and Tit. 1.7 and 11 and 1 Pet. 5.2, 3: *feed the flock of God, which is in your keeping... not for shameful profit but with an eager heart.* It is hardly allowable for a Christian man to go to law with anyone, even about his own property, Matt. 5.39, 40; 1 Cor. 6.7. How disgraceful is it, then, for a man of the church to enter into litigation with his flock, or rather with a flock which is not strictly speaking his at all, for the sake of tithes, which are the property of others. This sort of thing does not go on in any reformed church except ours.[242] Tithes originated either in the spoils of war, or in the voluntary vow of some individual, or in that agrarian law which was not only abrogated long ago but which never had anything to do with us anyway. These were the things which once made it obligatory to pay tithes, though to ministers of another sect than ours, but now they should not be paid to anyone. If the flock does belong to the minister, how avaricious it is for him to be so eager to make a profit out of his holy office; and if it does not, how unjust his behavior is! How officious, to force his instruction upon those who do not want to be taught by him at all! How extortionate, to exact payment for teaching from a man who

239. Cp. *Likeliest Means* (Yale 7:318): "They are to be reviled and shamed, who cry out with the distinct voice of notorious hirelings, that if ye settle not our maintenance by law, farewell the gospel."

240. Cp. *Likeliest Means* (Yale 7:318): "How can any Christian object it to a Turk that his religion stands by force only and not justly fear from him this reply, 'yours both by force and money in the judgment of your own preachers.' "

241. The comparison of hirelings to wolves is a favorite of Milton's. See *PL* 4.183–93; 12.507–11; *History of Britain* (Yale 5:175); *2Def* (Yale 4:650); *Likeliest Means* (Yale 7:280).

242. Cp. *Likeliest Means* (Yale 7:281): "Under the gospel as under the law, say our English divines, and they only of all Protestants, ... tithes."

rejects you as a teacher and whom you would reject as a pupil if it were not for the money! For *the hireling, to whom the sheep do not belong, runs away because he is a hireling and because he does not care for the sheep,* John 10.12, 13. Nowadays there are a great many who answer to this description. They run away and jump about from flock to flock on the slightest pretext, not so much because they are afraid of wolves as because they themselves become wolves whenever the prey of a more lucrative living in some other parish appears. Unlike real shepherds, they are continually chasing after richer pastures not for their flock but for themselves.[243]

BOOK 2

CHAPTER I

OF GOOD WORKS

The first book dealt with FAITH and THE KNOWLEDGE OF GOD. This second book is about THE WORSHIP OF GOD and CHARITY.

What chiefly constitutes the true worship of God is eagerness to do good works: Matt. 16.27: *then he will repay every man according to his work;* Rom. 2.13: *it is not those who hear the law that are just in God's sight; but it is those who do the law that shall be justified;* Phil. 1.11 [. . .], and 4.8 [. . .]; 2 Tim. 3.17 [. . .]; Tit. 2.11, 12 [. . .]; and 3.8 [. . .]; James 1.22 [. . .]; 2 Pet. 1.5, etc. [. . .].

GOOD WORKS are those which WE DO WHEN THE SPIRIT OF GOD WORKS WITHIN US, THROUGH TRUE FAITH, TO GOD'S GLORY, THE CERTAIN HOPE OF OUR OWN SALVATION, AND THE INSTRUCTION OF OUR NEIGHBOR.

WHEN THE SPIRIT OF GOD WORKS WITHIN US. John 3.21: *that his works may be made manifest, that they have been done in God;* 1 Cor. 15.10: *by the grace of God I am what I am, and his grace, which was bestowed upon me, was not in vain; on the contrary, I have worked more effectively than all of them—not I, though, but the grace of God which is with me;* and 2 Cor. 3.5 [. . .]; Gal. 5.22 [. . .]; Eph. 2.10 [. . .]; and 5.9 [. . .]; Phil. 2.13 [. . .].

THROUGH FAITH: John 15.5: *the man who abides in me, and in whom I abide bears much fruit; for without me you can do nothing;* Heb. 11.6 [. . .]; James 2.22: *you see that faith took a hand in his works, and by his works his faith was made perfect*—that is, faith, as form, gives form to the works, so that they can be good, and is itself brought to perfection by these same works, as by an end or fruit.

243. Cp. *Lyc* (114–15): "such as for their bellies' sake/Creep and intrude, and climb into the fold." In the rest of this chapter, Milton argues that ministers should support themselves by practicing trades, as did Christ and the apostles. He proposes that a church's members should be sufficiently knowledgeable in their faith to be able to test their ministers, and compares the self-sufficiency of individual Christian churches to the dependence of particular synagogues on the Jerusalem temple.

Some theologians insist that the form of good works is their conformity with the Ten Commandments, insofar as they are covered by the terms of the commandments. But I do not see how this can possibly be true under the gospel. Throughout the whole of his letter to the Romans, and elsewhere, Paul quite distinctly teaches that, Rom. 14.23: *whatever is not in accordance with faith, is sin.* Notice that he does not say *whatever is not in accordance with the Ten Commandments is sin,* but *whatever is not in accordance with faith.* So it is conformity with faith, not with the Ten Commandments, which must be considered as the form of good works. Thus if I keep the Sabbath, in accordance with the Ten Commandments, when my faith prompts me to do otherwise, my precise compliance with the commandments will be counted as sin and as ἀνομία or unlawful behavior. It is faith that justifies, not compliance with the commandments; and only that which justifies can make any work good. It follows that no work of ours can be good except through faith. Faith, then, is the form of good works, because the definition of *form* is *that through which a thing is what it is.*[244] As for passages like 1 John 2.4 and 3.24 and various others, where the keeping of God's commandments is mentioned, these should be understood as referring to the commandments of God in the gospel which always give faith precedence over the works of the law. If in the gospel faith is given precedence over the works of the law, it certainly ought to be given precedence over the commandments of the law, for the works are the end and fulfillment of these commandments. If anyone should, then, under the gospel, keep the commandments of the whole Mosaic Law with absolute scrupulousness, but have no faith, it would do him no good. So good works must obviously be defined with reference to faith, not to the commandments. Thus we ought to consider the form of good works to be conformity not with the written but with the unwritten law, that is, with the law of the Spirit which the Father has given us to lead us into truth. For the works of the faithful are the works of the Holy Spirit itself. These never run contrary to the love of God and of our neighbor, which is the sum of the law. They may, however, sometimes deviate from the letter even of the gospel precepts (particularly those which are special rather than general), in pursuance of their over-riding motive, which is charity.[245] Christ himself showed this by his abolition of the observance of the Sabbath, and on several other occasions. See above, Book 1, Chapter 27, on the gospel.[246]

244. Cp. *Art of Logic* (Yale 8:232): "*The form is the cause through which a thing is what it is.*" Also *Tetrachordon* (Yale 2:608): "the *form* by which the thing is what it is."

245. Cp. *Tetrachordon* (p. 240): "Christ having cancelled the handwriting of ordinances which was against us (Col. 2.14) and interpreted the fulfilling of all through charity, hath in that respect set us over law."

246. The remainder of this chapter scripturally elaborates the rest of Milton's definition of good works, and proceeds to consider the idea of "supererogation," that is, good works in excess of what the law prescribes.

CHAPTER 6[247]

OF ZEAL

I have called the first part of true religion, dealt with so far, INVOCATION. There remains the second part, THE SANCTIFICATION OF THE DIVINE NAME IN EVERY CIRCUMSTANCE OF OUR LIFE.

An eager desire to sanctify the divine name, together with a feeling of indignation against things which tend to the violation or contempt of religion, is called ZEAL.

[. . .].[248]

It is a fact, however, that all Greek writers, sacred as well as profane, use the word *blasphemy* in a general sense to mean any kind of evil-speaking, directed against any person. Jewish writers use the corresponding Hebrew words, which I mentioned, in the same general sense. Thus in Isa. 43.28: *I shall expose Israel to curses,* and in 51.7: *do not grow alarmed because of their abuse,* and in Ezek. 5.15: *a reproach and a taunt,* that is, to the Jews; and in Zeph. 2.8: *the taunts of the Ammonites, with which they insulted my people*—in all these passages the same word is employed, and it means blasphemy. Similarly in Matt. 15.19: *false witnesses, curses* (in the Greek: *blasphemies*), and in Mark 7.22 and 1 Tim. 6.1: *that God's name and doctrine be not blasphemed;* and again in Tit. 2.5 and 2 Pet. 2.10: *they are not afraid to insult dignitaries* (Greek: *blaspheme*), and 2.11: *whereas the angels themselves bring no evil-speaking* (Greek: *blasphemous judgment*) *against them before the Lord.* I repeat, even writers of religious works applied the Greek word *blasphemy* to any kind of evil-speaking. I think, therefore, that it was misleading and ill-advised of certain authors to introduce this foreign word into the Latin language, and to limit what had been a general term to mean only evil-speaking against God, while at the same time extending its meaning in one particular direction so that, since people generally no longer understood the term, these authors should be able to denounce out of hand as blasphemy pretty well any opinion about God or religious matters which did not tally with their own.[249] In this they resemble the lawyers in Matt. 9.3 who, when Christ had simply said, 9.2: *your sins are forgiven,* immediately *said to themselves, This man blasphemes.* In fact, though, to blaspheme God is, as the above examples make clear, nothing more nor less than to curse or abuse God openly and *high-handedly,* Num. 15.30. There is also Matt. 15.19:

247. Chapters 2–5 concern the immediate causes of good works (e.g., good habits), virtues related to worship of God (e.g., love of God), external worship or religion (e.g., religious rituals), and finally, oath taking and casting of lots. Milton considers the last three topics as they pertain to the proper invocation or religious adoration of God. The present chapter discusses how to infuse the rest of one's life with the same worshipful attitude.

248. The deleted passage lists relevant scriptural examples of ZEAL and of its opposite, blasphemy. In *Paradise Lost,* when Satan argues that the angels should not adore or submit to the Son, zealous Abdiel characterizes his position as "blasphemous, false and proud!" (5.809).

249. Milton similarly objects to the narrow definition of blasphemy in *Of Civil Power* (Yale 7:246). On the politics of blasphemy in Milton's era, see Loewenstein 1998, 176–98.

blasphemies come from the heart—meaning blasphemies against God or against men. Those who, in all sincerity, and with no desire to stir up controversy, teach or discuss some doctrine concerning the deity which they have quite apparently, as they see it, learned from the Holy Scriptures, are in no sense guilty of the sin of blasphemy. But if the meaning of *blasphemy* is to be derived from the Hebrew, it will be very extensive indeed: every obstinate sinner, in fact, will be guilty of blasphemy and thus, as some insist, of a capital offence: Num. 15.30: *the soul which behaves high-handedly, abuses* or *blasphemes Jehovah and that soul will, without fail, be extirpated from among his people;* Ezek. 20.27, 28: *yet in this your fathers have abused* (Vulgate: *blasphemed*) *me, trespassing against me, for they saw each hill* . . . .

[. . .].[250]

CHAPTER 13[251]

OF THE SECOND CLASS OF SPECIAL DUTIES TOWARDS ONE'S NEIGHBOR

[. . .].

Falsehood is usually defined as the EXPRESSION OF AN UNTRUTH, EITHER BY WORDS OR ACTIONS, WITH DECEITFUL INTENT. In practice, however, it frequently happens that not only to disguise or conceal the truth, but actually to tell lies with deceitful intent makes for the safety or advantage of one's neighbor. We must therefore turn our attention to producing a better definition of falsehood. Homicide and various other activities which I shall discuss later have to be considered with reference not so much to the act itself as to the end and object. I do not see why the same cannot be said of falsehood. Who but a madman would deny that we are absolutely justified in concluding that some people ought to be deceived? What about children, or lunatics, or people who are ill, or drunk, or hostile, or themselves deceitful? What about thieves? In the words of the old adage, *You cannot wrong a wrongdoer.* Is it really a religious duty to tell the truth even to these people? According to the above definition we must not deceive them either by word or deed. But I should certainly not give back to a madman a sword or other weapon which he had left with me while he was sane. So why should I reveal the truth to someone who never left it with me, and is quite unfit to receive it, and will turn it to evil ends? What is more, if giving an answer which is intended to deceive to

250. The rest of the chapter includes standard discussions of martyrdom and of consecration to the glory of God.

251. In chapter 12 of Book 2, Milton addressed the first class of "special virtues or duties towards one's neighbor," defined as those that affect his "internal well-being." These include "harmlessness," "gentleness," and "placability" (Yale 6:753–54). The second class of such virtues Milton defines as those that affect the neighbor's "reputation" or "fortune." In the excerpt included here, Milton works out a practical definition of falsehood as a wicked counterpart to veracity.

someone who asks you a question must always be accounted falsehood, then nothing was more common for the saints and prophets than to tell falsehoods.

So what about defining falsehood like this: FALSEHOOD must arise from EVIL INTENT and entails EITHER THE DELIBERATE MISREPRESENTATION OF THE TRUTH OR THE TELLING OF AN ACTUAL LIE TO SOMEONE, WHOEVER HE MAY BE, TO WHOM IT IS THE SPEAKER'S DUTY TO BE TRUTHFUL? Thus the devil, when he took the form of the serpent, was the first liar, Gen. 3.4. Cain, too, was a liar, 4.9; and Sarah, 18.15, who did not apologize and frankly confess her fault to the angels, who were rightly put out; also Abraham 12.13 and 20, whose story about Sarah being his sister, though it was intended only to save his own life, was, as he might have learned from his previous experience in Egypt, likely to lead men who did not know the truth into sin and unlawful desire; also David, 1 Sam. 21.3, who, when he was running away from Saul, ought not to have exposed his host, Abimelech, to such great danger by concealing from him how matters stood between himself and the king; also Ananias and Sapphira, Acts 5.

It is evident from this definition, as indeed from the previous one I quoted, that parables, hyperboles, fables and the various uses of irony are not falsehoods since they are calculated not to deceive but to instruct: 1 Kings 18.27: *that Elijah mocked them and said, Shout loudly, for he is a God . . . ,* and 22.15: *he said to him, Go on and prosper, for Jehovah will deliver it into the hand of the king.* It is evident, secondly, that, in the proper sense of the word "deceit," no one can be deceived unless he is, at the same time, injured in some way. If, then, we do not injure him in any way but, on the contrary, either assist him, or prevent him from inflicting or suffering injury, we do not really deceive him, not even if we tell him a thousand lies, but rather do him a service of which he is unaware. Thirdly, everyone agrees that the strategems and tactics of warfare, provided they do not involve treachery or perjury, do not constitute falsehood. Once this is granted it is obviously fatal to the first definition I quoted. For hardly any of the ambushes or surprise-tactics common in warfare can be carried out without the telling of a great many flagrant untruths which are quite specifically designed to deceive. If the first definition is correct, they cannot be cleared of the charge of falsehood. We ought rather to conclude, then, that strategems are allowable, even when they entail falsehood, because if it is not our duty to tell someone the truth, it does not matter if we lie to him whenever it is convenient. Moreover I do not see why this should apply to peace any less than to war, especially when we may, by a salutary and commendable falsehood, save ourselves or our neighbor from harm or danger.

The scriptural texts which are cited condemning falsehood must be understood, then, to refer to that kind of falsehood which evidently injures our neighbor or detracts from the glory of God. Texts of this sort, besides those quoted above, are Lev. 19.11: *do not tell lies or deal falsely with your neighbor;* Ps. 101.7: *a man who practices deception shall not dwell in my house, and he that speaks falsehoods shall not stand in my sight;* Prov. 6.16, 17 [. . .]; Jer. 9.5 [. . .]. These and similar texts command us to speak the truth: but to whom? Not to enemies, or madmen, or thugs, or murderers, but to our neighbor—one with whom we are at peace, and whose lawful society we enjoy. If, then, we are commanded to speak the truth only to our neighbor, it is clear that we are not forbidden to tell lies, as often as need be, to those who have not earned the name of neighbor. If anyone disagrees I should like to ask him which of the Ten Commandments forbids falsehood. No doubt he will reply, the ninth. Right then, let him repeat the words of that commandment, and he will no longer disagree with me. For what that commandment forbids is presented as an injury to one's neighbor, so if a falsehood does not injure one's neighbor it is certainly not forbidden by that commandment.

Thus we may absolve all those holy men who, according to the common judgment of theologians, are guilty of falsehood: Abraham, for example, Gen. 22.5. When he told his servants that he would come back with his son he intended to deceive them so that they would not suspect anything. He himself was quite sure that his son would be sacrificed and left behind. Had he not been sure of this, what sort of trial of his faith would there have been? But he was an intelligent man and he realized that it was not his servants' concern to know what was going on, and that it was convenient that they should not know for the time being. Rebecca and Jacob, Gen. 27, come in the same category. Their prudence, adroitness and circumspection made accessible to Jacob that birthright which his brother had sold for so poor a price—a birthright which was, indeed, already Jacob's both by prophetic prediction and by right of purchase. But, you will say, he deceived his father. Say rather that he corrected, and not before time, the error of his father who was swayed by his absurd passion for Esau. Joseph too, if the usual definition holds good, was obviously guilty of a great many falsehoods, Gen. 42.7, etc. How many lies he told to deceive his brothers! His intentions, however, were not evil but very much to his brothers' advantage. The Hebrew midwives may also be mentioned, Ex. 1.19, etc., whose conduct earned the approval of God himself, in that though they deceived Pharaoh they did him not an injury but a service because they deprived him of an opportunity for committing a crime. Moses may be added to the list, Ex. 3, for he was commanded by God himself to ask Pharaoh for permission to make a three days' journey into the desert, ostensibly for religious purposes but really with the intention of pulling the wool over Pharaoh's eyes. Thus he alleged a quite false reason for their departure, or at least substituted what was only an invented reason for the true one. Indeed the Israelites as a whole may be included, Ex. 11 and 12. It was, once more, at God's command that they borrowed gold and utensils and costly clothes from the Egyptians, no doubt promising to pay them back, though intending to deceive them—and why not, when they were enemies of God and violators of hospitality who had for years been robbing the Israelites? Rahab is another example, Josh. 2.45: she lied nobly and not dishonestly because she deceived those whom God wished to be deceived, though they were her fellow-countrymen and magistrates, and saved those he wished to be saved, rightly preferring religious to civil duty. Then, too, there was Ehud who deceived Eglon with a double lie, Judges 3.19, 20 (and justifiably, since Eglon was an enemy and Ehud acted upon divine prompting): and there was Jael who enticed Sisera to his death when he sought refuge with her, Judges 4.18, 19, though he was God's enemy rather than hers. (Junius claims that she achieved this by a pious fraud rather than by falsehood—as if there were any difference!).[252] Then there was Jonathan who at his friend David's request gave his father an invented reason for David's absence, 1 Sam. 20.6, 28. He had more regard for the safety of an innocent man than for his father's cruelty. It was more in keeping with charity that he should protect the life of his innocent friend, though at the cost of a lie, than that he should assist in the commission of a crime and gratify his father by a confession of the truth which could only do harm. So we see that my more accurate inquiry into this question of falsehood rescues the above-mentioned, plus a great many other very saintly men, from that limbo to which the old definition had condemned them.

[. . .][253]

URBANITY entails not only elegance and wit (of a decent kind) in conversation, but also the ability to discourse and to reply in an acute and apposite way. Prov. 24.26: *he will kiss the lips of the man who answers aptly,* and 25.11: *like golden apples placed on silverwork is an apposite word;* 1 Kings 18.27 [. . .]; Col. 4.6 [. . .].

Opposed to this are scurrility and banter. Eph. 4.29: *let no bad language come from your mouth,* and 5.4: [. . .]; Col. 3.8: *have done with all these things: anger . . . obscene talk.* Strictly speaking no word or thing is obscene. The obscenity is in the dirty mind of the man who perverts words or things out of prurience or to get a laugh. Thus those words in the Hebrew Bible for which the Jewish commentators offer marginal equivalents, which they consider more decent, are not to be thought of as obscene.[254] Their presence is to be attributed, rather, to the vehemence or indignation of the speaker.[255] Nor is there anything obscene about those words in Deut. 22.17: *they shall spread out the sheet before the elders.*

[. . .][256]

252. Cp. *SA* (989–90), where Dalila, to excuse her betrayal of Samson, cites Jael as precedent: "who with inhospitable guile/Smote Sisera sleeping through the temples nailed." In the Junius-Tremellius translation, the explanation of Jael's action as a "pious fraud" occurs in a note to Judg. 4.20.

253. In the deleted passage, Milton lists and cites biblical examples of behavior opposed to candor, such as "evil suspicion," "prying," "calumny," "abuse and disparagement," "litigiousness," and "at the other extreme," "flattery" and "unjustified praise or blame." He goes on to discuss "candor" in the now obsolete sense of "sweetness of temper" or "freedom from malice." Of various traits that Milton goes on to name as allied or opposed to candor in this now obsolete sense, we include two particularly characteristic of him.

254. See *Areop,* n. 66.

255. Milton defends himself similarly from criticism of his rough language in controversy. Cp. *Defense of Himself* (Yale 4:744–45).

256. In the deleted passage, Milton cites biblical examples of "frankness" (the virtue that "makes us speak the truth fearlessly") and its opposite, "timidity." He continues in the same way to define "admonitoriness" (the virtue that "makes us warn all sinners of their danger frankly and fearlessly"), a virtue not to be exercised on "stubborn sinners" or those who will "only scoff at such a warning."

CHAPTER 14

MORE ABOUT THE SECOND CLASS OF SPECIAL DUTIES TOWARDS ONE'S NEIGHBOR

[. . .][257]

It is a violation of justice to charge excessive interest on loans, and if the loan is made to a poor man, any interest at all is excessive. Ex. 22.25: *do not lend money at interest to a poor man;* Lev. 25.35–37: *when your brother is in straitened circumstances and his hand shakes before you, then you shall encourage him to live with you, even if he is a foreigner or a stranger; and you shall not take any interest from him, but you shall fear your God . . . so that your brother may live with you.* This is the meaning of Deut. 23.19: *do not lend to your brother at interest, interest of money or of food or of anything which is lent at interest.*

There are many conflicting opinions about usury, however, and as the controversy is of some relevance to this section let us now take a quick look at the rights and wrongs of the matter.

Most people agree that usury is not always illicit, and that in judging it we should take into account the usurer's motives, the rate of interest, and the borrower.

As for the borrower, they agree that it is legitimate to take interest from anyone who is well enough off to pay it.

They agree too, that the rate should square with justice, if not with charity.

They agree that, where motive is concerned, the usurer should have some consideration for his neighbor as well as for himself.

Given these conditions, they maintain, no fault can be found with usury—and they are certainly right about the conditions, for unless they are observed pretty well all business transactions are illicit. Usury, then, is no more reprehensible in itself than any other kind of lawful commerce. The proof of this is, in the first place, that if it were blameworthy in itself God would not have let the Israelites take interest from foreigners, Deut. 23.20, especially as he elsewhere instructs them to do no injury to foreigners but rather to assist them in all kindness, particularly those in need. Secondly, if we may make a profit out of cattle, land, houses and the like, why should we not out of money? When money is borrowed, as it often is, not to relieve hardship but simply for the purpose of gain, it tends to be more profitable to the borrower than to the lender. It is true that God did not wish the Israelites to devote the produce of their land to usury, but this was for purely ceremonial reasons, as was his desire that they

257. In the deleted passage, Milton discusses virtues by which one shows "regard for our neighbor' fortune," that is, "honesty and generosity." The excerpt printed here concerns usury, which comes under the heading of "commutative justice," which concerns "buying and selling, hiring, lending and borrowing, and the retention and restoration of deposits." Milton's father lent money for interest, and Milton occasionally aided him in this part of his business. Roman Catholic orthodoxy forbade usury.

should not sell their land permanently, Lev. 25.23. We see, then, that usury is only to be condemned if it is practiced at the expense of the poor, or solely out of avarice, or to an uncharitable and unjust extent; and these conditions apply to every kind of profit-making transaction just as much as they do to usury. Any transaction which disregards these conditions deserves, just as much as does usury, to be called נֶשֶׁךְ, "a bite." It is this kind of usury which is forbidden in Ex. 22.25: *if you lend money to one of my people, to one of the poor among you, do not be like a usurer to him . . .*, and Lev. 25.35–7, as above. Since these two passages are the very first to deal with the subject, they certainly ought to throw light upon later passages, and that exception which they contain must be inferred elsewhere; for example, in Deut. 23.19, as above; Ps. 15.5: *who does not put out his money to usury;* Prov. 28: *he who increases his capital by usury, will amass a fortune for one who will give generously to the poor;* Ezek. 18.8 [. . .].

[. . .][258]

CHAPTER 17[259]

OF PUBLIC DUTIES TOWARDS OUR NEIGHBOR

[. . .].

Above all it is the duty of magistrates to foster religion and the worship—particularly the public worship—of God, and to respect the church. Isa. 49.23: *kings will be your foster-fathers, and their queens your nurses; they will bow down their faces to the earth in your honor, and lick up the dust at your feet.* But churches do not need the supervision of magistrates. Provided that there is peace, they are perfectly well able to rule themselves according to their own laws and discipline, and also to enlarge themselves. There is evidence for this assertion in Acts 9.31: *the churches throughout the whole of Judea and Galilee and Samaria enjoyed peace and built up their strength; and progressing in the fear of the Lord and with the comfort of the Holy Ghost, they grew more numerous.*

Thus magistrates should protect religion, not enforce it, Josh. 24.15: *if it seems evil in your eyes . . . choose today whom you will serve . . . but I and my family will serve Jehovah;* Ps. 105. 14: *he did not allow anyone to oppress them; he even reproved kings for*

258. After a brief discussion of deposits, Milton defines and cites scriptural examples of "moderation" and "generosity," the latter including "liberality" and "munificence" and opposed by "niggardliness" and "prodigality." He concludes with a brief mention of the corresponding virtue of "gratitude" and its opposite, "ingratitude."

259. In chapters 15 and 16 of Book 2, Milton addresses "reciprocal duties toward his neighbor, particularly private duties" (Yale 6:781). Chapter 15 primarily concerns duties toward family and quasi-family members; chapter 16, "duties toward those not of your own household" (Yale 6:789) The section of the final chapter included here addresses church-state relations, freedom of conscience, ethical limits on the subject's obedience to a ruler, and international affairs.

their sake, saying, Do not touch my anointed, or do my prophets harm. If kings are here forbidden to subject religious persons to any kind of compulsion, then a king must certainly not force the consciences of such people in the matter of religion itself (particularly over controversial issues where a king or magistrate can be—and often is—just as mistaken as the Pope), unless he wants to be called antichrist as the Pope, chiefly for this reason, is. It is true that, in ancient times, the kings and magistrates of the Jews gave judgments in matters of religion, and even enforced their execution. This happened, however, only when the law of God was absolutely explicit, so that the magistrate's decision could be unquestionably correct. Nowadays, on the other hand, Christians are often persecuted or punished over things which are controversial, or permitted by Christian liberty, or about which the gospel says nothing explicit.[260] Magistrates who do this sort of thing are Christians in name alone, and there are plenty of Jewish and heathen magistrates who can be cited as evidence against them: Pontius Pilate himself, to begin with. He had enough respect for the Jews to go outside and talk to them, though he was a proconsul, when they would not enter the praetorium because of their religion, John 18.28, 29: also Gamaliel, Acts 5.39: *but if it is from God, your hands have not the power . . . ;* and Gallio, Acts 18.15: *I will not be a judge of these things.*

Even an ecclesiastical minister does not have the right to domineer over the church, let alone a magistrate. 2 Cor. 1.24: *not that we may domineer over your faith, but that we may contribute to your happiness; for you stand by faith;* Col. 2.18 [. . .]; 1 Pet. 5.3 [. . .]; Rom. 14.4 [. . .]; similarly James 4.12. Further proof may be found in my first book, in the discussions of Christ's kingdom, faith, the gospel, Christian liberty and church-government and its object. We may be sure that, since Christ's kingdom is not of this world, it does not stand by force and constraint, the constituents of worldly authority. So the gospel should not be made a matter of compulsion, and faith, liberty and conscience cannot be. These are the concern of ecclesiastical discipline, and are quite outside the province of civil jurisdiction. To compel religious people to profess a religion of which they do not approve, and to compel the profane, whom God keeps from holy things, to take part in public worship, are equally senseless and impious acts. Ps. 1.16, 17; *God says to the wicked man, What business have you to tell of my decrees or take my covenant in your mouth . . . ?;* Prov. 15.8 and 21.27: *the sacrifice of the wicked is an abomination, and much more so when he offers it impiously.*

THE DUTIES OF THE PEOPLE TOWARDS THE MAGISTRATE are prescribed in Ex. 22.28: *you shall not revile the magistrates, or curse the ruler of your*

260. Cp. *Of Civil Power* (Yale 7:259): "Now is the state of grace, manhood, freedom and faith; to which belongs willingness and reason, not force; the law was then written on tables of stone, and to be performed according to the letter, willingly or unwillingly; the gospel, our new covenant, upon the heart of every believer, to be interpreted only by the sense of charity and inward persuasion."

people; 2 Sam. 21.17 [. . .]; Prov. 24.21, 22 [. . .], and 29.26 [. . .]; Eccles. 8.2, etc. [. . .]; Matt. 22.21 [. . .]; Rom. 13.1, etc. [. . .]; 1 Tim. 2.1, 2 [. . .]; Tit. 3.1: *prompt them to be submissive to the government and the authorities, to be obedient, to be ready for any good work;* 1 Pet. 2.13, etc.: *submit to every human ordinance, for the sake of the Lord.*

Even towards unjust magistrates: Matt. 17.26, 27: *their own citizens are free: but so that we shall not cause difficulty, go . . . ;* Acts 23.3, etc. [. . .].

Except in things which are unlawful. Ex. 1.17: *but the midwives feared God, and did not do as the king of Egypt had told them;* Ex. 2.2 [. . .]; 1 Sam. 14.45, etc. [. . .], and 20.2, etc. [. . .], and 22.17 [. . .]; Josh. 1.17 [. . .]; 2 Chron. 21.10 [. . .], and 26.18 [. . .]; Esther 3.2–4 [. . .]; Dan. 3.16 [. . .], and 3.18 [. . .], and 6.11 [. . .]; Acts 4.19: *decide for yourselves whether it is right in the sight of God to obey you rather than God;* Heb. 11.23: *through faith Moses was hidden for three months by his parents, and they were not afraid of the king's edict.*

Opposed to this is rebellion: Num. 16.1, etc.: *but Korah took men . . . ;* 2 Sam. 20.1, etc. [. . .].

And obedience in unlawful things. 1 Sam. 22.18: *so Doeg turned . . . .*

Some maintain that magistrates must be obeyed not only when they are god-fearing but also when they are tyrannical and when their commands are wicked. There is, however, no divine authority for such an opinion. When 1 Pet. 2.13 talks about obeying *every human ordinance,* it means every kind of human ordinance which can legitimately be obeyed, as the next verse makes perfectly clear. As for 2.18, it is addressed to slaves, and has nothing to do with the duties of free peoples, who must be judged by standards quite different from those which apply to slaves, serfs and mercenaries. Again, the Israelites obeyed Pharaoh. True: but was their obedience willing or unwilling, right or wrong? Who knows? We read nowhere that they were commanded to obey him or praised for doing so. And as for Daniel's behavior in captivity, it, too, is irrelevant to the argument. What else could he do? He was a prisoner. Look at Ps. 60.4: *you have given a banner to those who fear you, to be used mightily in the service of truth.*

I do not deny that in lawful matters it may be prudent to obey even a tyrant, or at any rate to be a time-server, in the interest of public peace and personal safety.

The duties of magistrate and people TOWARDS NEIGHBORING STATES concern either peace or war.

The duties of PEACE include the making of treaties. In order to know whether it is right or wrong to make treaties with the wicked, we must first understand the reasons for which treaties are concluded, namely: to strengthen the existing peace, or to ensure mutual defense and reinforce the friendship between neighboring states.

Of the first class are the treaties made by Abraham with the natives and with Abimelech, Gen. 14.13 and 21.27; that of Isaac with Abimelech, 26.29–31; and that of Solomon with Hiram, 1 Kings 5.12. These examples place the lawfulness of such treaties beyond question.

Of the second class are the treaties made by Asa with Benhadad, 1 Kings 15.19, and with Baasha, 2 Chron. 16.7; by Jehoshaphat with the house of Ahab, 18.1 compared with 19.2, etc.; by Amaziah with the Israelites, 25.7, 8; by Ahaz with the Assyrians, 2 Kings 16.7; and the treaty which the Jews attempted to make with the Egyptians, Isa. 30.2, etc. Each of these was forbidden and had an unhappy outcome: Ex. 23.32, 33: *you shall not make a treaty with them* . . . , and 34.12 [. . .], similarly 34.15; Deut. 7.4 [. . .]; Ezek. 16.26, etc. [. . .]; 2 Cor. 6.14: *do not couple with unbelievers, it is an unequal match; for what has righteousness to do with wickedness, and what have light and darkness in common?.*

Examples of treaty-breakers are Asa, 2 Chron. 16.3, and Zedekiah, 36.13. See also Ezek. 17.

Num. 34 and 35.15, and Deut. 23.15 deal with the subject of asylum.

As for WAR, we are instructed, in the first place, that it is to be undertaken only after extremely careful consideration, Prov. 20.18 and 24.6; Luke 14.31 [. . .].; secondly, that it is to be waged knowledgeably and skillfully, 1 Sam. 14.29 [. . .], and 23.22 [. . .]; Prov. 21.22 [. . .]; and thirdly, with moderation, Deut. 20.19: *you shall not destroy its trees . . . ;* and fourthly, in holiness, Deut. 23. 9, etc.: *when the army goes out against your enemies, then beware of anything evil* . . . , and 32.29, 30 [. . .]; 1 Sam. 7.9 [. . .]; Isa. 31.6, etc. [. . .]; Amos 1.13 [. . .]; fifthly, that a cruel enemy should not be spared, 1 Sam. 15.33 [. . .]; Ps. 18.42, 43 [. . .], and 60.10 [. . .]; Jer. 48.10: *cursed is the man who keeps his sword from blood;* sixthly, that we should not trust in the strength of our forces, but in God alone, Ex. 14.17, 18 [. . .]; Deut. 20.1, etc. [. . .]; 1 Sam. 14.6 [. . .], and 17.47 [. . .]; Ps. 33.16, 17 [. . .], and 44.3, etc. [. . .], and 60.1, 2, etc. [. . .], and 127.1 [. . .], and 144.1, 2: *blessed be Jehovah, my rock, who teaches my hands battle* . . . , and 147.10 [. . .], and 147.13 [. . .]; Prov. 21.31: *the horse is prepared for the day of battle, but safety is Jehovah's;* 2 Chron. 14.11 [. . .], and 20.21 [. . .], and 24.24 [. . .]; Isa. 5.26, etc. [. . .]; Jer. 21.4 [. . .], and 37.10 [. . .]; Ezek. 13.5 [. . .]; Zech. 10.4–6 [. . .]; Amos 2.11 [. . .]; seventhly, that the spoil should be divided equally and fairly, Num. 31.27, etc.: *that you divide the booty between those who fought this battle, and marched out to war, and the whole assembly . . . ;* Deut. 20.14 [. . .]; Josh. 22.8, etc. [. . .]; 1 Sam. 30.24 [. . .].

There is no reason why war should be any less lawful now than it was in the time of the Jews. It is not forbidden in the New Testament. Ps. 149.6: *with a two-edged sword in their hand* . . . Two centurions, Cornelius and the man from Capernaum, are included among the faithful, Matt. 8, Acts 10; and it was not against war but against unjust plunder and rapine that John warned the soldiers, Luke 3.14: *he said to the soldiers, Do not bully anyone to extort money . . . ;* 1 Cor. 9.7 [. . .]; Paul availed himself of a military bodyguard, Acts 23.17 [. . .].

Obedience to God's commandments makes nations prosperous in every respect; see Lev. 26. It makes them fortunate, wealthy and victorious, Deut. 15.4–6, and lords over other nations; see Deut. 15.6 and 26.17–19, and particularly 28.1, etc.—a passage which politicians should read over and over again. See also Deut. 29 and 4; Judges 2 and 3; Ps. 33.12: *blessed is the nation whose God is Jehovah;* Prov. 11.11 [. . .], and 14.34 [. . .], and 28.2 [. . .]; Isa. 3 and 24 and 48.18: *if only you had listened . . . ;* Jer. 5; Ezek. 7.

The converse is also true, Isa. 3.8: *in my house there is neither bread nor clothing, do not make me a ruler of the people*. . . , and 57.13, 14, 17 [. . .]; Hos. 5.13 [. . .], and 7.11, 12 [. . .], and 12.2 [. . .]; Habak. 2.12 [. . .].

[. . .][261]

261. The rest of the chapter addresses duties of ministers toward the church as a whole and toward individual believers as well as the duties of the church and believers toward ministers.

Works Cited

I. Editions of Milton

Darbishire, Helen. *The Manuscript of Milton's Paradise Lost Book I.* Clarendon Press, 1931.

Dzelzainis, Martin. *John Milton: Political Writings.* Cambridge Univ. Press, 1991.

Hughes, Merritt Y. *Complete Poems and Major Prose.* Odyssey Press, 1957.

Tillyard, Phyllis B., and E. M. W. Tillyard. *Milton: Private Correspondence and Academic Exercises.* Cambridge Univ. Press, 1932.

Wolfe, Don M., et al. *The Complete Prose Works of John Milton.* 7 vols. Yale Univ. Press, 1953–82.

Wright, B. A. *Shorter Poems of John Milton.* Macmillan, 1938.

Wright, William A. *Poems Reproduced in Facsimile from the Manuscript in Trinity College, Cambridge, with a Transcript.* Scolar Press, 1972.

II. Critical and Historical Works

Amesii, Guilielmi [Ames, William]. *Medulla Theologica* [*Marrow of Sacred Divinity*]. Ioannem Ianssonium, 1623.

Aquinas, Thomas. *Summa Theologica.* Trans. Fathers of the English Dominican Province. 5 vols. Christian Classics, 1981.

Aubrey, John. *Aubrey's Brief Lives.* Ed. Oliver Lawson Dick. Secker and Warburg, 1950.

Barker, Arthur. *Milton and the Puritan Dilemma.* Univ. of Toronto Press, 1942.

Basil. *Opera.* 2 Vols. [+Appendix Vol. 3]. Michaelem Sonnium, 1618.

Bauman, Michael. "Heresy in Paradise and the Ghost of Readers Past," *College Language Association Journal* 30 (1986): 59–68.

______. *Milton's Arianism.* Peter Lang, 1987.

______. *A Scripture Index to John Milton's De Doctrina Christiana.* Medieval and Renaissance Texts Society, 1989.

Bennett, Joan S. *Reviving Liberty: Radical Christian Humanism in Milton's Great Poems.* Cambridge Univ. Press, 1989.

Boesky, Amy. "The Maternal Shape of Mourning: A Reconsideration of *Lycidas*," *Modern Philology* 95 (1998): 463–83.

Buchanan, George. *Rerum Scoticarum Historia.* Arbuthnetum. 1582.

Camden, William. *Annales Rerum Anglicanarum et Hibernicarum.* Simonis Watersonus. 1615.

Campbell, Gordon, Thomas N. Corns, John K. Hale, David I. Holmes, and Fiona

Tweedie. "The Provenance of *De Doctrina Christiana*," *Milton Quarterly* 31 (1997): 67–117.

Campbell, Gordon, Thomas N. Corns, John K. Hale, Fiona J. Tweedie. *Milton and the Manuscript of "De Doctrina Christiana."* Oxford Univ. Press, 2007.

Chaplin, Gregory. "Beyond Sacrifice: Milton and the Atonement." *PMLA* 125 (2010): 354–69.

Chrysostom, John. *Opera.* 5 vols. Signum Spei, 1549.

Corns, Thomas N. *The Development of Milton's Prose Style.* Oxford Univ. Press, 1982.

Corns, Thomas N., David I Holmes, and Fiona J. Tweedie. "The Provenance of *De doctrina Christiana.*" *Literary and Linguistic Computing* 13 (1998): 77–87.

Costanzo, Angelo di. *Historia.* Gioseppe Cacchio. 1581.

Cyprian. *Opera.* Joannes le Preux. 1593.

Danielson, Dennis. *Milton's Good God: A Study in Literary Theodicy.* Cambridge Univ. Press, 1982.

Dante Alighieri. *Dante con l'espositione di M. Bernardino Daniello da Lucca.* Pietro da Fino. 1568.

Darbishire, Helen. *Early Lives of Milton.* Oxford Univ. Press, 1932.

D'Israeli, Isaac. *Curiosities of Literature.* Routledge, 1859.

Dobranski, Stephen B., and John P. Rumrich, eds. *Milton and Heresy.* Cambridge Univ. Press, 1998.

Fallon, Stephen M. "'To Act or Not': Milton's Conception of Divine Freedom," *Journal of the History of Ideas* 49 (1988): 425–49.

______. "'Elect Above the Rest': Theology as Self-Representation in Milton." In *Milton and Heresy,* ed. Stephen B. Dobranski and John Rumrich, pp. 93–116. Cambridge Univ. Press, 1998.

______. "Milton's Arminianism and the Authorship of De Doctrina Christiana," *Texas Studies in Literature and Language* 41 (1999): 103–27.

______. "'The Spur of Self-Concernment': Milton in His Divorce Tracts." In *John Milton: The Writer in His Works, Milton Studies* 38, ed. Albert C. Labiola and Michael Lieb, pp. 220–42. Univ. of Pittsburgh Press, 2000.

______. "Alexander More Reads Milton." In *Milton and the Terms of Liberty,* ed. Graham Parry and Joad Raymond, pp. 111–24. D. S. Brewer, 2002.

______. *Milton's Peculiar Grace: Self-representation and Authority.* Cornell Univ. Press, 2007.

Foran, Gregory. "*Macbeth* and the Political Uncanny in *The Tenure of Kings and Magistrates.*" Milton Studies 51 (2010): 1–20.

Fulton, Thomas. *Historical Milton: Manuscript, Print, and Political Culture in Revolutionary England.* Univ. of Massachusetts Press, 2010.

Grotius, Hugo. *Of the Rights of Peace and War.* Trans. William Evats. M.W., 1682.

Halkett, John. *Milton and the Idea of Matrimony: A Study of the Divorce Tracts and Paradise Lost.* Yale Univ. Press, 1970.

Hanford, James Holly. "The Chronology of Milton's Private Studies," *Publications of the Modern Language Association* 36 (1921): 251–314.

Haskin, Dayton. *Milton's Burden of Interpretation.* Univ. of Pennsylvania Press, 1994.

Hawkes, David. "The Politics of Character in John Milton's Divorce Tracts," *Journal of the History of Ideas* 62 (2001): 141–60.

Hill, Christopher. "Professor William B. Hunter, Bishop Burgess, and John Milton," *Studies in English Literature* 34 (1994): 165–93.

Hoxby, Blair. *Mammon's Music: Literature and Economics in the Age of Milton.* Yale Univ. Press, 2002.

Hunter, William B. "Milton's Power of Matter," *Journal of the History of Ideas* 13 (1952): 551–62.

______. "Milton's Arianism Reconsidered," *Harvard Theological Review* 52 (1959): 9–35.

Hunter, William B., Barbara K. Lewalski, and John T. Shawcross. "Forum: Milton's *Christian Doctrine.*" *Studies in English Literature,* 1500–1900. 32 (1992): 143–66.

Johnson, Samuel. *Lives of the English Poets.* Ed. George Birkbeck Hill. 3 vols. Clarendon Press, 1905.

Jovius, Paulus. *Opera.* P. Pernae. 2 vols. 1578.

Justin Martyr. *Opera.* C. Morellum. 1615.

Kelley, Maurice. "Milton's Arianism Again Considered," *Harvard Theological Review* 54 (1961): 195–205.

______. "The Provenance of John Milton's Christian Doctrine: A Reply to William B. Hunter." *Studies in English Literature,* 1500–1900 34 (1994): 153–63.

Kerrigan, William. *The Prophetic Milton.* Univ. Press of Virginia, 1974.

______. *The Sacred Complex: On the Psychogenesis of Paradise Lost.* Harvard Univ. Press, 1983.

Knoppers, Laura Lunger. "*The Readie and Easie Way* and the English Jeremiad." In *Politics, Poetics, and Hermeneutics in Milton's Prose,* David Loewenstein and James Grantham Turner, eds., pp. 213–25. Cambridge Univ. Press, 1990.

______. "Late Political Prose." Thomas N. Corns, ed., *A Companion to Milton,* pp. 309–25. Blackwell, 2002.

LaBreche, Ben. "Espousing Liberty: The Gender of Liberalism and the Politics of Miltonic Divorce." *ELH* 77 (2010): 969–94.

Lactantius. *Opera.* Ed. Onorato Fascitelli. Joannes Tornesius & Guilielmus Gazeius, 1548.

Lewalski, Barbara Kiefer. *Milton's Brief Epic: The Genre, Meaning, and Art of Paradise Regained.* Brown Univ. Press, 1966.

______. "Milton and *De Doctrina Christiana*: Evidences of Authorship," *Milton Studies* 36 (1998): 203–28.

______. *The Life of John Milton: A Critical Biography.* Blackwell, 2000.

Loewenstein, David. *Milton and the Drama of History.* Cambridge Univ. Press, 1990.

______. "Treason Against God and State." In Stephen B. Dobranski and John Rumrich, eds., *Milton and Heresy,* pp. 176–98. Cambridge Univ. Press, 1998.

Machiavelli, Niccolo. *Tutte le Opere.* [n. p.] 1550.

Masson, David. *The Life of John Milton.* 6 vols. Peter Smith, 1965.

Merrill, R. V. "Eros and Anteros," *Speculum* 19 (1944): 265–84.

Mohl, Ruth. *John Milton and His Commonplace Book.* Frederick Ungar, 1969.

Mueller, Janel. "Milton on Heresy," in *Milton and Heresy,* ed. Stephen B. Dobranski and John Rumrich, pp. 21–38. Cambridge Univ. Press, 1998.

Ng, Su Fang. *Literature and the Politics of Family in Seventeenth-Century England.* Cambridge Univ. Press, 2007.

Nichols, Jennifer. "Milton's Claim for Self and Freedom in the Divorce Tracts." *Milton Studies* 49 (2009): 192–211.

Norbrook, David. *Writing the English Republic.* Cambridge Univ. Press, 1999.

Parker, William R. *Milton: A Biography.* 2 vols. Clarendon Press, 1968.

Patterson, Annabel. "No Meer Amatorious Novel." In *Politics, Poetics, and Hermeneutics in*

Milton's Prose, ed. David Loewenstein and James Grantham Turner, pp. 88–95. Cambridge Univ. Press, 1990.

Photius. *Bibliotheca.* Augustae Vindelicorum, 1606.

Poole, William. "The Genres of Milton's Commonplace Book." *Oxford Handbook of Milton.* Ed. Nicholas McDowell and Nigel Smith. Oxford University Press, 2009.

Prestige, G. L. *God in Patristic Thought.* SPCK, 1952.

Rumrich, John Peter. "Milton's Concept of Substance," *ELN* 19 (1982): 218–33.

______. *Matter of Glory: A New Preface to Paradise Lost.* Univ. of Pittsburgh Press, 1987.

______. "Milton's God and the Matter of Chaos," *PMLA* 110 (1995): 1035–46.

______. *Milton Unbound: Controversy and Reinterpretation.* Cambridge Univ. Press, 1996.

______. "The Erotic Milton," *Texas Studies in Literature and Language* 41 (1999): 128–41.

______. "Milton's *Theanthropos*: The Body of Christ in *Paradise Regained,*" *Milton Studies* 42 (2003): 50–67.

______. "The Provenance of *De Doctrina Christiana*: A View of the Present State of the Controversy." In Michael Lieb and John Shawcross, eds., *Milton and the Grounds of Contention,* pp. 214–33. Duquesne Univ. Press, 2004.

Schwartz, Regina M. *Remembering and Repeating: Biblical Creation in Paradise Lost.* Cambridge Univ. Press, 1988.

Selden, John. *De Dis Syris.* Guilielmus Stansbeins, 1617.

Sidonius, Carolus. *De Occidentali Imperio.* 1618.

Sinibaldus, Johann Benedict. *Geanthropeia, sive de hominis generatione decateuchon.* F. Caballus. 1642.

Sleidan, John [Sleidanus, Johannes]. *Commentaries* [*De statu religionis et reipublicae, Carolo Quinto Caesare, commentarii*]. Wendelin Rihel [Vuendelinus Riheilius], 1555.

Smith, Thomas. *The Common-wealth of England and the Maner of government thereof.* William Stansby for John Smethwicke. 1621.

Stoll, Abraham. *Milton and Monotheism.* Duquesne University Press, 2009.

Suh, Hong-Won. "Of Milton's Reformation." *Prose Studies: History, Theory, Criticism* 23 (2000) 23–42.

Tertullian. *Opera.* Ed. N. Rigaltius. Lutetiae, 1634.

Theodoret, et al. *Historia Ecclesiastica.* Petri le Petit, 1673.

Thuanus, Jacobus Augustus. *Historia Sui Temporis.* 3 vols. Aurelianae. 1620.

Turner, James Grantham. *One Flesh: Paradisal Marriage and Sexual Relations in the Age of Milton.* Oxford Univ. Press, 1987.

Williams, Arnold. *The Common Expositor: An Account of the Commentaries on Genesis 1527–1633.* Univ. of North Carolina Press, 1948.

Index

This index includes names of historical persons and authors to whom Milton refers, or who are mentioned in the accompanying text and footnotes. Names of mythological characters are omitted. Milton's name and the titles of his works are not indexed; however, his Milton and Phillips relatives are included.

About the Editors

William Kerrigan is the author of many books, including *The Sacred Complex: On the Psychogenesis of Paradise Lost,* for which he won the James Holly Hanford Award of the Milton Society of America. A former president of the Milton Society, he has also earned numerous honors and distinctions from that group, including its award for lifetime achievement. He is professor emeritus at the University of Massachusetts.

John Rumrich is the author of *Matter of Glory: A New Preface to Paradise Lost* and *Milton Unbound: Controversy and Reinterpretation.* An award-winning editor and writer, he is A. J. and W. D. Thaman Professor of English at the University of Texas at Austin, where he teaches early modern British literature.

Stephen M. Fallon is the author of *Milton's Peculiar Grace: Self-Representation and Authority* and *Milton among the Philosophers: Poetry and Materialism in Seventeenth-Century England,* winner of the Milton Society's Hanford Award. He is Cavanaugh Professor of the Humanities at the University of Notre Dame.

A Note on the Type

The principal text of this Modern Library edition was set in a digitized version of Janson, a typeface that dates from about 1690 and was cut by Nicholas Kis, a Hungarian working in Amsterdam. The original matrices have survived and are held by the Stempel foundry in Germany. Hermann Zapf redesigned some of the weights and sizes for Stempel, basing his revisions on the original design.

Also available from the Modern Library

The Complete Poetry and Essential Prose of John Milton

Edited by William Kerrigan, John Rumrich, and Stephen M. Fallon

"A model of its kind: well [illegible] and attractive [illegible] [illegible] introductions to the major works. [illegible] [illegible] to be [illegible] [illegible]."

—*The Wall Street Journal*

"This [illegible] edition [illegible] read Milton intelligently [illegible] [illegible]."

—William H. Pritchard, Amherst College

Printed in the United States
by Baker & Taylor Publisher Services

Printed in the United States
by Baker & Taylor Publisher Services